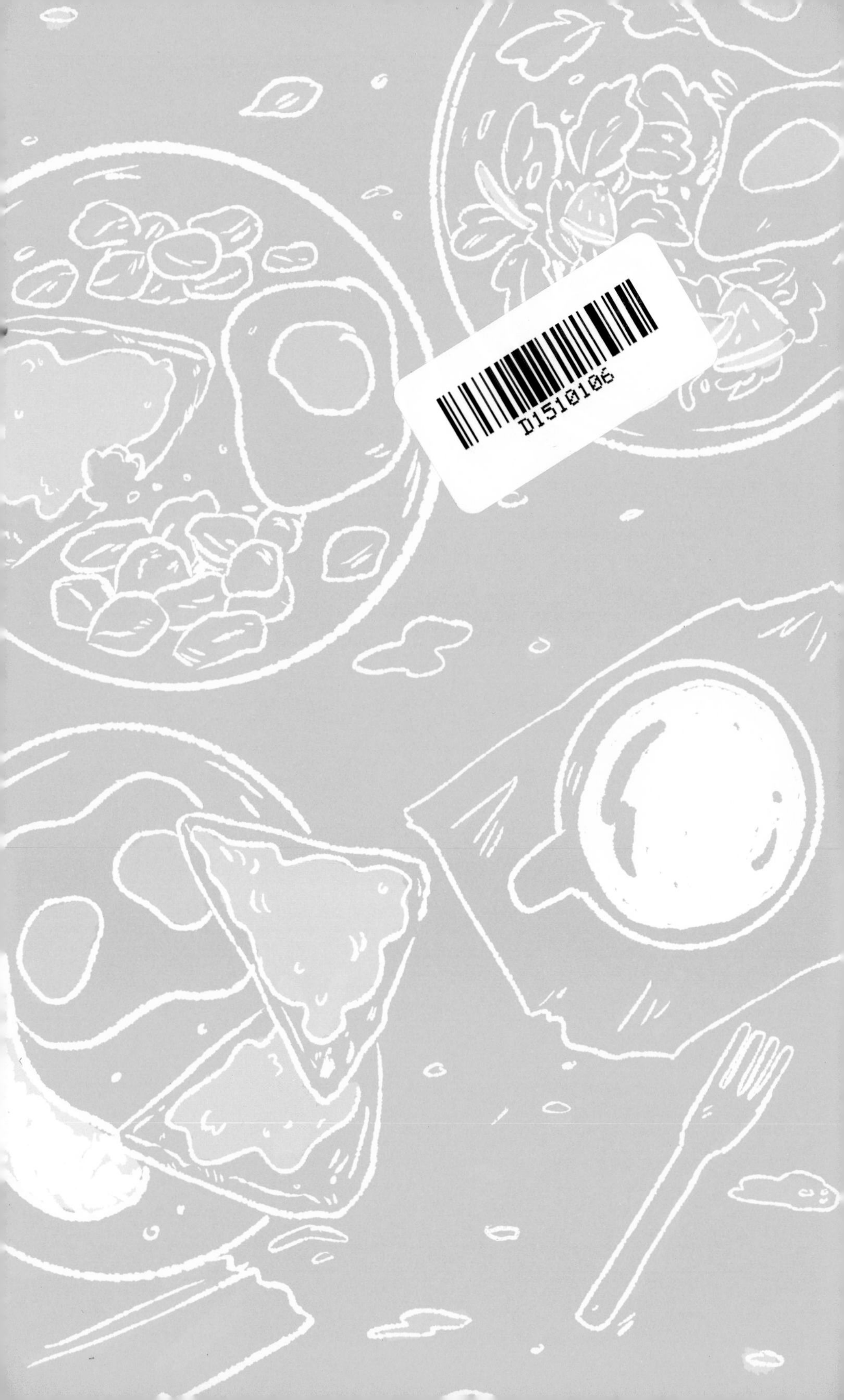

MiMOSA

MiMOSA

ARCHIE BONGIOVANNI

ABRAMS COMICARTS SURELY · NEW YORK

SURELY PUBLISHES LGBTQIA+ STORIES BY LGBTQIA+ CREATORS, WITH A FOCUS
ON NEW STORIES, NEW VOICES, AND UNTOLD HISTORIES, IN WORKS THAT SPAN
FICTION AND NONFICTION, INCLUDING MEMOIR, HORROR, COMEDY, AND FANTASY.
SURELY AIMS TO PUBLISH BOOKS FOR TEENS AND ADULTS THAT LEND CONTEXT
AND PERSPECTIVE TO OUR CURRENT STRUGGLES AND VICTORIES, AND TO SUPPORT
THOSE CREATORS UNDERREPRESENTED IN THE CURRENT PUBLISHING WORLD.
WE ARE BOLD, BRAVE, LOUD, UNEXPECTED, DARING, UNIQUE.

SURELY CURATOR: MARIKO TAMAKI
EDITOR: CHARLOTTE GREENBAUM
EDITORIAL ASSISTANT: LAUREN WHITE-JACKSON
DESIGNER: ANDREA MILLER
MANAGING EDITOR: MARIE OISHI
PRODUCTION MANAGER: ALISON GERVAIS

LIBRARY OF CONGRESS CONTROL NUMBER 2022932879

ISBN 978-1-4197-5243-8

TEXT AND ILLUSTRATIONS © 2023 ARCHIE BONGIOVANNI

PRINTED AND BOUND IN CHINA
10 9 8 7 6 5 4 3 2 1

ABRAMS COMICARTS BOOKS ARE AVAILABLE AT SPECIAL DISCOUNTS
WHEN PURCHASED IN QUANTITY FOR PREMIUMS AND PROMOTIONS AS WELL
AS FUNDRAISING OR EDUCATIONAL USE. SPECIAL EDITIONS CAN ALSO BE CREATED
TO SPECIFICATION. FOR DETAILS, CONTACT SPECIALSALES@ABRAMSBOOKS.COM
OR THE ADDRESS BELOW.

ABRAMS The Art of Books
195 Broadway, New York, NY 10007
abramsbooks.com

DEDICATED TO,
IN THE MOST EXPANSIVE
MEANING OF THE TERM,
MY FAMILY

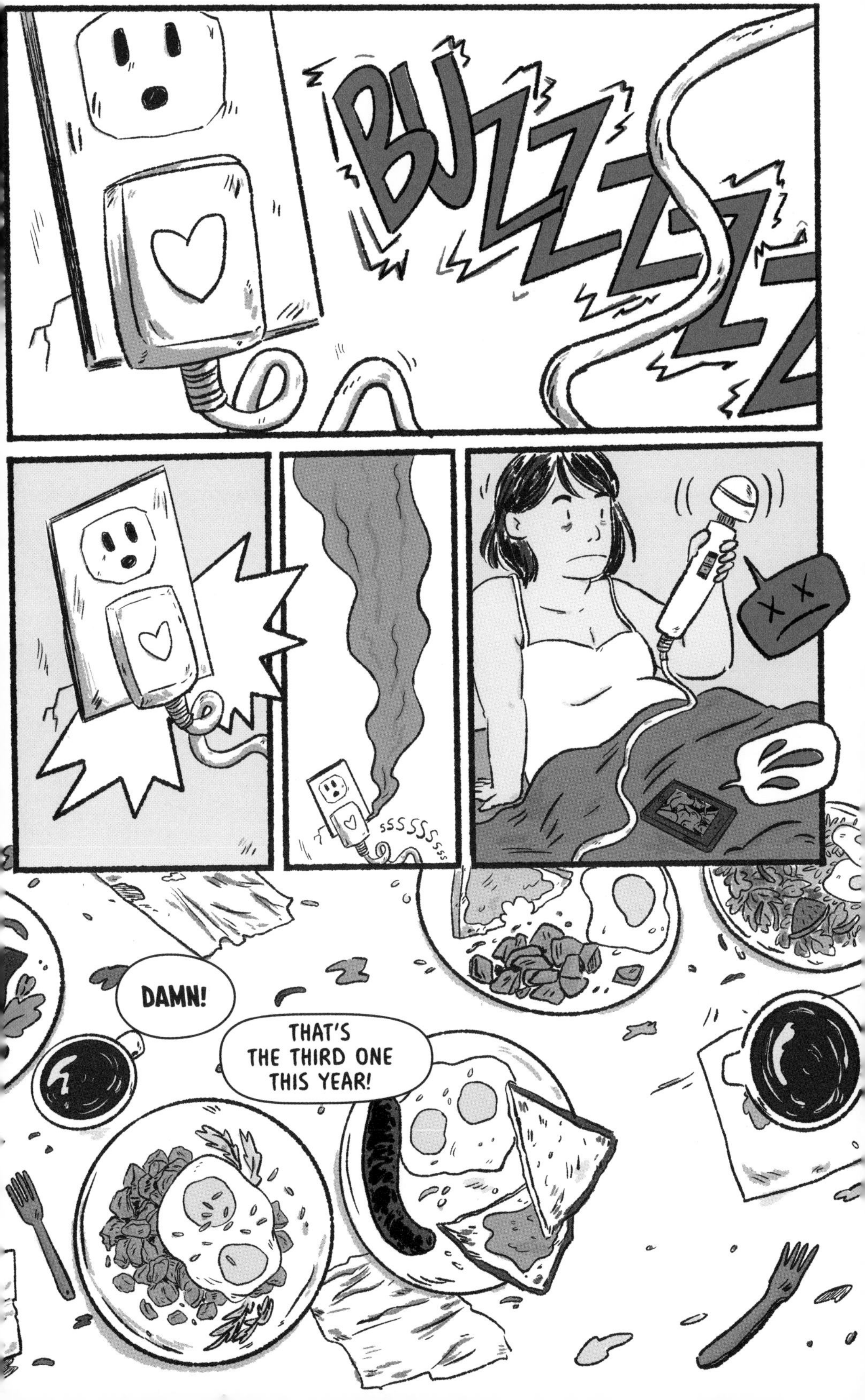
BUZZZZZ
SSSSSSsss
DAMN!
THAT'S THE THIRD ONE THIS YEAR!

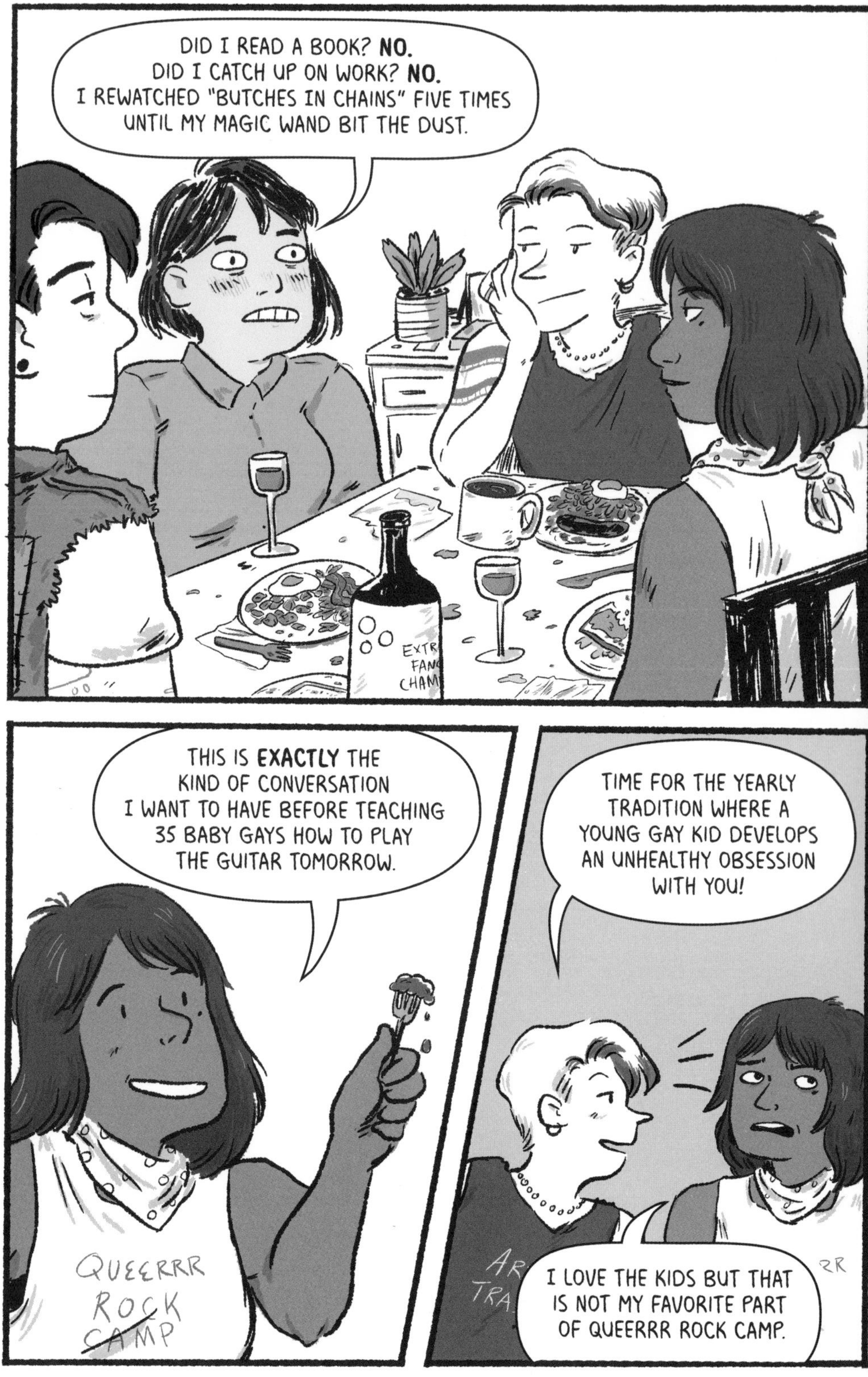
DID I READ A BOOK? **NO.** DID I CATCH UP ON WORK? **NO.** I REWATCHED "BUTCHES IN CHAINS" FIVE TIMES UNTIL MY MAGIC WAND BIT THE DUST.
THIS IS **EXACTLY** THE KIND OF CONVERSATION I WANT TO HAVE BEFORE TEACHING 35 BABY GAYS HOW TO PLAY THE GUITAR TOMORROW.
QUEERRR ROCK CAMP
TIME FOR THE YEARLY TRADITION WHERE A YOUNG GAY KID DEVELOPS AN UNHEALTHY OBSESSION WITH YOU!
I LOVE THE KIDS BUT THAT IS NOT MY FAVORITE PART OF QUEERRR ROCK CAMP.

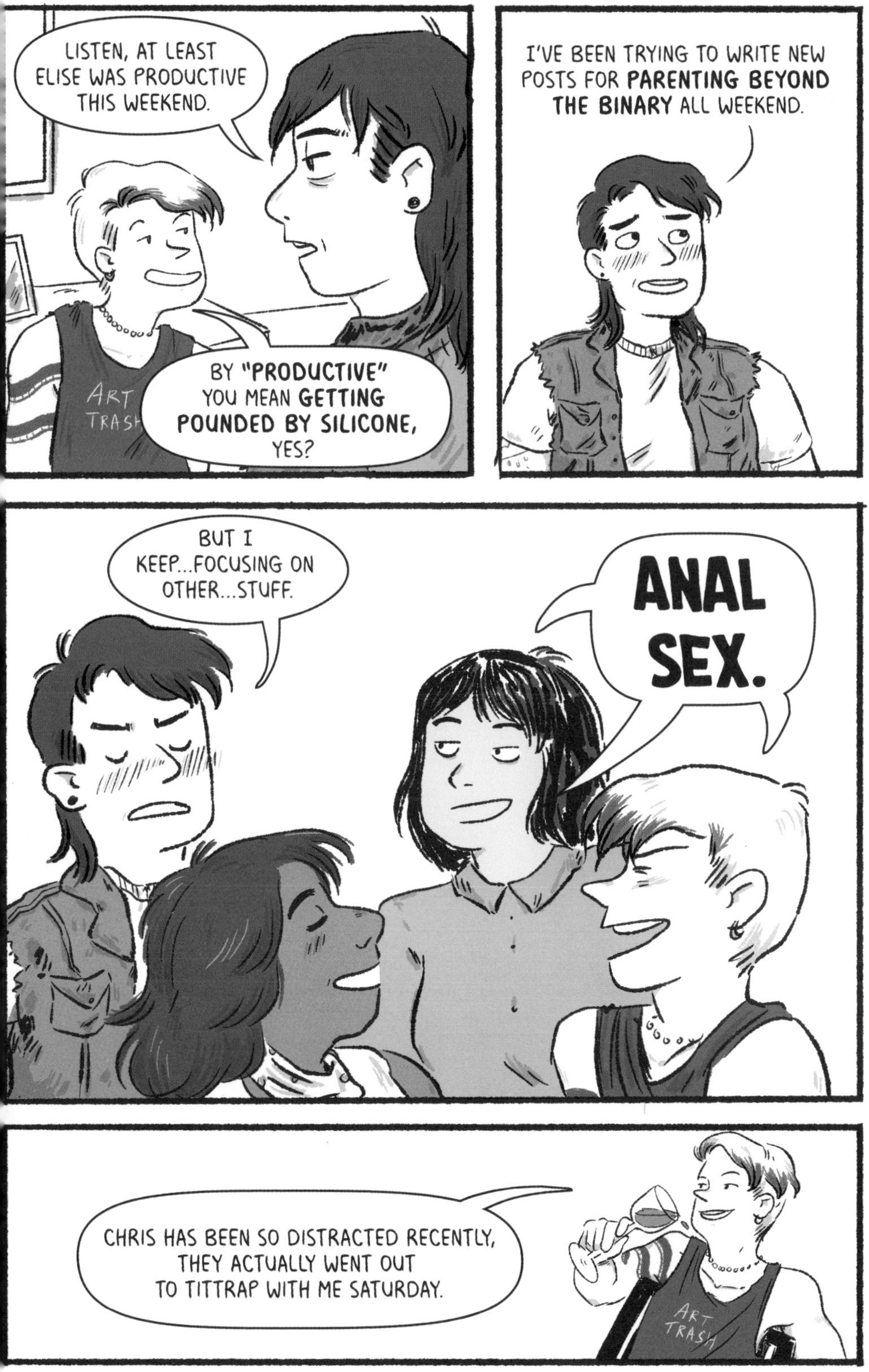
LISTEN, AT LEAST ELISE WAS PRODUCTIVE THIS WEEKEND.
BY **"PRODUCTIVE"** YOU MEAN **GETTING POUNDED BY SILICONE,** YES?
I'VE BEEN TRYING TO WRITE NEW POSTS FOR **PARENTING BEYOND THE BINARY** ALL WEEKEND.
ART TRASH
BUT I KEEP...FOCUSING ON OTHER...STUFF.
ANAL SEX.
CHRIS HAS BEEN SO DISTRACTED RECENTLY, THEY ACTUALLY WENT OUT TO TITTRAP WITH ME SATURDAY.
ART TRASH

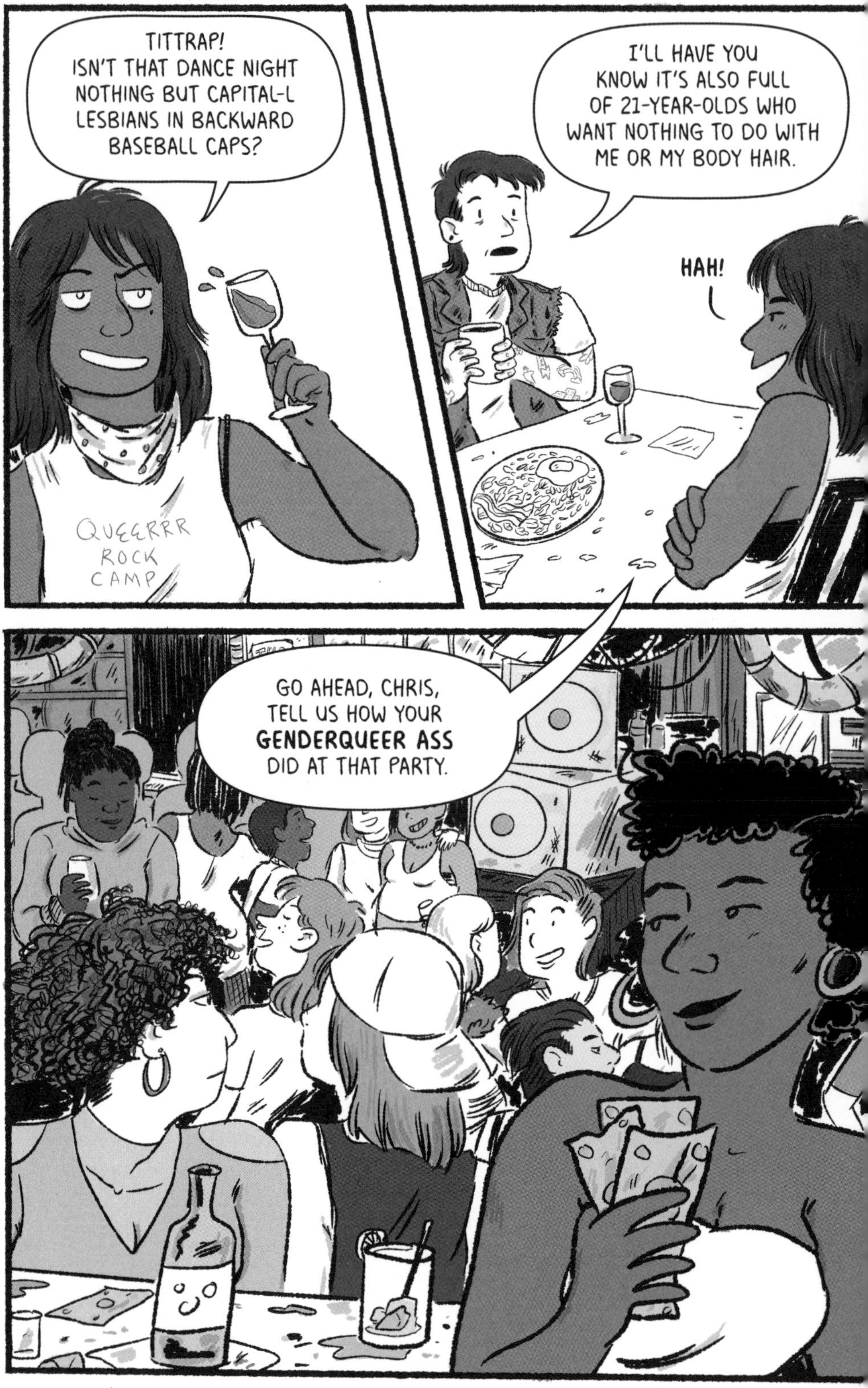
TITTRAP! ISN'T THAT DANCE NIGHT NOTHING BUT CAPITAL-L LESBIANS IN BACKWARD BASEBALL CAPS?
QUEERRR ROCK CAMP
I'LL HAVE YOU KNOW IT'S ALSO FULL OF 21-YEAR-OLDS WHO WANT NOTHING TO DO WITH ME OR MY BODY HAIR.
HAH!
GO AHEAD, CHRIS, TELL US HOW YOUR **GENDERQUEER ASS** DID AT THAT PARTY.

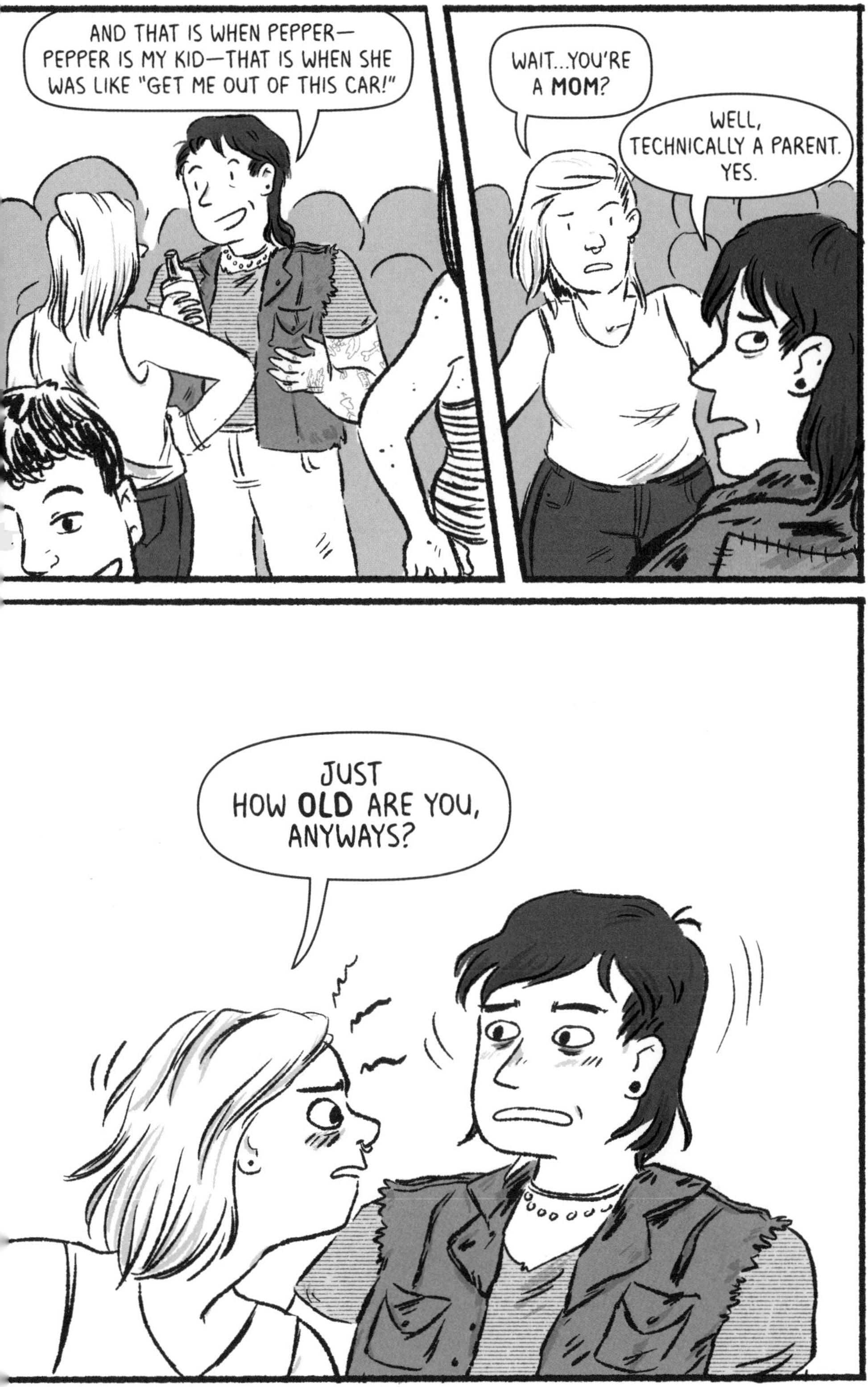
AND THAT IS WHEN PEPPER—PEPPER IS MY KID—THAT IS WHEN SHE WAS LIKE "GET ME OUT OF THIS CAR!"
WAIT...YOU'RE A **MOM**?
WELL, TECHNICALLY A PARENT. YES.
JUST HOW **OLD** ARE YOU, ANYWAYS?

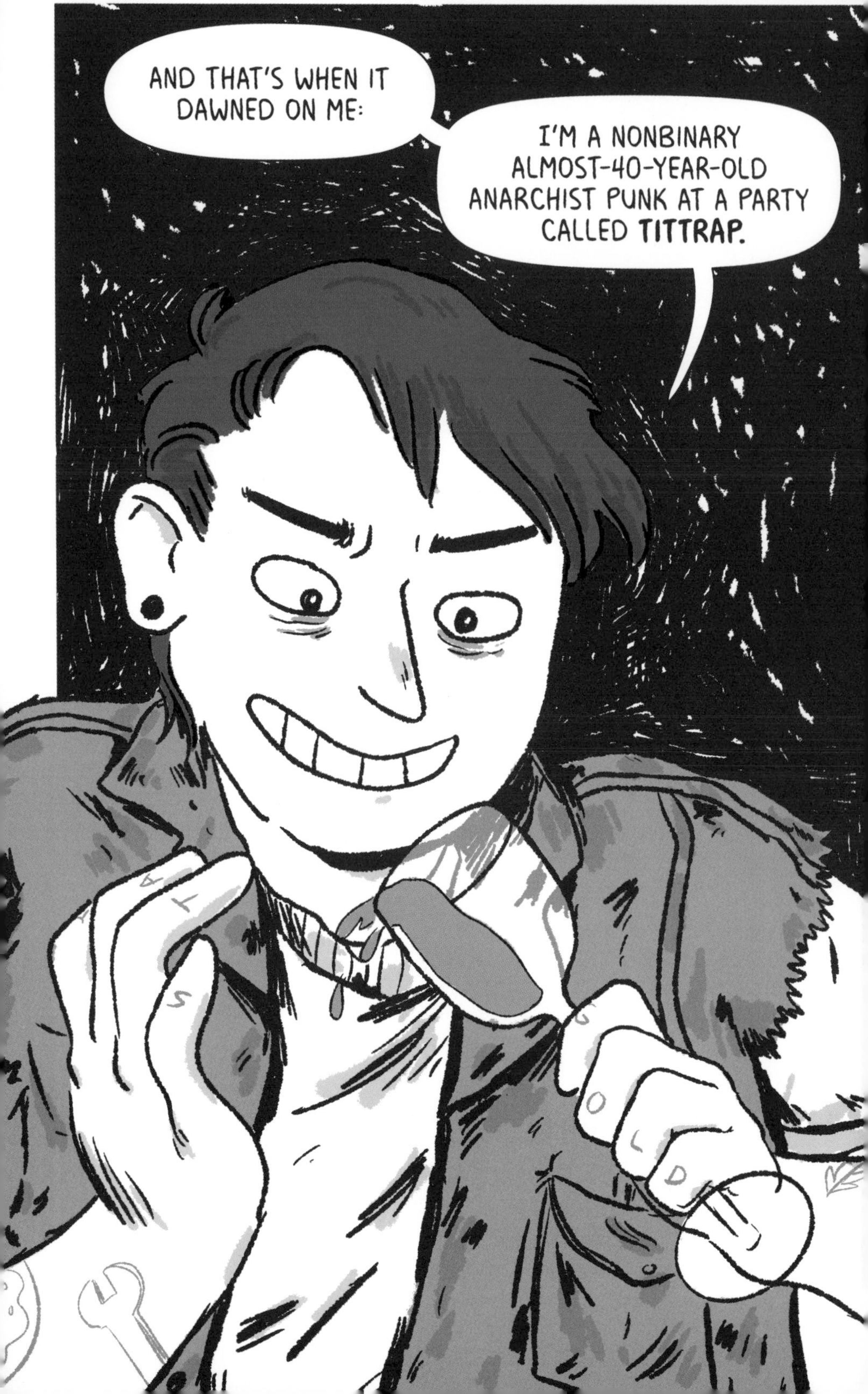

AND THAT'S WHEN IT DAWNED ON ME:
I'M A NONBINARY ALMOST-40-YEAR-OLD ANARCHIST PUNK AT A PARTY CALLED **TITTRAP.**

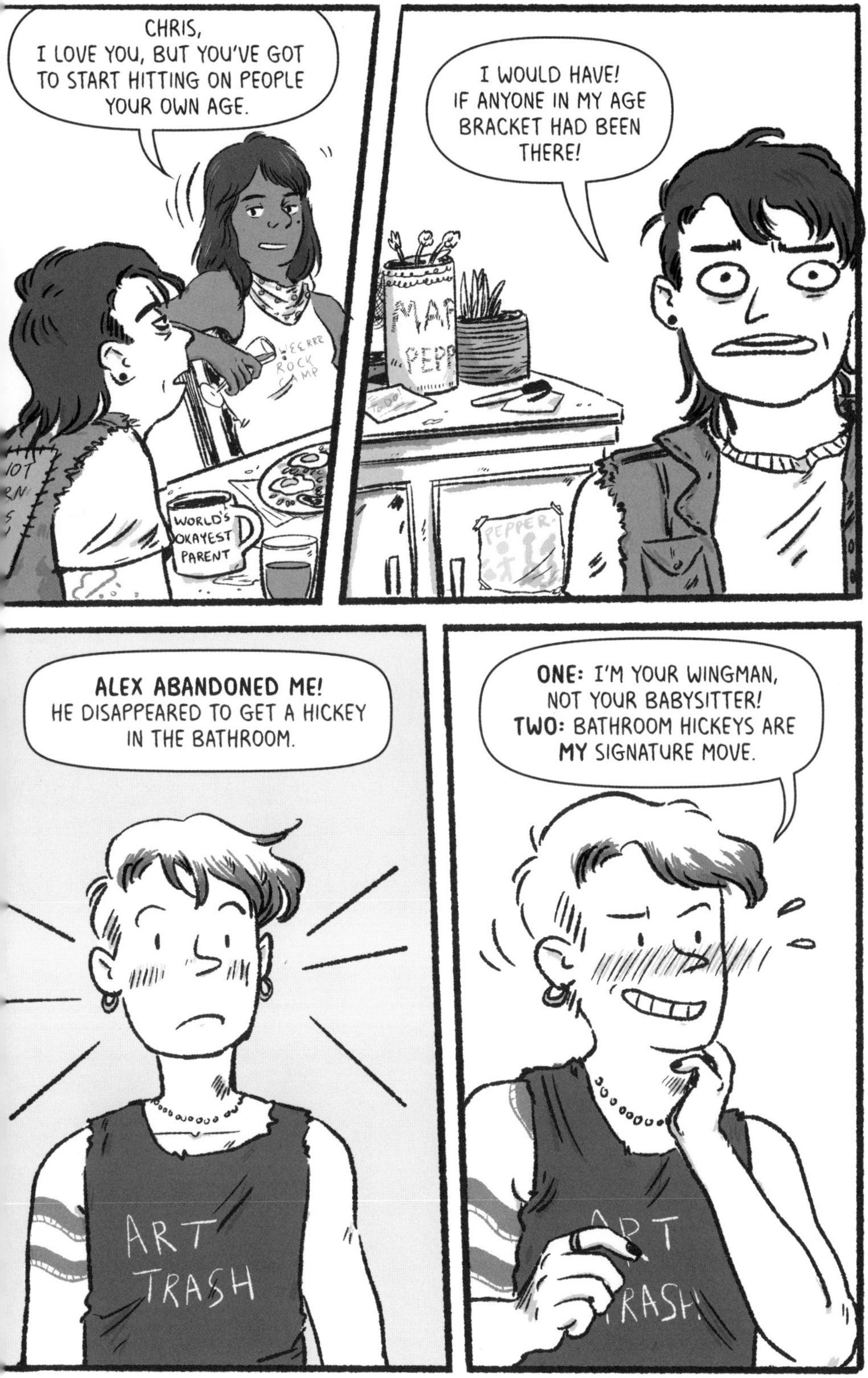

CHRIS,
I LOVE YOU, BUT YOU'VE GOT TO START HITTING ON PEOPLE YOUR OWN AGE.
WEERRR ROCK CAMP
WORLD'S OKAYEST PARENT
I WOULD HAVE! IF ANYONE IN MY AGE BRACKET HAD BEEN THERE!
PEPPER
ALEX ABANDONED ME! HE DISAPPEARED TO GET A HICKEY IN THE BATHROOM.
ART TRASH
ONE: I'M YOUR WINGMAN, NOT YOUR BABYSITTER! TWO: BATHROOM HICKEYS ARE MY SIGNATURE MOVE.

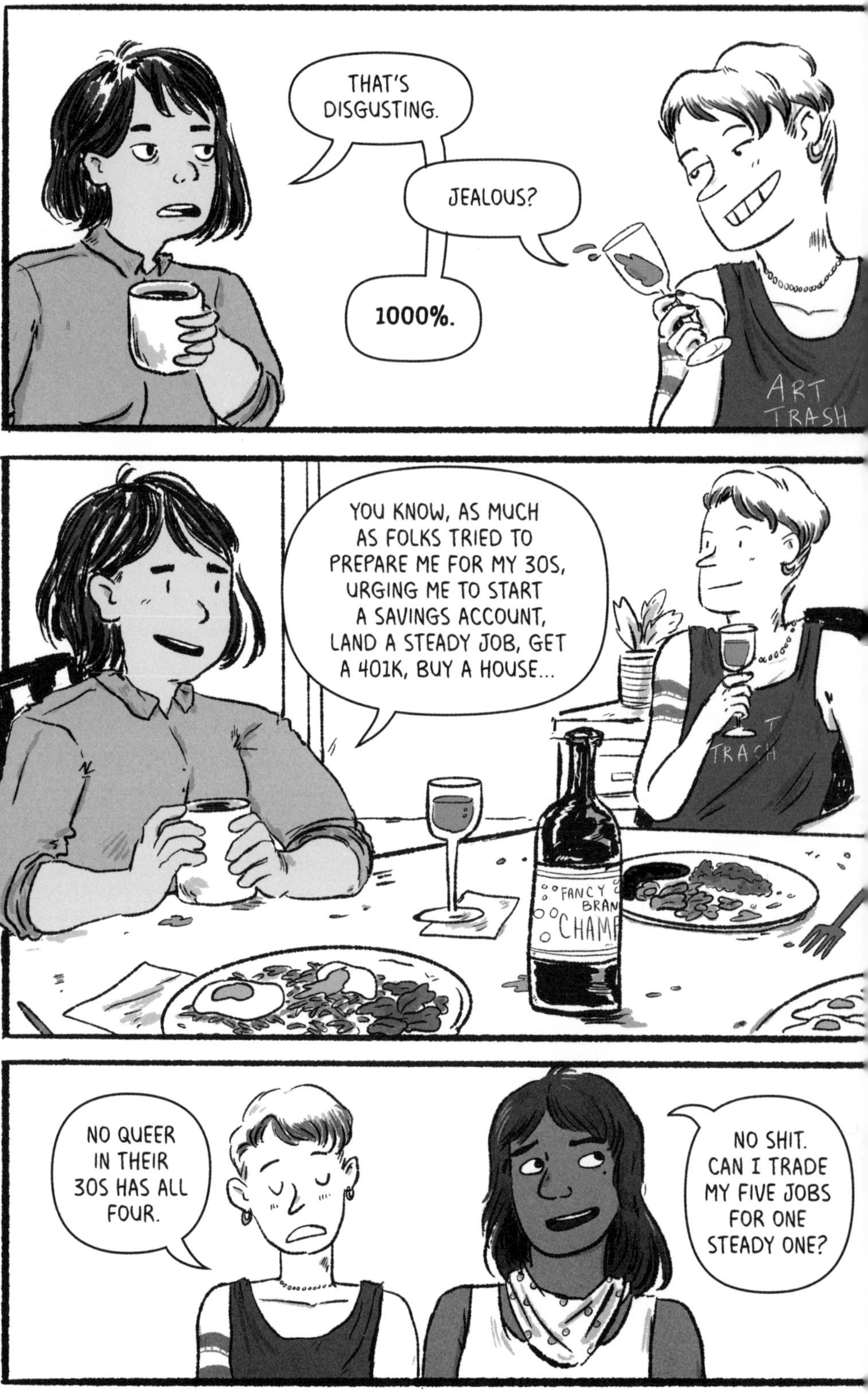
THAT'S DISGUSTING.
JEALOUS?
1000%.
ART TRASH
YOU KNOW, AS MUCH AS FOLKS TRIED TO PREPARE ME FOR MY 30S, URGING ME TO START A SAVINGS ACCOUNT, LAND A STEADY JOB, GET A 401K, BUY A HOUSE...
NO QUEER IN THEIR 30S HAS ALL FOUR.
NO SHIT. CAN I TRADE MY FIVE JOBS FOR ONE STEADY ONE?

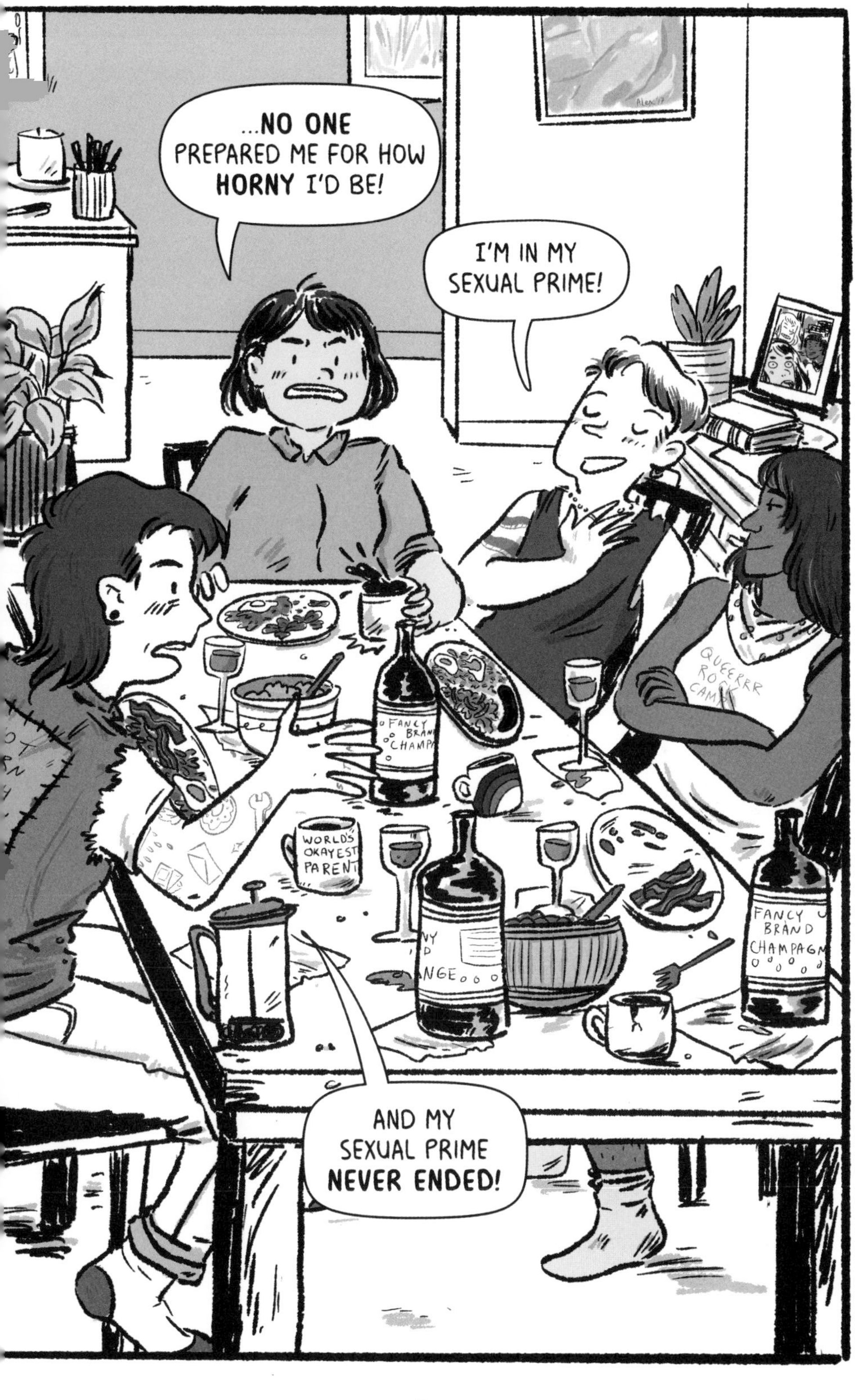

...NO ONE PREPARED ME FOR HOW HORNY I'D BE!
I'M IN MY SEXUAL PRIME!
AND MY SEXUAL PRIME NEVER ENDED!
WORLD'S OKAYEST PARENT
FANCY BRAND CHAMPAGN
QUEERRR ROCK CAMP

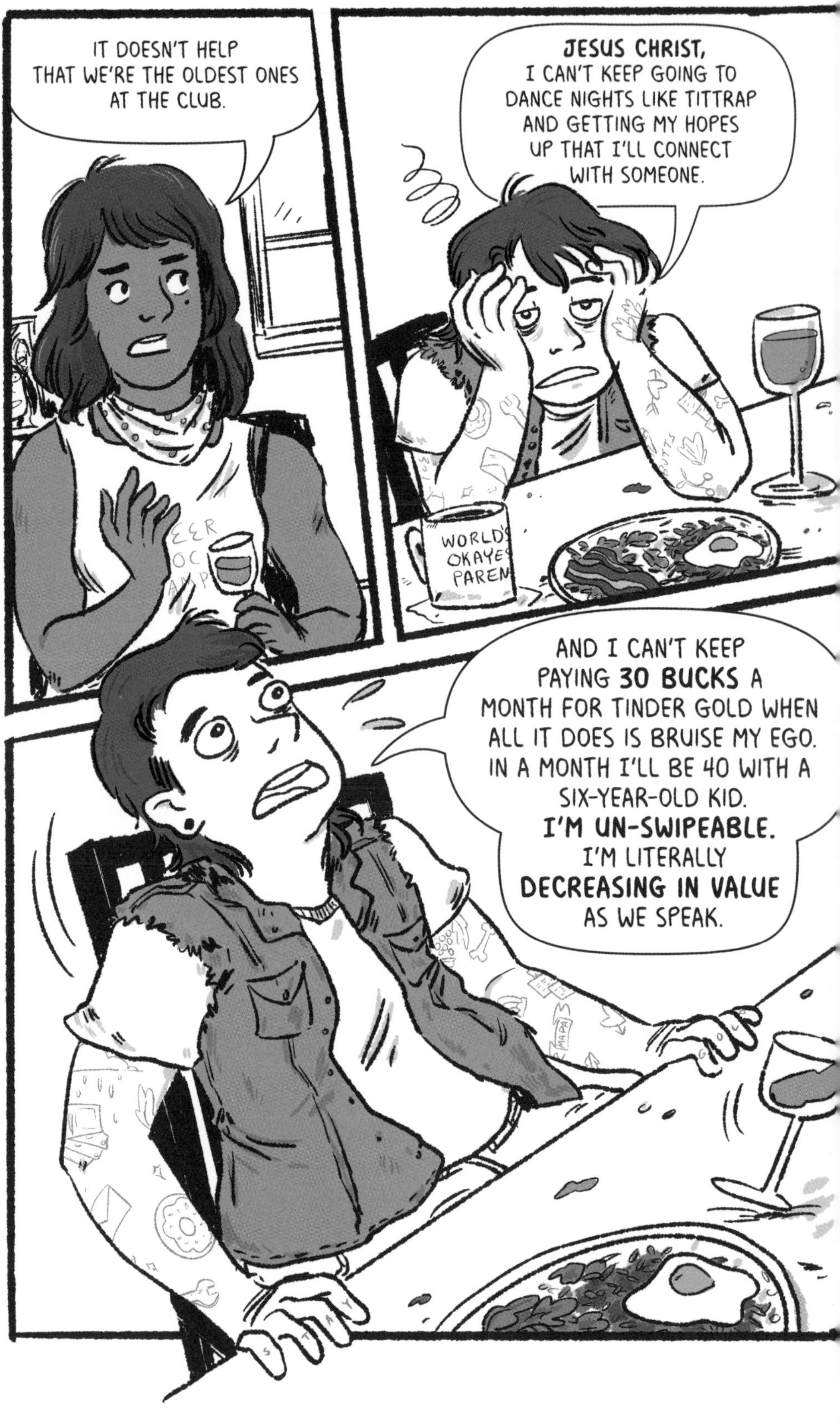
IT DOESN'T HELP THAT WE'RE THE OLDEST ONES AT THE CLUB.
JESUS CHRIST, I CAN'T KEEP GOING TO DANCE NIGHTS LIKE TITTRAP AND GETTING MY HOPES UP THAT I'LL CONNECT WITH SOMEONE.
WORLD'S OKAYEST PARENT
AND I CAN'T KEEP PAYING 30 BUCKS A MONTH FOR TINDER GOLD WHEN ALL IT DOES IS BRUISE MY EGO. IN A MONTH I'LL BE 40 WITH A SIX-YEAR-OLD KID. I'M UN-SWIPEABLE. I'M LITERALLY DECREASING IN VALUE AS WE SPEAK.

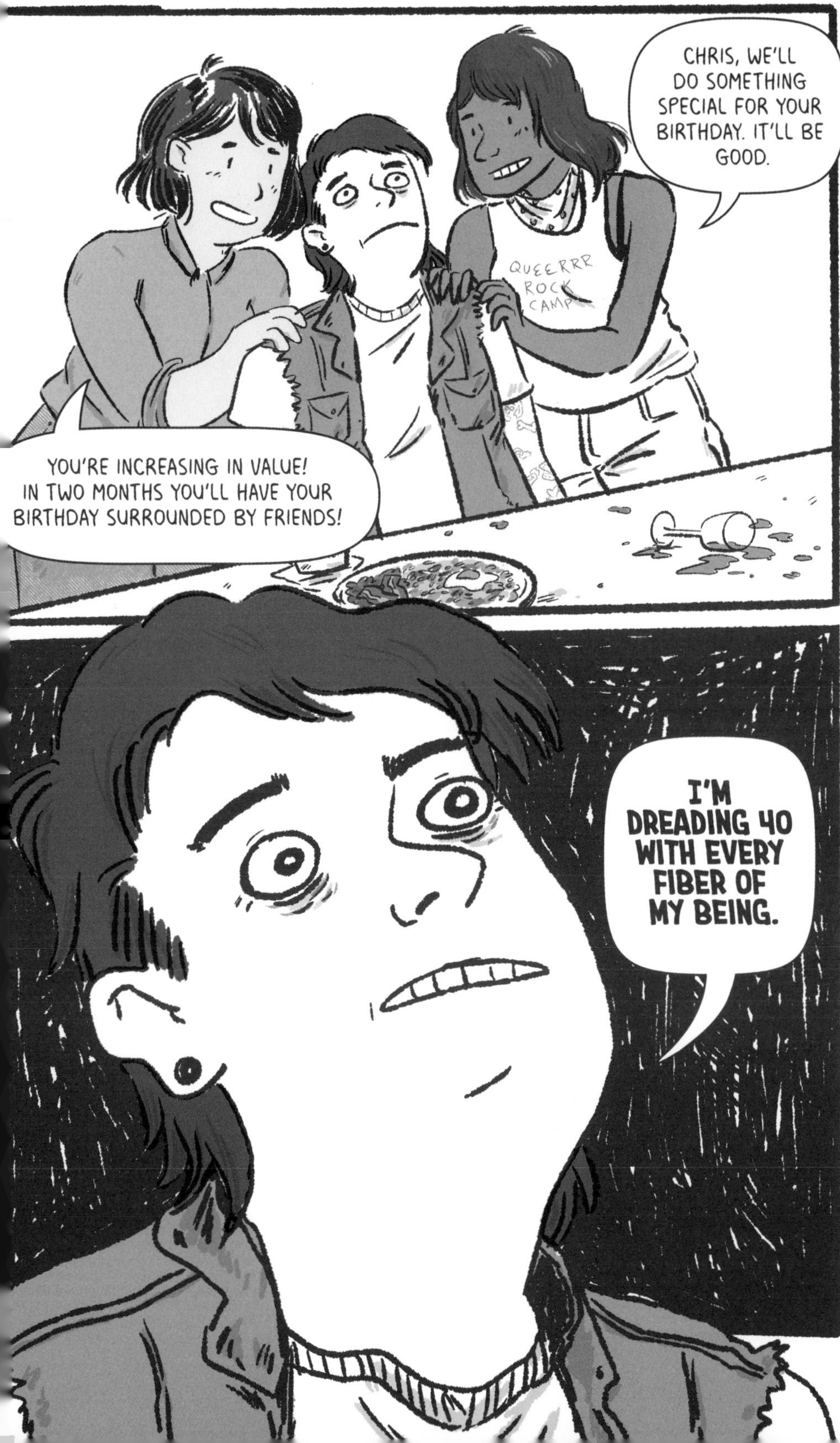
CHRIS, WE'LL DO SOMETHING SPECIAL FOR YOUR BIRTHDAY. IT'LL BE GOOD.
QUEERRR ROCK CAMP
YOU'RE INCREASING IN VALUE! IN TWO MONTHS YOU'LL HAVE YOUR BIRTHDAY SURROUNDED BY FRIENDS!
I'M DREADING 40 WITH EVERY FIBER OF MY BEING.

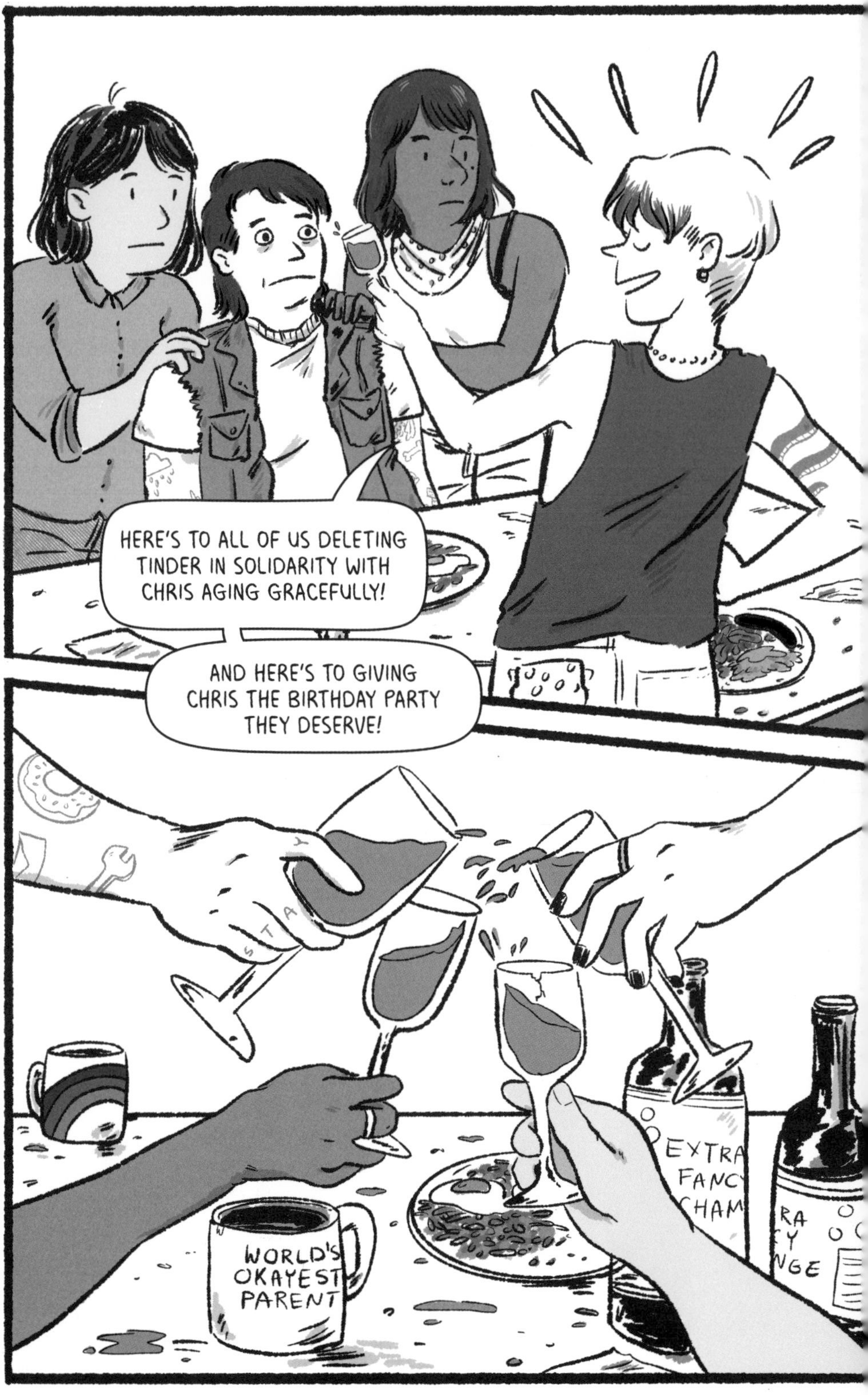
HERE'S TO ALL OF US DELETING TINDER IN SOLIDARITY WITH CHRIS AGING GRACEFULLY!
AND HERE'S TO GIVING CHRIS THE BIRTHDAY PARTY THEY DESERVE!
WORLD'S OKAYEST PARENT
EXTRA FANCY CHAM

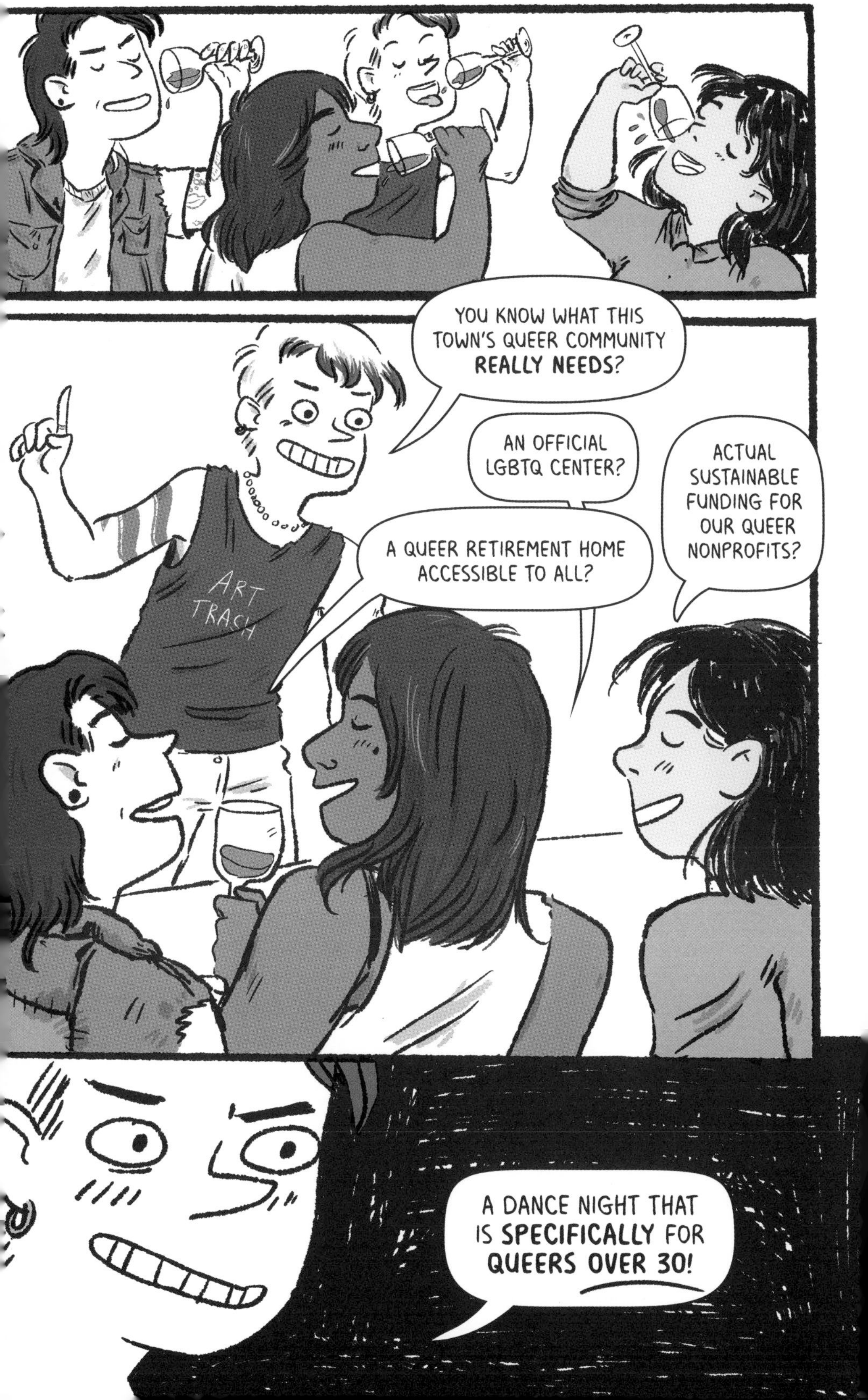
YOU KNOW WHAT THIS TOWN'S QUEER COMMUNITY **REALLY NEEDS**?
AN OFFICIAL LGBTQ CENTER?
ACTUAL SUSTAINABLE FUNDING FOR OUR QUEER NONPROFITS?
A QUEER RETIREMENT HOME ACCESSIBLE TO ALL?
ART TRASH
A DANCE NIGHT THAT IS **SPECIFICALLY** FOR **QUEERS OVER 30**!

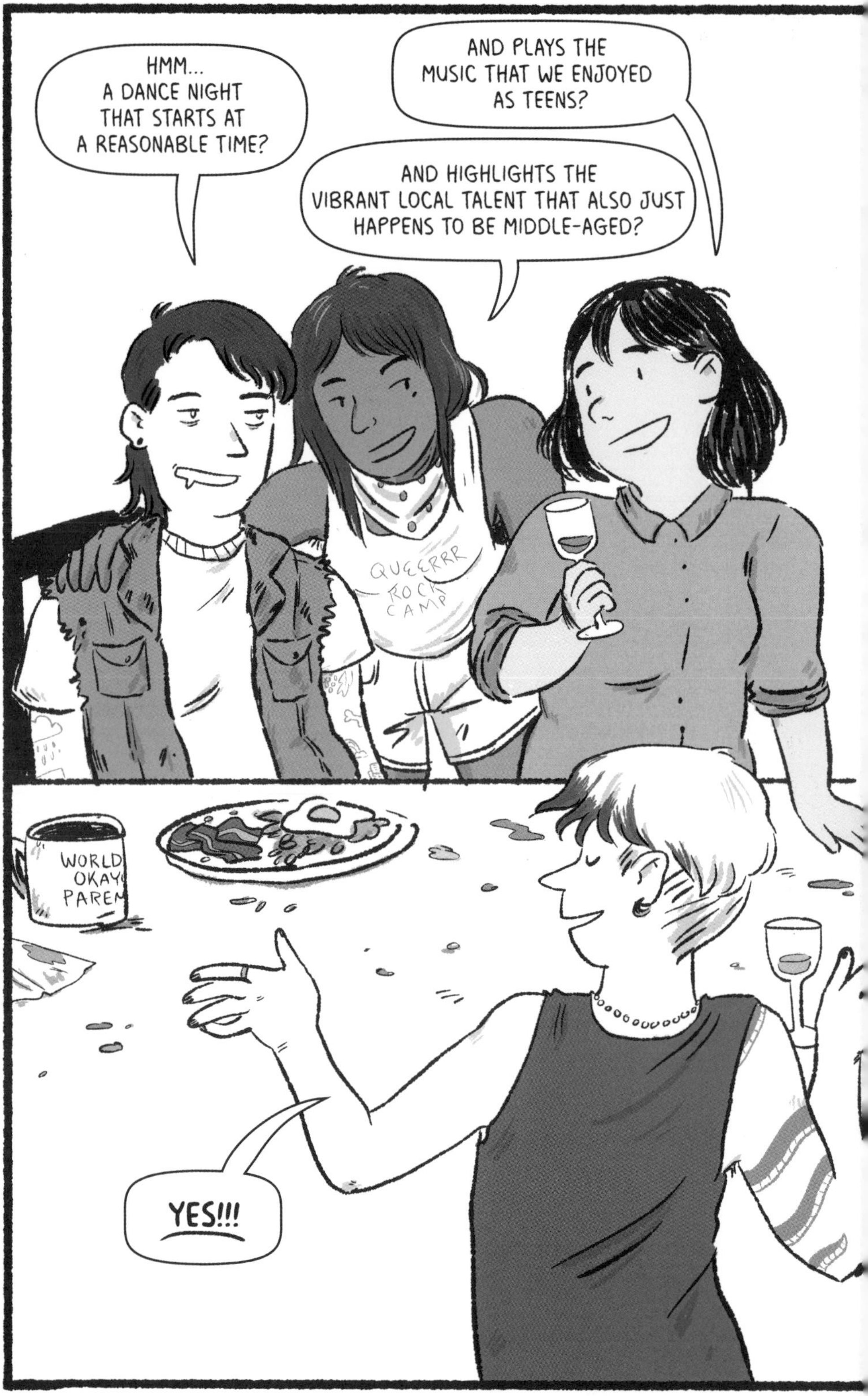
HMM...
A DANCE NIGHT
THAT STARTS AT
A REASONABLE TIME?
AND PLAYS THE
MUSIC THAT WE ENJOYED
AS TEENS?
AND HIGHLIGHTS THE
VIBRANT LOCAL TALENT THAT ALSO JUST
HAPPENS TO BE MIDDLE-AGED?
QUEERRR
ROCK
CAMP
WORLD
OKAY
PAREN
YES!!!

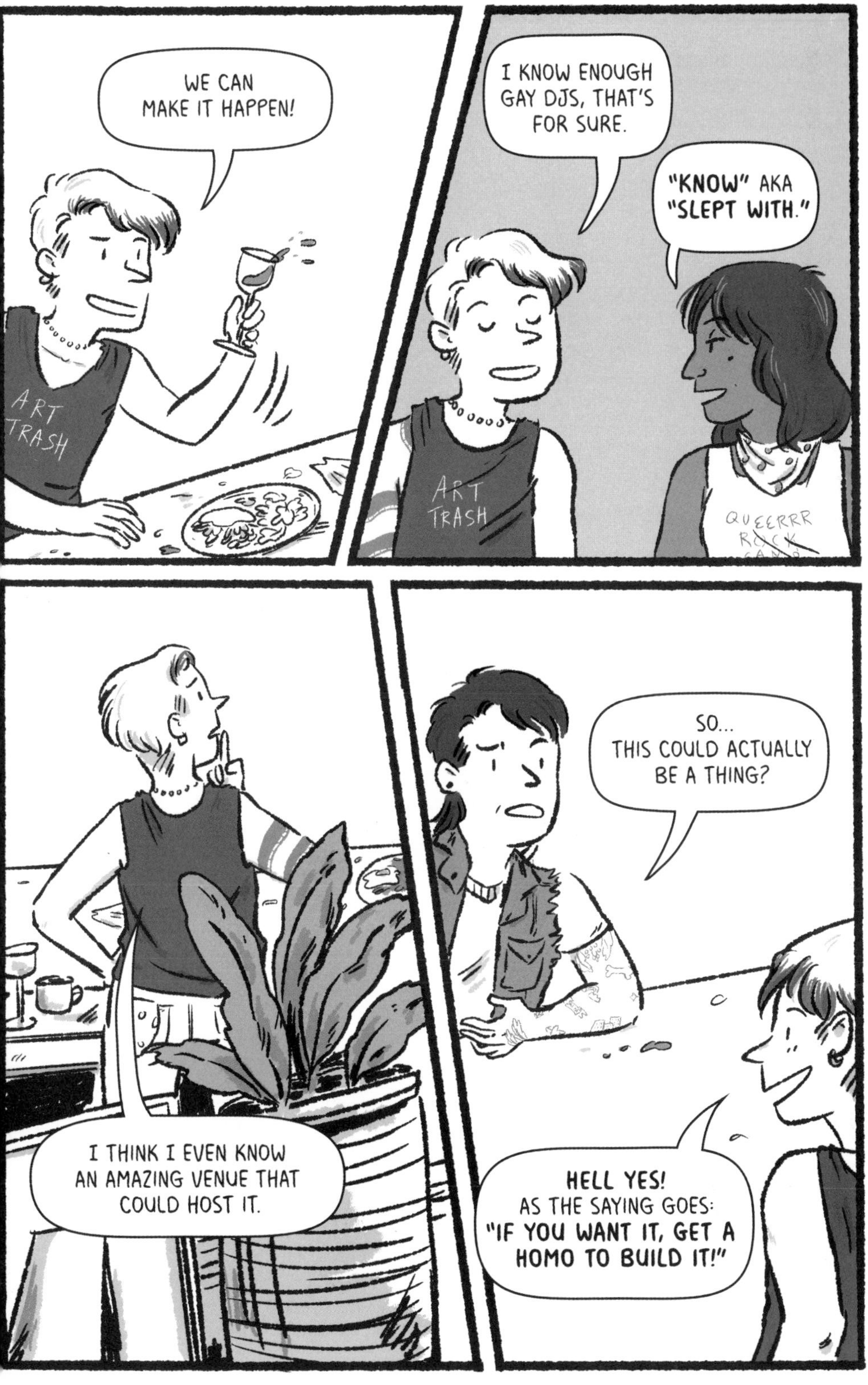
WE CAN MAKE IT HAPPEN!
ART TRASH
I KNOW ENOUGH GAY DJS, THAT'S FOR SURE.
"KNOW" AKA "SLEPT WITH."
ART TRASH
QUEERRR
I THINK I EVEN KNOW AN AMAZING VENUE THAT COULD HOST IT.
SO... THIS COULD ACTUALLY BE A THING?
HELL YES! AS THE SAYING GOES: "IF YOU WANT IT, GET A HOMO TO BUILD IT!"

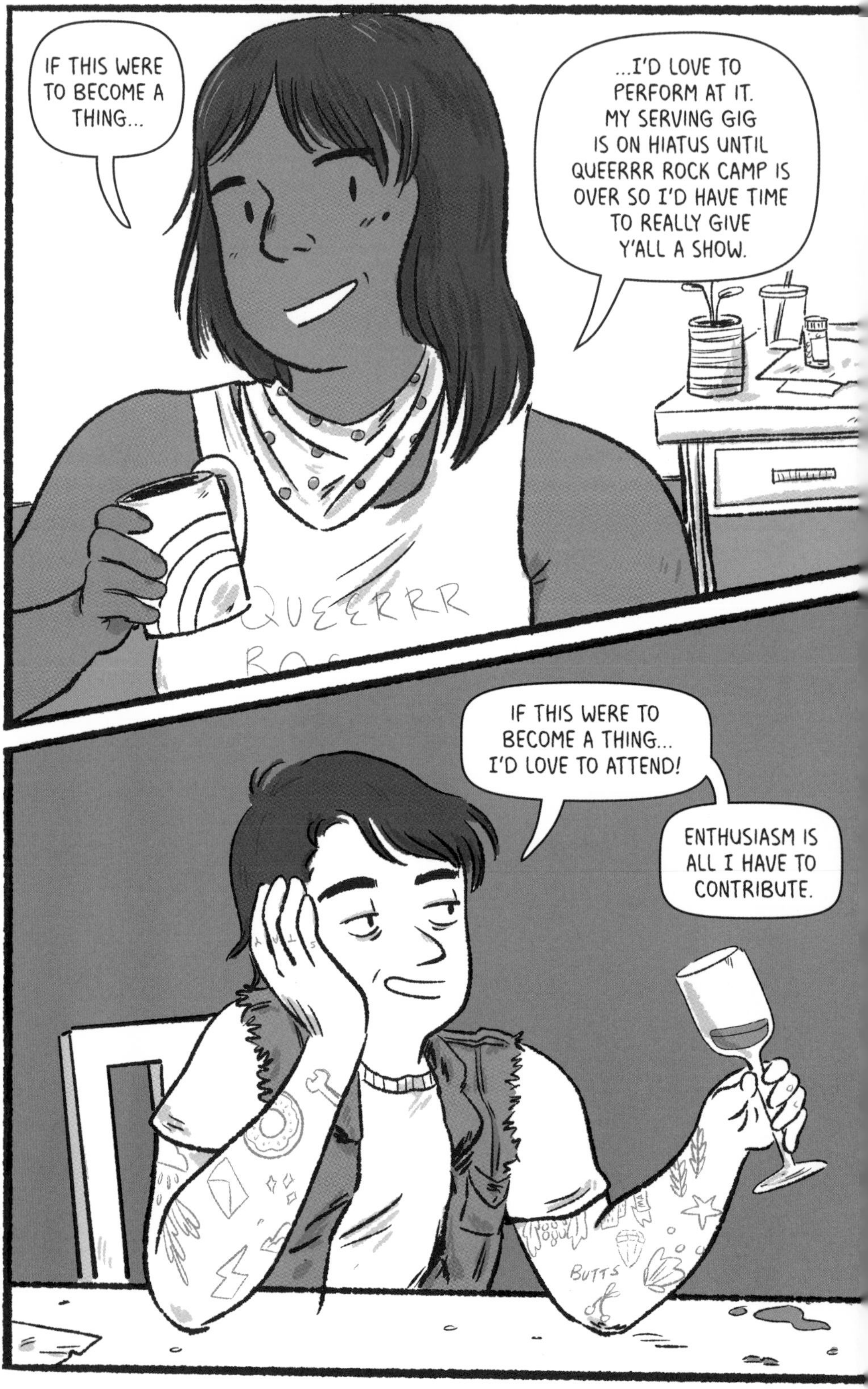
IF THIS WERE TO BECOME A THING...
...I'D LOVE TO PERFORM AT IT. MY SERVING GIG IS ON HIATUS UNTIL QUEERRR ROCK CAMP IS OVER SO I'D HAVE TIME TO REALLY GIVE Y'ALL A SHOW.
QUEERRR
IF THIS WERE TO BECOME A THING... I'D LOVE TO ATTEND!
ENTHUSIASM IS ALL I HAVE TO CONTRIBUTE.
BUTTS

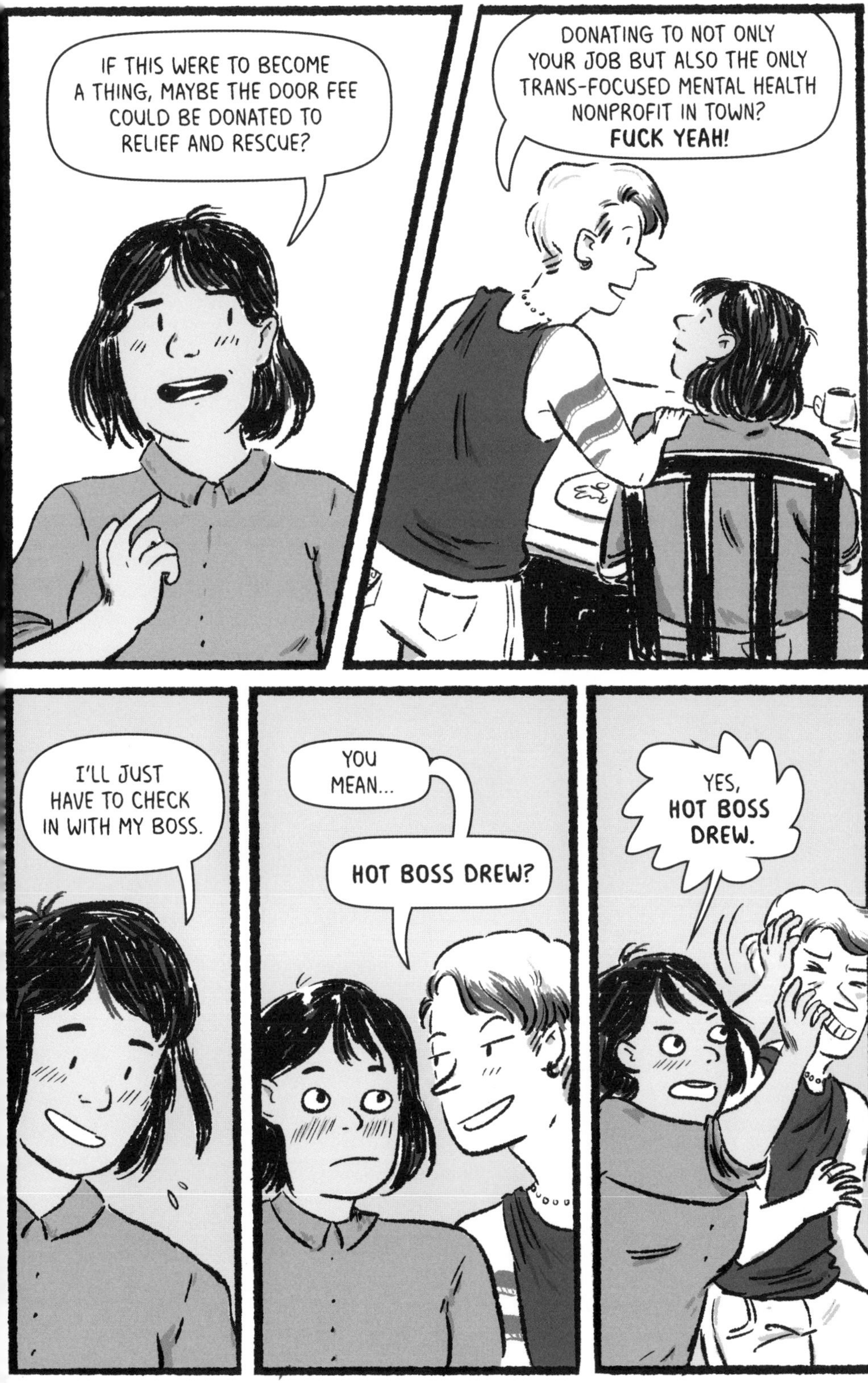
IF THIS WERE TO BECOME A THING, MAYBE THE DOOR FEE COULD BE DONATED TO RELIEF AND RESCUE?
DONATING TO NOT ONLY YOUR JOB BUT ALSO THE ONLY TRANS-FOCUSED MENTAL HEALTH NONPROFIT IN TOWN? FUCK YEAH!
I'LL JUST HAVE TO CHECK IN WITH MY BOSS.
YOU MEAN...
HOT BOSS DREW?
YES, HOT BOSS DREW.

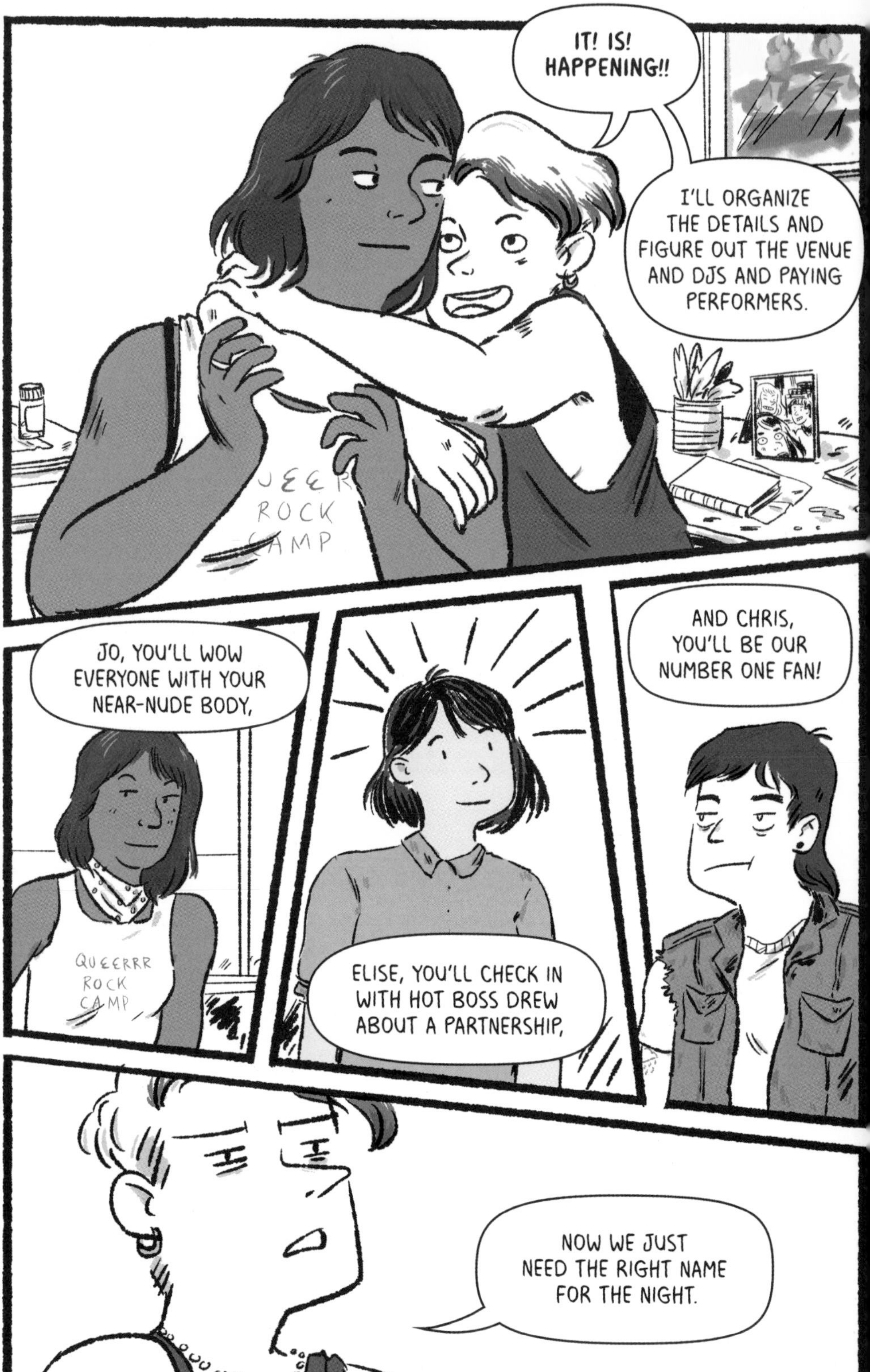
IT! IS! HAPPENING!!
I'LL ORGANIZE THE DETAILS AND FIGURE OUT THE VENUE AND DJS AND PAYING PERFORMERS.
QUEER ROCK CAMP
JO, YOU'LL WOW EVERYONE WITH YOUR NEAR-NUDE BODY,
QUEERRR ROCK CAMP
ELISE, YOU'LL CHECK IN WITH HOT BOSS DREW ABOUT A PARTNERSHIP,
AND CHRIS, YOU'LL BE OUR NUMBER ONE FAN!
NOW WE JUST NEED THE RIGHT NAME FOR THE NIGHT.

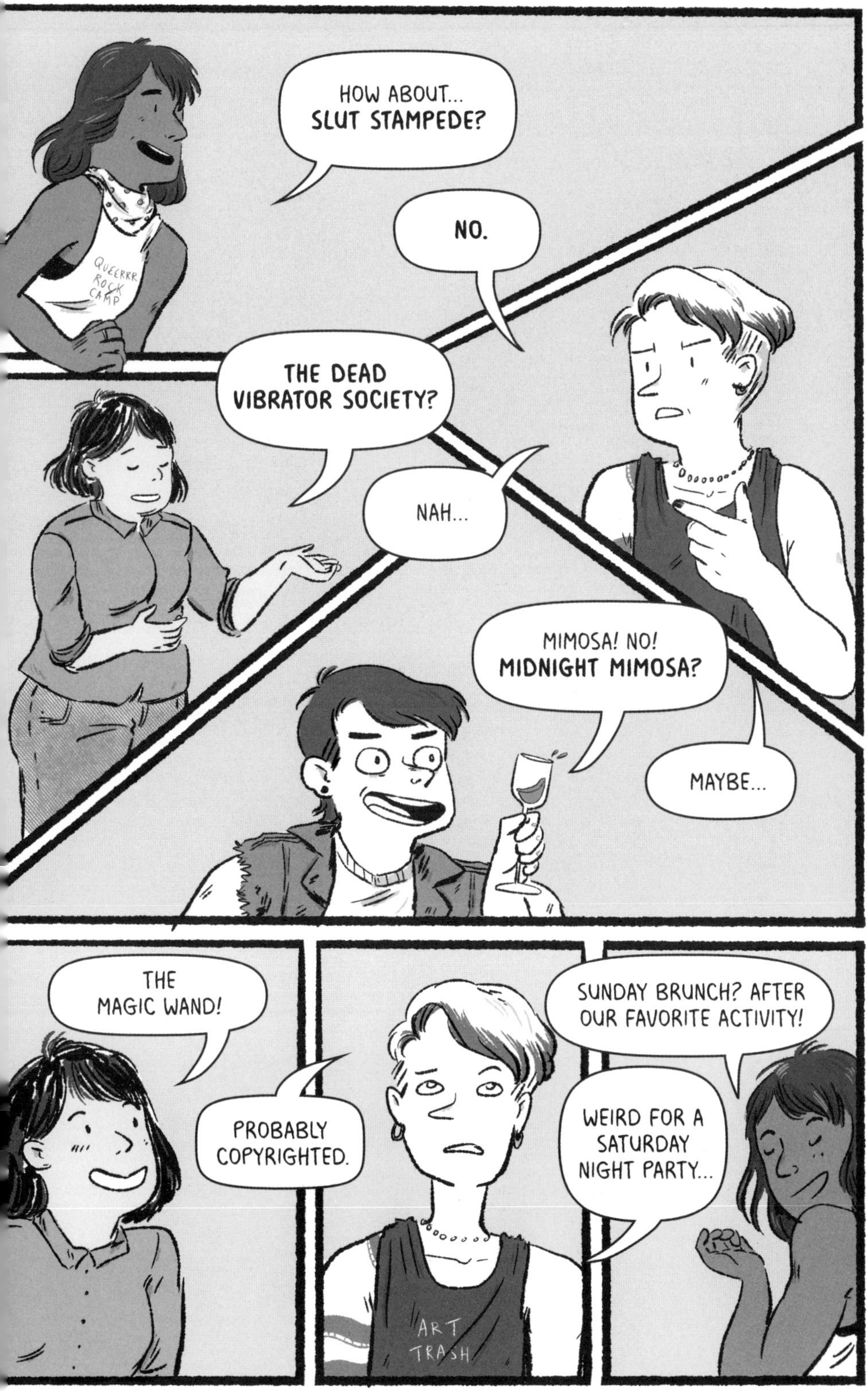
HOW ABOUT... SLUT STAMPEDE?
QUEERRR ROCK CAMP
NO.
THE DEAD VIBRATOR SOCIETY?
NAH...
MIMOSA! NO! MIDNIGHT MIMOSA?
MAYBE...
THE MAGIC WAND!
PROBABLY COPYRIGHTED.
SUNDAY BRUNCH? AFTER OUR FAVORITE ACTIVITY!
WEIRD FOR A SATURDAY NIGHT PARTY...
ART TRASH

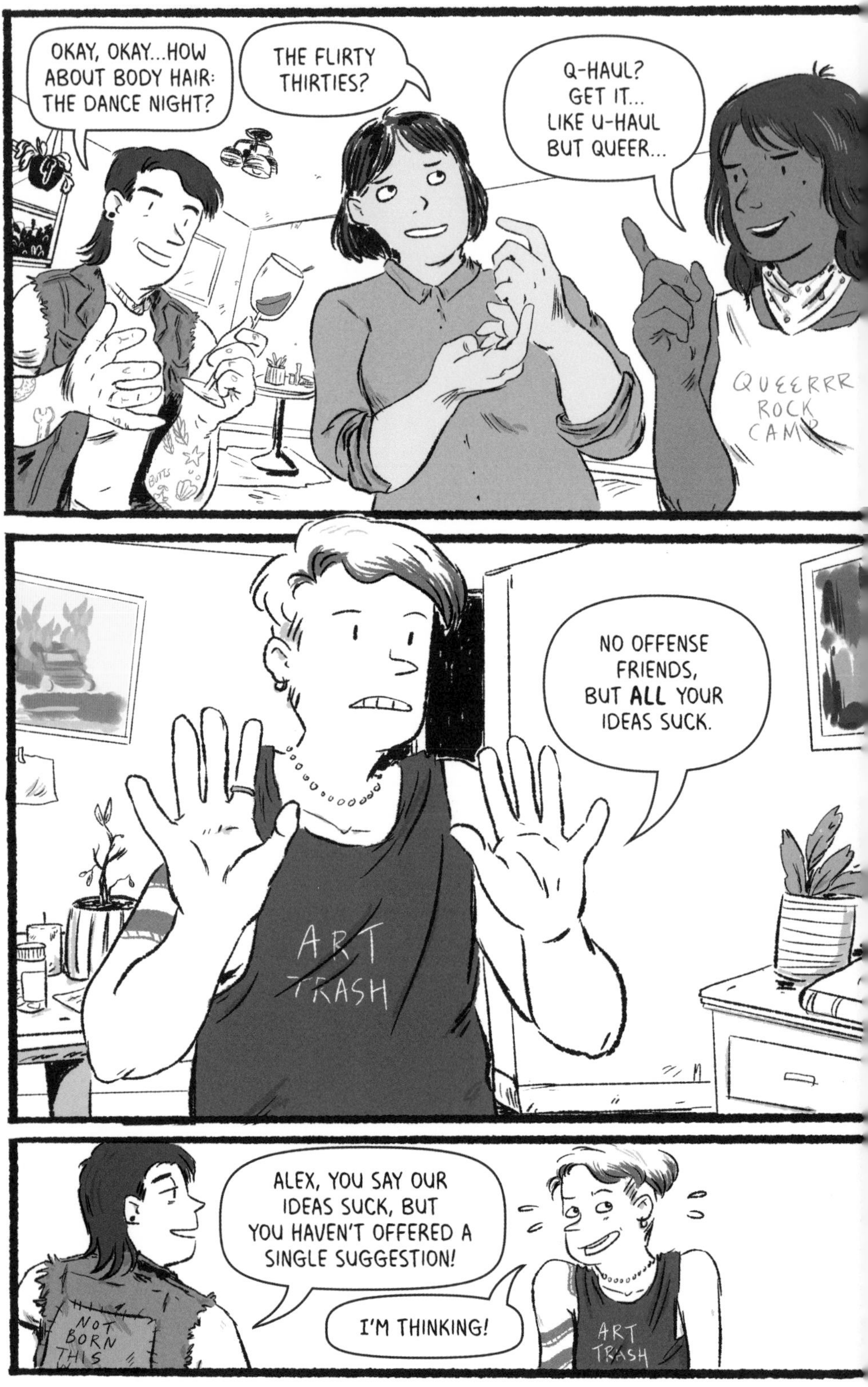
OKAY, OKAY...HOW ABOUT BODY HAIR: THE DANCE NIGHT?
THE FLIRTY THIRTIES?
Q-HAUL? GET IT... LIKE U-HAUL BUT QUEER...
QUEERRR ROCK CAMP
BUTTS
NO OFFENSE FRIENDS, BUT **ALL** YOUR IDEAS SUCK.
ART TRASH
ALEX, YOU SAY OUR IDEAS SUCK, BUT YOU HAVEN'T OFFERED A SINGLE SUGGESTION!
I'M THINKING!
NOT BORN THIS
ART TRASH

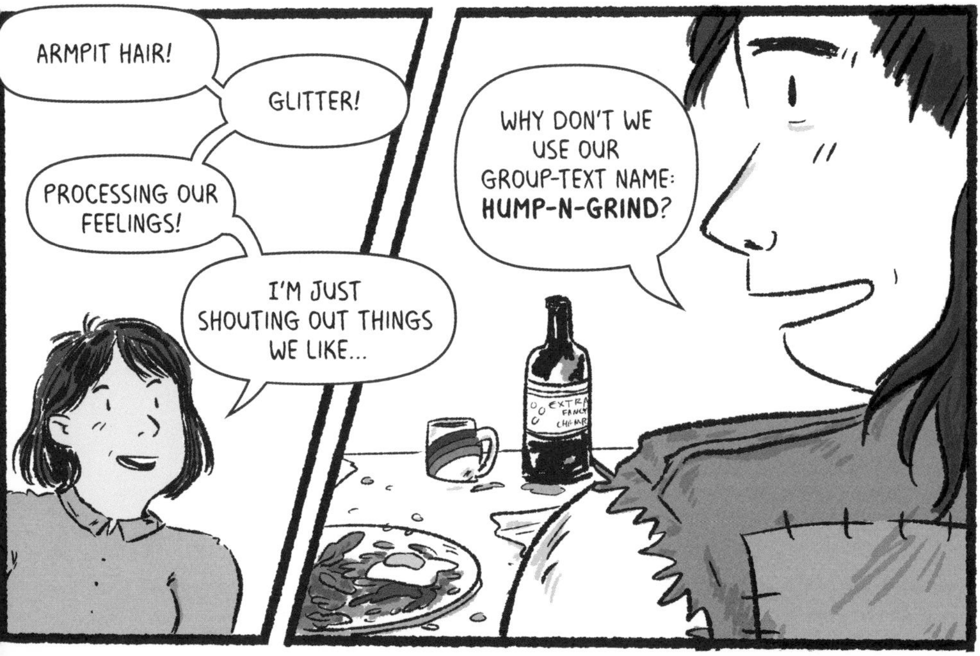
ARMPIT HAIR!
GLITTER!
PROCESSING OUR FEELINGS!
I'M JUST SHOUTING OUT THINGS WE LIKE...
WHY DON'T WE USE OUR GROUP-TEXT NAME: **HUMP-N-GRIND**?
EXTRA FANCY CHAMP

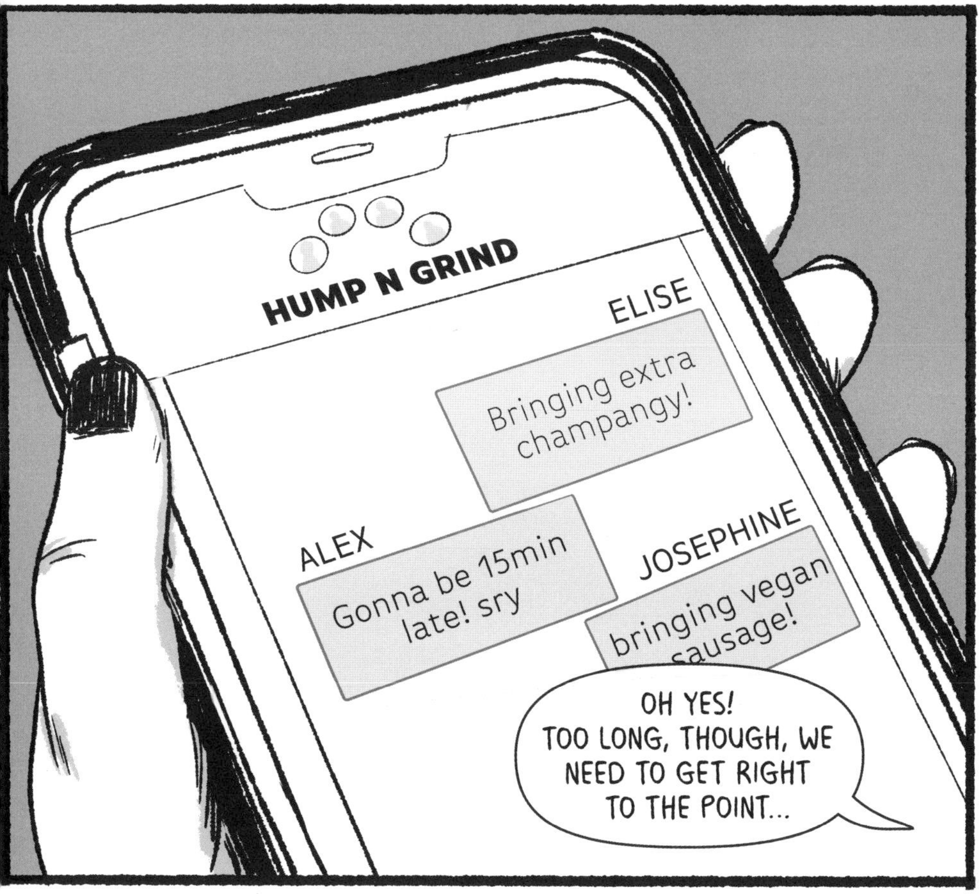
HUMP N GRIND
ELISE
Bringing extra champangy!
ALEX
Gonna be 15min late! sry
JOSEPHINE
bringing vegan sausage!
OH YES! TOO LONG, THOUGH, WE NEED TO GET RIGHT TO THE POINT...

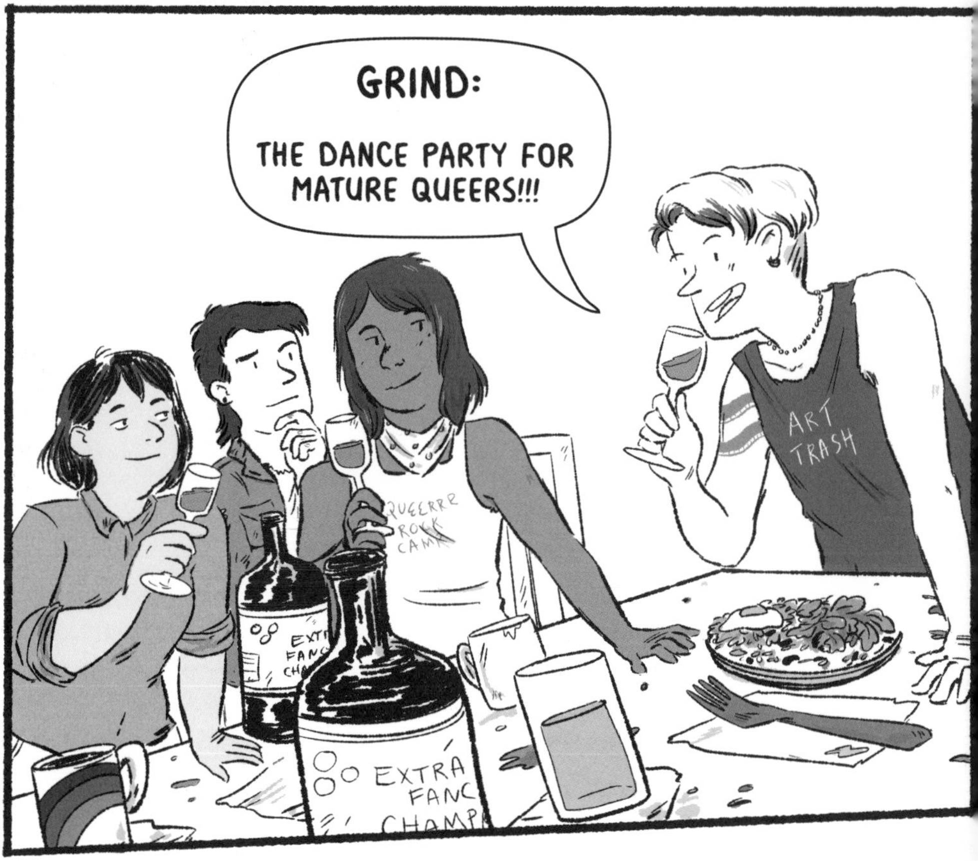
GRIND:
THE DANCE PARTY FOR MATURE QUEERS!!!
QUEERRR ROCK CAMP
ART TRASH
EXTRA FANC CHAMP

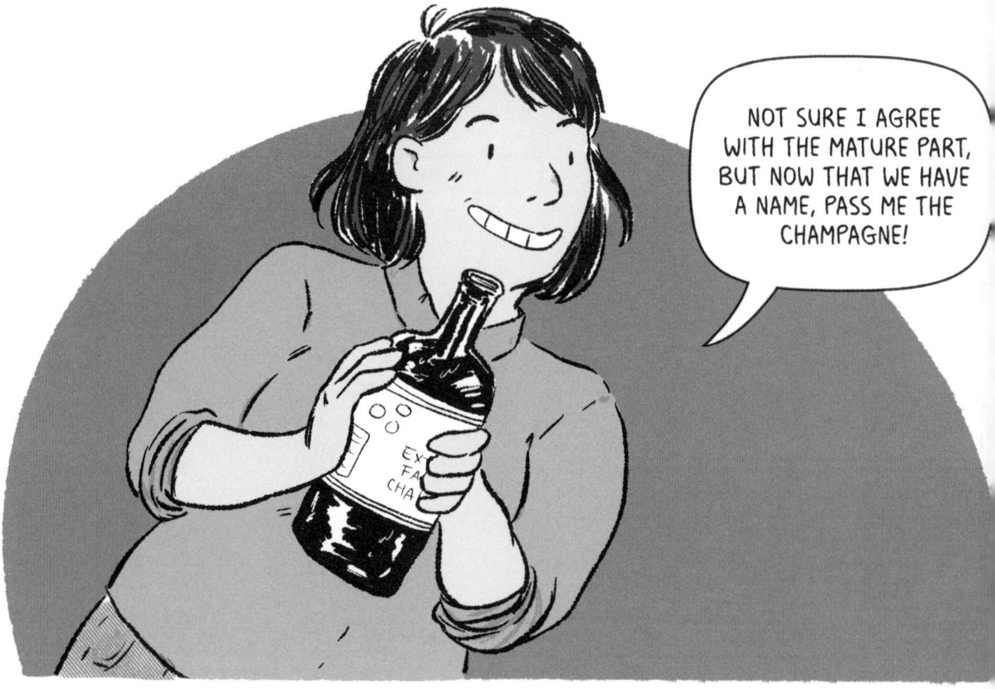
NOT SURE I AGREE WITH THE MATURE PART, BUT NOW THAT WE HAVE A NAME, PASS ME THE CHAMPAGNE!

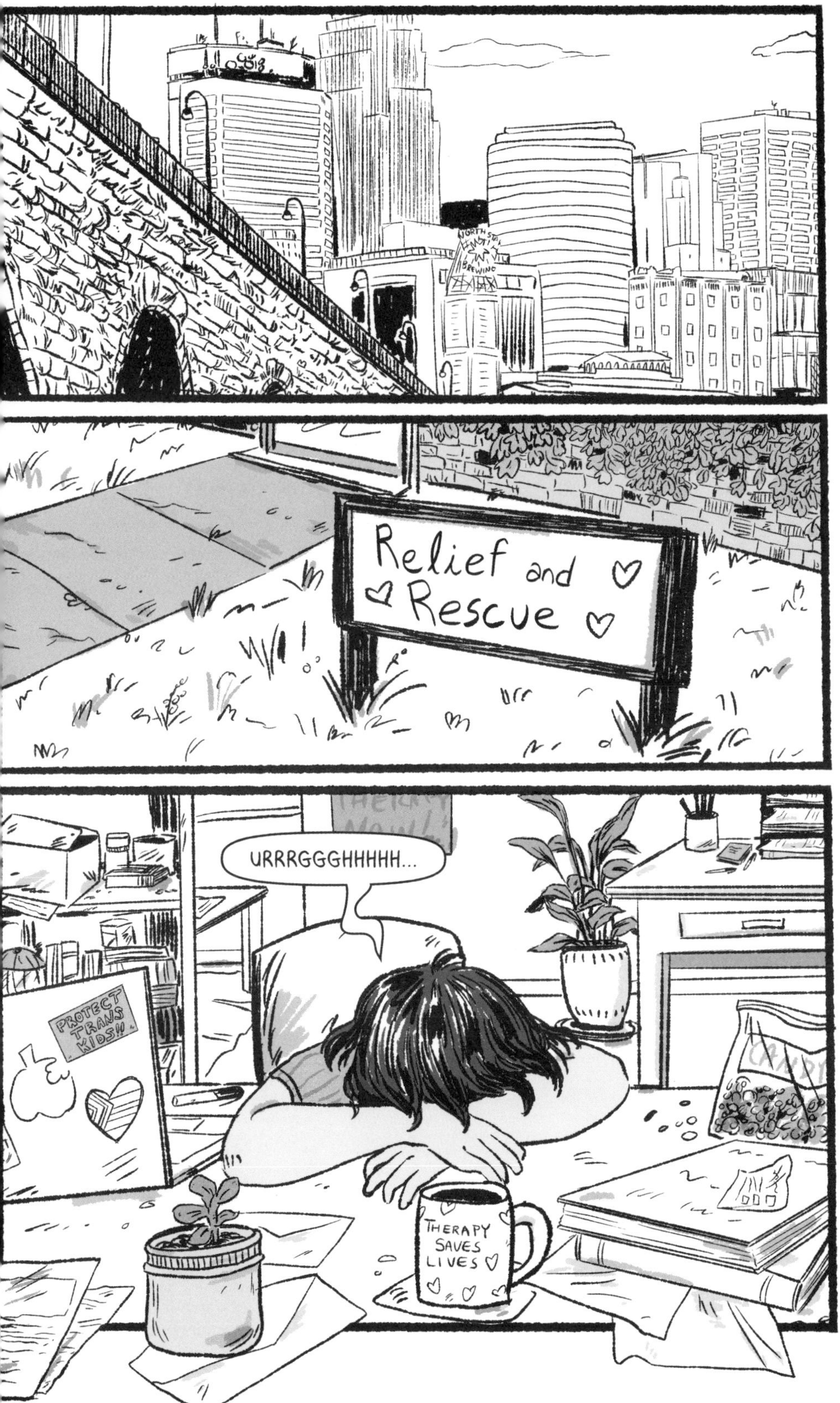
Relief and Rescue
URRRGGGHHHHH...
PROTECT TRANS KIDS!!
THERAPY SAVES LIVES

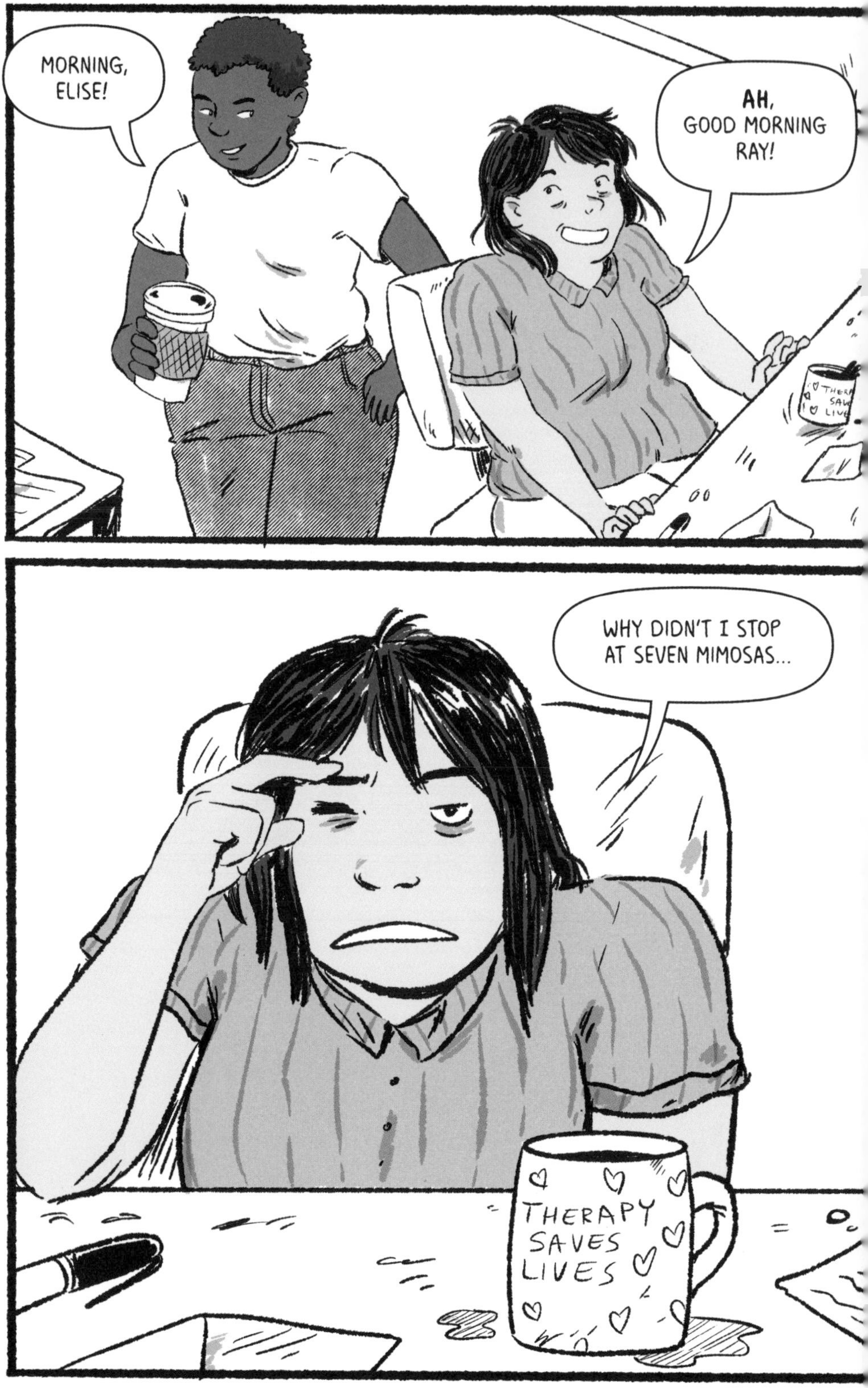
MORNING, ELISE!
AH, GOOD MORNING RAY!
THERAPY SAVES LIVES
WHY DIDN'T I STOP AT SEVEN MIMOSAS...
THERAPY SAVES LIVES

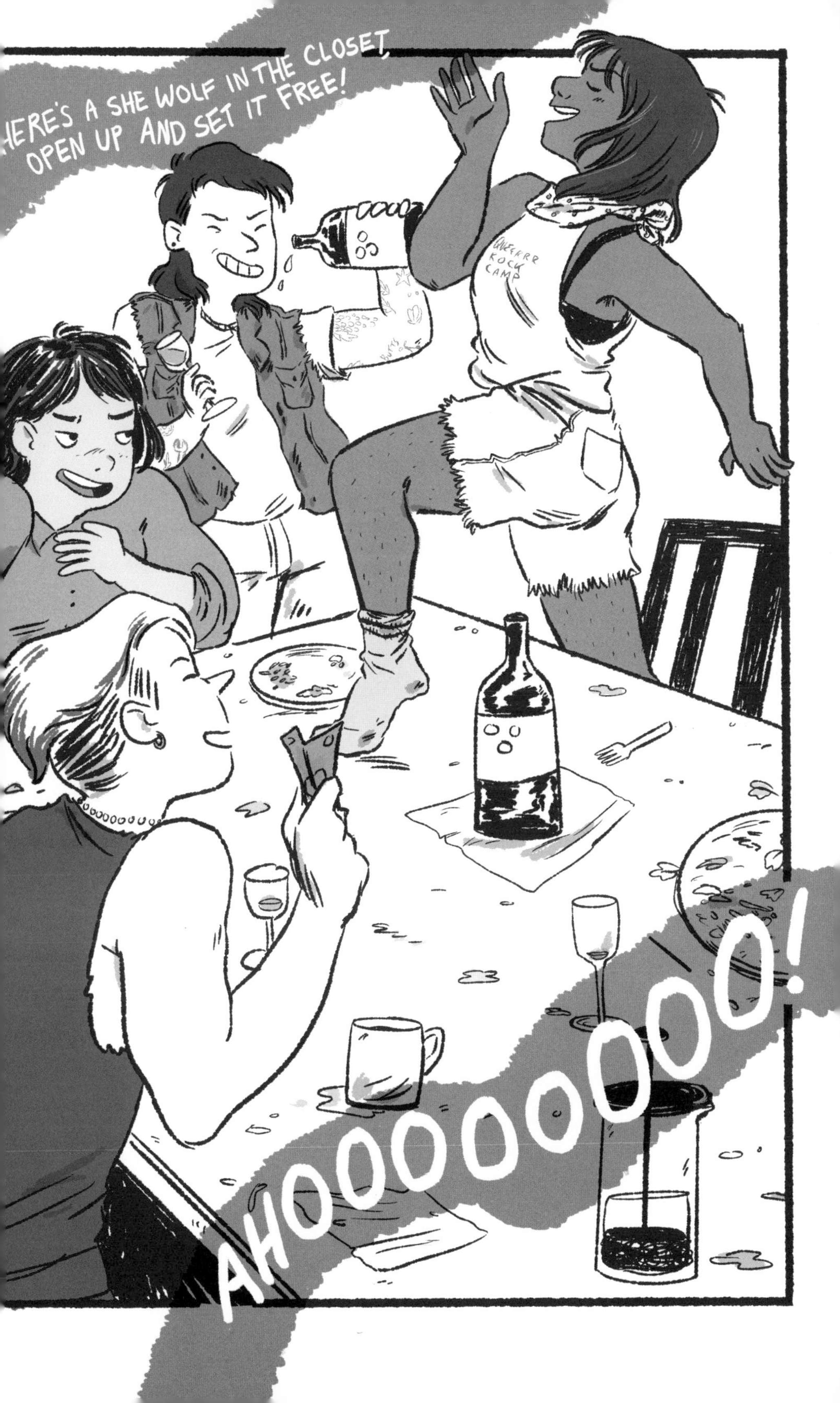
HERE'S A SHE WOLF IN THE CLOSET, OPEN UP AND SET IT FREE!
QUEERRR ROCK CAMP
AHOOOOOOOOO!

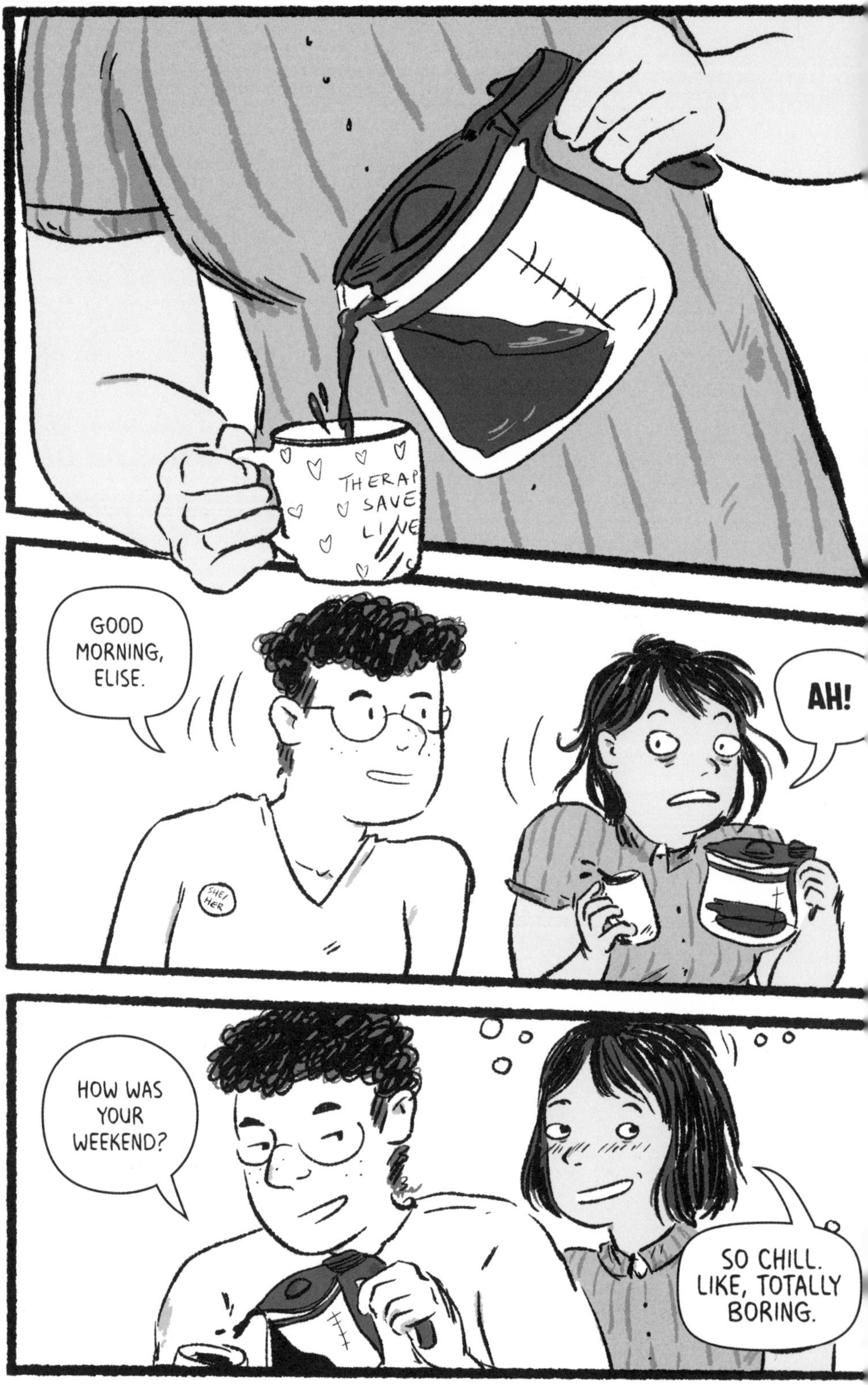

GOOD MORNING, ELISE.
AH!
SHE/HER
HOW WAS YOUR WEEKEND?
SO CHILL. LIKE, TOTALLY BORING.

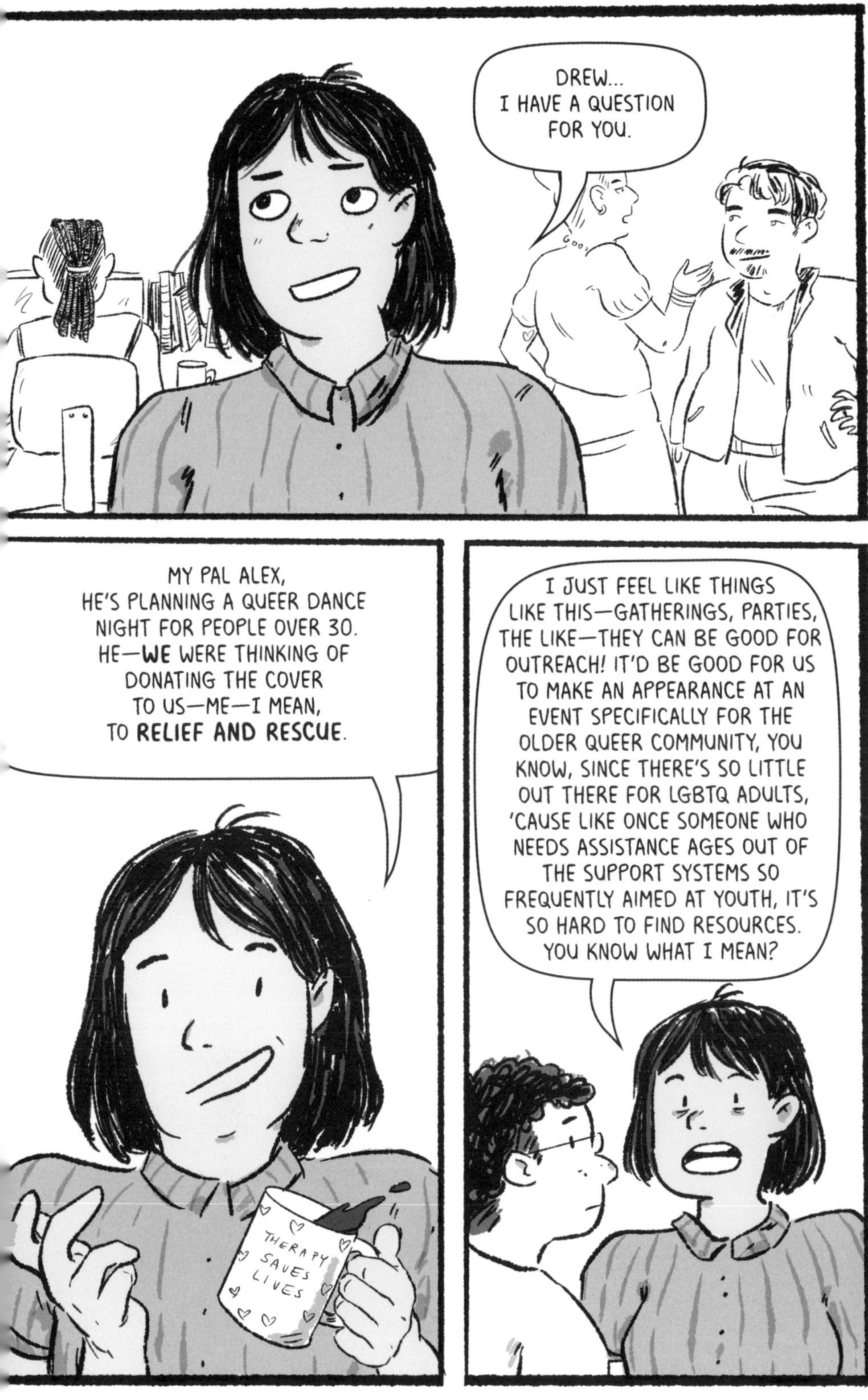
DREW... I HAVE A QUESTION FOR YOU.
MY PAL ALEX, HE'S PLANNING A QUEER DANCE NIGHT FOR PEOPLE OVER 30. HE—**WE** WERE THINKING OF DONATING THE COVER TO US—ME—I MEAN, TO **RELIEF AND RESCUE**.
THERAPY SAVES LIVES
I JUST FEEL LIKE THINGS LIKE THIS—GATHERINGS, PARTIES, THE LIKE—THEY CAN BE GOOD FOR OUTREACH! IT'D BE GOOD FOR US TO MAKE AN APPEARANCE AT AN EVENT SPECIFICALLY FOR THE OLDER QUEER COMMUNITY, YOU KNOW, SINCE THERE'S SO LITTLE OUT THERE FOR LGBTQ ADULTS, 'CAUSE LIKE ONCE SOMEONE WHO NEEDS ASSISTANCE AGES OUT OF THE SUPPORT SYSTEMS SO FREQUENTLY AIMED AT YOUTH, IT'S SO HARD TO FIND RESOURCES. YOU KNOW WHAT I MEAN?

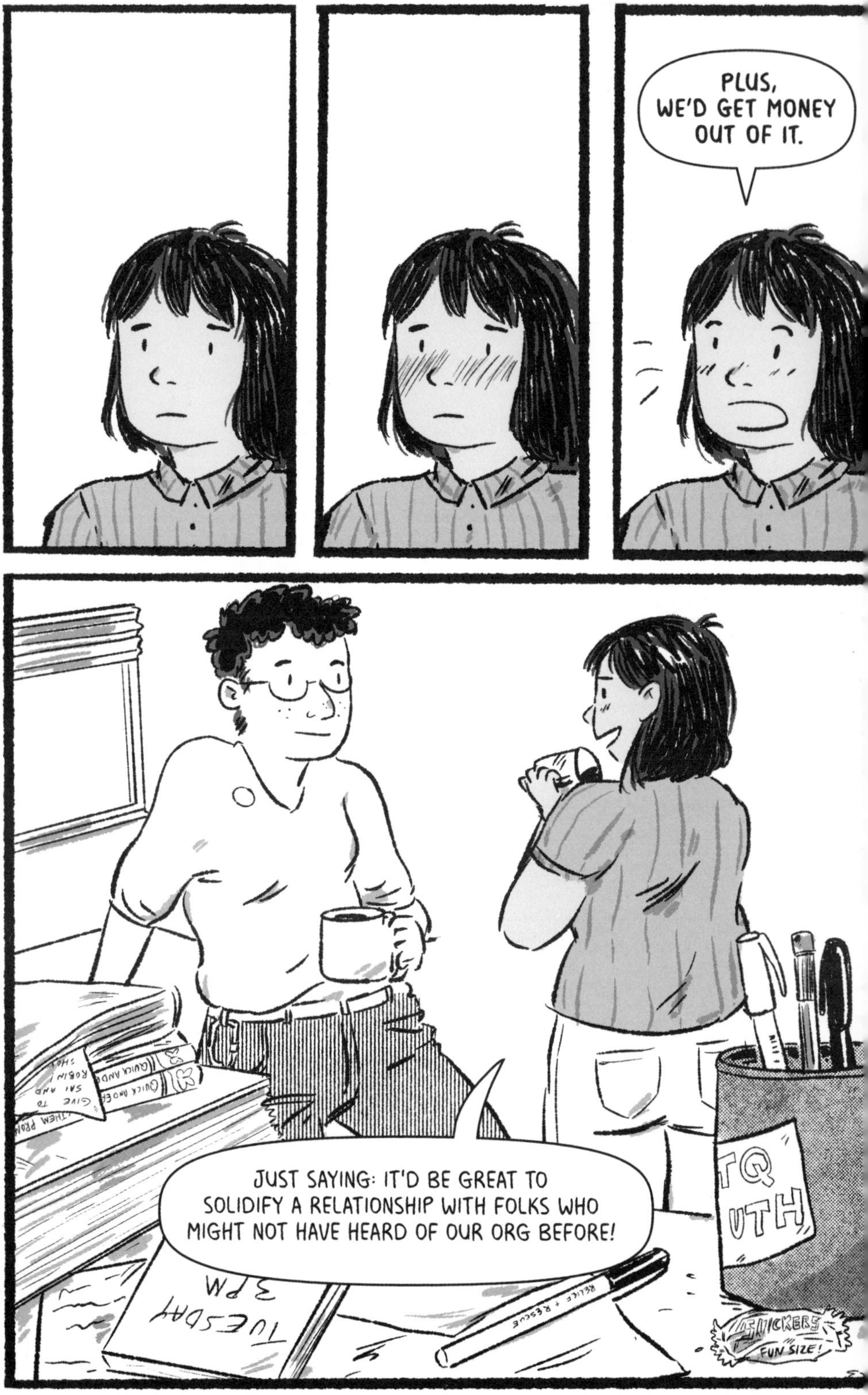
PLUS, WE'D GET MONEY OUT OF IT.
JUST SAYING: IT'D BE GREAT TO SOLIDIFY A RELATIONSHIP WITH FOLKS WHO MIGHT NOT HAVE HEARD OF OUR ORG BEFORE!
FUN SIZE!

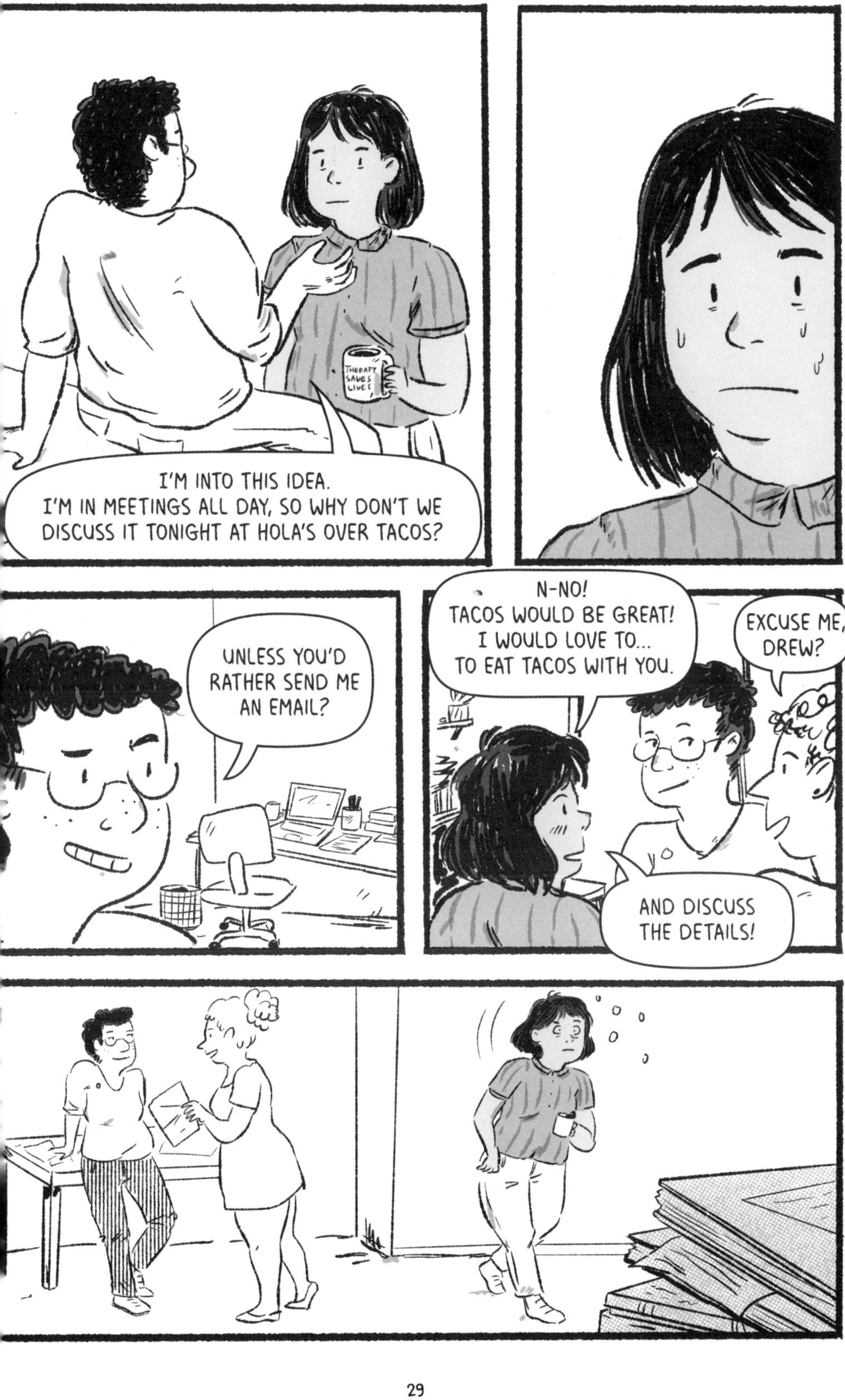
THERAPY SAVES LIVES
I'M INTO THIS IDEA. I'M IN MEETINGS ALL DAY, SO WHY DON'T WE DISCUSS IT TONIGHT AT HOLA'S OVER TACOS?
UNLESS YOU'D RATHER SEND ME AN EMAIL?
N-NO! TACOS WOULD BE GREAT! I WOULD LOVE TO... TO EAT TACOS WITH YOU.
AND DISCUSS THE DETAILS!
EXCUSE ME, DREW?

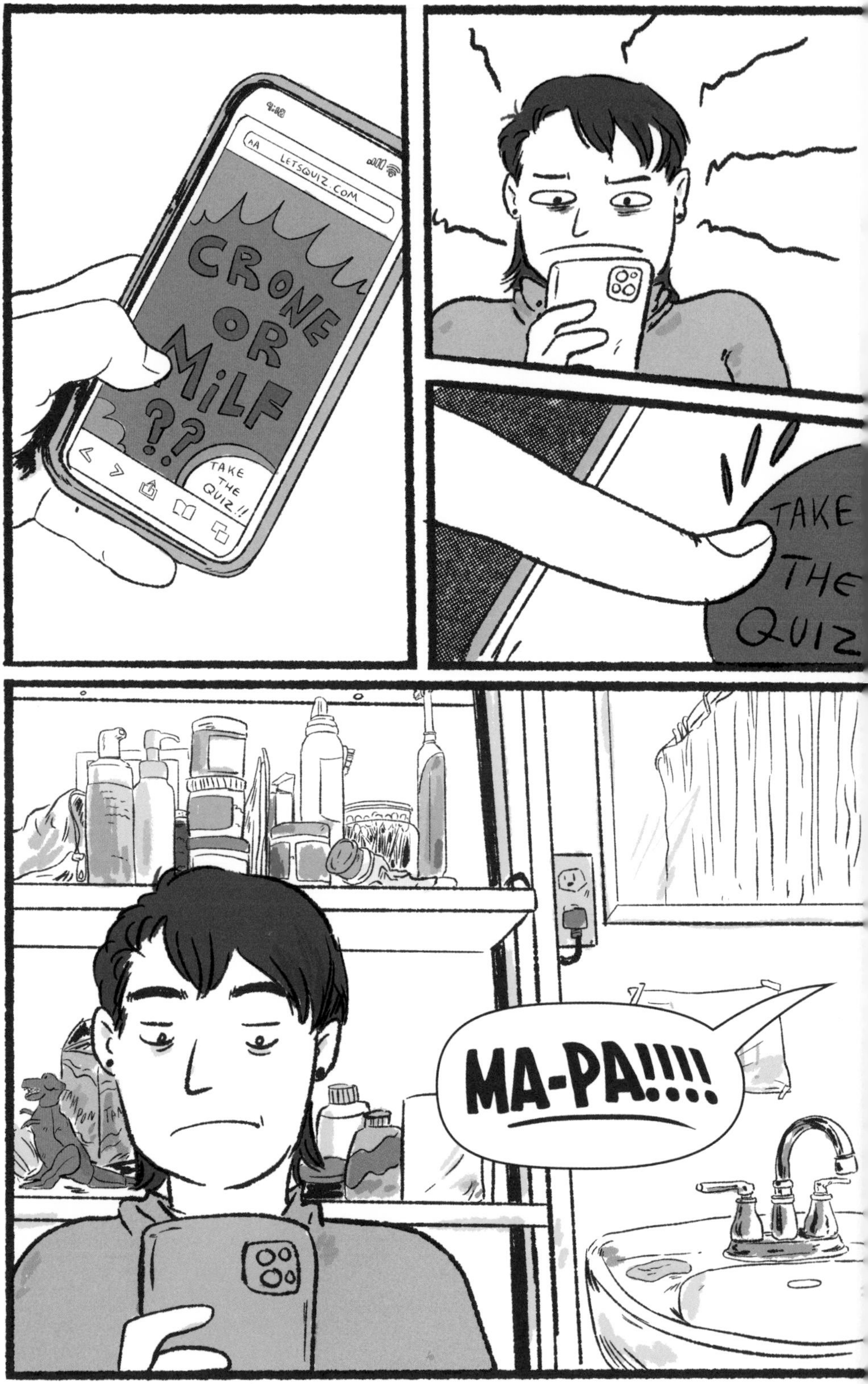
9:18
LETSQUIZ.COM
CRONE OR MILF ??
TAKE THE QUIZ!!
TAKE THE QUIZ
TAMPON
MA-PA!!!!

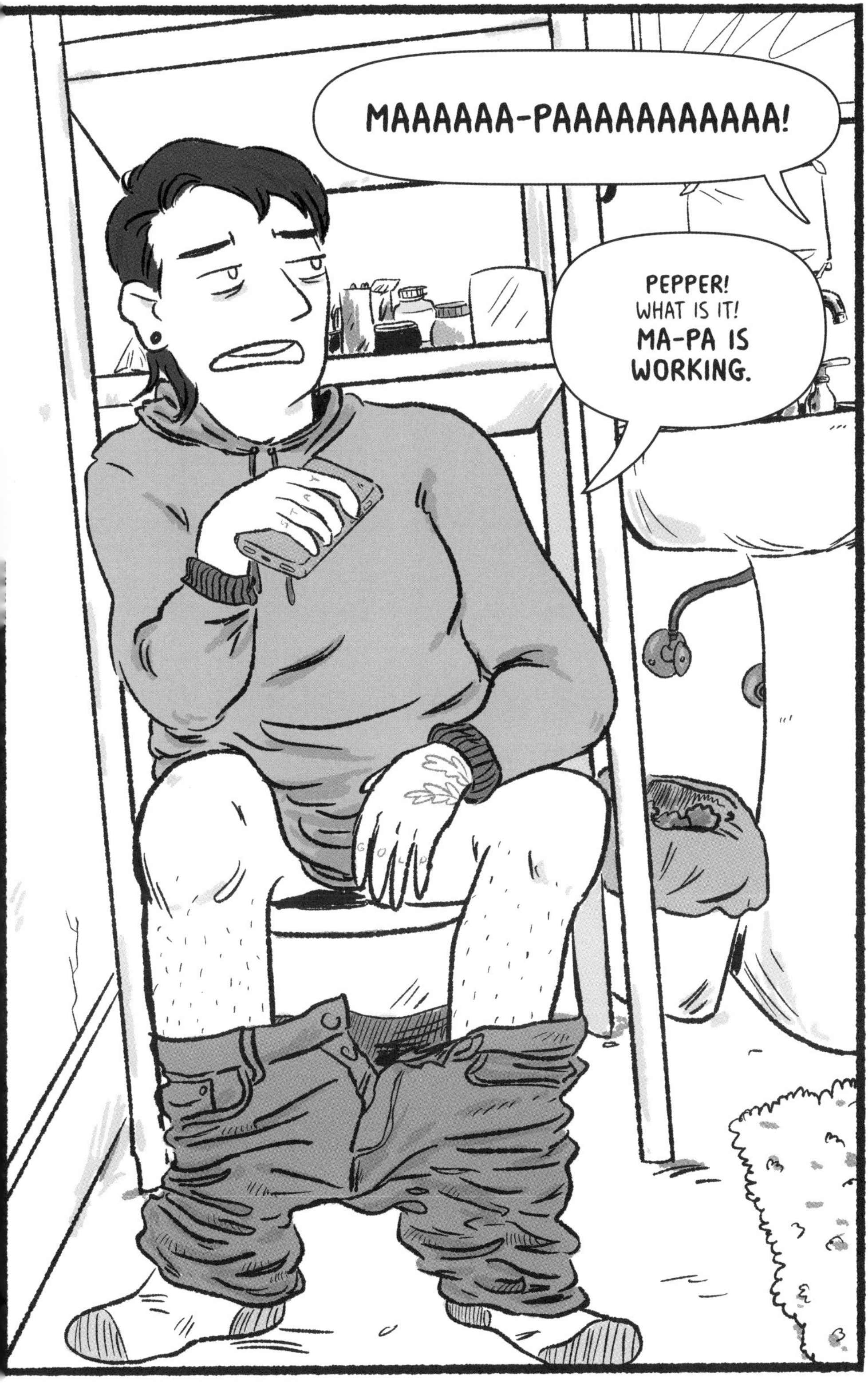
MAAAAAA-PAAAAAAAAAAA!
PEPPER! WHAT IS IT! MA-PA IS WORKING.

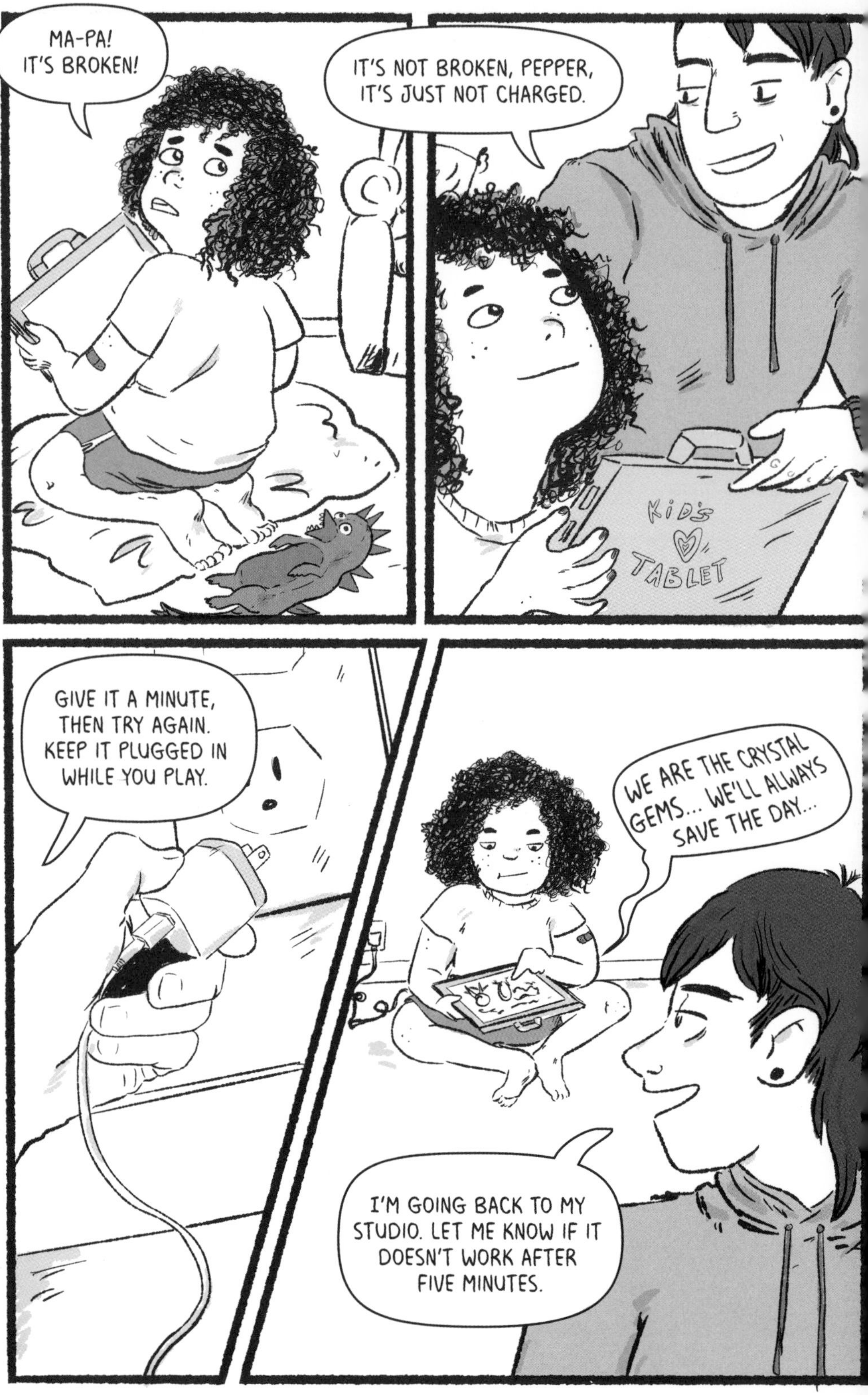
MA-PA! IT'S BROKEN!
IT'S NOT BROKEN, PEPPER, IT'S JUST NOT CHARGED.
KID'S TABLET
GIVE IT A MINUTE, THEN TRY AGAIN. KEEP IT PLUGGED IN WHILE YOU PLAY.
WE ARE THE CRYSTAL GEMS... WE'LL ALWAYS SAVE THE DAY...
I'M GOING BACK TO MY STUDIO. LET ME KNOW IF IT DOESN'T WORK AFTER FIVE MINUTES.

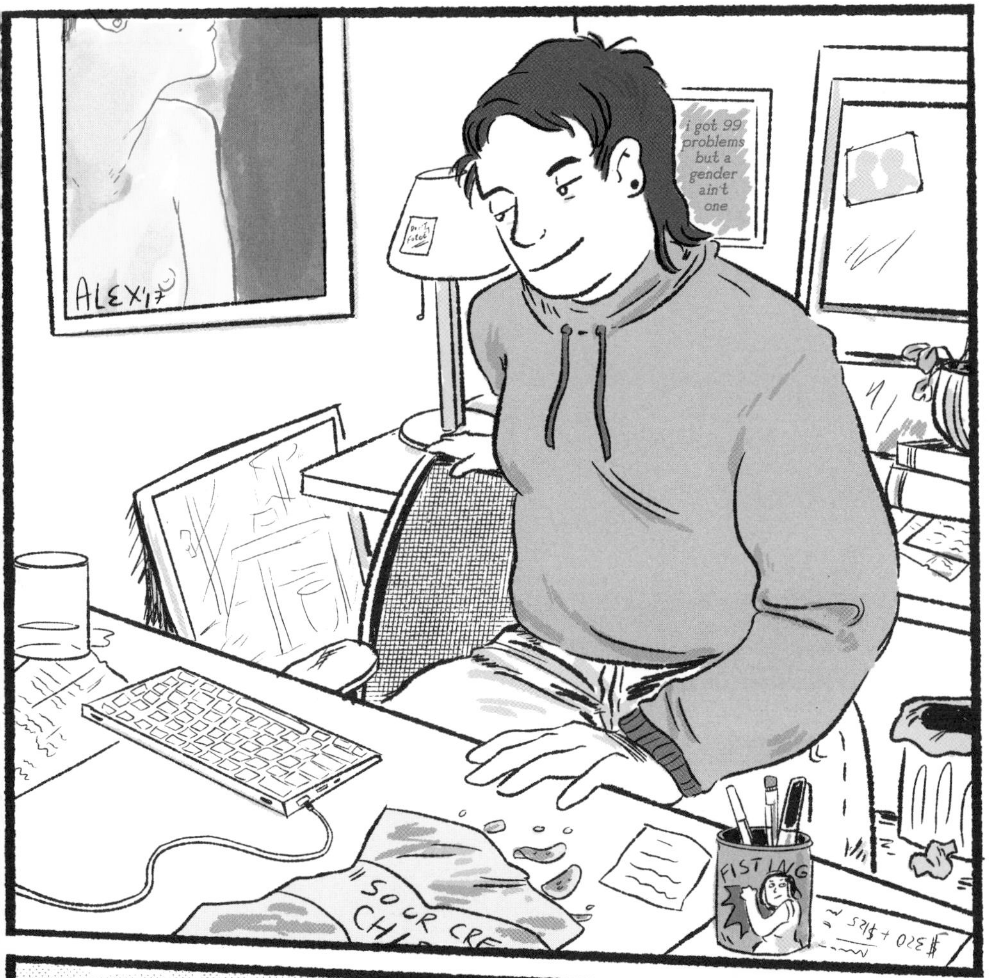

ALEX'17
i got 99 problems but a gender ain't one
FISTING

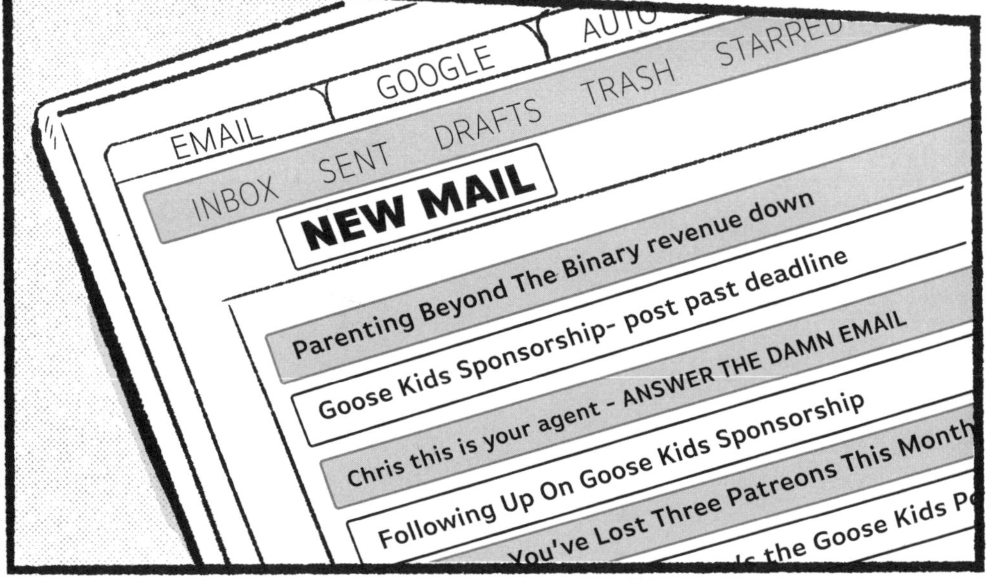

EMAIL
GOOGLE
INBOX
SENT
DRAFTS
TRASH
STARRED
NEW MAIL
Parenting Beyond The Binary revenue down
Goose Kids Sponsorship- post past deadline
Chris this is your agent - ANSWER THE DAMN EMAIL
Following Up On Goose Kids Sponsorship
You've Lost Three Patreons This Month

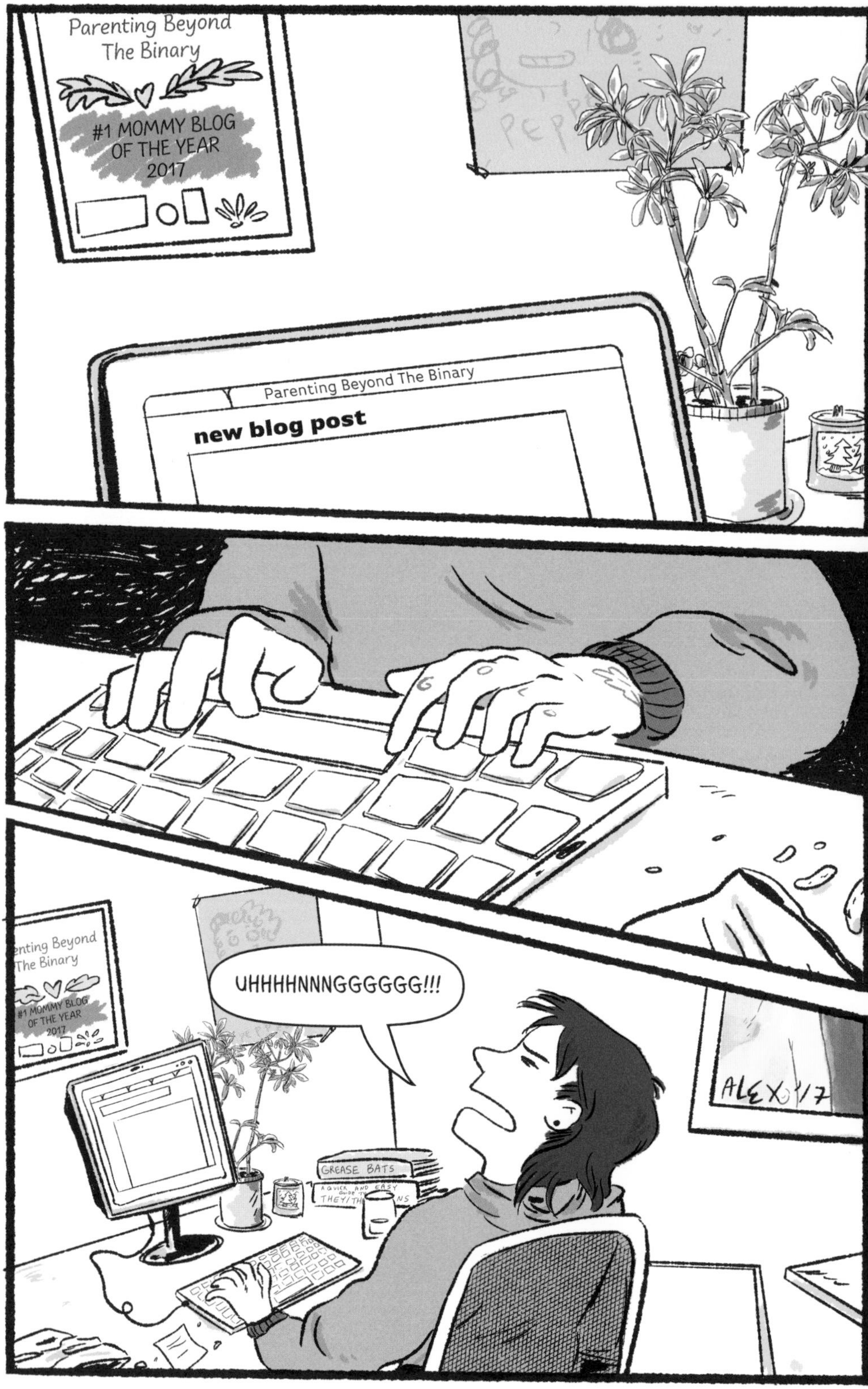

Parenting Beyond The Binary
#1 MOMMY BLOG OF THE YEAR 2017
Parenting Beyond The Binary
new blog post
UHHHHNNNGGGGGG!!!
GREASE BATS
ALEX '17

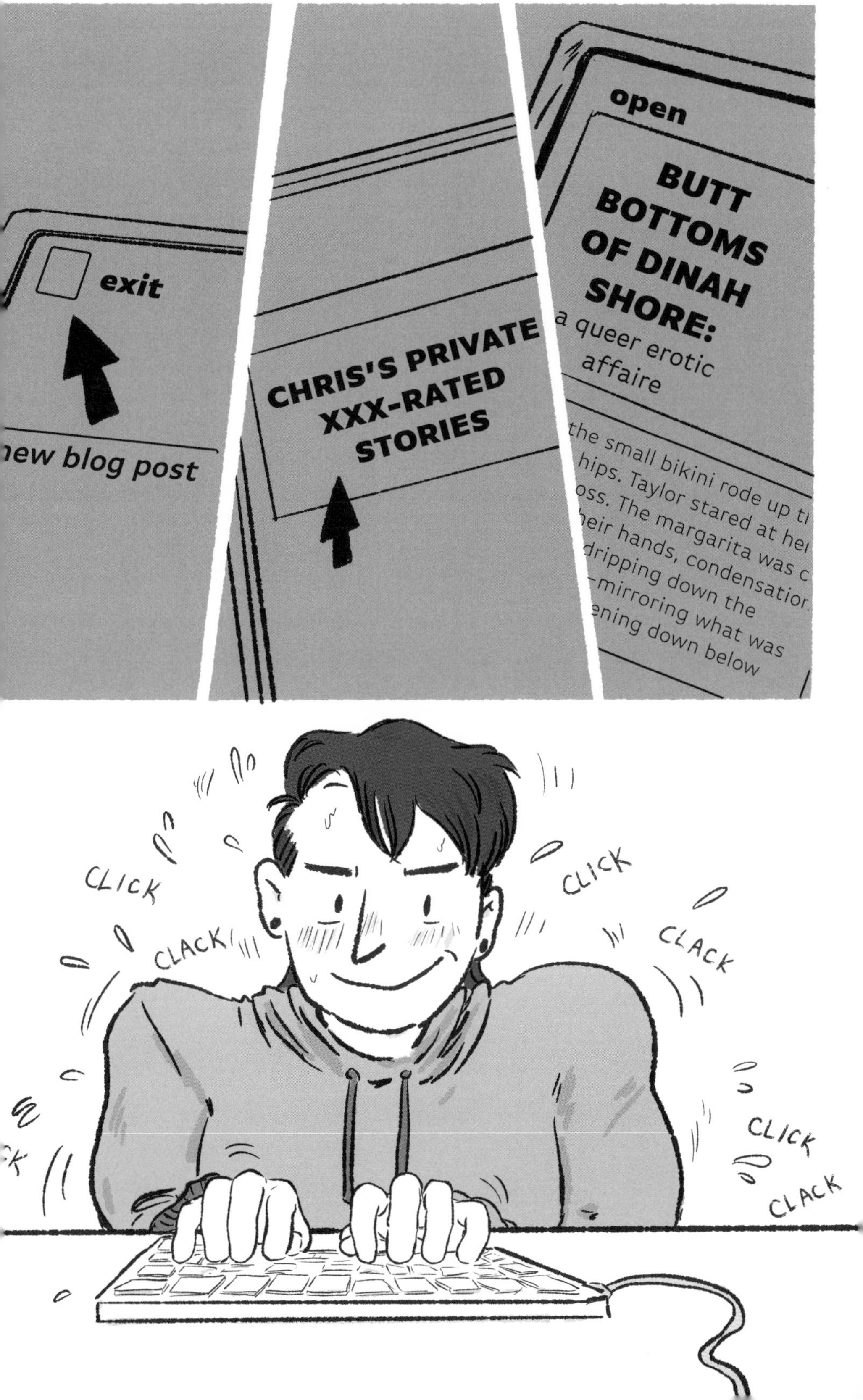
exit
new blog post
CHRIS'S PRIVATE XXX-RATED STORIES
open
BUTT BOTTOMS OF DINAH SHORE:
a queer erotic affaire
CLICK
CLACK
CLICK
CLACK
CLICK
CLACK

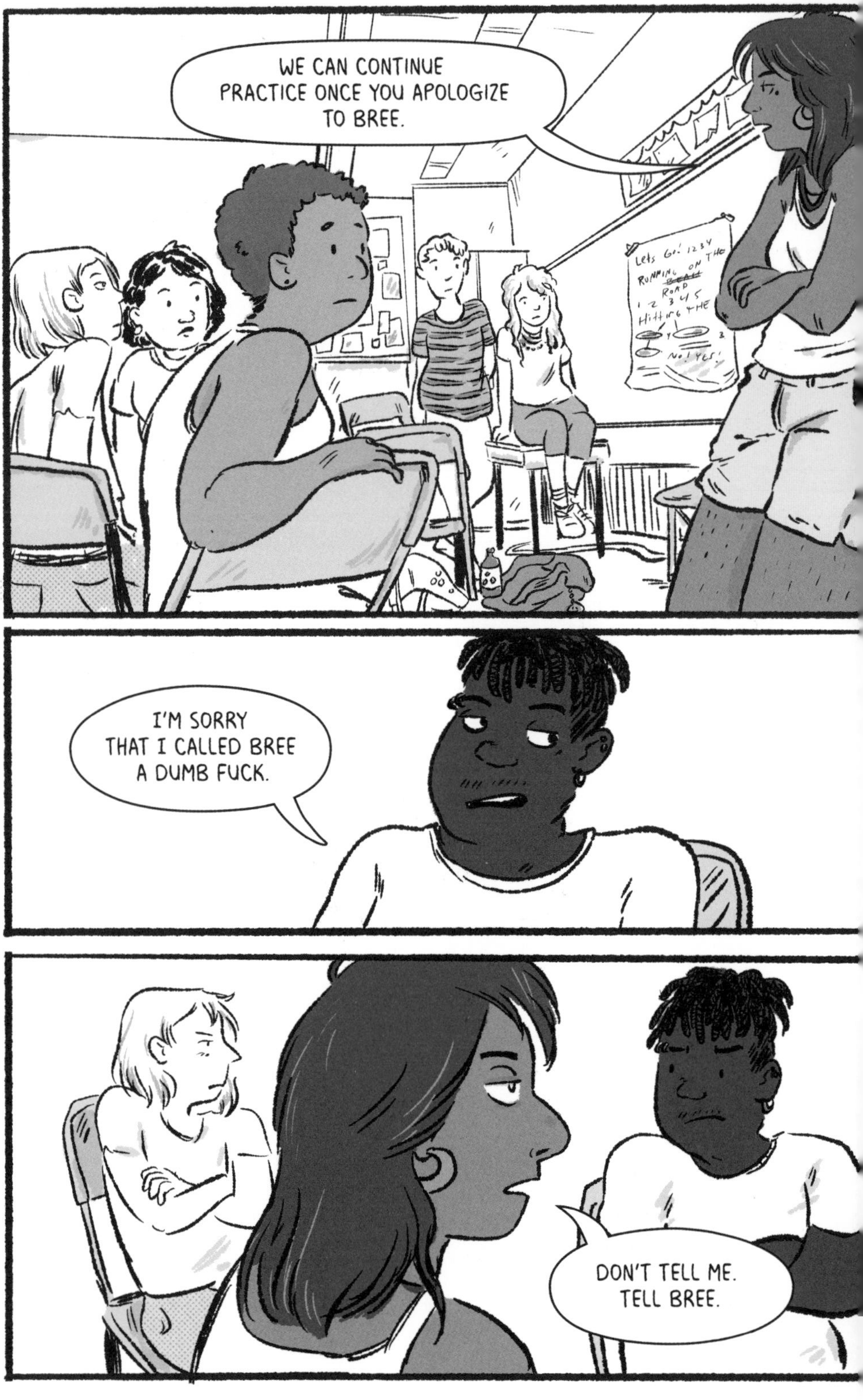
WE CAN CONTINUE PRACTICE ONCE YOU APOLOGIZE TO BREE.
I'M SORRY THAT I CALLED BREE A DUMB FUCK.
DON'T TELL ME. TELL BREE.

I'M SORRY I CALLED YOU A DUMB FUCK.

THAT'S GOOD ENOUGH, I GUESS.

QUEERRR ROCK CAMP ISN'T JUST TO LEARN MUSIC, IT'S A WAY FOR US TO PRACTICE BEING IN COMMUNITY WITH EACH OTHER! IT'S A CHANCE FOR US TO CREATE A CHOSEN FAMILY!

I WOULDN'T JUST BE WHO I AM TODAY WITHOUT MY FRIENDS—I WOULDN'T **BE**, PERIOD.

RIGHT?

AND WE'RE GONNA START BY LEARNING TRUE TRANS SOUL REBEL!

YES!!!!

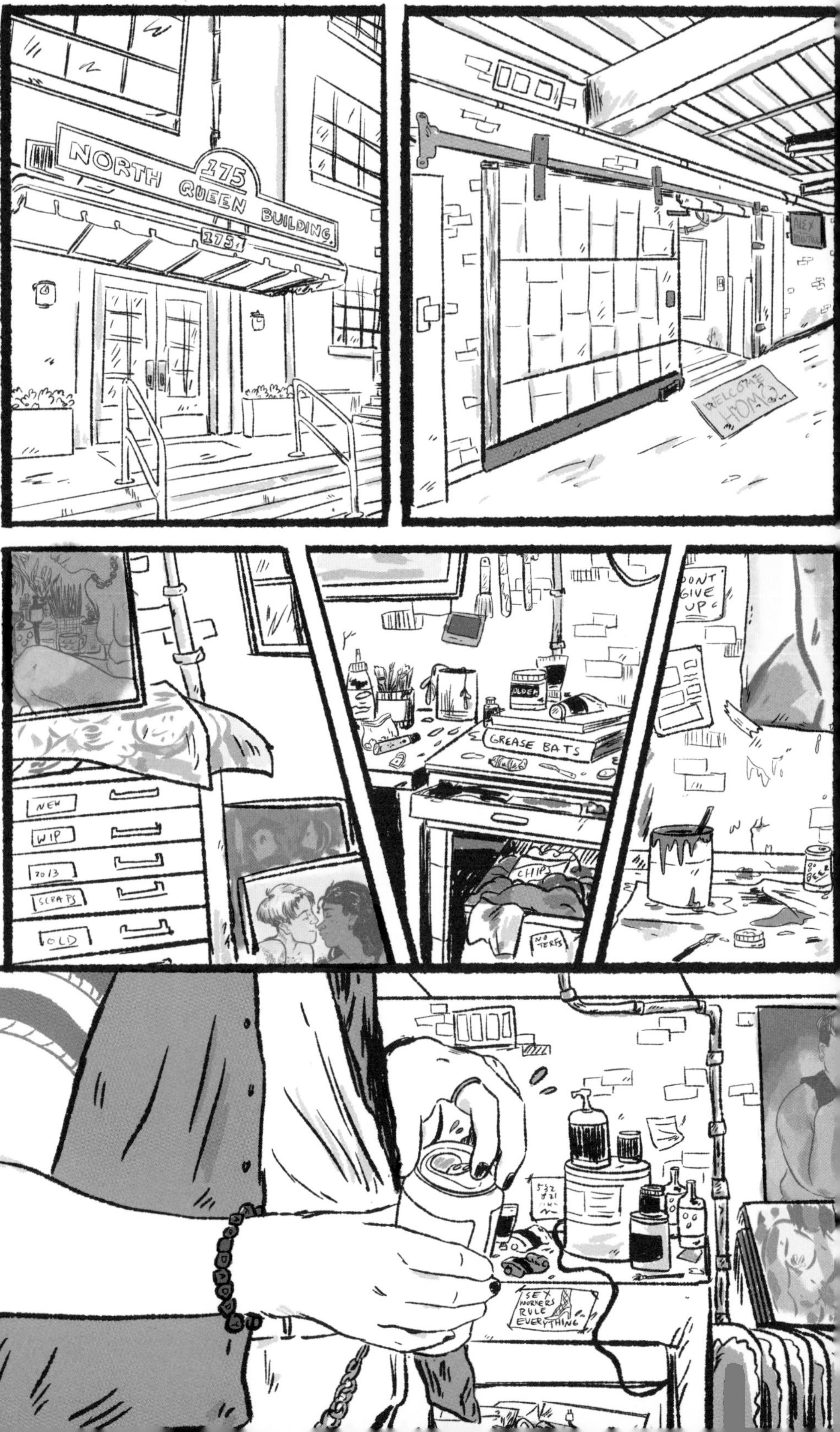
NORTH 175 QUEEN BUILDING
175
WELCOME HOMO
NEW
WIP
2013
SCRAPS
OLD
GREASE BATS
CHIP
NO TERFS
DONT GIVE UP
BEER
SEX WORKERS RULE EVERYTHING

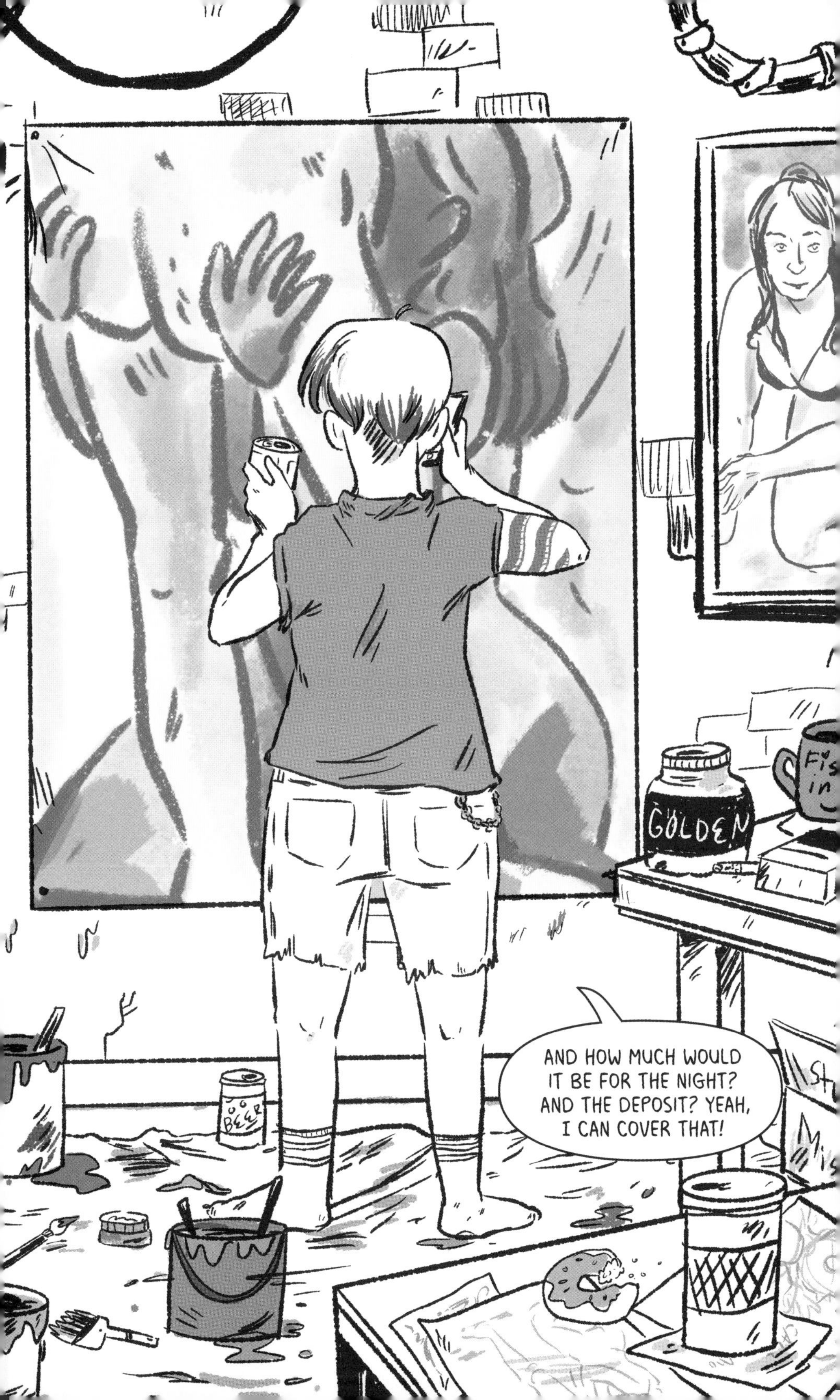
GOLDEN
BEER
AND HOW MUCH WOULD IT BE FOR THE NIGHT? AND THE DEPOSIT? YEAH, I CAN COVER THAT!

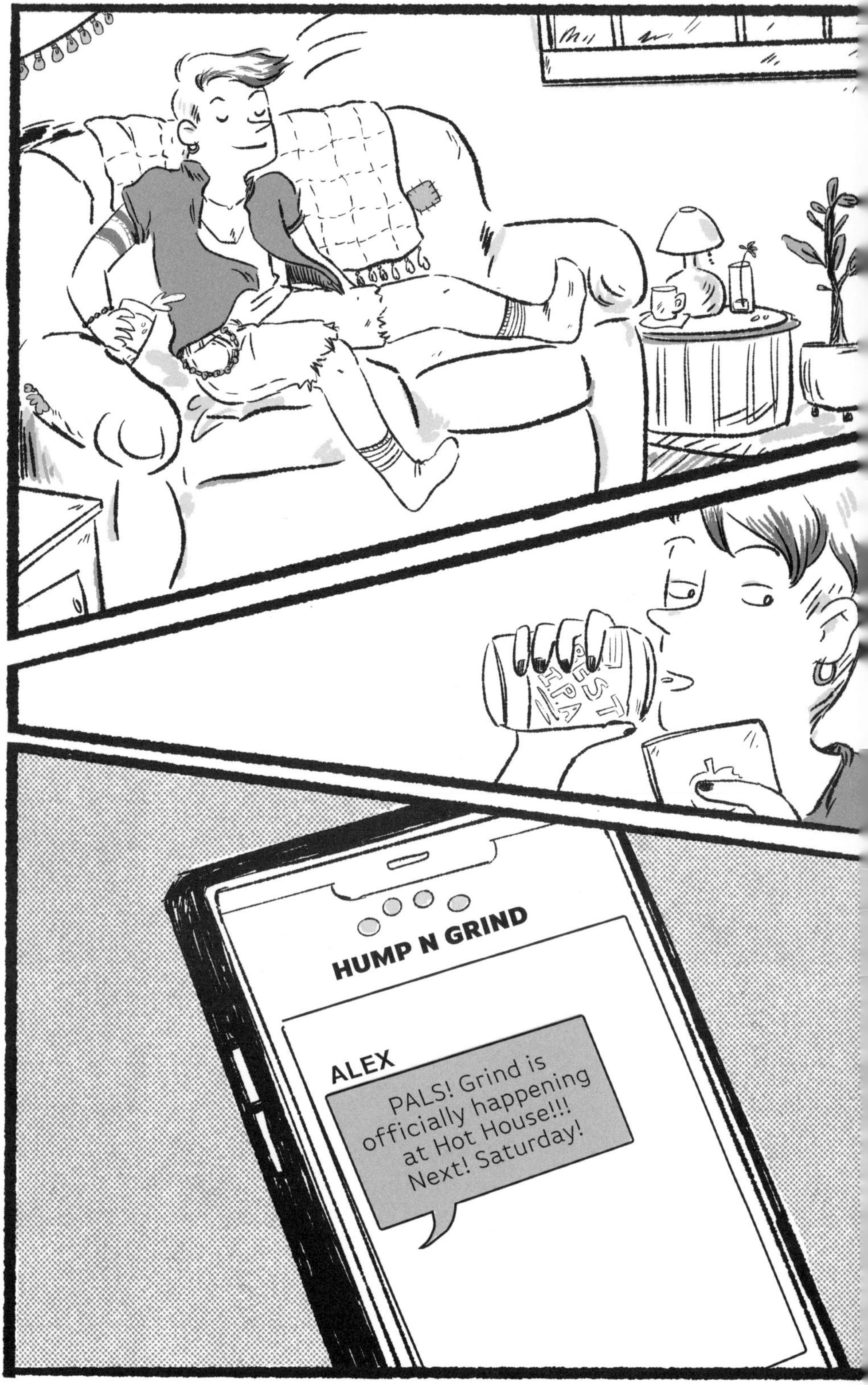

HUMP N GRIND
ALEX
PALS! Grind is officially happening at Hot House!!! Next! Saturday!

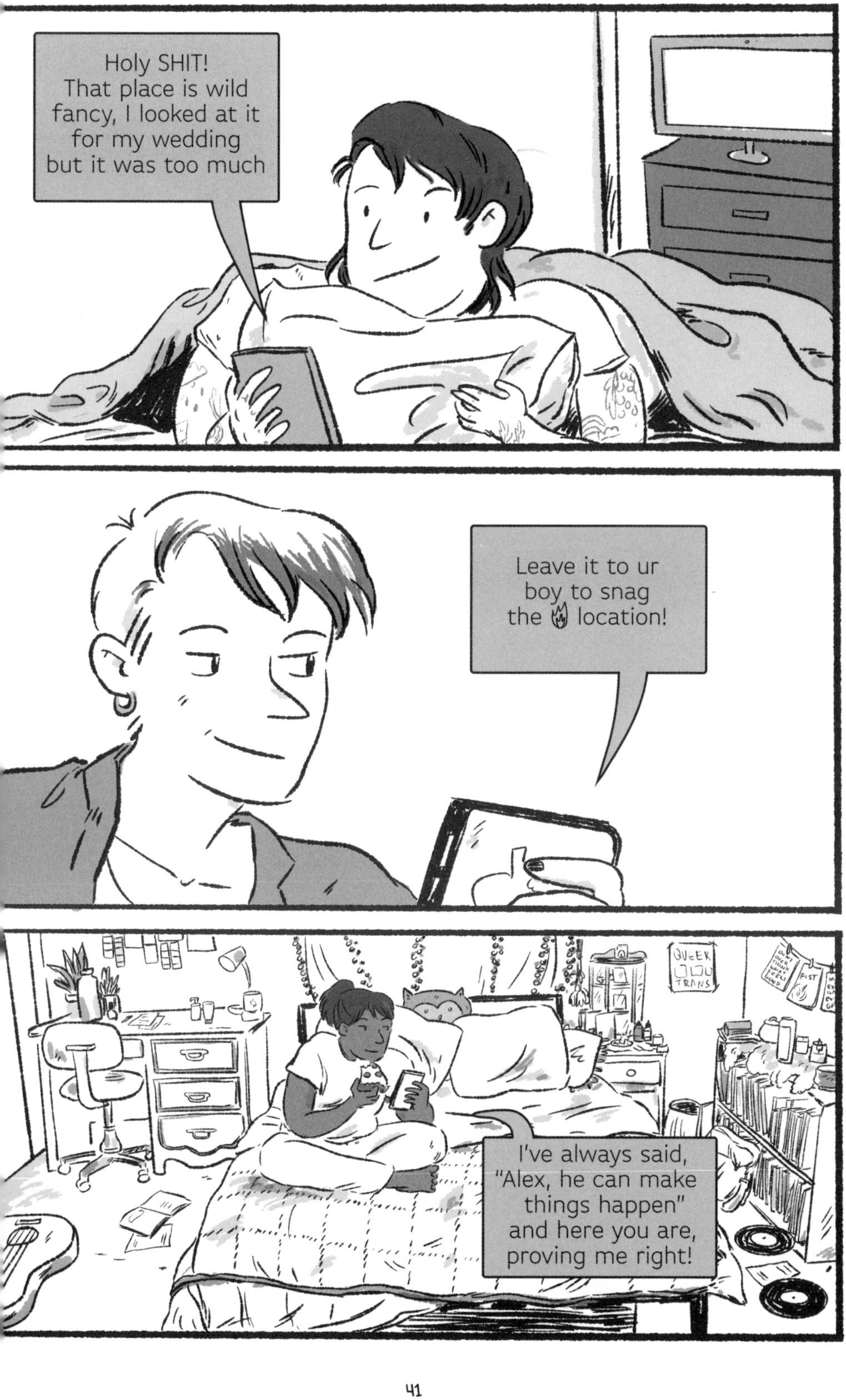
Holy SHIT! That place is wild fancy, I looked at it for my wedding but it was too much
Leave it to ur boy to snag the 🔥 location!
I've always said, "Alex, he can make things happen" and here you are, proving me right!

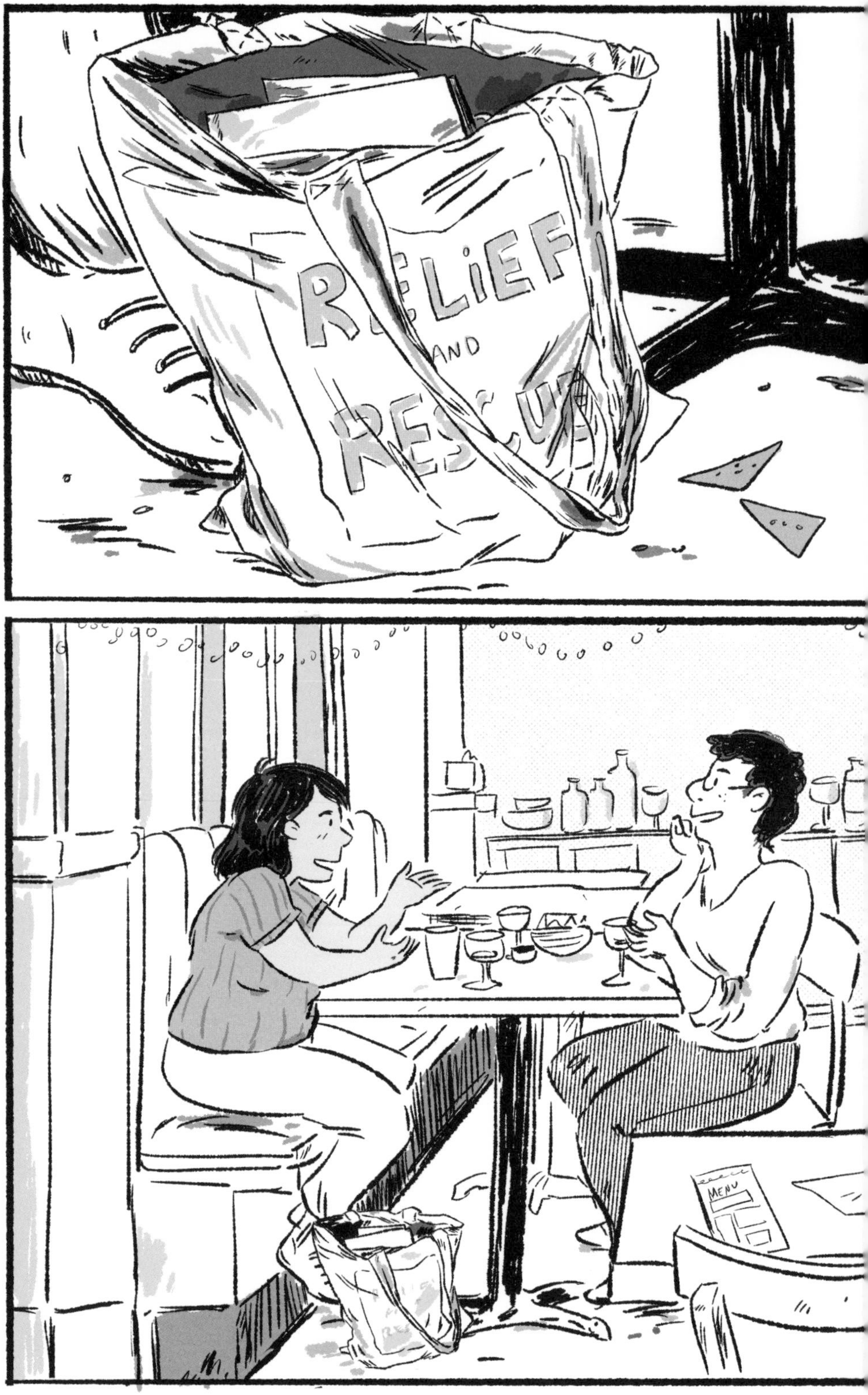
RELiEF
AND
RESCUE
MENU

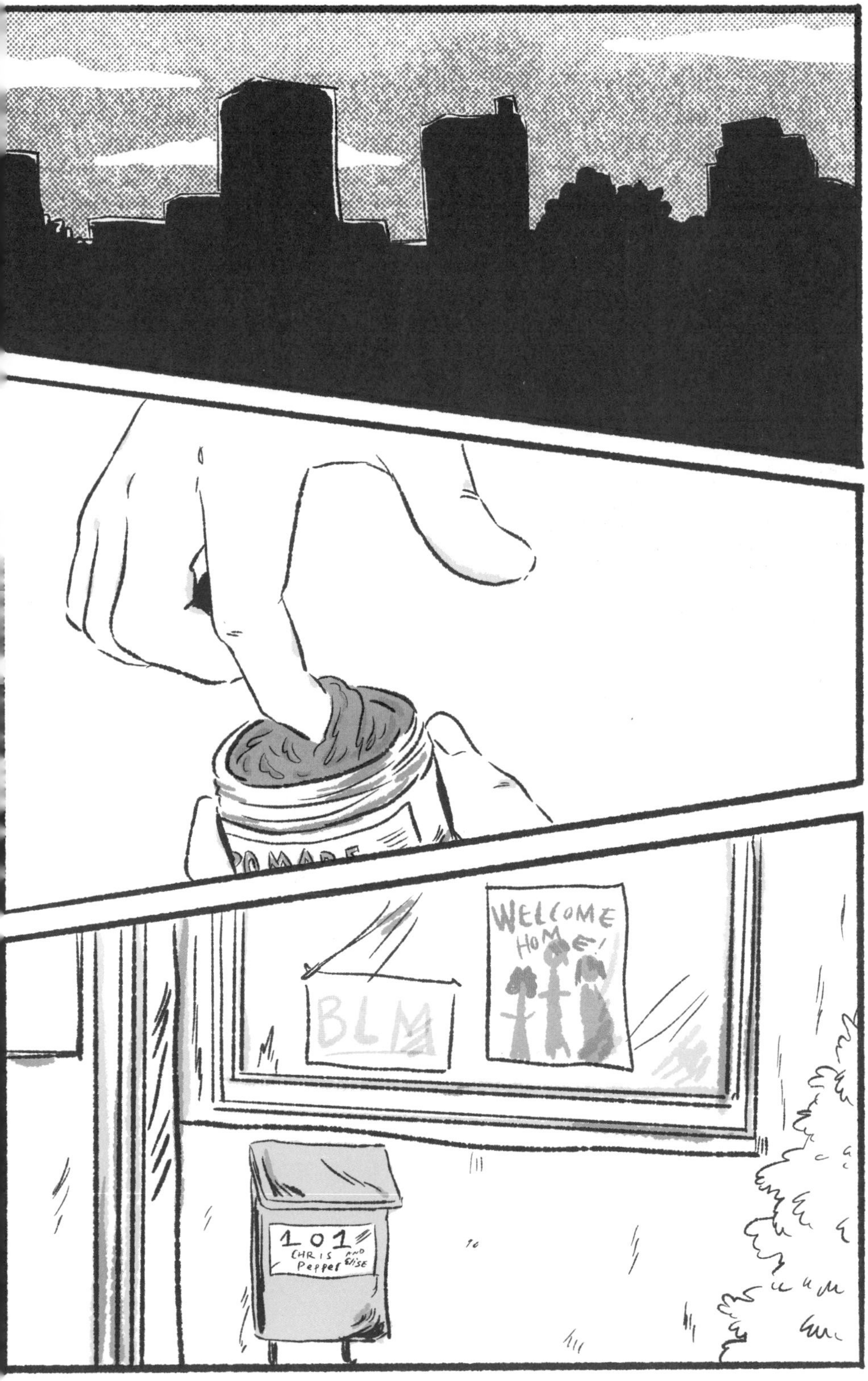
POMADE
BLM
WELCOME HOME!
101
CHRIS Pepper AND Elise

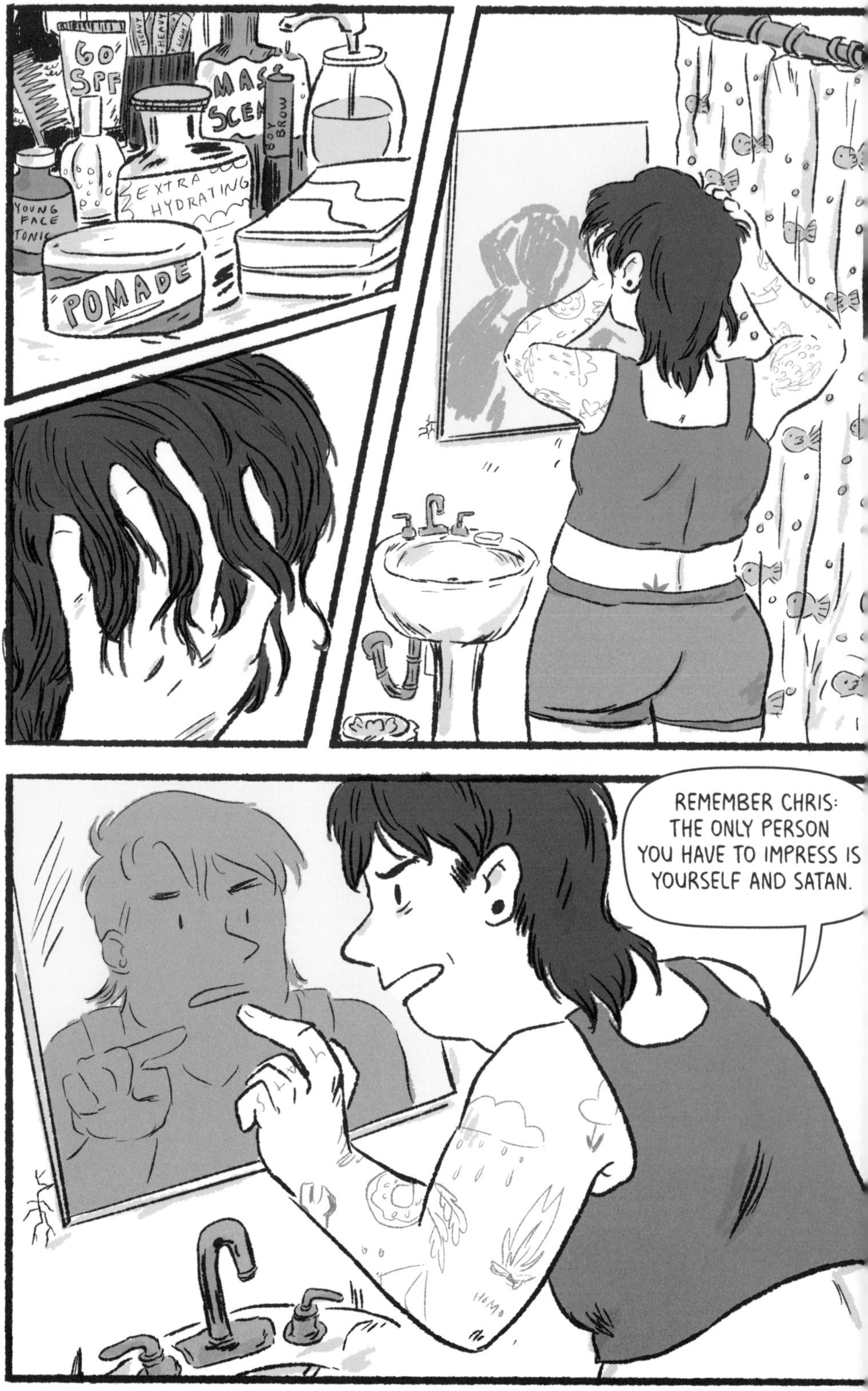
60 SPF
HEAVY
HEAVY
LIGHT
MASS
SCEN
BOY BROW
EXTRA HYDRATING
YOUNG FACE TONIC
POMADE
REMEMBER CHRIS: THE ONLY PERSON YOU HAVE TO IMPRESS IS YOURSELF AND SATAN.
HOMO

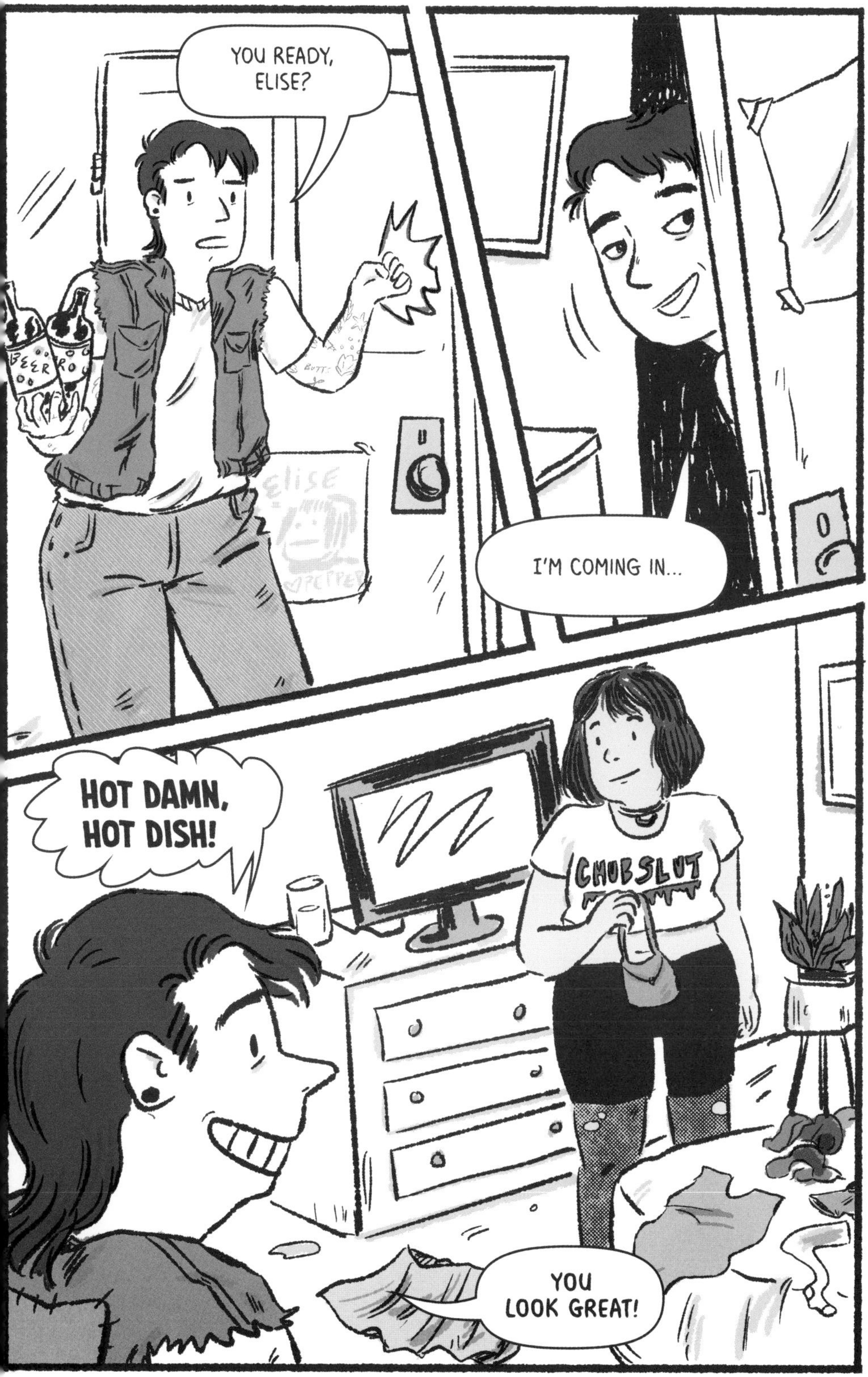
YOU READY, ELISE?
I'M COMING IN...
ELISE
HOT DAMN, HOT DISH!
CHUBSLUT
YOU LOOK GREAT!

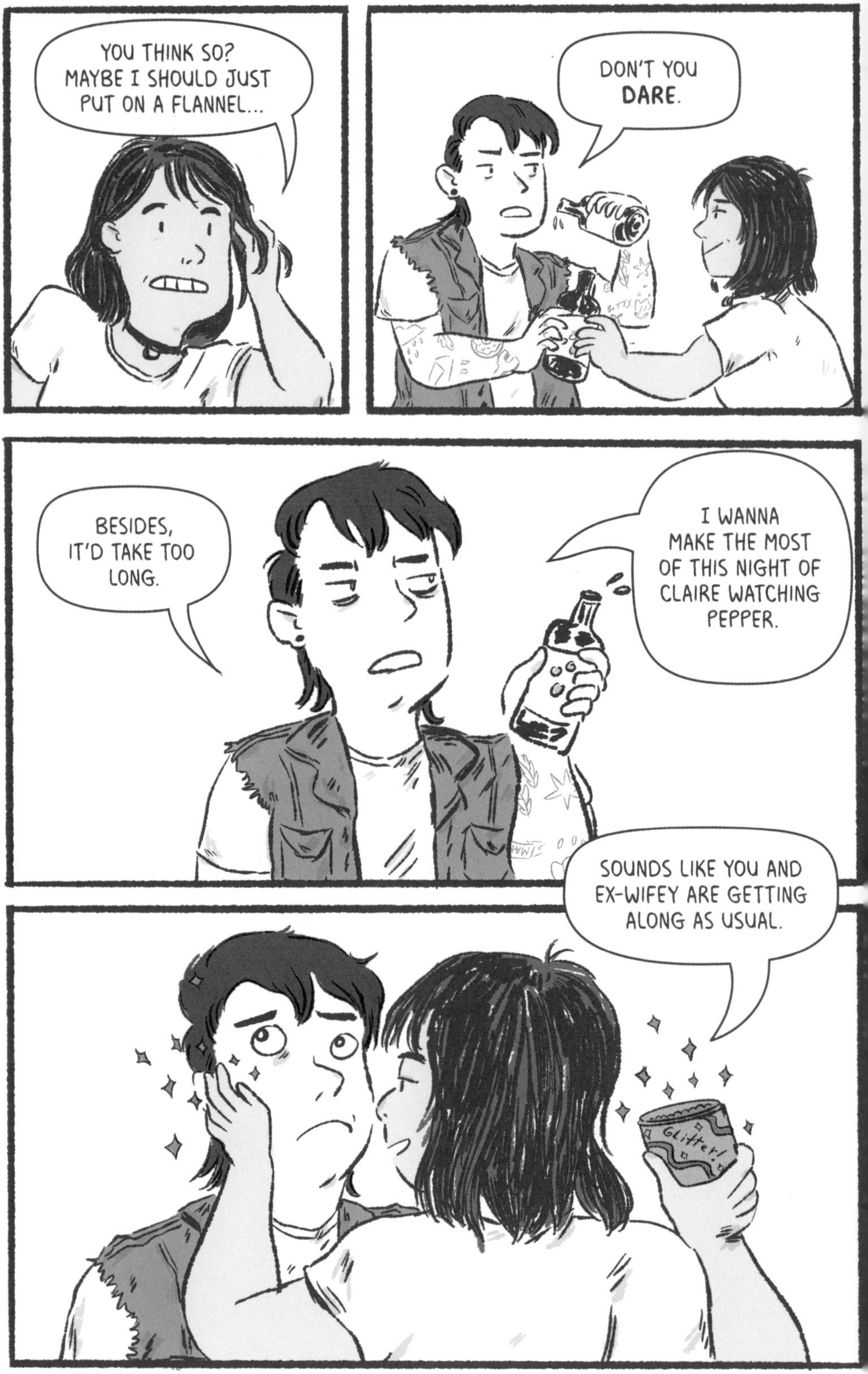
YOU THINK SO? MAYBE I SHOULD JUST PUT ON A FLANNEL...
DON'T YOU **DARE**.
BESIDES, IT'D TAKE TOO LONG.
I WANNA MAKE THE MOST OF THIS NIGHT OF CLAIRE WATCHING PEPPER.
SOUNDS LIKE YOU AND EX-WIFEY ARE GETTING ALONG AS USUAL.
Glitter!

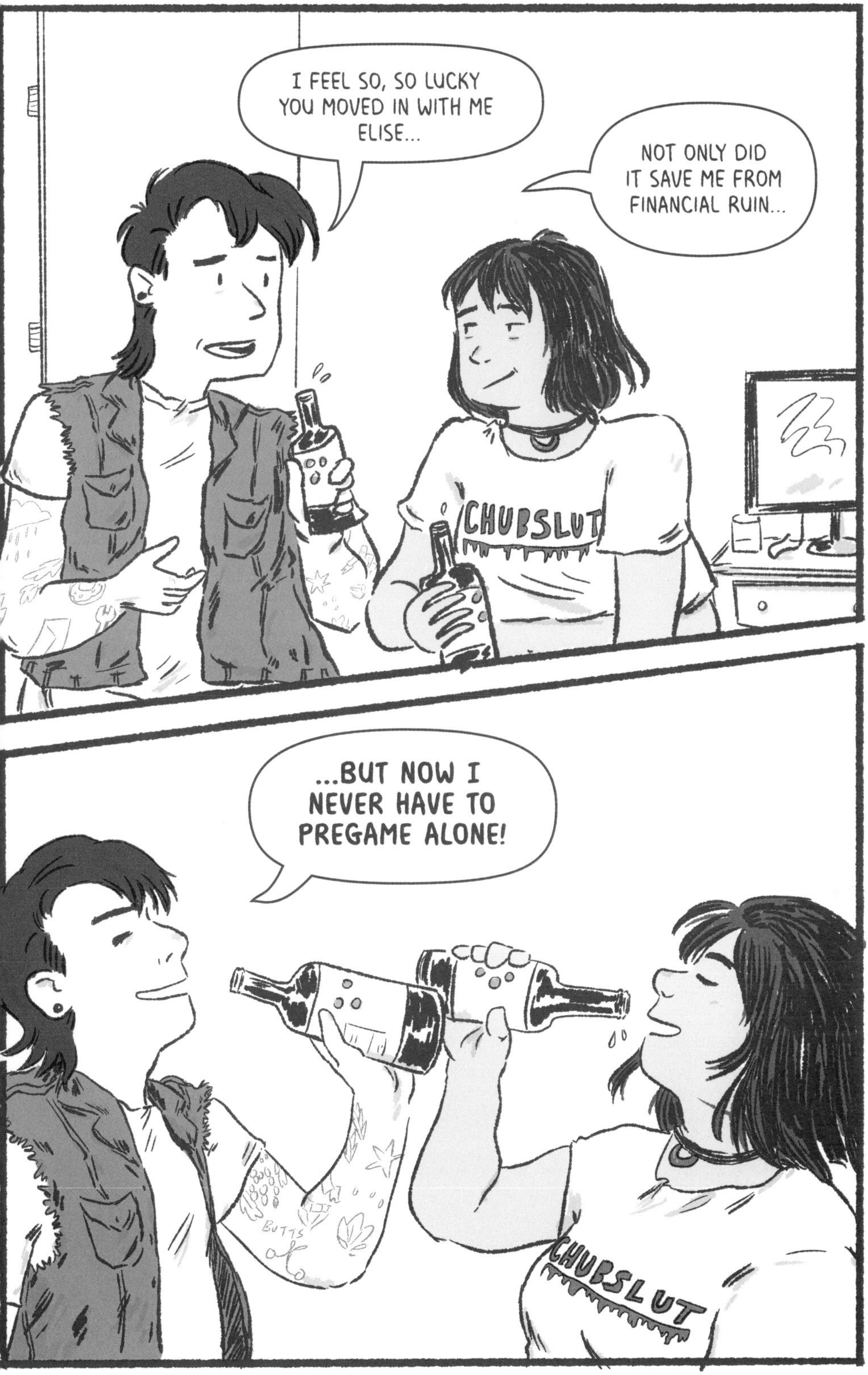
I FEEL SO, SO LUCKY YOU MOVED IN WITH ME ELISE...
NOT ONLY DID IT SAVE ME FROM FINANCIAL RUIN...
CHUBSLUT
...BUT NOW I NEVER HAVE TO PREGAME ALONE!
BUTTS
CHUBSLUT

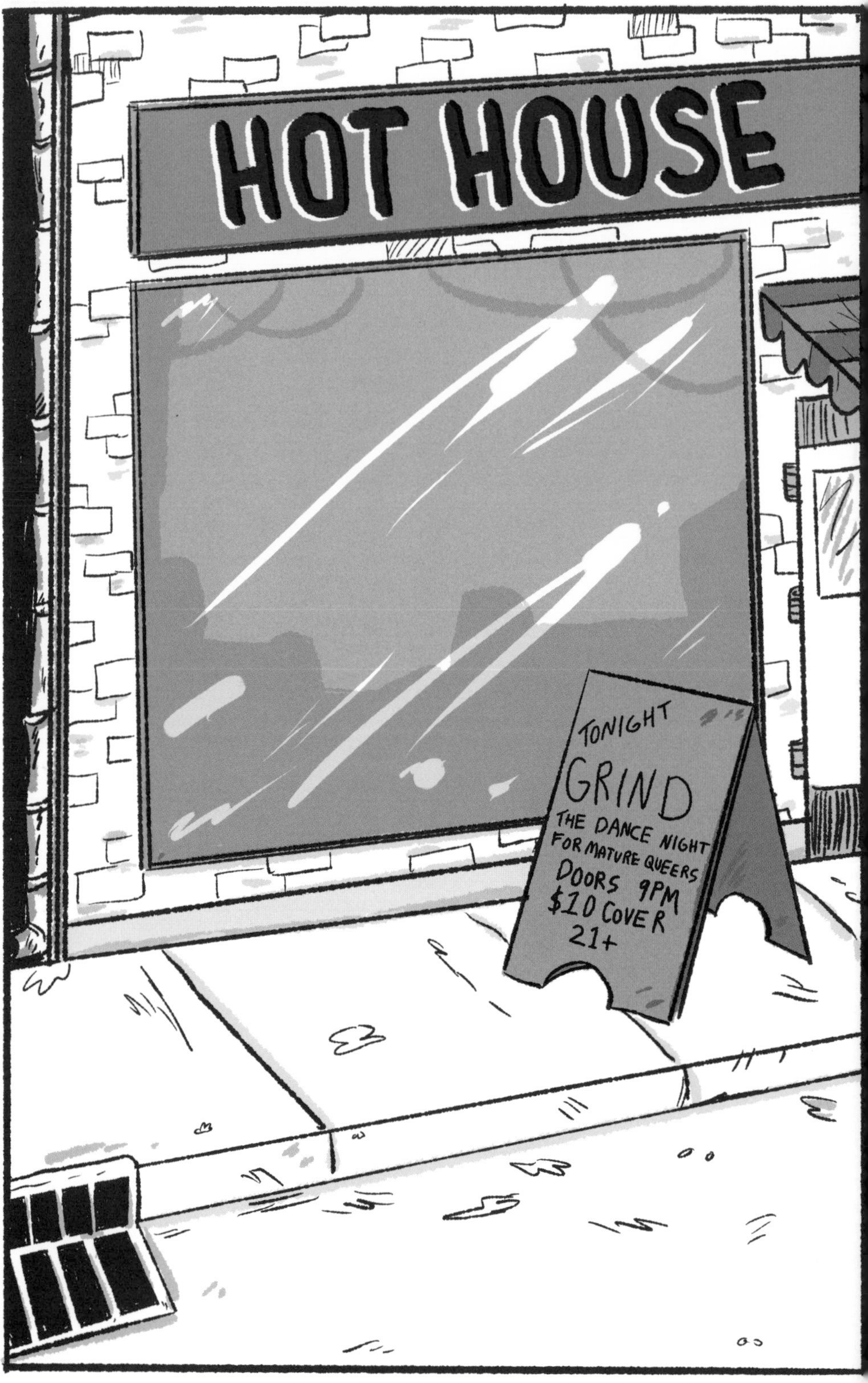
HOT HOUSE
TONIGHT
GRIND
THE DANCE NIGHT
FOR MATURE QUEERS
DOORS 9PM
$10 COVER
21+

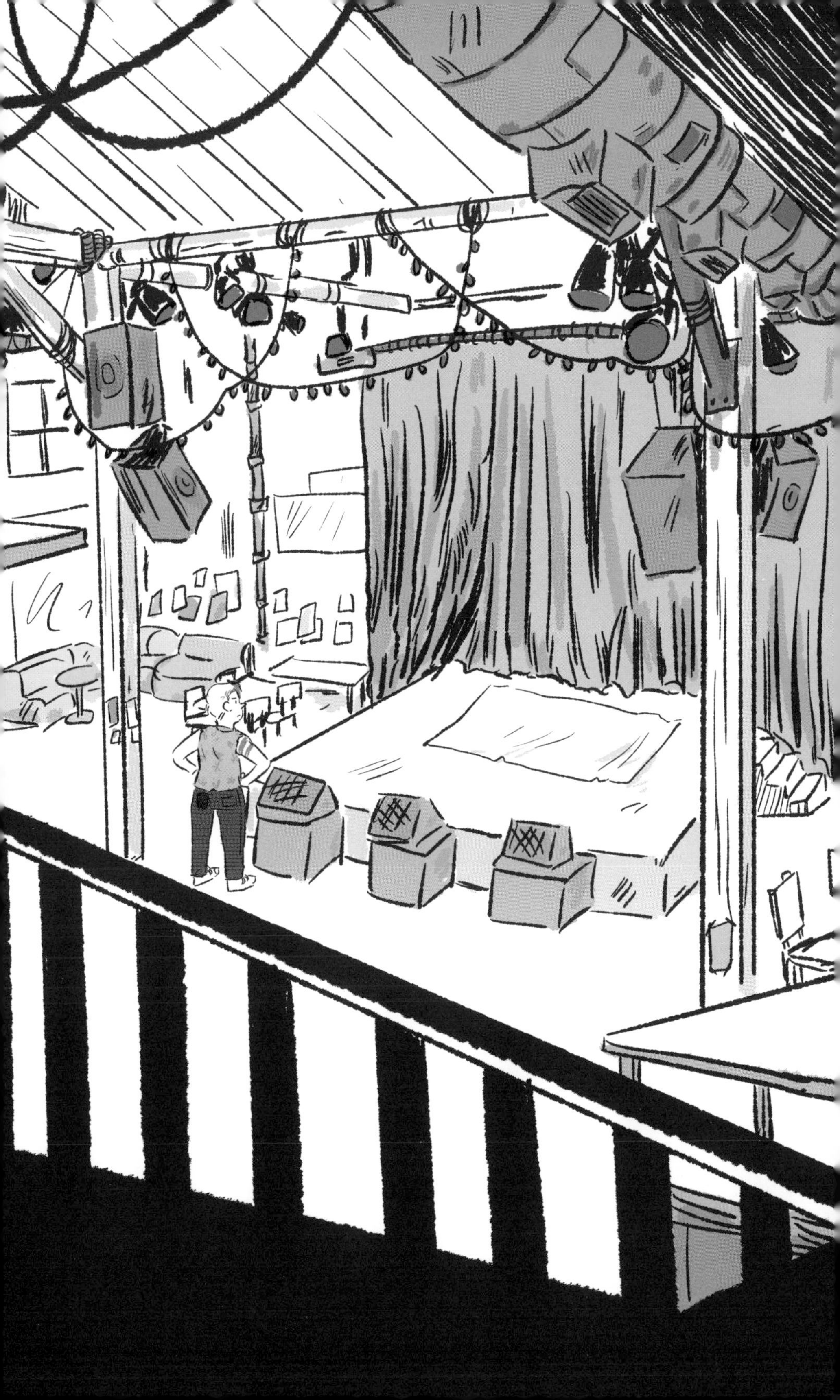

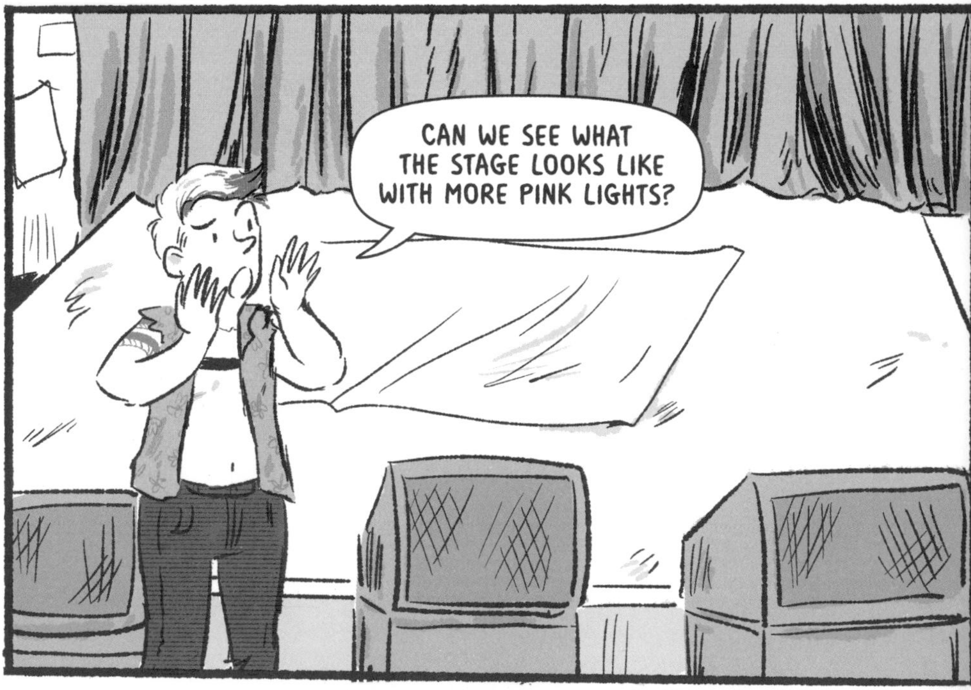
CAN WE SEE WHAT THE STAGE LOOKS LIKE WITH MORE PINK LIGHTS?

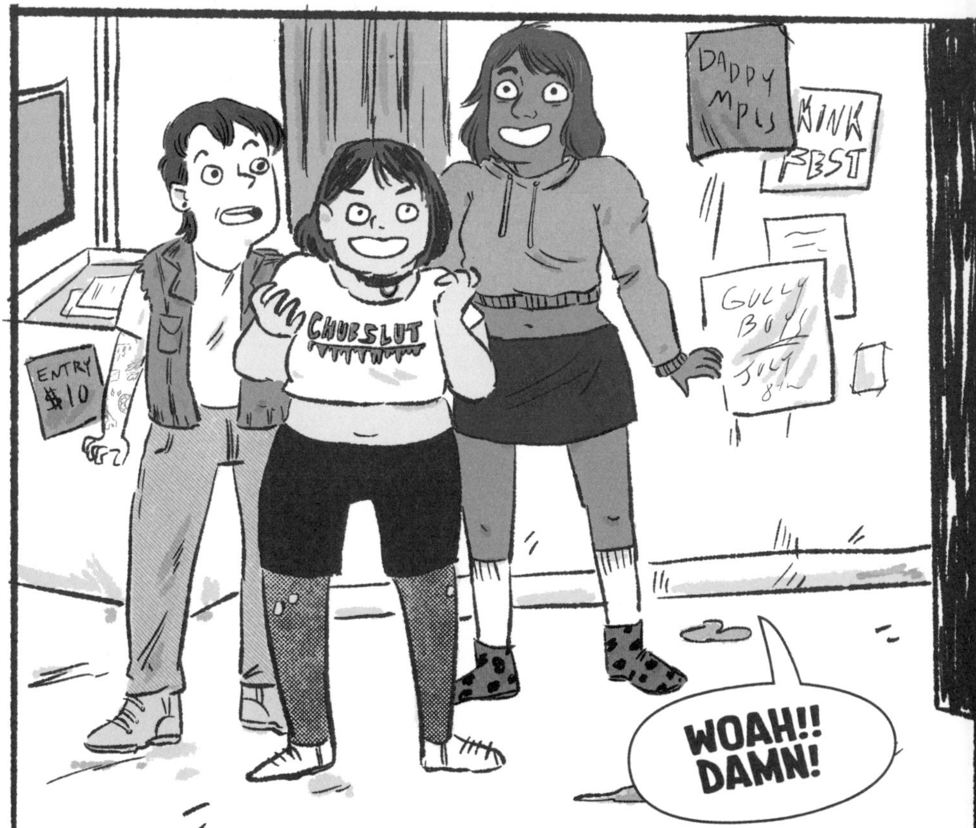
DADDY MPLS
KINK FEST
CHUBSLUT
ENTRY $10
GULLY BOYS
WOAH!! DAMN!

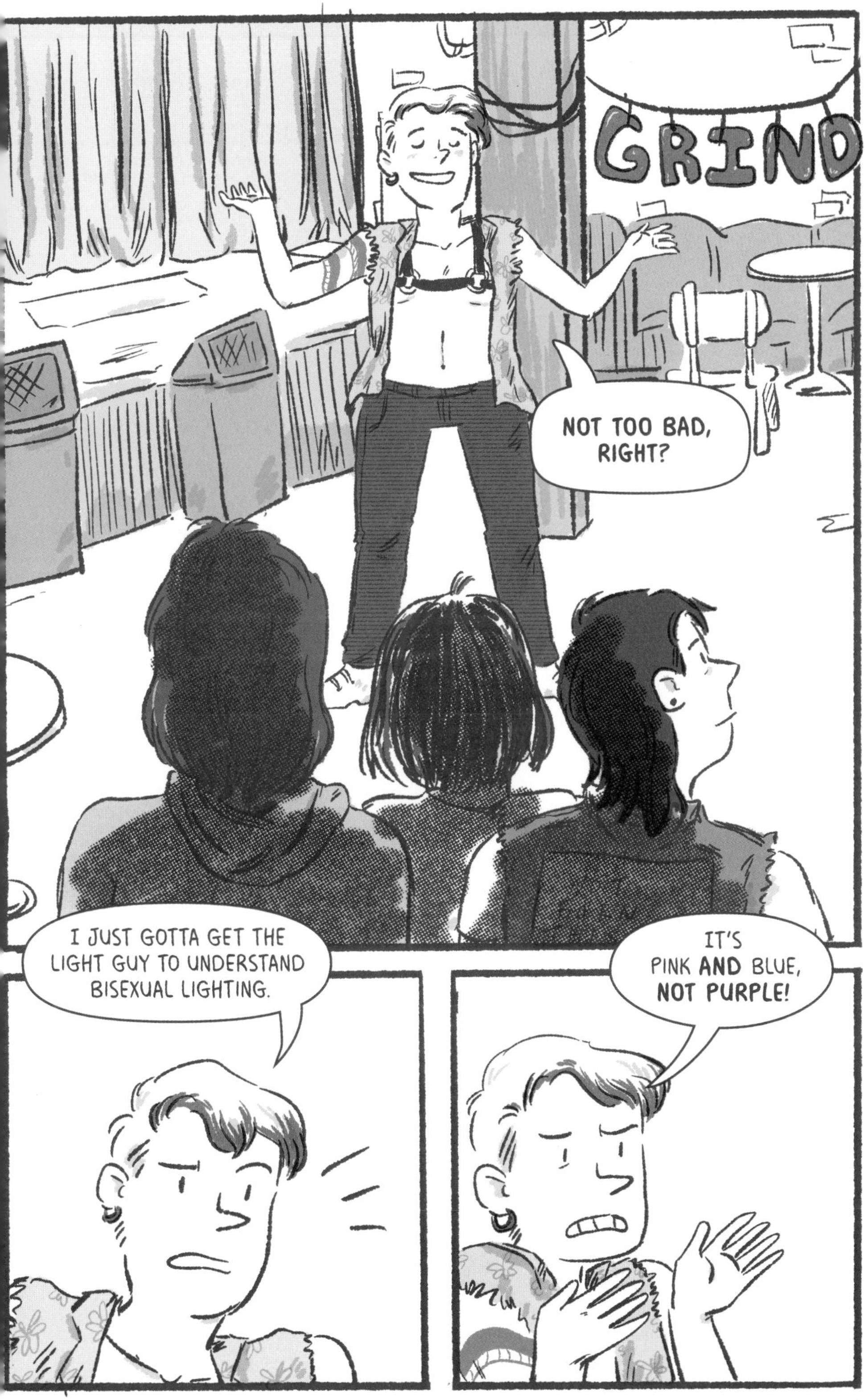
GRIND
NOT TOO BAD, RIGHT?
I JUST GOTTA GET THE LIGHT GUY TO UNDERSTAND BISEXUAL LIGHTING.
IT'S PINK AND BLUE, NOT PURPLE!

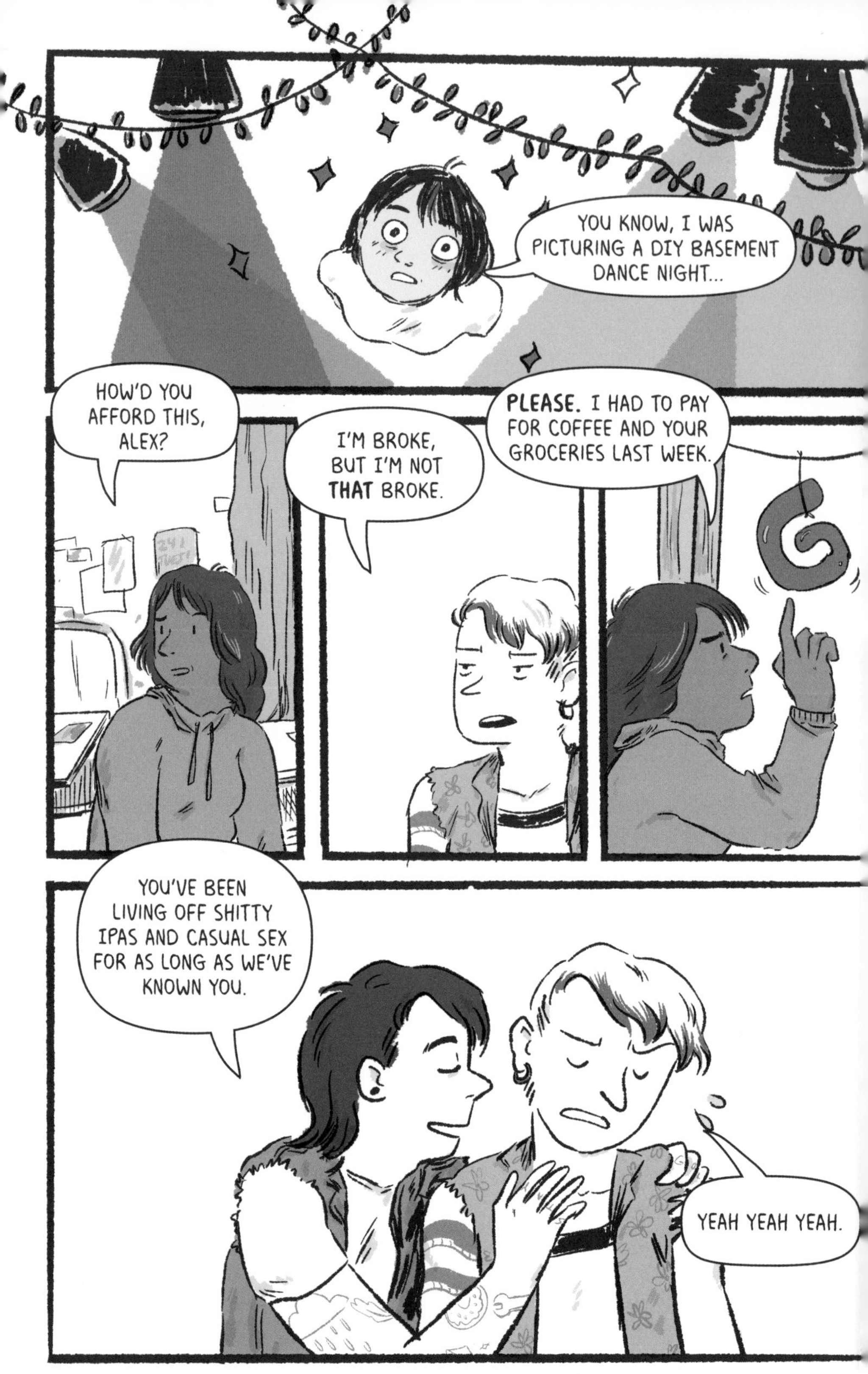
YOU KNOW, I WAS PICTURING A DIY BASEMENT DANCE NIGHT...
HOW'D YOU AFFORD THIS, ALEX?
I'M BROKE, BUT I'M NOT **THAT** BROKE.
PLEASE. I HAD TO PAY FOR COFFEE AND YOUR GROCERIES LAST WEEK.
YOU'VE BEEN LIVING OFF SHITTY IPAS AND CASUAL SEX FOR AS LONG AS WE'VE KNOWN YOU.
YEAH YEAH YEAH.

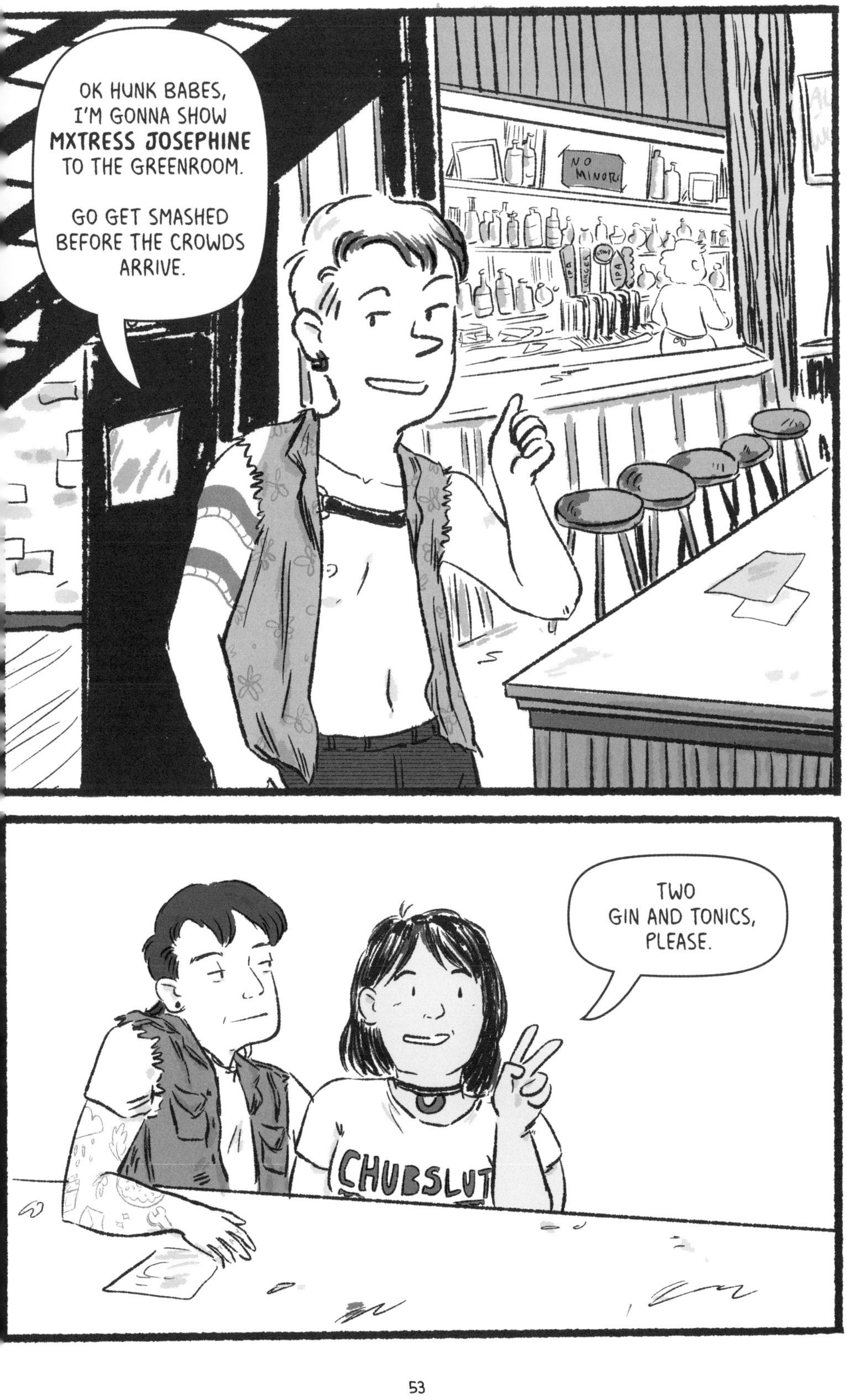
OK HUNK BABES, I'M GONNA SHOW **MXTRESS JOSEPHINE** TO THE GREENROOM.
GO GET SMASHED BEFORE THE CROWDS ARRIVE.
TWO GIN AND TONICS, PLEASE.
CHUBSLUT

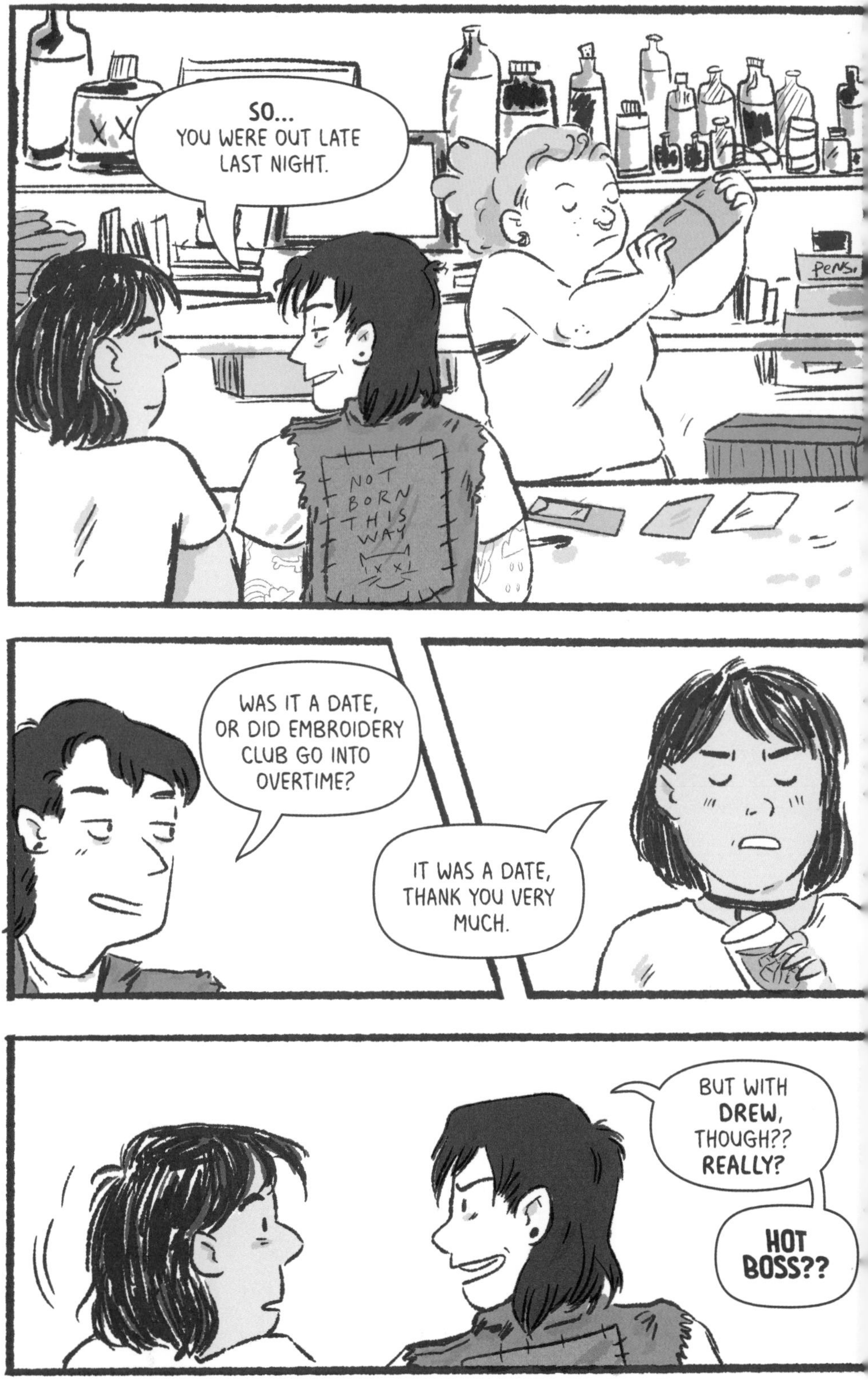

SO...
YOU WERE OUT LATE LAST NIGHT.
PENS.
NOT BORN THIS WAY
WAS IT A DATE, OR DID EMBROIDERY CLUB GO INTO OVERTIME?
IT WAS A DATE, THANK YOU VERY MUCH.
BUT WITH DREW, THOUGH?? REALLY?
HOT BOSS??

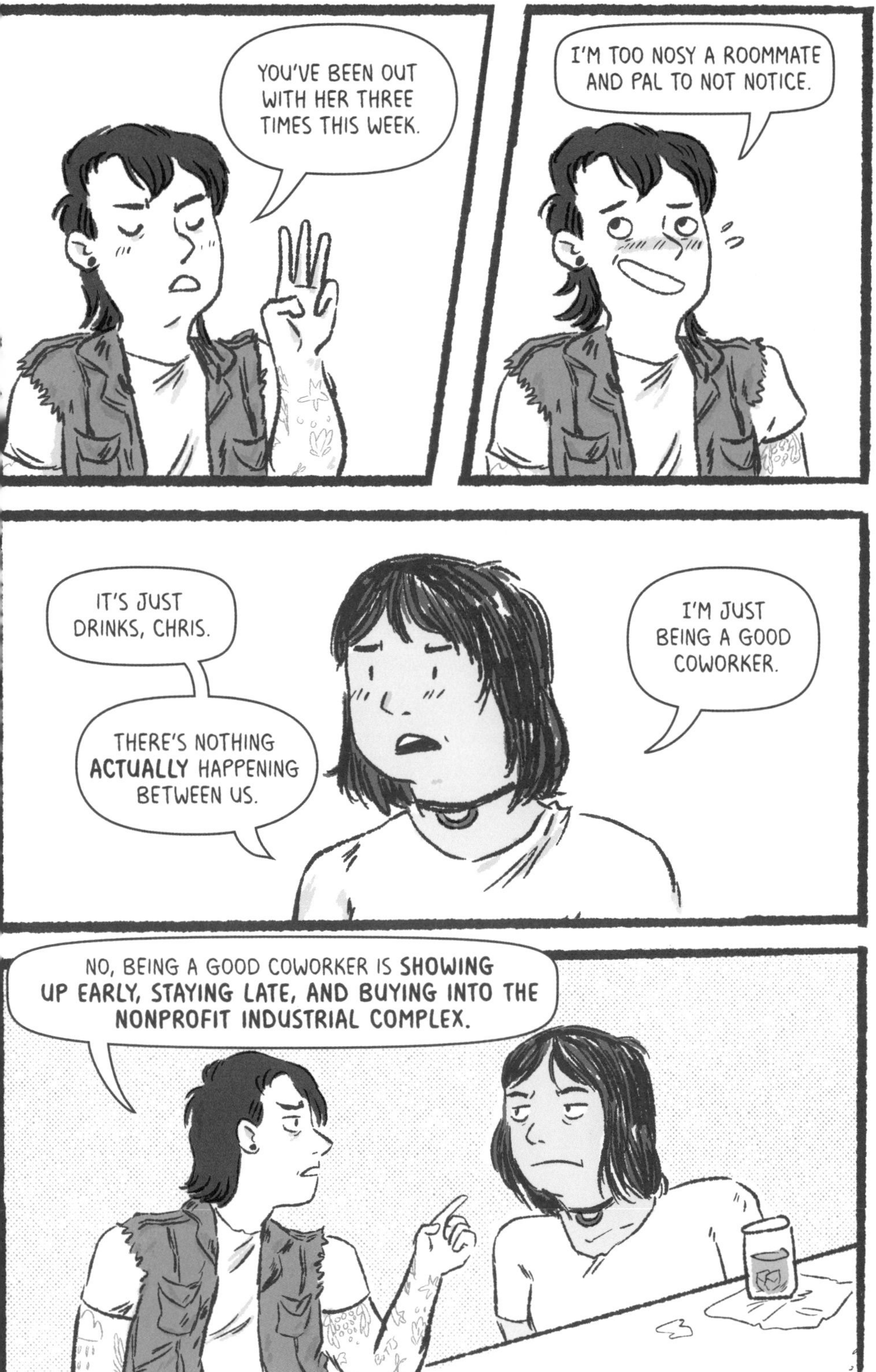
YOU'VE BEEN OUT WITH HER THREE TIMES THIS WEEK.
I'M TOO NOSY A ROOMMATE AND PAL TO NOT NOTICE.
IT'S JUST DRINKS, CHRIS.
THERE'S NOTHING ACTUALLY HAPPENING BETWEEN US.
I'M JUST BEING A GOOD COWORKER.
NO, BEING A GOOD COWORKER IS SHOWING UP EARLY, STAYING LATE, AND BUYING INTO THE NONPROFIT INDUSTRIAL COMPLEX.

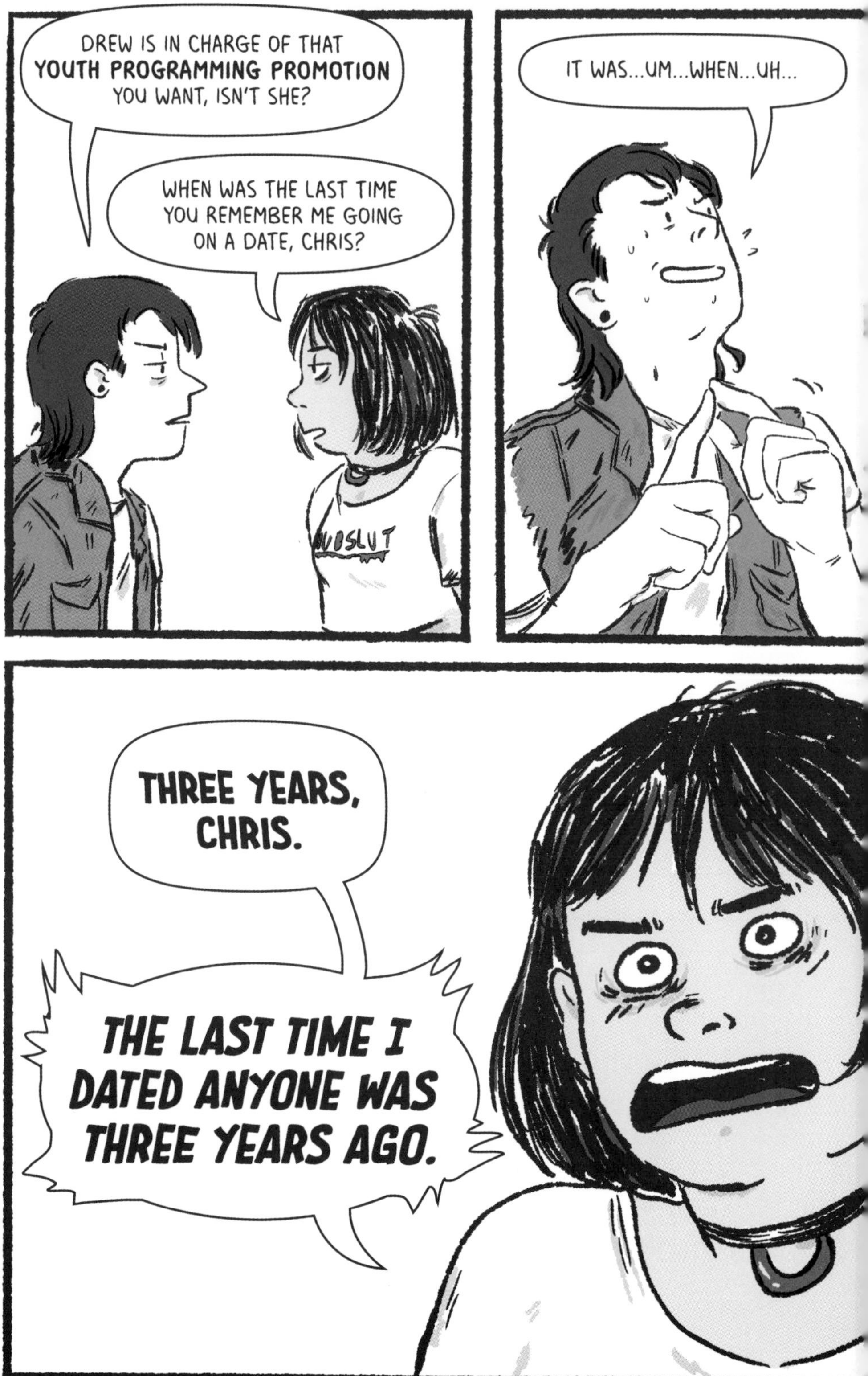
DREW IS IN CHARGE OF THAT **YOUTH PROGRAMMING PROMOTION** YOU WANT, ISN'T SHE?
WHEN WAS THE LAST TIME YOU REMEMBER ME GOING ON A DATE, CHRIS?
IT WAS...UM...WHEN...UH...
THREE YEARS, CHRIS.
THE LAST TIME I DATED ANYONE WAS THREE YEARS AGO.

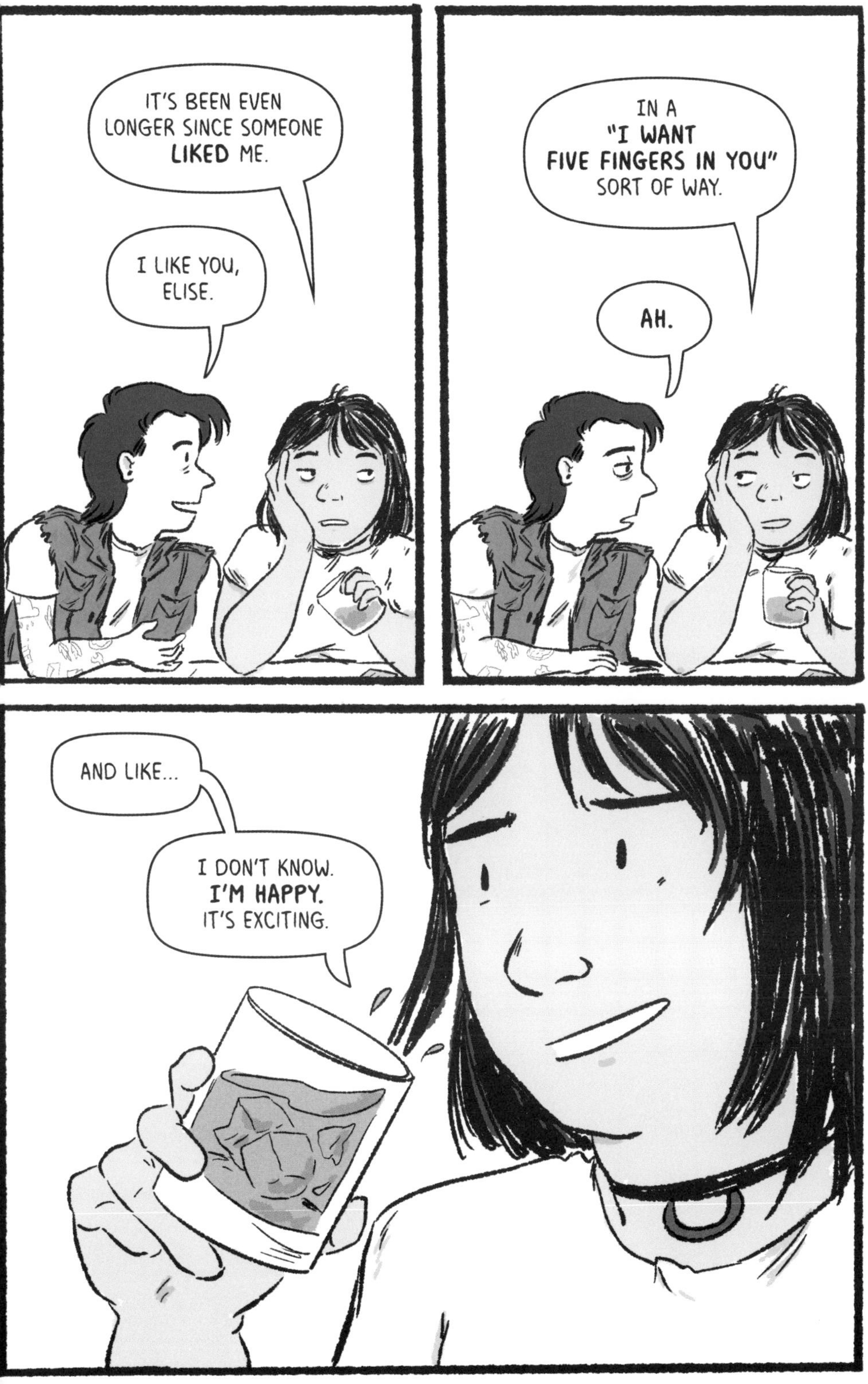

IT'S BEEN EVEN LONGER SINCE SOMEONE **LIKED** ME.
I LIKE YOU, ELISE.
IN A **"I WANT FIVE FINGERS IN YOU"** SORT OF WAY.
AH.
AND LIKE...
I DON'T KNOW. **I'M HAPPY.** IT'S EXCITING.

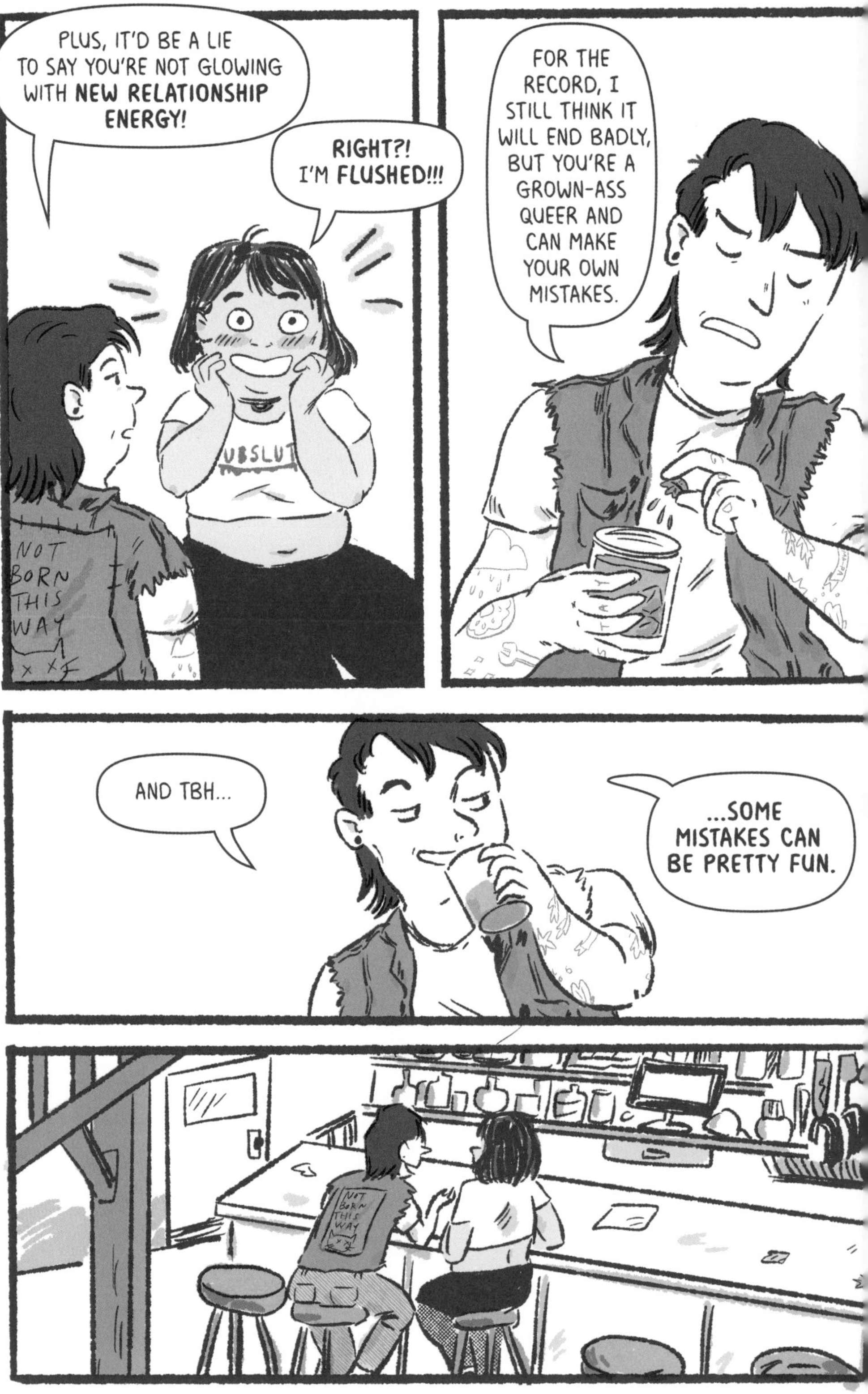
PLUS, IT'D BE A LIE TO SAY YOU'RE NOT GLOWING WITH **NEW RELATIONSHIP ENERGY!**
RIGHT?! I'M **FLUSHED!!!**
NOT BORN THIS WAY
FOR THE RECORD, I STILL THINK IT WILL END BADLY, BUT YOU'RE A GROWN-ASS QUEER AND CAN MAKE YOUR OWN MISTAKES.
AND TBH...
...SOME MISTAKES CAN BE PRETTY FUN.
NOT BORN THIS WAY

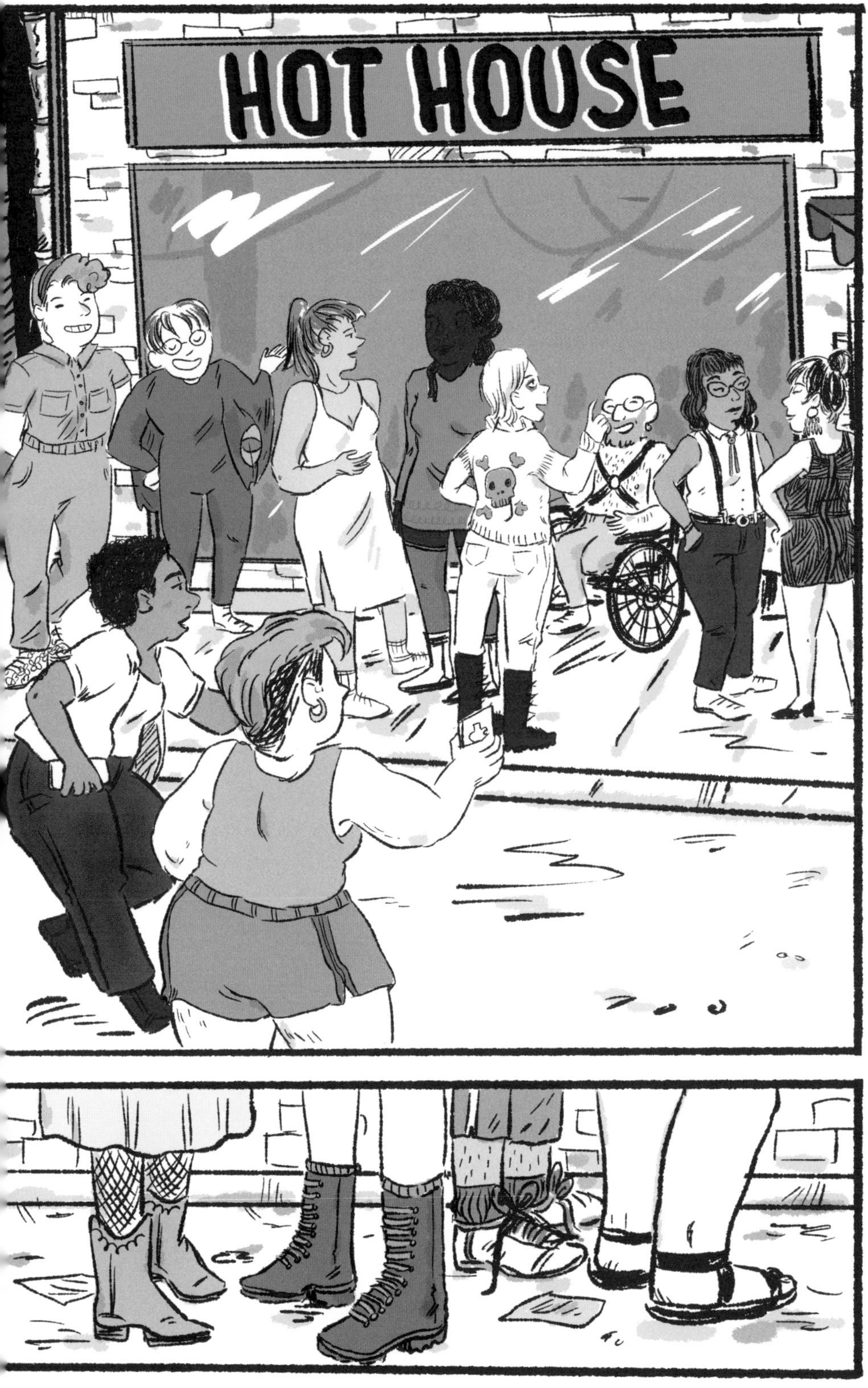
HOT HOUSE

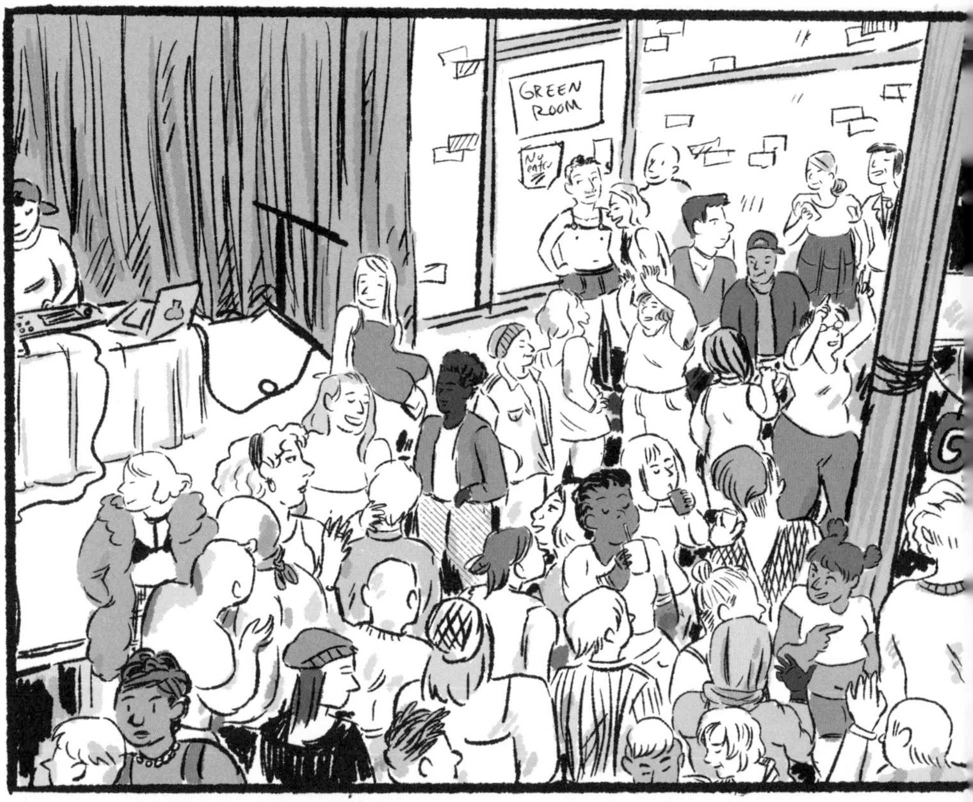
GREEN ROOM
No entry

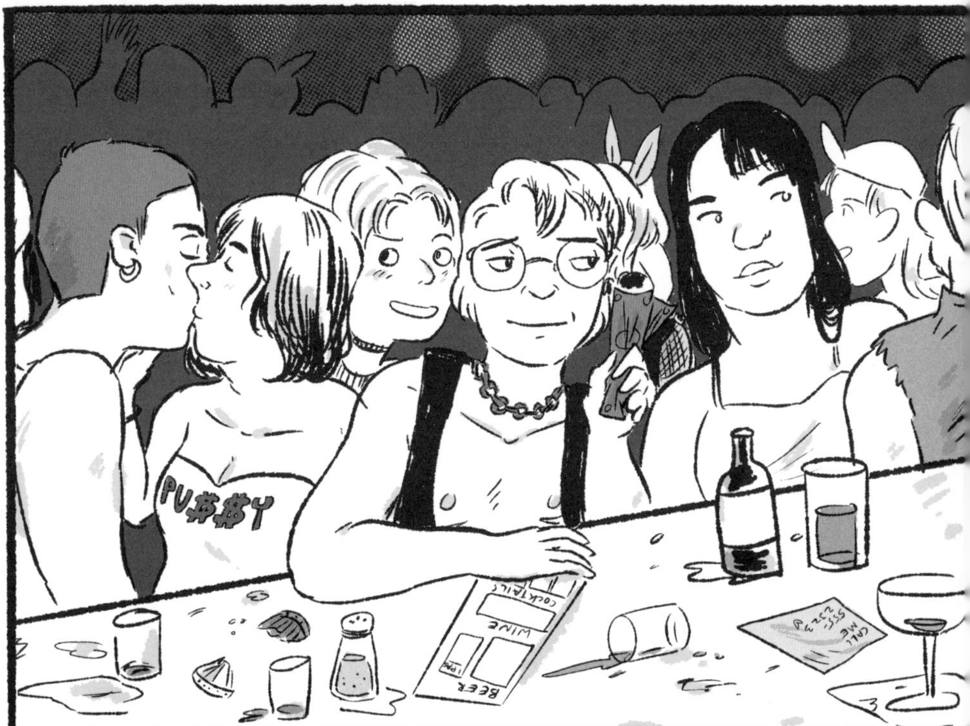
PU$$Y
COCKTAILS
WINE
BEER
CALL ME

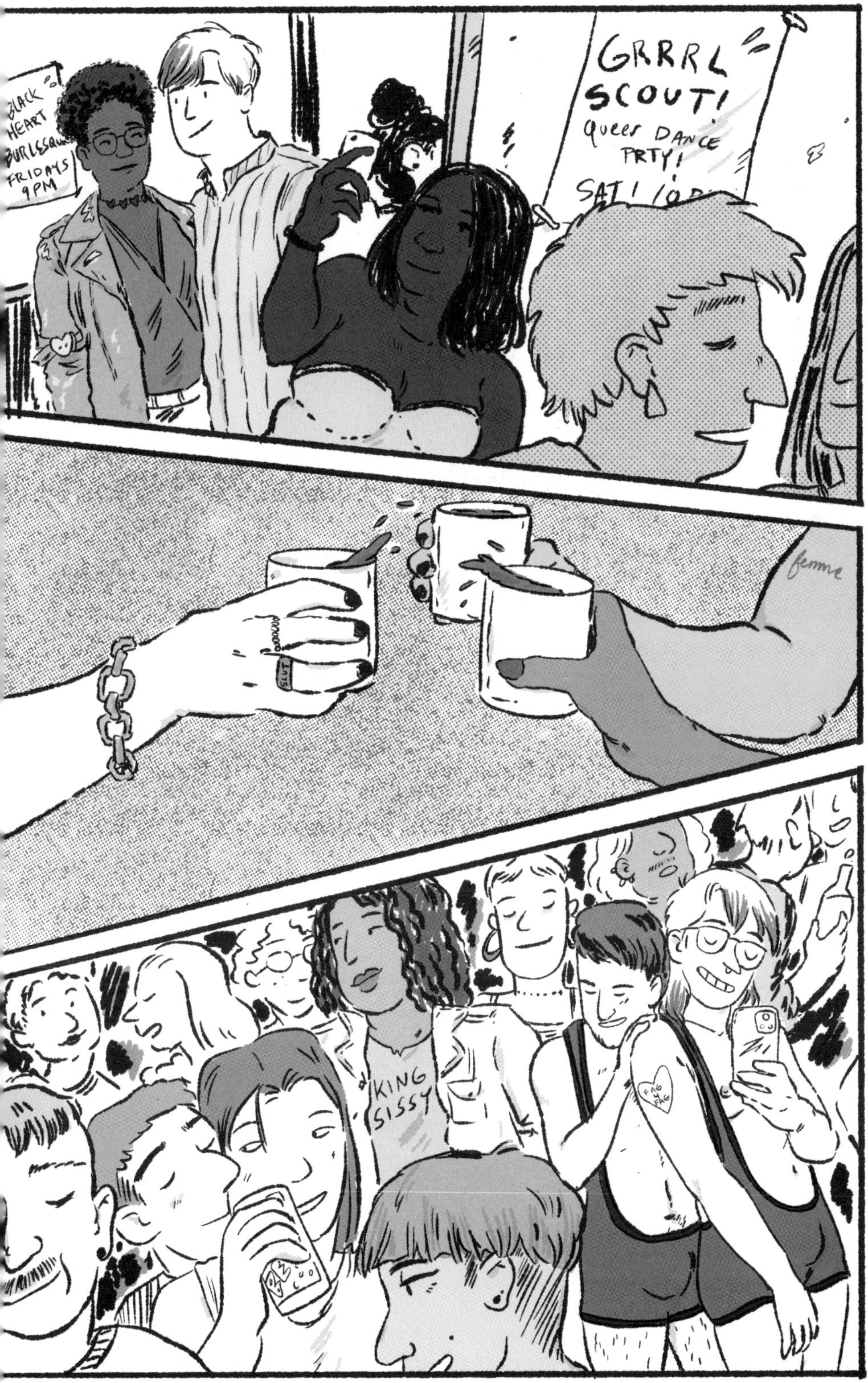
BLACK HEART BURLESQUE FRIDAYS 9PM
GRRRL SCOUT! Queer DANCE PRTY! SAT
femme
SLUT
KING SISSY
FAG 4 FAG

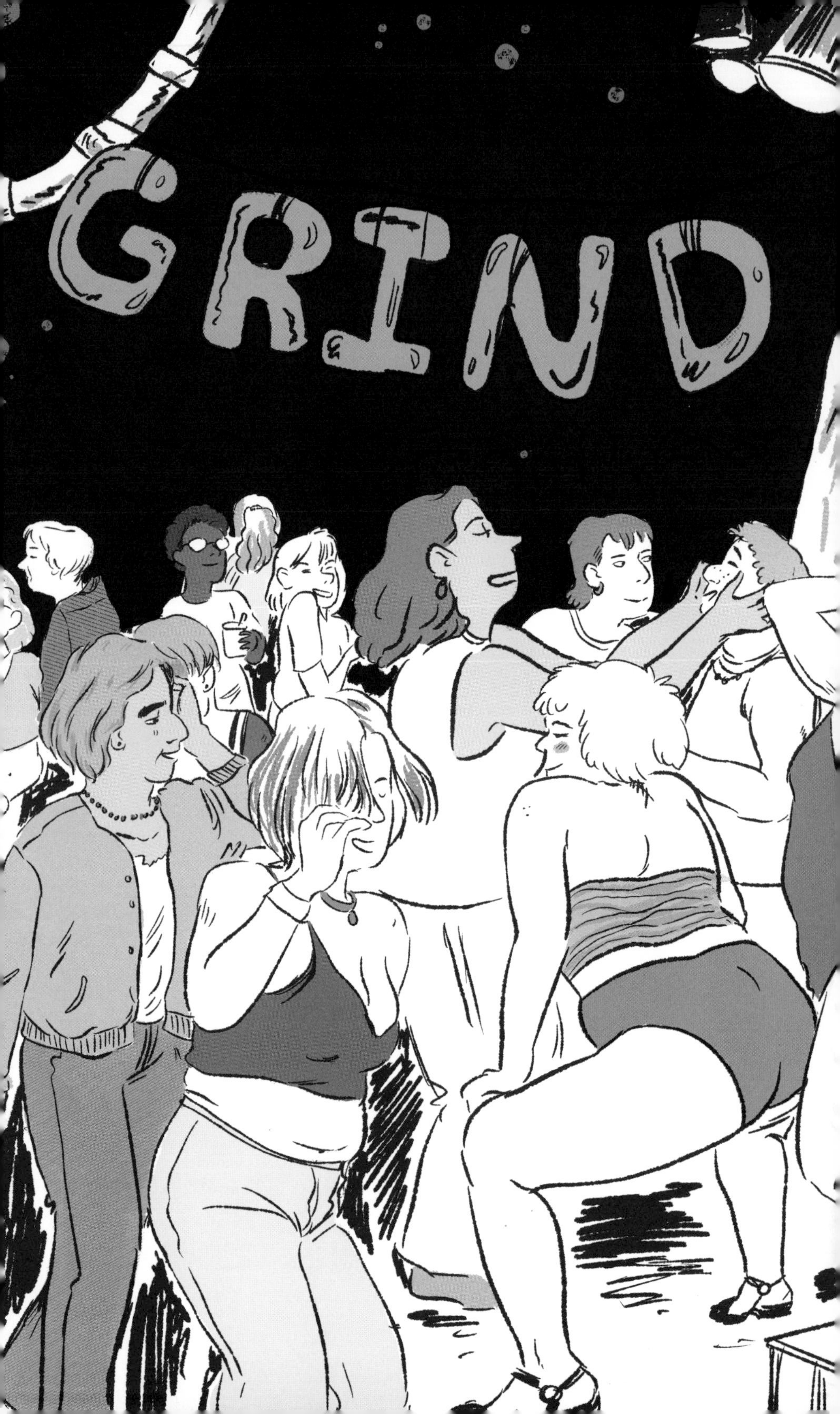
GRIND

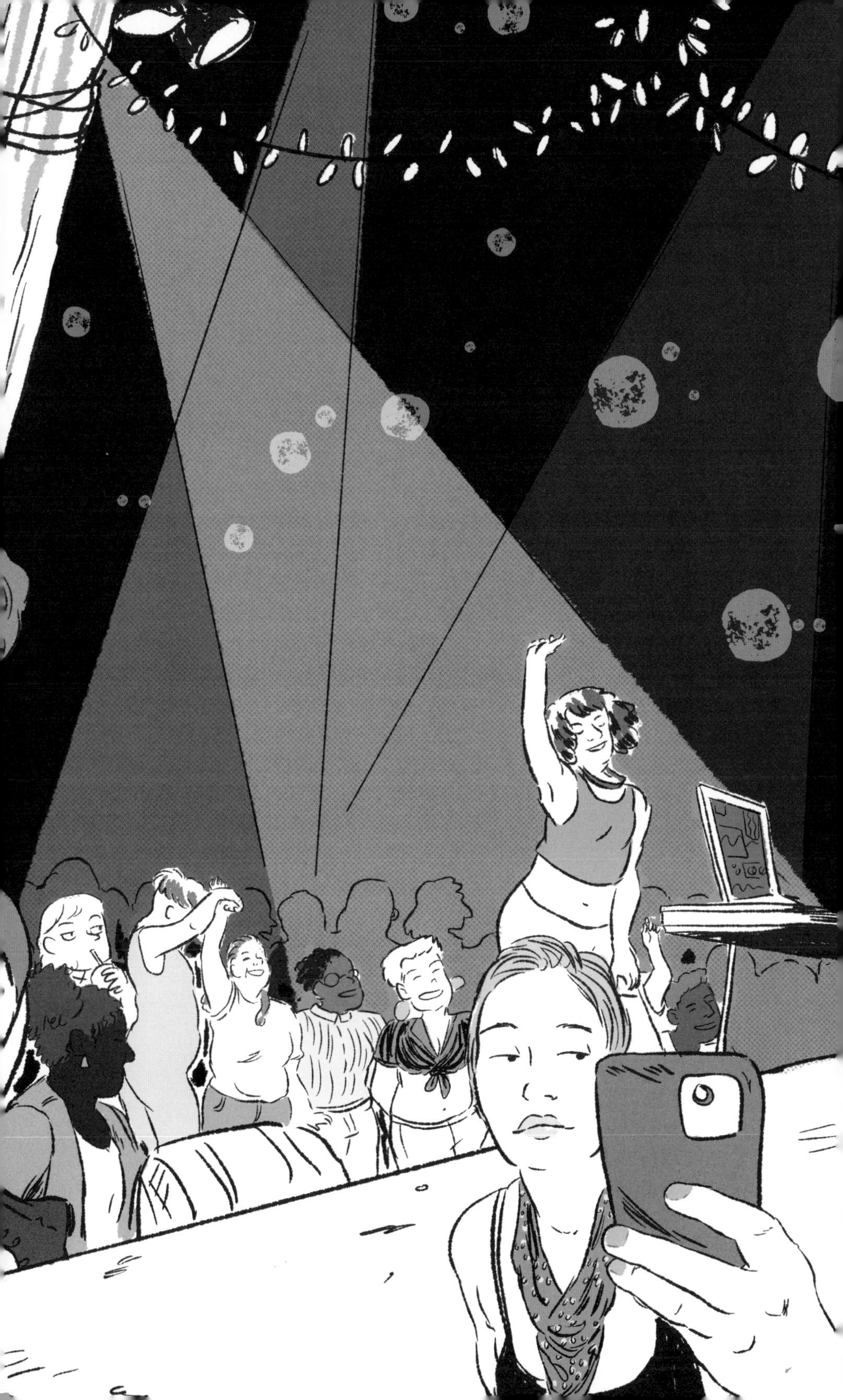

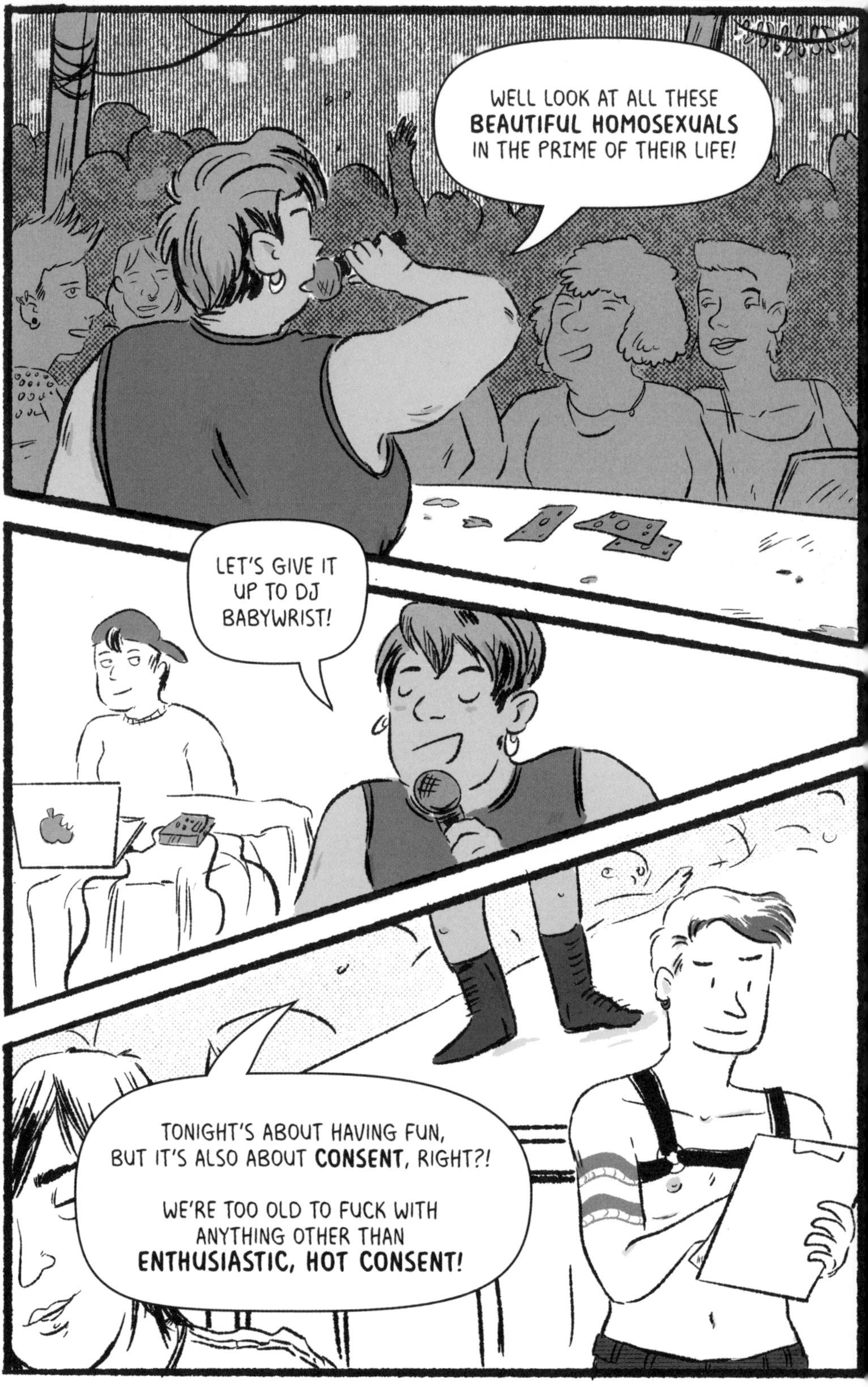
WELL LOOK AT ALL THESE **BEAUTIFUL HOMOSEXUALS** IN THE PRIME OF THEIR LIFE!
LET'S GIVE IT UP TO DJ BABYWRIST!
TONIGHT'S ABOUT HAVING FUN, BUT IT'S ALSO ABOUT **CONSENT**, RIGHT?!
WE'RE TOO OLD TO FUCK WITH ANYTHING OTHER THAN **ENTHUSIASTIC, HOT CONSENT!**

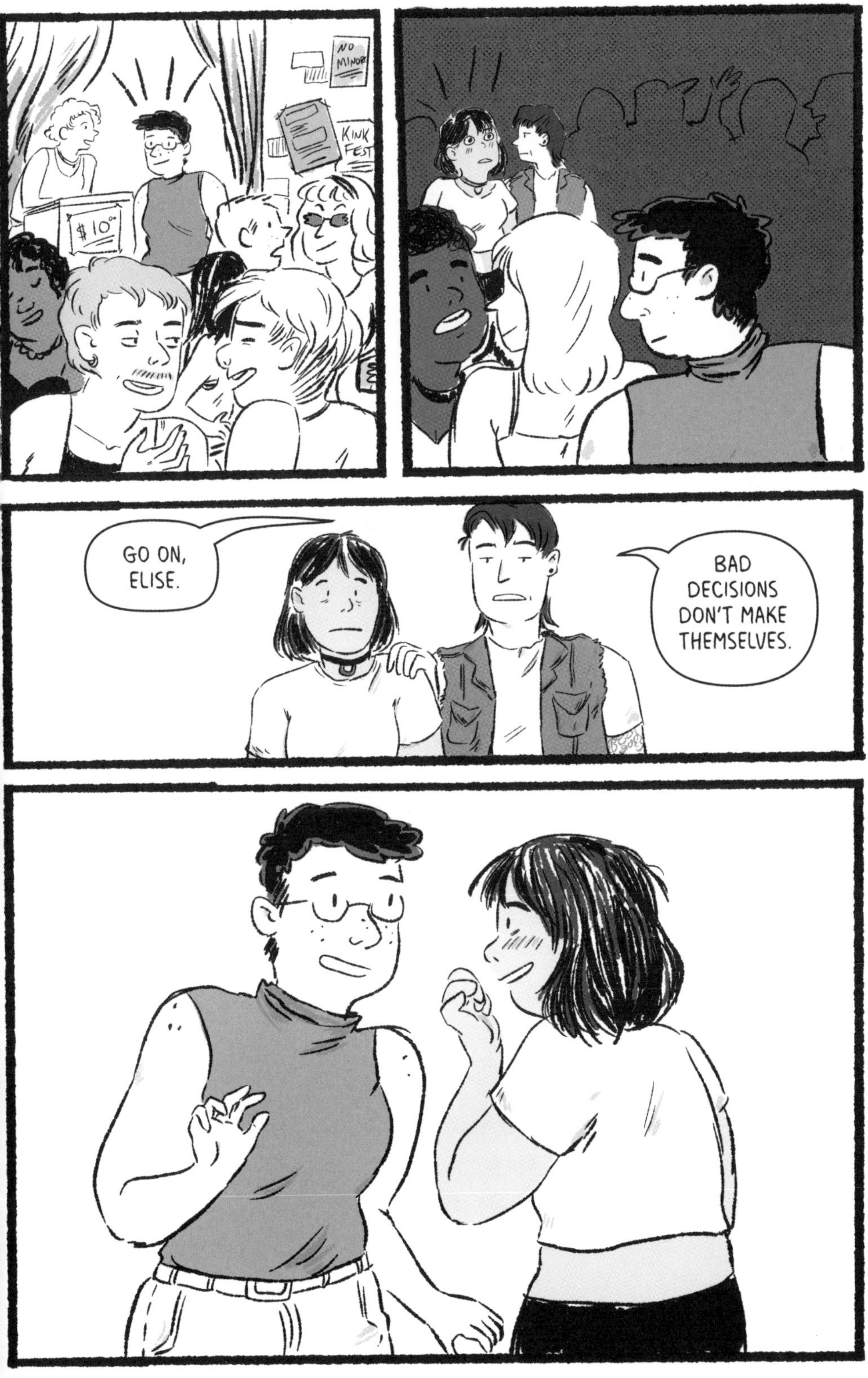
NO MINORS
KINK FEST
$10
GO ON, ELISE.
BAD DECISIONS DON'T MAKE THEMSELVES.

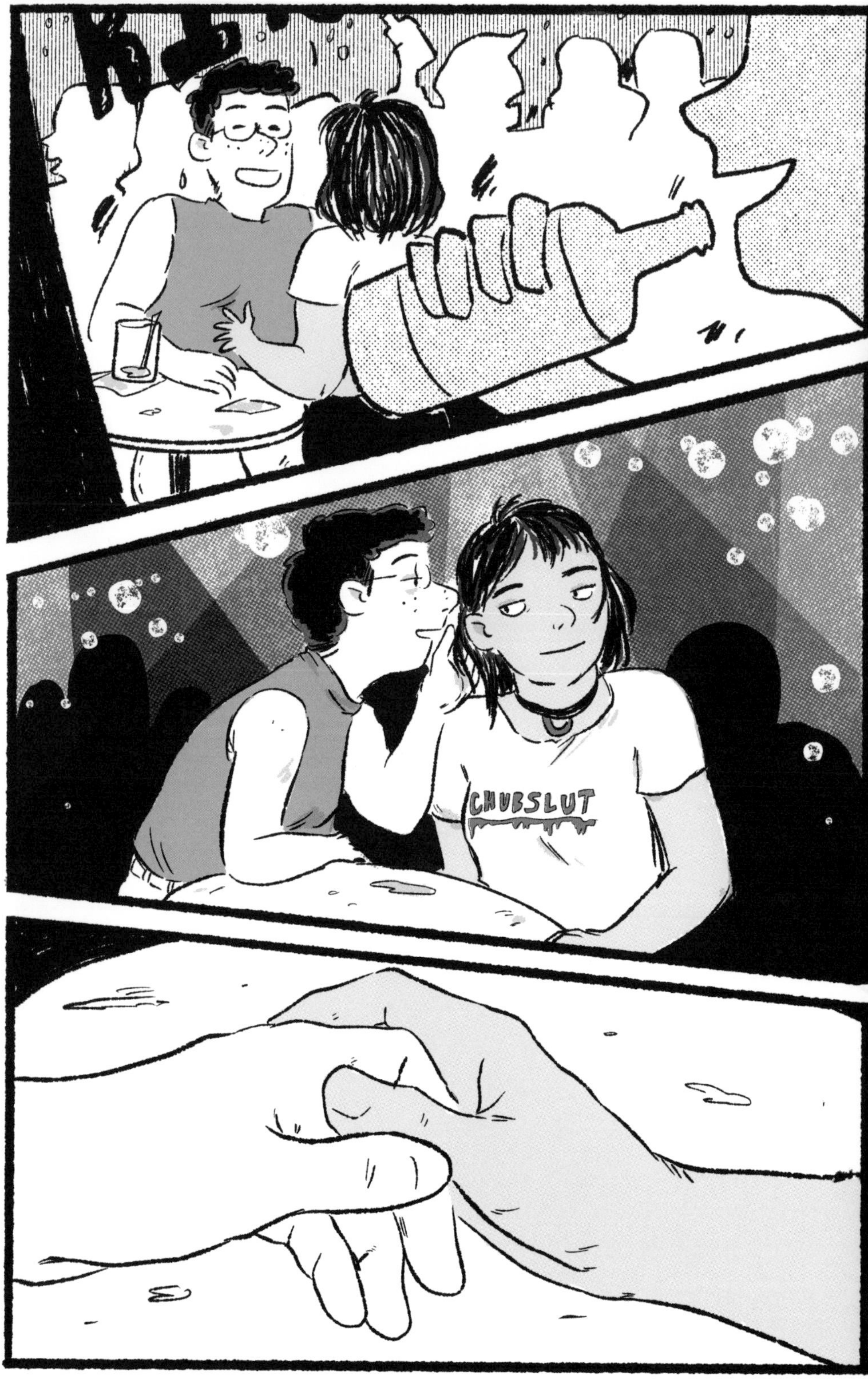
CHUBSLUT

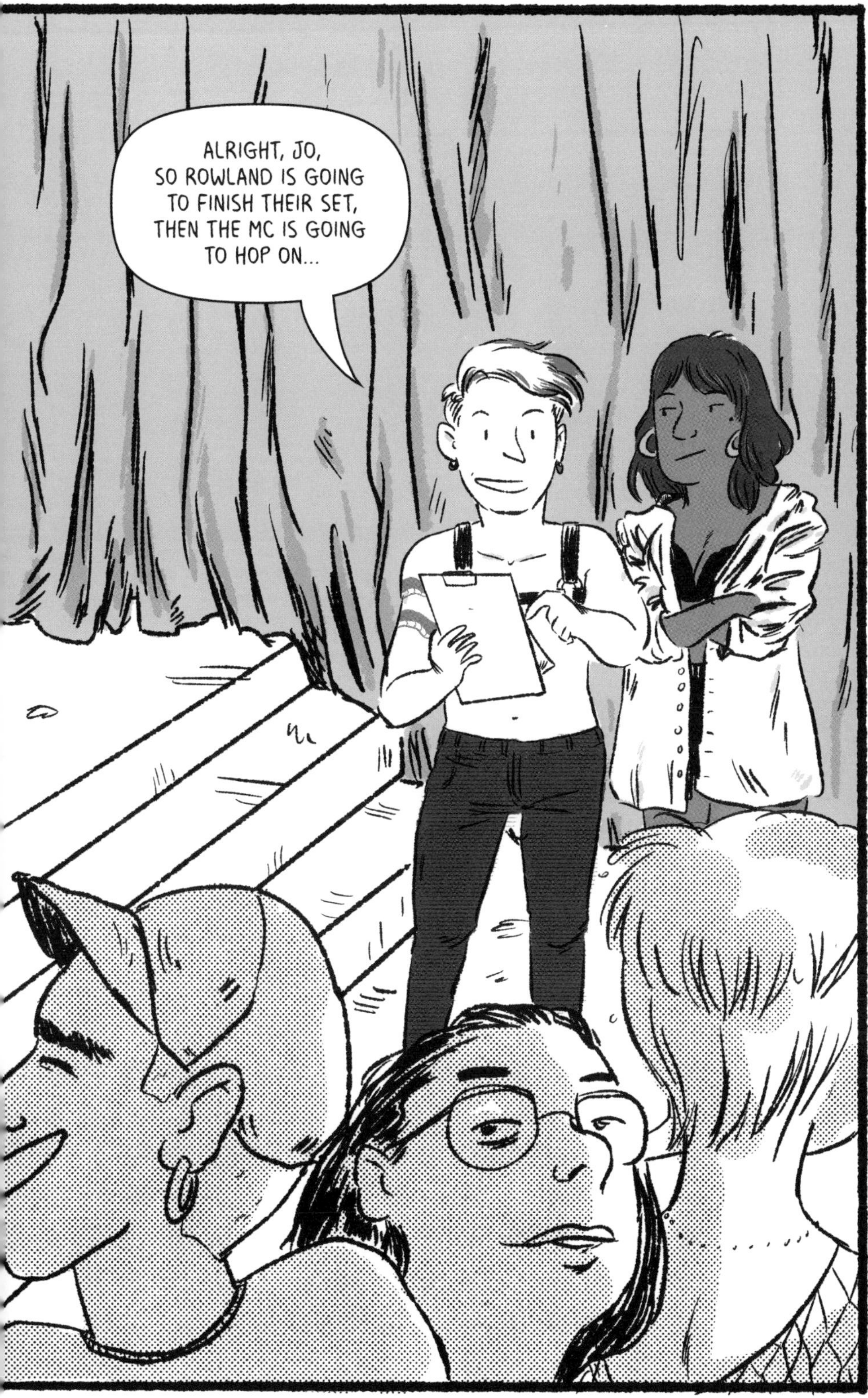
ALRIGHT, JO,
SO ROWLAND IS GOING
TO FINISH THEIR SET,
THEN THE MC IS GOING
TO HOP ON...

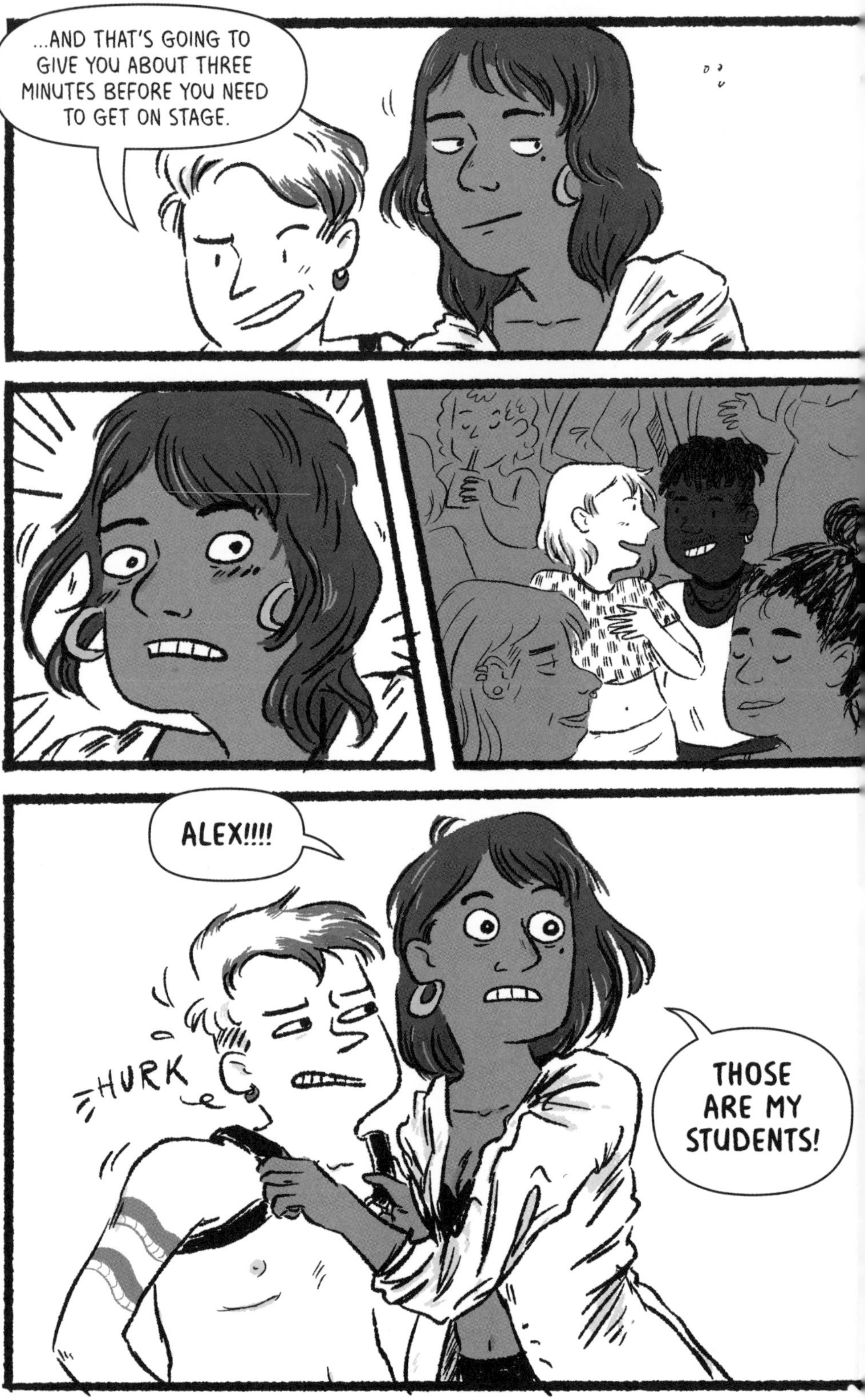
...AND THAT'S GOING TO GIVE YOU ABOUT THREE MINUTES BEFORE YOU NEED TO GET ON STAGE.
ALEX!!!!
HURK
THOSE ARE MY STUDENTS!

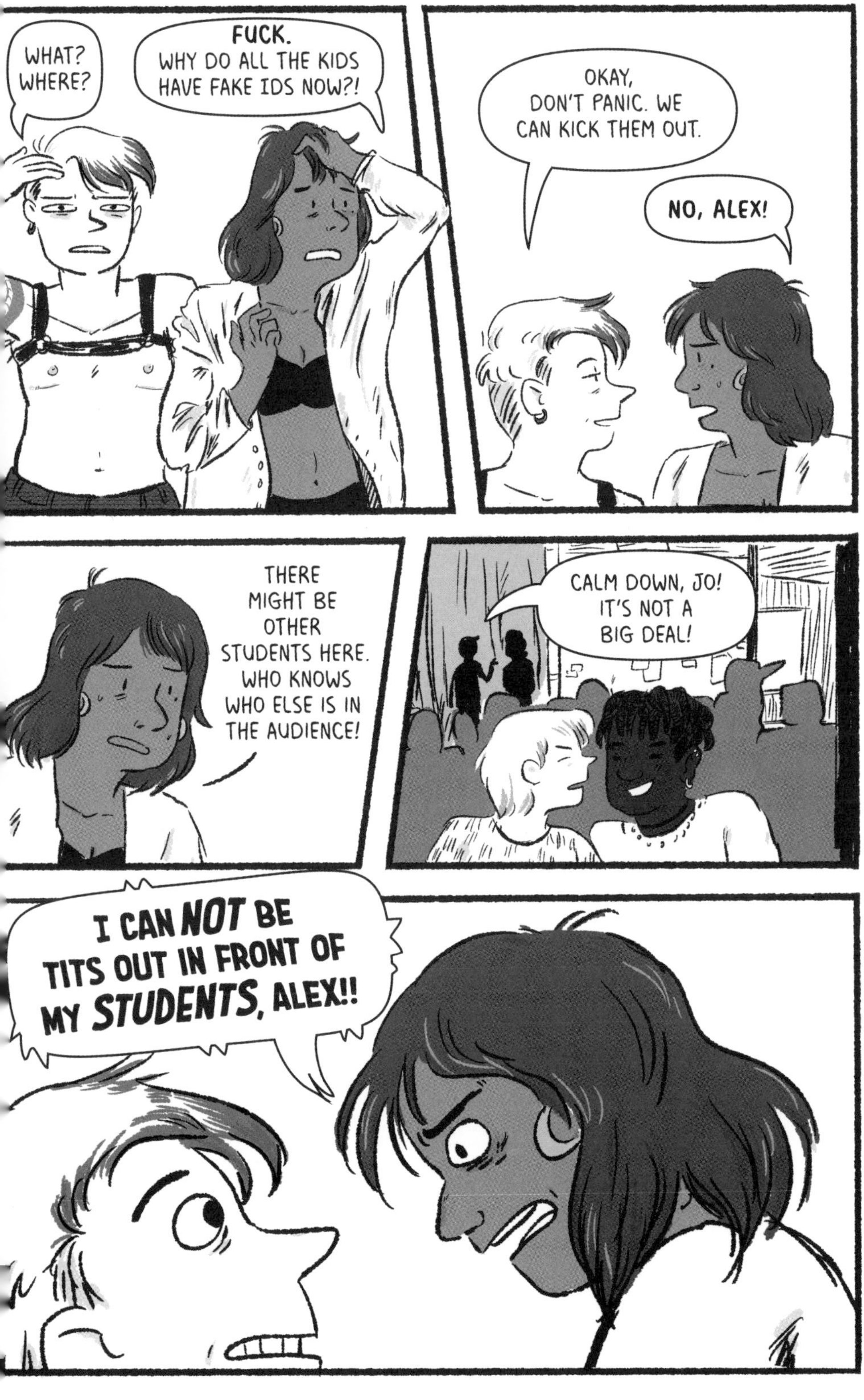

WHAT? WHERE?
FUCK. WHY DO ALL THE KIDS HAVE FAKE IDS NOW?!
OKAY, DON'T PANIC. WE CAN KICK THEM OUT.
NO, ALEX!
THERE MIGHT BE OTHER STUDENTS HERE. WHO KNOWS WHO ELSE IS IN THE AUDIENCE!
CALM DOWN, JO! IT'S NOT A BIG DEAL!
I CAN NOT BE TITS OUT IN FRONT OF MY STUDENTS, ALEX!!

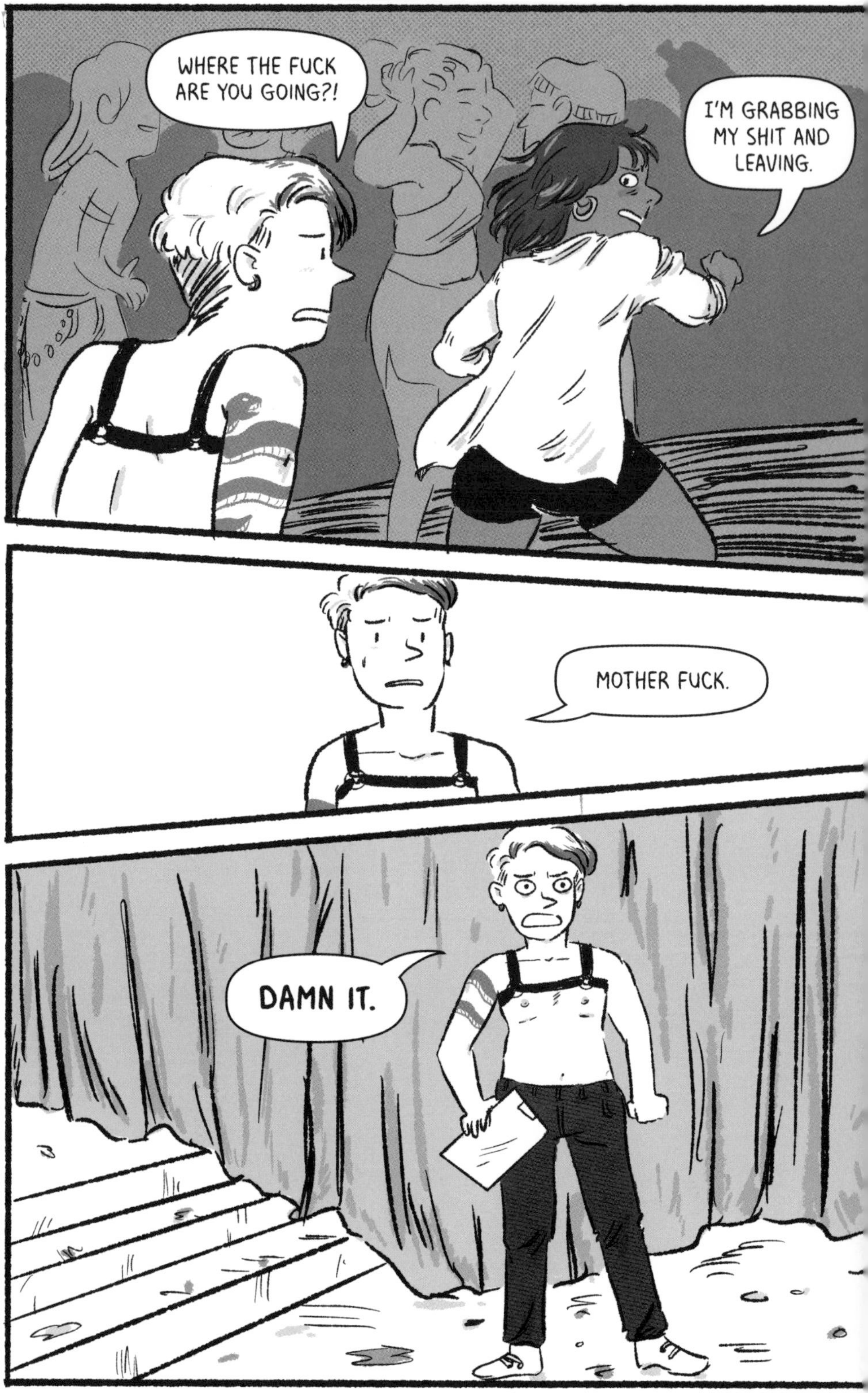
WHERE THE FUCK ARE YOU GOING?!
I'M GRABBING MY SHIT AND LEAVING.
MOTHER FUCK.
DAMN IT.

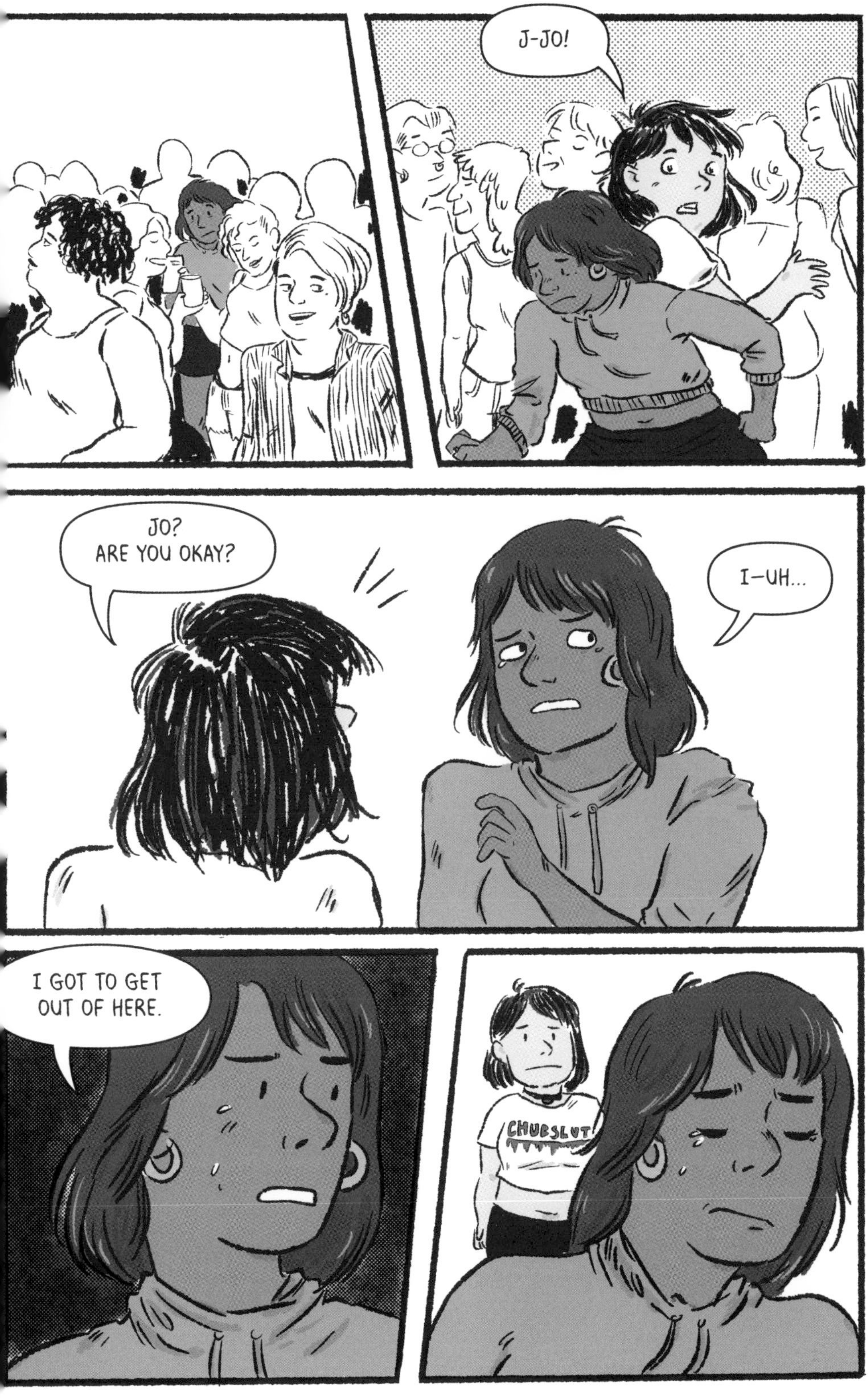
J-JO!
JO? ARE YOU OKAY?
I—UH...
I GOT TO GET OUT OF HERE.
CHUBSLUT

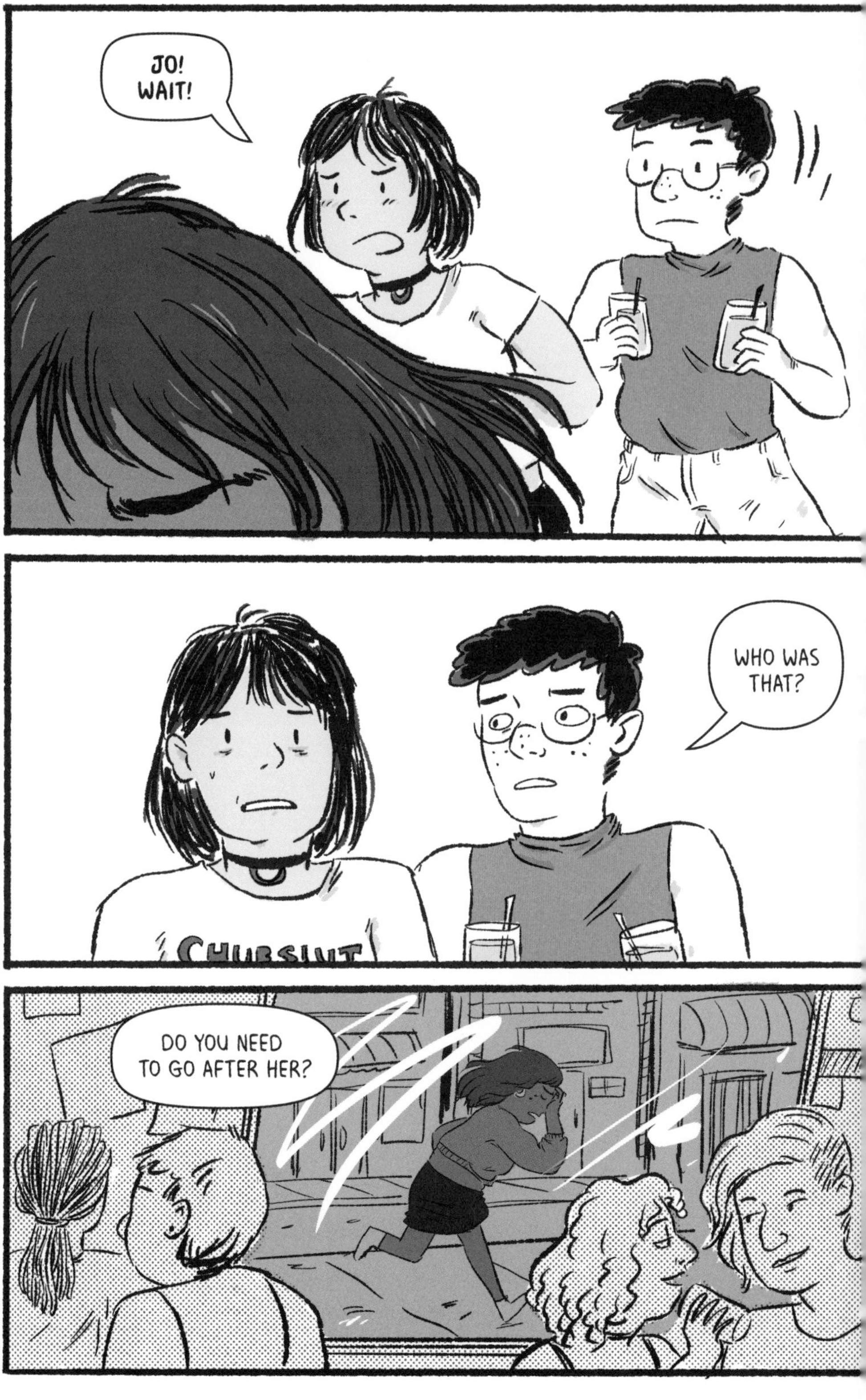
JO! WAIT!
WHO WAS THAT?
CHUBSLUT
DO YOU NEED TO GO AFTER HER?

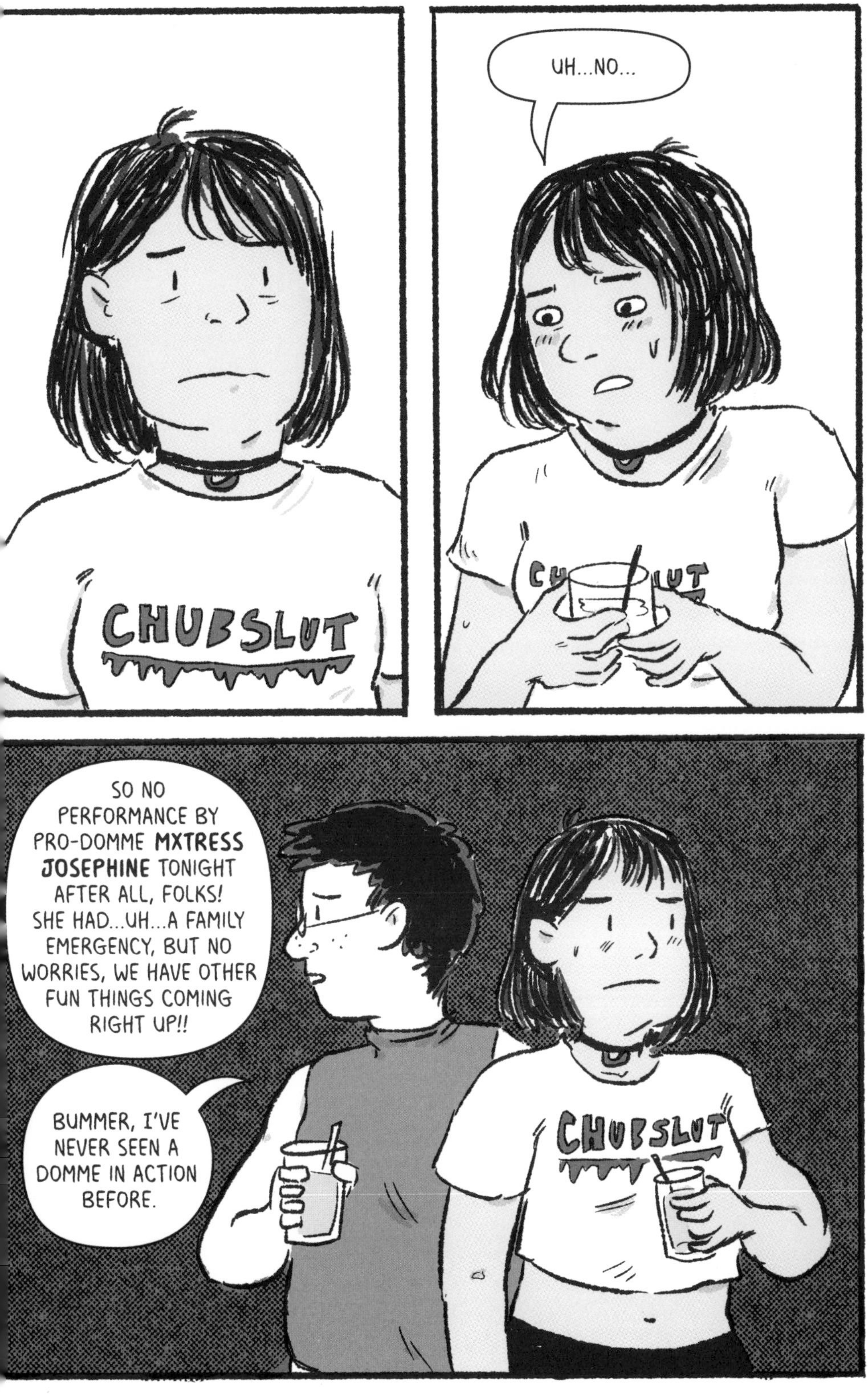
CHUBSLUT
UH...NO...
CHUBSLUT
SO NO PERFORMANCE BY PRO-DOMME **MXTRESS JOSEPHINE** TONIGHT AFTER ALL, FOLKS! SHE HAD...UH...A FAMILY EMERGENCY, BUT NO WORRIES, WE HAVE OTHER FUN THINGS COMING RIGHT UP!!
BUMMER, I'VE NEVER SEEN A DOMME IN ACTION BEFORE.
CHUBSLUT

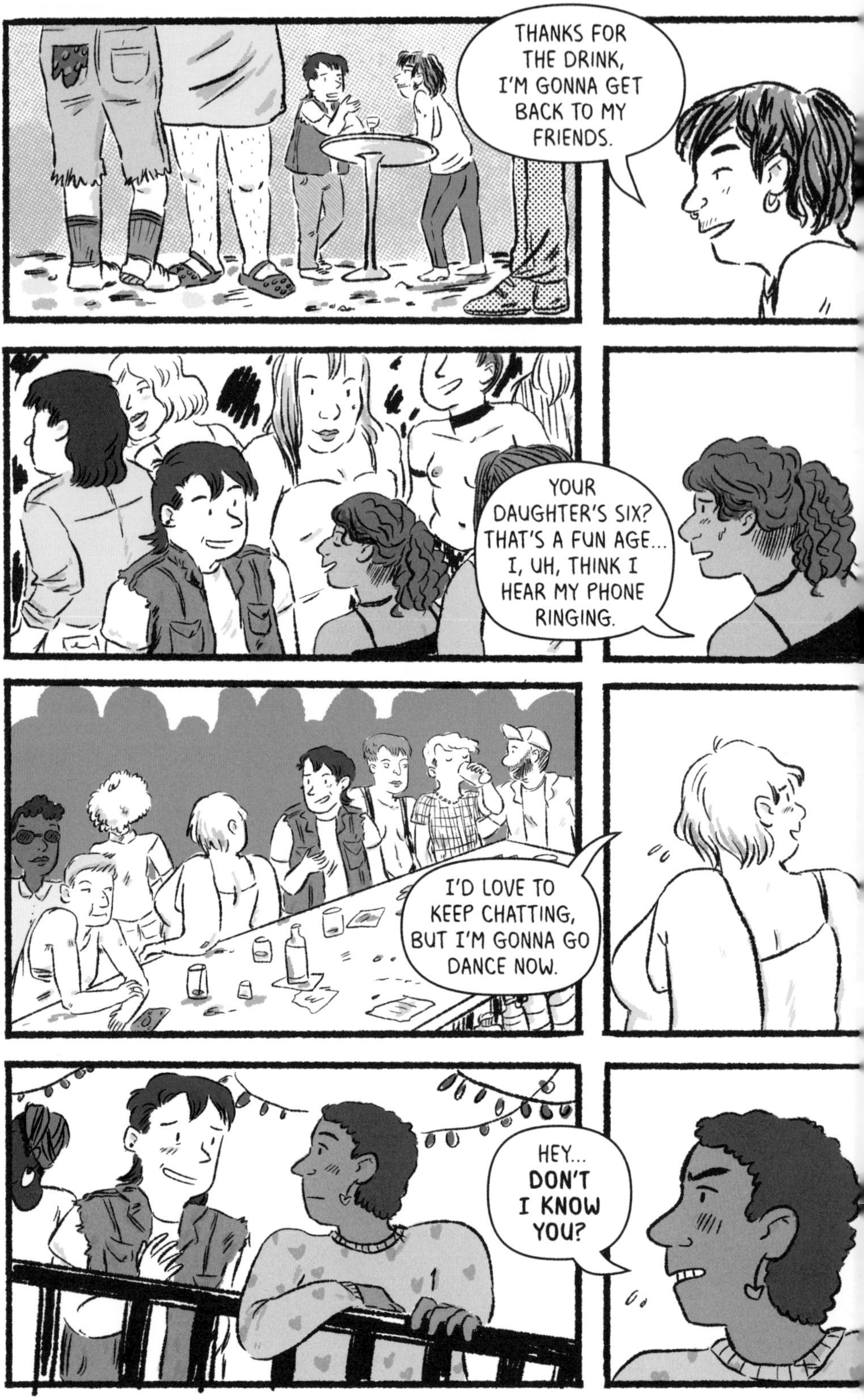
THANKS FOR THE DRINK, I'M GONNA GET BACK TO MY FRIENDS.
YOUR DAUGHTER'S SIX? THAT'S A FUN AGE... I, UH, THINK I HEAR MY PHONE RINGING.
I'D LOVE TO KEEP CHATTING, BUT I'M GONNA GO DANCE NOW.
HEY... **DON'T I KNOW YOU?**

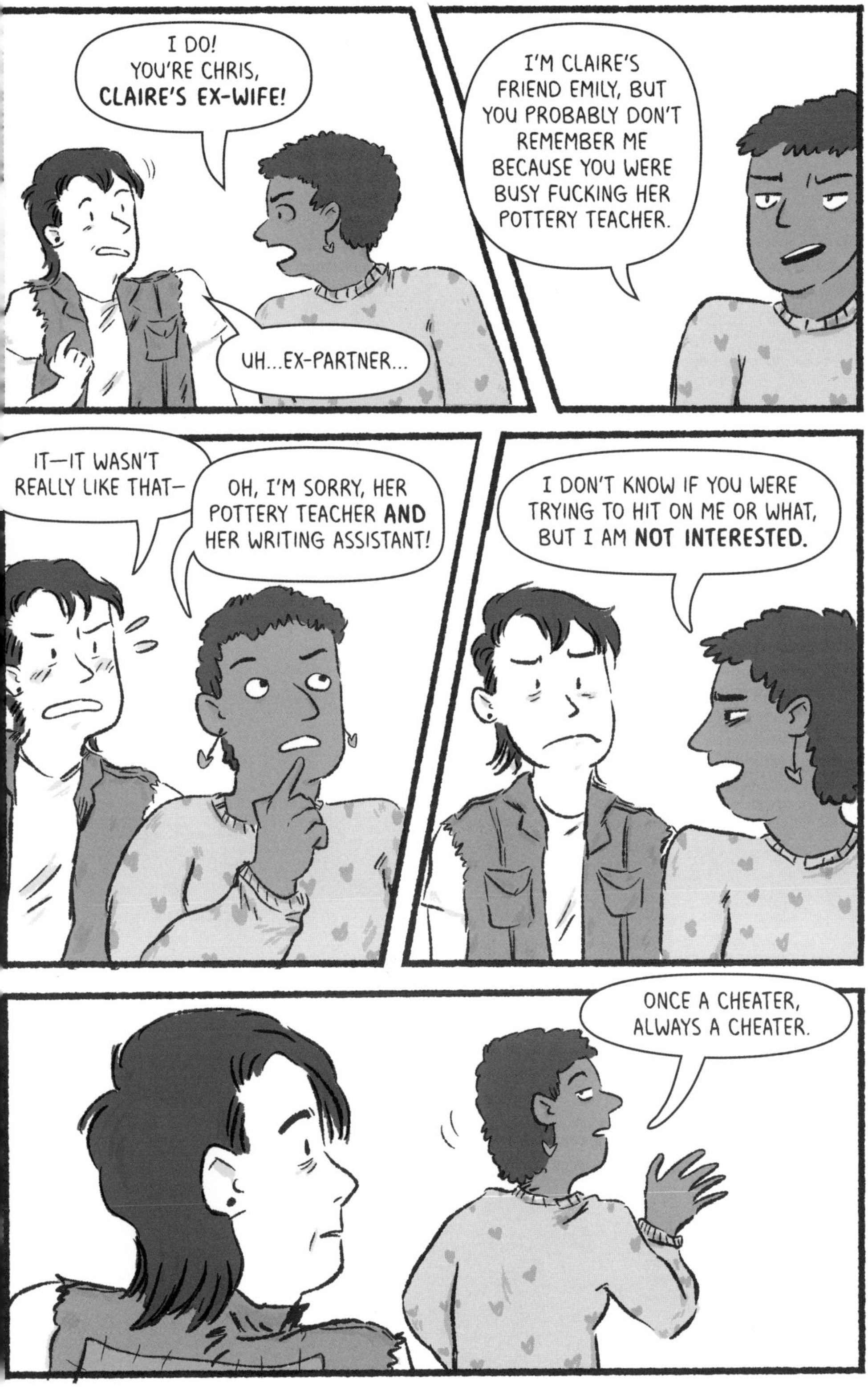
I DO! YOU'RE CHRIS, **CLAIRE'S EX-WIFE!**
UH...EX-PARTNER...
I'M CLAIRE'S FRIEND EMILY, BUT YOU PROBABLY DON'T REMEMBER ME BECAUSE YOU WERE BUSY FUCKING HER POTTERY TEACHER.
IT—IT WASN'T REALLY LIKE THAT—
OH, I'M SORRY, HER POTTERY TEACHER **AND** HER WRITING ASSISTANT!
I DON'T KNOW IF YOU WERE TRYING TO HIT ON ME OR WHAT, BUT I AM **NOT INTERESTED.**
ONCE A CHEATER, ALWAYS A CHEATER.

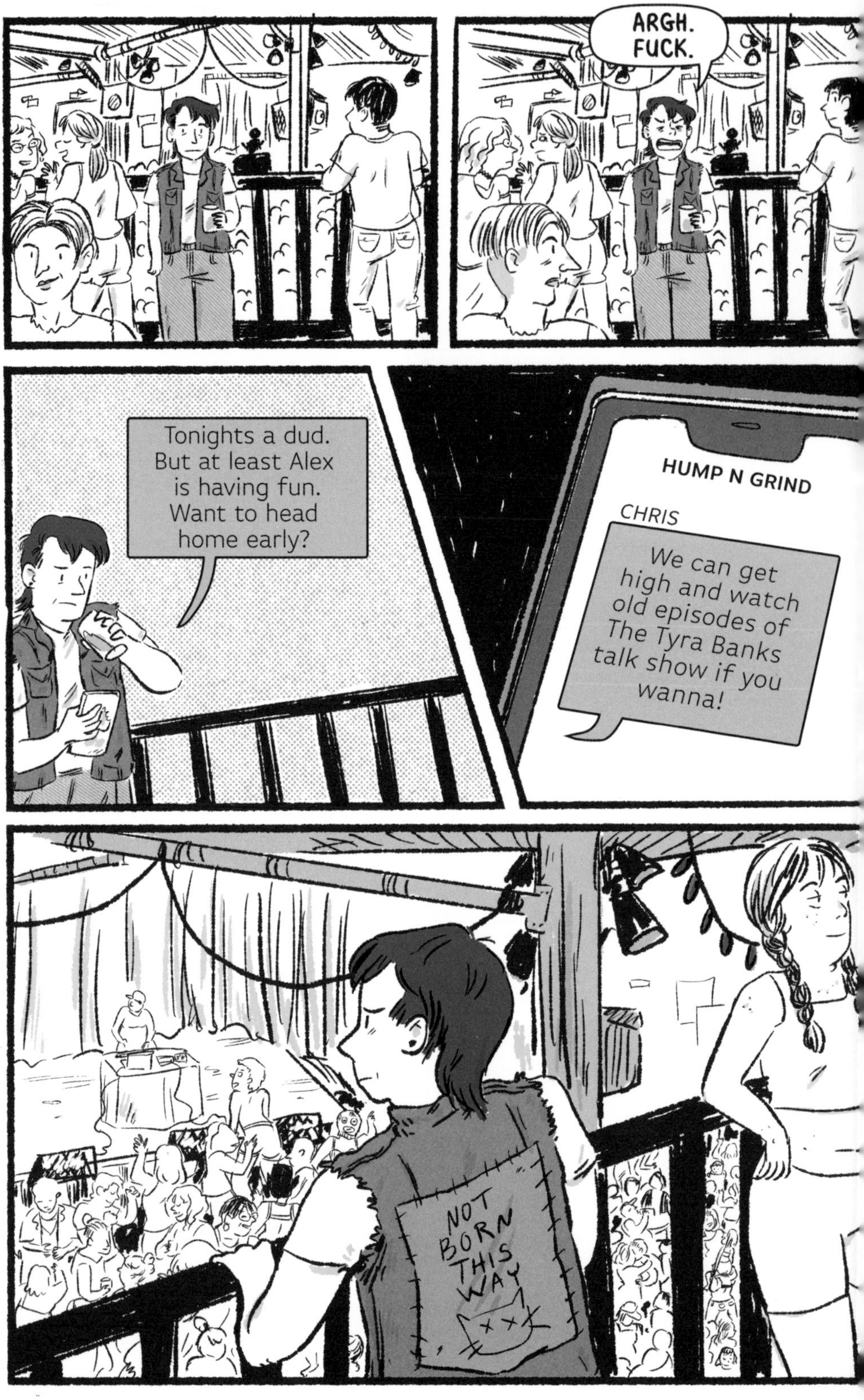
ARGH. FUCK.
Tonights a dud. But at least Alex is having fun. Want to head home early?
HUMP N GRIND
CHRIS
We can get high and watch old episodes of The Tyra Banks talk show if you wanna!
NOT BORN THIS WAY

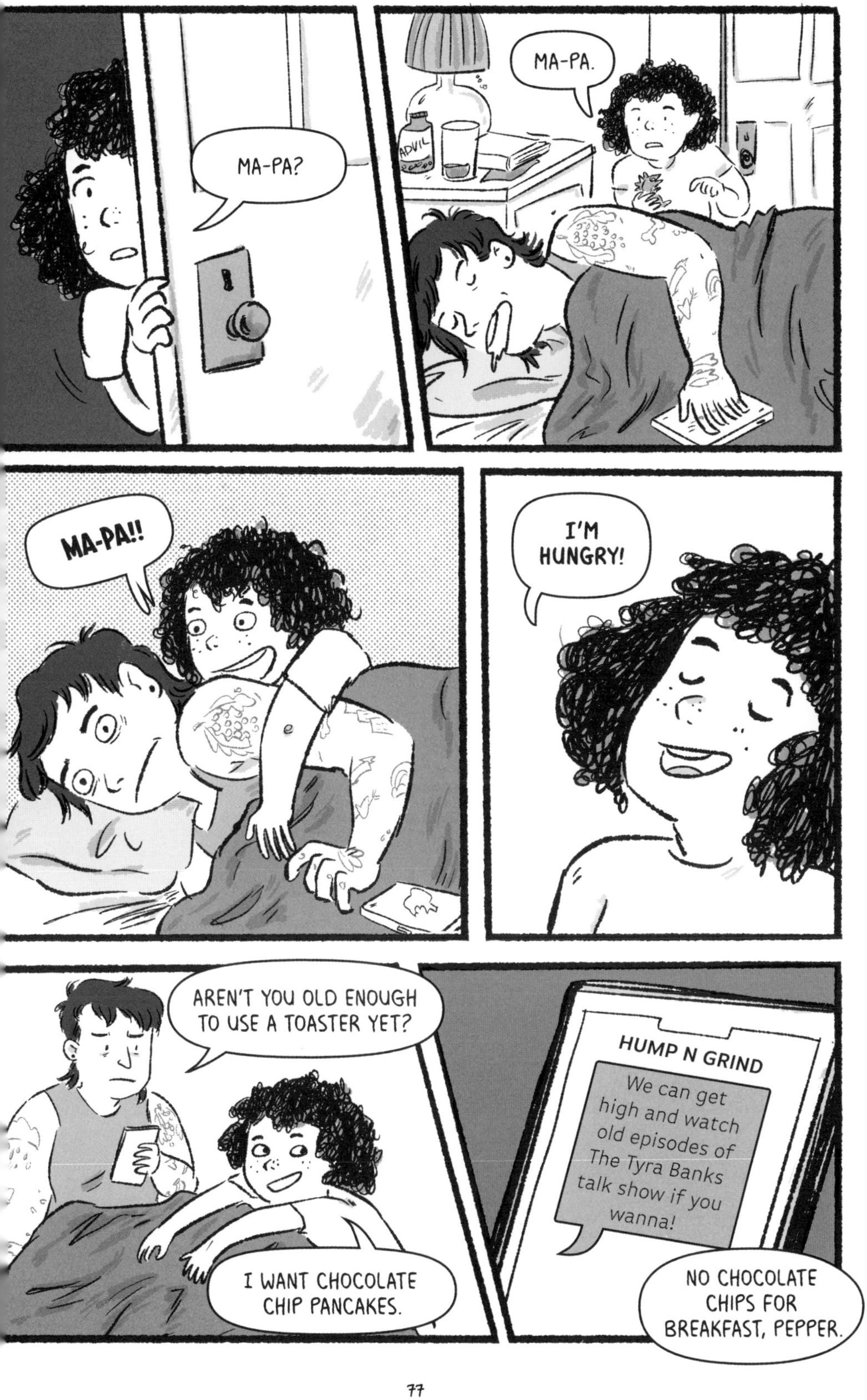

MA-PA?
MA-PA.
MA-PA!!
I'M HUNGRY!
AREN'T YOU OLD ENOUGH TO USE A TOASTER YET?
I WANT CHOCOLATE CHIP PANCAKES.
ADVIL
HUMP N GRIND
We can get high and watch old episodes of The Tyra Banks talk show if you wanna!
NO CHOCOLATE CHIPS FOR BREAKFAST, PEPPER.

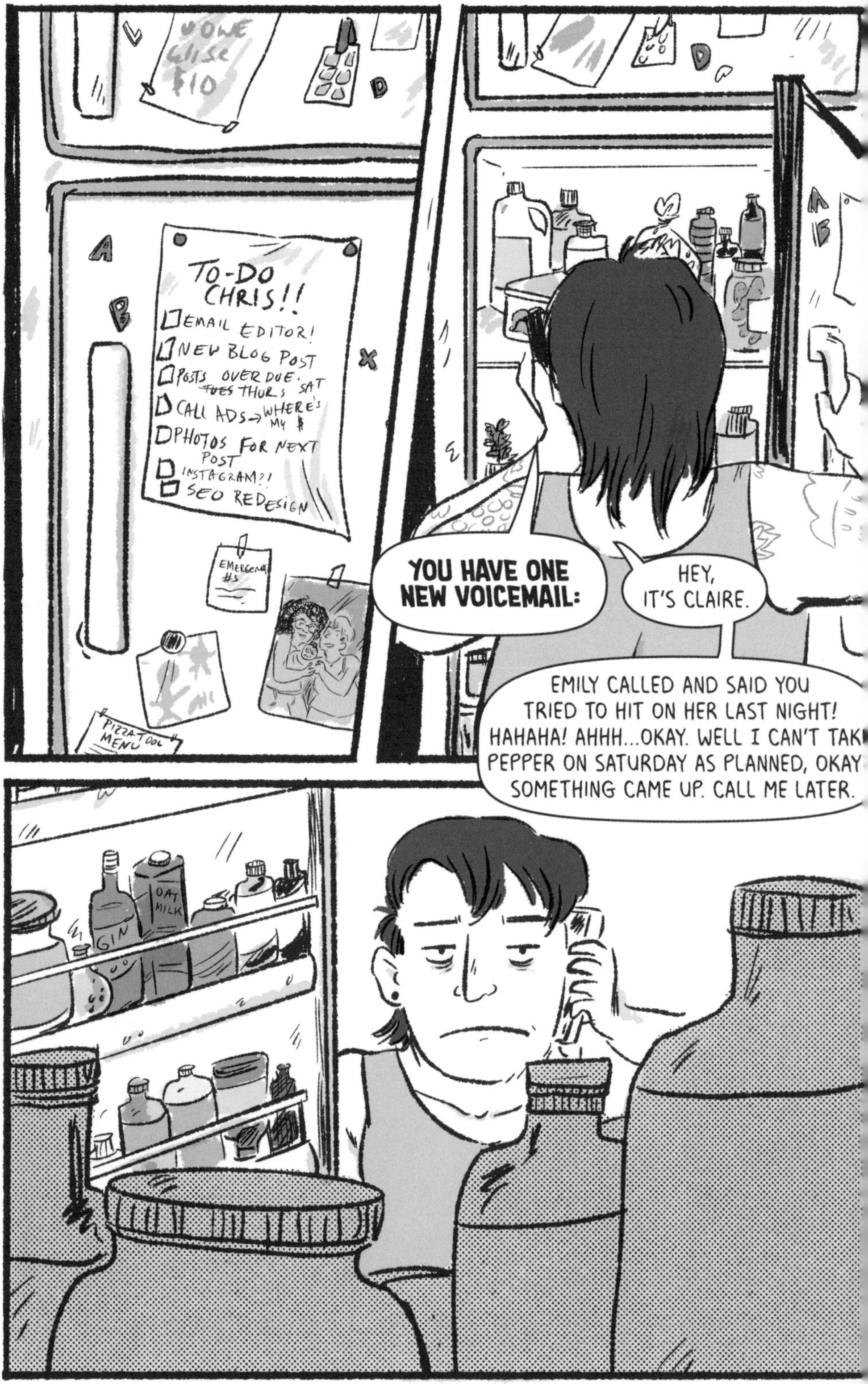
TO-DO CHRIS!!
EMAIL EDITOR!
NEW BLOG POST
POSTS OVERDUE. TUES THURS SAT
CALL ADS → WHERE'S MY $
PHOTOS FOR NEXT POST
INSTAGRAM?!
SEO REDESIGN
EMERGENCY #S
PIZZA TOOL MENU
YOU HAVE ONE NEW VOICEMAIL:
HEY, IT'S CLAIRE.
EMILY CALLED AND SAID YOU TRIED TO HIT ON HER LAST NIGHT! HAHAHA! AHHH...OKAY. WELL I CAN'T TAK PEPPER ON SATURDAY AS PLANNED, OKAY SOMETHING CAME UP. CALL ME LATER.
GIN
OAT MILK

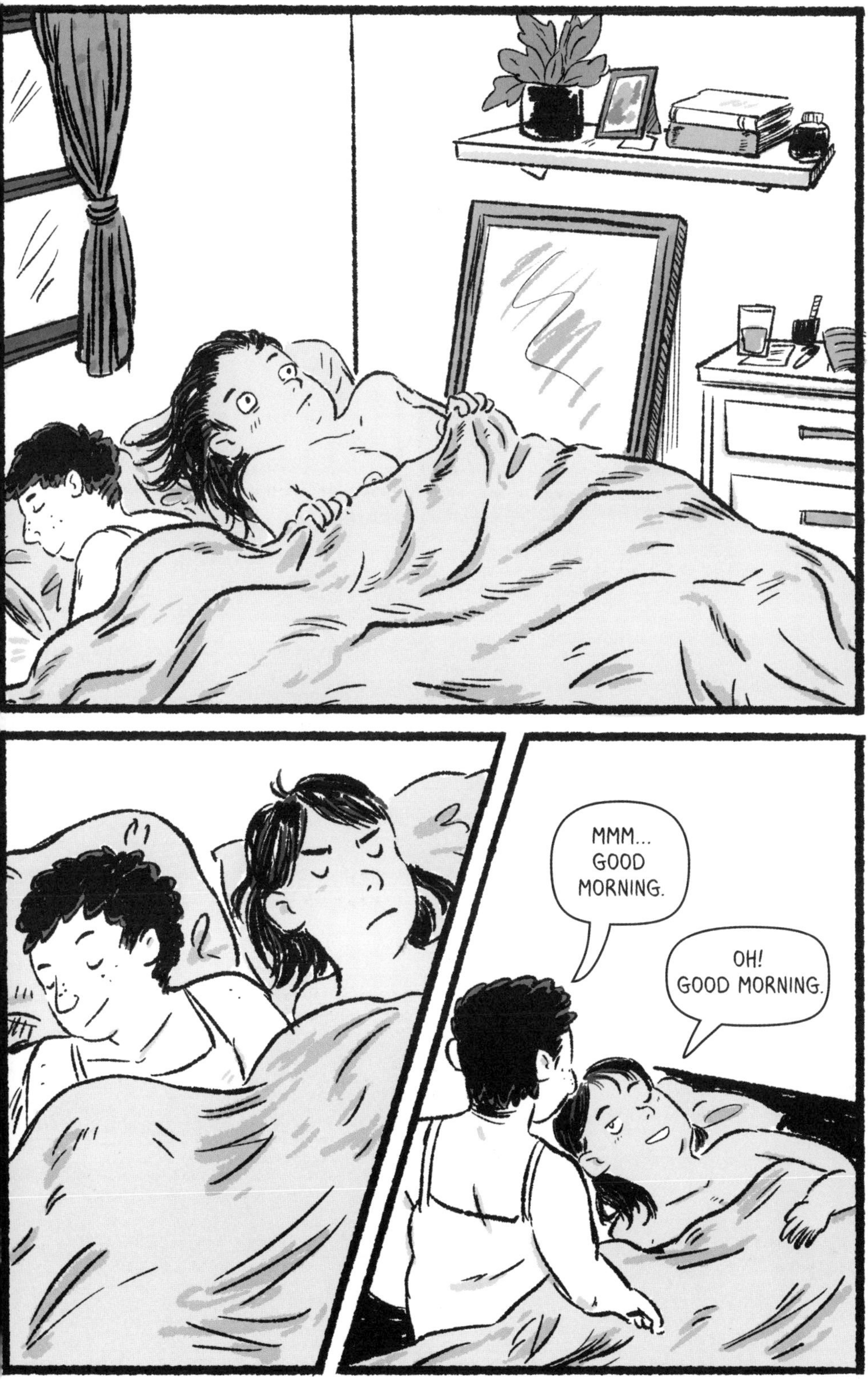
MMM... GOOD MORNING.
OH! GOOD MORNING.

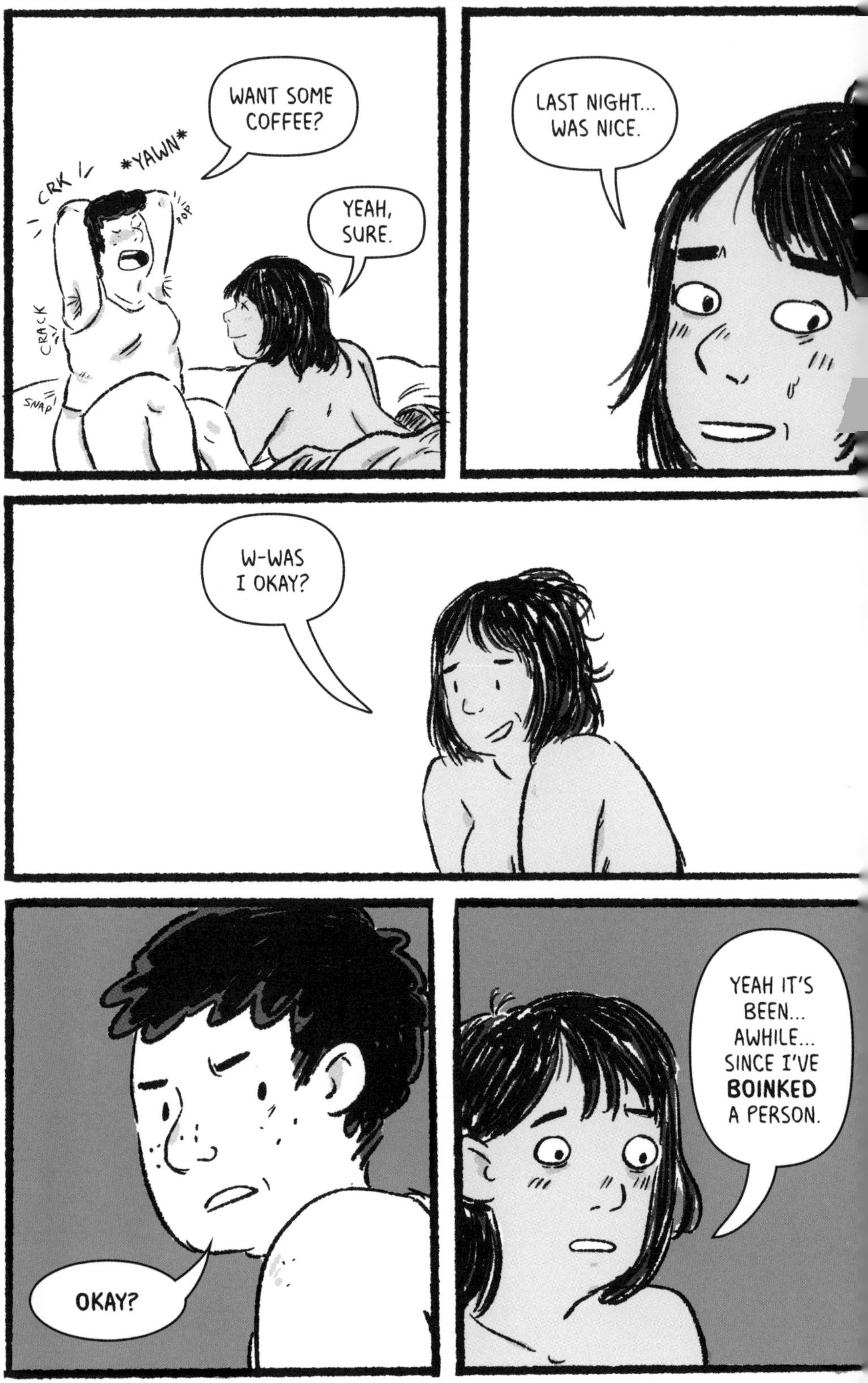
CRK
YAWN
WANT SOME COFFEE?
POP
CRACK
SNAP
YEAH, SURE.
LAST NIGHT... WAS NICE.
W-WAS I OKAY?
OKAY?
YEAH IT'S BEEN... AWHILE... SINCE I'VE **BOINKED** A PERSON.

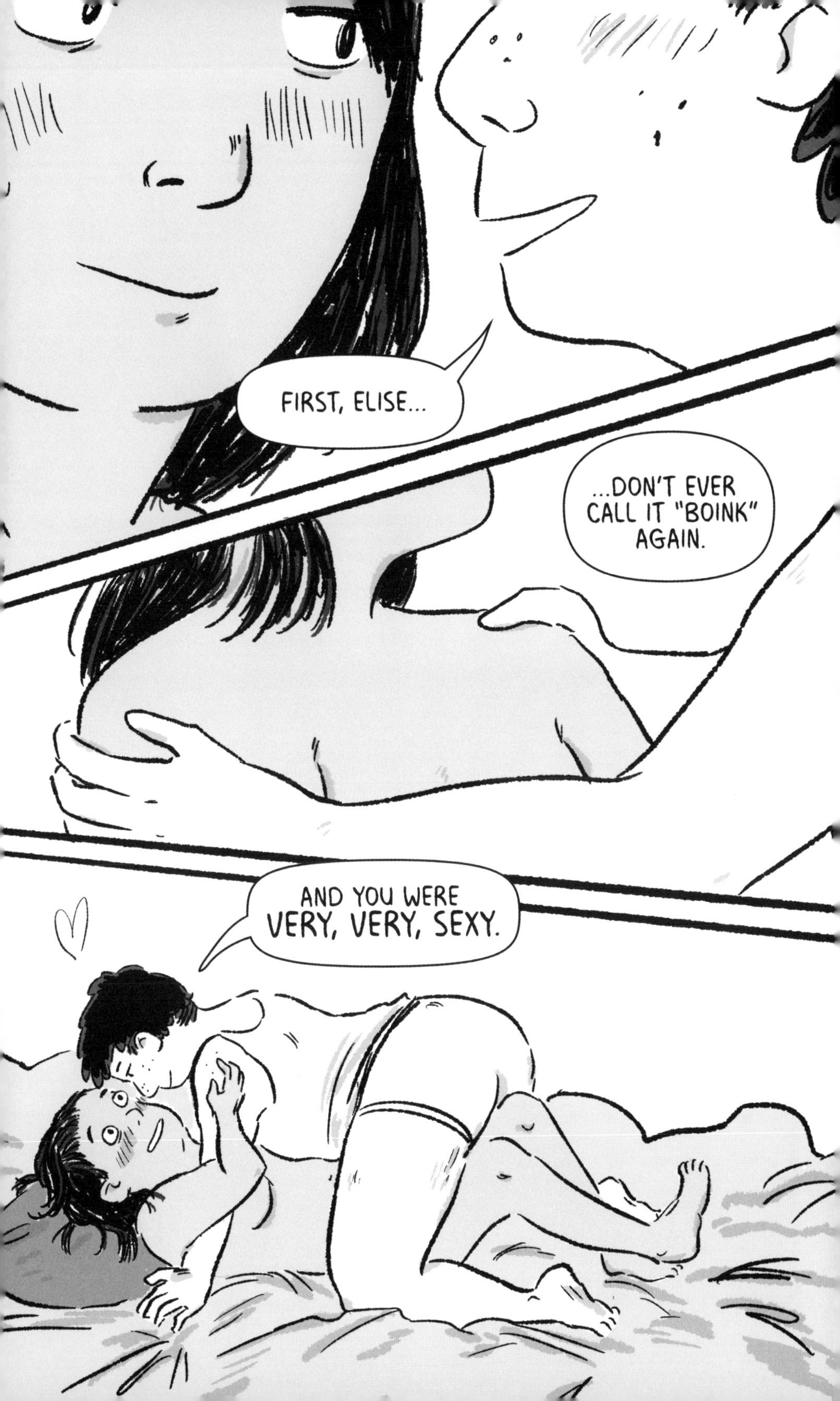
FIRST, ELISE...
...DON'T EVER CALL IT "BOINK" AGAIN.
AND YOU WERE VERY, VERY, SEXY.

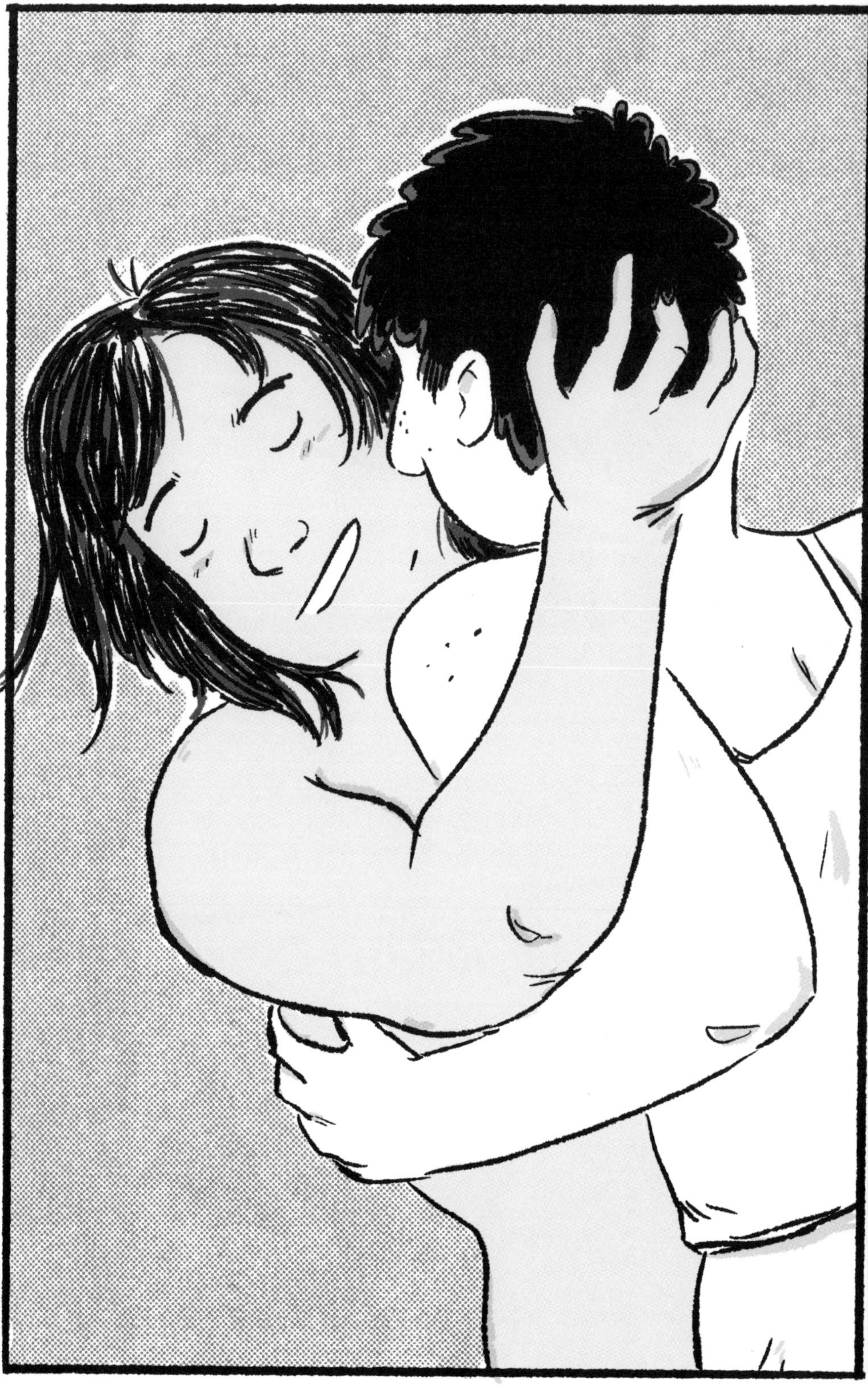

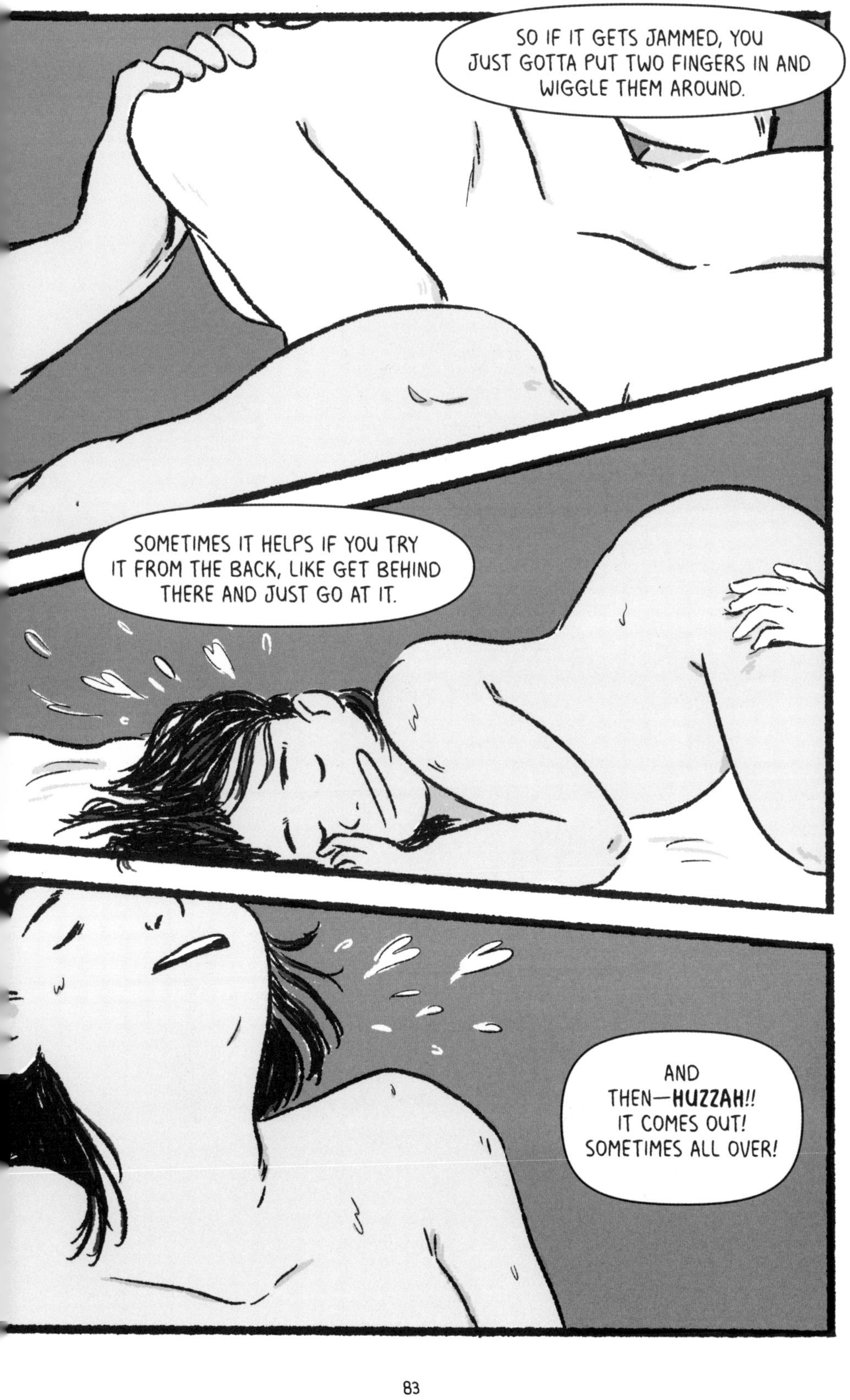
SO IF IT GETS JAMMED, YOU JUST GOTTA PUT TWO FINGERS IN AND WIGGLE THEM AROUND.
SOMETIMES IT HELPS IF YOU TRY IT FROM THE BACK, LIKE GET BEHIND THERE AND JUST GO AT IT.
AND THEN—**HUZZAH**!! IT COMES OUT! SOMETIMES ALL OVER!

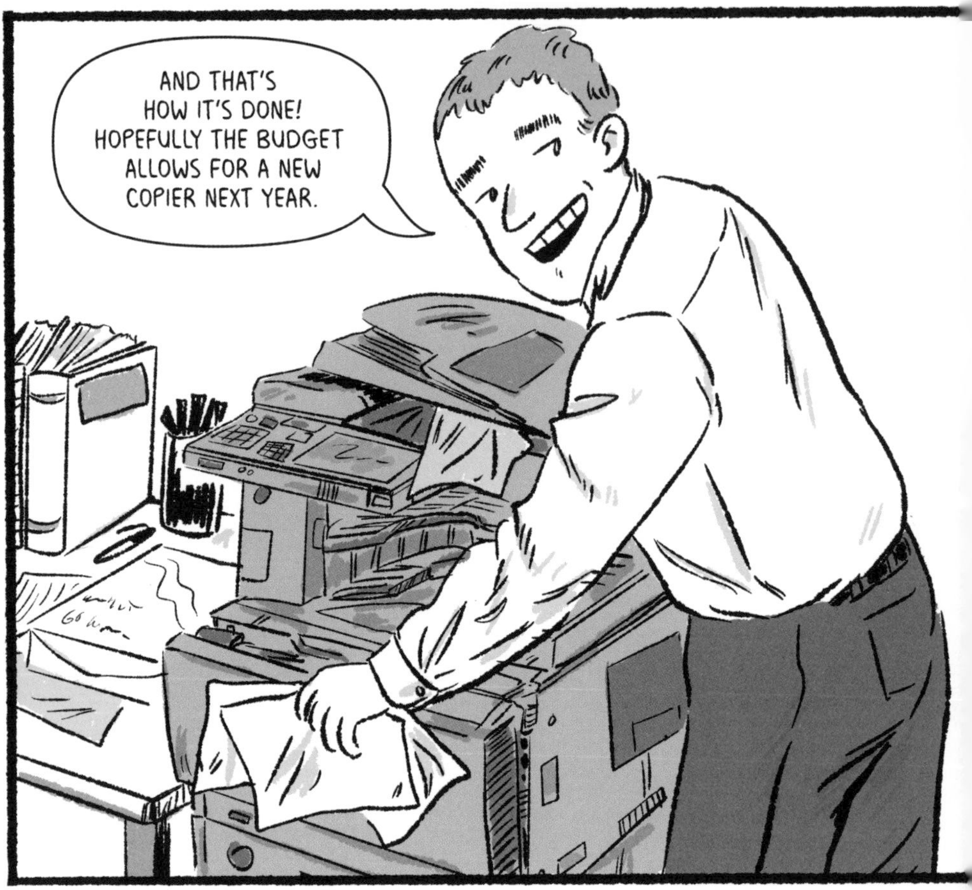
AND THAT'S HOW IT'S DONE! HOPEFULLY THE BUDGET ALLOWS FOR A NEW COPIER NEXT YEAR.

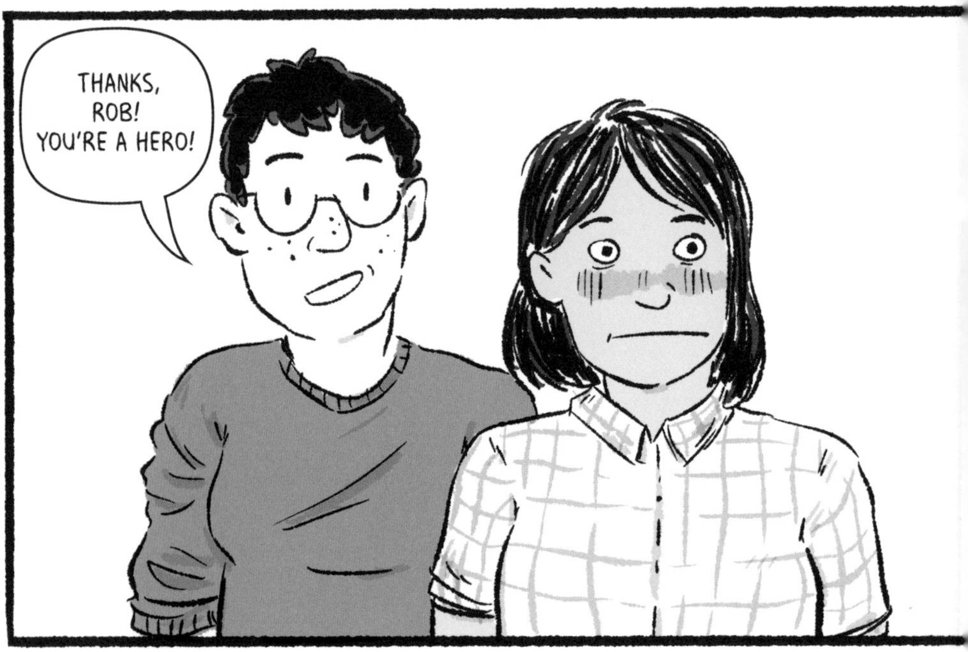
THANKS, ROB! YOU'RE A HERO!

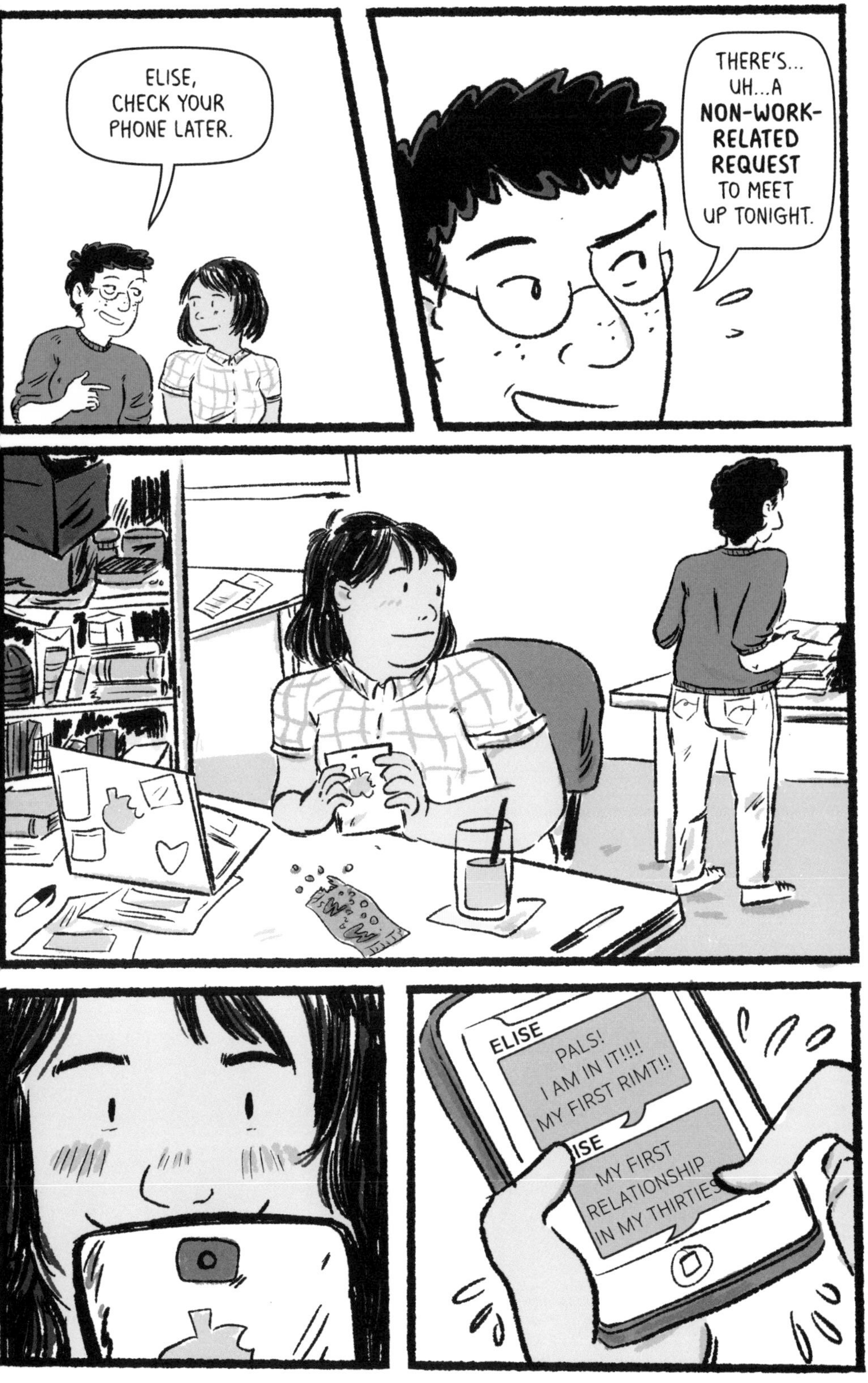
ELISE, CHECK YOUR PHONE LATER.
THERE'S... UH...A **NON-WORK-RELATED REQUEST** TO MEET UP TONIGHT.
ELISE
PALS! I AM IN IT!!!! MY FIRST RIMT!!
ISE
MY FIRST RELATIONSHIP IN MY THIRTIES

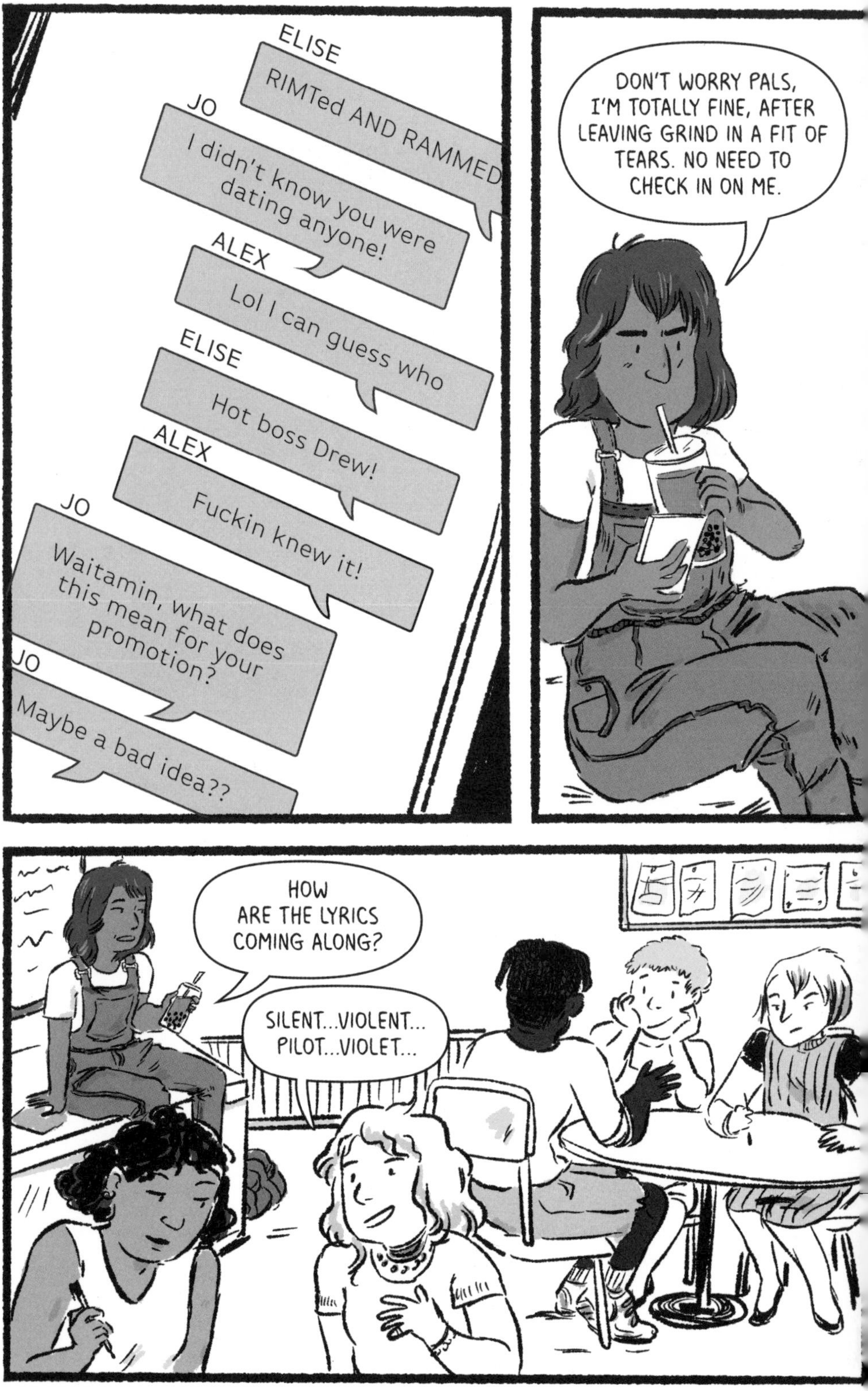
ELISE
RIMTed AND RAMMED
JO
I didn't know you were dating anyone!
ALEX
Lol I can guess who
ELISE
Hot boss Drew!
ALEX
Fuckin knew it!
JO
Waitamin, what does this mean for your promotion?
JO
Maybe a bad idea??
DON'T WORRY PALS, I'M TOTALLY FINE, AFTER LEAVING GRIND IN A FIT OF TEARS. NO NEED TO CHECK IN ON ME.
HOW ARE THE LYRICS COMING ALONG?
SILENT...VIOLENT... PILOT...VIOLET...

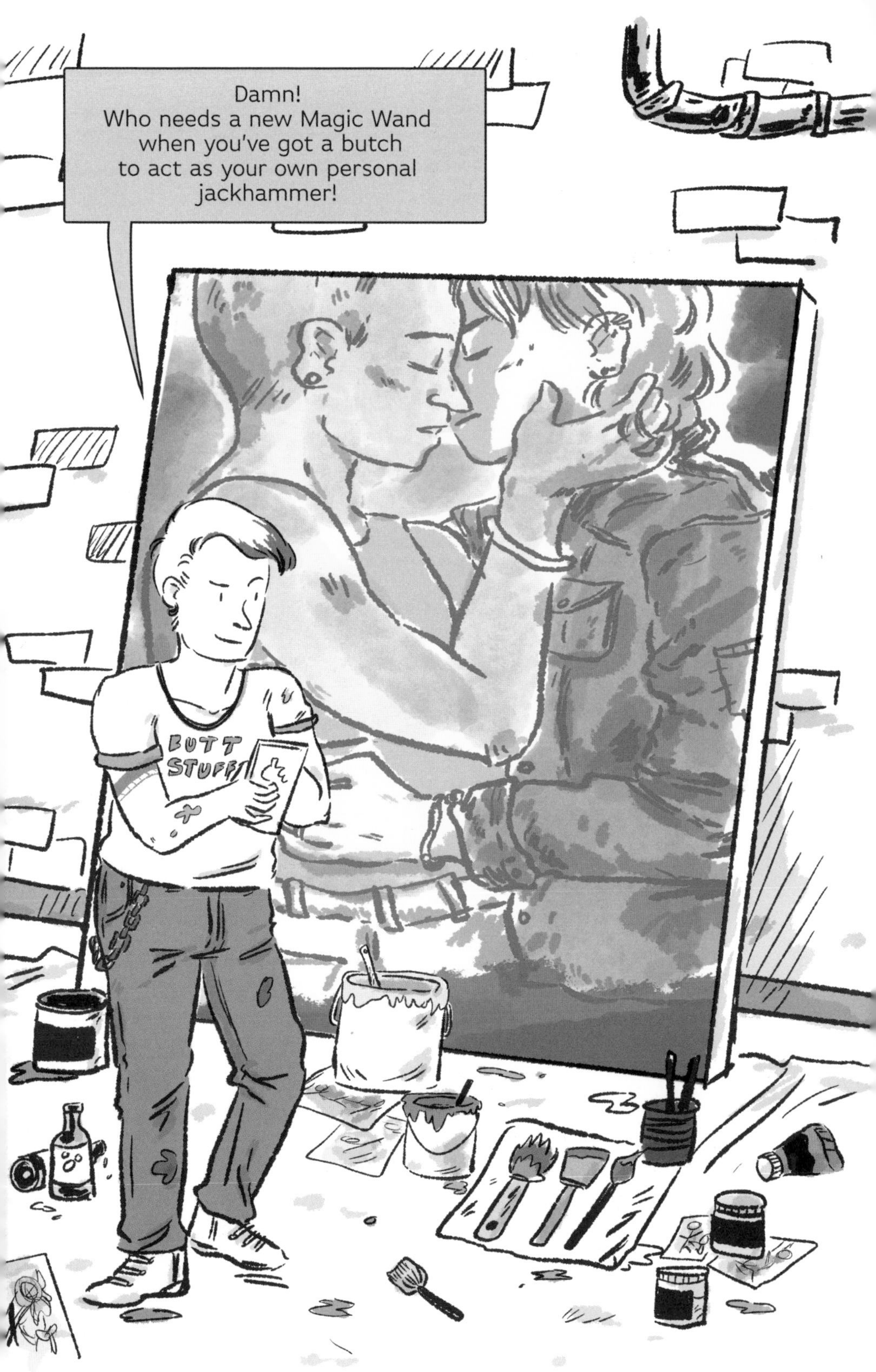
Damn!
Who needs a new Magic Wand
when you've got a butch
to act as your own personal
jackhammer!
BUTT STUFF

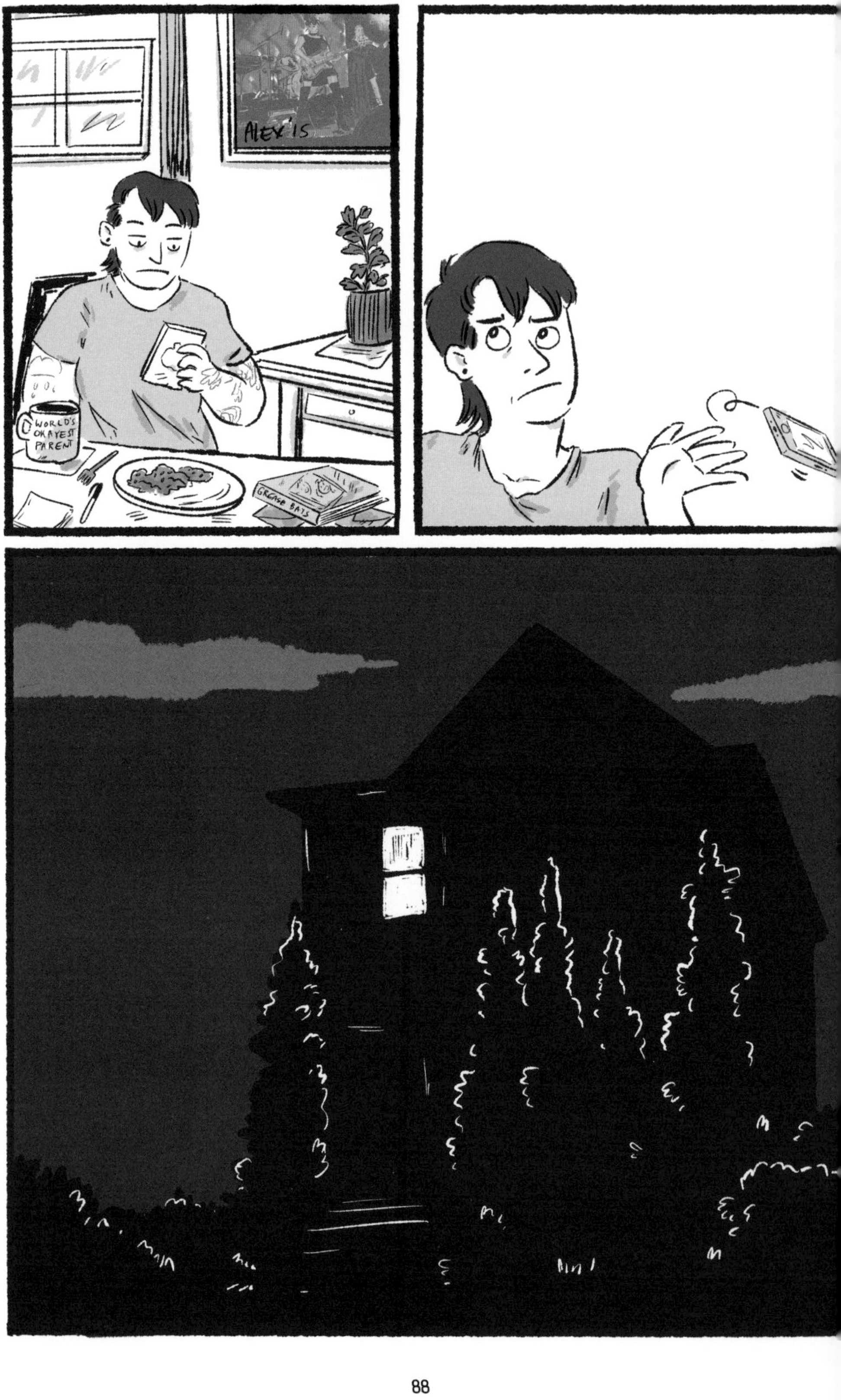
ALEX '15
WORLD'S OKAYEST PARENT
GREASE BATS

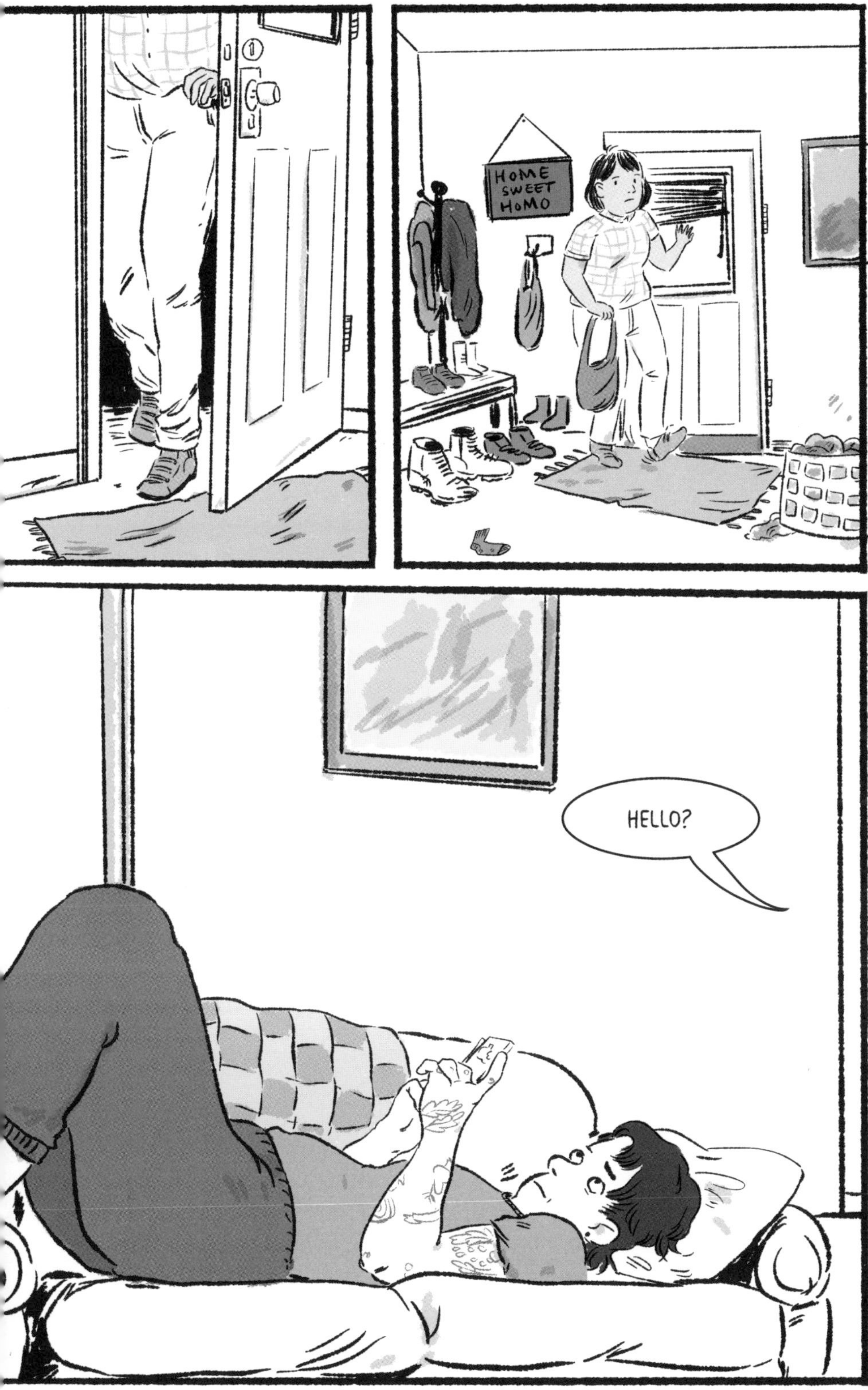
HOME
SWEET
HOMO
HELLO?

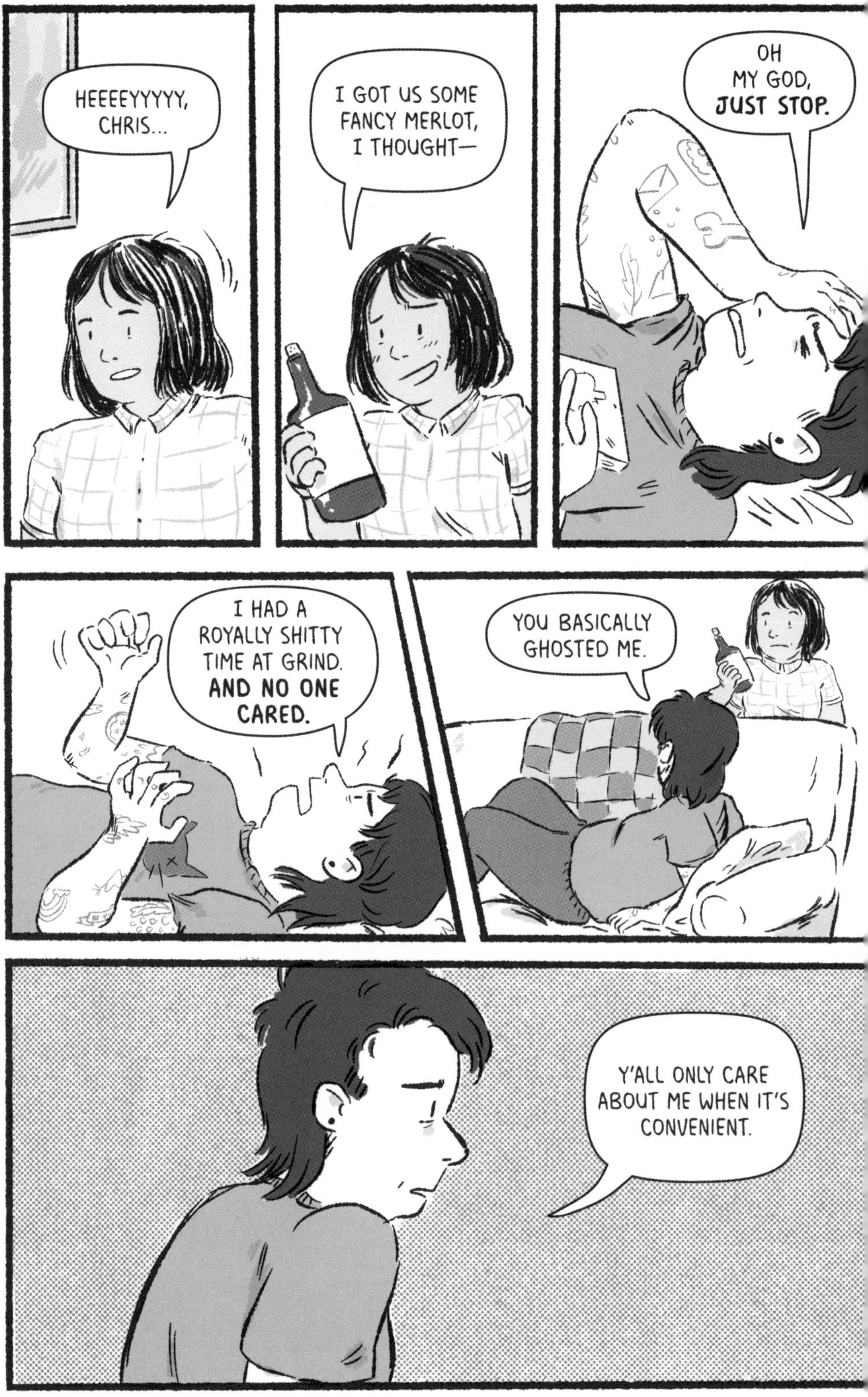
HEEEEYYYYY, CHRIS...
I GOT US SOME FANCY MERLOT, I THOUGHT—
OH MY GOD, **JUST STOP.**
I HAD A ROYALLY SHITTY TIME AT GRIND. **AND NO ONE CARED.**
YOU BASICALLY GHOSTED ME.
Y'ALL ONLY CARE ABOUT ME WHEN IT'S CONVENIENT.

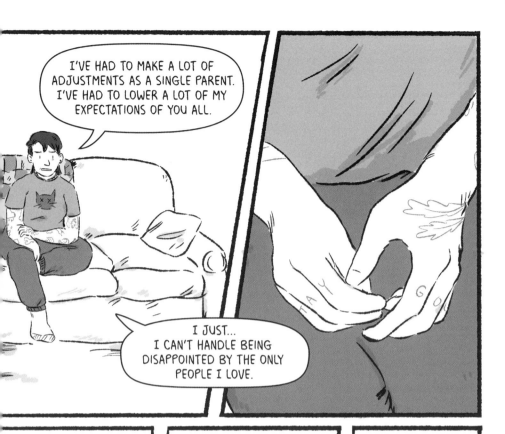

I'VE HAD TO MAKE A LOT OF ADJUSTMENTS AS A SINGLE PARENT. I'VE HAD TO LOWER A LOT OF MY EXPECTATIONS OF YOU ALL.

I JUST... I CAN'T HANDLE BEING DISAPPOINTED BY THE ONLY PEOPLE I LOVE.

I'M SORRY YOU DIDN'T GET LAID AT GRIND.

AND I'M SORRY I WAS TOO BUSY GETTING LAID TO TEXT YOU BACK.

AND MOST OF ALL, I'M SORRY I WASN'T THERE TO WATCH TYRA WITH YOU.

OKAY, I GET IT.

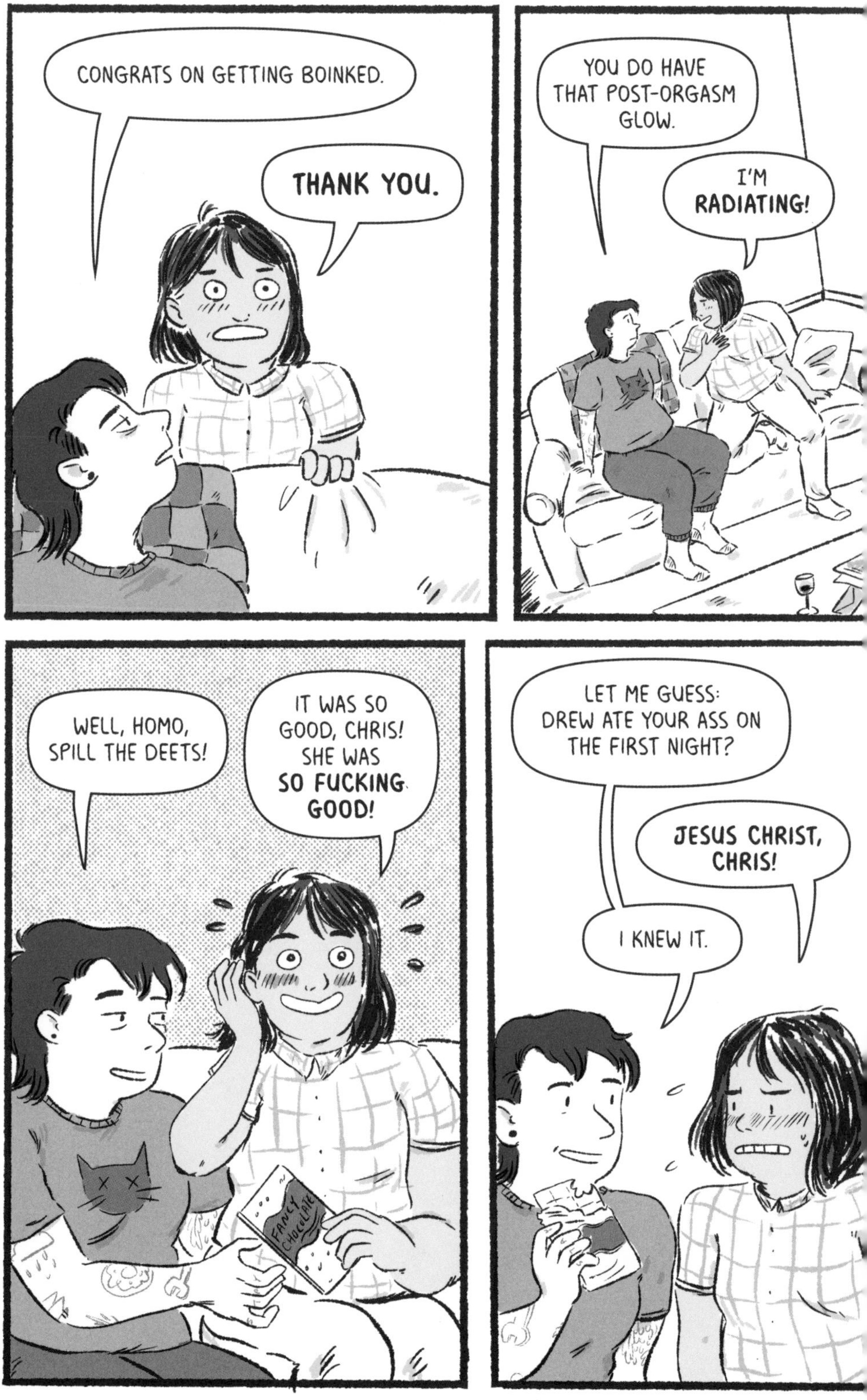
CONGRATS ON GETTING BOINKED.
THANK YOU.
YOU DO HAVE THAT POST-ORGASM GLOW.
I'M RADIATING!
WELL, HOMO, SPILL THE DEETS!
IT WAS SO GOOD, CHRIS! SHE WAS SO FUCKING GOOD!
FANCY CHOCOLATE
LET ME GUESS: DREW ATE YOUR ASS ON THE FIRST NIGHT?
JESUS CHRIST, CHRIS!
I KNEW IT.

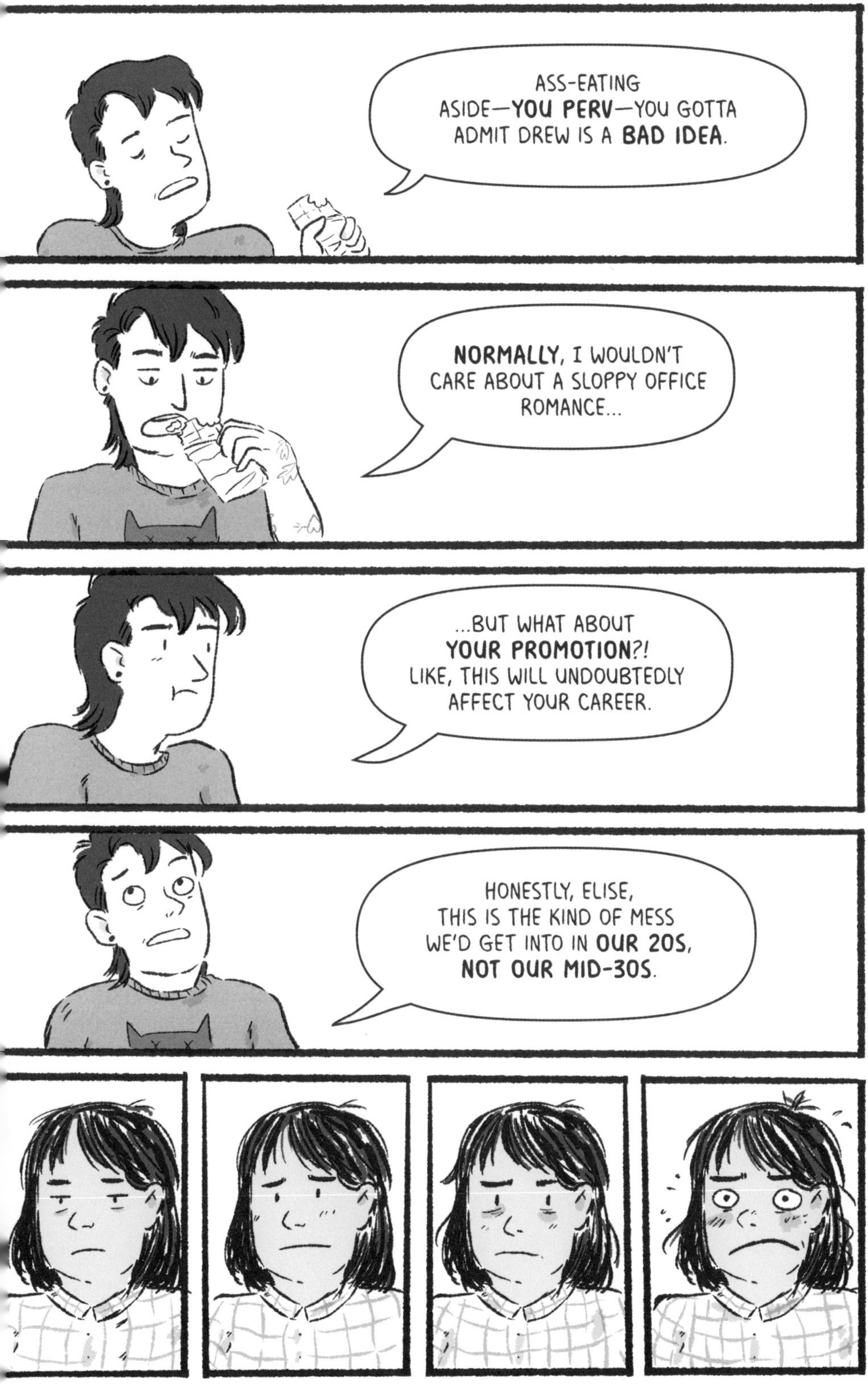
ASS-EATING ASIDE—**YOU PERV**—YOU GOTTA ADMIT DREW IS A **BAD IDEA**.
NORMALLY, I WOULDN'T CARE ABOUT A SLOPPY OFFICE ROMANCE...
...BUT WHAT ABOUT **YOUR PROMOTION**?! LIKE, THIS WILL UNDOUBTEDLY AFFECT YOUR CAREER.
HONESTLY, ELISE, THIS IS THE KIND OF MESS WE'D GET INTO IN **OUR 20S, NOT OUR MID-30S**.

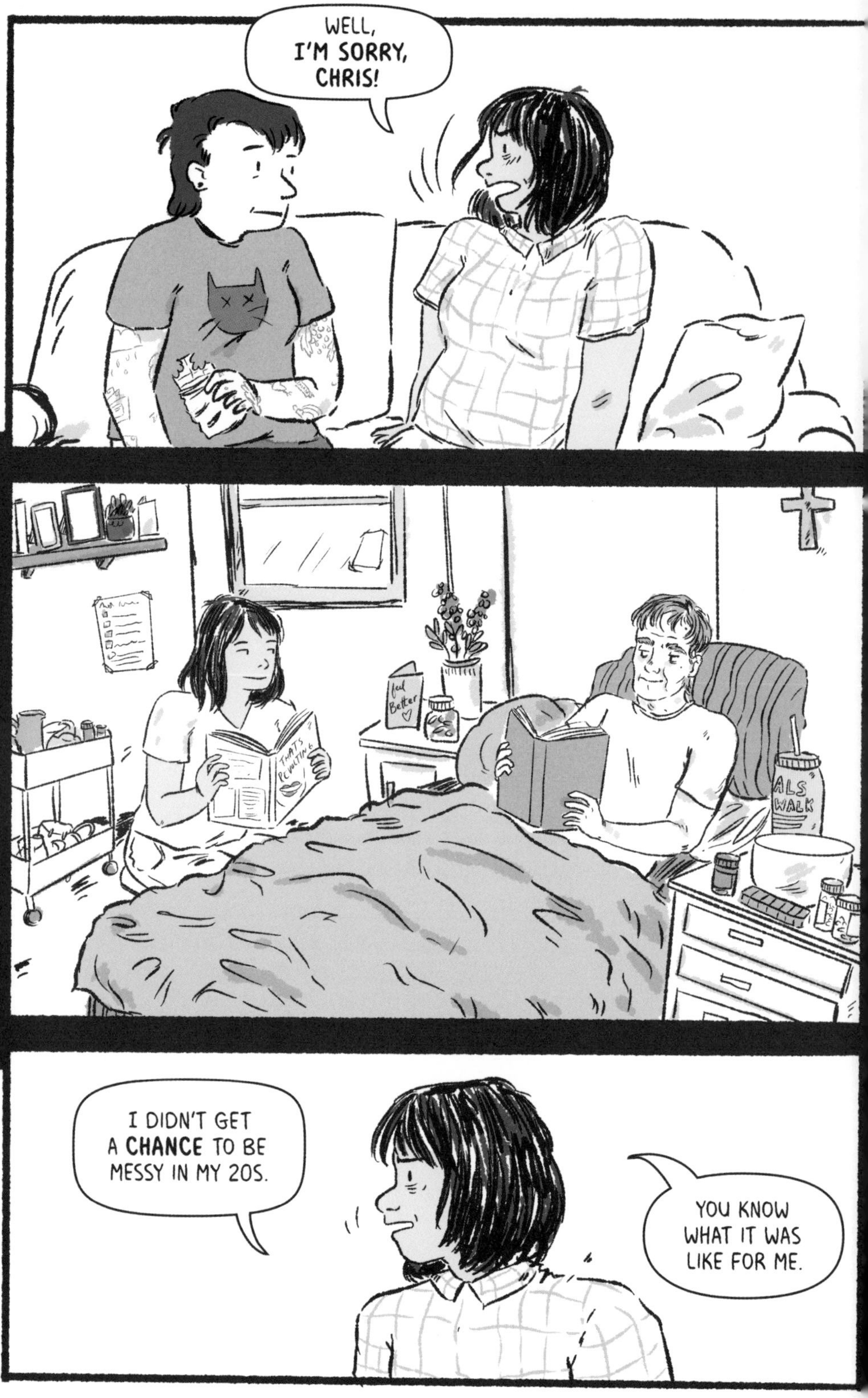
WELL, **I'M SORRY, CHRIS!**
feel Better
THAT'S REVOLTING
ALS WALK
I DIDN'T GET A **CHANCE** TO BE MESSY IN MY 20S.
YOU KNOW WHAT IT WAS LIKE FOR ME.

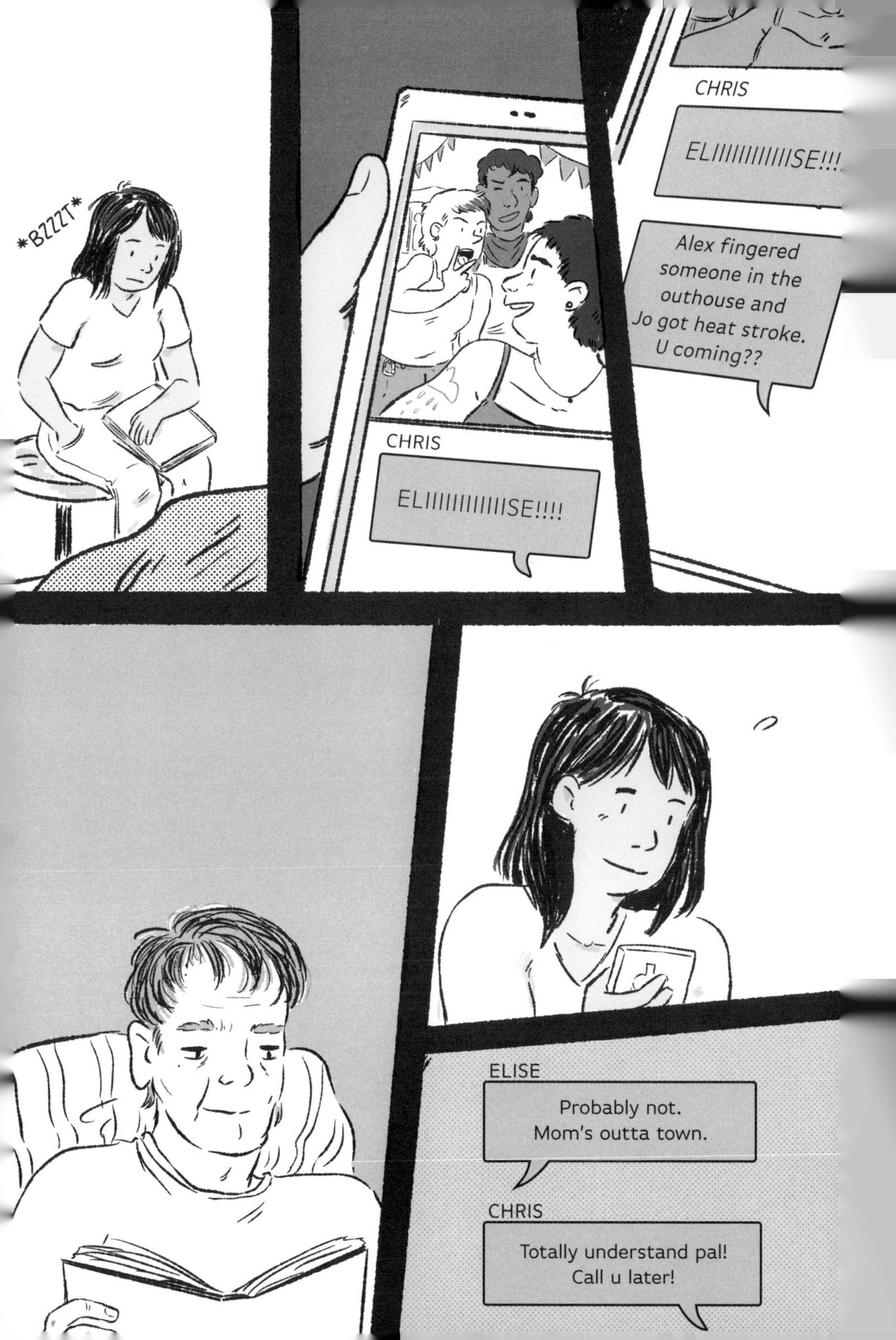
BZZZT
CHRIS
ELIIIIIIIIIIIISE!!!!
CHRIS
ELIIIIIIIIIIIISE!!!
Alex fingered someone in the outhouse and Jo got heat stroke. U coming??
ELISE
Probably not. Mom's outta town.
CHRIS
Totally understand pal! Call u later!

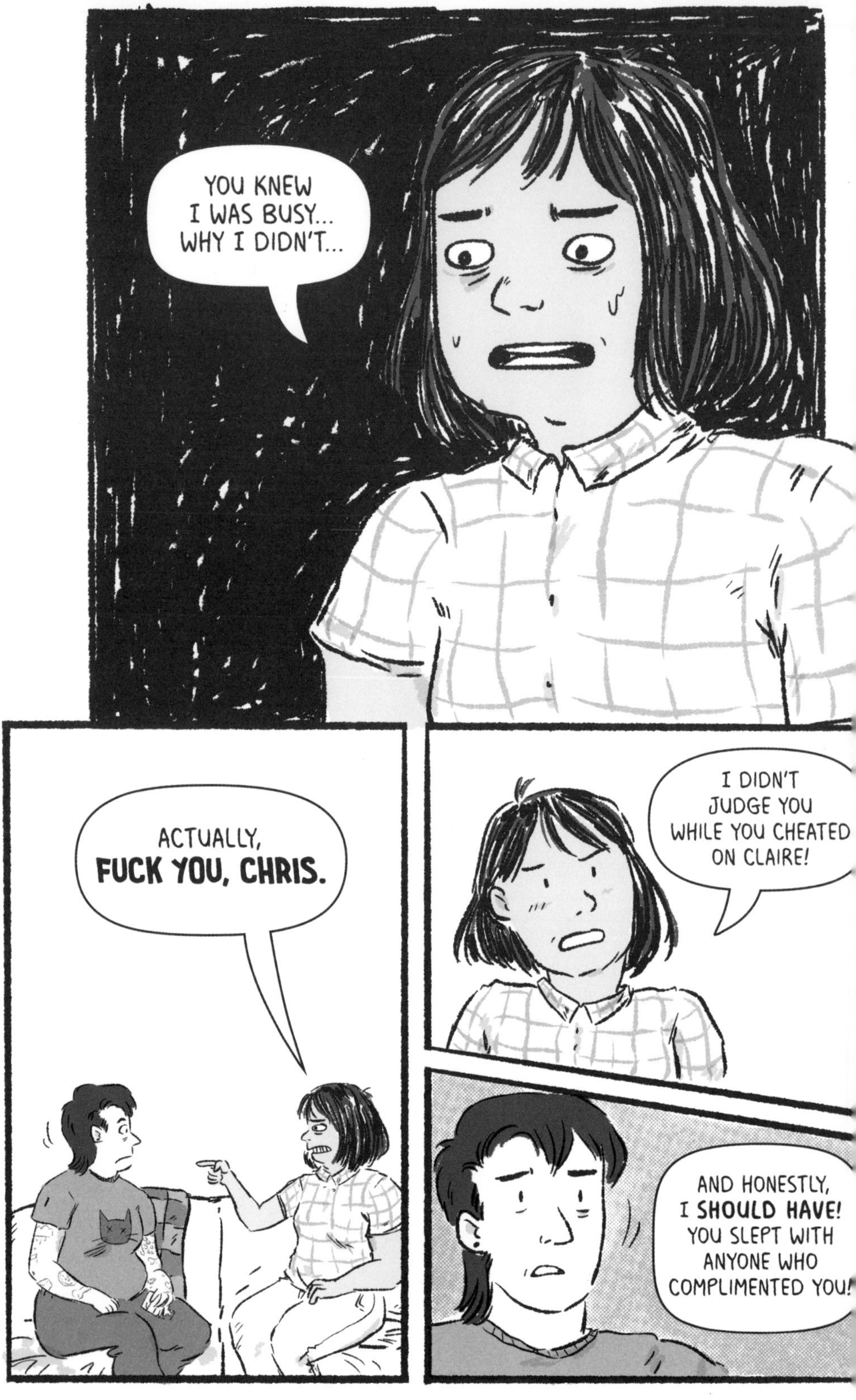
YOU KNEW I WAS BUSY... WHY I DIDN'T...
ACTUALLY, **FUCK YOU, CHRIS.**
I DIDN'T JUDGE YOU WHILE YOU CHEATED ON CLAIRE!
AND HONESTLY, I **SHOULD HAVE!** YOU SLEPT WITH ANYONE WHO COMPLIMENTED YOU!

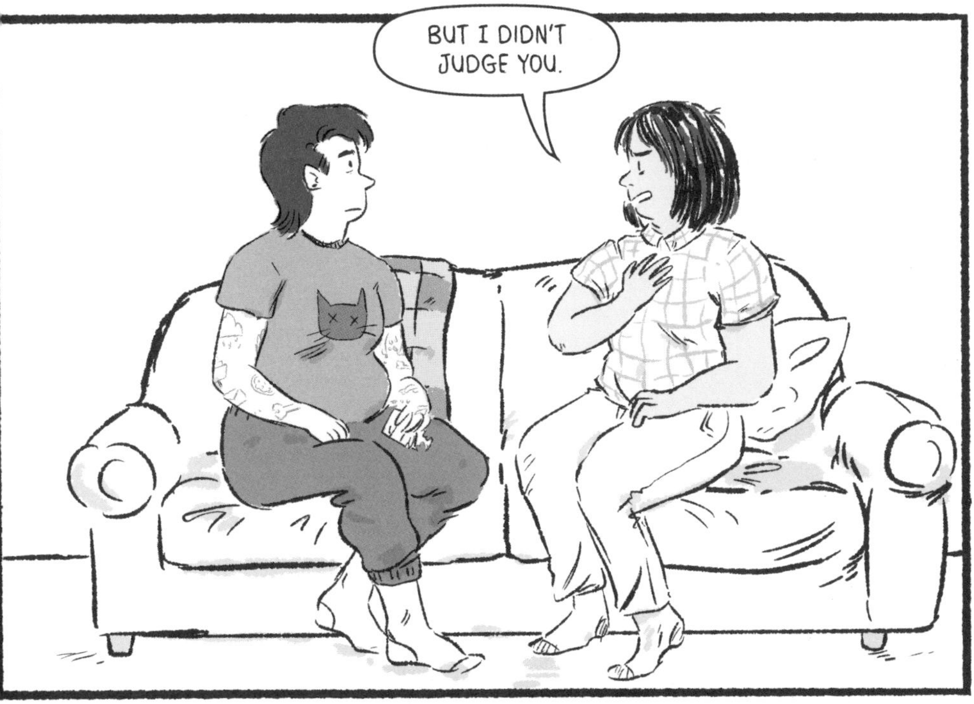
BUT I DIDN'T JUDGE YOU.

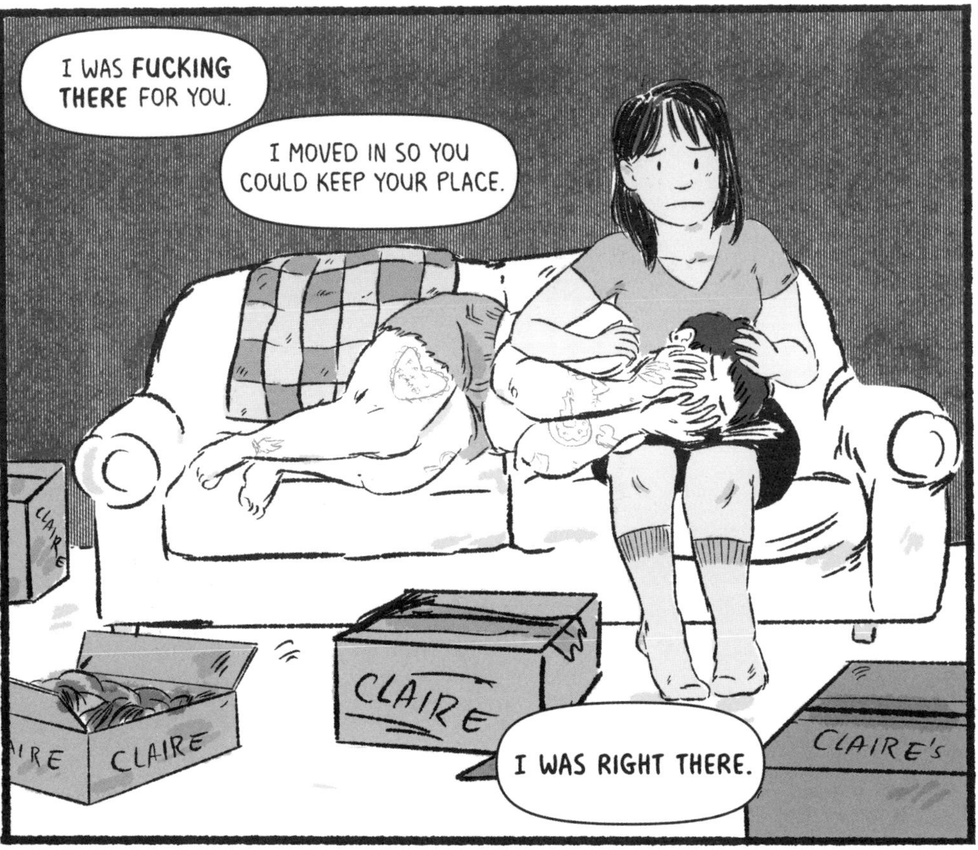
I WAS **FUCKING THERE** FOR YOU.
I MOVED IN SO YOU COULD KEEP YOUR PLACE.
CLAIRE
IRE
CLAIRE
CLAIRE
CLAIRE's
I WAS RIGHT THERE.

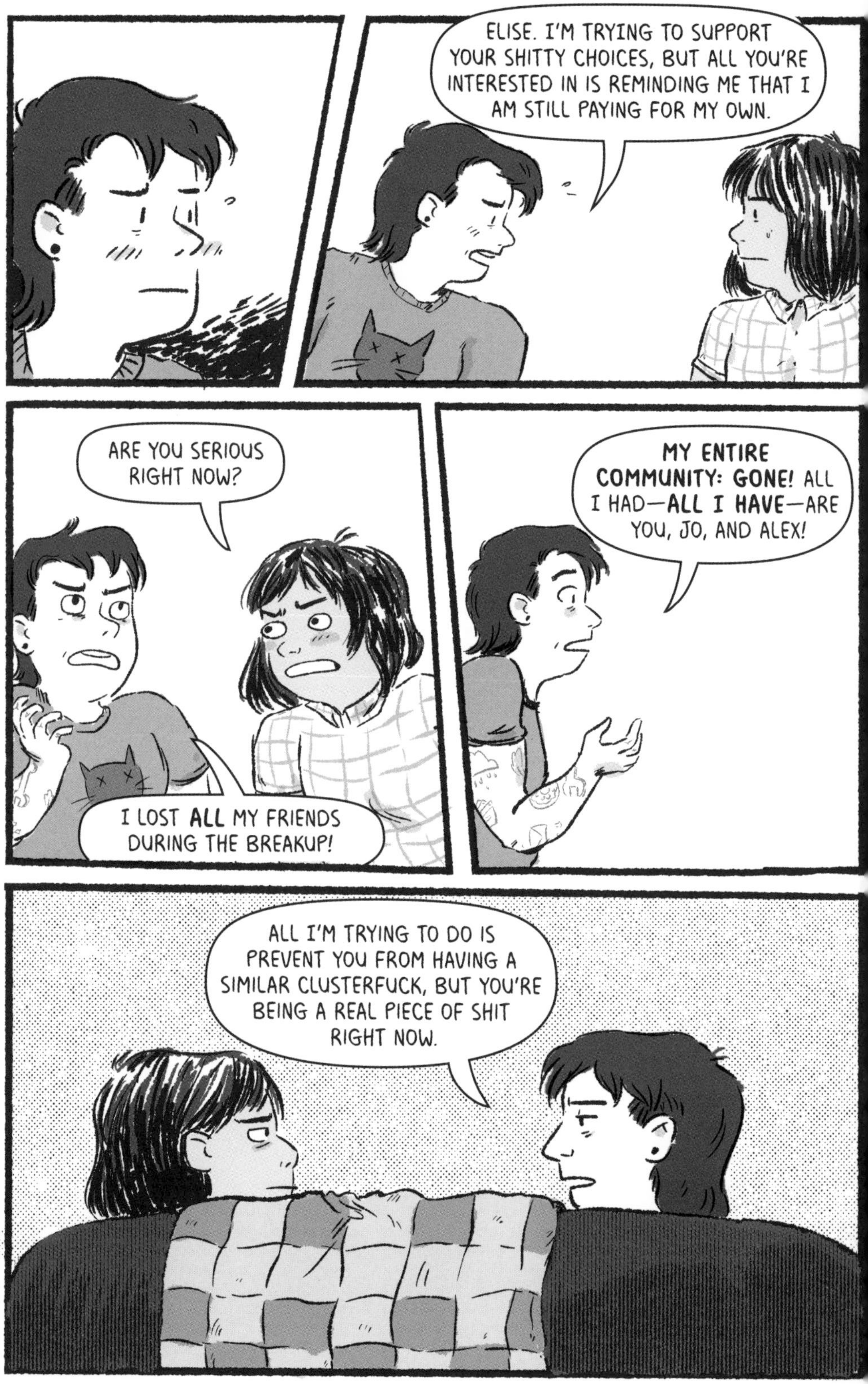
ELISE. I'M TRYING TO SUPPORT YOUR SHITTY CHOICES, BUT ALL YOU'RE INTERESTED IN IS REMINDING ME THAT I AM STILL PAYING FOR MY OWN.
ARE YOU SERIOUS RIGHT NOW?
I LOST ALL MY FRIENDS DURING THE BREAKUP!
MY ENTIRE COMMUNITY: GONE! ALL I HAD—ALL I HAVE—ARE YOU, JO, AND ALEX!
ALL I'M TRYING TO DO IS PREVENT YOU FROM HAVING A SIMILAR CLUSTERFUCK, BUT YOU'RE BEING A REAL PIECE OF SHIT RIGHT NOW.

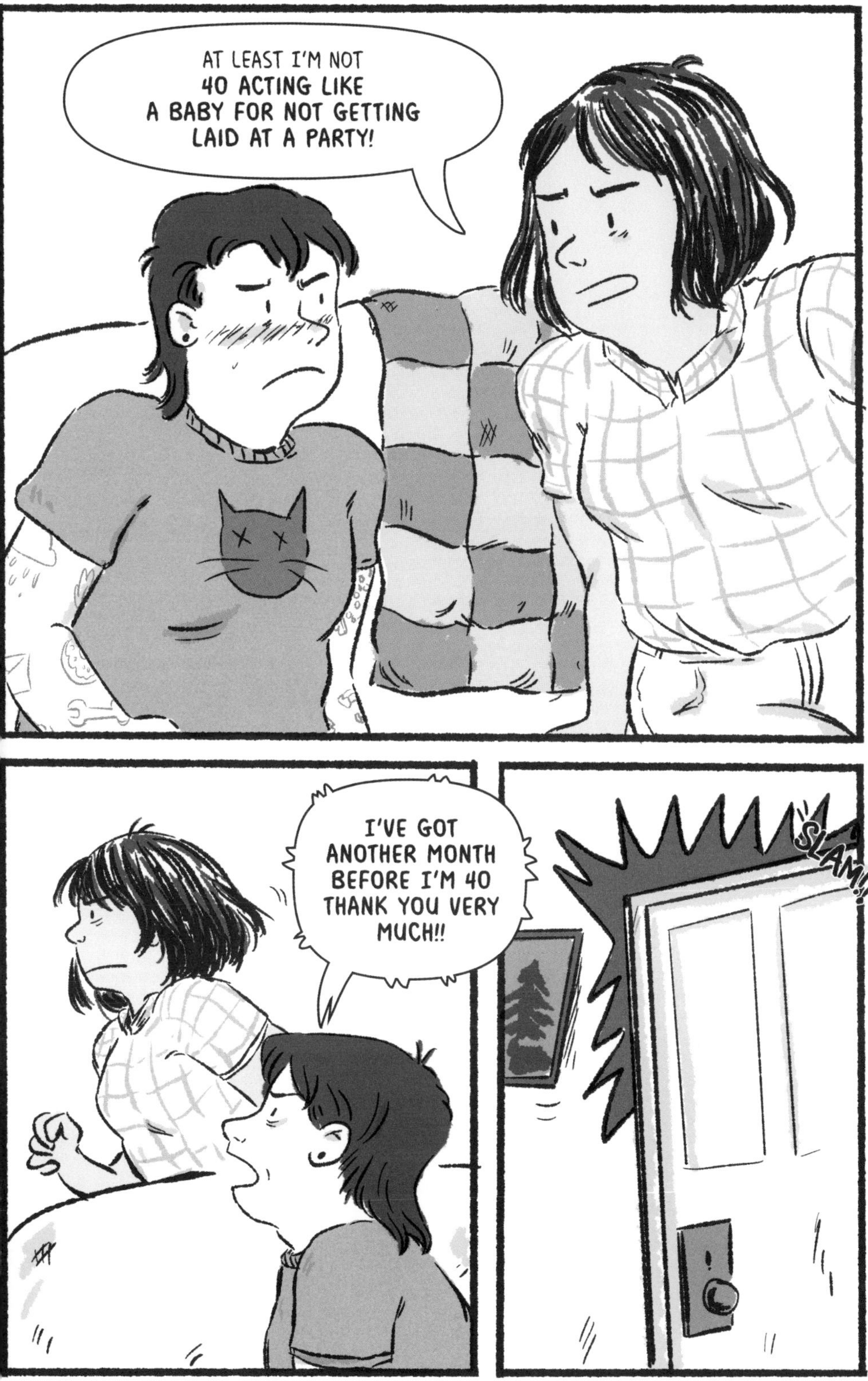
AT LEAST I'M NOT
40 ACTING LIKE
A BABY FOR NOT GETTING
LAID AT A PARTY!
I'VE GOT
ANOTHER MONTH
BEFORE I'M 40
THANK YOU VERY
MUCH!!
SLAM!!

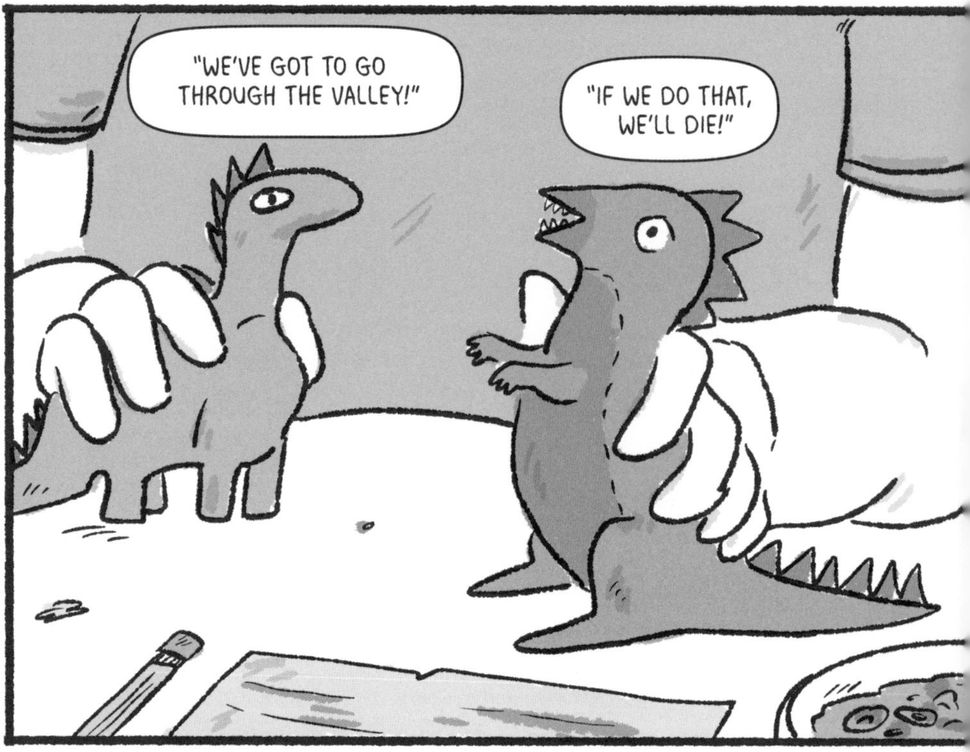
"WE'VE GOT TO GO THROUGH THE VALLEY!"
"IF WE DO THAT, WE'LL DIE!"

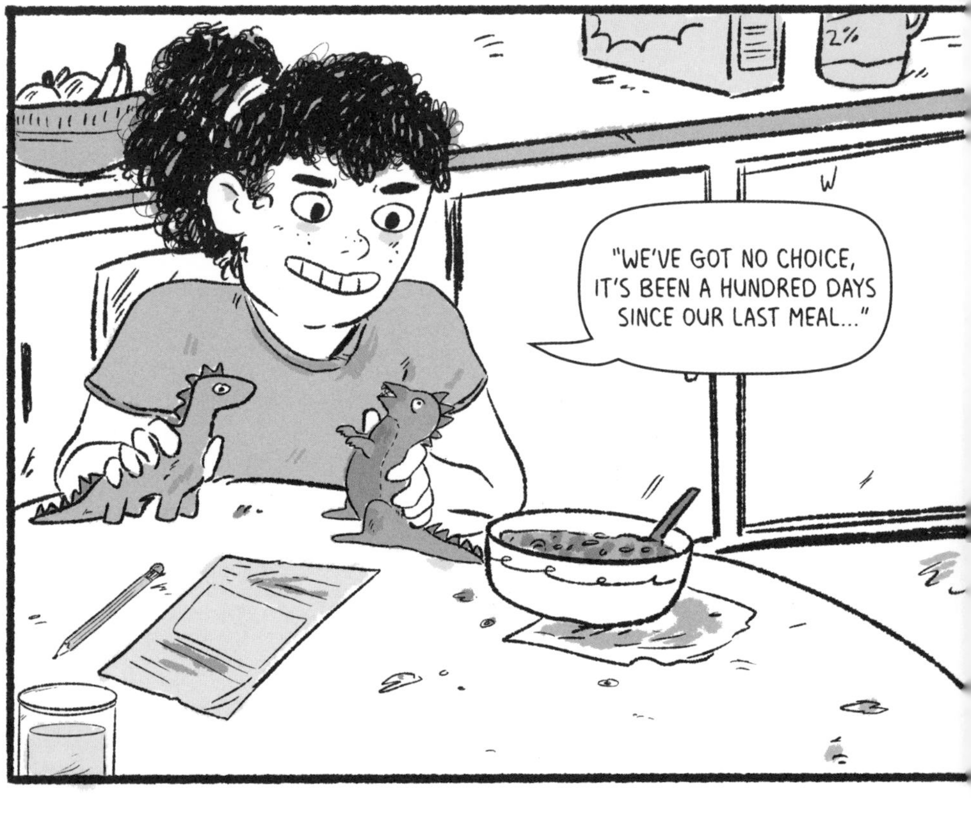
"WE'VE GOT NO CHOICE, IT'S BEEN A HUNDRED DAYS SINCE OUR LAST MEAL..."

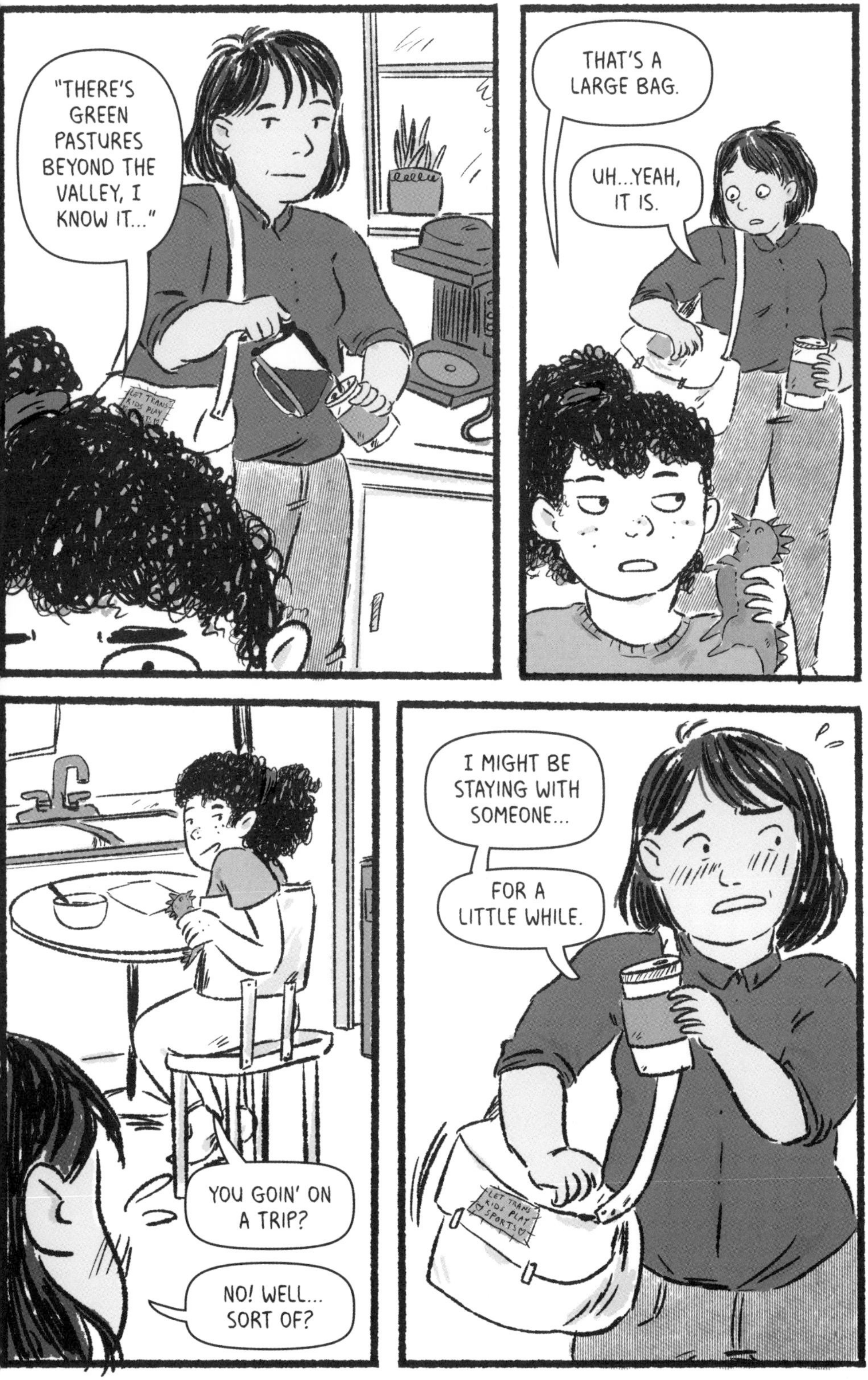
"THERE'S GREEN PASTURES BEYOND THE VALLEY, I KNOW IT..."
LET TRANS KIDS PLAY SPORTS
THAT'S A LARGE BAG.
UH...YEAH, IT IS.
YOU GOIN' ON A TRIP?
NO! WELL... SORT OF?
I MIGHT BE STAYING WITH SOMEONE...
FOR A LITTLE WHILE.
LET TRANS KIDS PLAY SPORTS

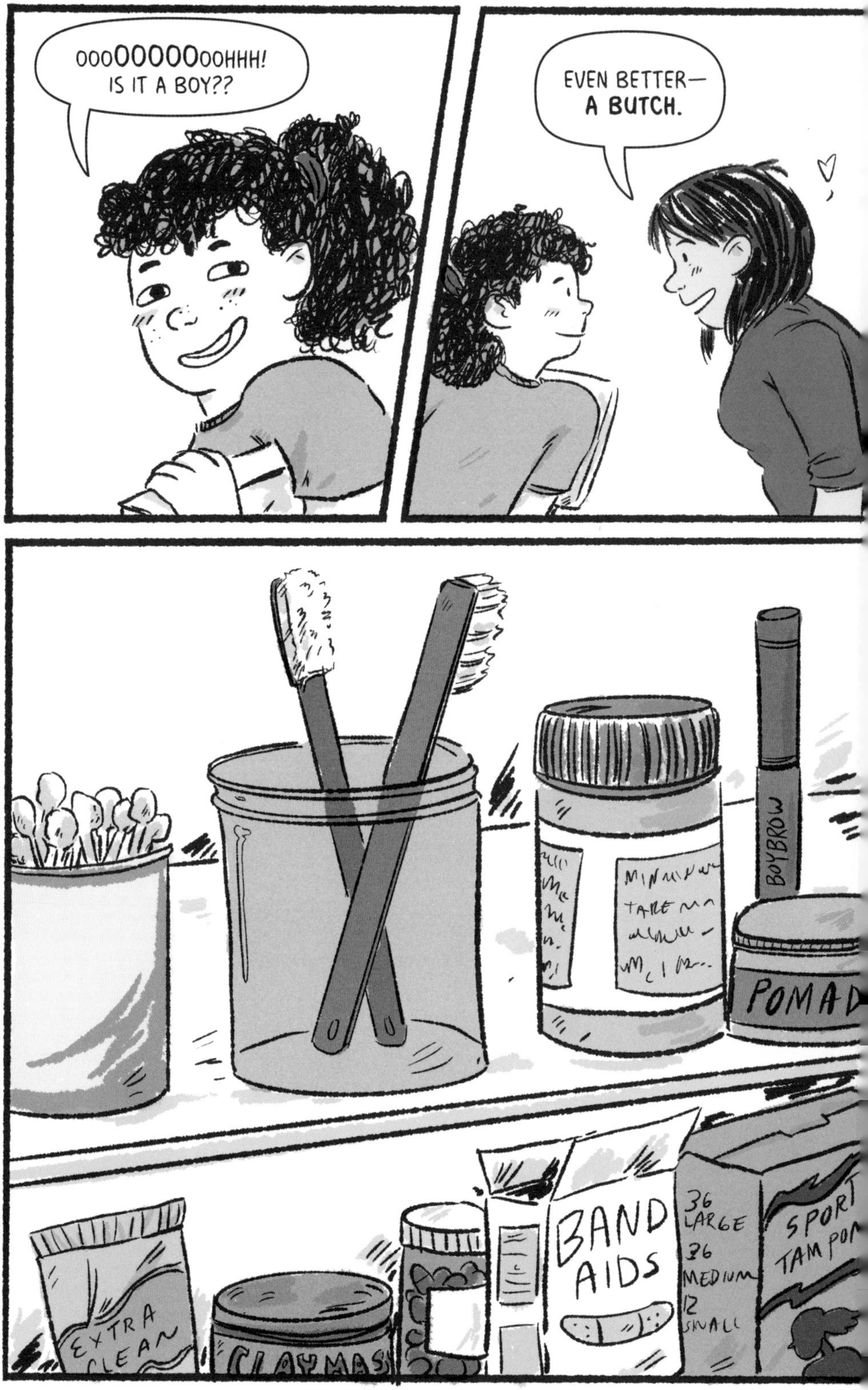

oooOOOOOOoohhh! IS IT A BOY??
EVEN BETTER— A BUTCH.
BOYBROW
POMAD
BAND AIDS
36 LARGE 36 MEDIUM 12 SMALL
SPORT TAMPON
EXTRA CLEAN
CLAYMAS

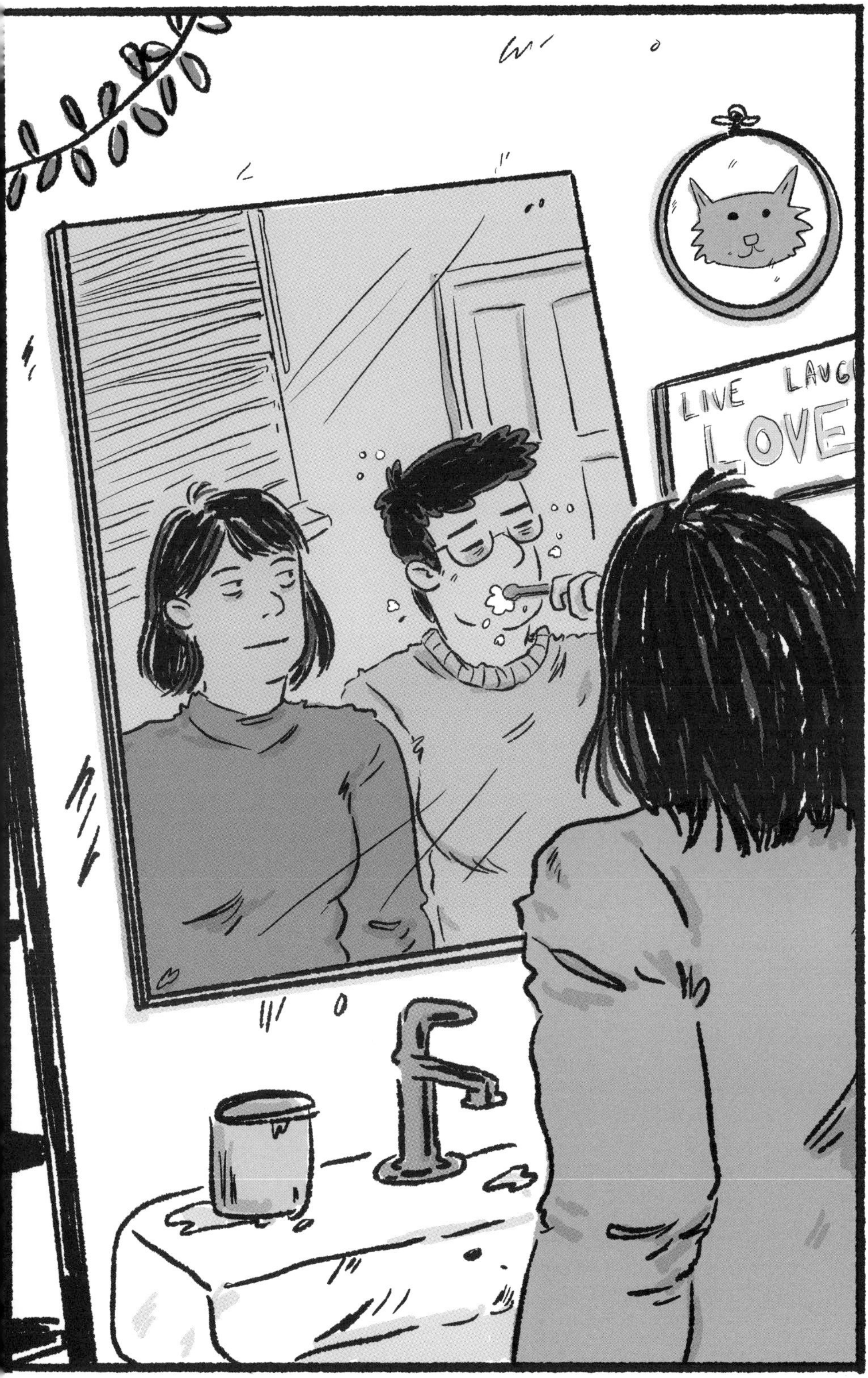
LIVE LAUG
LOVE

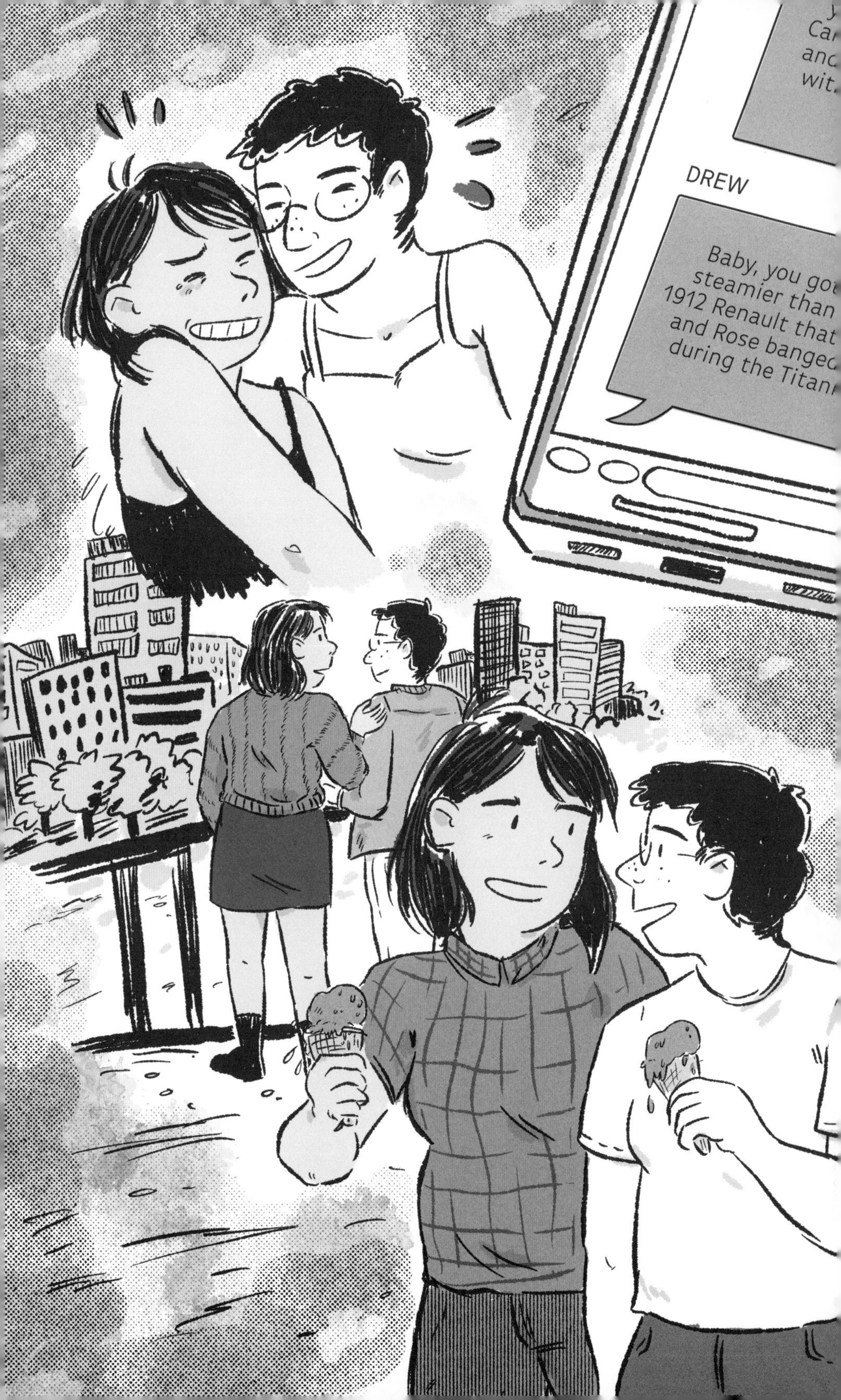
DREW
Baby, you go
steamier than
1912 Renault that
and Rose banged
during the Titan

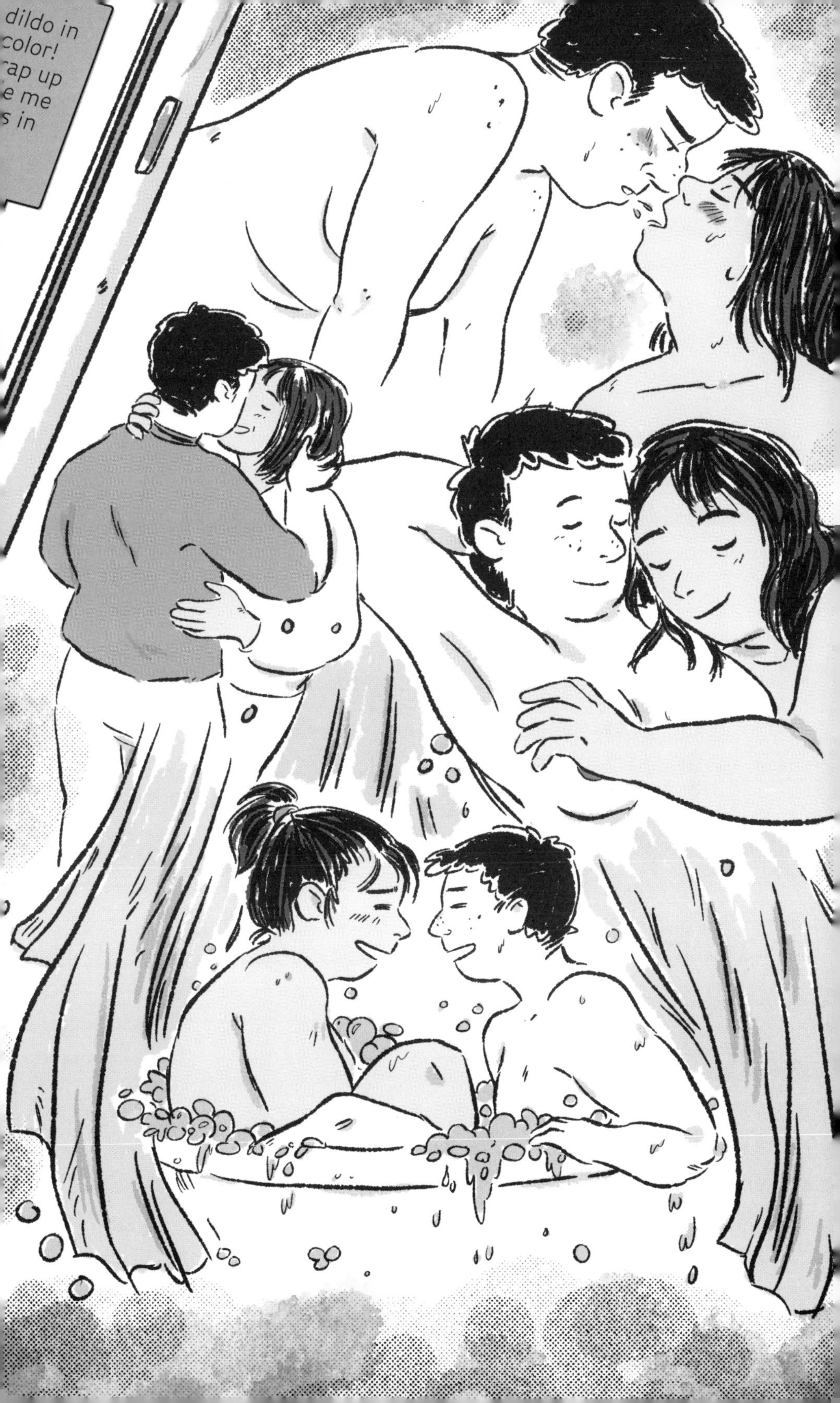
dildo in
color!
rap up
e me
s in

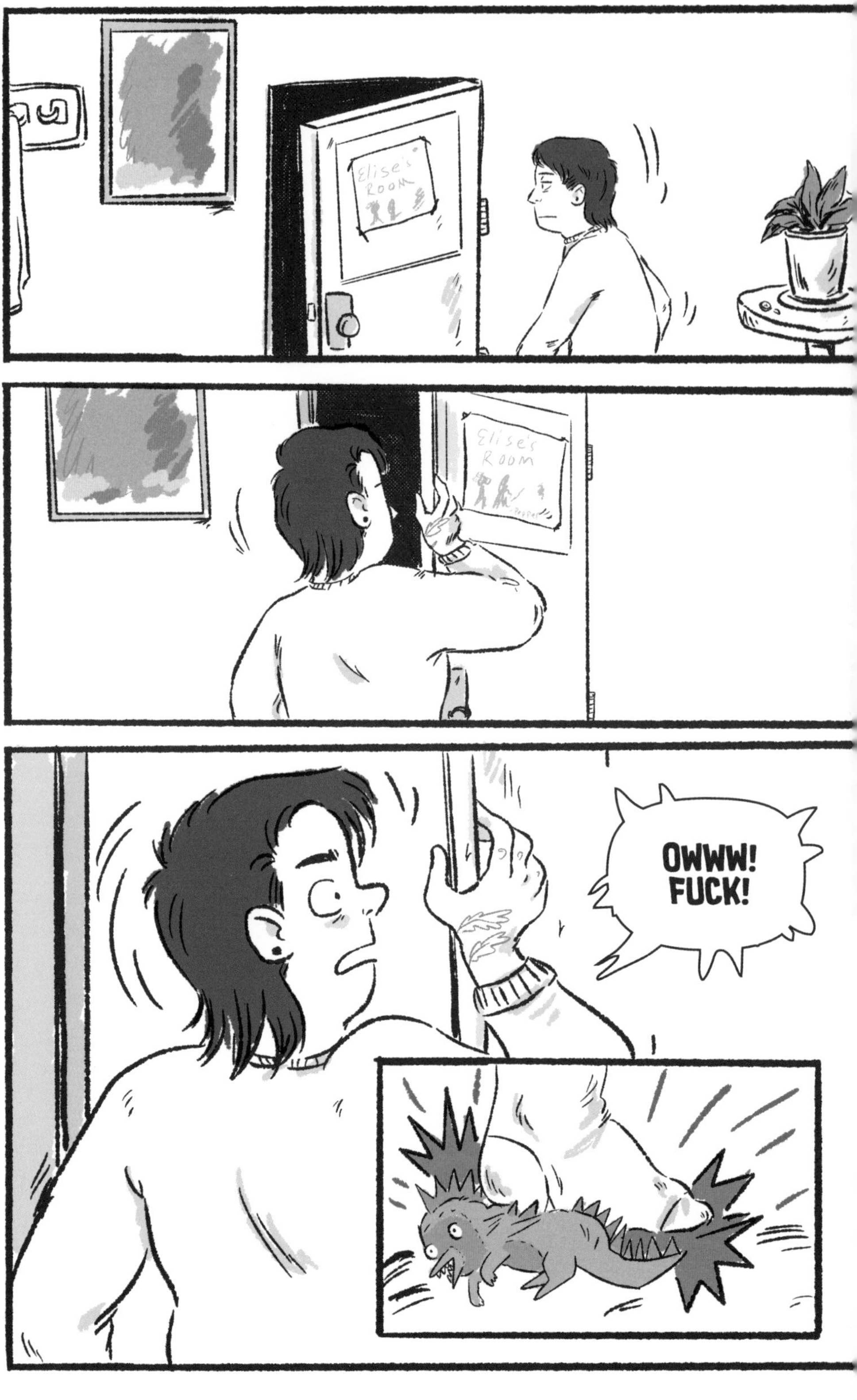
Elise's Room
Elise's Room
OWWW! FUCK!

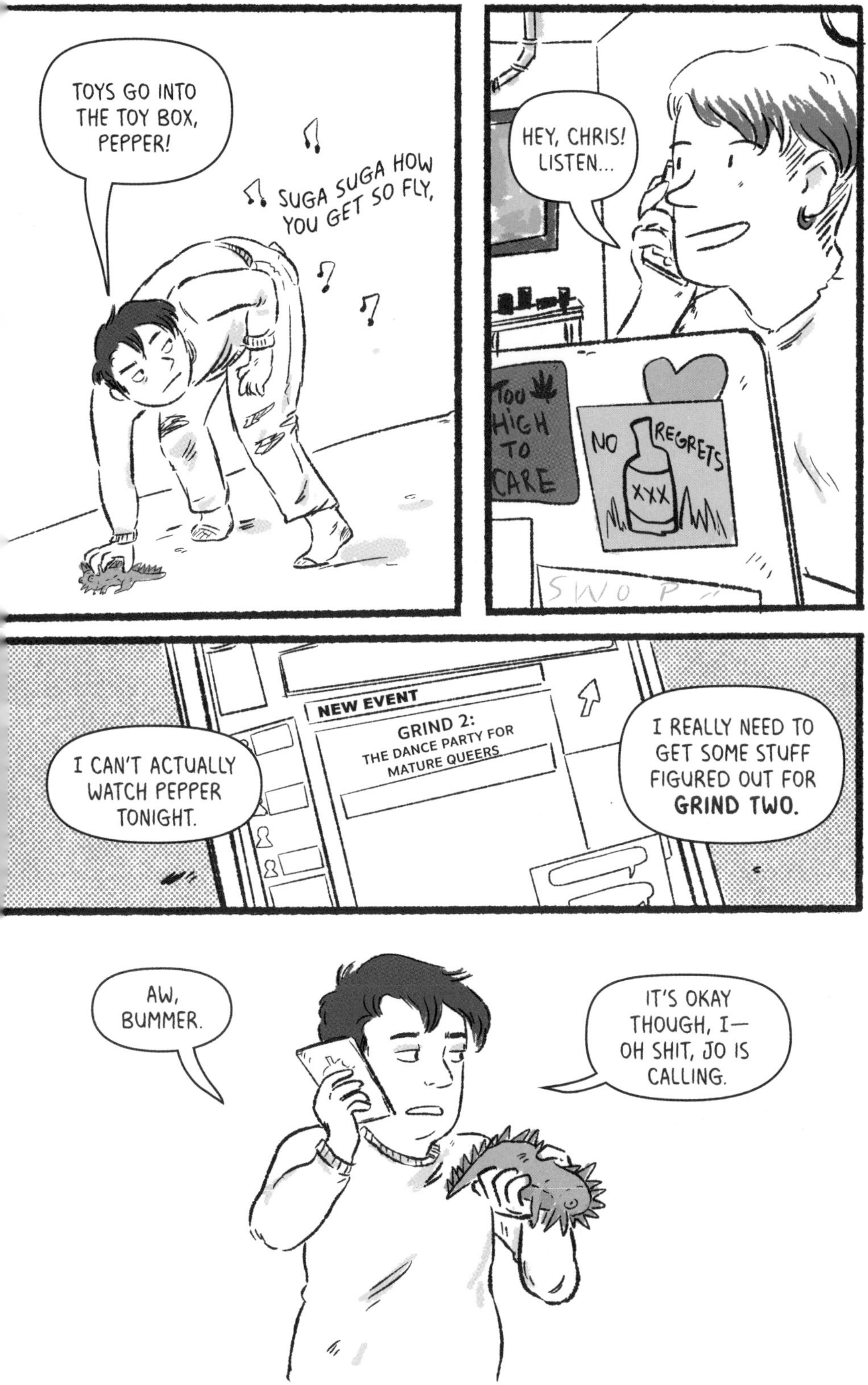
TOYS GO INTO THE TOY BOX, PEPPER!
SUGA SUGA HOW YOU GET SO FLY,
HEY, CHRIS! LISTEN...
TOO HIGH TO CARE
NO REGRETS
XXX
NEW EVENT
GRIND 2:
THE DANCE PARTY FOR MATURE QUEERS
I CAN'T ACTUALLY WATCH PEPPER TONIGHT.
I REALLY NEED TO GET SOME STUFF FIGURED OUT FOR **GRIND TWO.**
AW, BUMMER.
IT'S OKAY THOUGH, I— OH SHIT, JO IS CALLING.

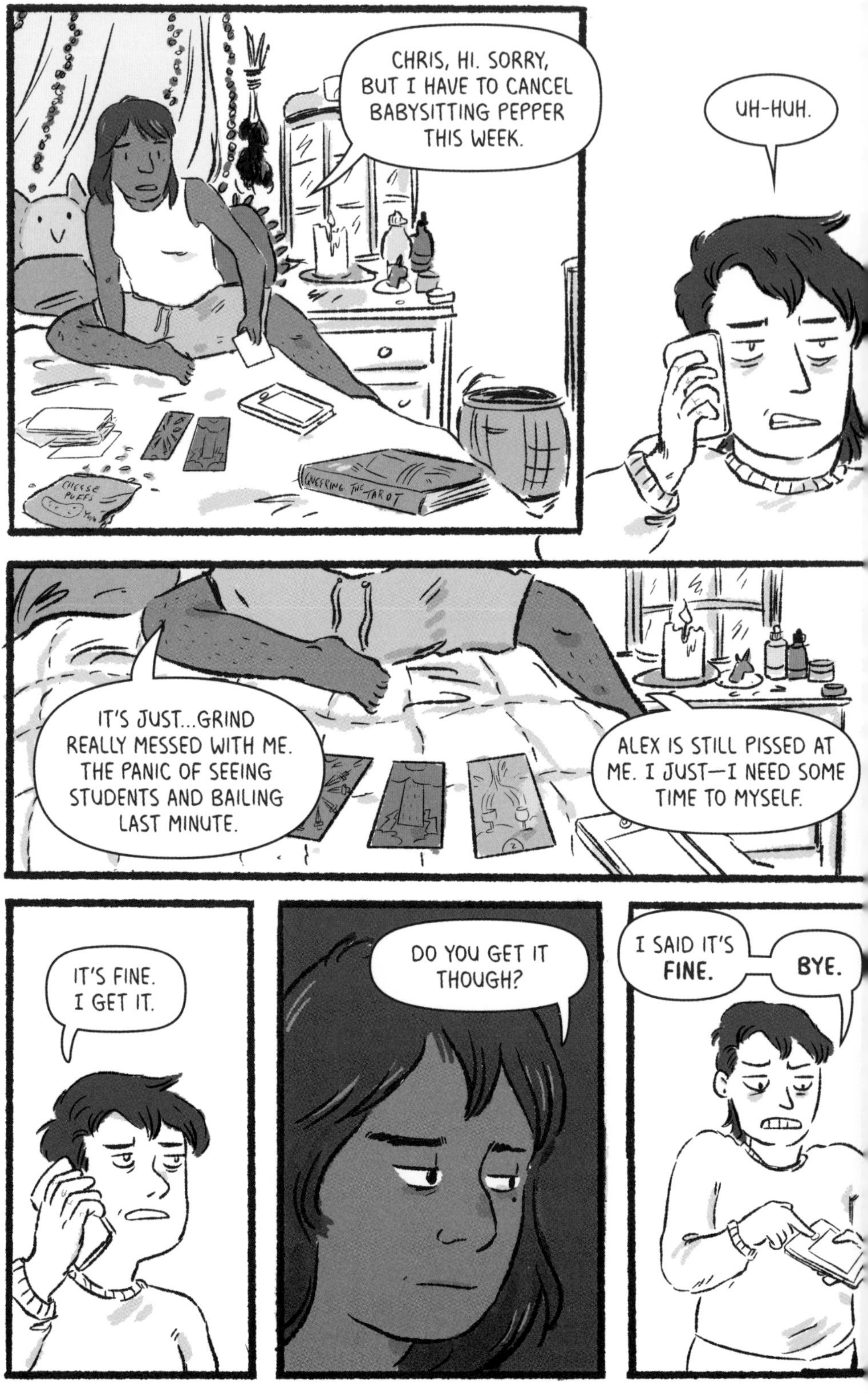

CHRIS, HI. SORRY, BUT I HAVE TO CANCEL BABYSITTING PEPPER THIS WEEK.
UH-HUH.
QUEERING THE TAROT
CHEESE PUFFS
IT'S JUST...GRIND REALLY MESSED WITH ME. THE PANIC OF SEEING STUDENTS AND BAILING LAST MINUTE.
ALEX IS STILL PISSED AT ME. I JUST—I NEED SOME TIME TO MYSELF.
IT'S FINE. I GET IT.
DO YOU GET IT THOUGH?
I SAID IT'S **FINE.**
BYE.

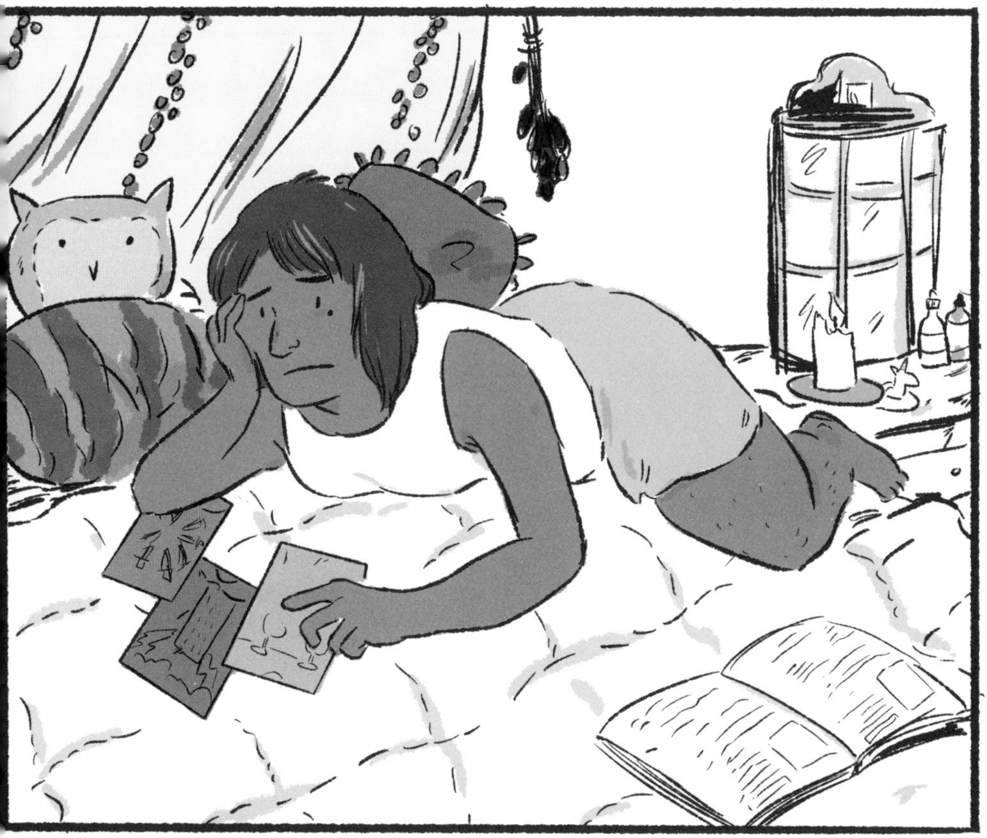

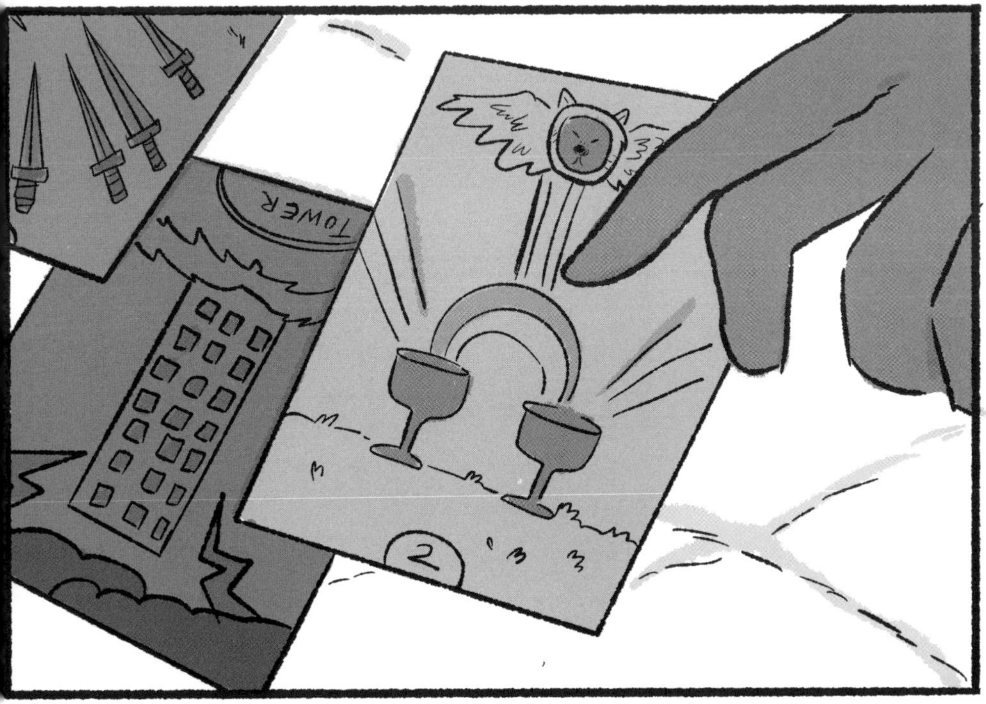
TOWER
2

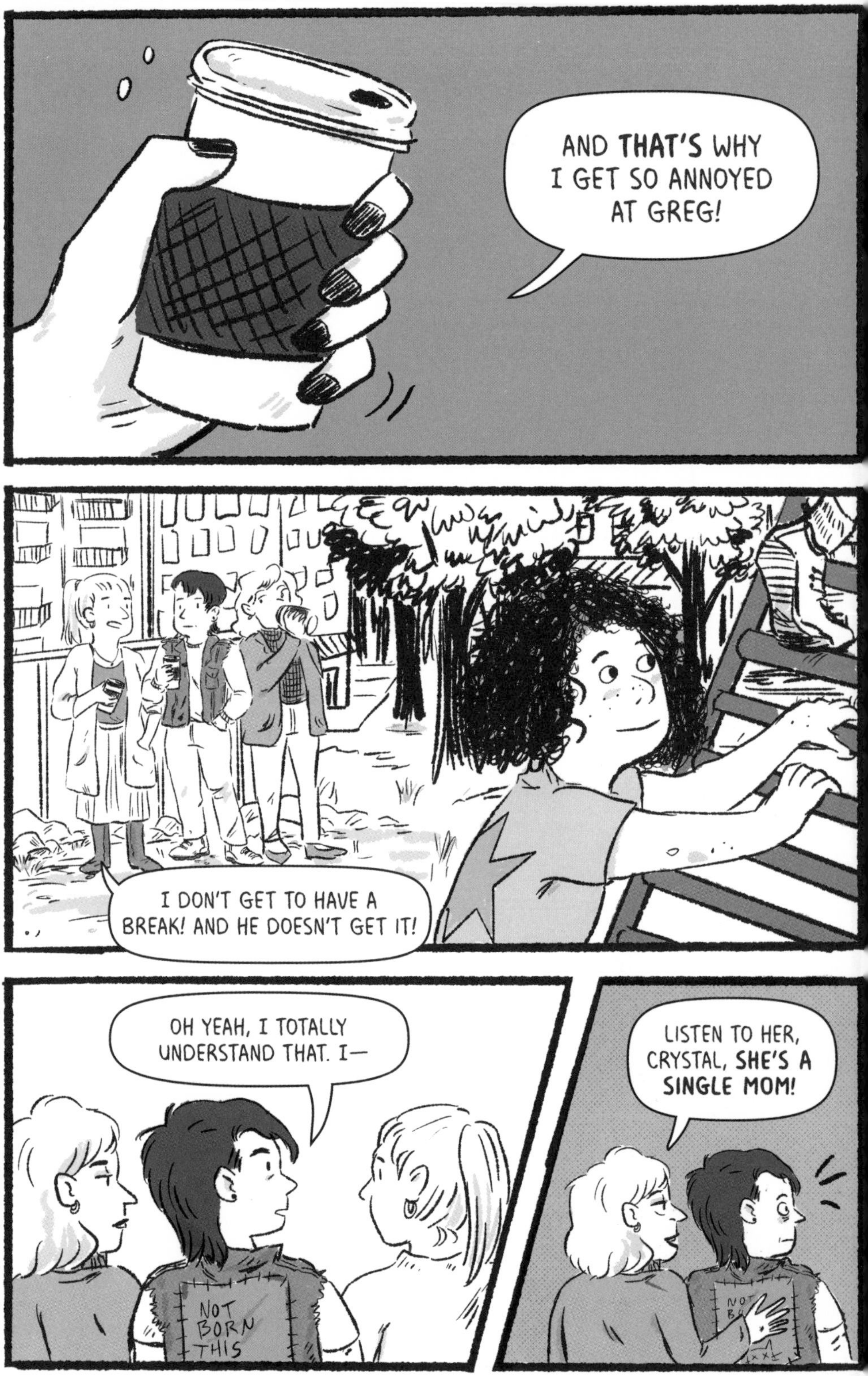
AND **THAT'S** WHY I GET SO ANNOYED AT GREG!
I DON'T GET TO HAVE A BREAK! AND HE DOESN'T GET IT!
OH YEAH, I TOTALLY UNDERSTAND THAT. I—
NOT BORN THIS
LISTEN TO HER, CRYSTAL, **SHE'S A SINGLE MOM!**

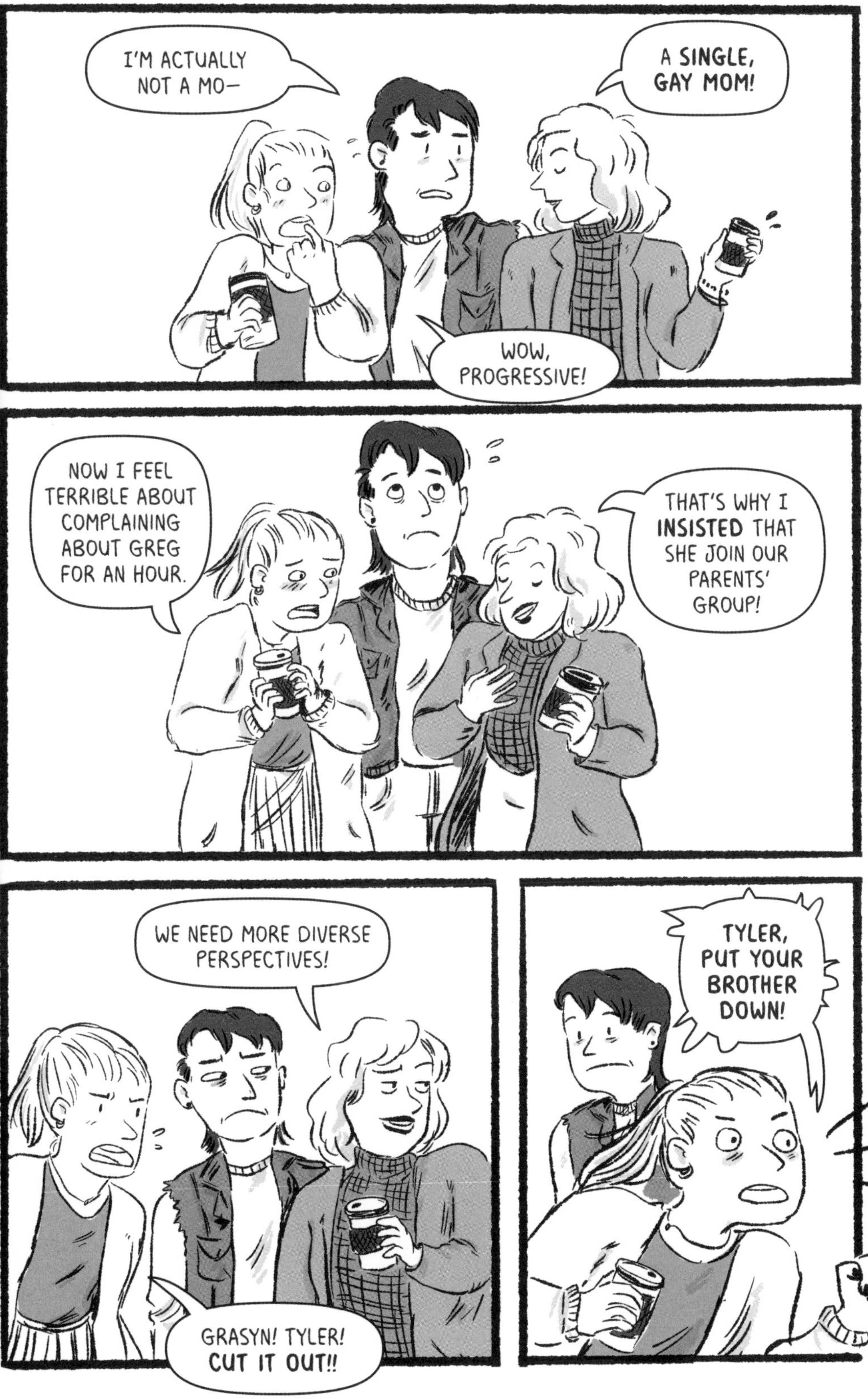
I'M ACTUALLY NOT A MO—
A SINGLE, GAY MOM!
WOW, PROGRESSIVE!
NOW I FEEL TERRIBLE ABOUT COMPLAINING ABOUT GREG FOR AN HOUR.
THAT'S WHY I INSISTED THAT SHE JOIN OUR PARENTS' GROUP!
WE NEED MORE DIVERSE PERSPECTIVES!
GRASYN! TYLER! CUT IT OUT!!
TYLER, PUT YOUR BROTHER DOWN!

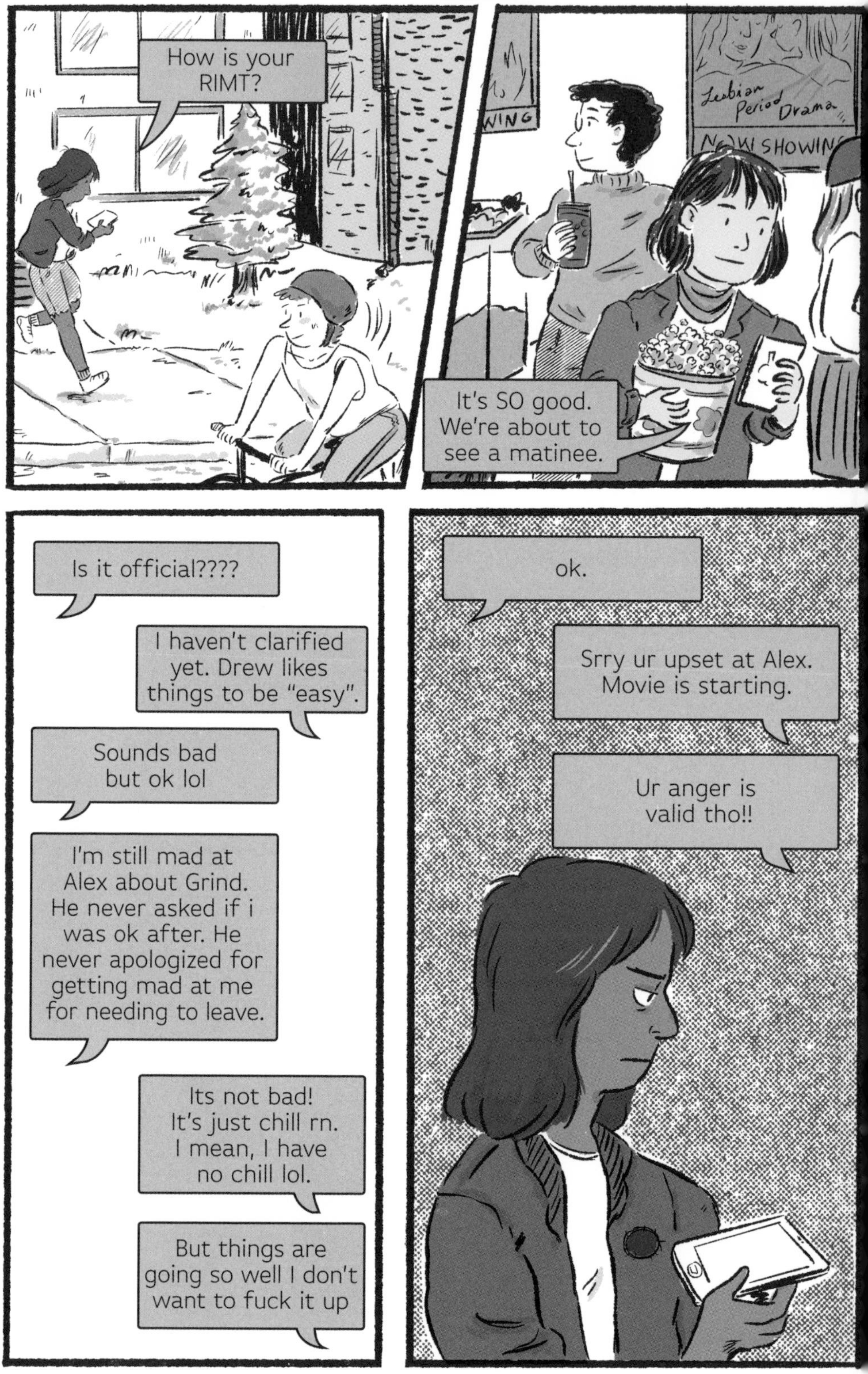

How is your RIMT?
Lesbian Period Drama
NOW SHOWING
It's SO good. We're about to see a matinee.
Is it official????
I haven't clarified yet. Drew likes things to be "easy".
Sounds bad but ok lol
I'm still mad at Alex about Grind. He never asked if i was ok after. He never apologized for getting mad at me for needing to leave.
Its not bad! It's just chill rn. I mean, I have no chill lol.
But things are going so well I don't want to fuck it up
ok.
Srry ur upset at Alex. Movie is starting.
Ur anger is valid tho!!

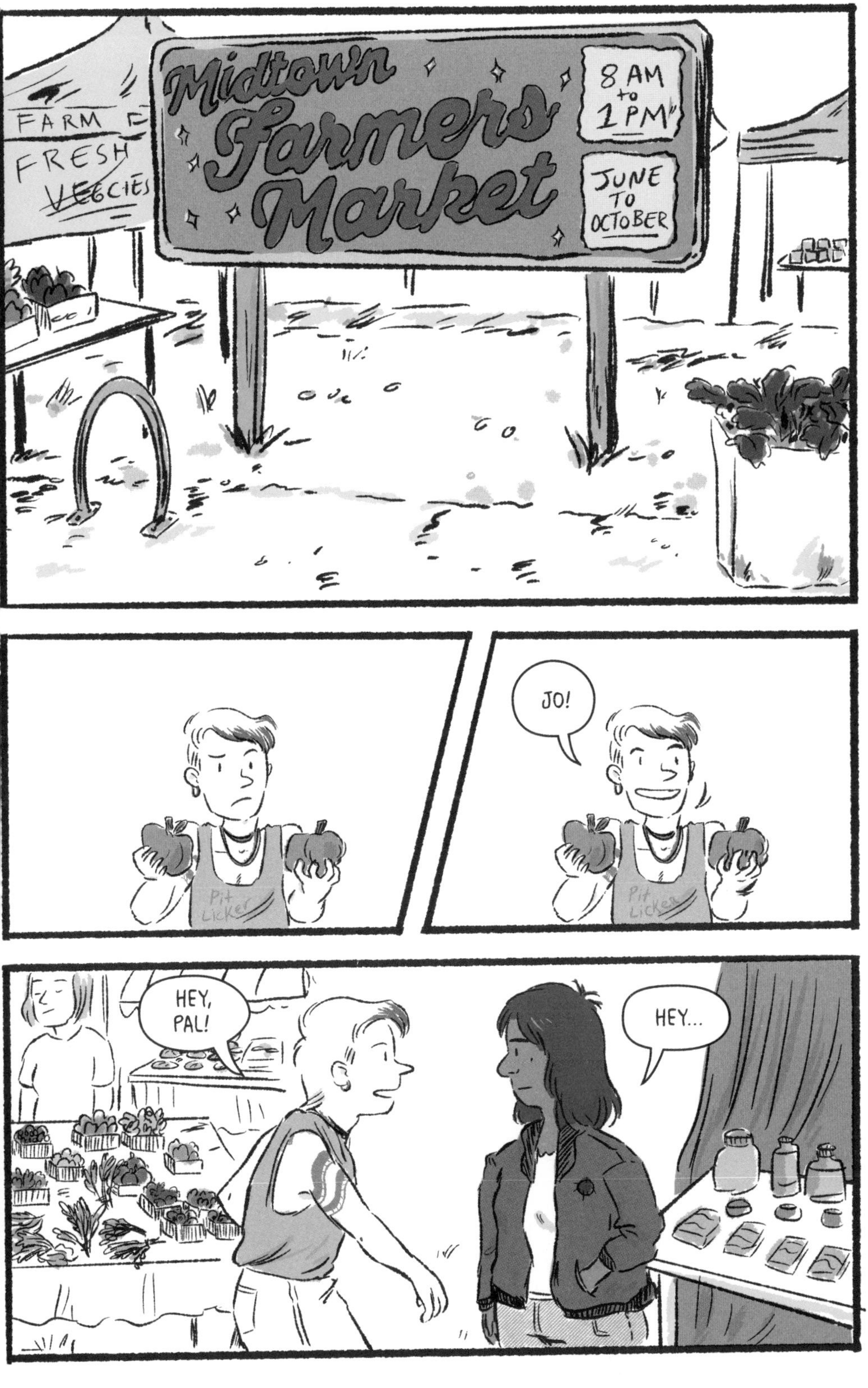
FARM
FRESH
VEGGIES
Midtown Farmers' Market
8 AM to 1 PM
JUNE TO OCTOBER
Pit Licker
JO!
Pit Licker
HEY, PAL!
HEY...

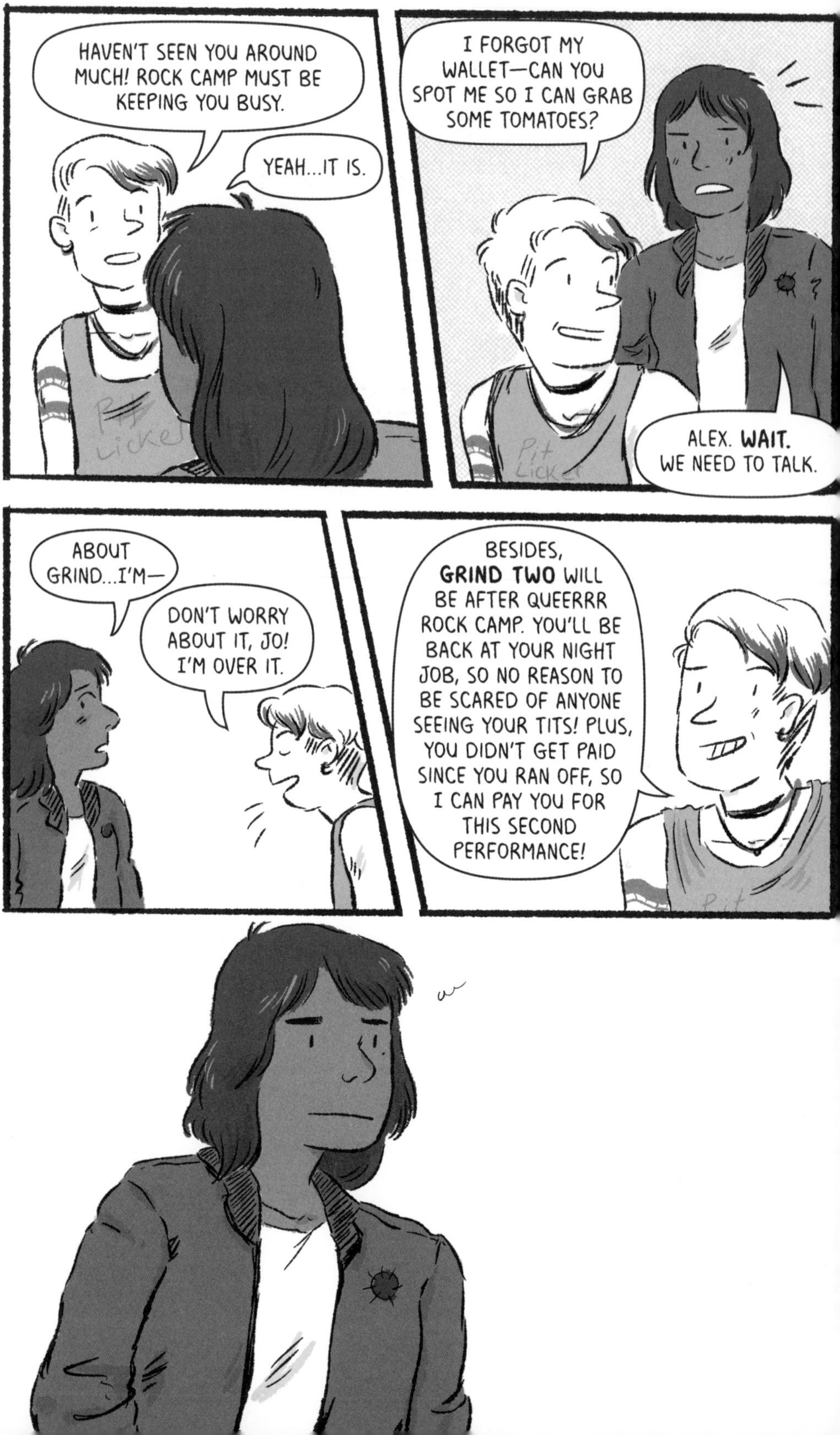
HAVEN'T SEEN YOU AROUND MUCH! ROCK CAMP MUST BE KEEPING YOU BUSY.
YEAH...IT IS.
Pit Licker
I FORGOT MY WALLET—CAN YOU SPOT ME SO I CAN GRAB SOME TOMATOES?
Pit Licker
ALEX. **WAIT.** WE NEED TO TALK.
ABOUT GRIND...I'M—
DON'T WORRY ABOUT IT, JO! I'M OVER IT.
BESIDES, **GRIND TWO** WILL BE AFTER QUEERRR ROCK CAMP. YOU'LL BE BACK AT YOUR NIGHT JOB, SO NO REASON TO BE SCARED OF ANYONE SEEING YOUR TITS! PLUS, YOU DIDN'T GET PAID SINCE YOU RAN OFF, SO I CAN PAY YOU FOR THIS SECOND PERFORMANCE!

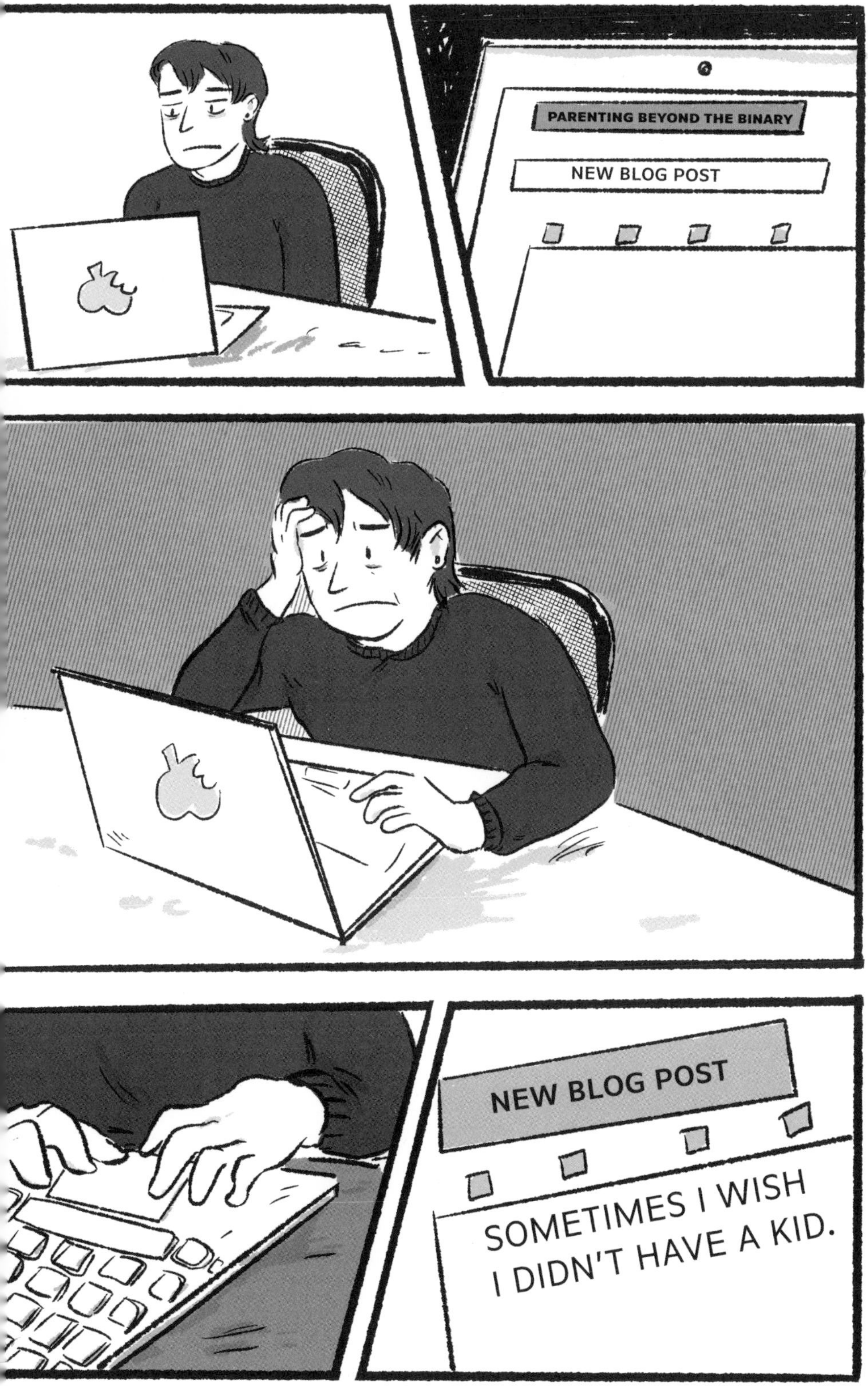
PARENTING BEYOND THE BINARY
NEW BLOG POST
NEW BLOG POST
SOMETIMES I WISH
I DIDN'T HAVE A KID.

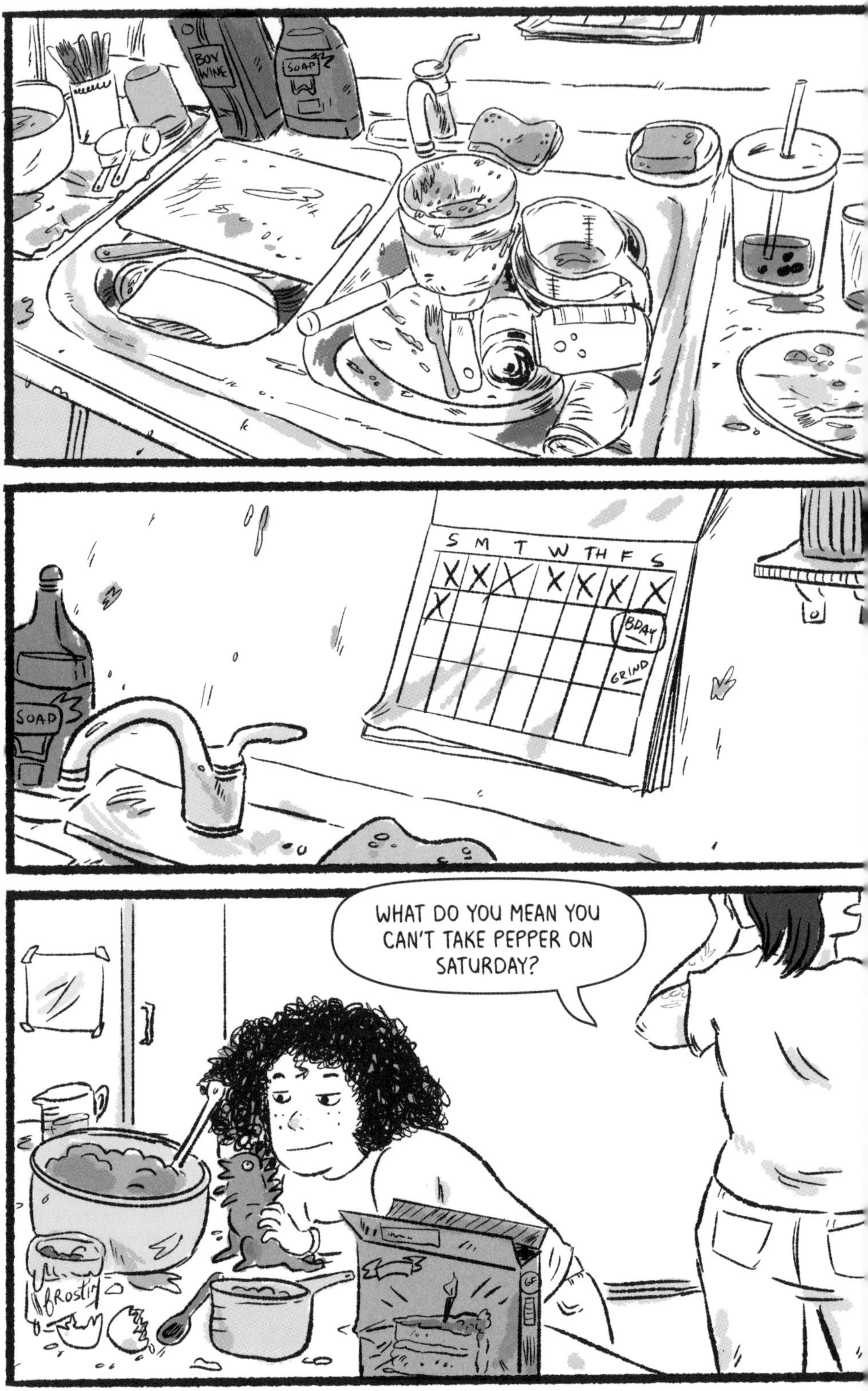
BOX WINE
SOAP
S M T W TH F S
BDAY
GRIND
SOAP
WHAT DO YOU MEAN YOU CAN'T TAKE PEPPER ON SATURDAY?
FROSTIN
GF

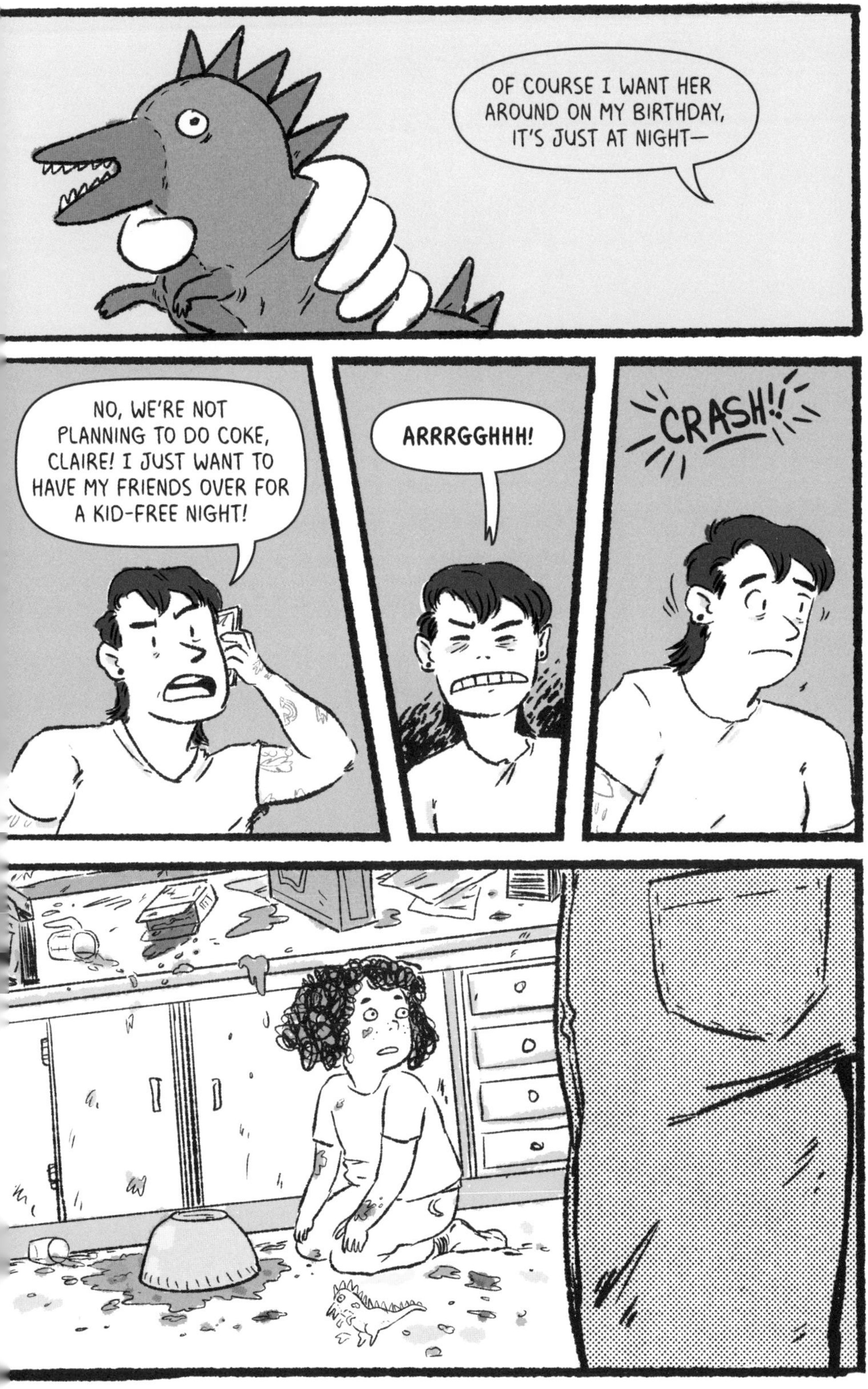
OF COURSE I WANT HER AROUND ON MY BIRTHDAY, IT'S JUST AT NIGHT—
NO, WE'RE NOT PLANNING TO DO COKE, CLAIRE! I JUST WANT TO HAVE MY FRIENDS OVER FOR A KID-FREE NIGHT!
ARRRGGHHH!
CRASH!!

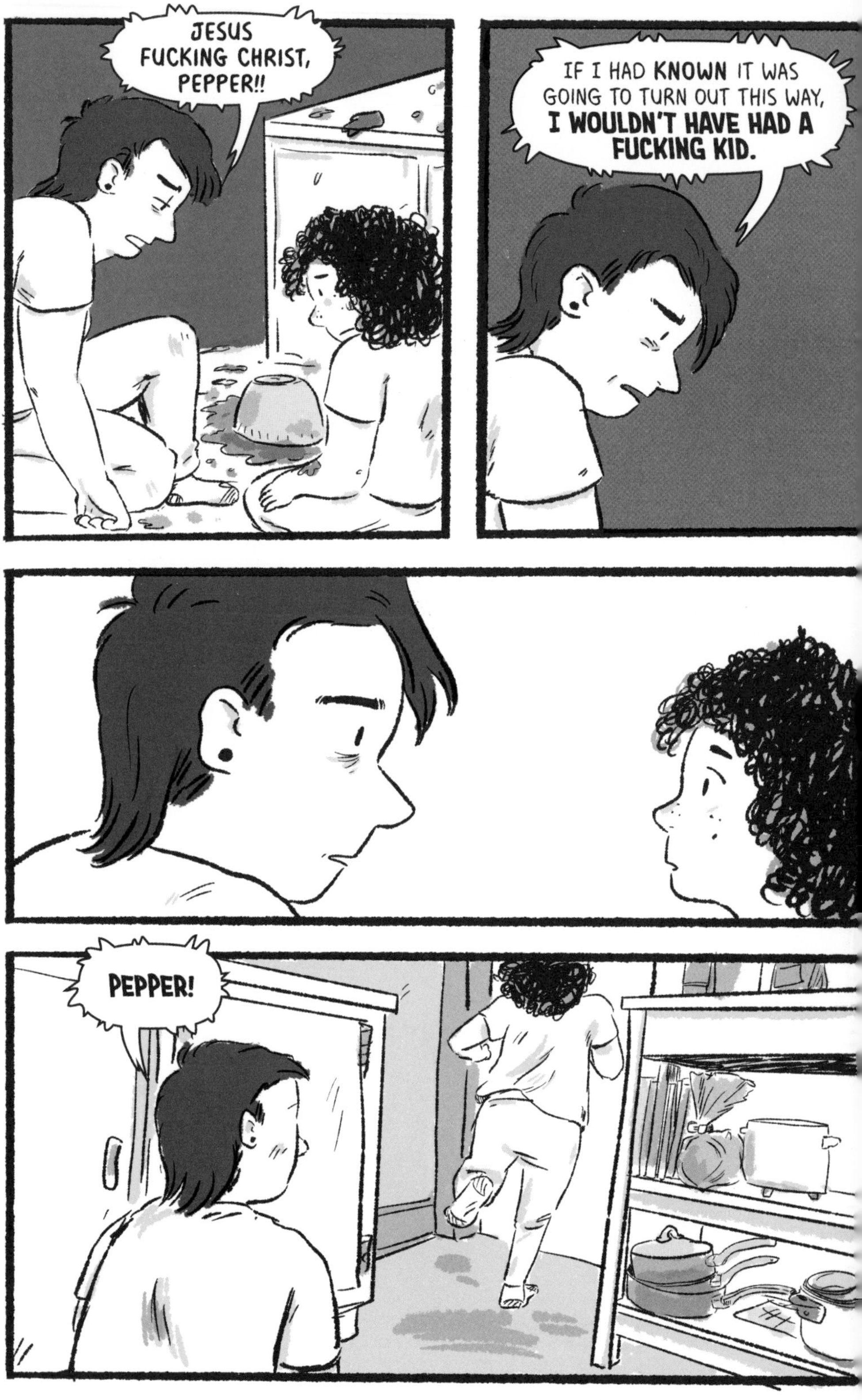
JESUS FUCKING CHRIST, PEPPER!!
IF I HAD KNOWN IT WAS GOING TO TURN OUT THIS WAY, I WOULDN'T HAVE HAD A FUCKING KID.
PEPPER!

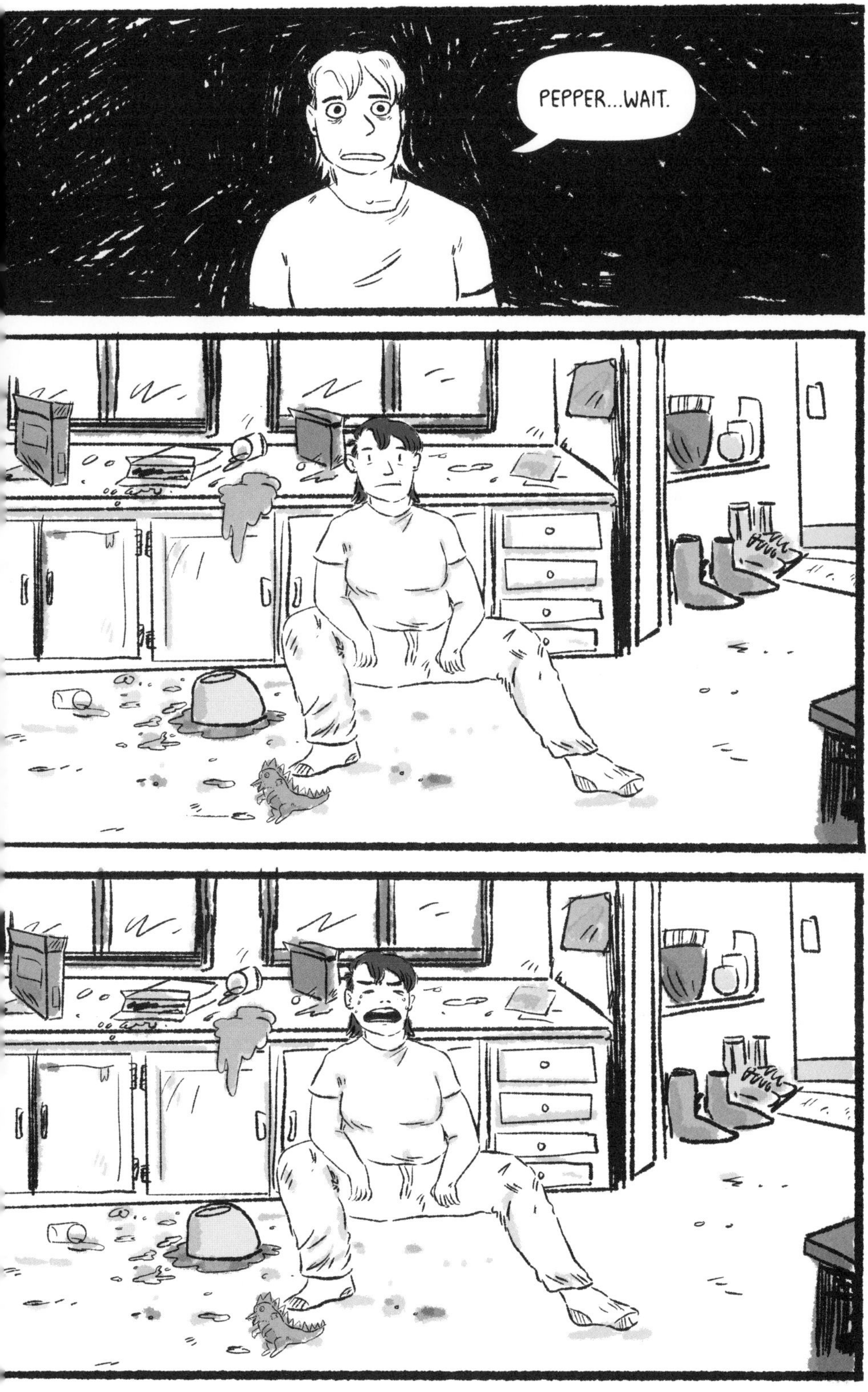
PEPPER...WAIT.

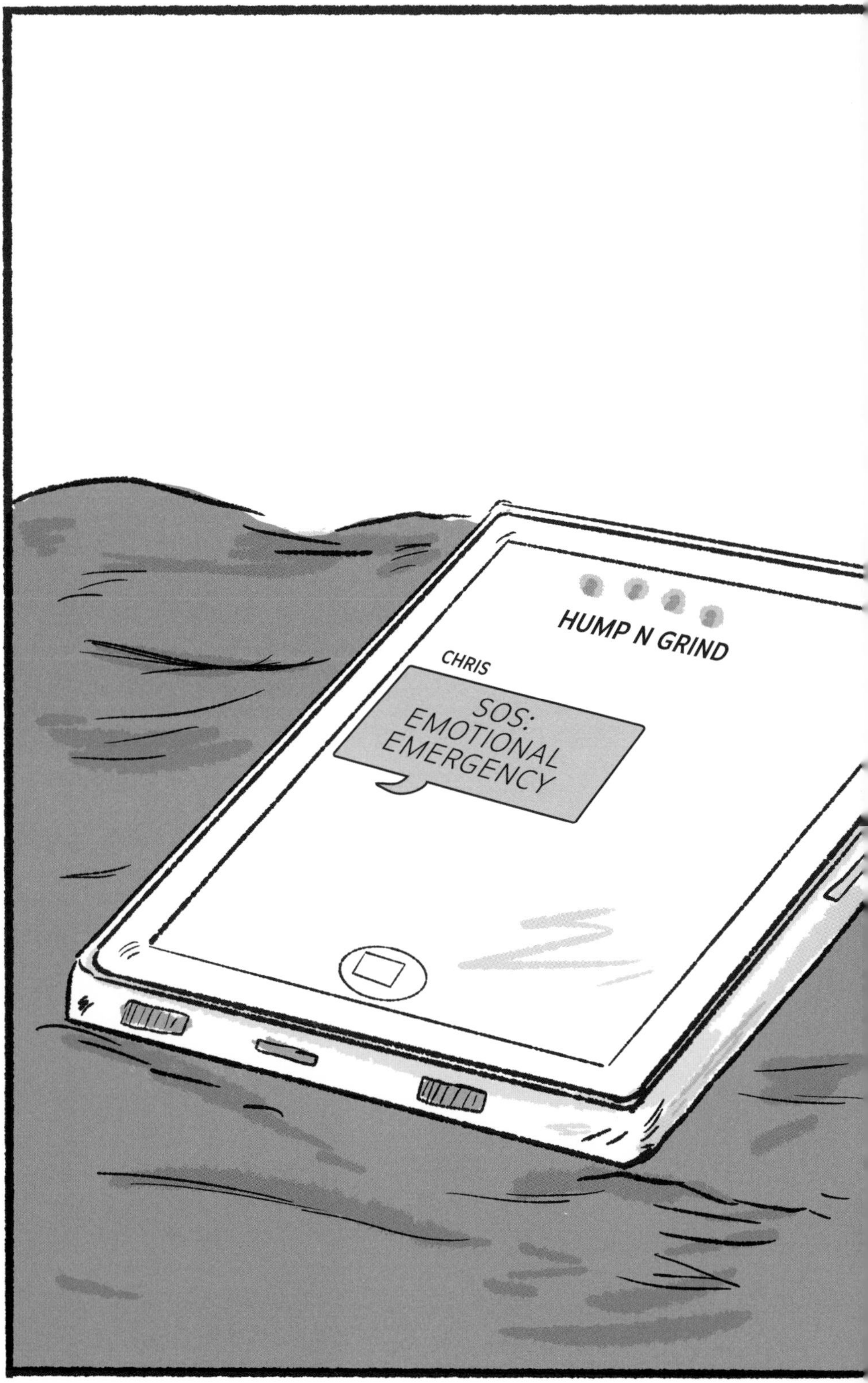
HUMP N GRIND
CHRIS
SOS: EMOTIONAL EMERGENCY

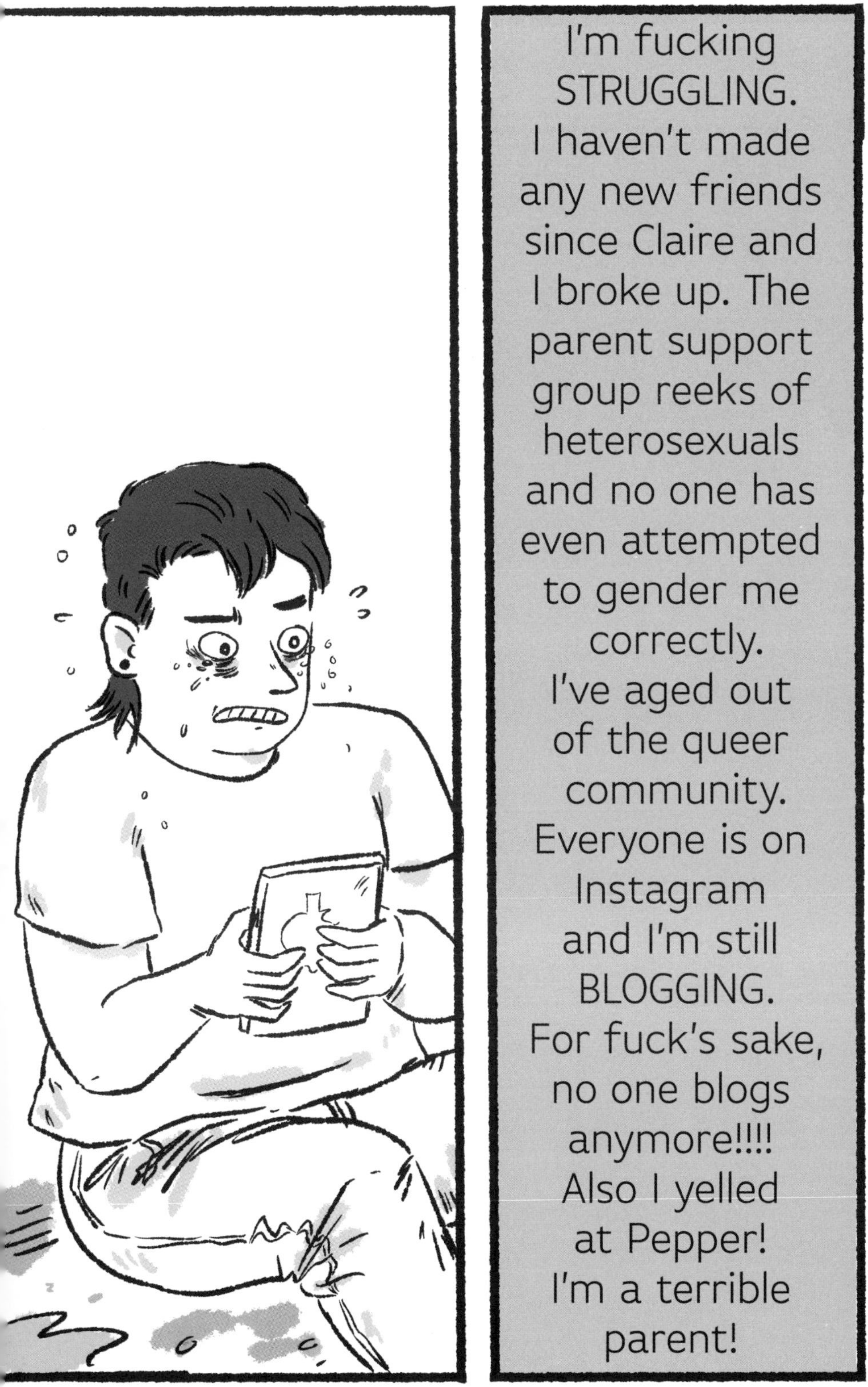

I'm fucking STRUGGLING. I haven't made any new friends since Claire and I broke up. The parent support group reeks of heterosexuals and no one has even attempted to gender me correctly. I've aged out of the queer community. Everyone is on Instagram and I'm still BLOGGING. For fuck's sake, no one blogs anymore!!!! Also I yelled at Pepper! I'm a terrible parent!

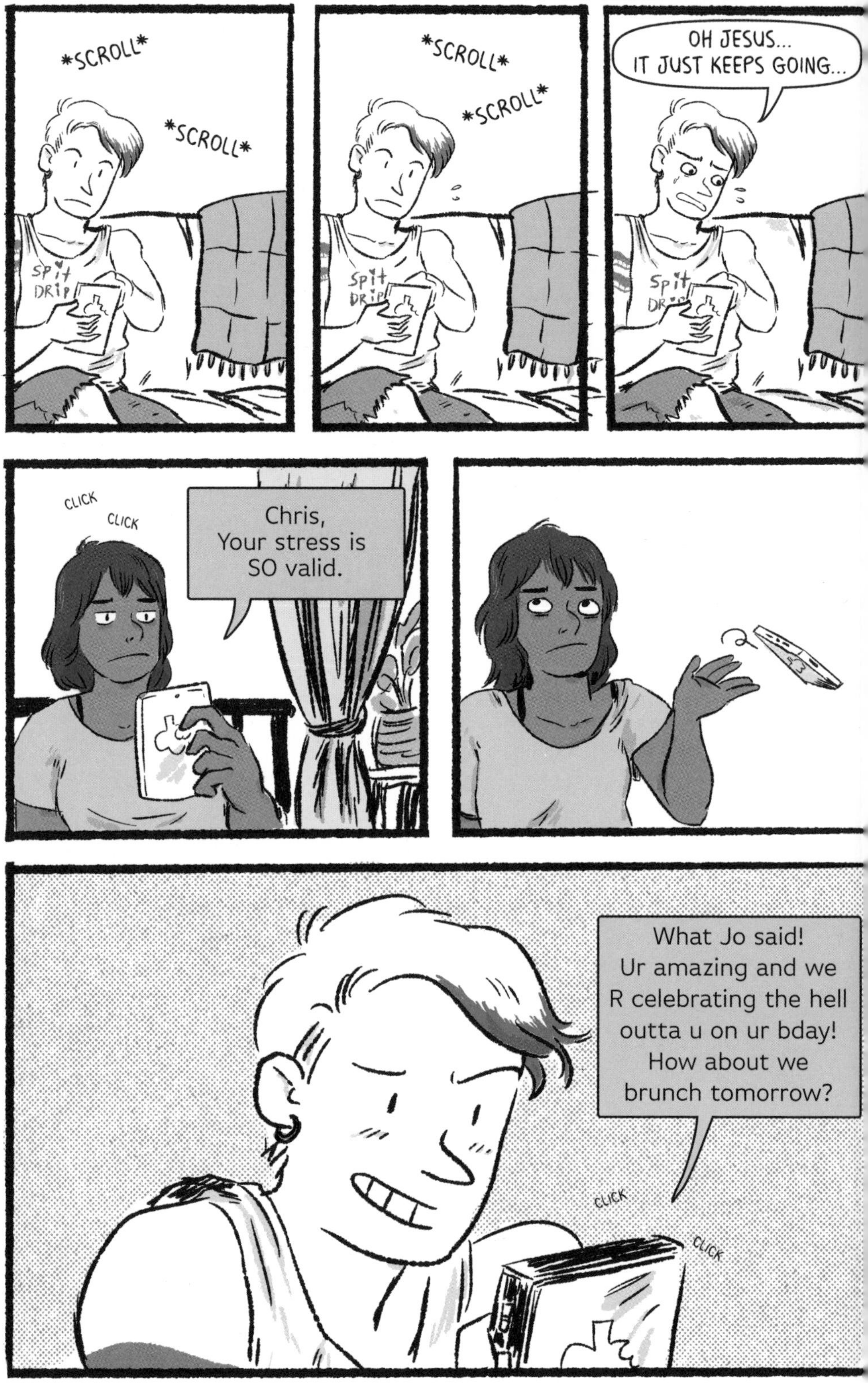
SCROLL
SCROLL
SPIT DRIP
SCROLL
SCROLL
OH JESUS...
IT JUST KEEPS GOING...
CLICK
CLICK
Chris,
Your stress is
SO valid.
What Jo said!
Ur amazing and we
R celebrating the hell
outta u on ur bday!
How about we
brunch tomorrow?
CLICK
CLICK

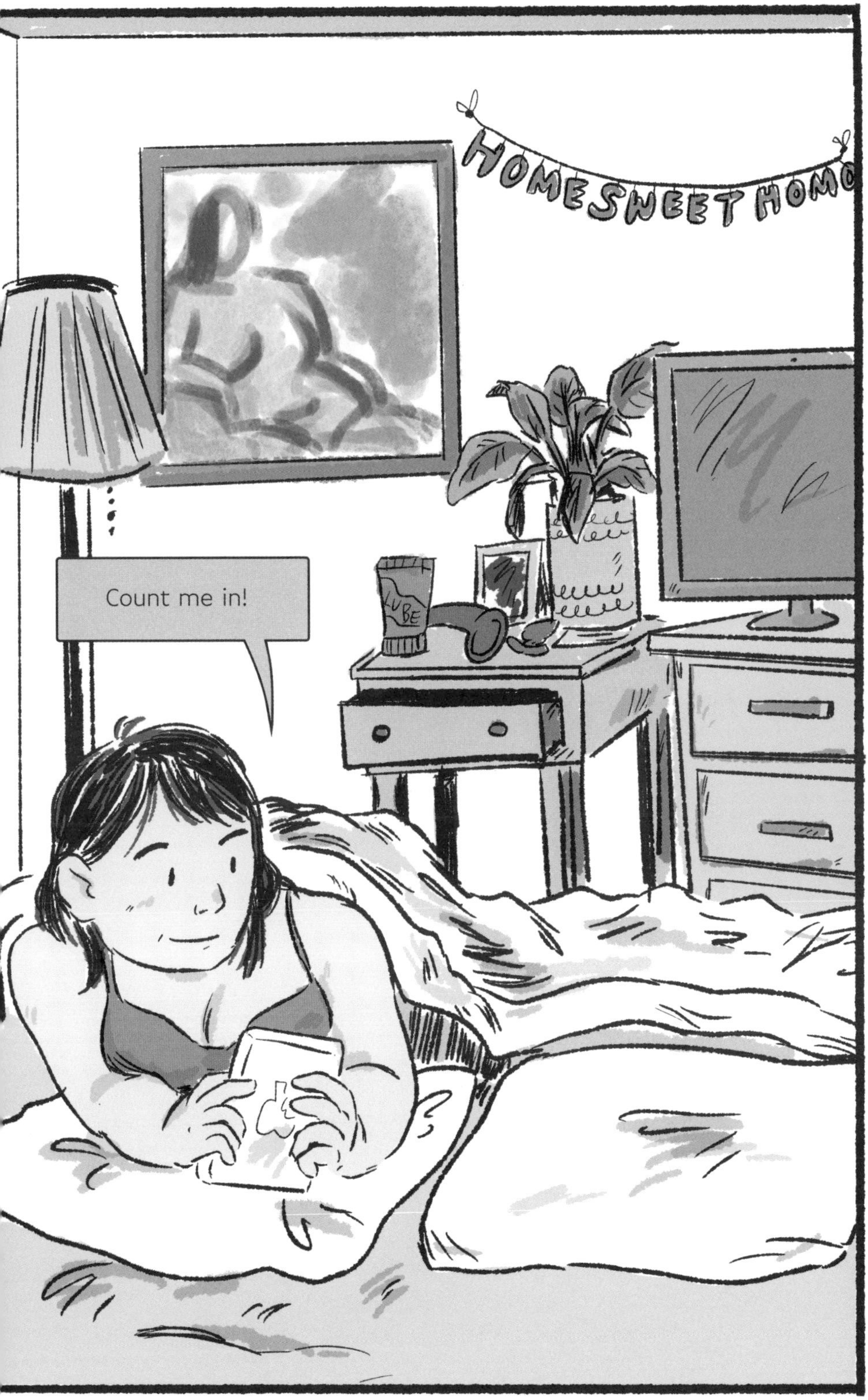
HOME SWEET HOMO
LUBE
Count me in!

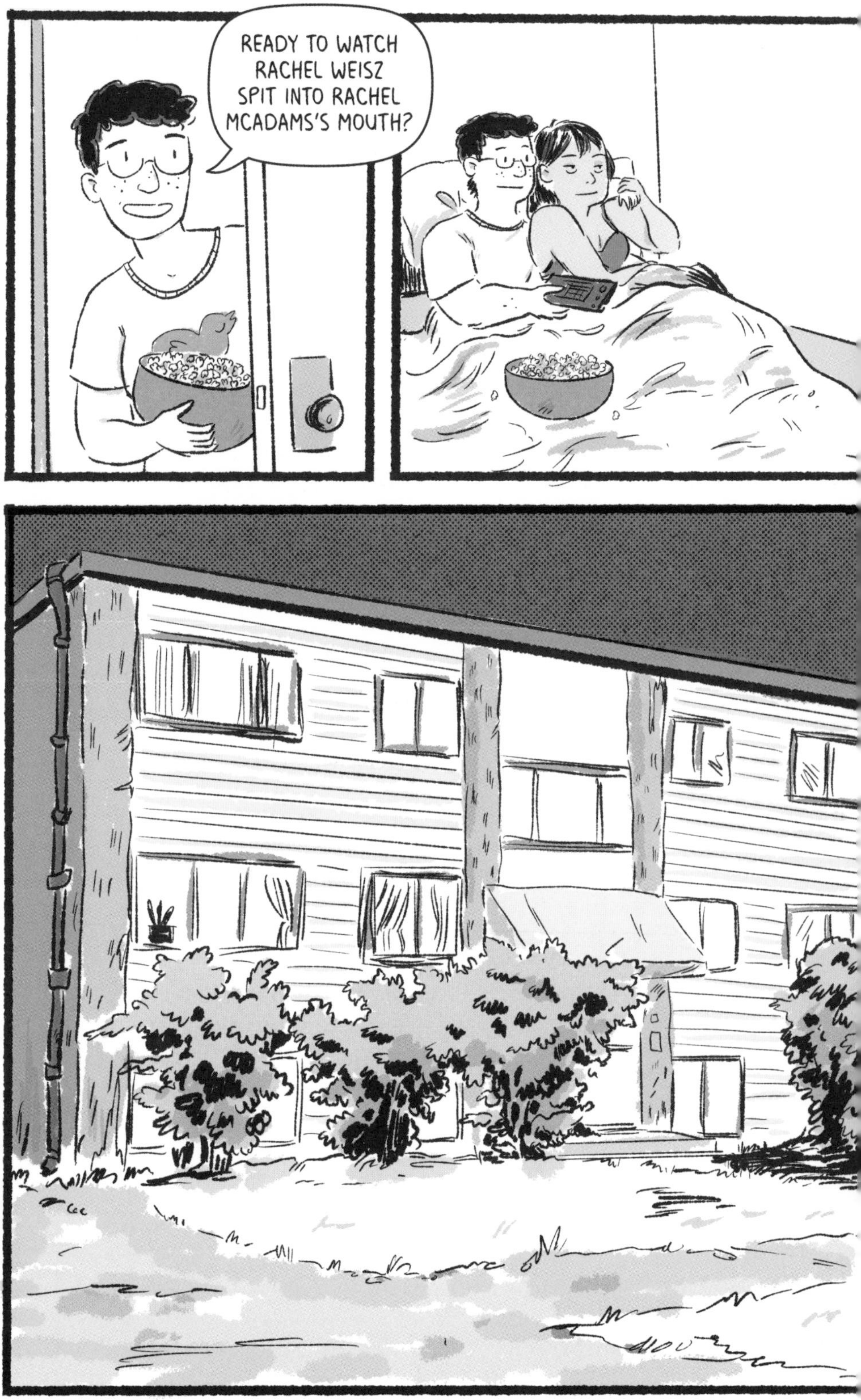
READY TO WATCH RACHEL WEISZ SPIT INTO RACHEL MCADAMS'S MOUTH?

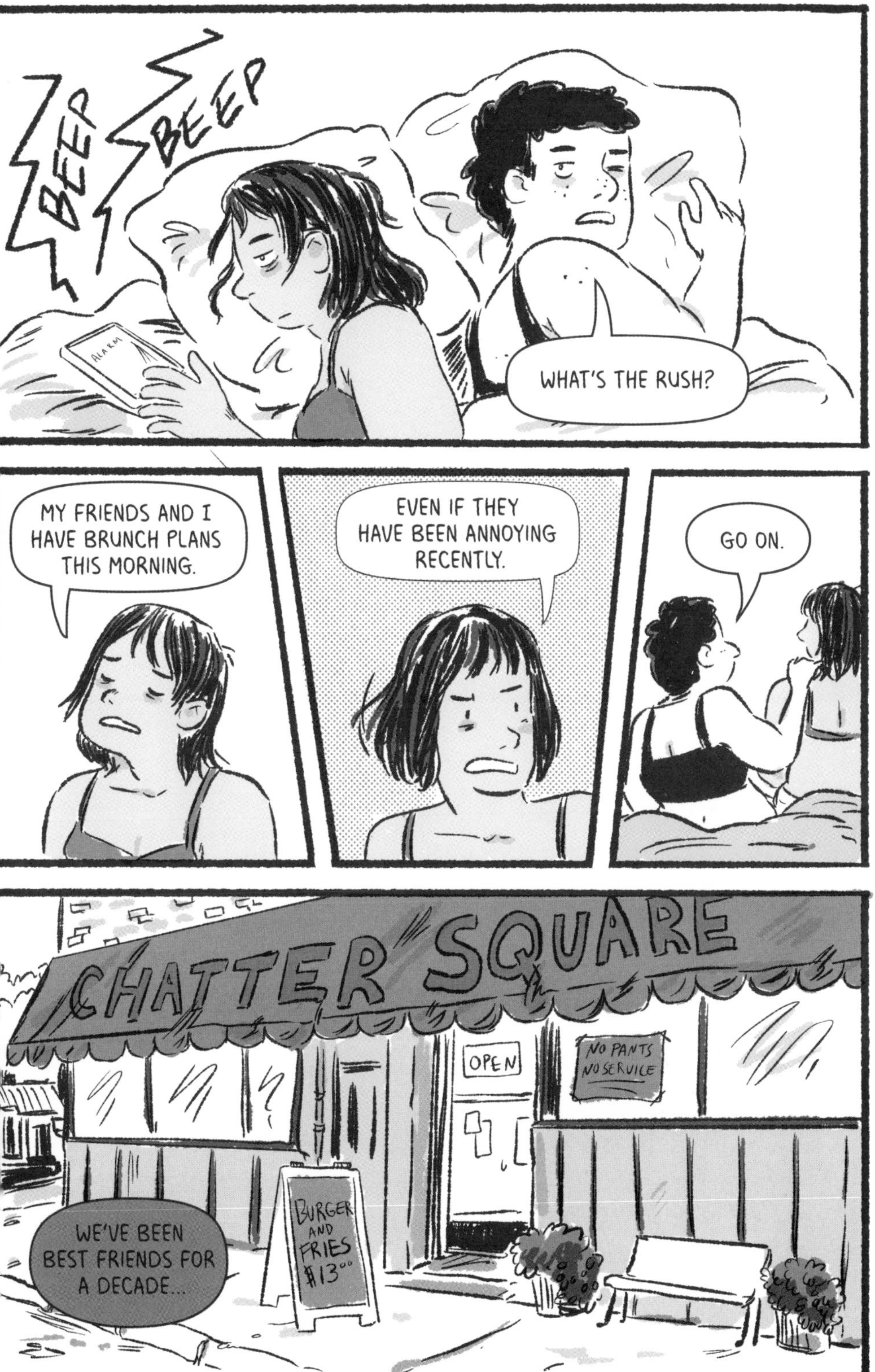
BEEP
BEEP
ALARM
WHAT'S THE RUSH?
MY FRIENDS AND I HAVE BRUNCH PLANS THIS MORNING.
EVEN IF THEY HAVE BEEN ANNOYING RECENTLY.
GO ON.
CHATTER SQUARE
OPEN
NO PANTS NO SERVICE
BURGER AND FRIES $13.00
WE'VE BEEN BEST FRIENDS FOR A DECADE...

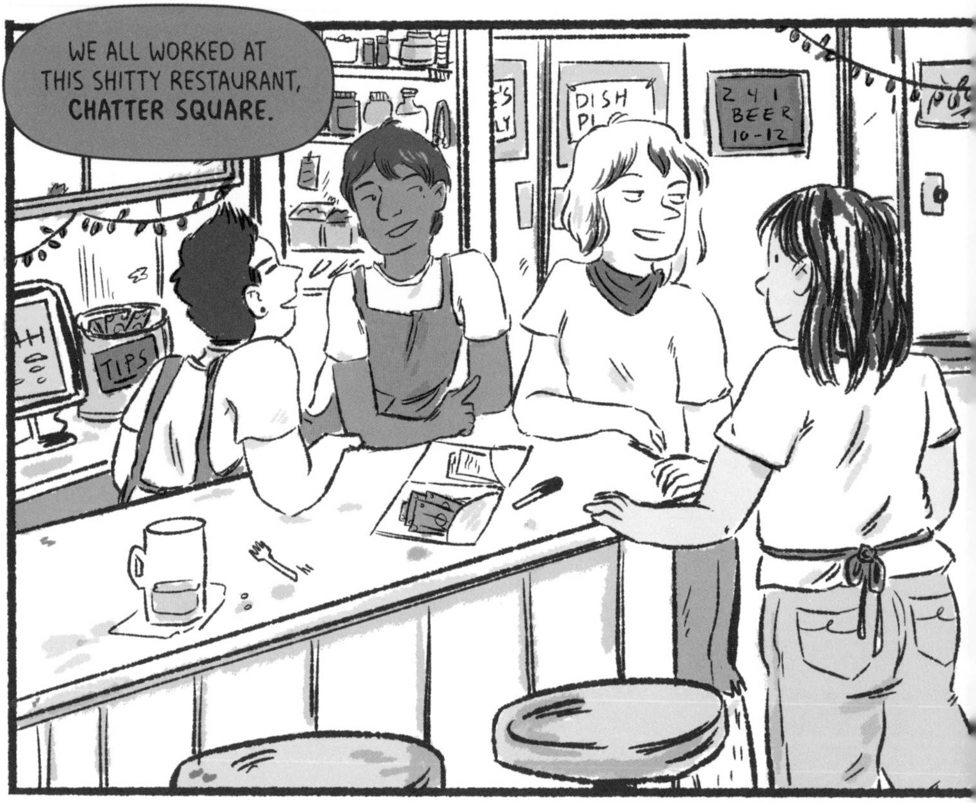
WE ALL WORKED AT THIS SHITTY RESTAURANT, **CHATTER SQUARE.**
DISH
2 4 1
BEER
10-12
TIPS

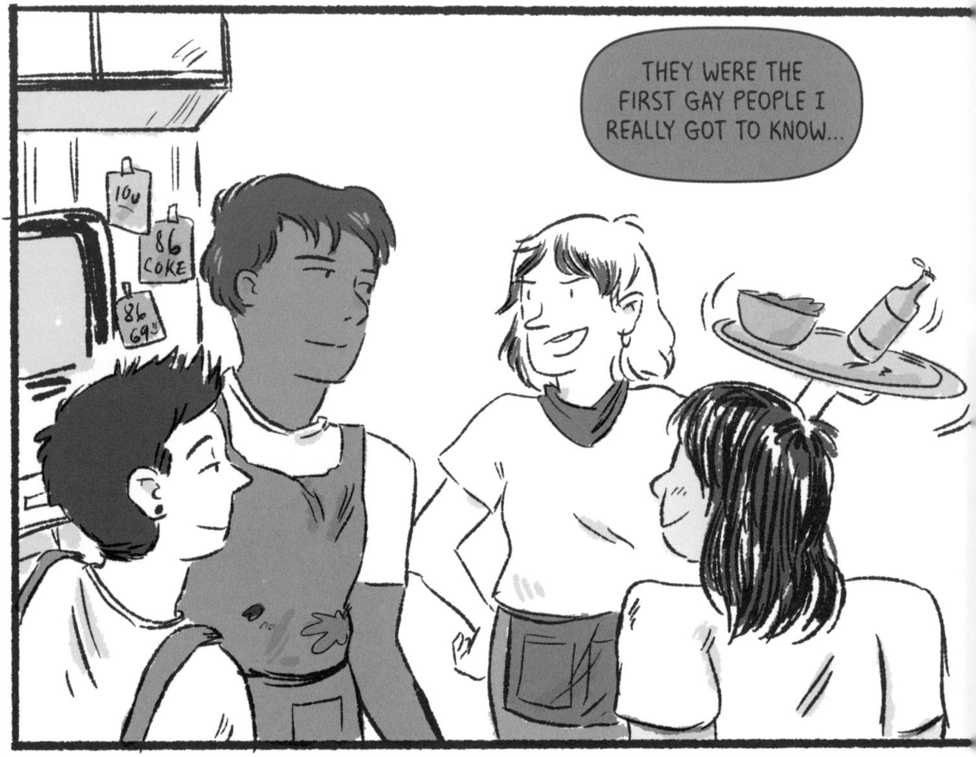
THEY WERE THE FIRST GAY PEOPLE I REALLY GOT TO KNOW...
86
COKE

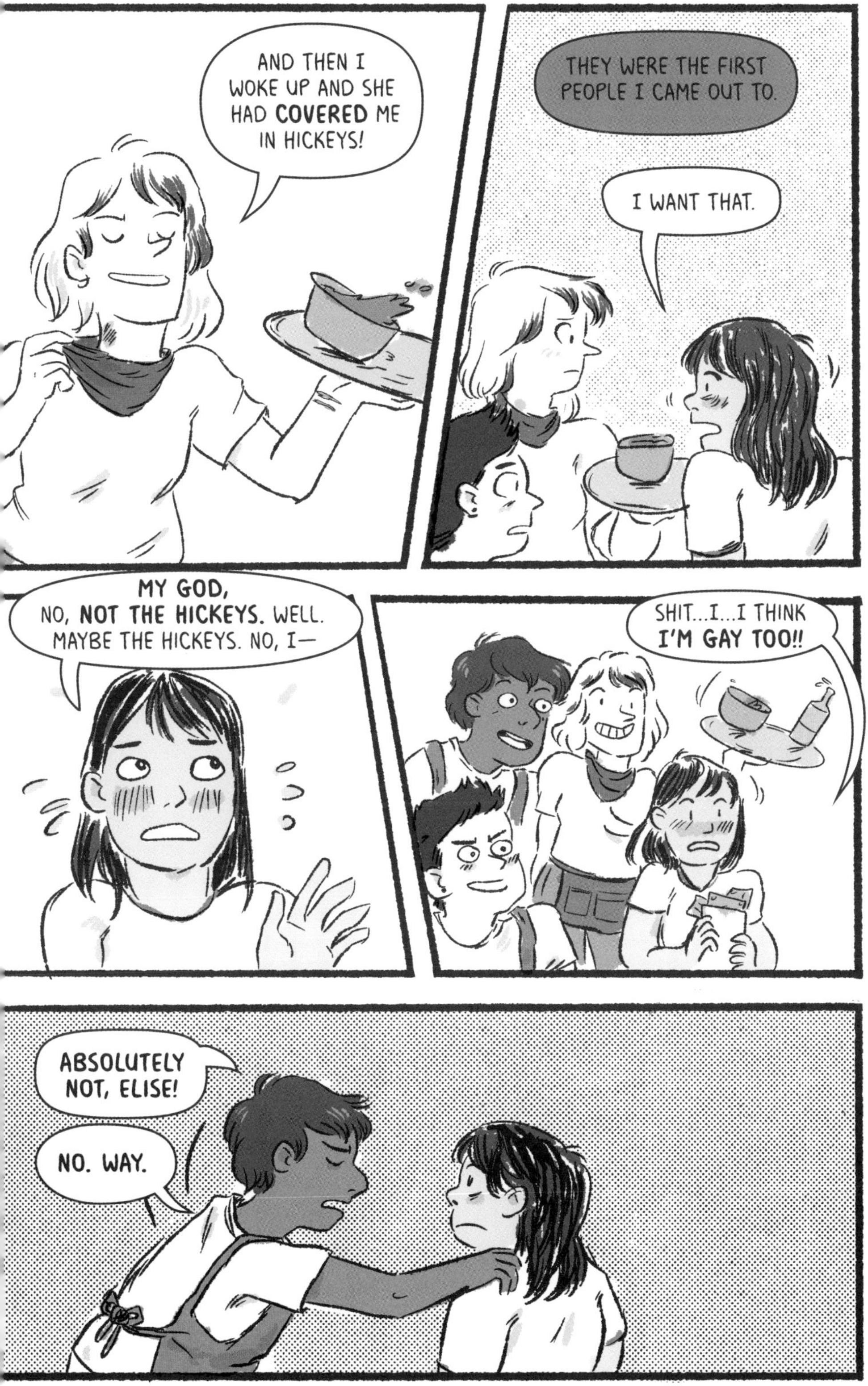
AND THEN I WOKE UP AND SHE HAD **COVERED** ME IN HICKEYS!
THEY WERE THE FIRST PEOPLE I CAME OUT TO.
I WANT THAT.
MY GOD, NO, **NOT THE HICKEYS.** WELL. MAYBE THE HICKEYS. NO, I—
SHIT...I...I THINK **I'M GAY TOO!!**
ABSOLUTELY NOT, ELISE!
NO. WAY.

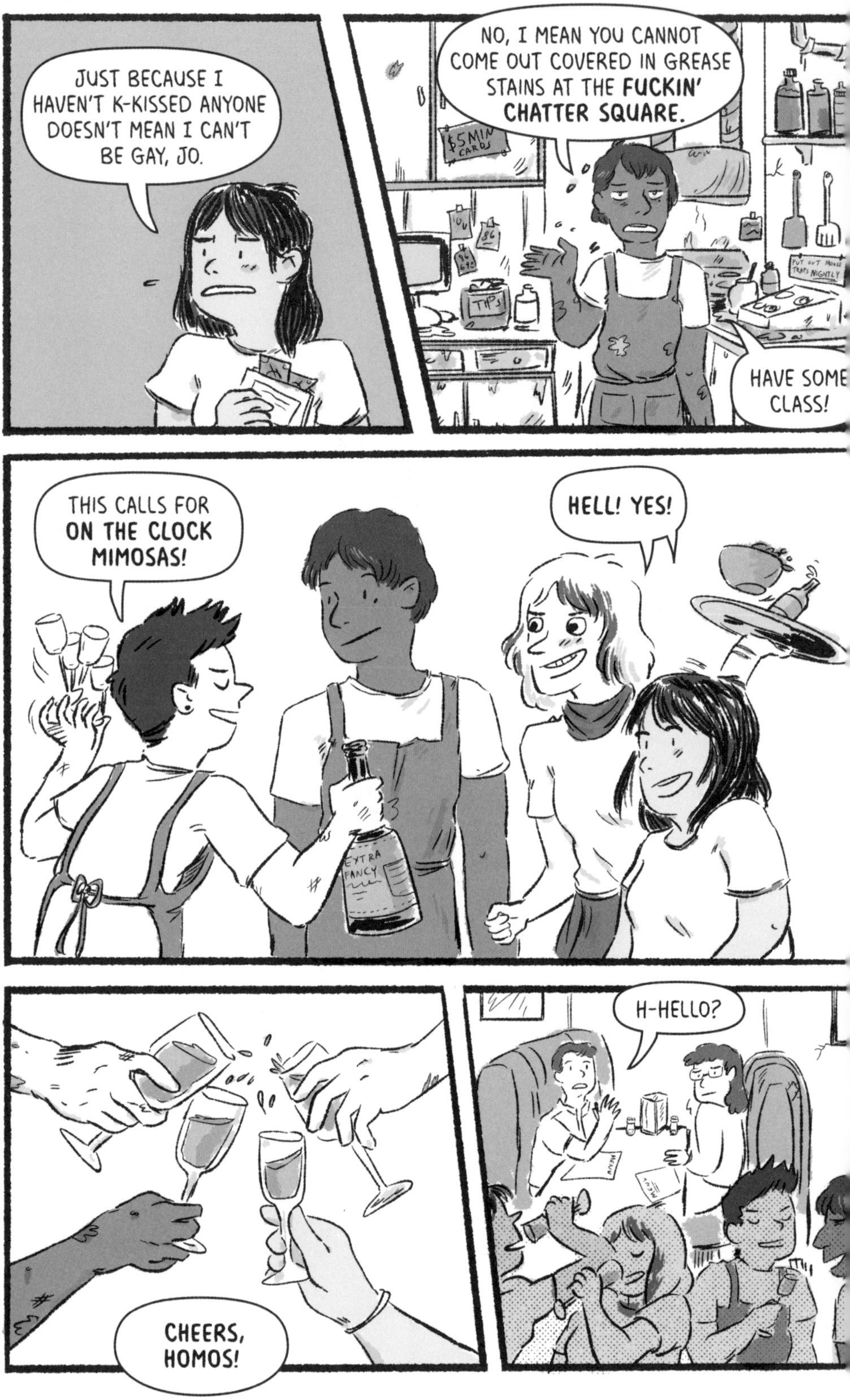
JUST BECAUSE I HAVEN'T K-KISSED ANYONE DOESN'T MEAN I CAN'T BE GAY, JO.
NO, I MEAN YOU CANNOT COME OUT COVERED IN GREASE STAINS AT THE **FUCKIN' CHATTER SQUARE.**
$5 MIN CARDS
TIPS
PUT OUT MOUSE TRAPS NIGHTLY
HAVE SOME CLASS!
THIS CALLS FOR **ON THE CLOCK MIMOSAS!**
HELL! YES!
EXTRA FANCY
CHEERS, HOMOS!
H-HELLO?
MENU

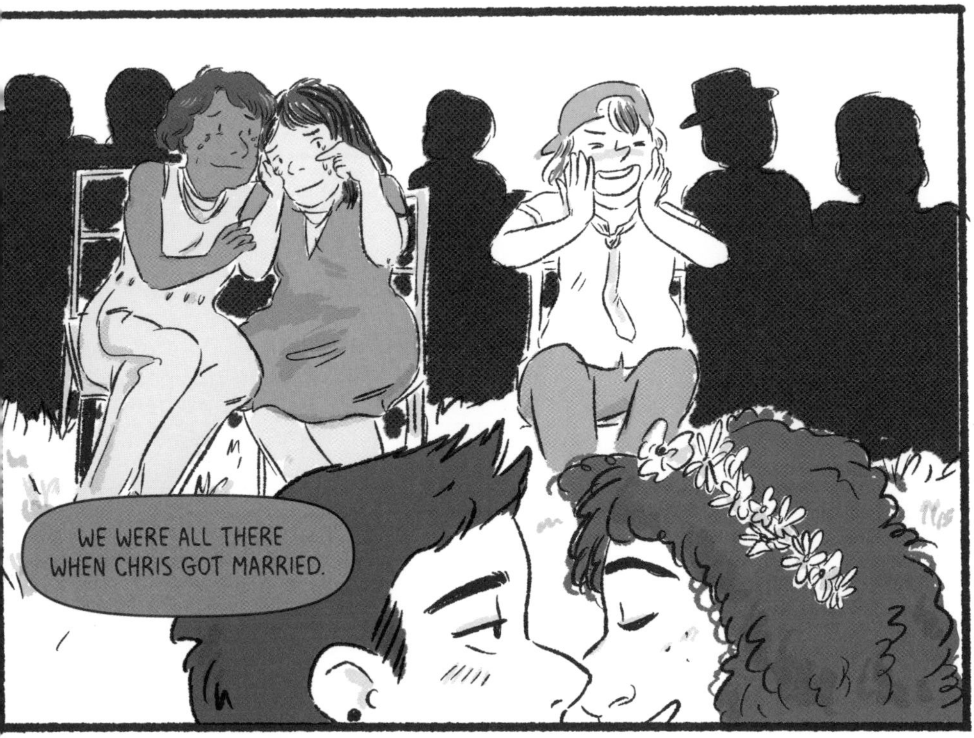
WE WERE ALL THERE WHEN CHRIS GOT MARRIED.

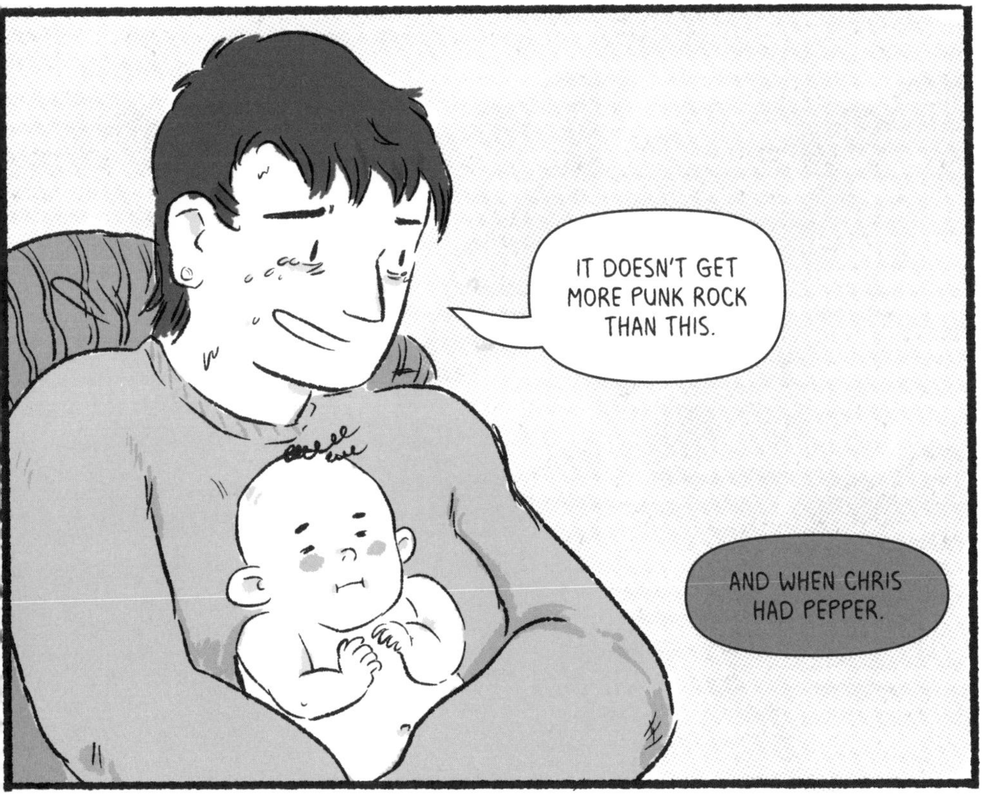
IT DOESN'T GET MORE PUNK ROCK THAN THIS.
AND WHEN CHRIS HAD PEPPER.

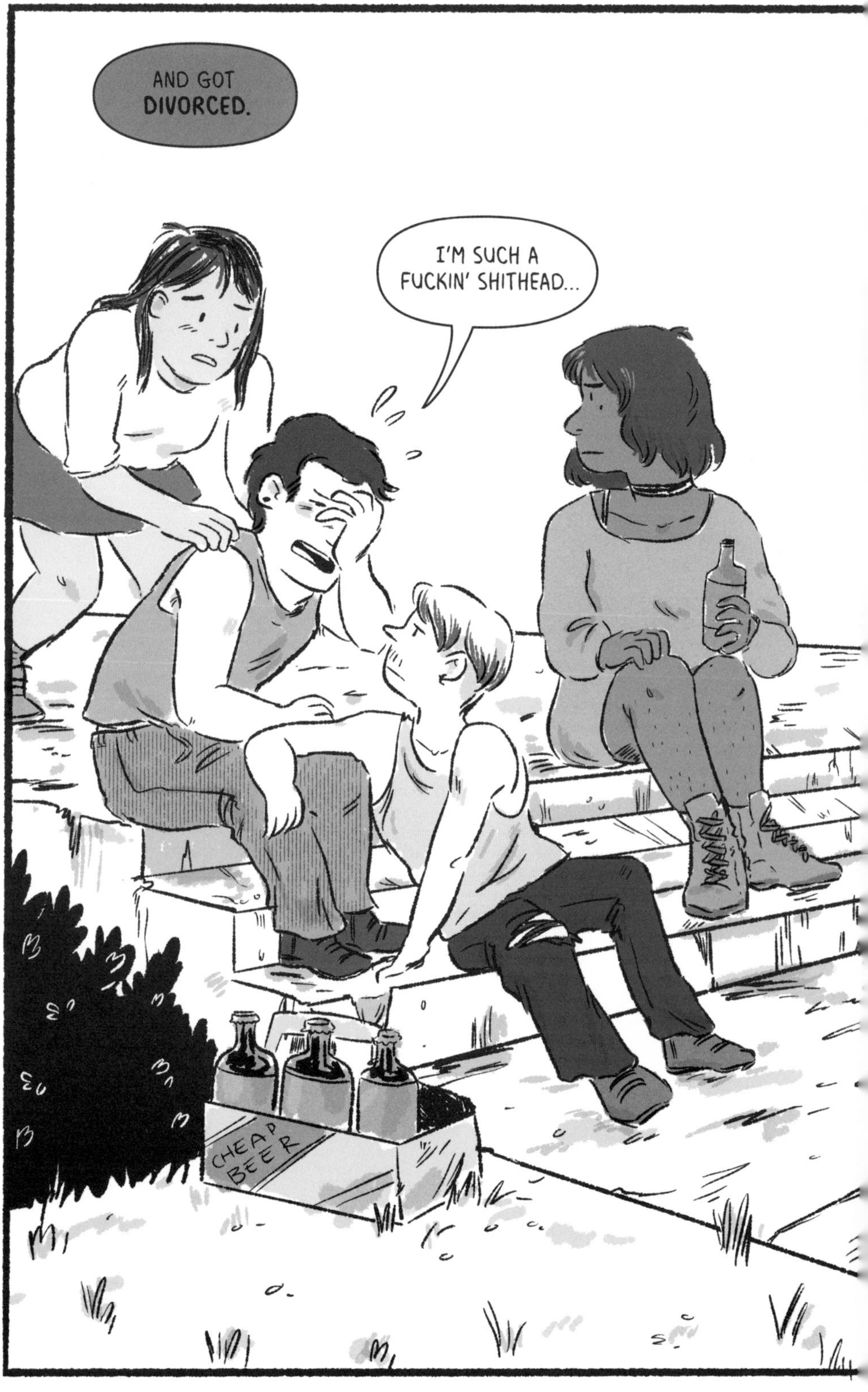
AND GOT DIVORCED.
I'M SUCH A FUCKIN' SHITHEAD...
CHEAP BEER

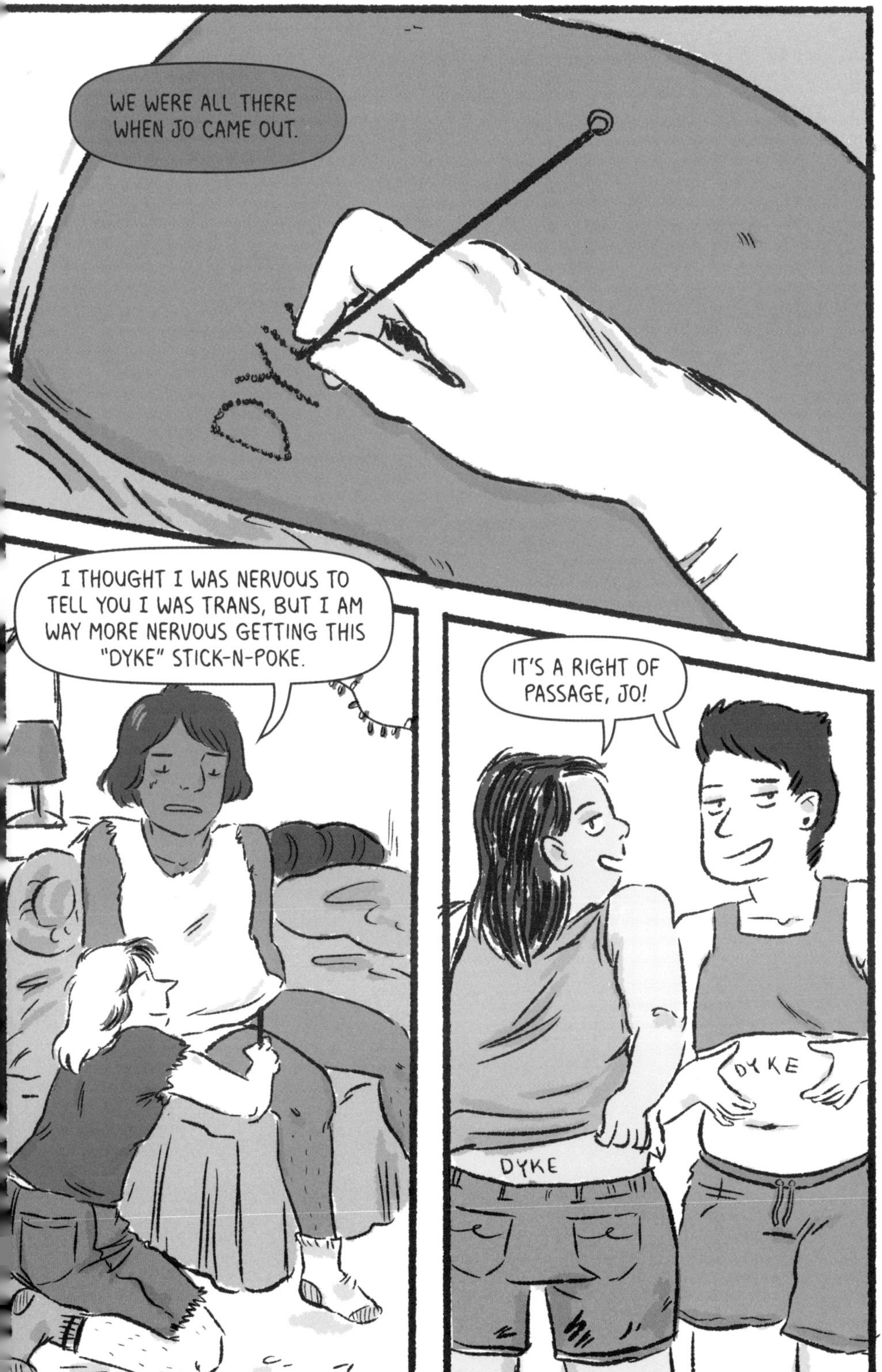
WE WERE ALL THERE WHEN JO CAME OUT.
I THOUGHT I WAS NERVOUS TO TELL YOU I WAS TRANS, BUT I AM WAY MORE NERVOUS GETTING THIS "DYKE" STICK-N-POKE.
IT'S A RIGHT OF PASSAGE, JO!
DYKE
DYKE

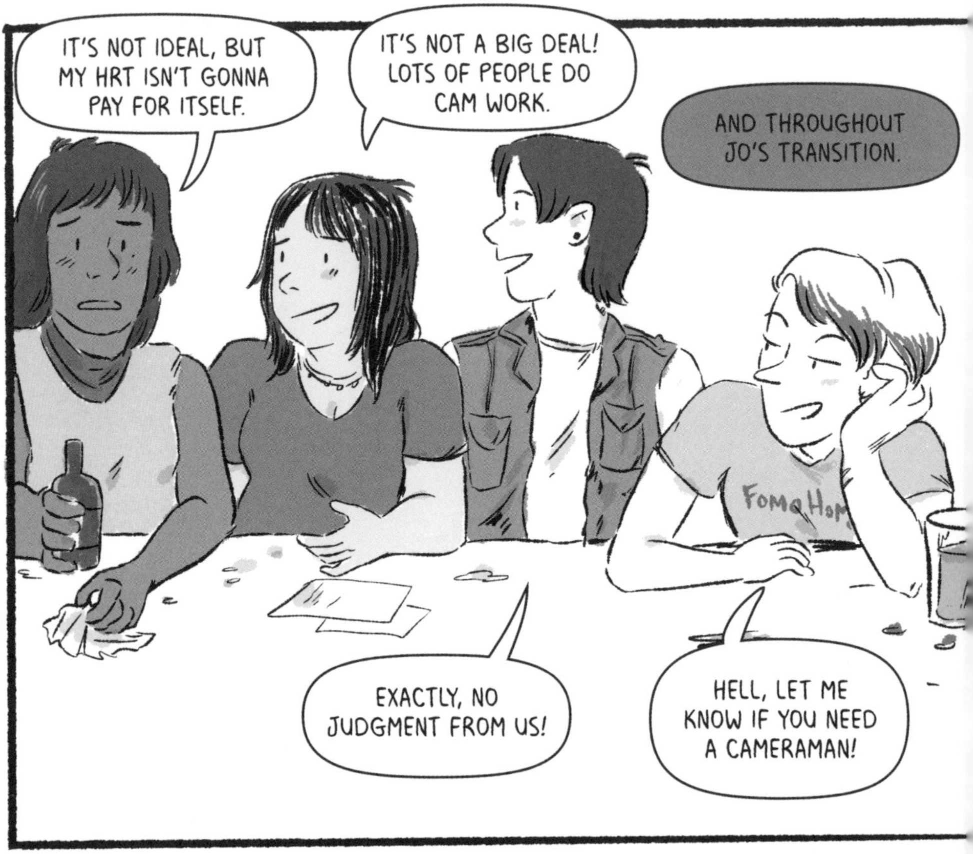
IT'S NOT IDEAL, BUT MY HRT ISN'T GONNA PAY FOR ITSELF.
IT'S NOT A BIG DEAL! LOTS OF PEOPLE DO CAM WORK.
AND THROUGHOUT JO'S TRANSITION.
FomaHom
EXACTLY, NO JUDGMENT FROM US!
HELL, LET ME KNOW IF YOU NEED A CAMERAMAN!

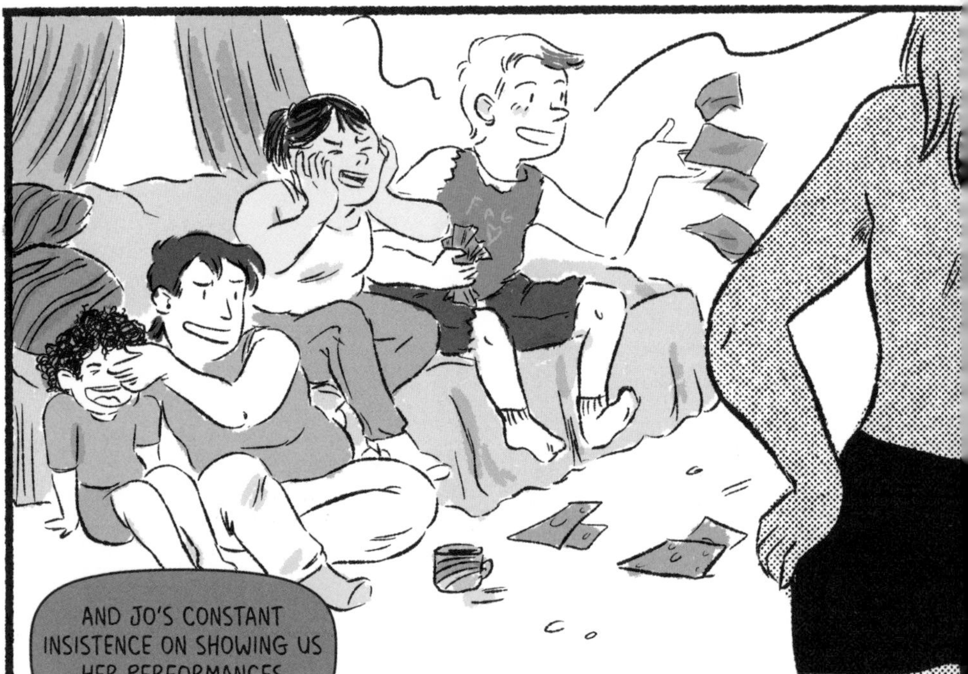
FAG
AND JO'S CONSTANT INSISTENCE ON SHOWING US HER PERFORMANCES.

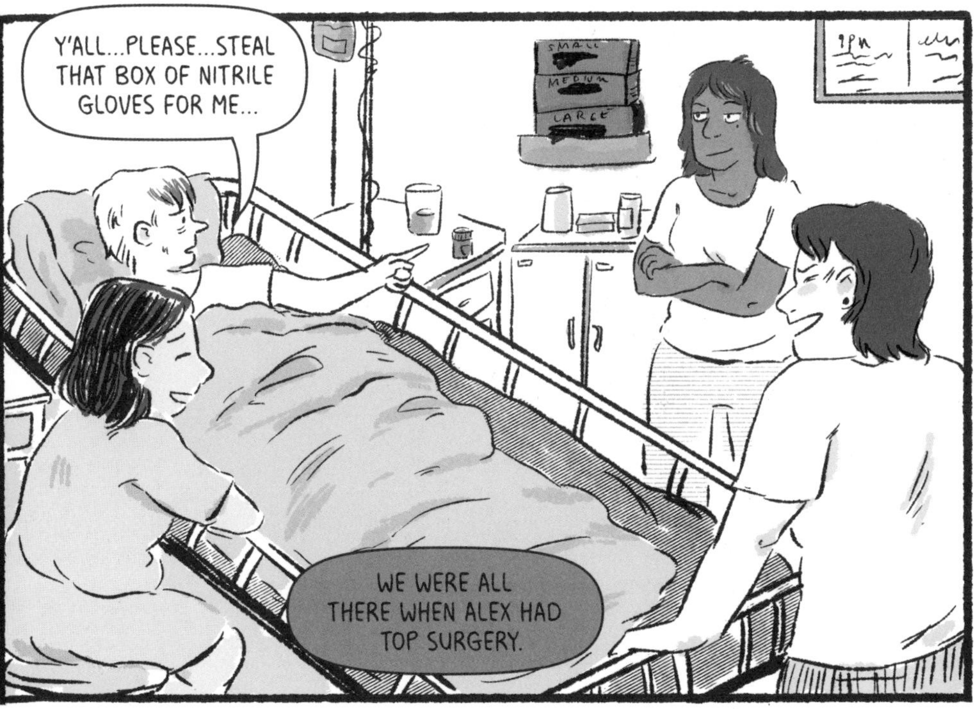
Y'ALL...PLEASE...STEAL THAT BOX OF NITRILE GLOVES FOR ME...
SMALL
MEDIUM
LARGE
WE WERE ALL THERE WHEN ALEX HAD TOP SURGERY.

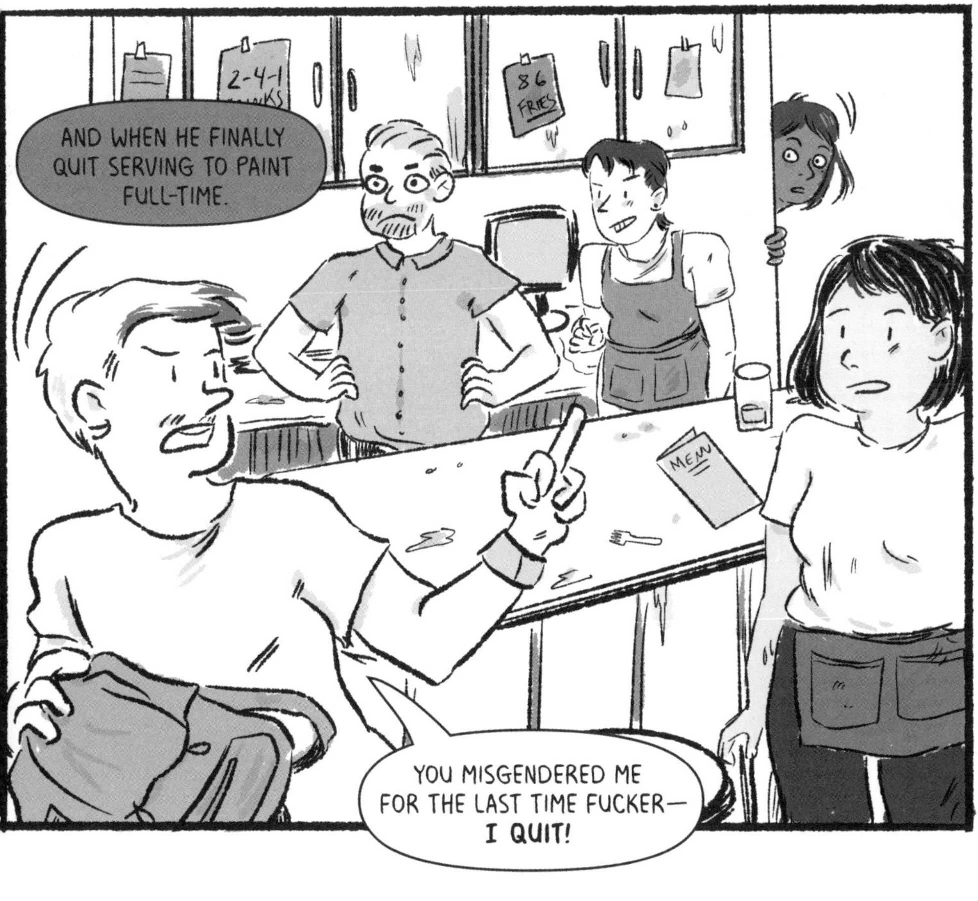
AND WHEN HE FINALLY QUIT SERVING TO PAINT FULL-TIME.
86 FRIES
MENU
YOU MISGENDERED ME FOR THE LAST TIME FUCKER—
I QUIT!

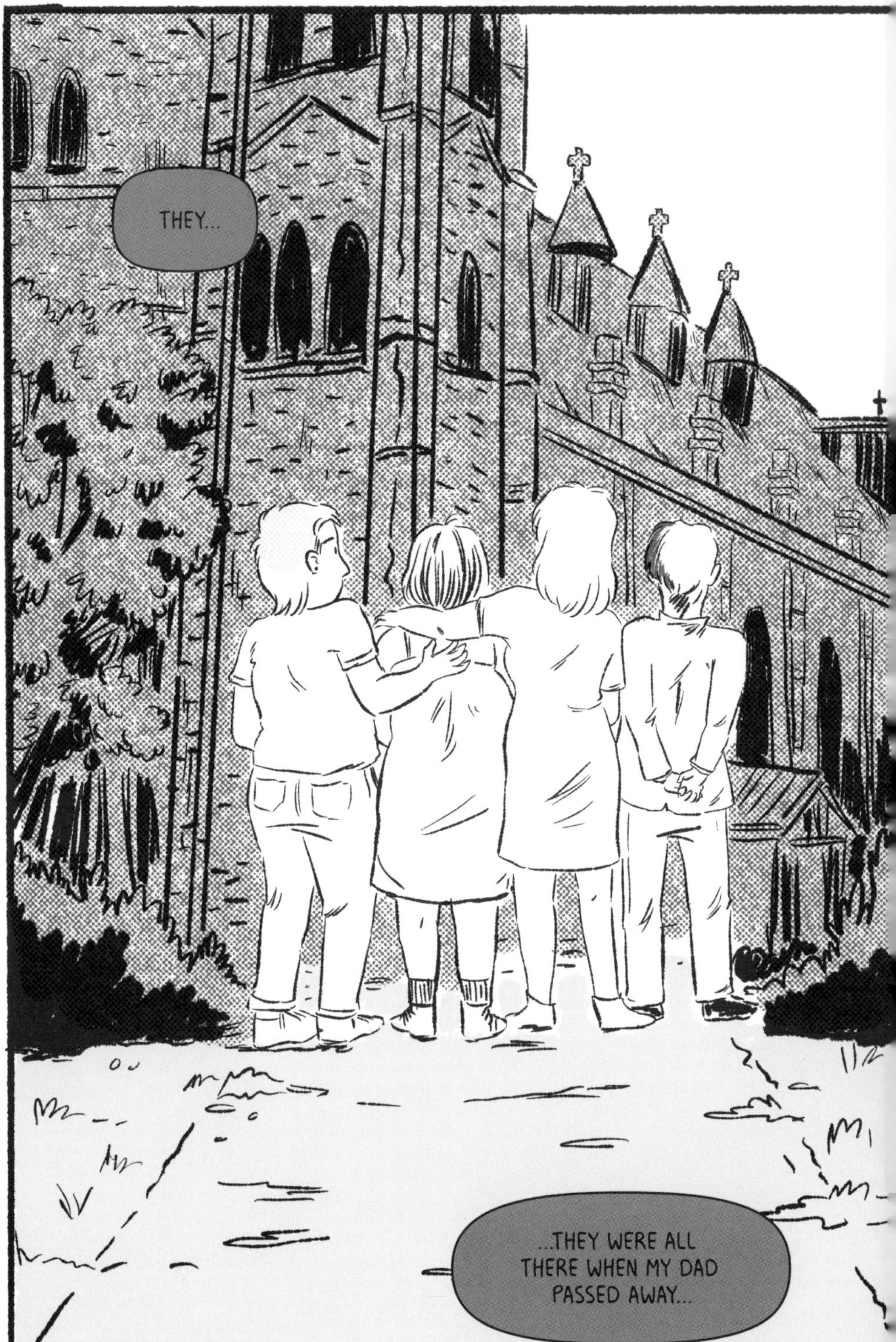
THEY...
...THEY WERE ALL
THERE WHEN MY DAD
PASSED AWAY...

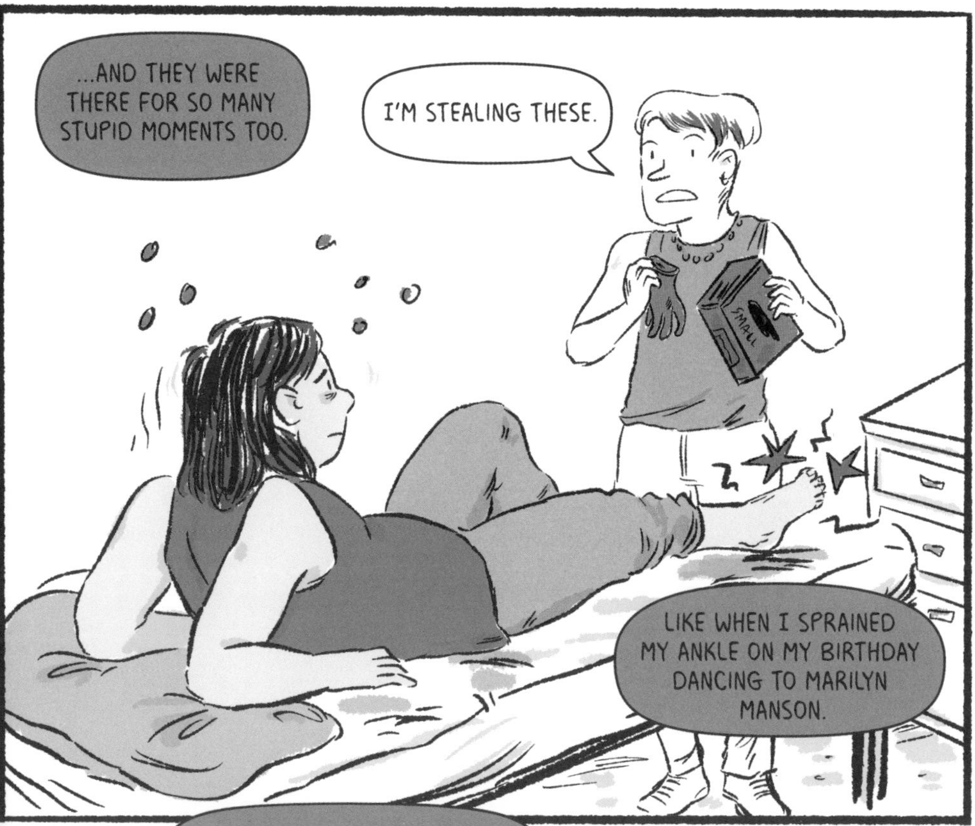
...AND THEY WERE THERE FOR SO MANY STUPID MOMENTS TOO.
I'M STEALING THESE.
SMALL
LIKE WHEN I SPRAINED MY ANKLE ON MY BIRTHDAY DANCING TO MARILYN MANSON.

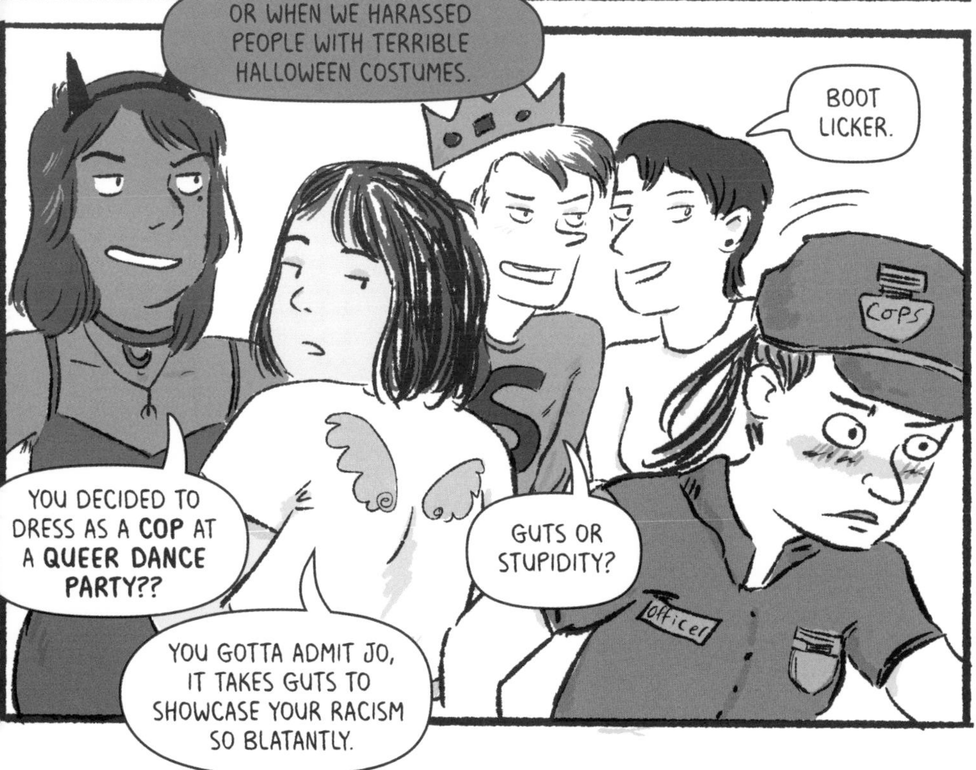
OR WHEN WE HARASSED PEOPLE WITH TERRIBLE HALLOWEEN COSTUMES.
BOOT LICKER.
COPS
YOU DECIDED TO DRESS AS A **COP** AT A **QUEER DANCE PARTY??**
GUTS OR STUPIDITY?
Officer
YOU GOTTA ADMIT JO, IT TAKES GUTS TO SHOWCASE YOUR RACISM SO BLATANTLY.

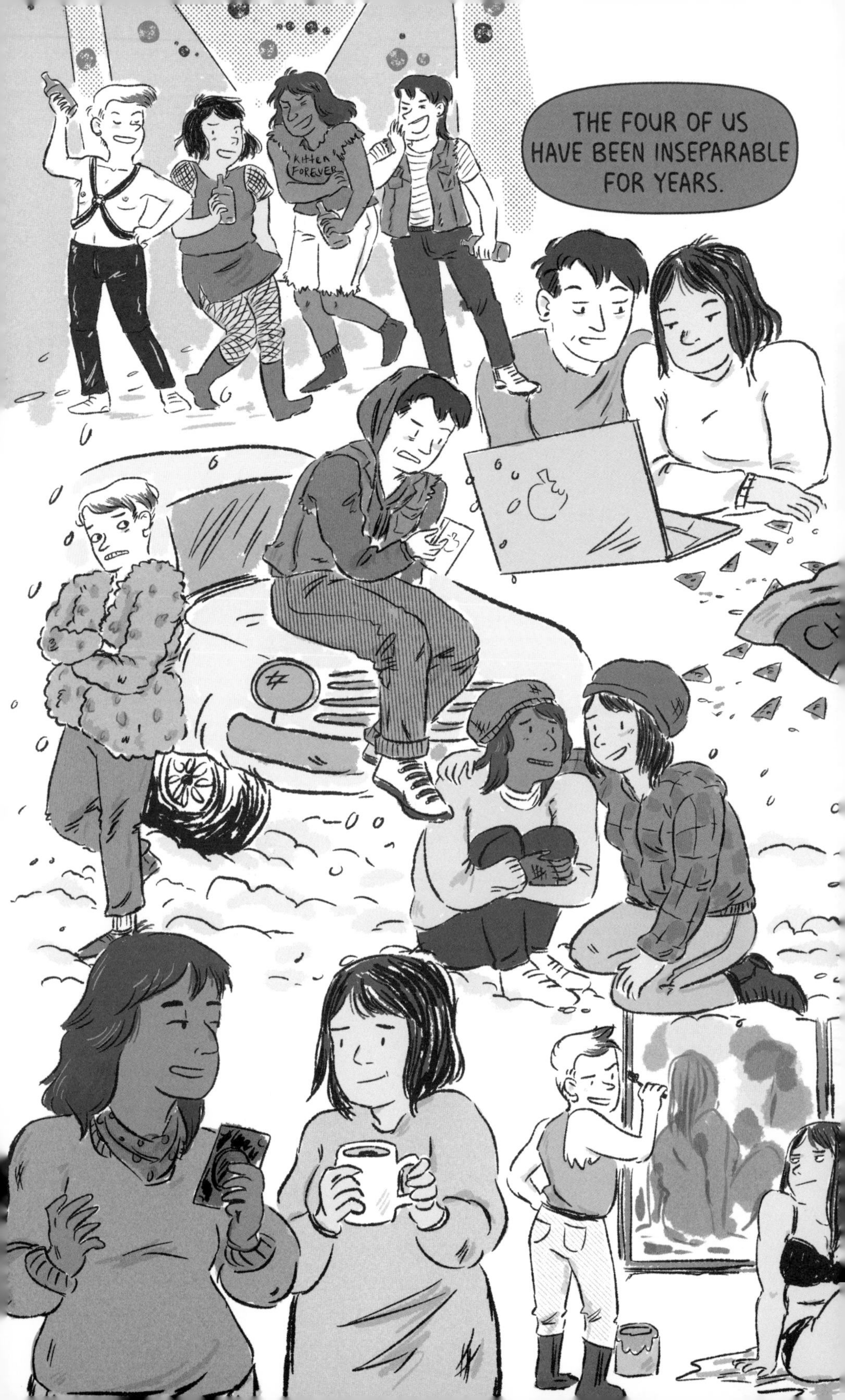
THE FOUR OF US HAVE BEEN INSEPARABLE FOR YEARS.
Kitten FOREVER

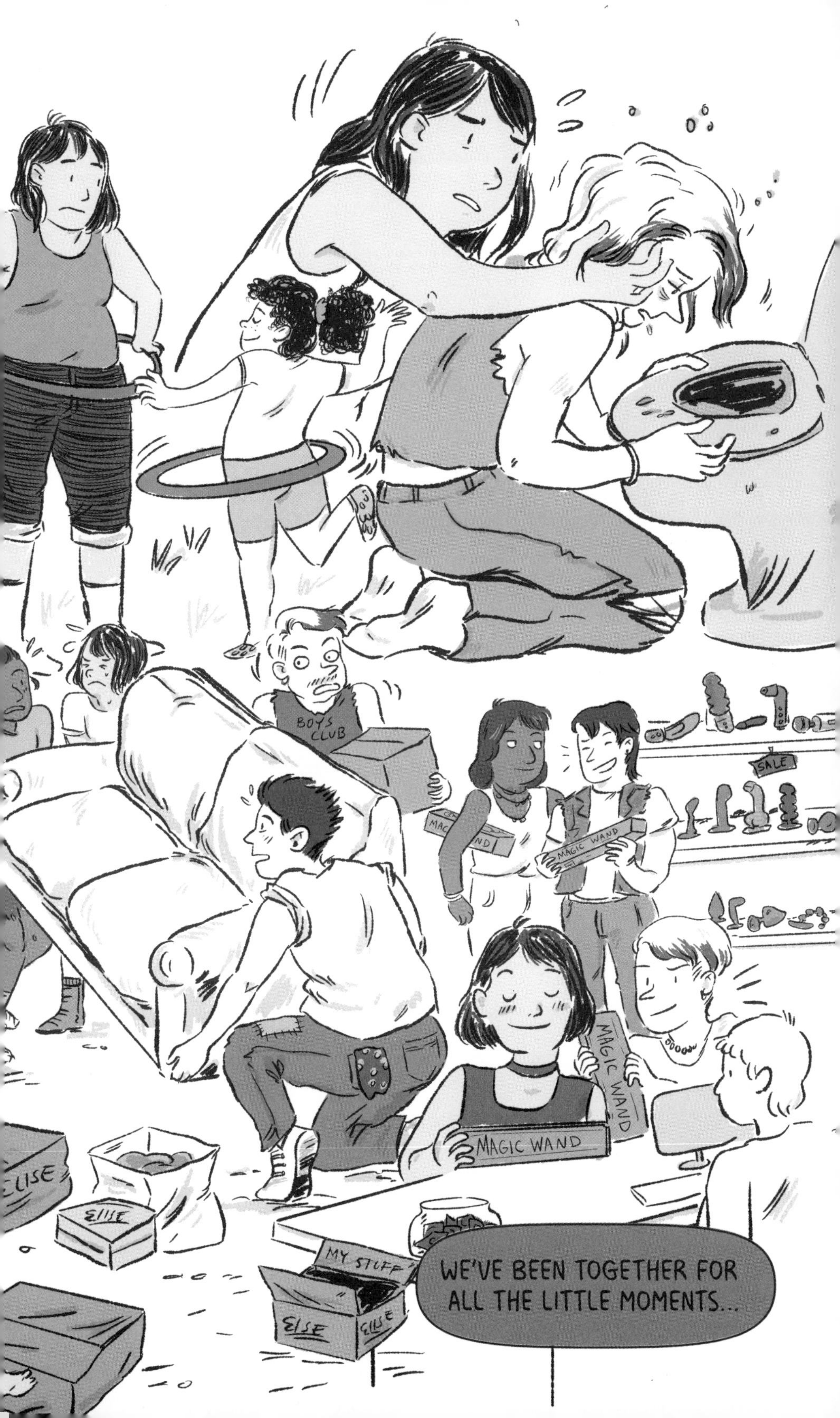
BOYS CLUB
SALE
MAGIC WAND
MAGIC WAND
MAGIC WAND
MAGIC WAND
ELISE
ELISE
MY STUFF
ELISE
ELISE
WE'VE BEEN TOGETHER FOR ALL THE LITTLE MOMENTS...

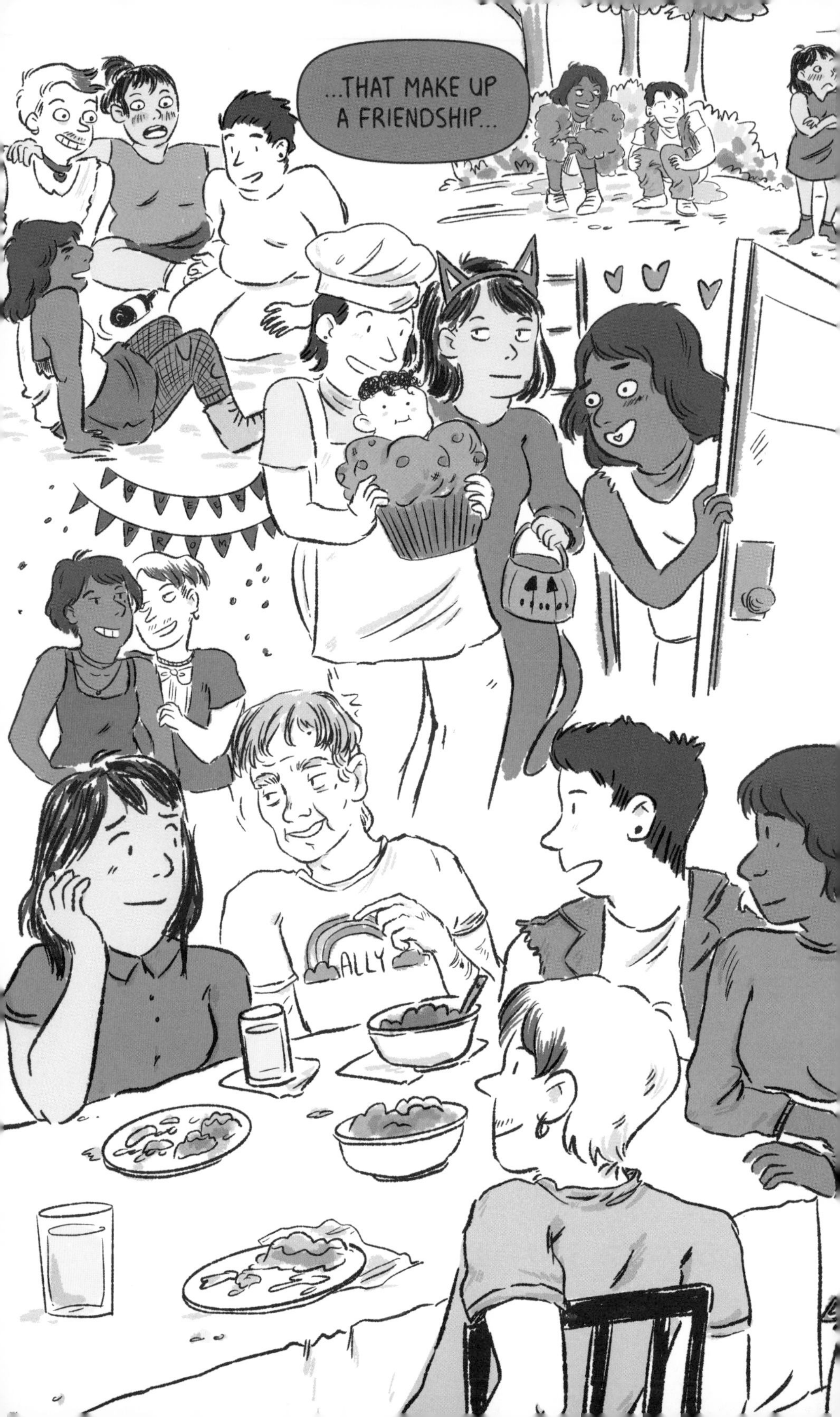
...THAT MAKE UP A FRIENDSHIP...
QUEER PROM
ALLY

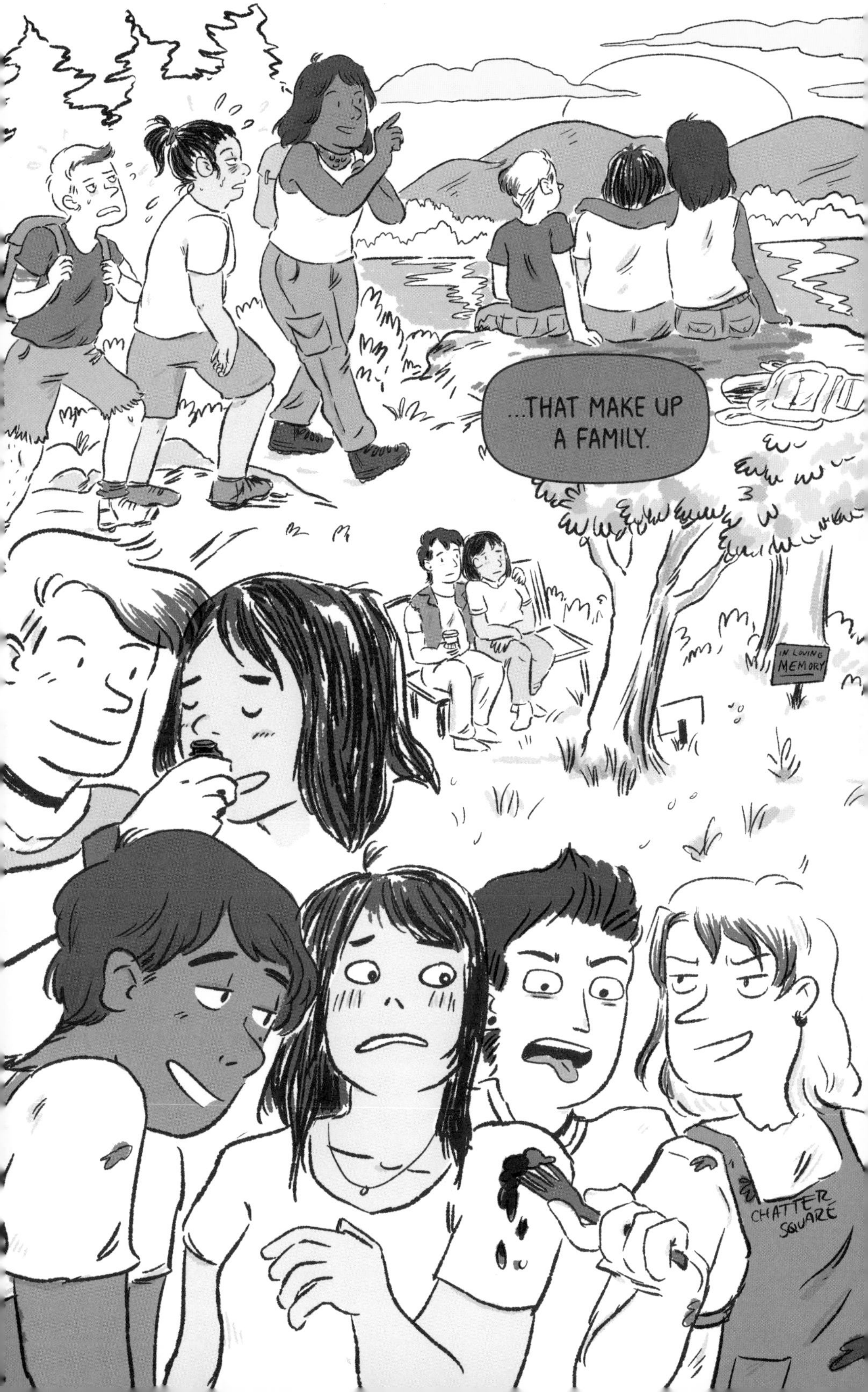
...THAT MAKE UP A FAMILY.
IN LOVING MEMORY
CHATTER SQUARE

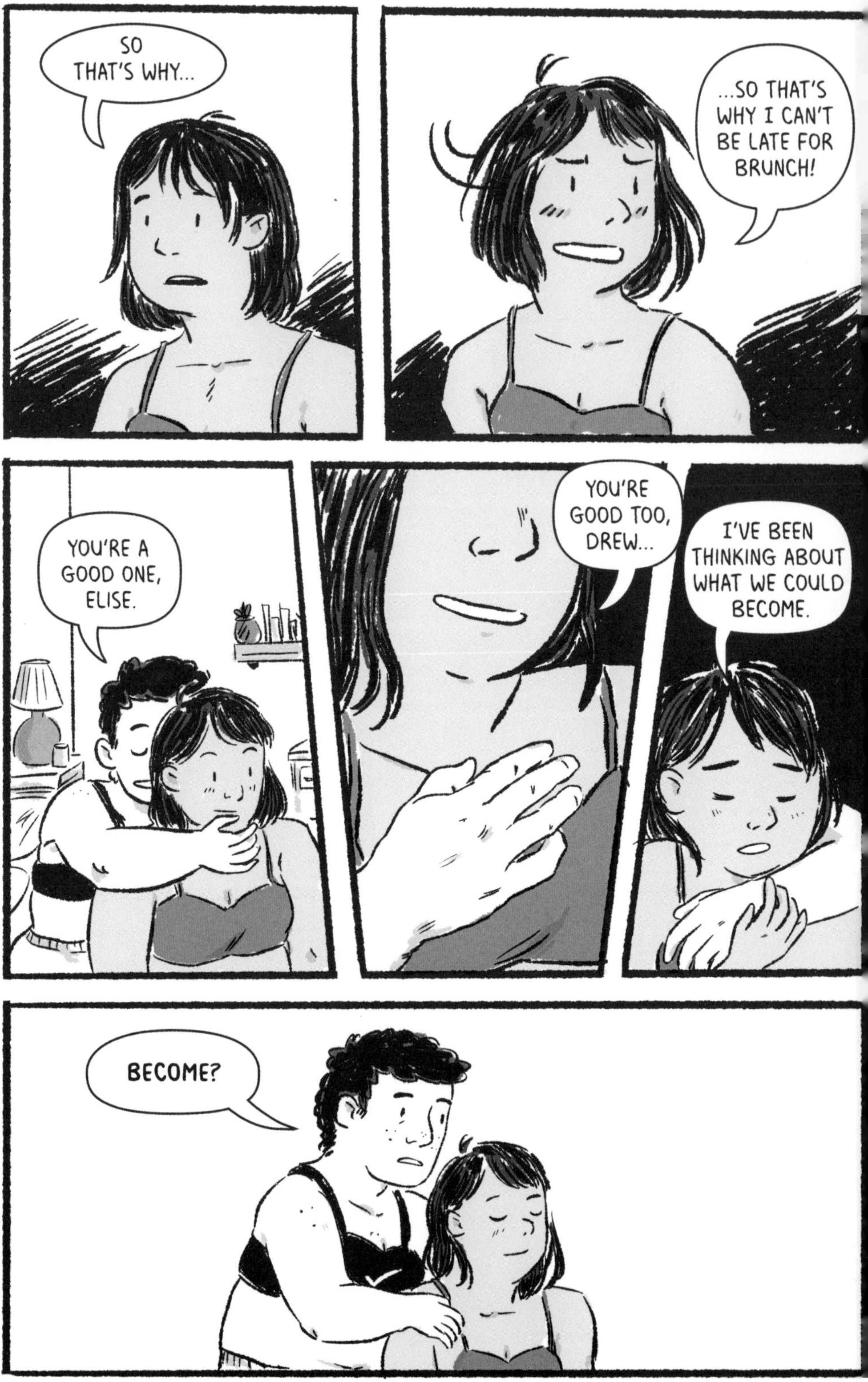
SO THAT'S WHY...
...SO THAT'S WHY I CAN'T BE LATE FOR BRUNCH!
YOU'RE A GOOD ONE, ELISE.
YOU'RE GOOD TOO, DREW...
I'VE BEEN THINKING ABOUT WHAT WE COULD BECOME.
BECOME?

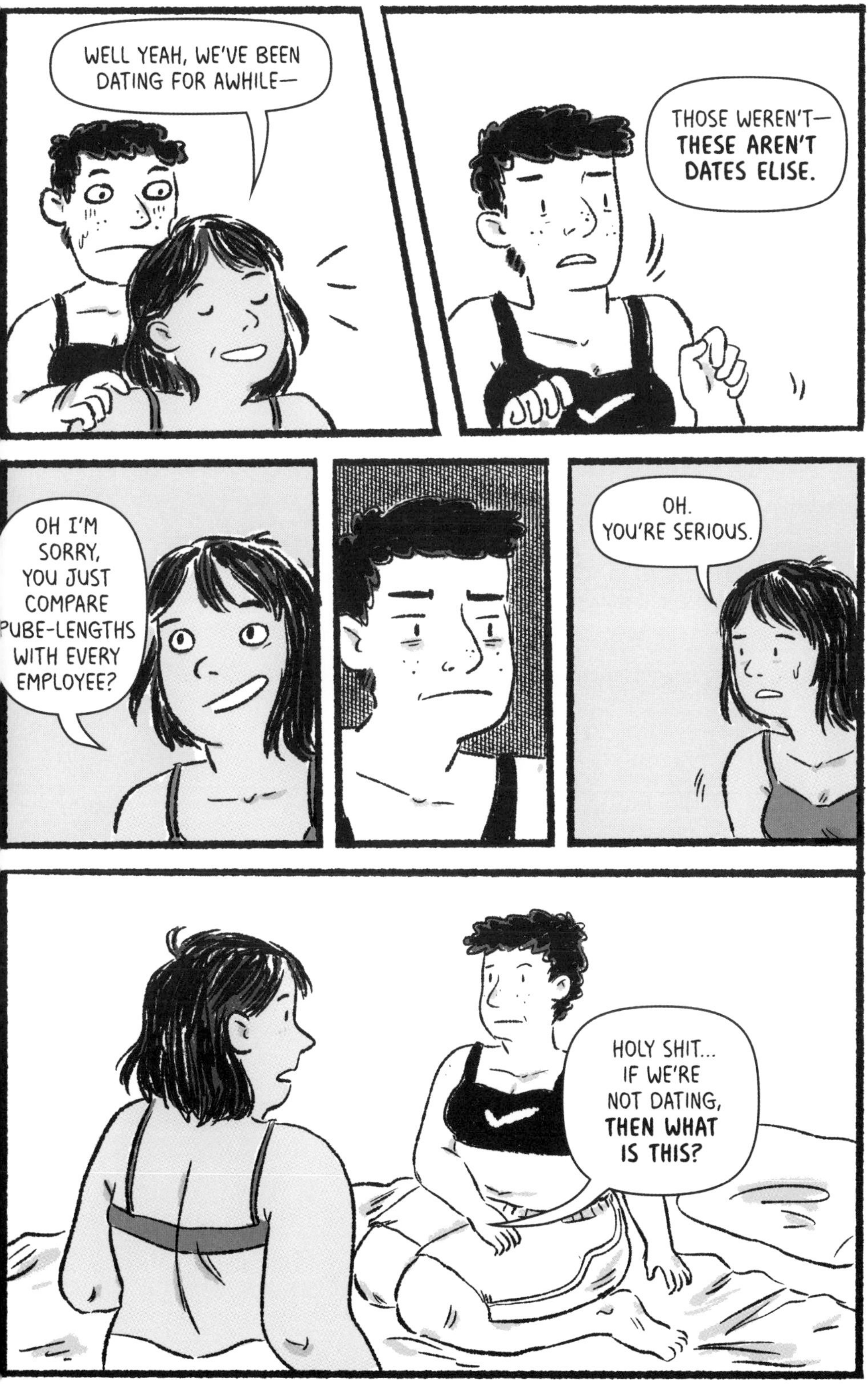

WELL YEAH, WE'VE BEEN DATING FOR AWHILE—
THOSE WEREN'T— **THESE AREN'T DATES ELISE.**
OH I'M SORRY, YOU JUST COMPARE PUBE-LENGTHS WITH EVERY EMPLOYEE?
OH. YOU'RE SERIOUS.
HOLY SHIT... IF WE'RE NOT DATING, **THEN WHAT IS THIS?**

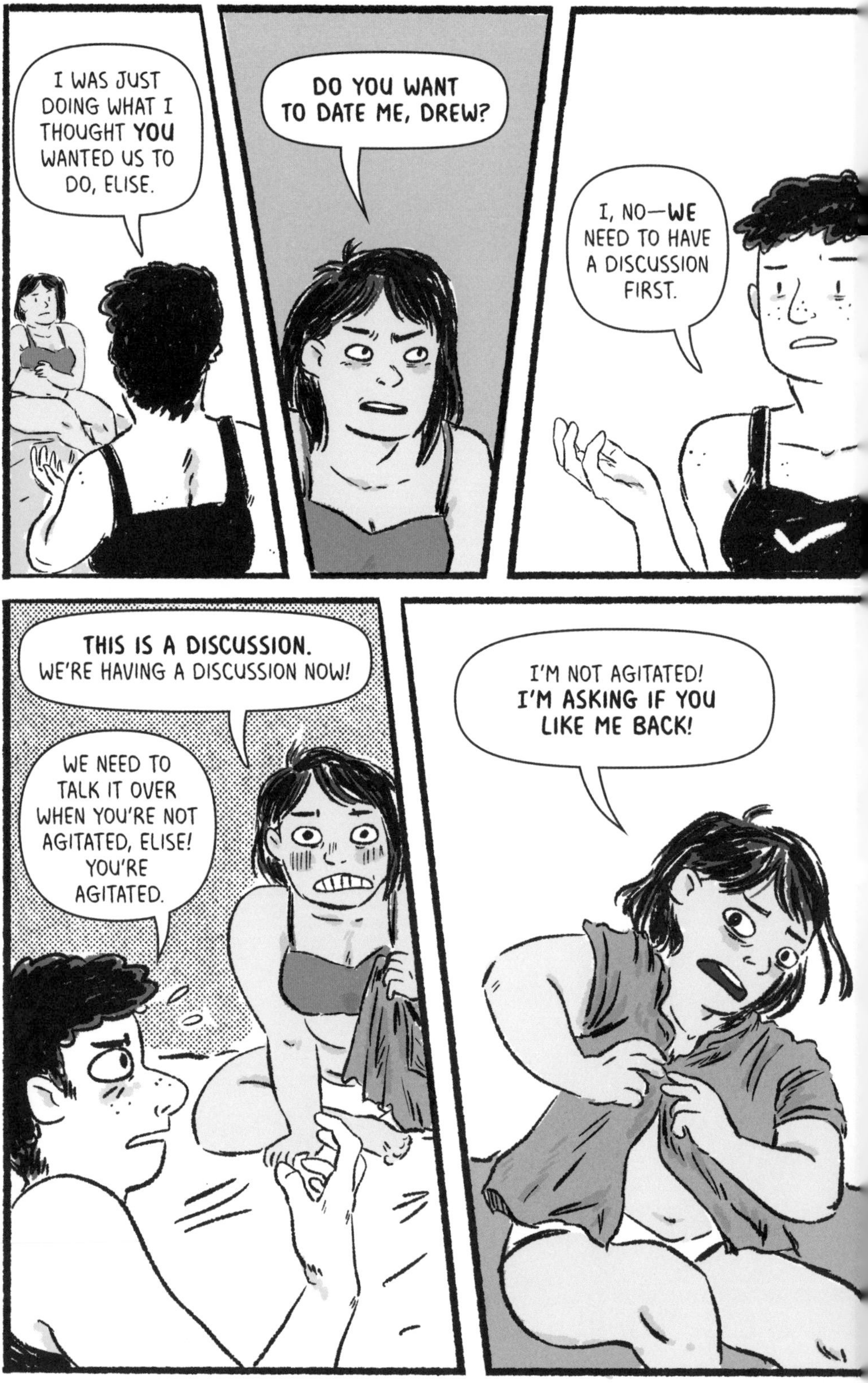
I WAS JUST DOING WHAT I THOUGHT **YOU** WANTED US TO DO, ELISE.
DO YOU WANT TO DATE ME, DREW?
I, NO—**WE** NEED TO HAVE A DISCUSSION FIRST.
THIS IS A DISCUSSION. WE'RE HAVING A DISCUSSION NOW!
WE NEED TO TALK IT OVER WHEN YOU'RE NOT AGITATED, ELISE! YOU'RE AGITATED.
I'M NOT AGITATED! **I'M ASKING IF YOU LIKE ME BACK!**

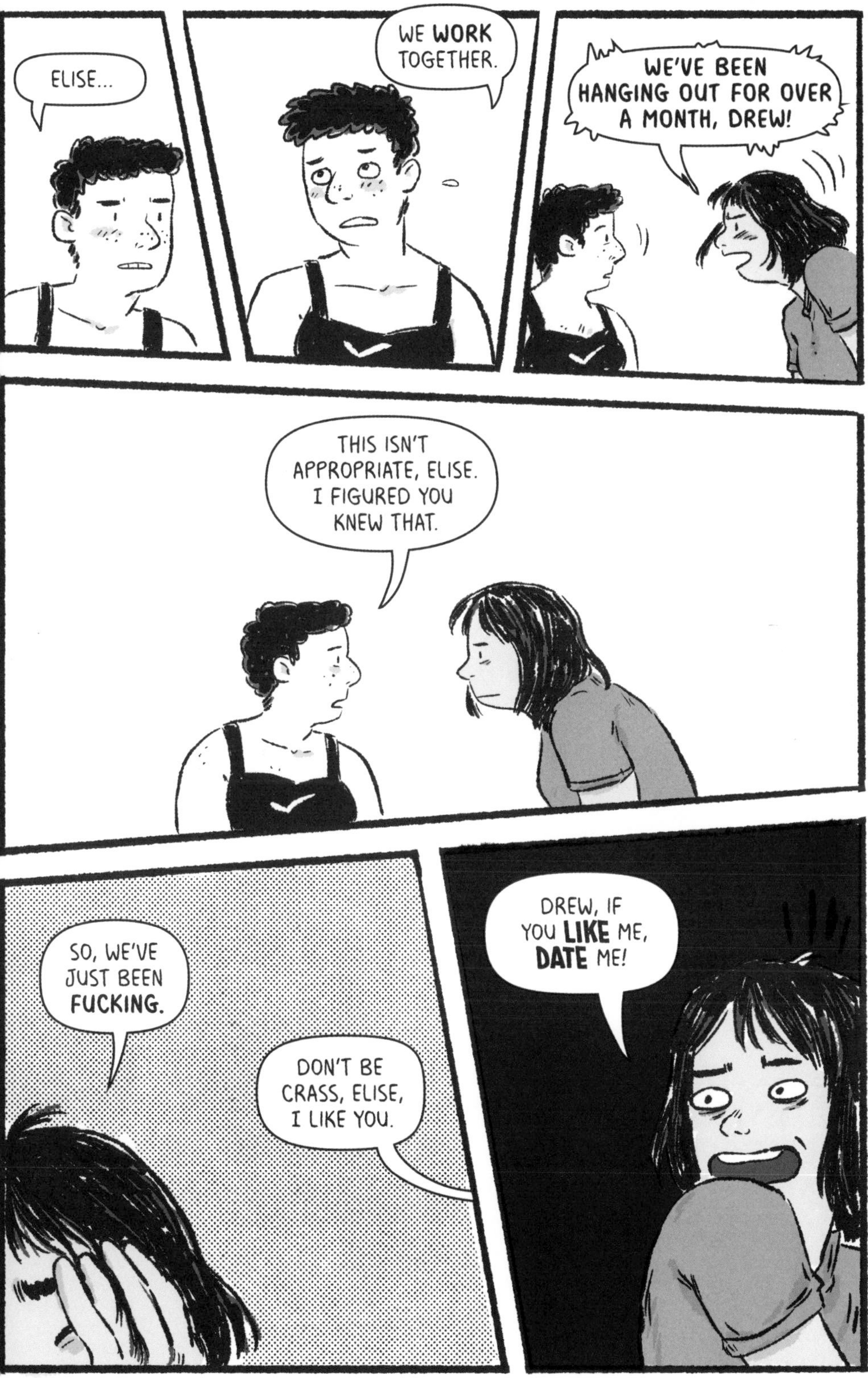
ELISE...
WE **WORK** TOGETHER.
WE'VE BEEN HANGING OUT FOR OVER A MONTH, DREW!
THIS ISN'T APPROPRIATE, ELISE. I FIGURED YOU KNEW THAT.
SO, WE'VE JUST BEEN **FUCKING.**
DON'T BE CRASS, ELISE, I LIKE YOU.
DREW, IF YOU **LIKE** ME, **DATE** ME!

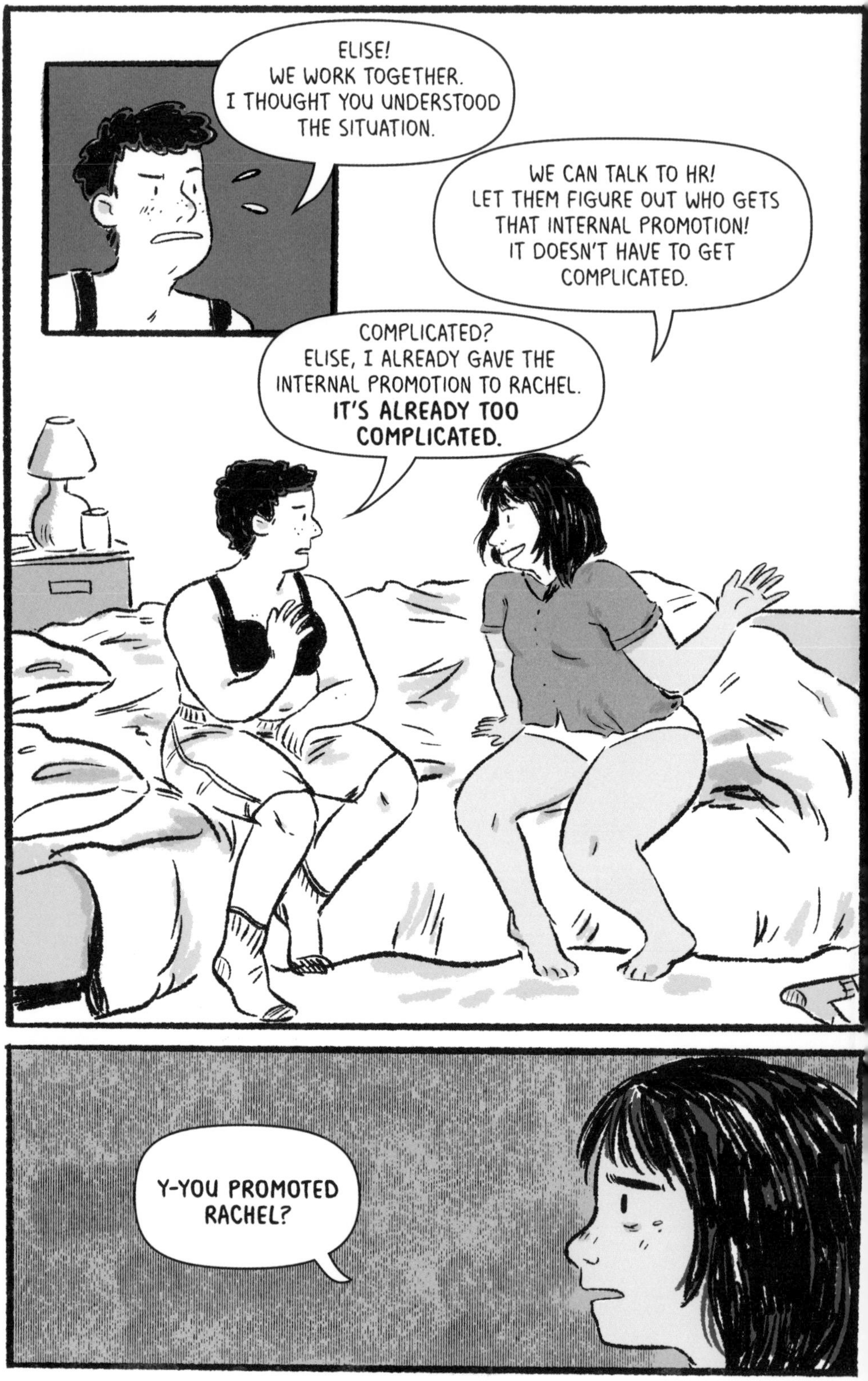
ELISE!
WE WORK TOGETHER.
I THOUGHT YOU UNDERSTOOD
THE SITUATION.
WE CAN TALK TO HR!
LET THEM FIGURE OUT WHO GETS
THAT INTERNAL PROMOTION!
IT DOESN'T HAVE TO GET
COMPLICATED.
COMPLICATED?
ELISE, I ALREADY GAVE THE
INTERNAL PROMOTION TO RACHEL.
IT'S ALREADY TOO
COMPLICATED.
Y-YOU PROMOTED
RACHEL?

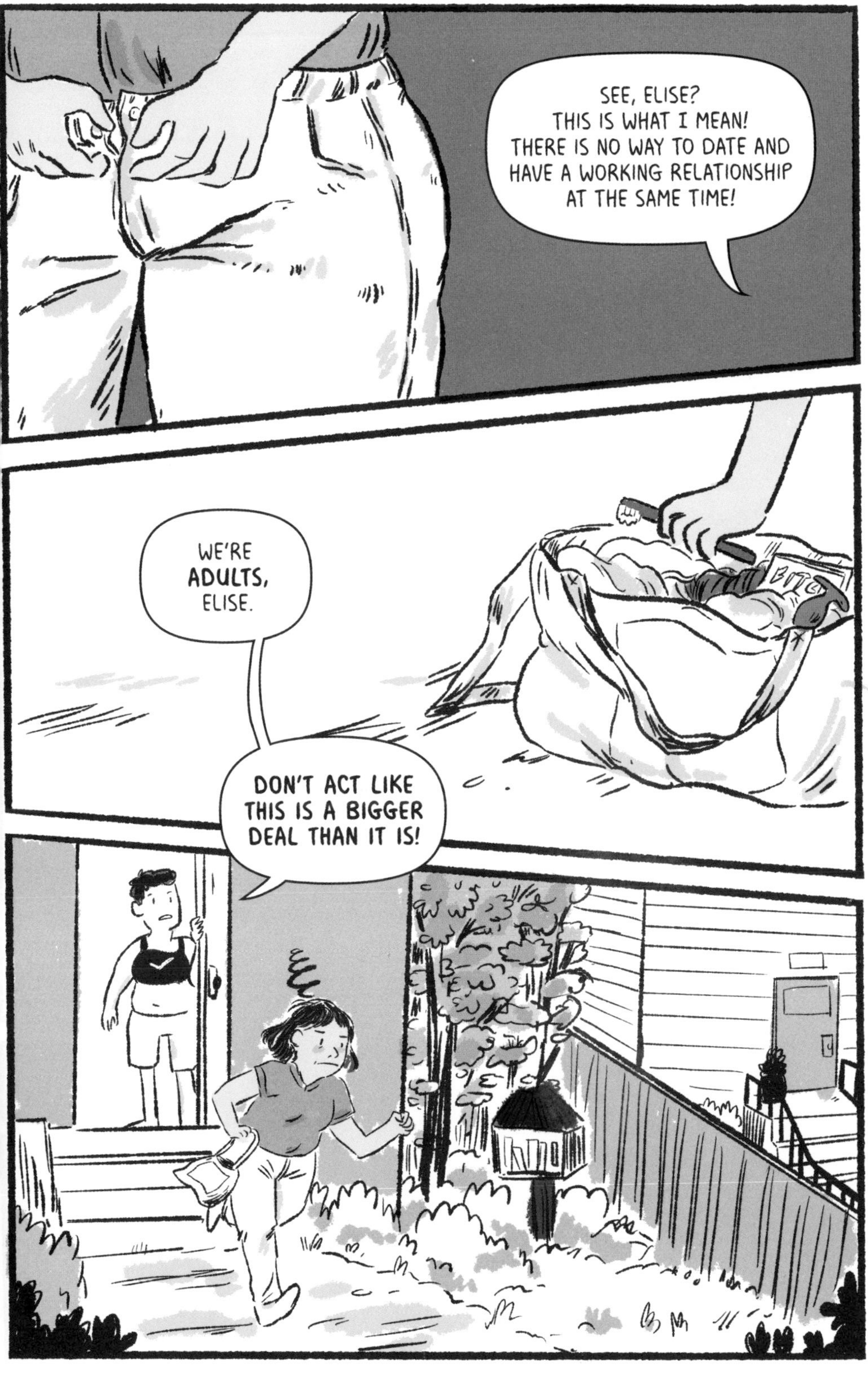
SEE, ELISE? THIS IS WHAT I MEAN! THERE IS NO WAY TO DATE AND HAVE A WORKING RELATIONSHIP AT THE SAME TIME!
WE'RE ADULTS, ELISE.
DON'T ACT LIKE THIS IS A BIGGER DEAL THAN IT IS!

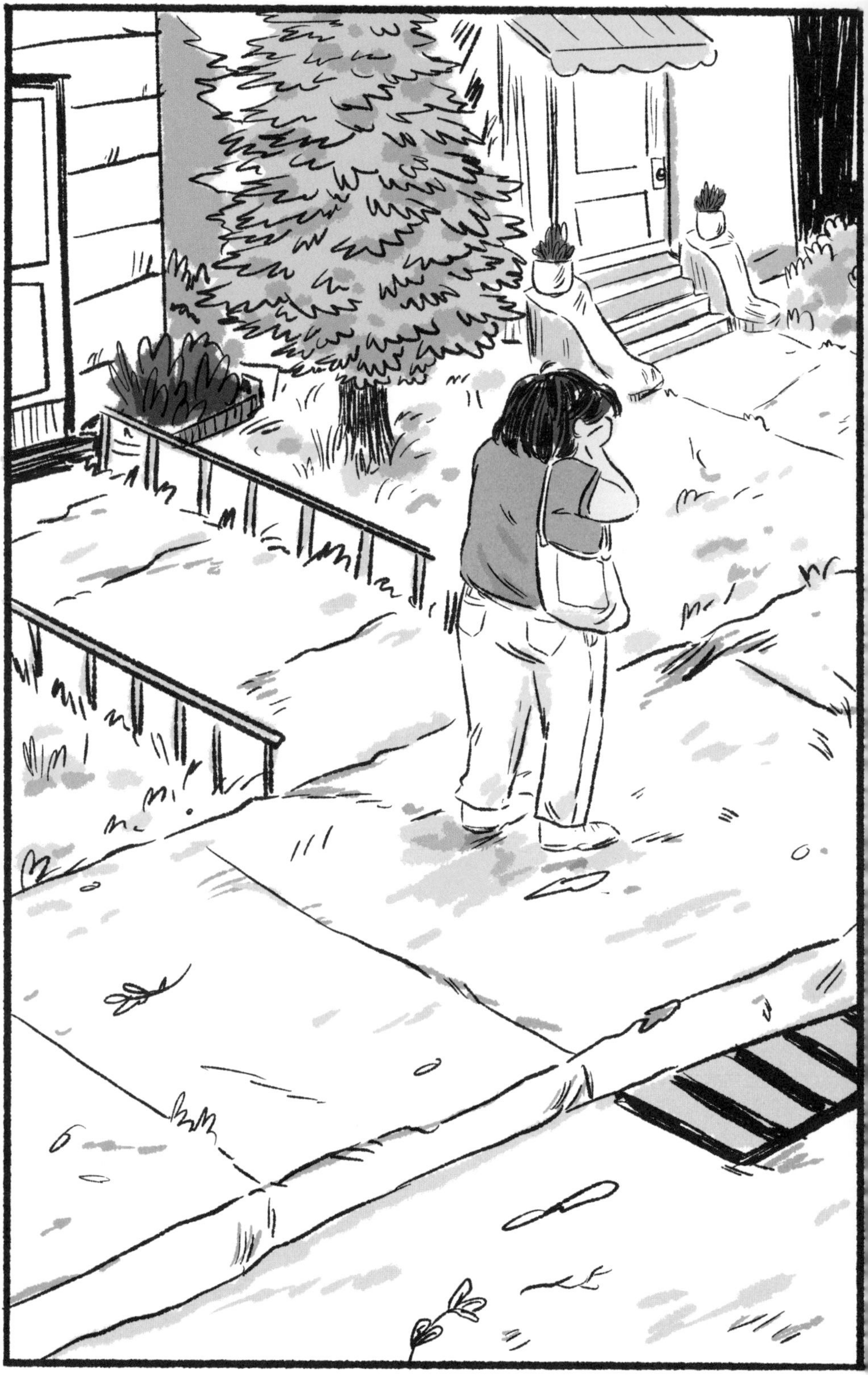

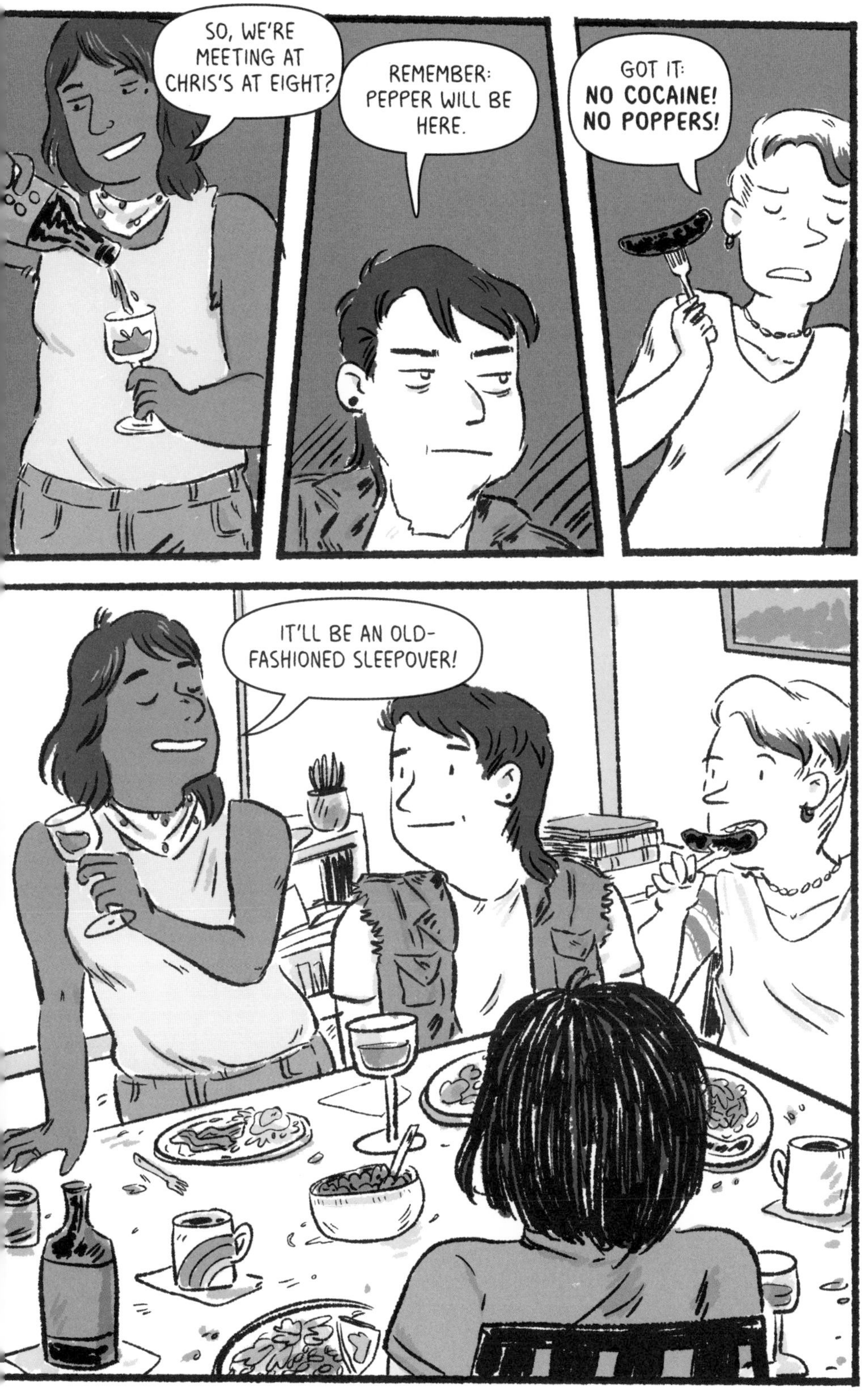
SO, WE'RE MEETING AT CHRIS'S AT EIGHT?
REMEMBER: PEPPER WILL BE HERE.
GOT IT: **NO COCAINE! NO POPPERS!**
IT'LL BE AN OLD-FASHIONED SLEEPOVER!

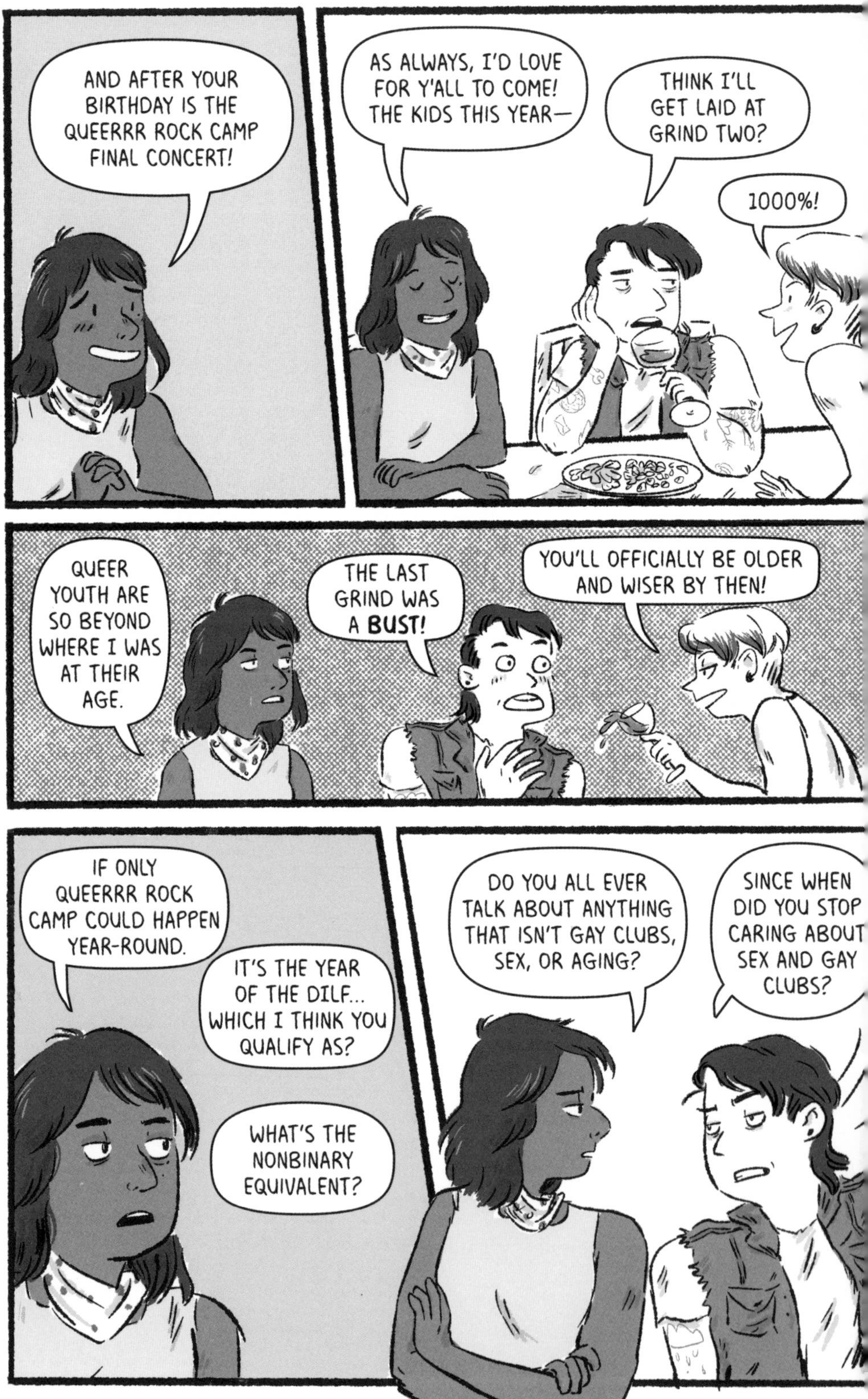
AND AFTER YOUR BIRTHDAY IS THE QUEERRR ROCK CAMP FINAL CONCERT!
AS ALWAYS, I'D LOVE FOR Y'ALL TO COME! THE KIDS THIS YEAR—
THINK I'LL GET LAID AT GRIND TWO?
1000%!
QUEER YOUTH ARE SO BEYOND WHERE I WAS AT THEIR AGE.
THE LAST GRIND WAS A **BUST!**
YOU'LL OFFICIALLY BE OLDER AND WISER BY THEN!
IF ONLY QUEERRR ROCK CAMP COULD HAPPEN YEAR-ROUND.
IT'S THE YEAR OF THE DILF... WHICH I THINK YOU QUALIFY AS?
WHAT'S THE NONBINARY EQUIVALENT?
DO YOU ALL EVER TALK ABOUT ANYTHING THAT ISN'T GAY CLUBS, SEX, OR AGING?
SINCE WHEN DID YOU STOP CARING ABOUT SEX AND GAY CLUBS?

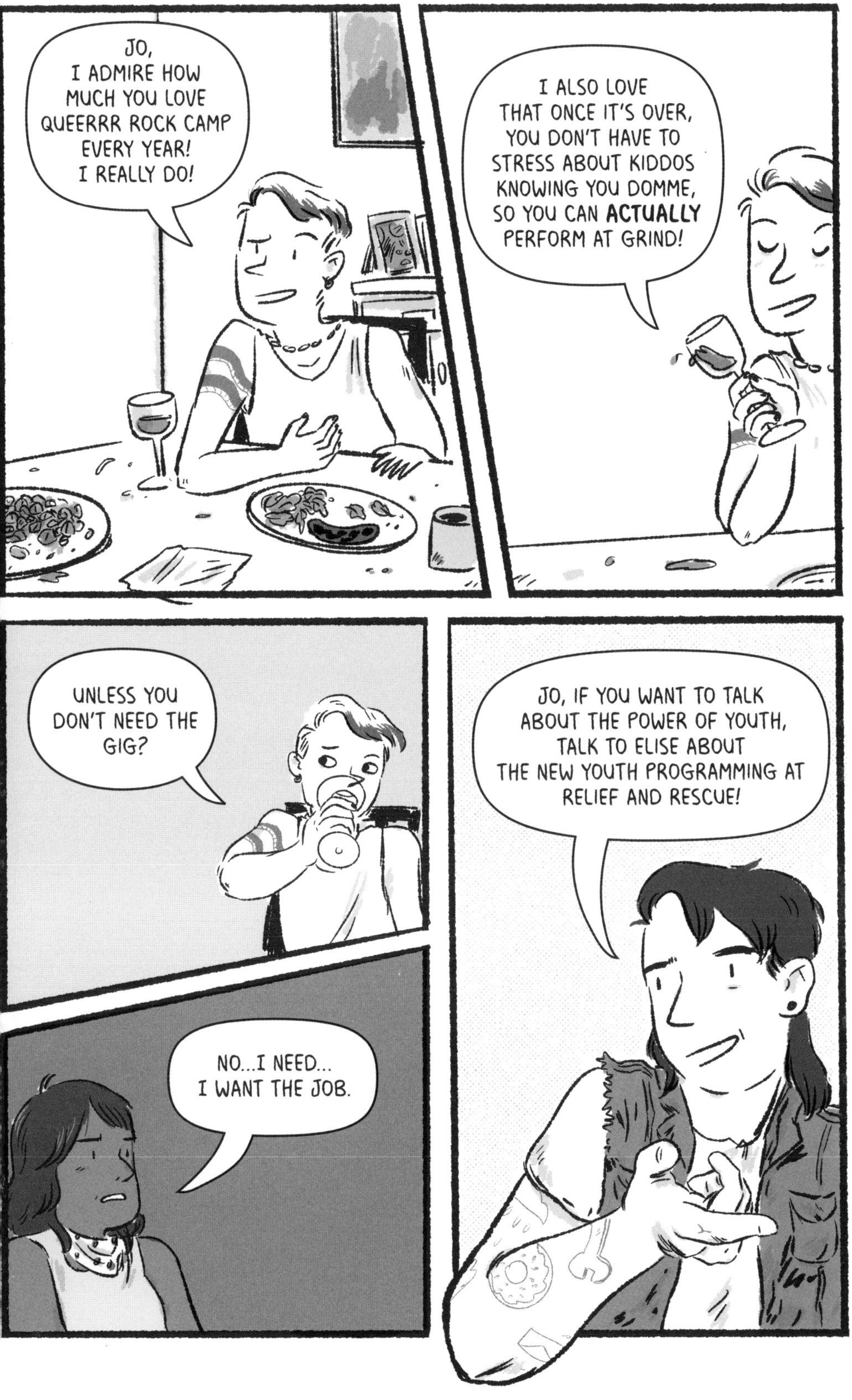
JO, I ADMIRE HOW MUCH YOU LOVE QUEERRR ROCK CAMP EVERY YEAR! I REALLY DO!
I ALSO LOVE THAT ONCE IT'S OVER, YOU DON'T HAVE TO STRESS ABOUT KIDDOS KNOWING YOU DOMME, SO YOU CAN **ACTUALLY** PERFORM AT GRIND!
UNLESS YOU DON'T NEED THE GIG?
NO...I NEED... I WANT THE JOB.
JO, IF YOU WANT TO TALK ABOUT THE POWER OF YOUTH, TALK TO ELISE ABOUT THE NEW YOUTH PROGRAMMING AT RELIEF AND RESCUE!

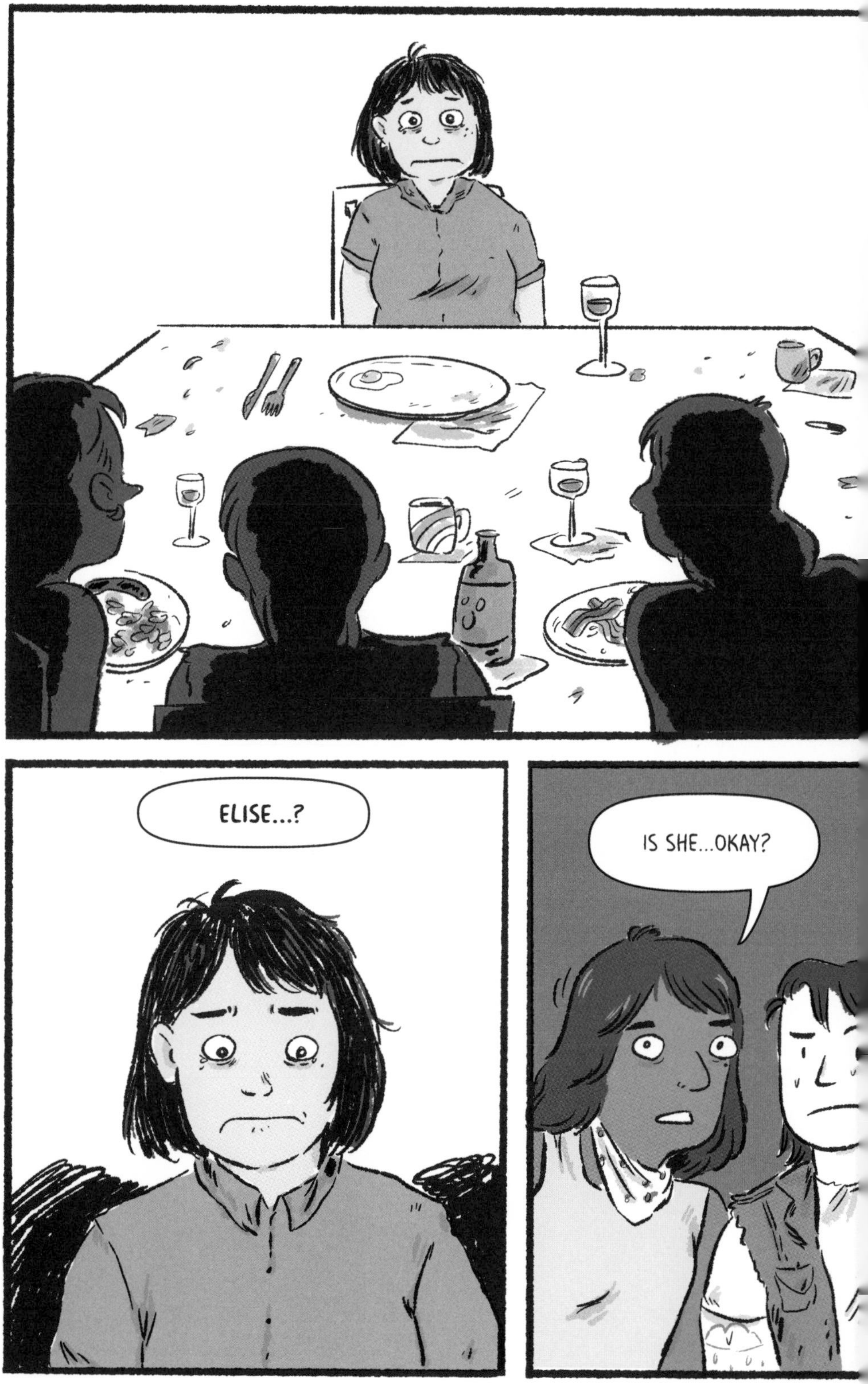
ELISE...?
IS SHE...OKAY?

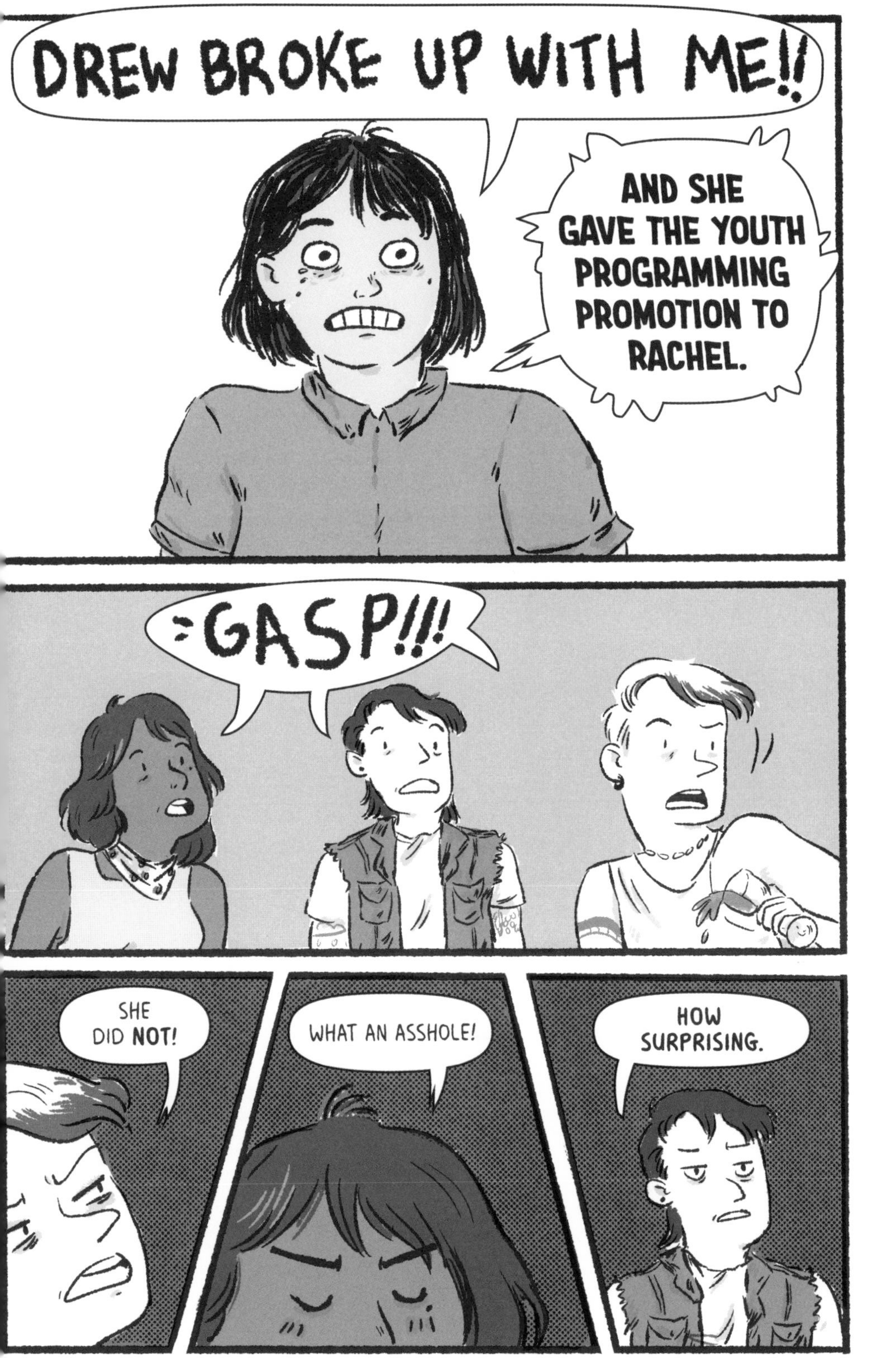
DREW BROKE UP WITH ME!!
AND SHE GAVE THE YOUTH PROGRAMMING PROMOTION TO RACHEL.
GASP!!!
SHE DID NOT!
WHAT AN ASSHOLE!
HOW SURPRISING.

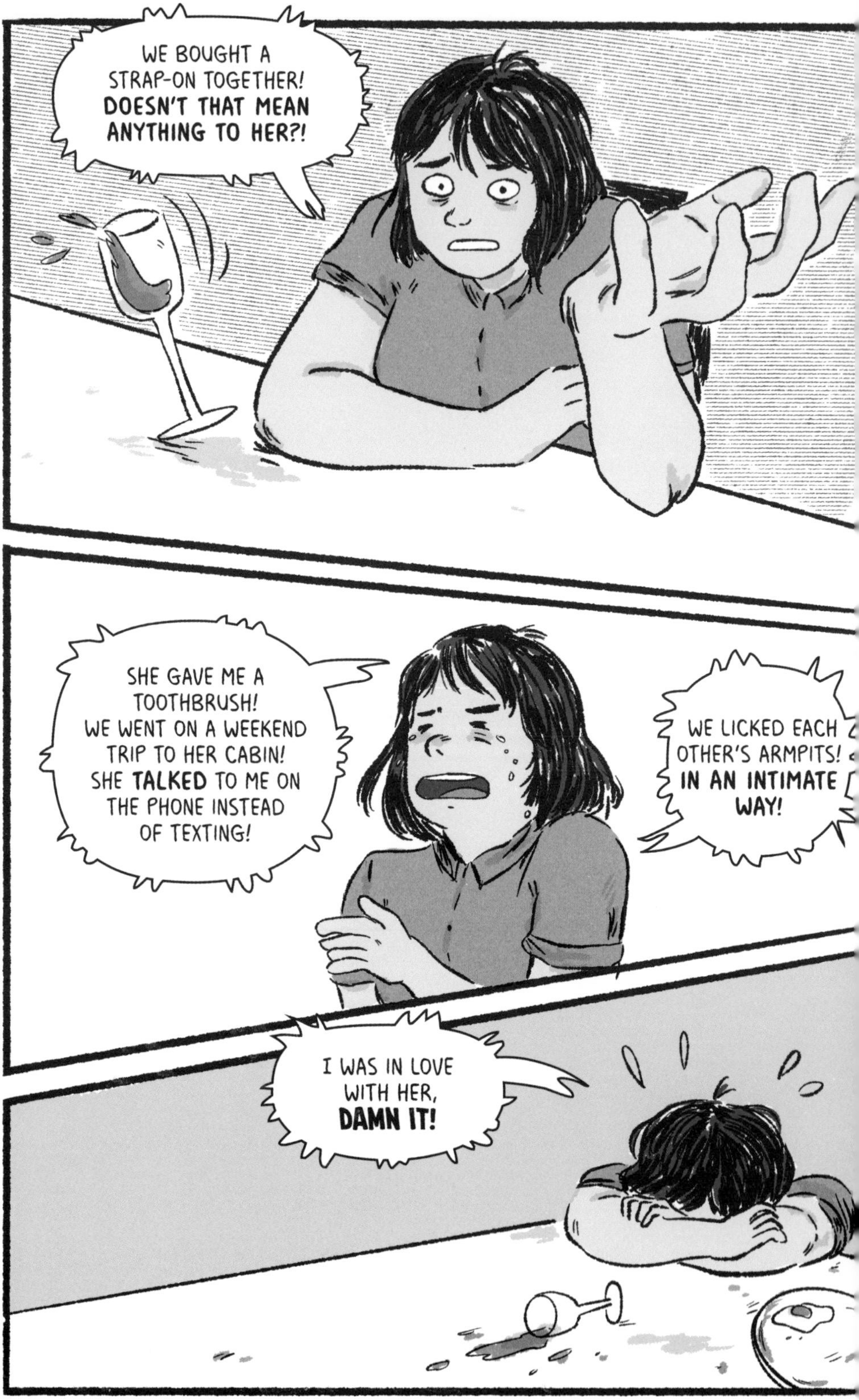
WE BOUGHT A STRAP-ON TOGETHER! **DOESN'T THAT MEAN ANYTHING TO HER?!**
SHE GAVE ME A TOOTHBRUSH! WE WENT ON A WEEKEND TRIP TO HER CABIN! SHE **TALKED** TO ME ON THE PHONE INSTEAD OF TEXTING!
WE LICKED EACH OTHER'S ARMPITS! **IN AN INTIMATE WAY!**
I WAS IN LOVE WITH HER, **DAMN IT!**

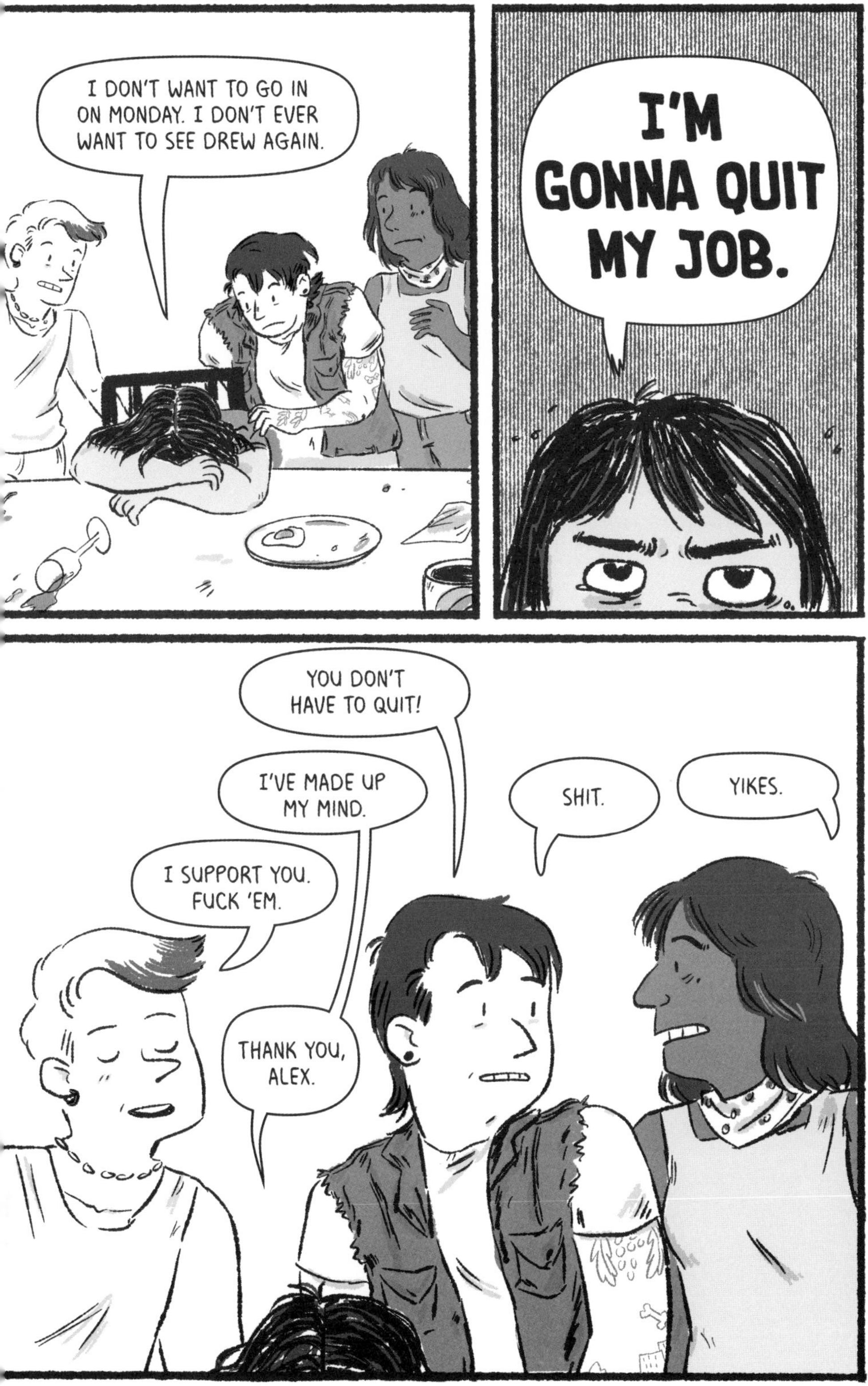
I DON'T WANT TO GO IN ON MONDAY. I DON'T EVER WANT TO SEE DREW AGAIN.
I'M GONNA QUIT MY JOB.
YOU DON'T HAVE TO QUIT!
I'VE MADE UP MY MIND.
I SUPPORT YOU. FUCK 'EM.
THANK YOU, ALEX.
SHIT.
YIKES.

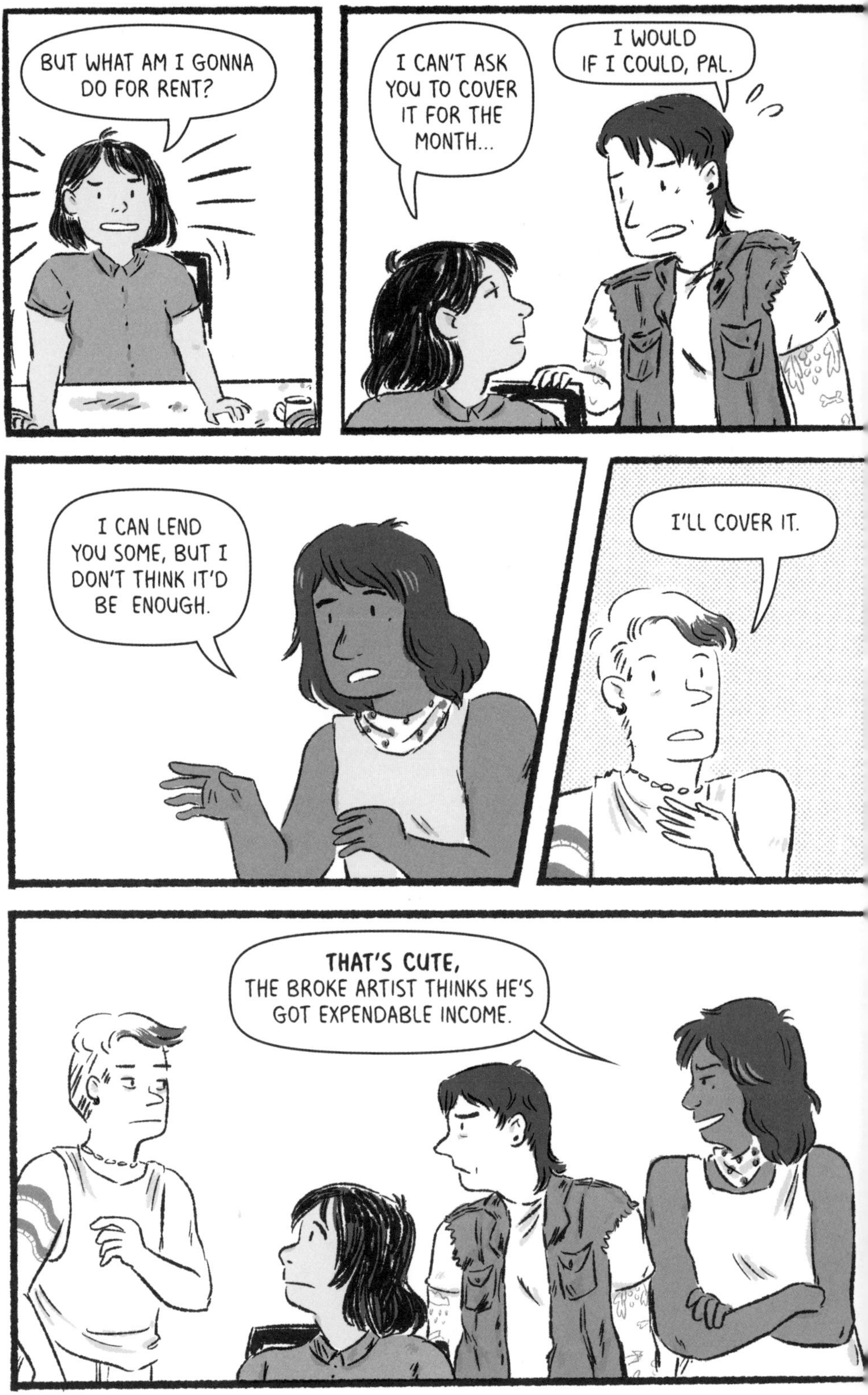
BUT WHAT AM I GONNA DO FOR RENT?
I CAN'T ASK YOU TO COVER IT FOR THE MONTH...
I WOULD IF I COULD, PAL.
I CAN LEND YOU SOME, BUT I DON'T THINK IT'D BE ENOUGH.
I'LL COVER IT.
THAT'S CUTE, THE BROKE ARTIST THINKS HE'S GOT EXPENDABLE INCOME.

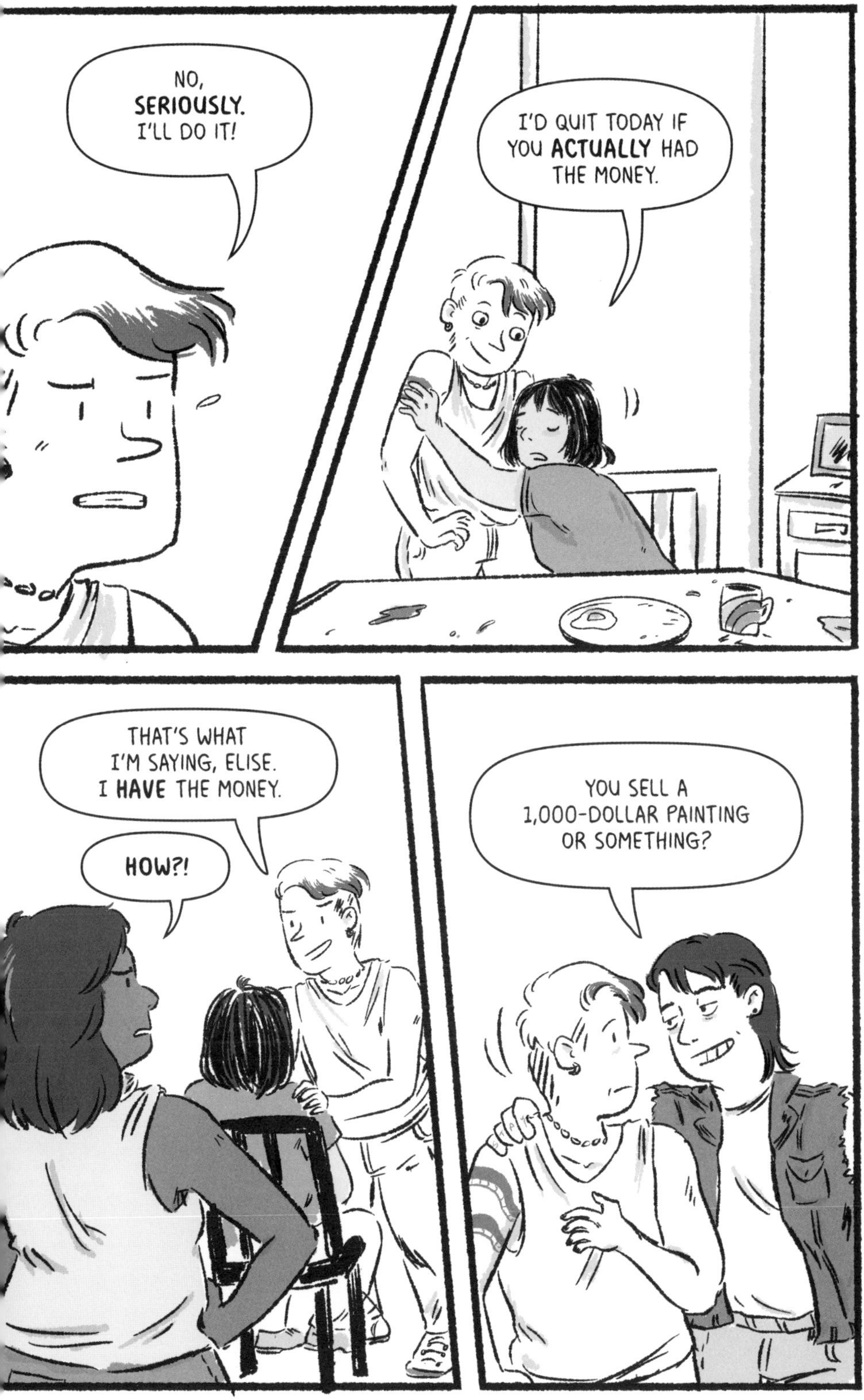
NO, SERIOUSLY. I'LL DO IT!
I'D QUIT TODAY IF YOU ACTUALLY HAD THE MONEY.
THAT'S WHAT I'M SAYING, ELISE. I HAVE THE MONEY.
HOW?!
YOU SELL A 1,000-DOLLAR PAINTING OR SOMETHING?

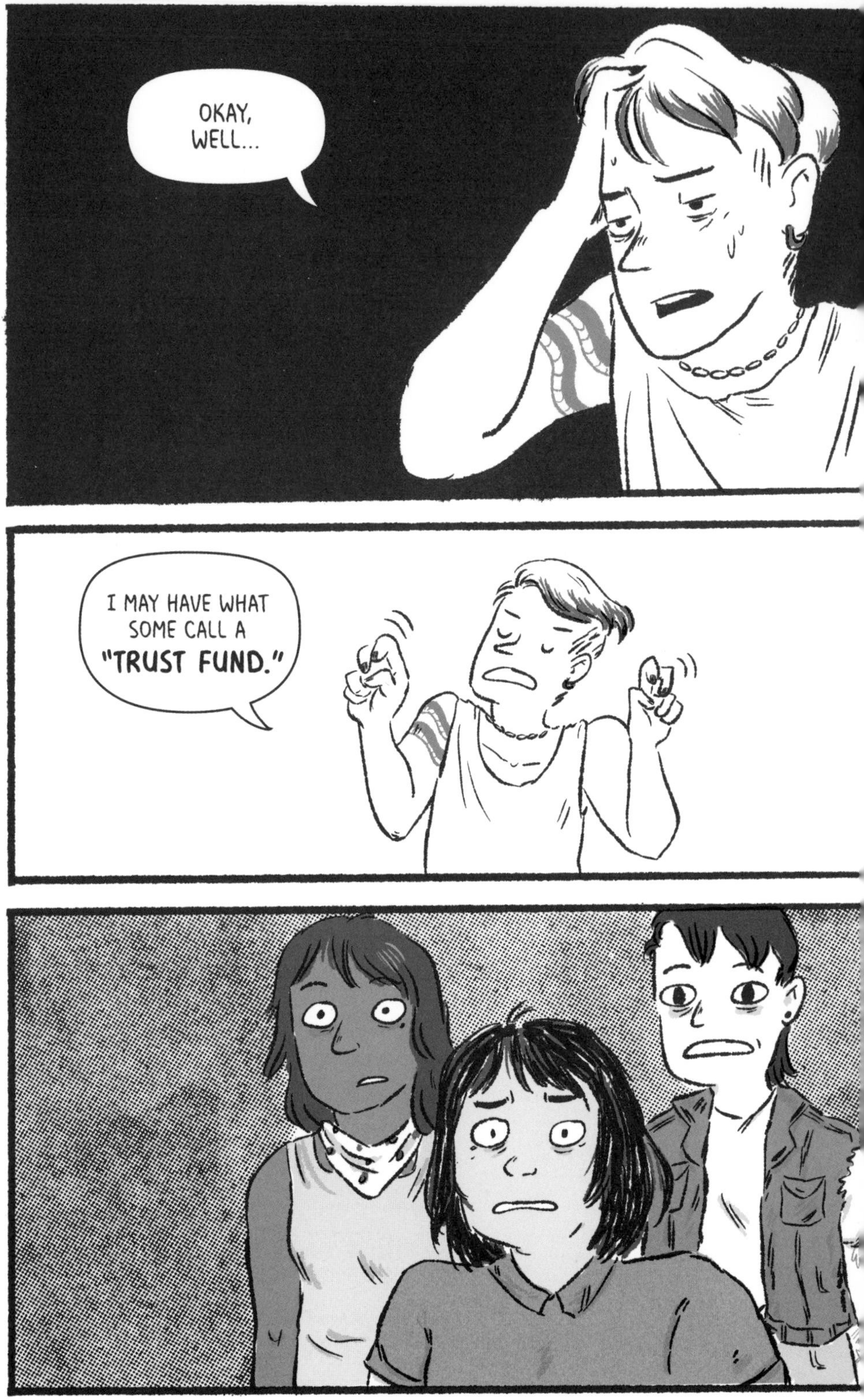
OKAY,
WELL...
I MAY HAVE WHAT SOME CALL A "TRUST FUND."

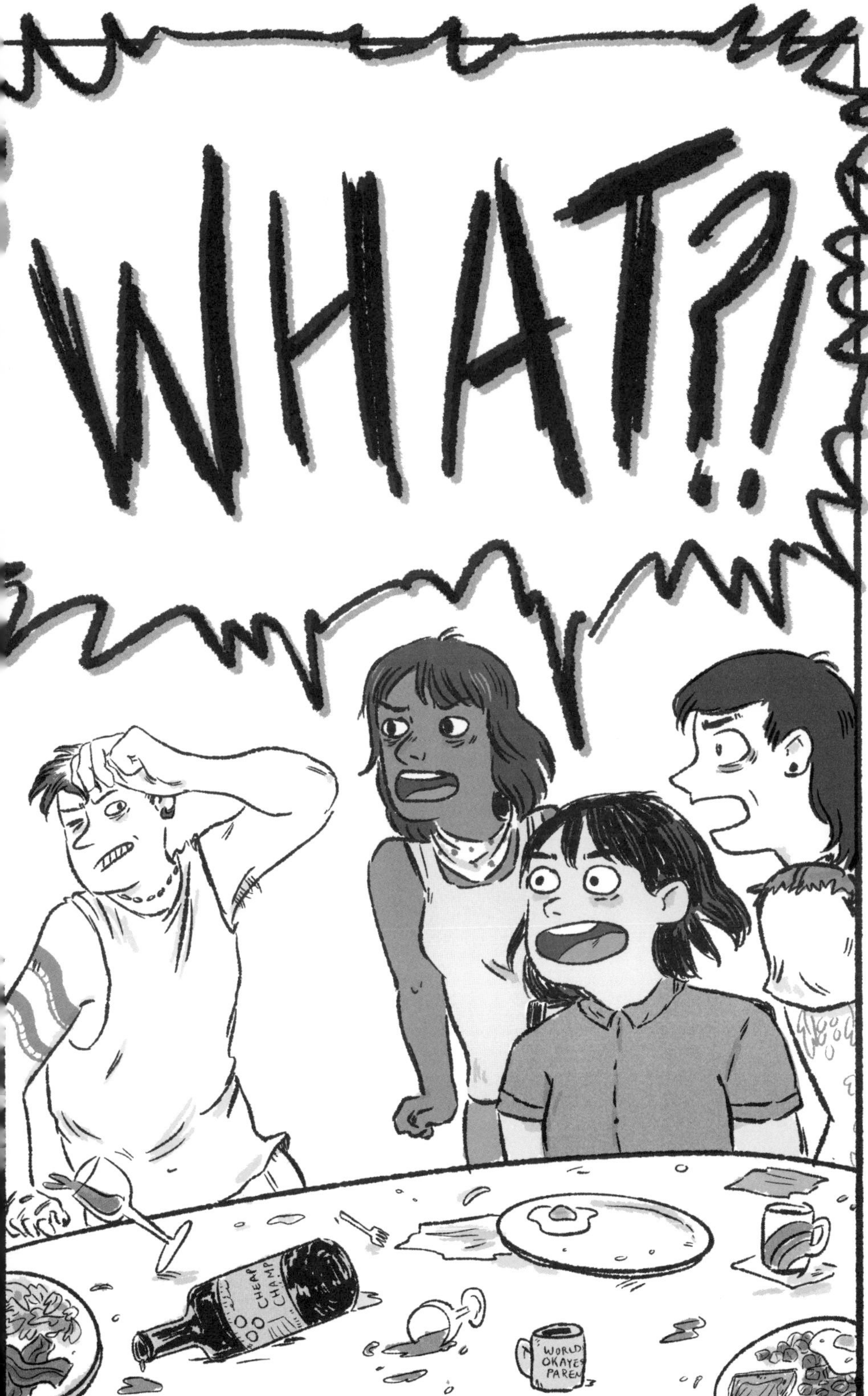
WHAT?!
CHEAP CHAMP
WORLD OKAYEST PARENT

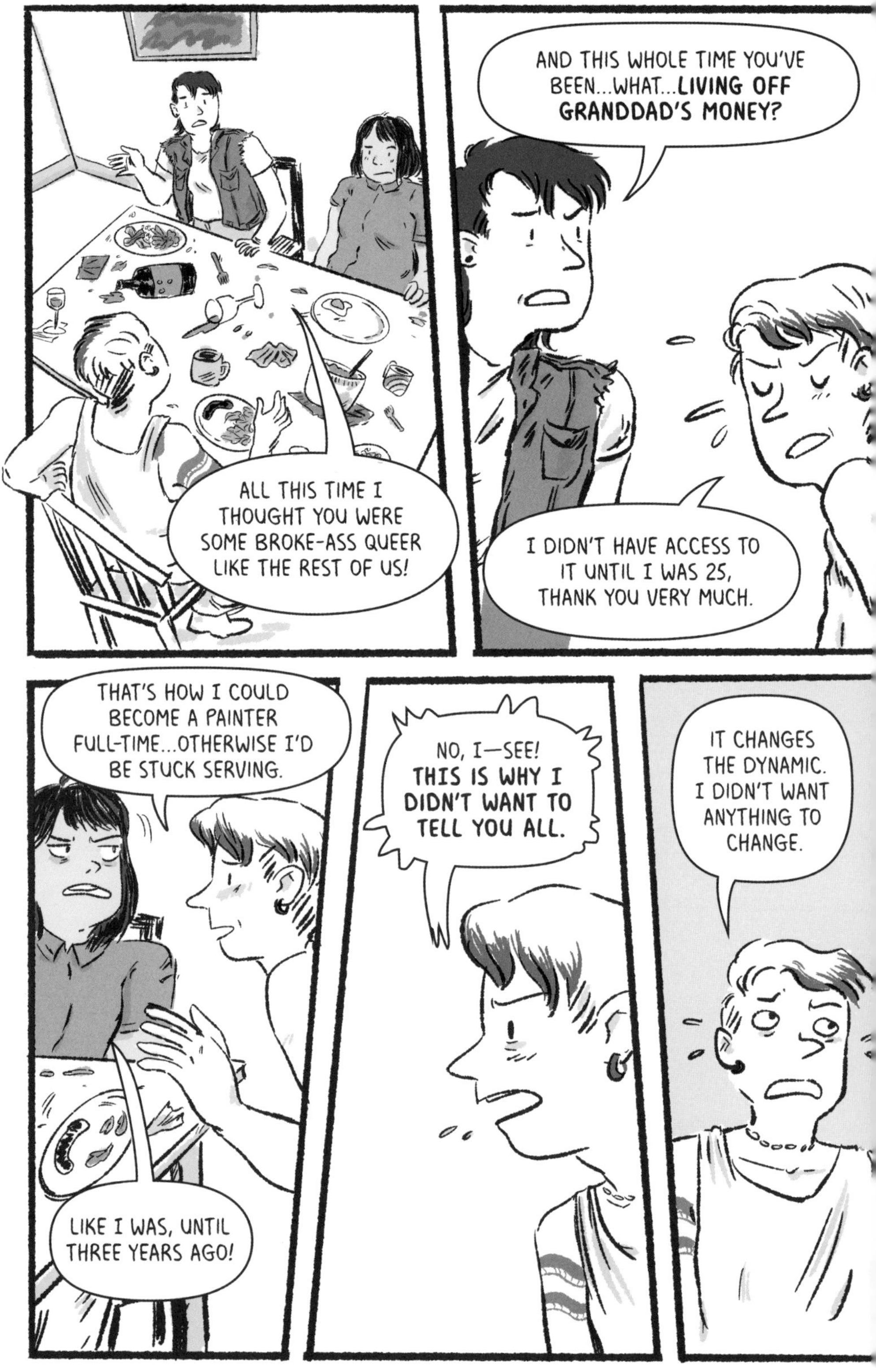
ALL THIS TIME I THOUGHT YOU WERE SOME BROKE-ASS QUEER LIKE THE REST OF US!
AND THIS WHOLE TIME YOU'VE BEEN...WHAT...**LIVING OFF GRANDDAD'S MONEY?**
I DIDN'T HAVE ACCESS TO IT UNTIL I WAS 25, THANK YOU VERY MUCH.
THAT'S HOW I COULD BECOME A PAINTER FULL-TIME...OTHERWISE I'D BE STUCK SERVING.
LIKE I WAS, UNTIL THREE YEARS AGO!
NO, I—SEE! **THIS IS WHY I DIDN'T WANT TO TELL YOU ALL.**
IT CHANGES THE DYNAMIC. I DIDN'T WANT ANYTHING TO CHANGE.

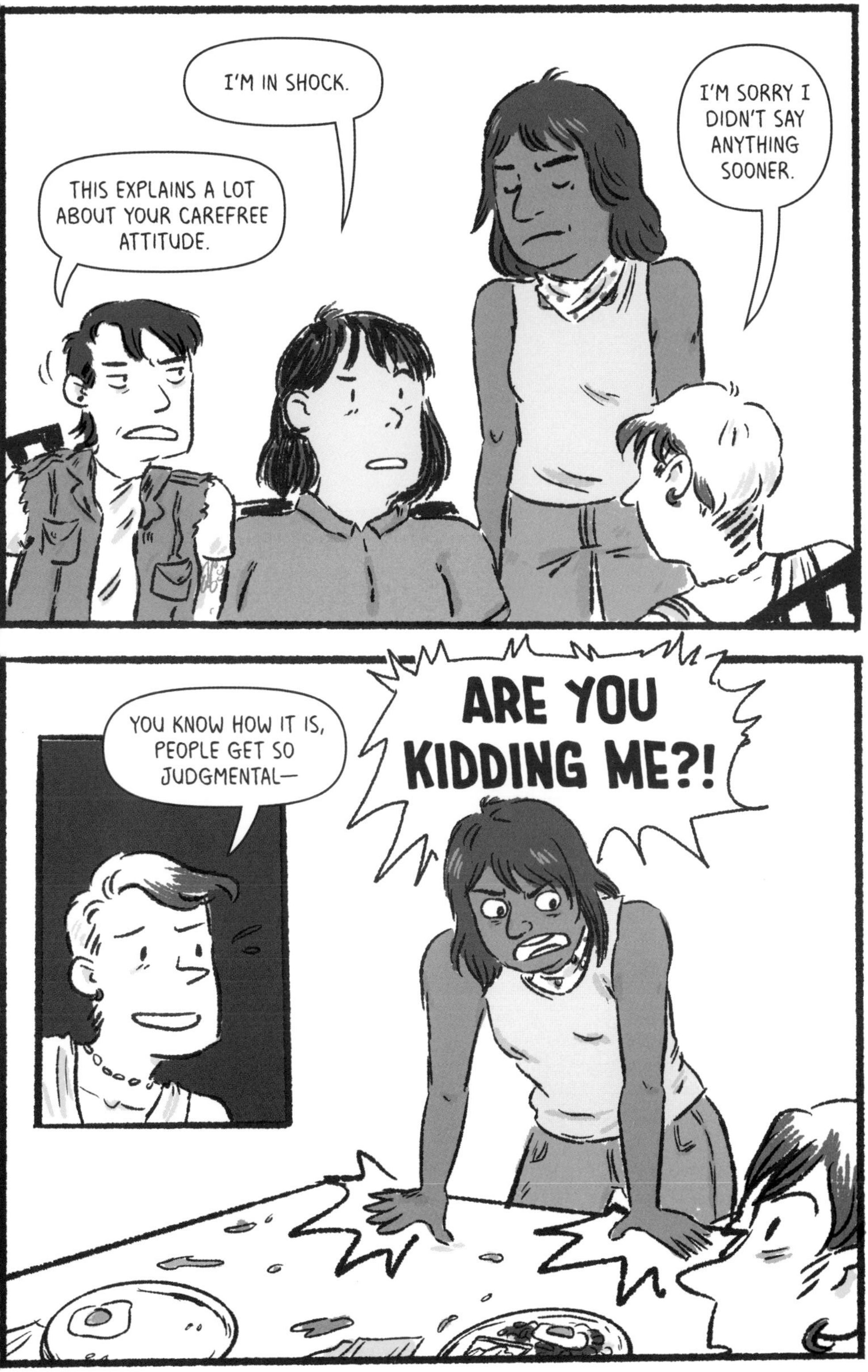
THIS EXPLAINS A LOT ABOUT YOUR CAREFREE ATTITUDE.
I'M IN SHOCK.
I'M SORRY I DIDN'T SAY ANYTHING SOONER.
YOU KNOW HOW IT IS, PEOPLE GET SO JUDGMENTAL—
ARE YOU KIDDING ME?!

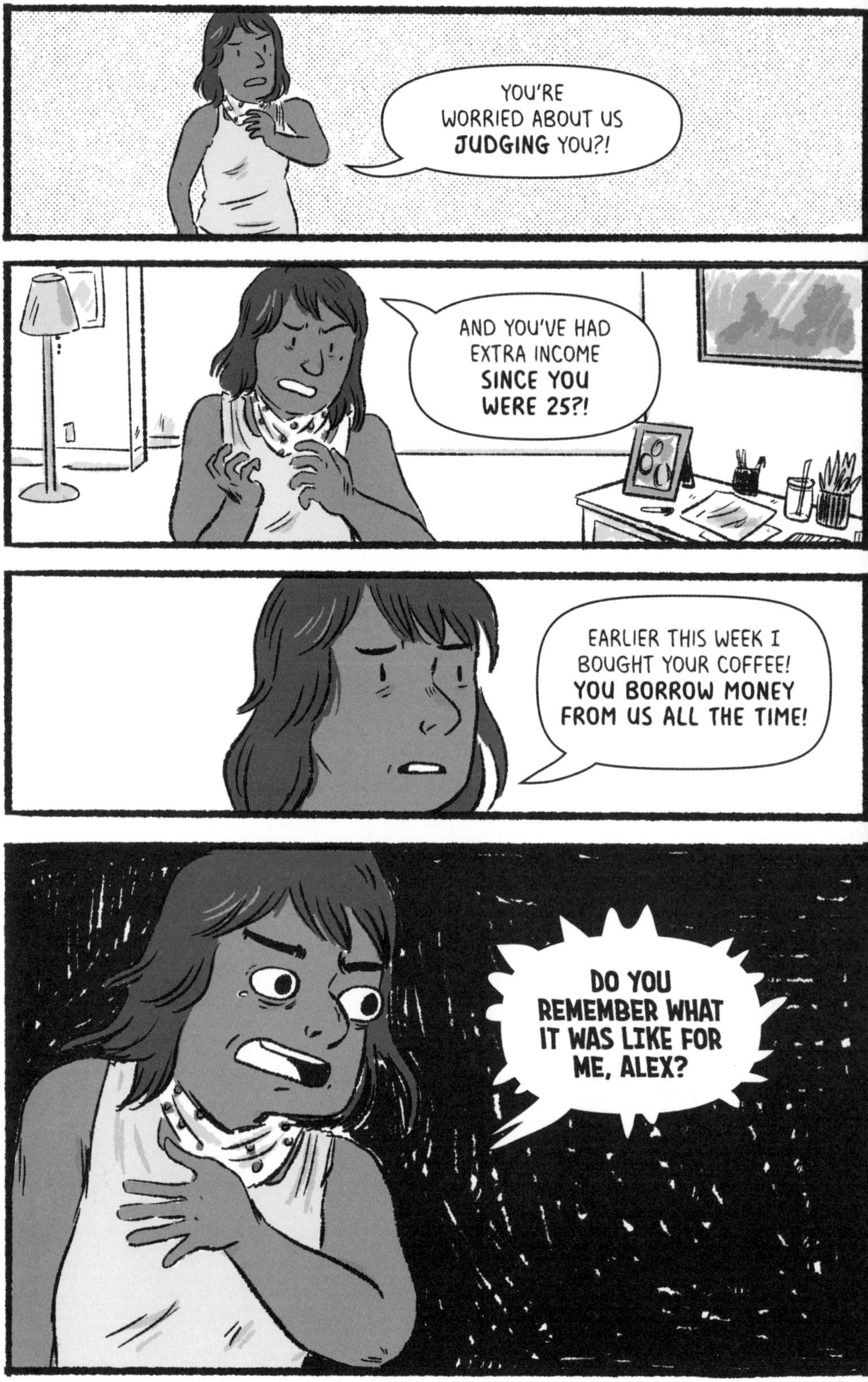
YOU'RE WORRIED ABOUT US **JUDGING** YOU?!
AND YOU'VE HAD EXTRA INCOME **SINCE YOU WERE 25?!**
EARLIER THIS WEEK I BOUGHT YOUR COFFEE! **YOU BORROW MONEY FROM US ALL THE TIME!**
DO YOU REMEMBER WHAT IT WAS LIKE FOR ME, ALEX?

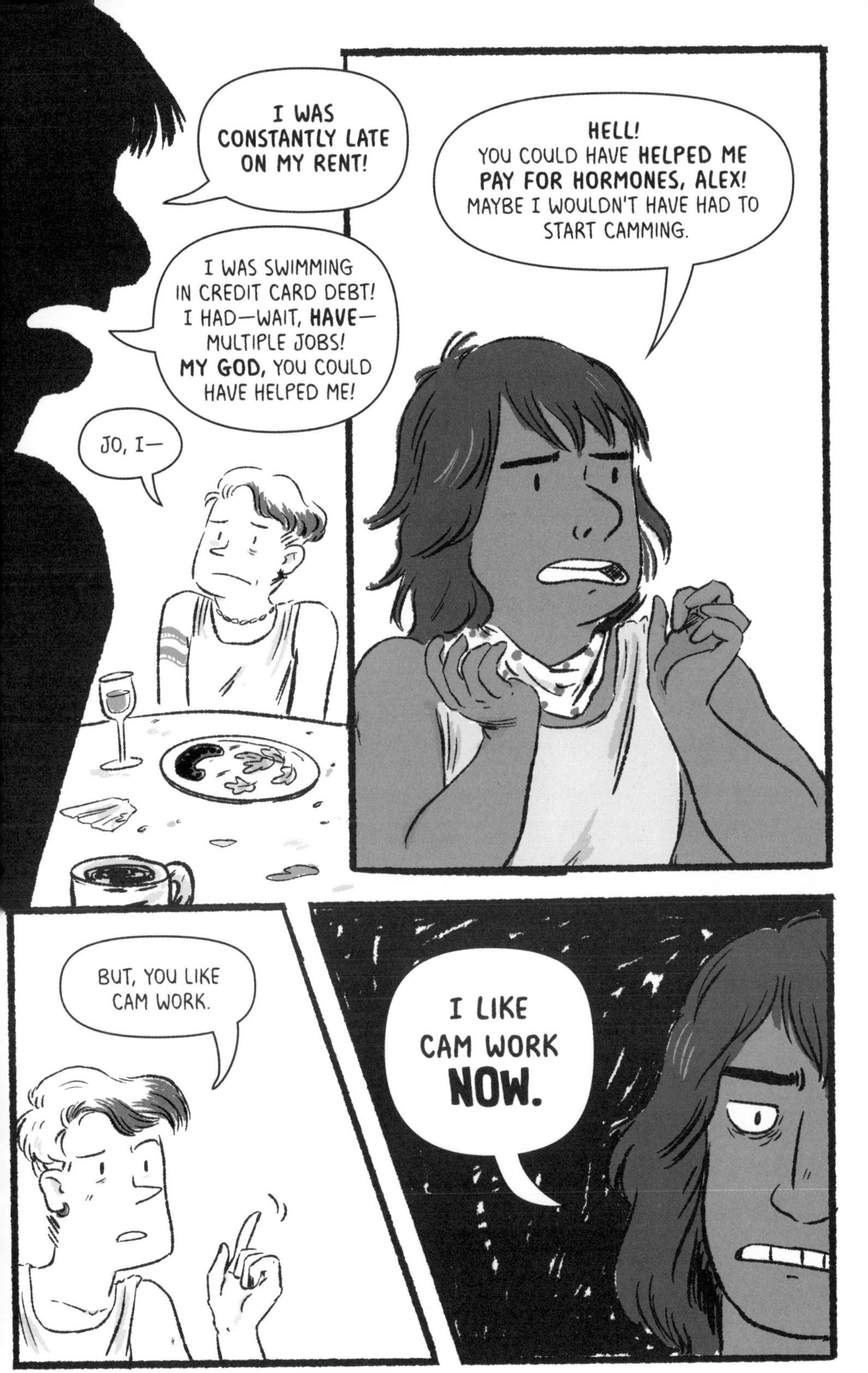

I WAS CONSTANTLY LATE ON MY RENT!
I WAS SWIMMING IN CREDIT CARD DEBT! I HAD—WAIT, HAVE—MULTIPLE JOBS! MY GOD, YOU COULD HAVE HELPED ME!
JO, I—
HELL! YOU COULD HAVE HELPED ME PAY FOR HORMONES, ALEX! MAYBE I WOULDN'T HAVE HAD TO START CAMMING.
BUT, YOU LIKE CAM WORK.
I LIKE CAM WORK NOW.

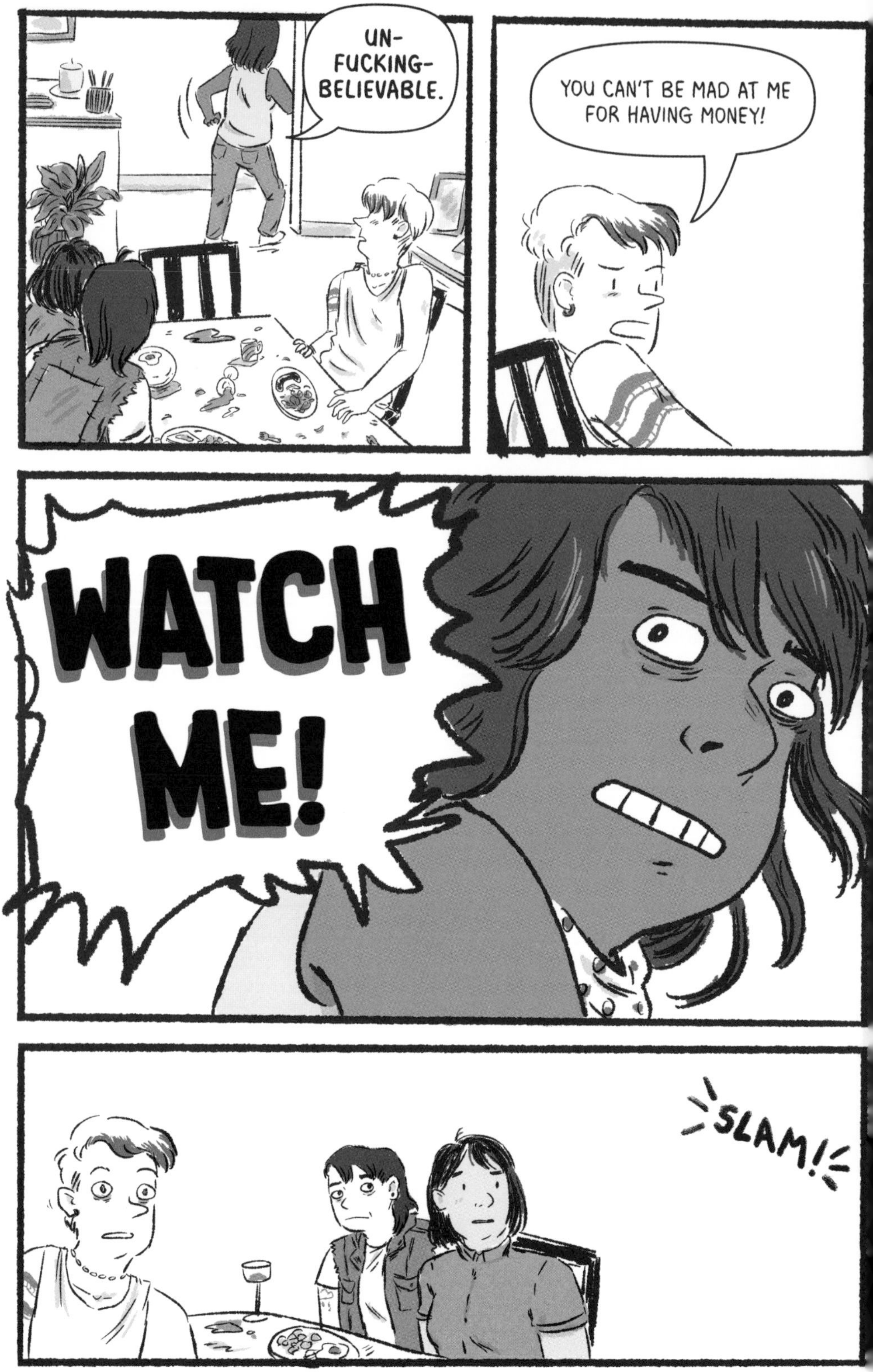
UN-FUCKING-BELIEVABLE.
YOU CAN'T BE MAD AT ME FOR HAVING MONEY!
WATCH ME!
SLAM!

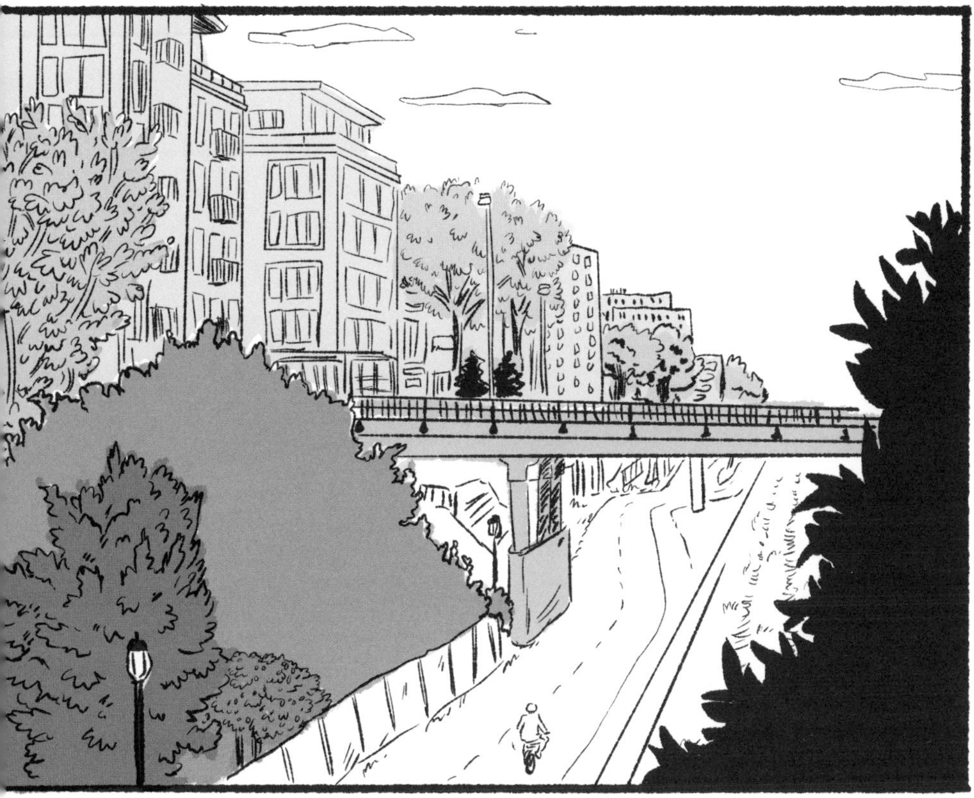

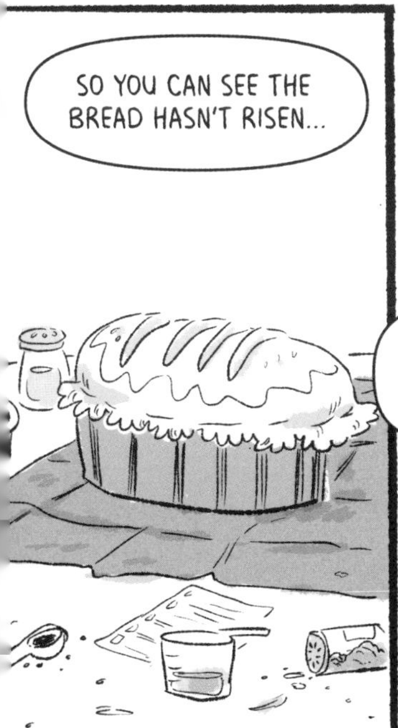
SO YOU CAN SEE THE BREAD HASN'T RISEN...

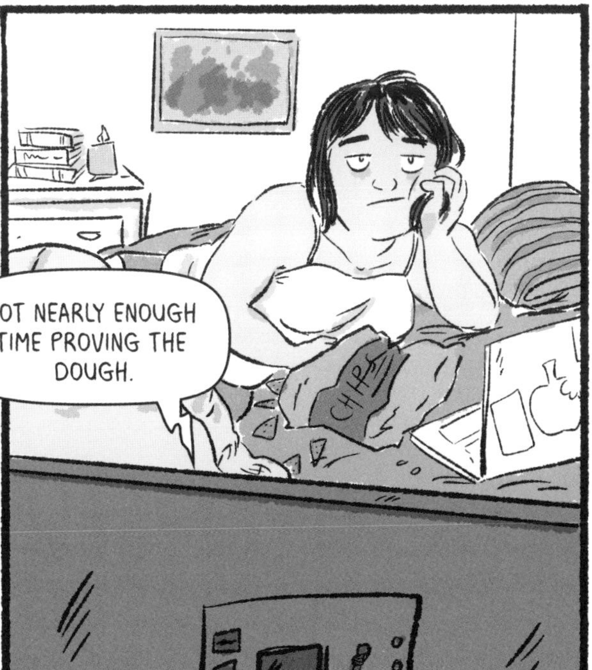
NOT NEARLY ENOUGH TIME PROVING THE DOUGH.
CHIPS

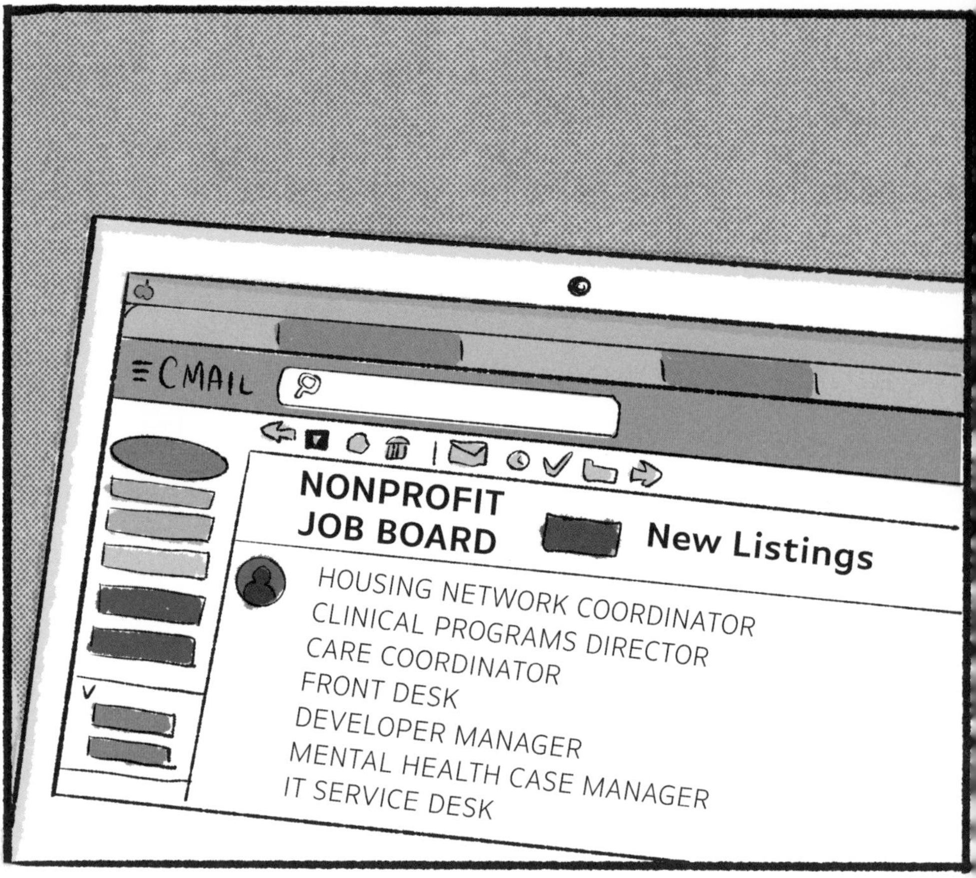
CMAIL
NONPROFIT
JOB BOARD
New Listings
HOUSING NETWORK COORDINATOR
CLINICAL PROGRAMS DIRECTOR
CARE COORDINATOR
FRONT DESK
DEVELOPER MANAGER
MENTAL HEALTH CASE MANAGER
IT SERVICE DESK

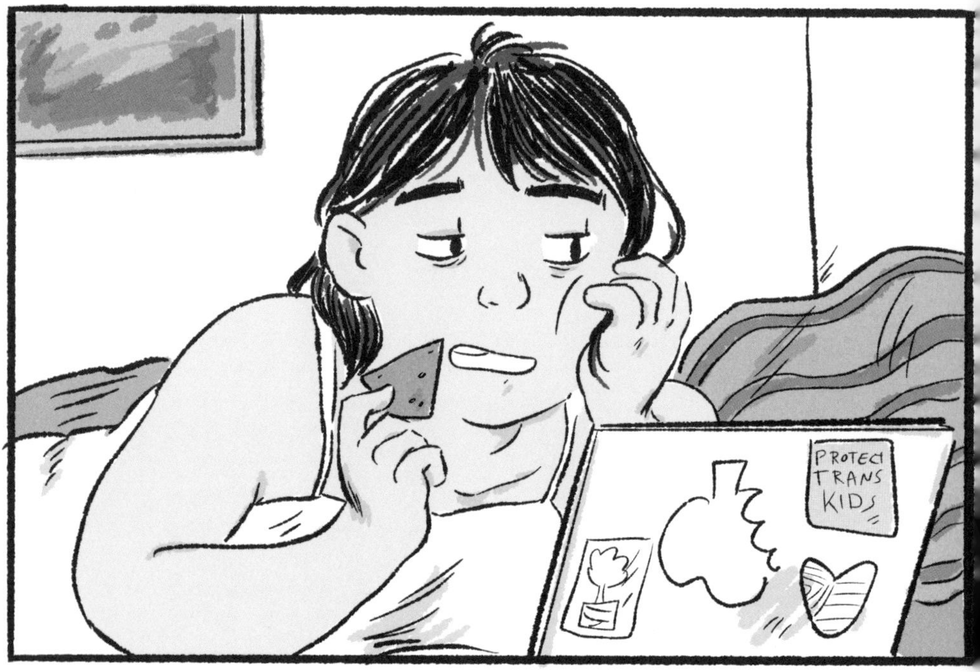
PROTECT
TRANS
KIDS

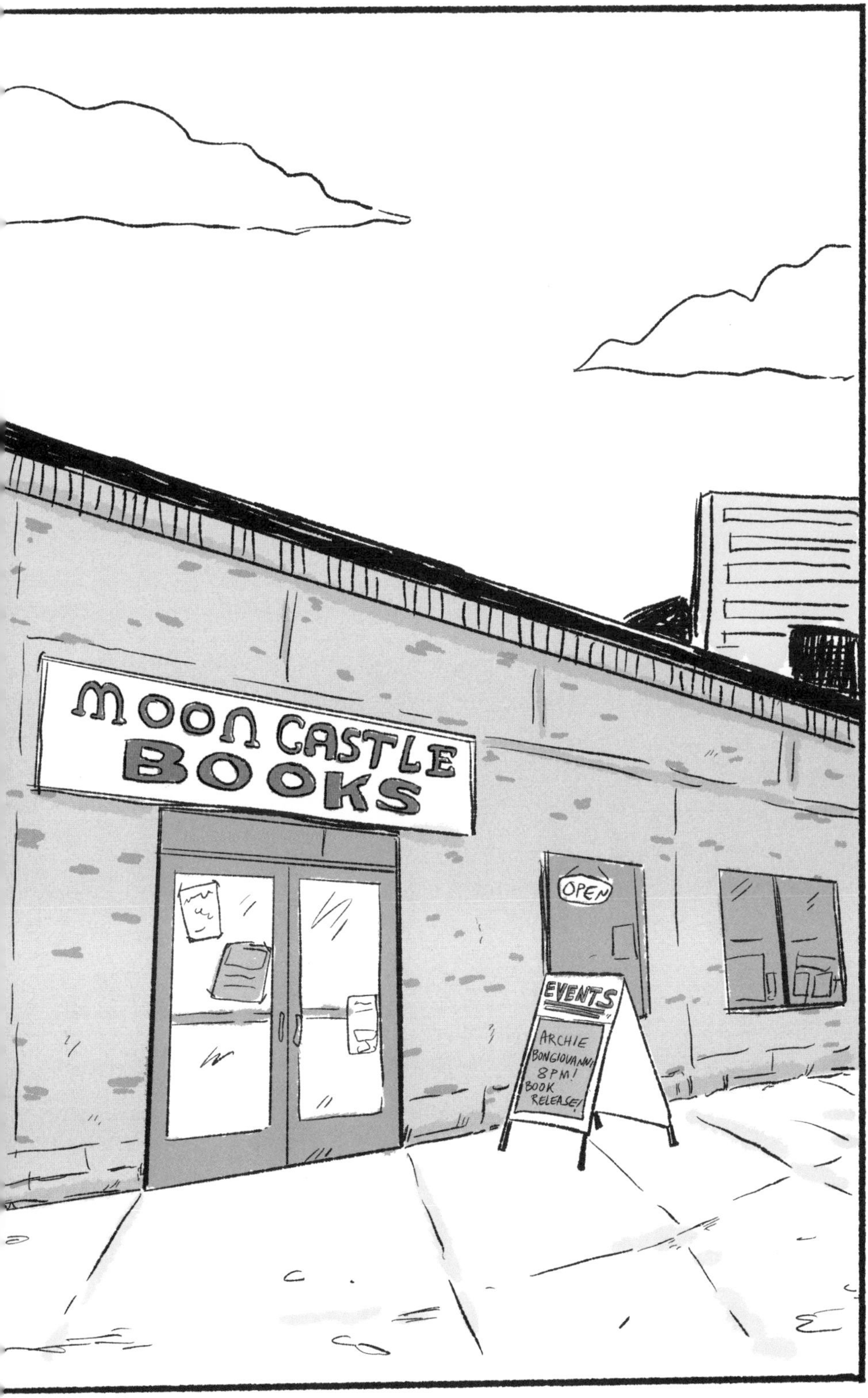
MOON CASTLE BOOKS
OPEN
EVENTS
ARCHIE BONGIOVANNI 8PM! BOOK RELEASE!

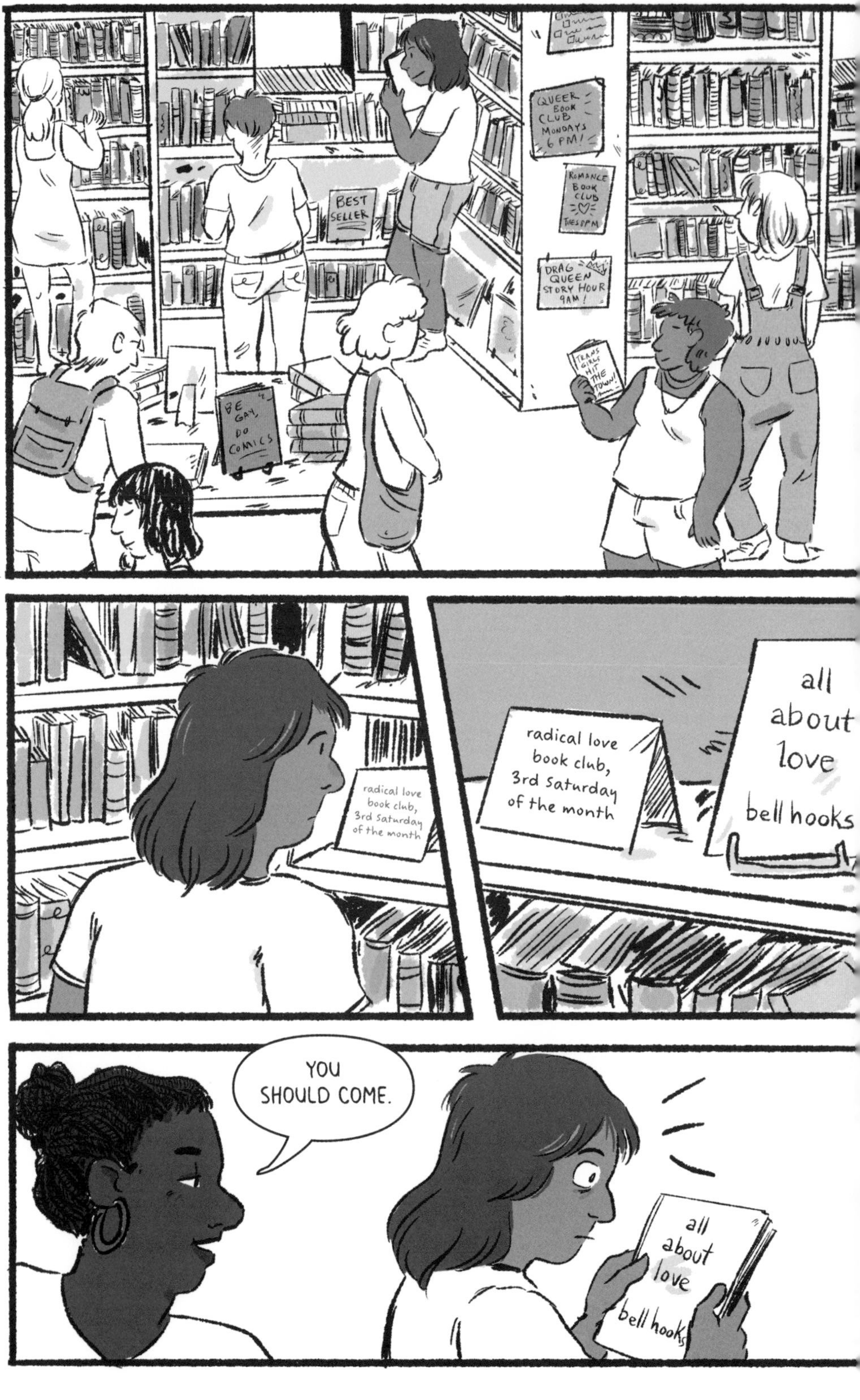
QUEER BOOK CLUB MONDAYS 6 PM!
ROMANCE BOOK CLUB
DRAG QUEEN STORY HOUR 9AM!
BEST SELLER
BE GAY, DO COMICS
TRANS GIRLS HIT THE TOWN!
radical love book club, 3rd Saturday of the month
radical love book club, 3rd Saturday of the month
all about love bell hooks
YOU SHOULD COME.
all about love bell hooks

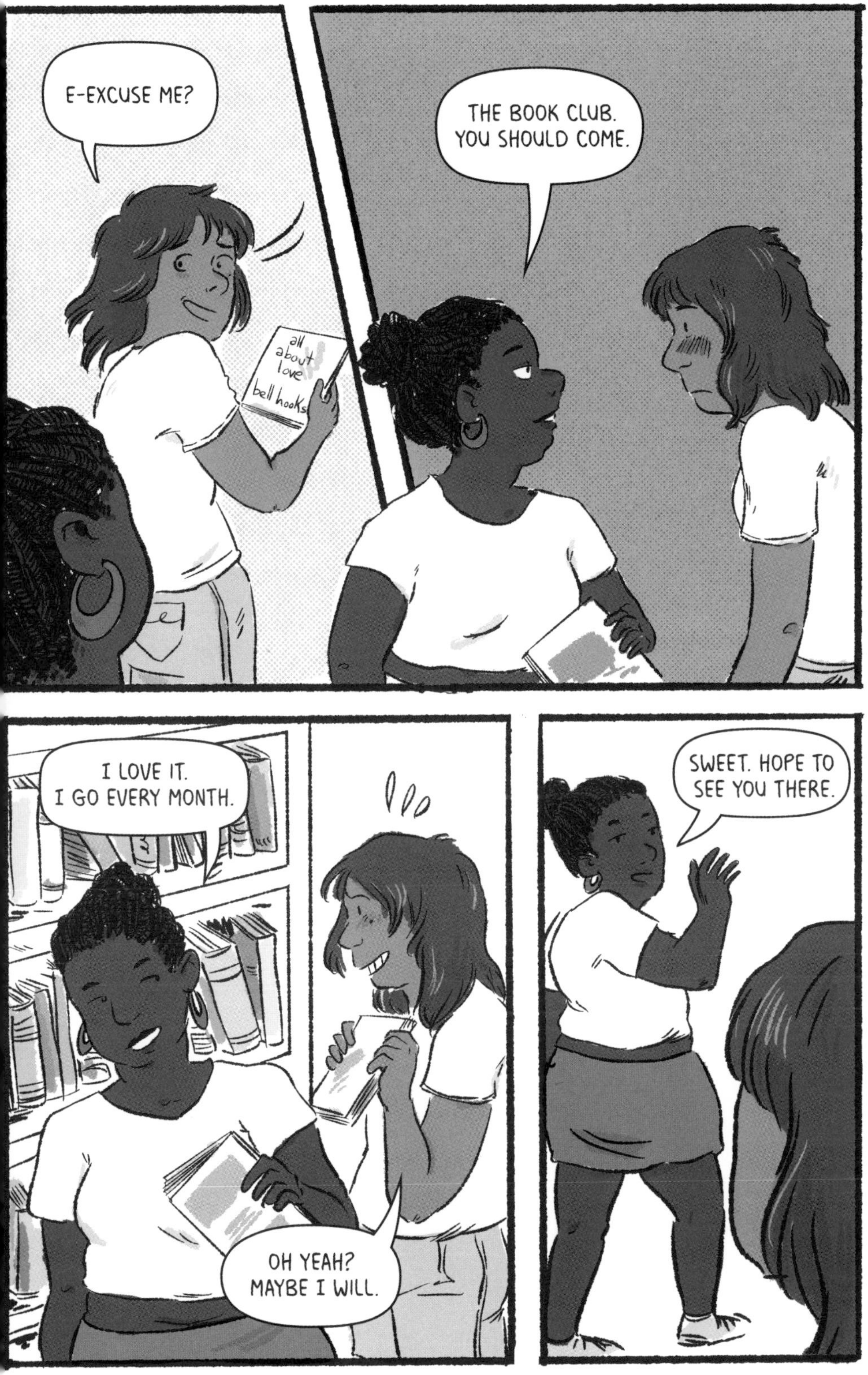
E-EXCUSE ME?
all about love
bell hooks
THE BOOK CLUB.
YOU SHOULD COME.
I LOVE IT.
I GO EVERY MONTH.
OH YEAH?
MAYBE I WILL.
SWEET. HOPE TO
SEE YOU THERE.

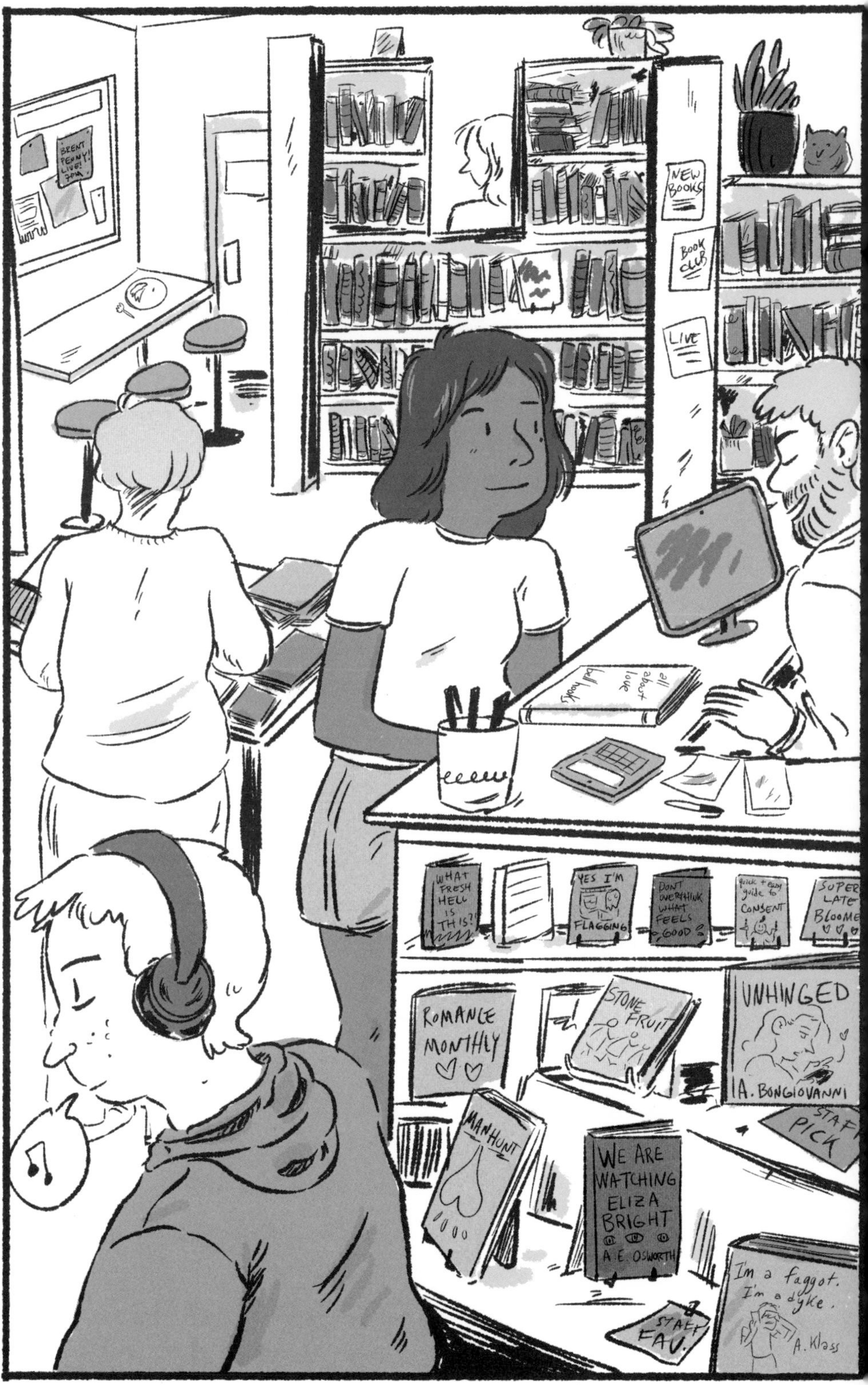
BRENT PENNY!! LIVE! 7PM
NEW BOOKS
BOOK CLUB
LIVE
all about love
bell hooks
WHAT FRESH HELL IS THIS?!
YES I'M FLAGGING
DON'T OVERTHINK WHAT FEELS GOOD
quick + easy guide to CONSENT
SUPER LATE BLOOME
ROMANCE MONTHLY
STONE FRUIT
UNHINGED
A. BONGIOVANNI
STAFF PICK
MANHUNT
WE ARE WATCHING ELIZA BRIGHT
A. E. OSWORTH
I'm a faggot. I'm a dyke.
A. Klass
STAFF FAV.

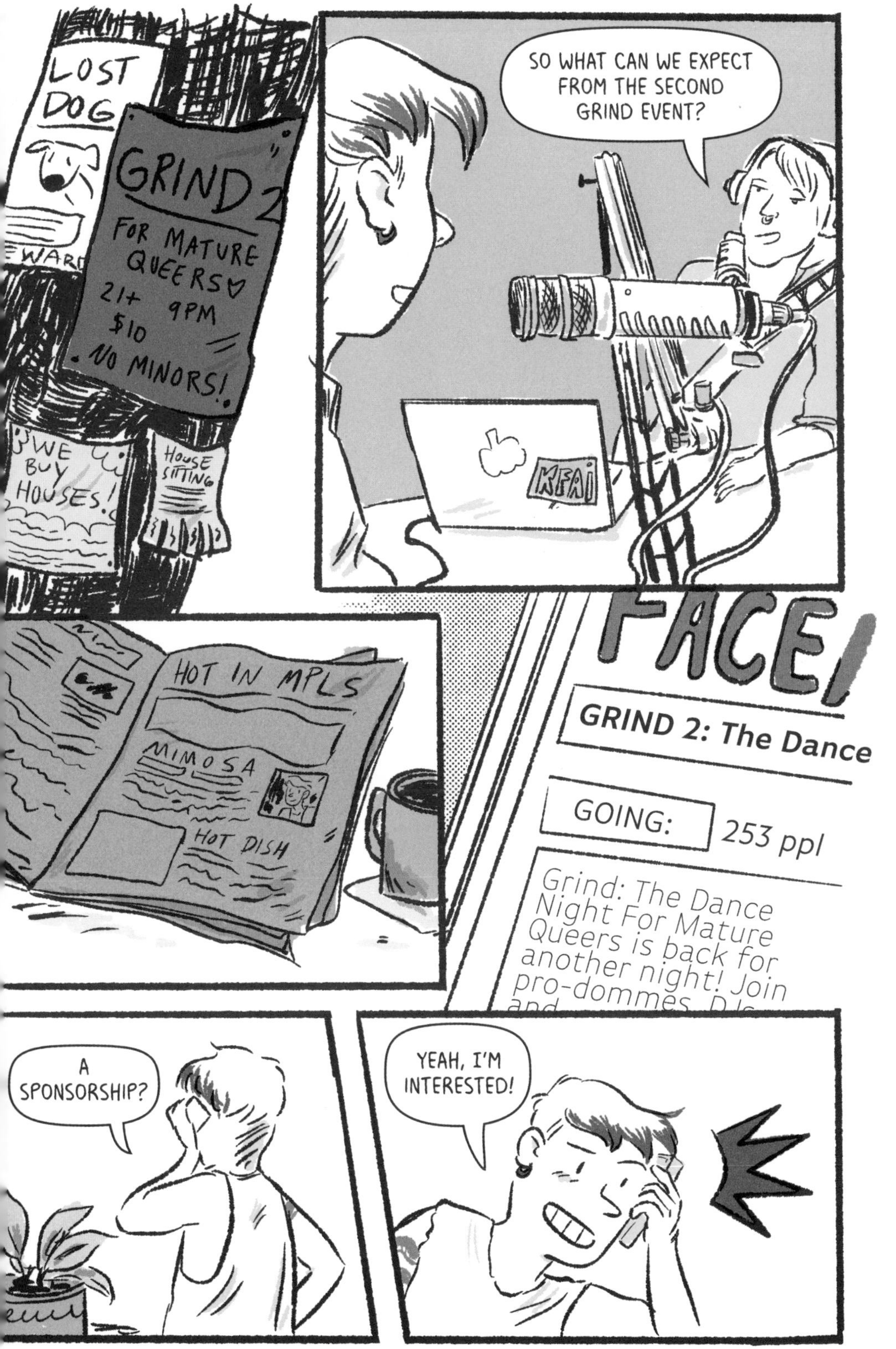
LOST DOG
GRIND 2
FOR MATURE QUEERS♡
21+ 9PM
$10
NO MINORS!
WE BUY HOUSES!
HOUSE SITTING
SO WHAT CAN WE EXPECT FROM THE SECOND GRIND EVENT?
KFAI
HOT IN MPLS
MIMOSA
HOT DISH
FACE
GRIND 2: The Dance
GOING:
253 ppl
Grind: The Dance Night For Mature Queers is back for another night! Join pro-dommes,
A SPONSORSHIP?
YEAH, I'M INTERESTED!

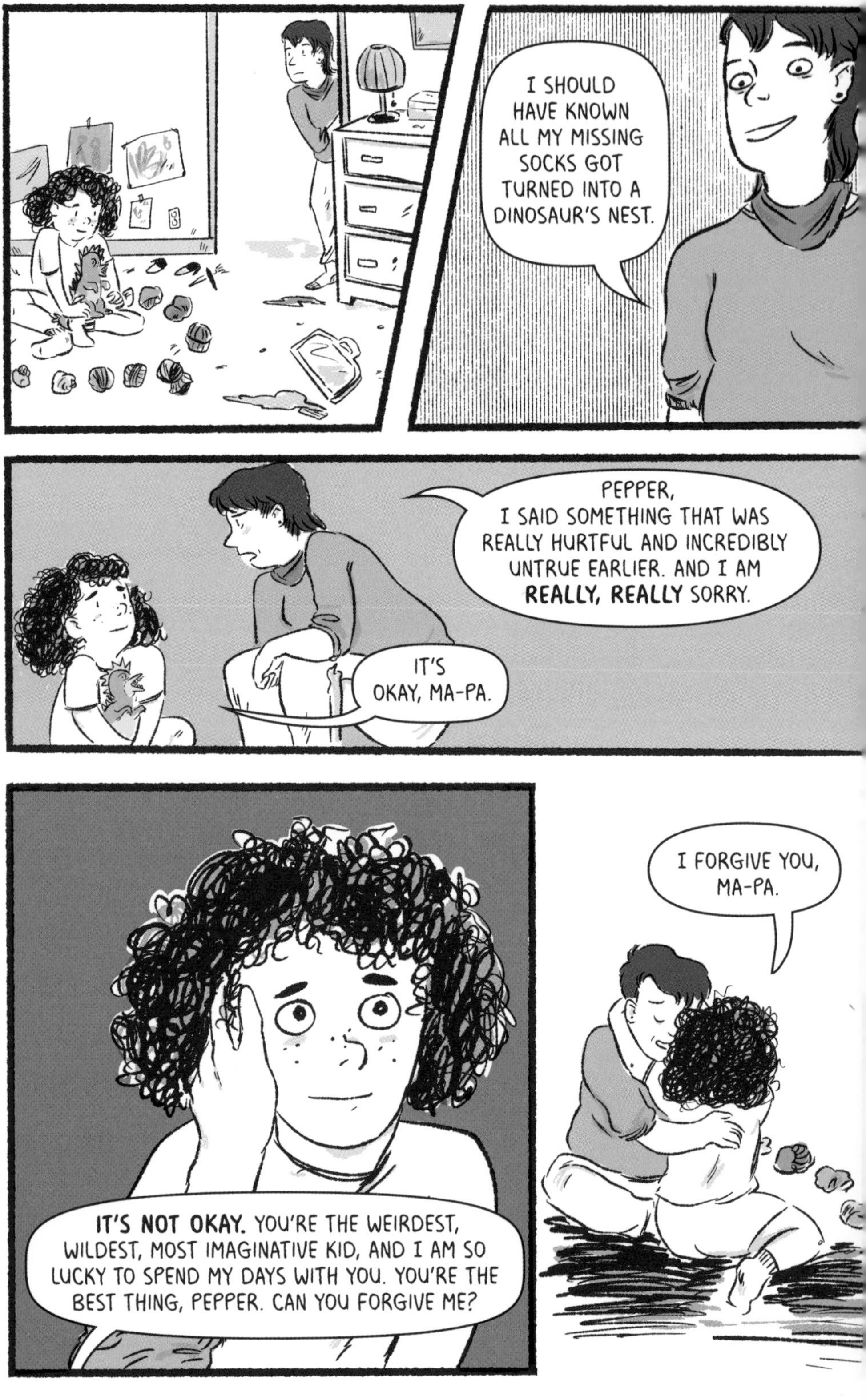
I SHOULD HAVE KNOWN ALL MY MISSING SOCKS GOT TURNED INTO A DINOSAUR'S NEST.
PEPPER, I SAID SOMETHING THAT WAS REALLY HURTFUL AND INCREDIBLY UNTRUE EARLIER. AND I AM **REALLY, REALLY** SORRY.
IT'S OKAY, MA-PA.
IT'S NOT OKAY. YOU'RE THE WEIRDEST, WILDEST, MOST IMAGINATIVE KID, AND I AM SO LUCKY TO SPEND MY DAYS WITH YOU. YOU'RE THE BEST THING, PEPPER. CAN YOU FORGIVE ME?
I FORGIVE YOU, MA-PA.

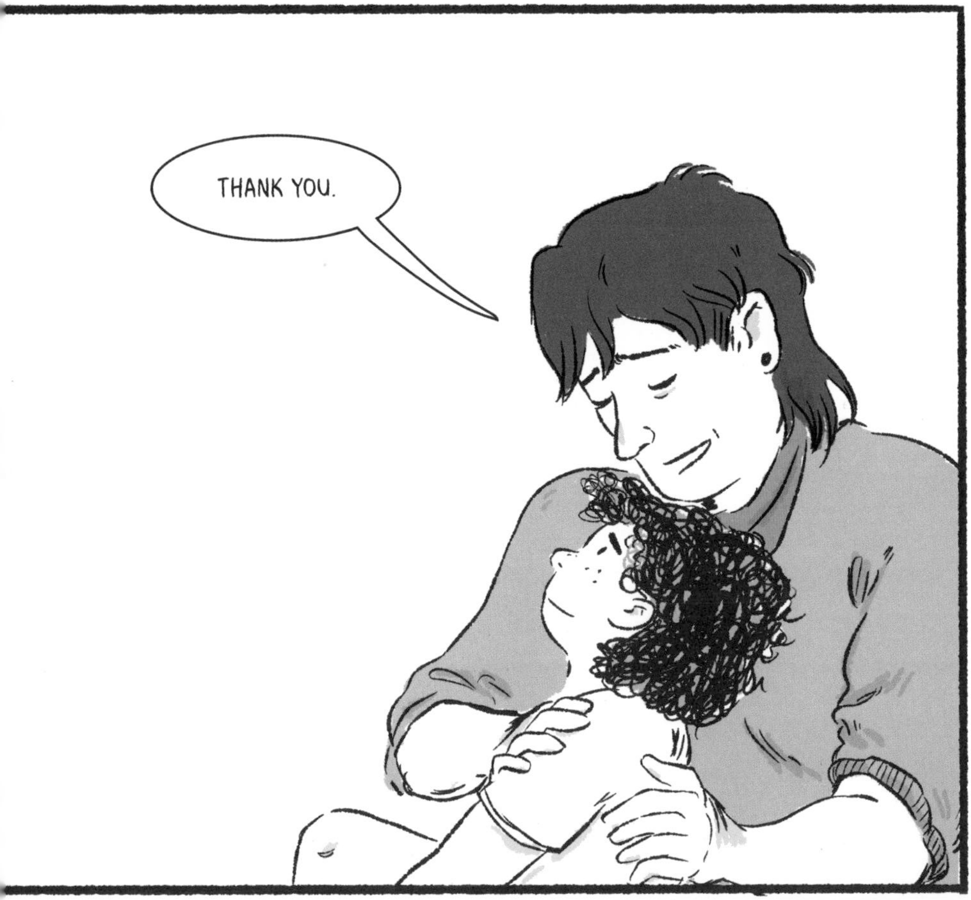
THANK YOU.

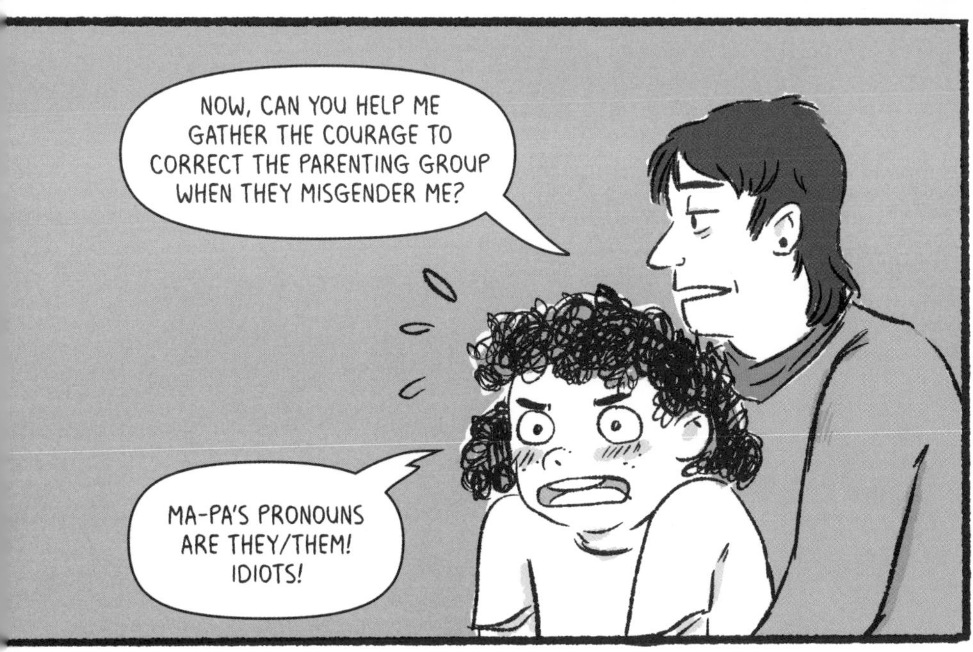
NOW, CAN YOU HELP ME GATHER THE COURAGE TO CORRECT THE PARENTING GROUP WHEN THEY MISGENDER ME?
MA-PA'S PRONOUNS ARE THEY/THEM! IDIOTS!

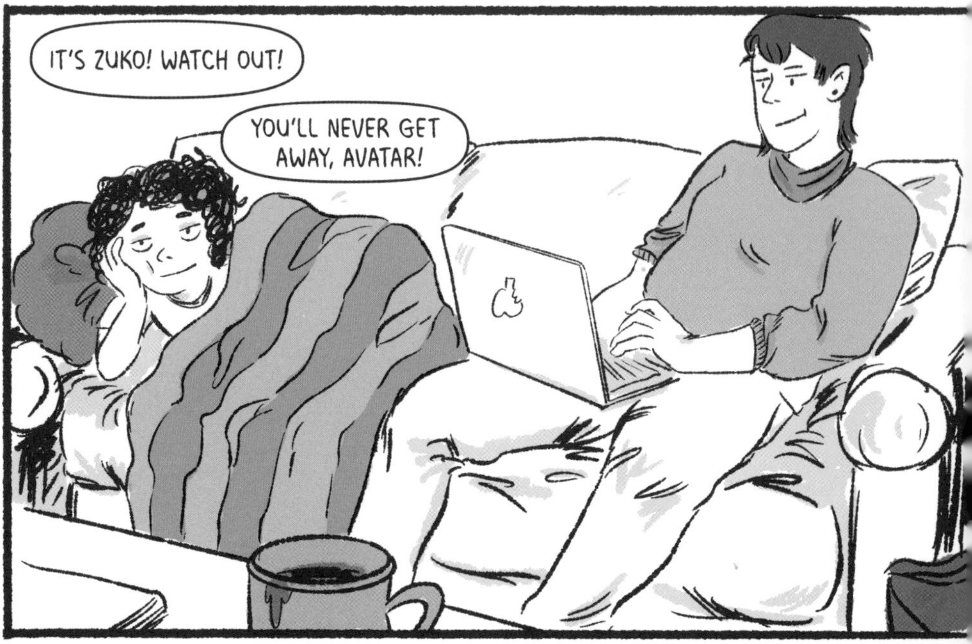
IT'S ZUKO! WATCH OUT!
YOU'LL NEVER GET AWAY, AVATAR!

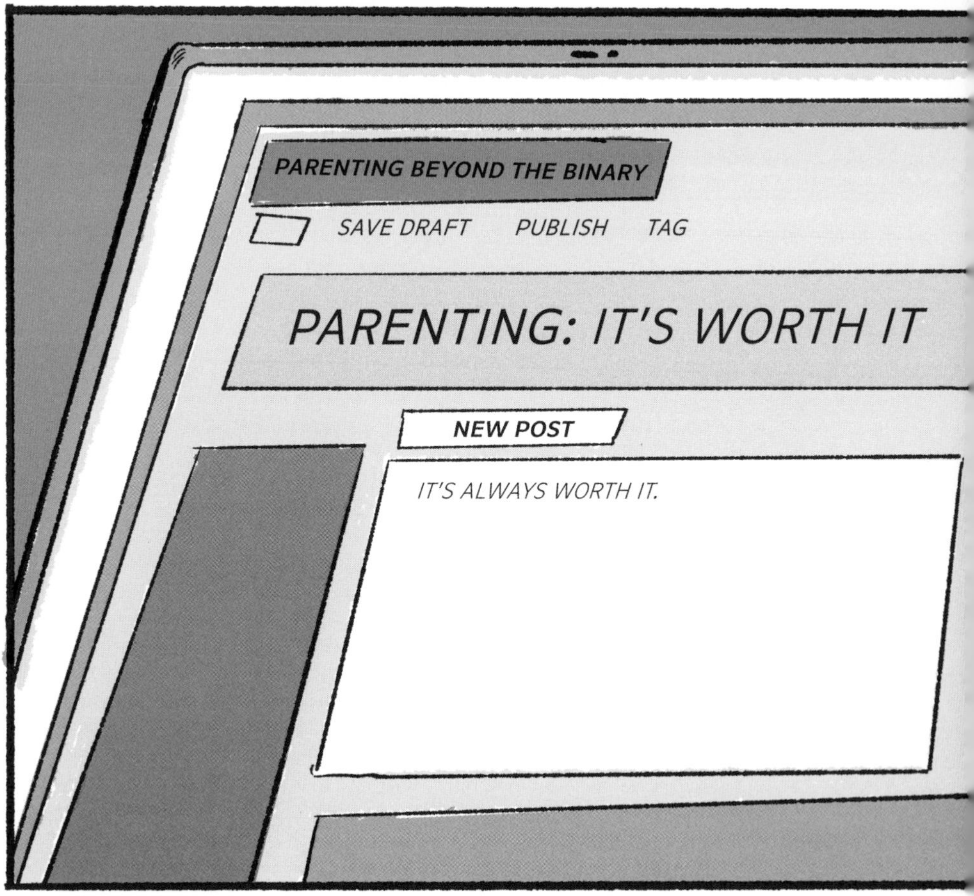
PARENTING BEYOND THE BINARY
SAVE DRAFT
PUBLISH
TAG
PARENTING: IT'S WORTH IT
NEW POST
IT'S ALWAYS WORTH IT.

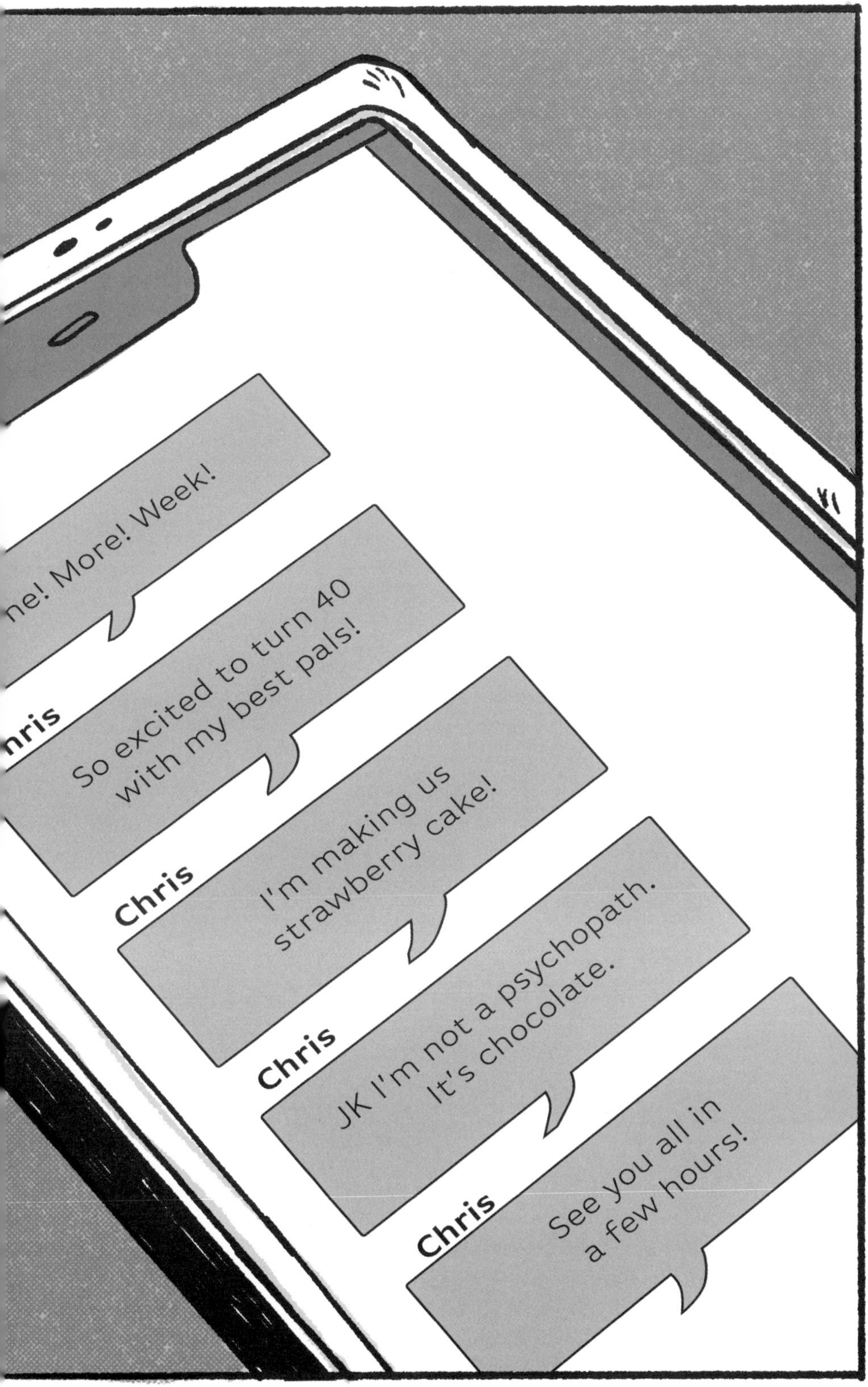

ne! More! Week!
hris
So excited to turn 40 with my best pals!
Chris
I'm making us strawberry cake!
Chris
JK I'm not a psychopath. It's chocolate.
Chris
See you all in a few hours!

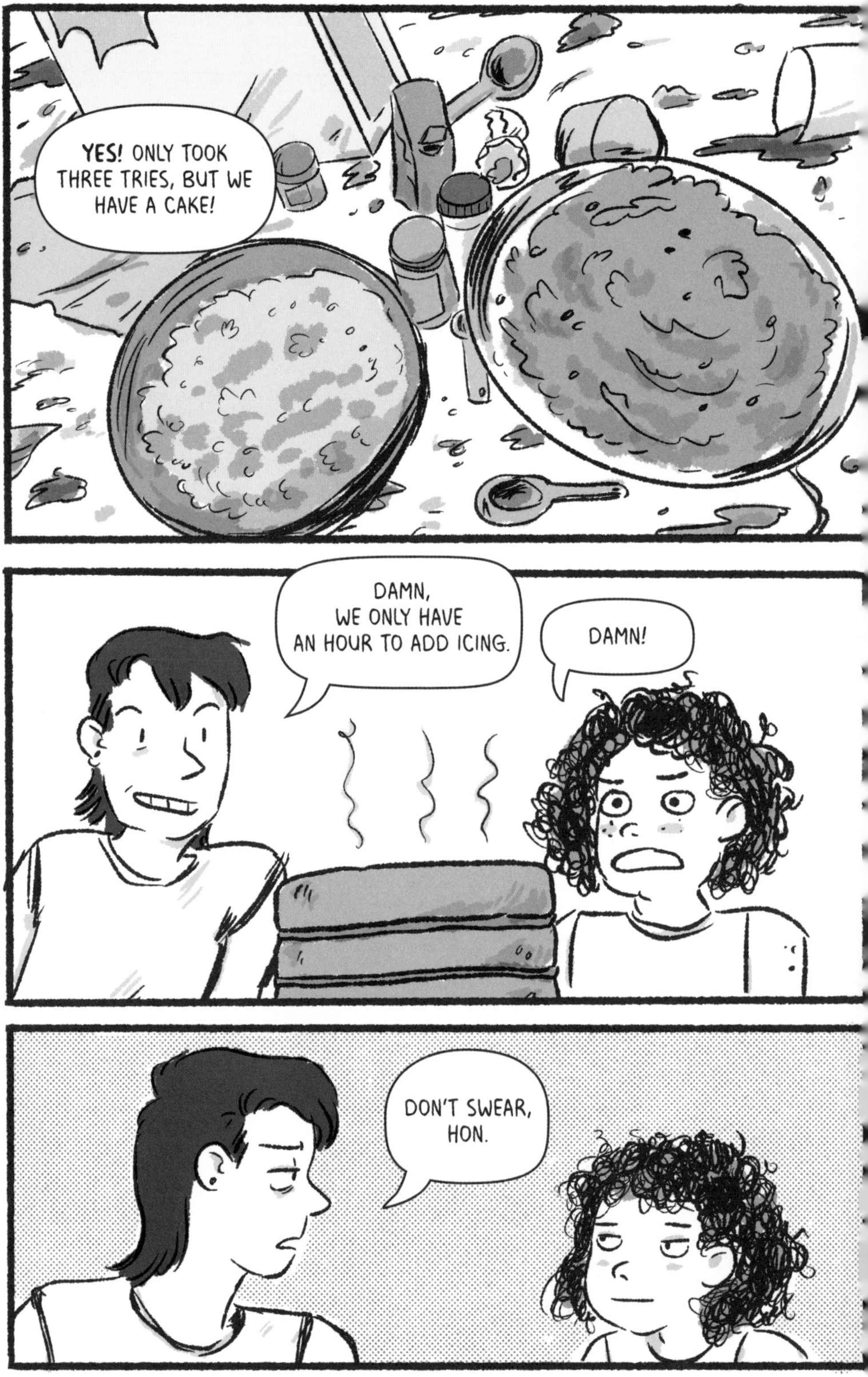
YES! ONLY TOOK THREE TRIES, BUT WE HAVE A CAKE!
DAMN, WE ONLY HAVE AN HOUR TO ADD ICING.
DAMN!
DON'T SWEAR, HON.

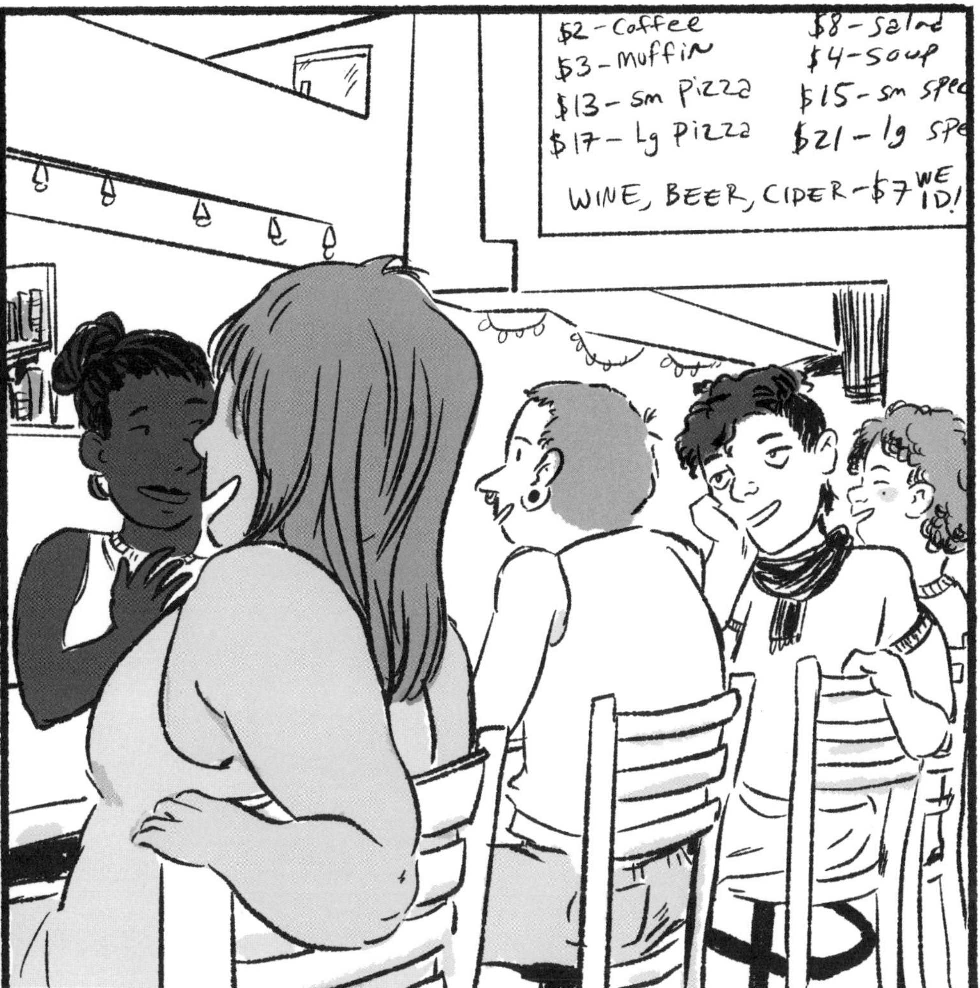
$2 - Coffee
$3 - muffin
$13 - sm pizza
$17 - lg pizza
$8 - Salad
$4 - Soup
$15 - sm spe
$21 - lg spe
WINE, BEER, CIDER - $7 WE ID!

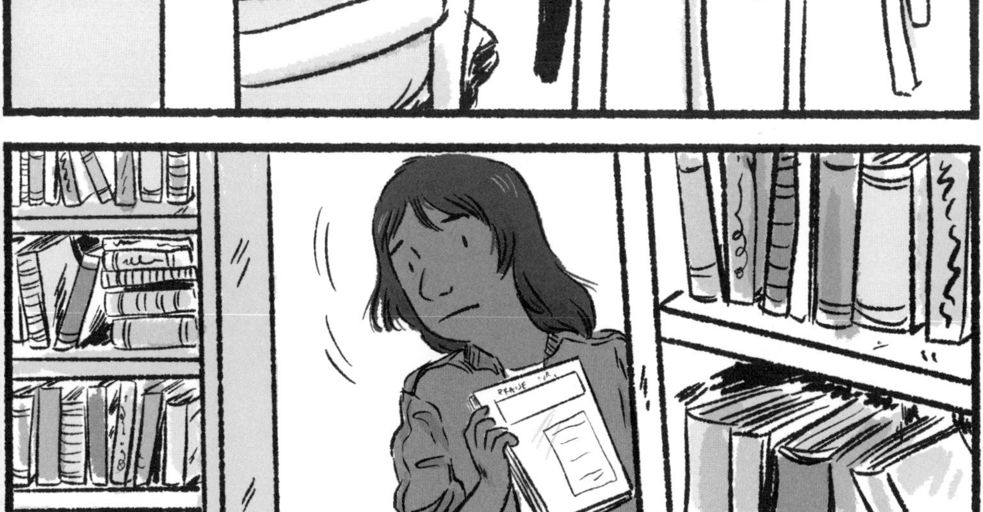

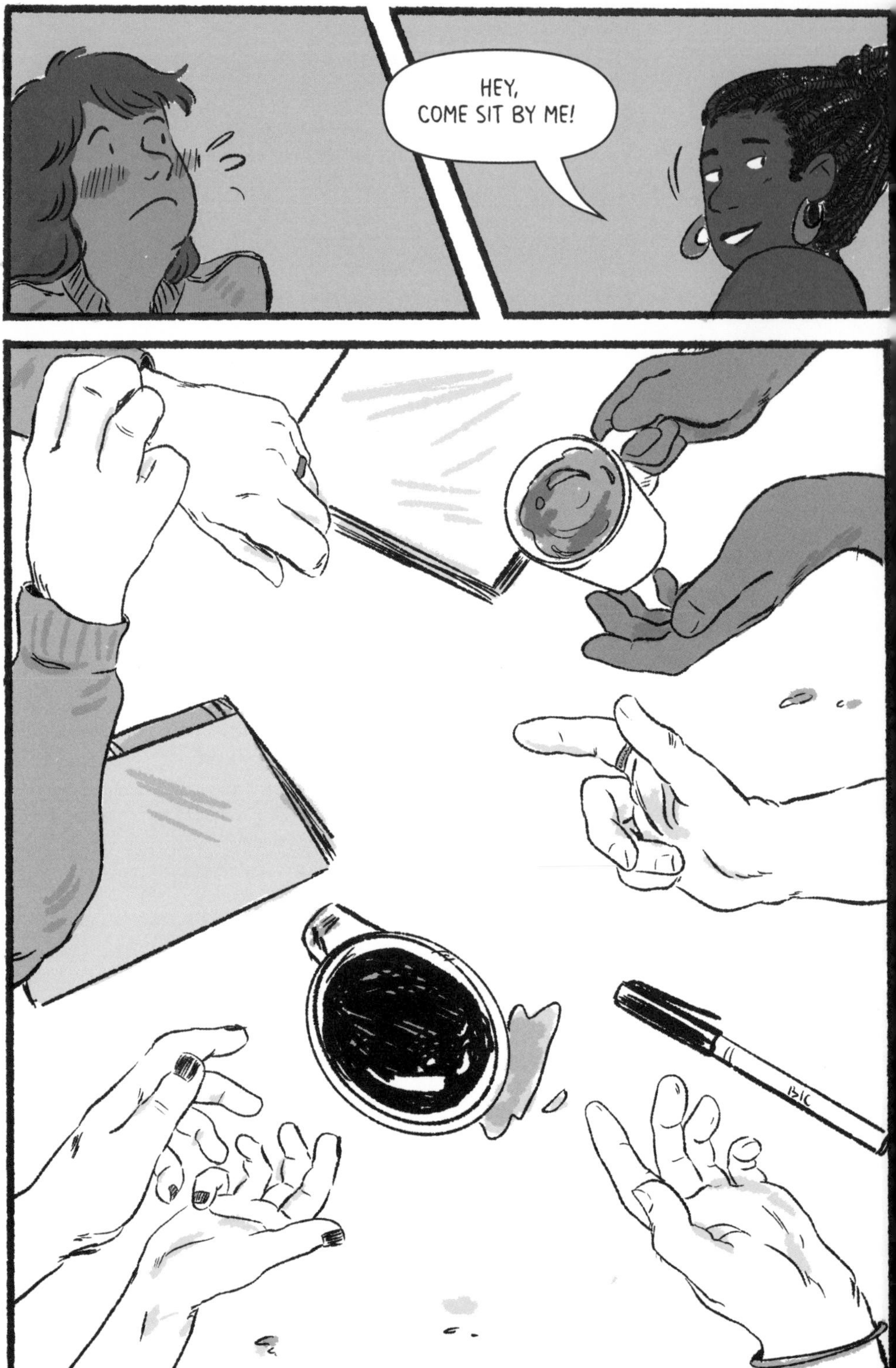
HEY,
COME SIT BY ME!
BIC

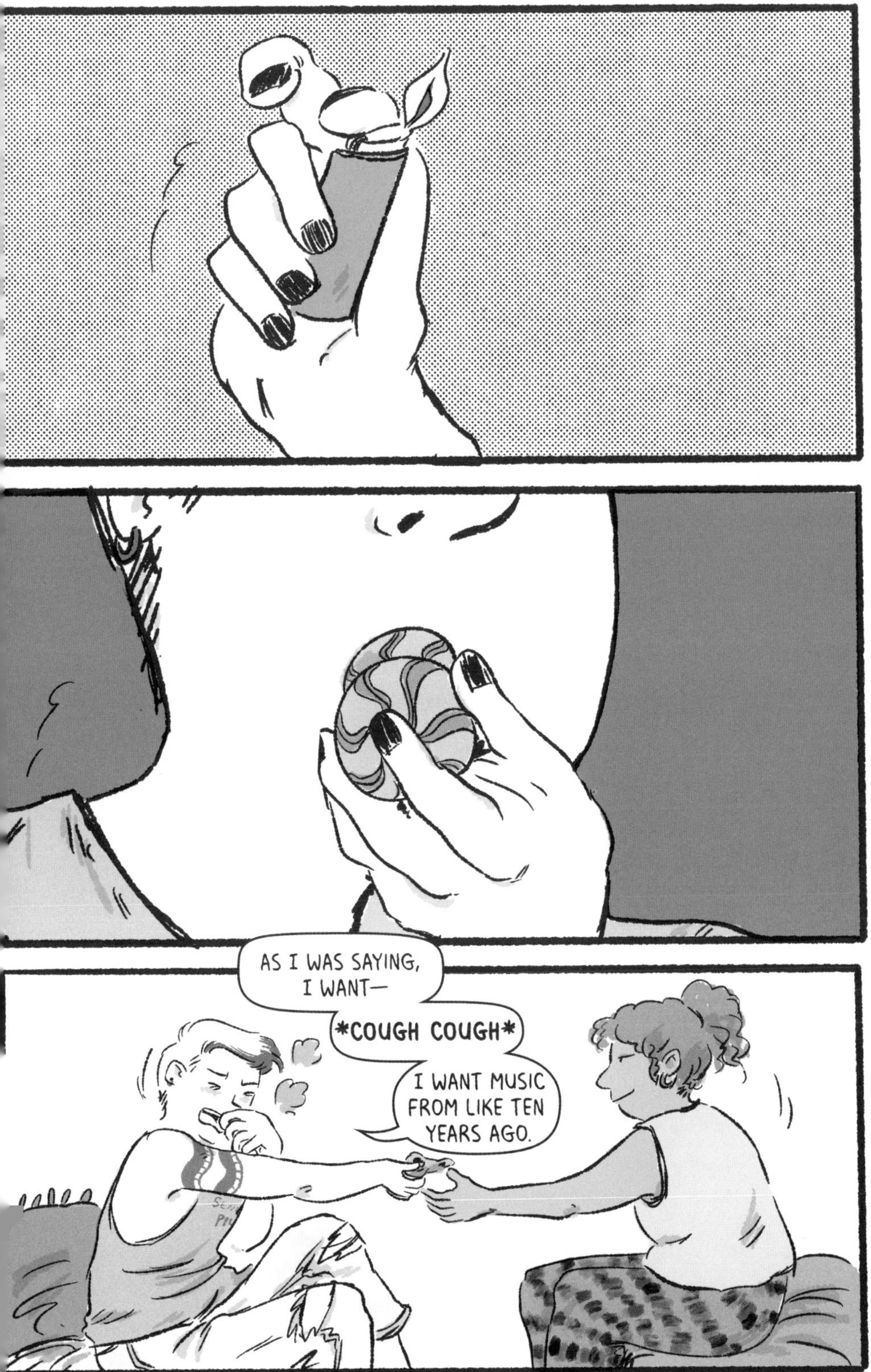
AS I WAS SAYING, I WANT—
COUGH COUGH
I WANT MUSIC FROM LIKE TEN YEARS AGO.

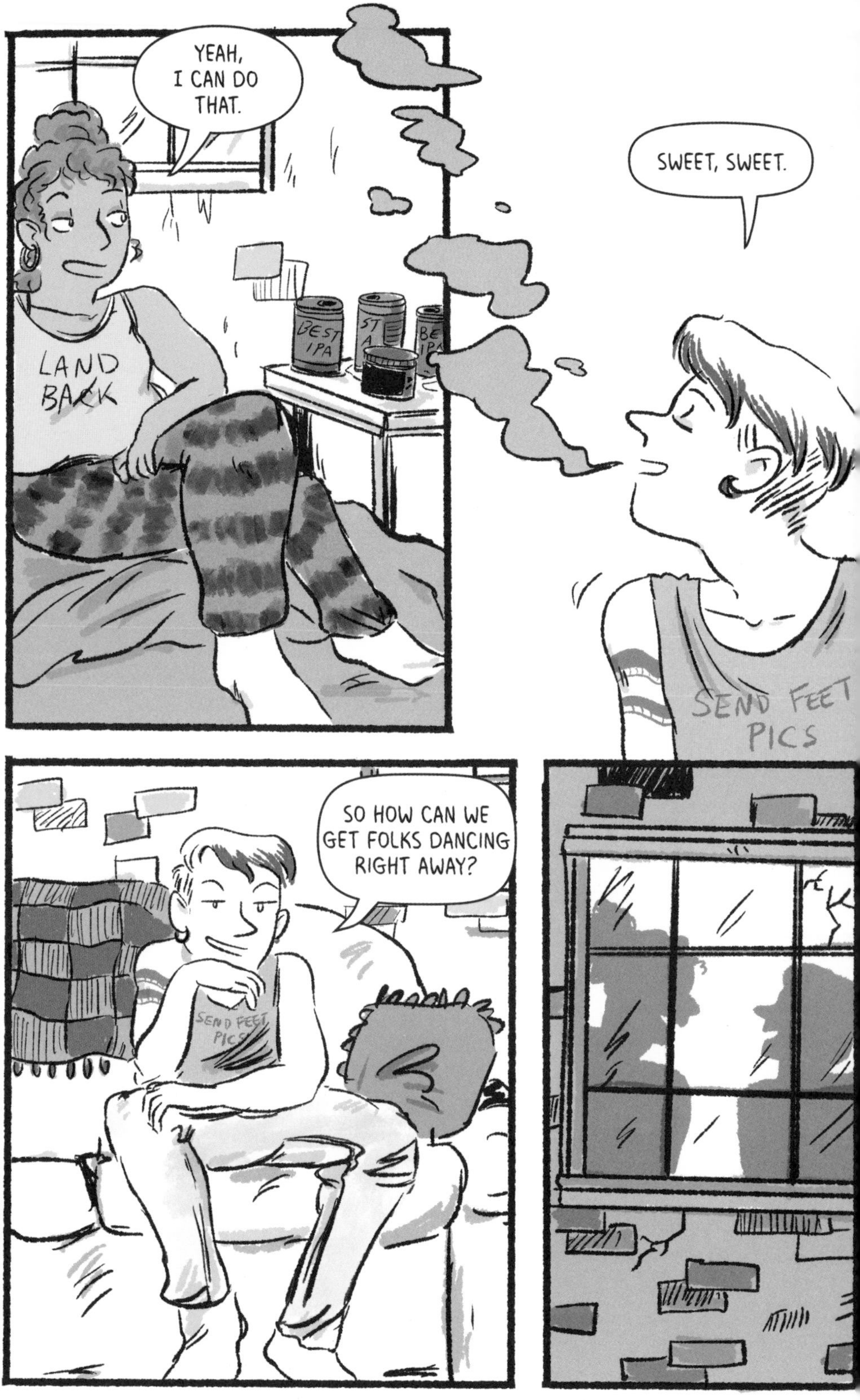
YEAH, I CAN DO THAT.
LAND BACK
BEST IPA
SWEET, SWEET.
SEND FEET PICS
SO HOW CAN WE GET FOLKS DANCING RIGHT AWAY?
SEND FEET PICS

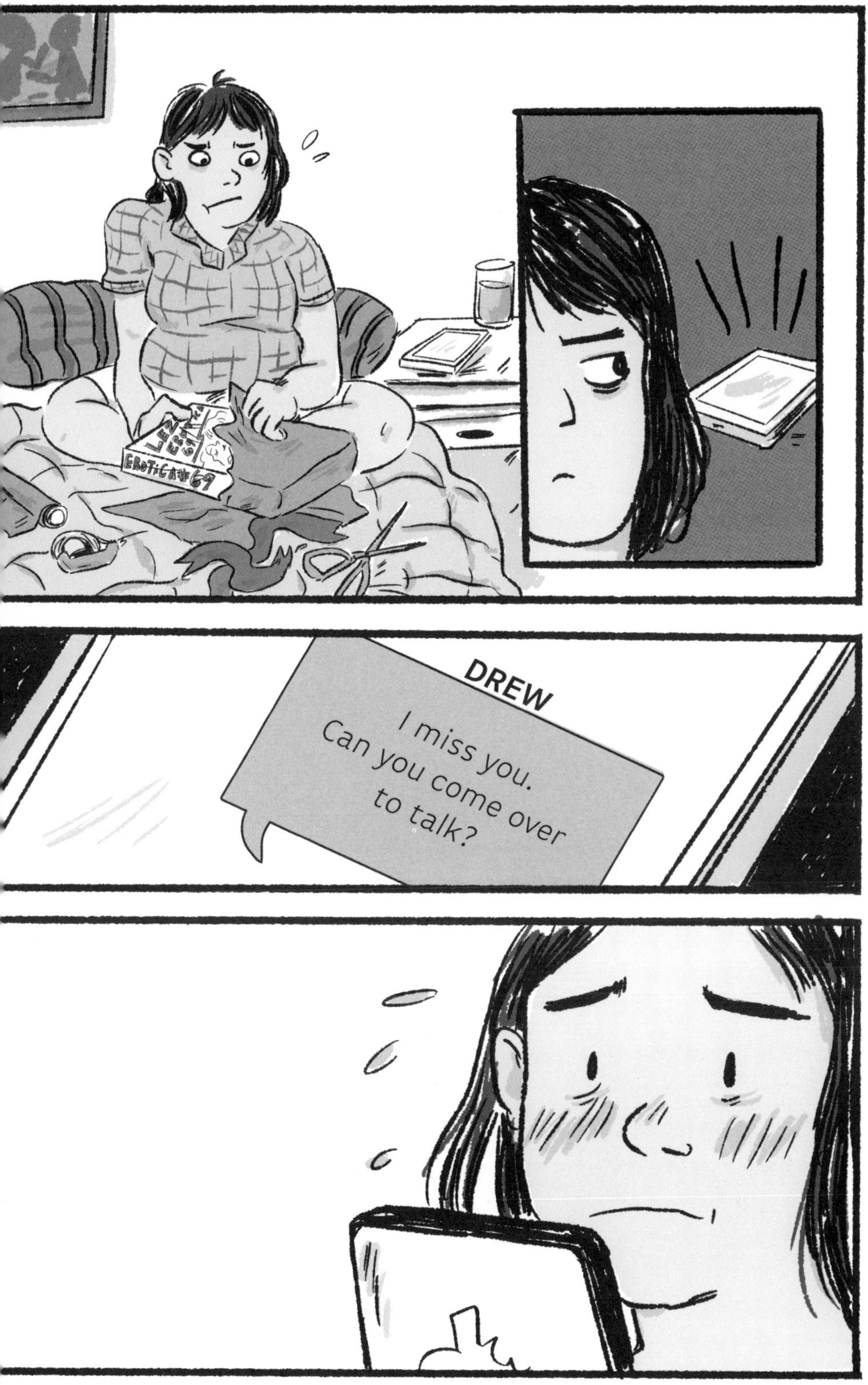
EROTICA#69
DREW
I miss you.
Can you come over
to talk?

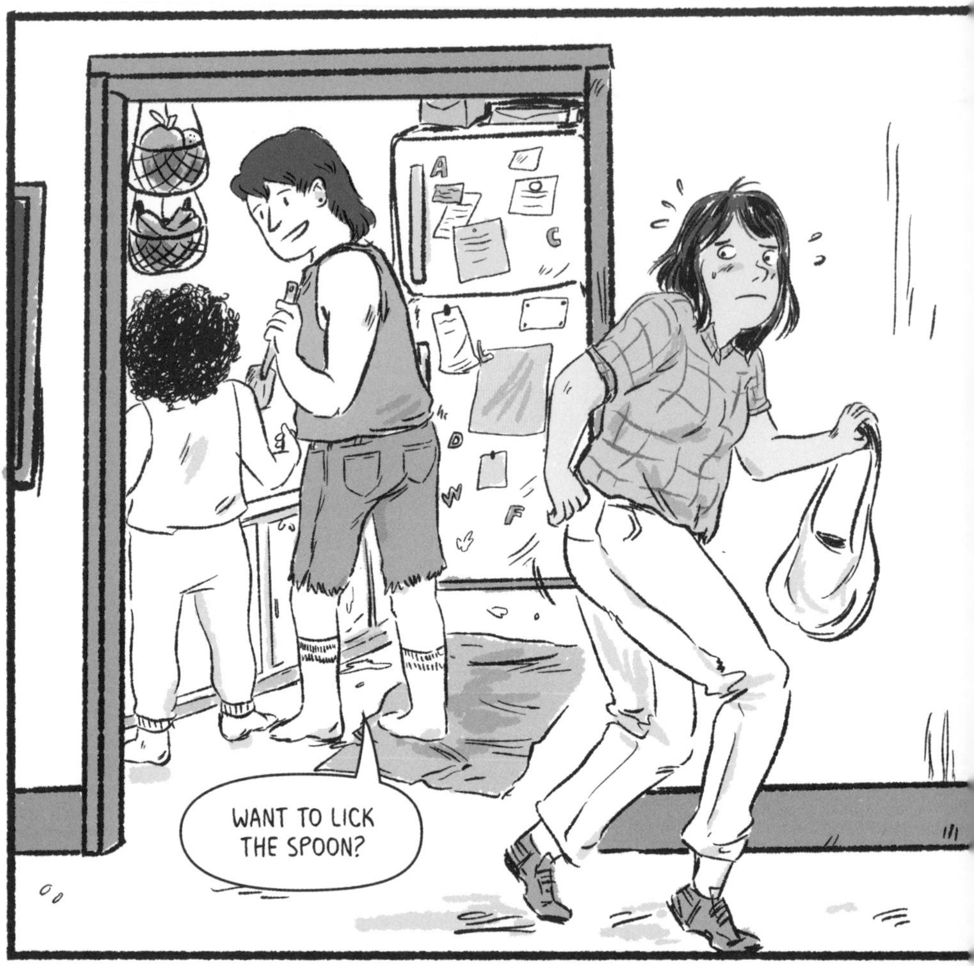
WANT TO LICK THE SPOON?

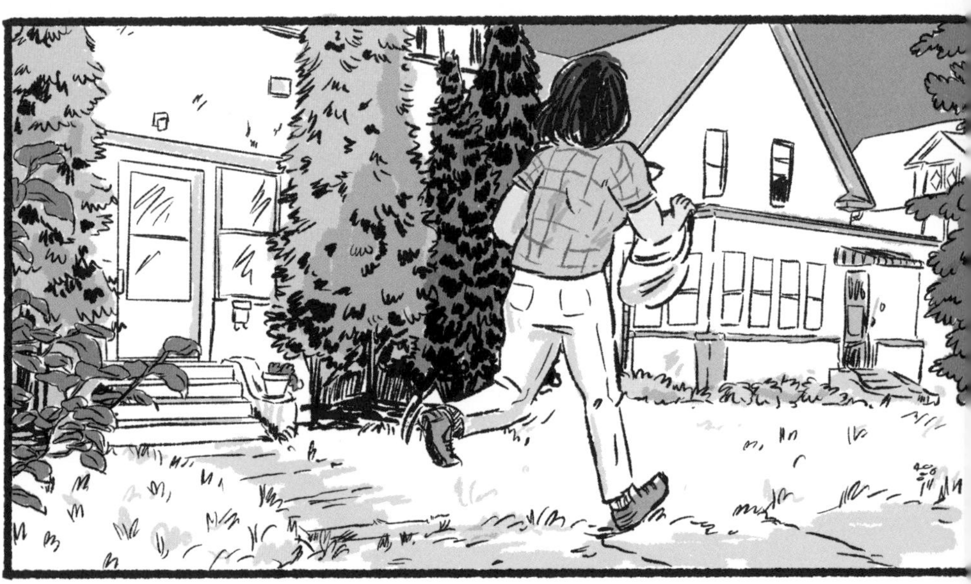

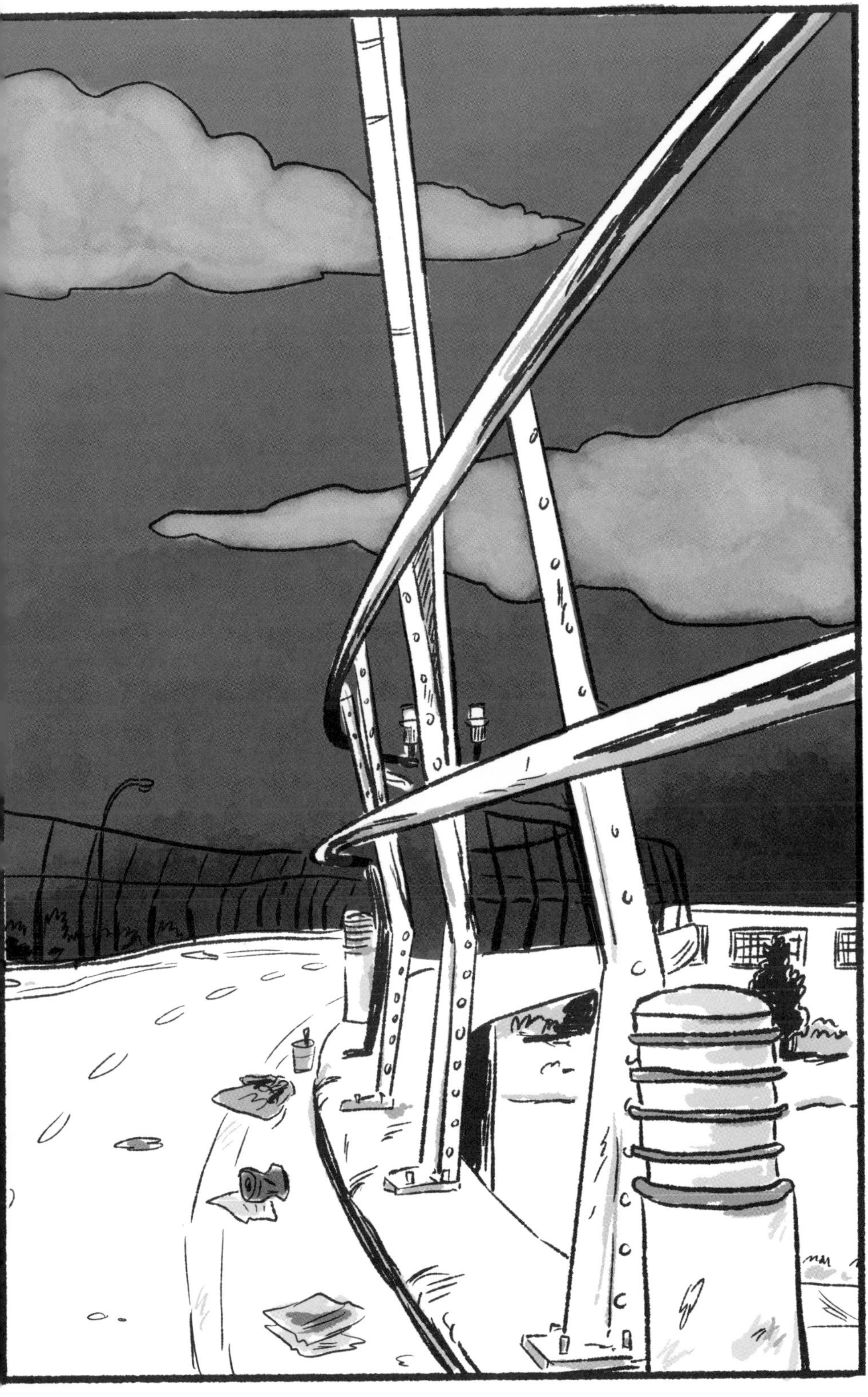

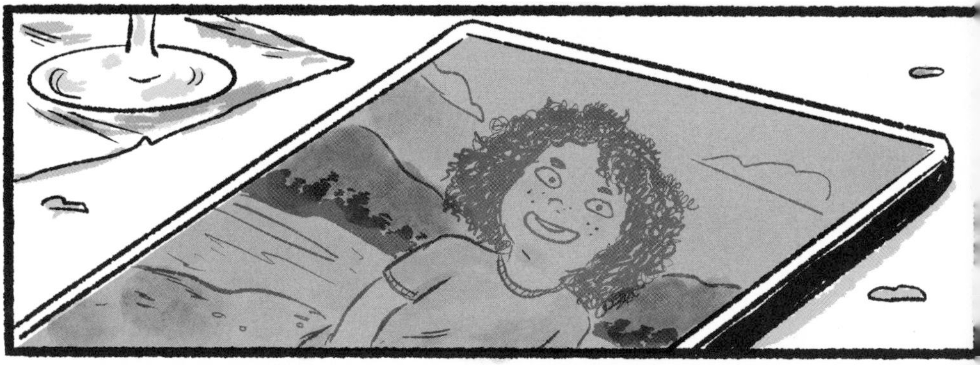

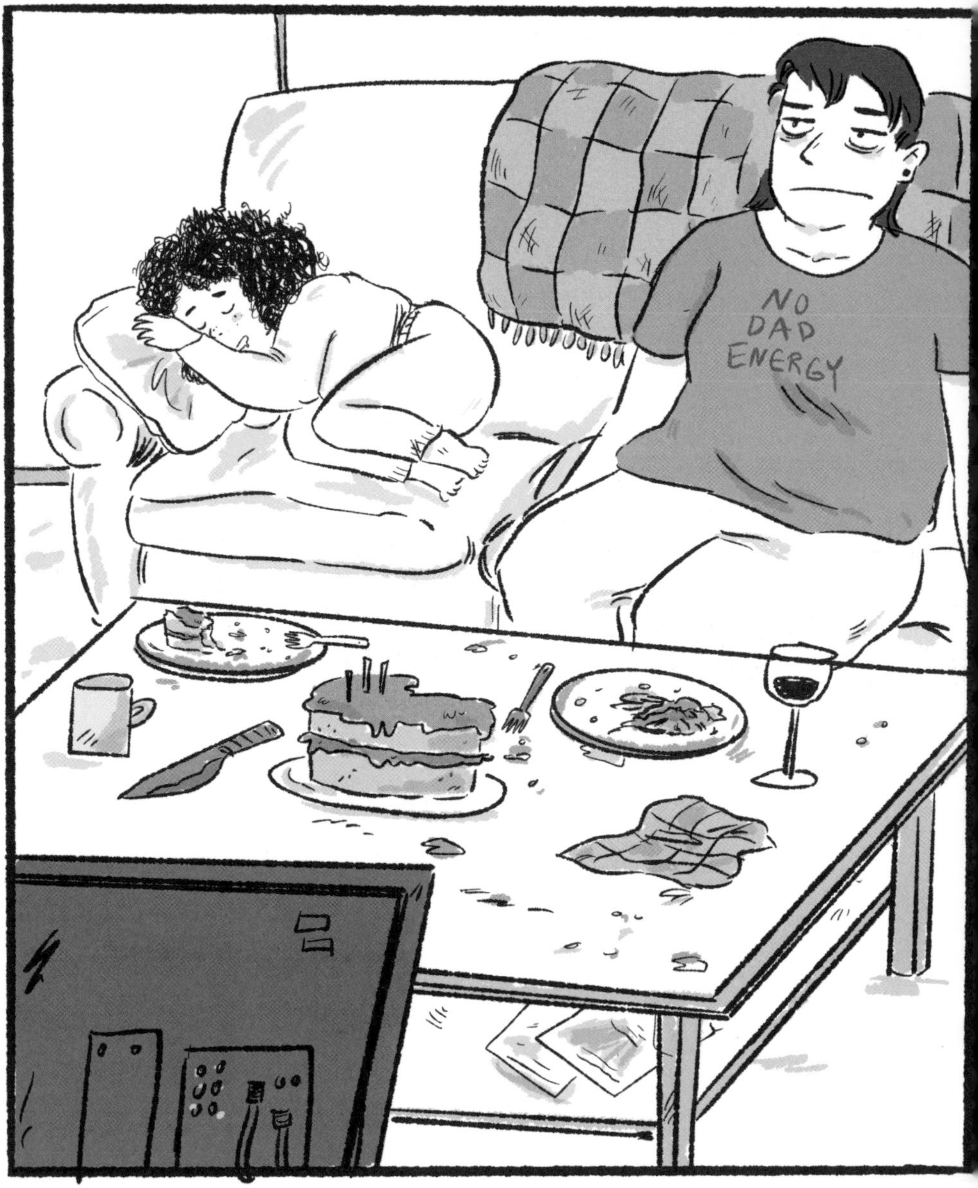
NO DAD ENERGY

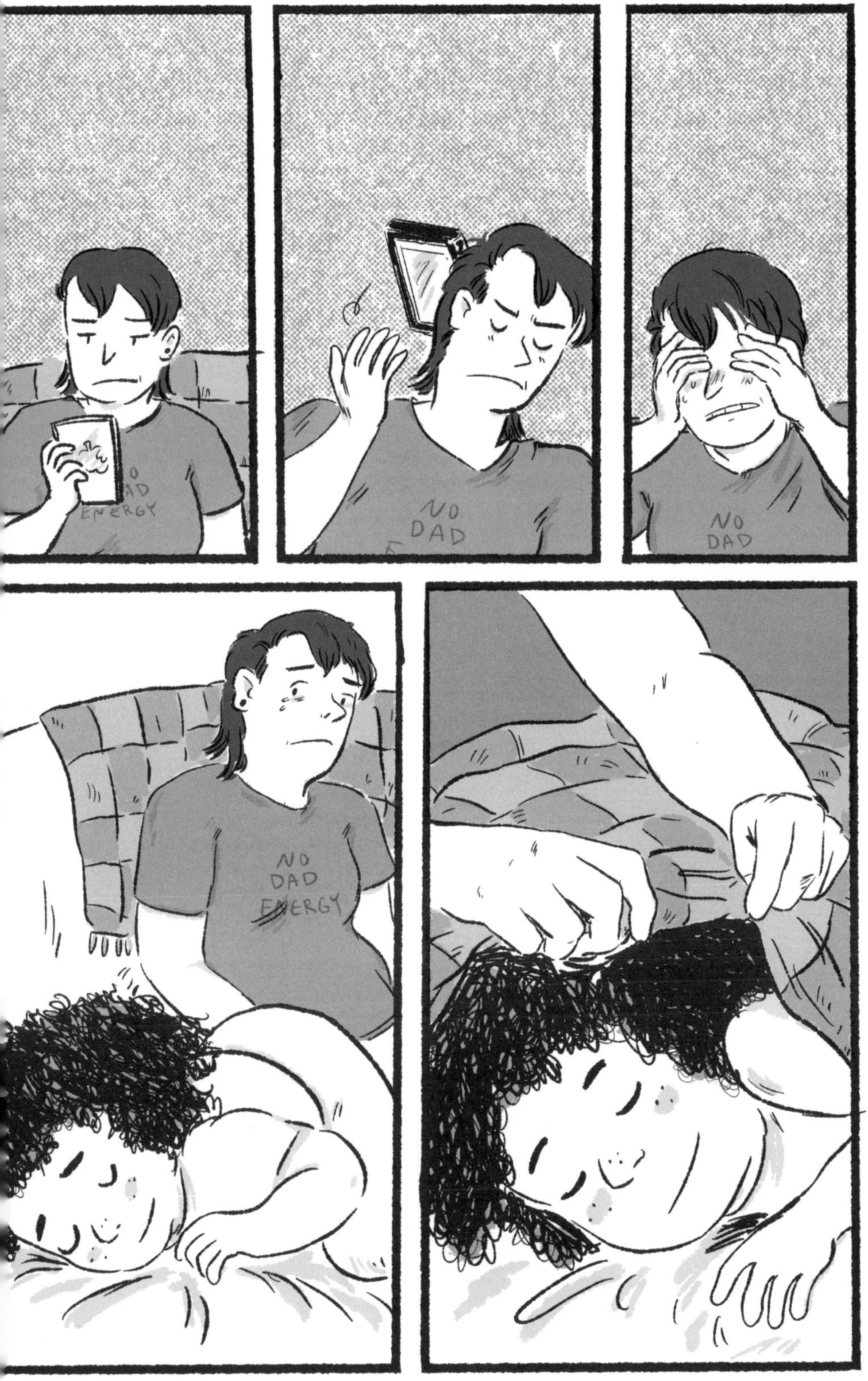
NO
DAD
ENERGY
NO
DAD
NO
DAD
NO
DAD
ENERGY

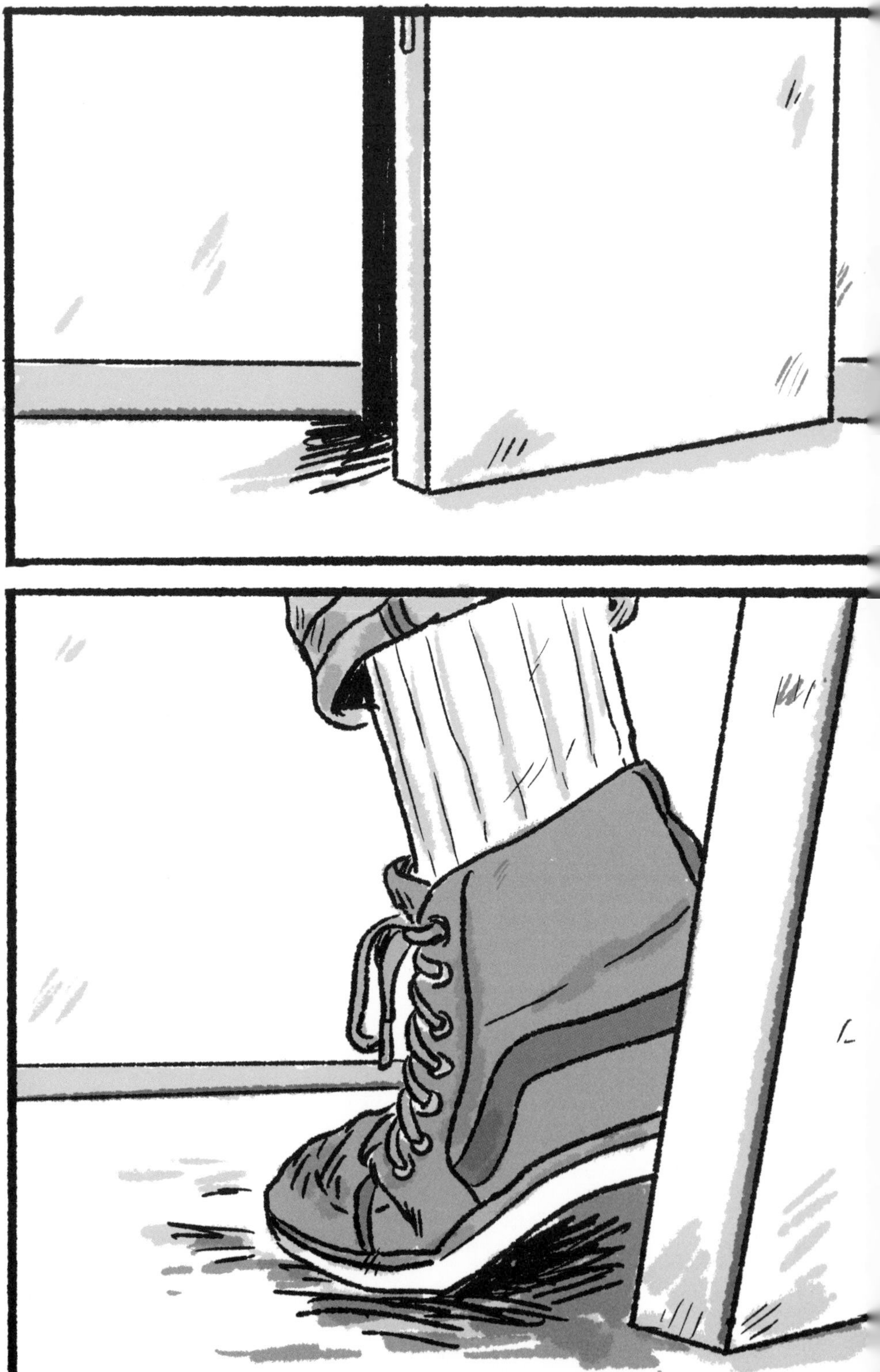

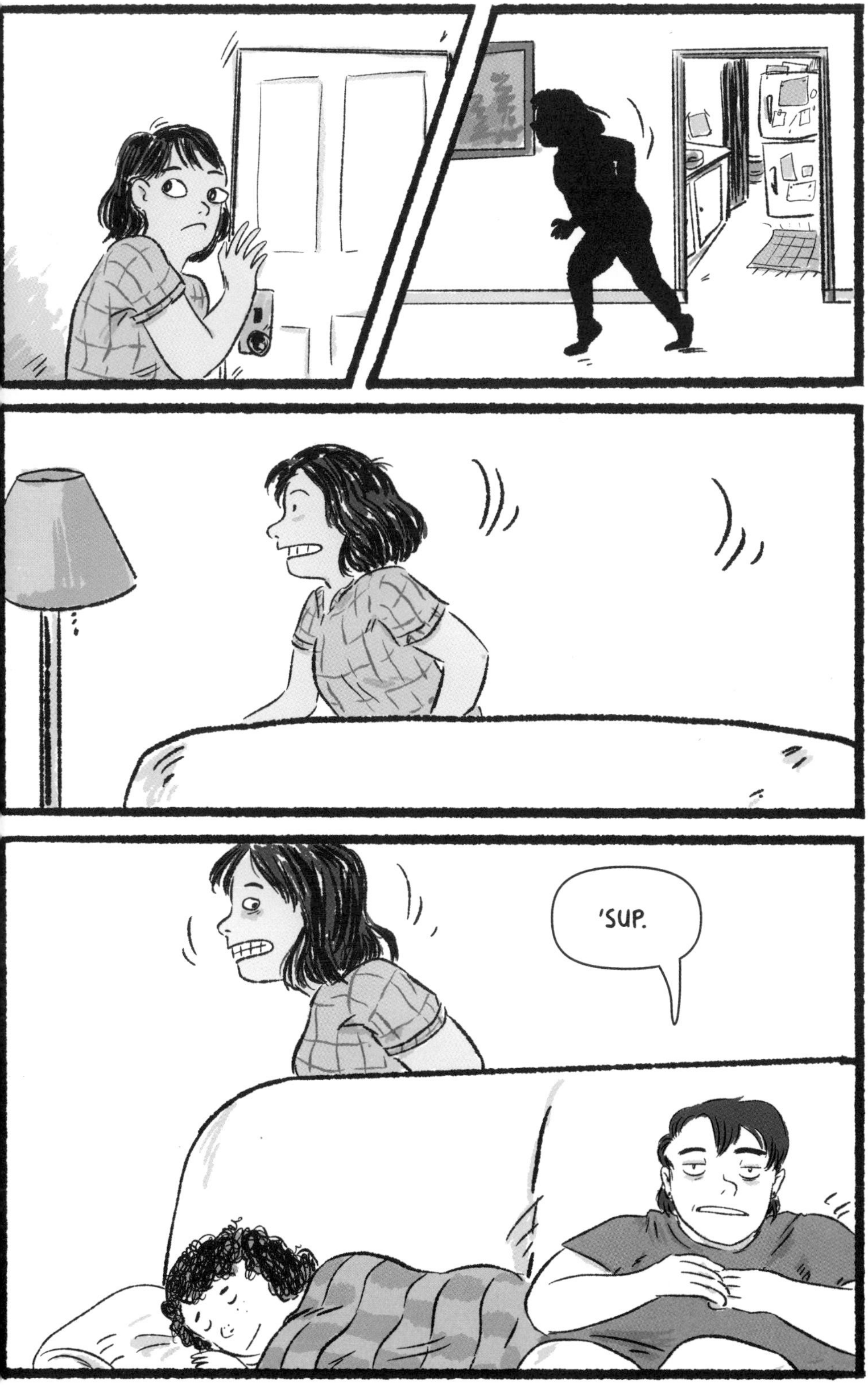
'SUP.

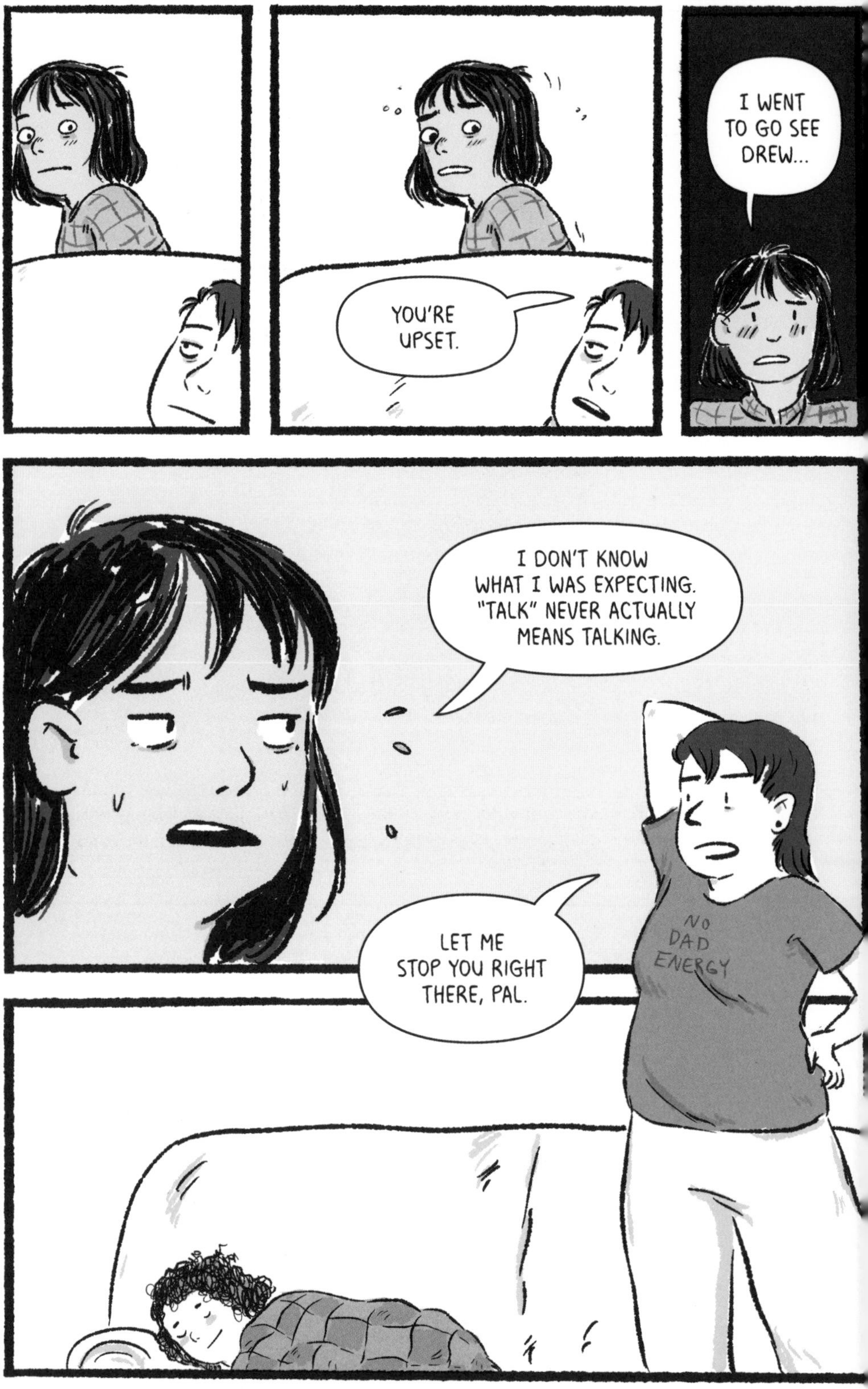
YOU'RE UPSET.
I WENT TO GO SEE DREW...
I DON'T KNOW WHAT I WAS EXPECTING. "TALK" NEVER ACTUALLY MEANS TALKING.
LET ME STOP YOU RIGHT THERE, PAL.
NO DAD ENERGY

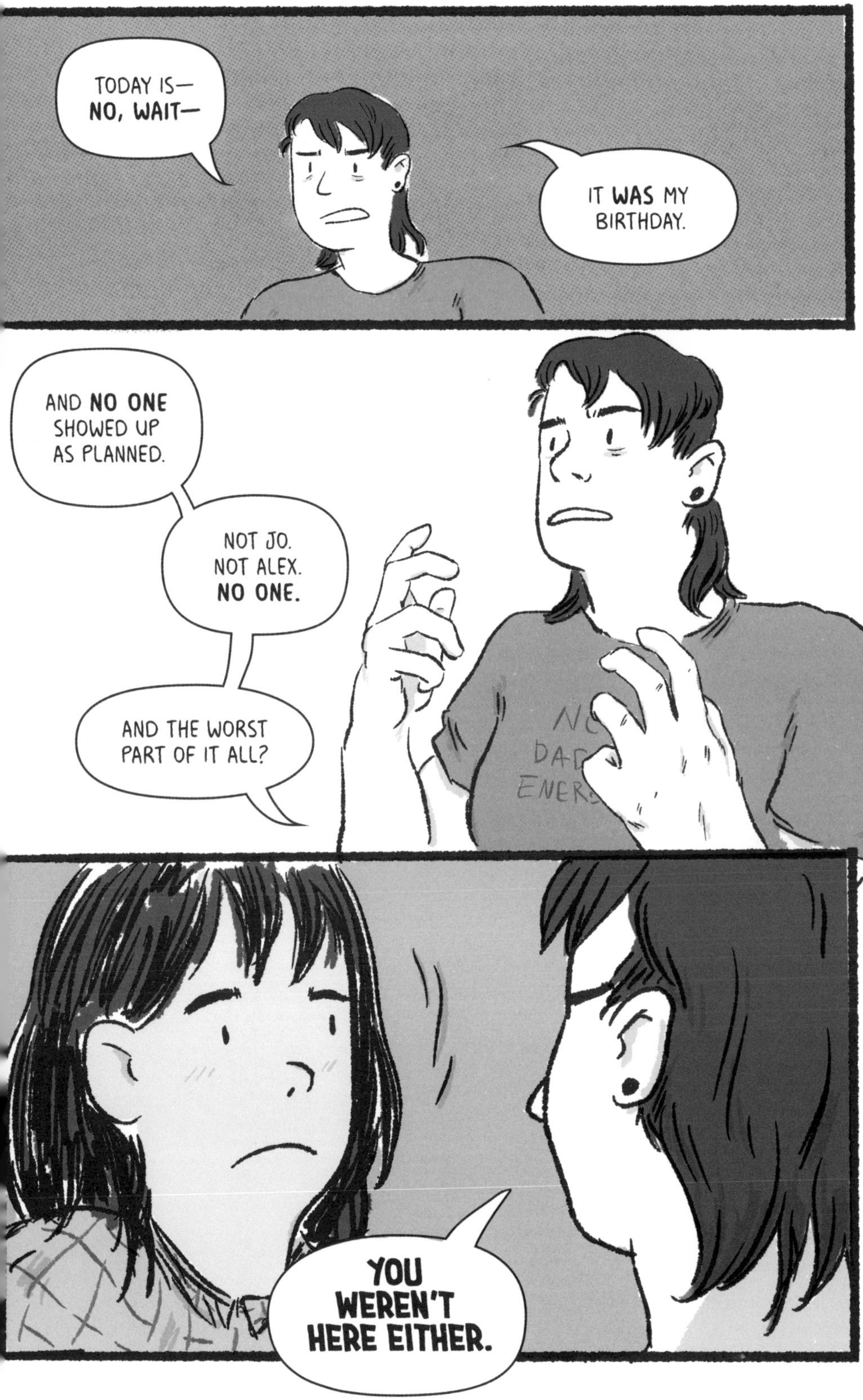
TODAY IS—
NO, WAIT—
IT WAS MY BIRTHDAY.
AND NO ONE SHOWED UP AS PLANNED.
NOT JO. NOT ALEX. NO ONE.
AND THE WORST PART OF IT ALL?
YOU WEREN'T HERE EITHER.

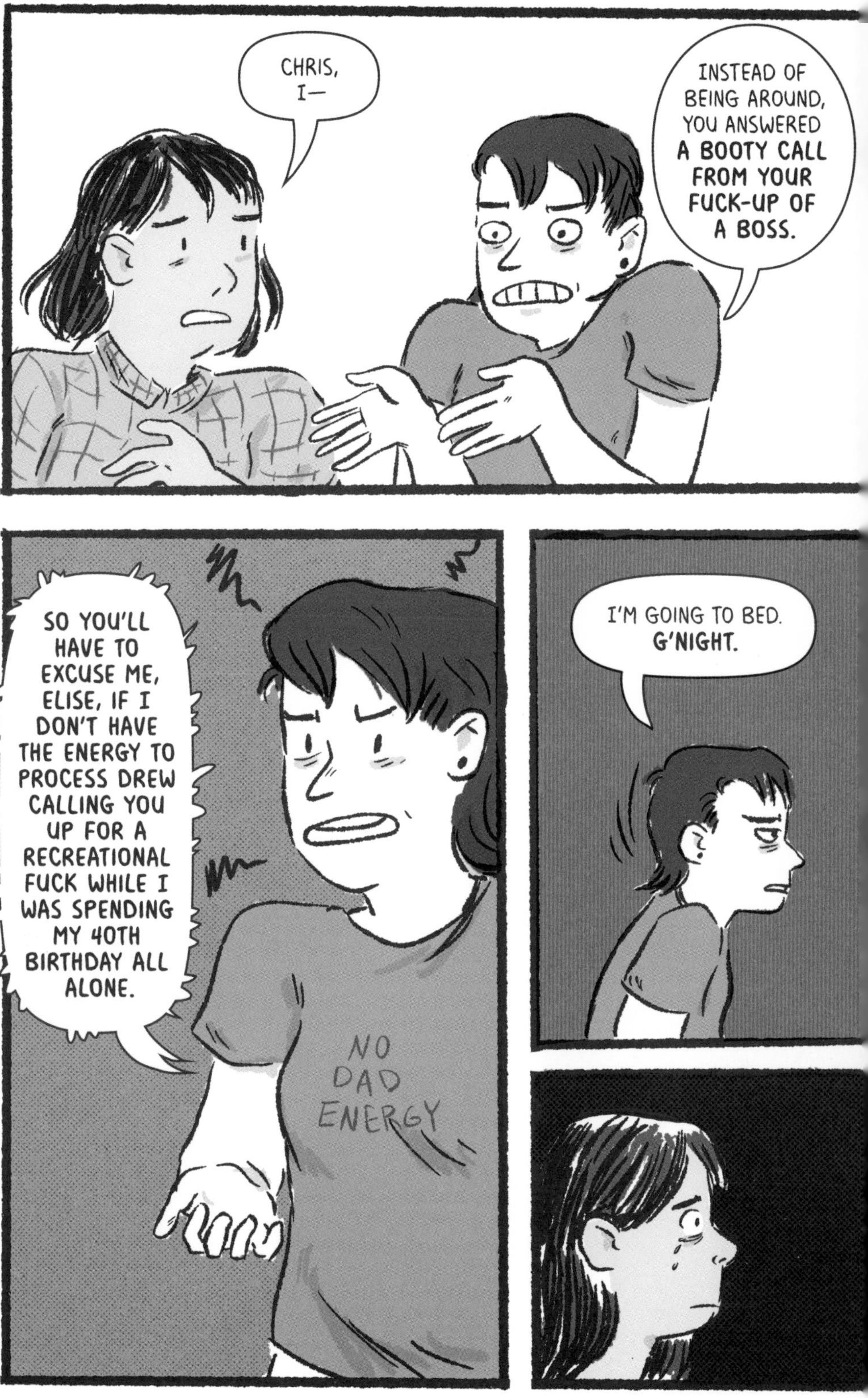
CHRIS, I—
INSTEAD OF BEING AROUND, YOU ANSWERED A BOOTY CALL FROM YOUR FUCK-UP OF A BOSS.
SO YOU'LL HAVE TO EXCUSE ME, ELISE, IF I DON'T HAVE THE ENERGY TO PROCESS DREW CALLING YOU UP FOR A RECREATIONAL FUCK WHILE I WAS SPENDING MY 40TH BIRTHDAY ALL ALONE.
NO DAD ENERGY
I'M GOING TO BED. G'NIGHT.

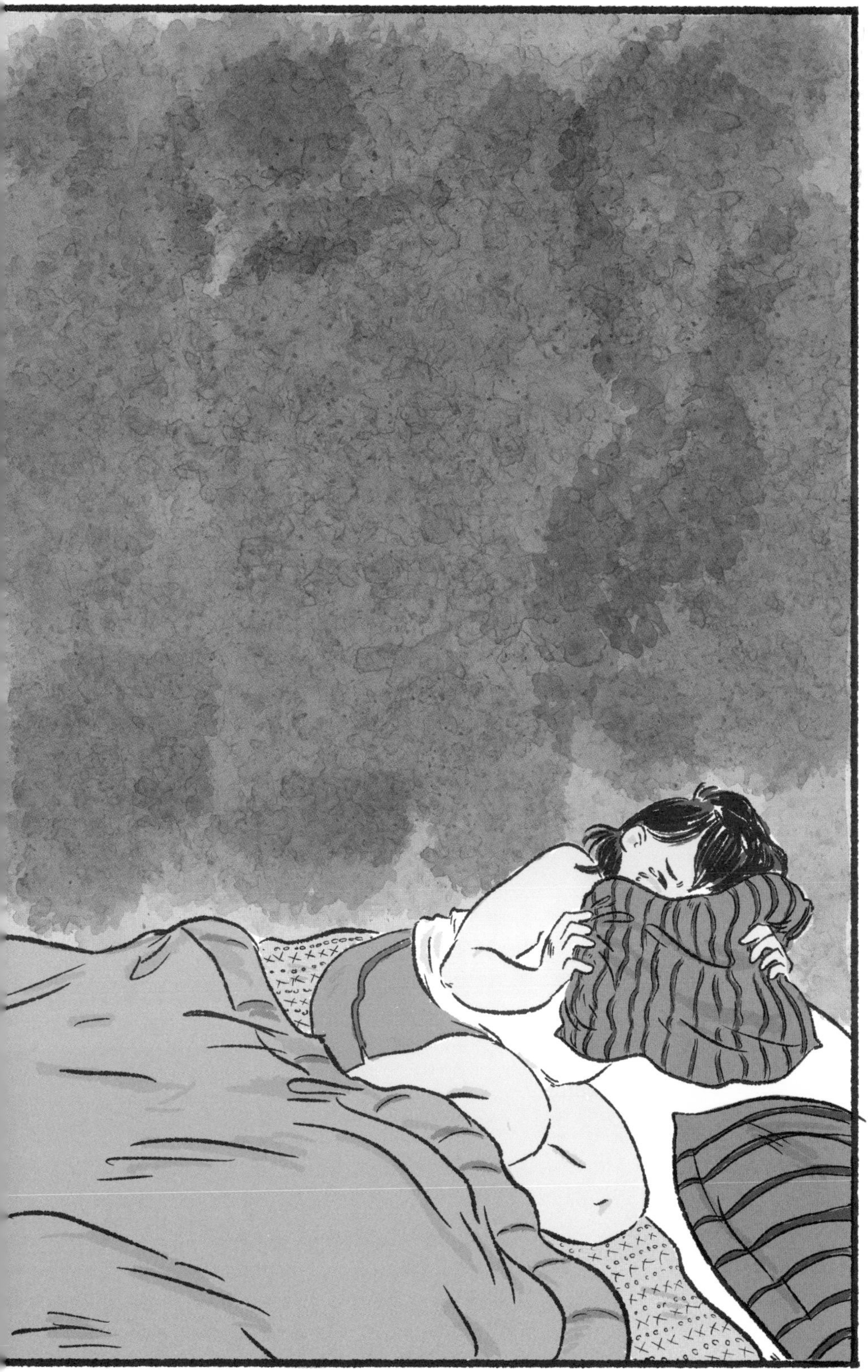

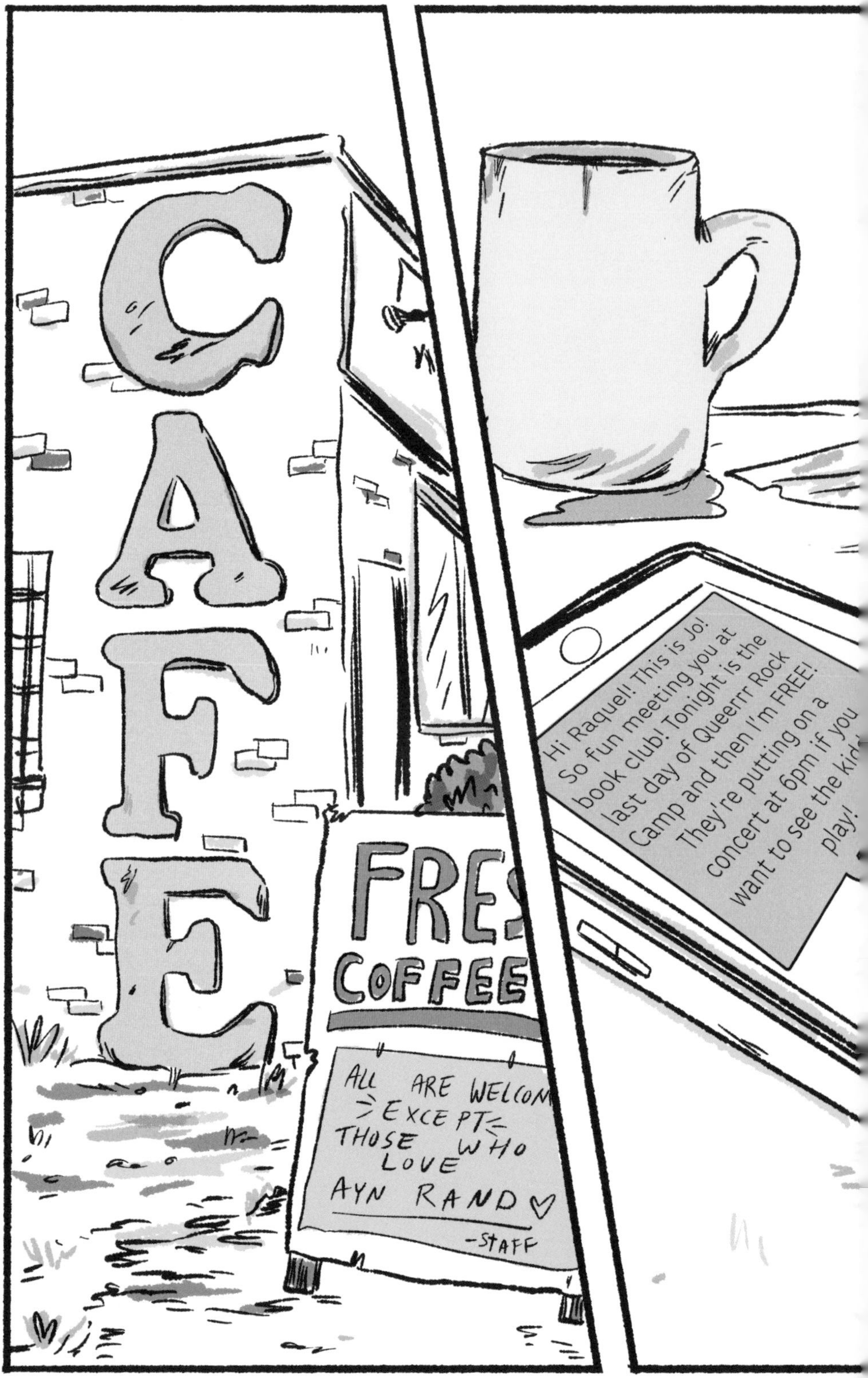
CAFE
FRES
COFFEE
ALL ARE WELCOM
EXCEPT
THOSE WHO LOVE
AYN RAND
-STAFF
Hi Raquel! This is Jo! So fun meeting you at book club! Tonight is the last day of Queerrr Rock Camp and then I'm FREE! They're putting on a concert at 6pm if you want to see the kid play!

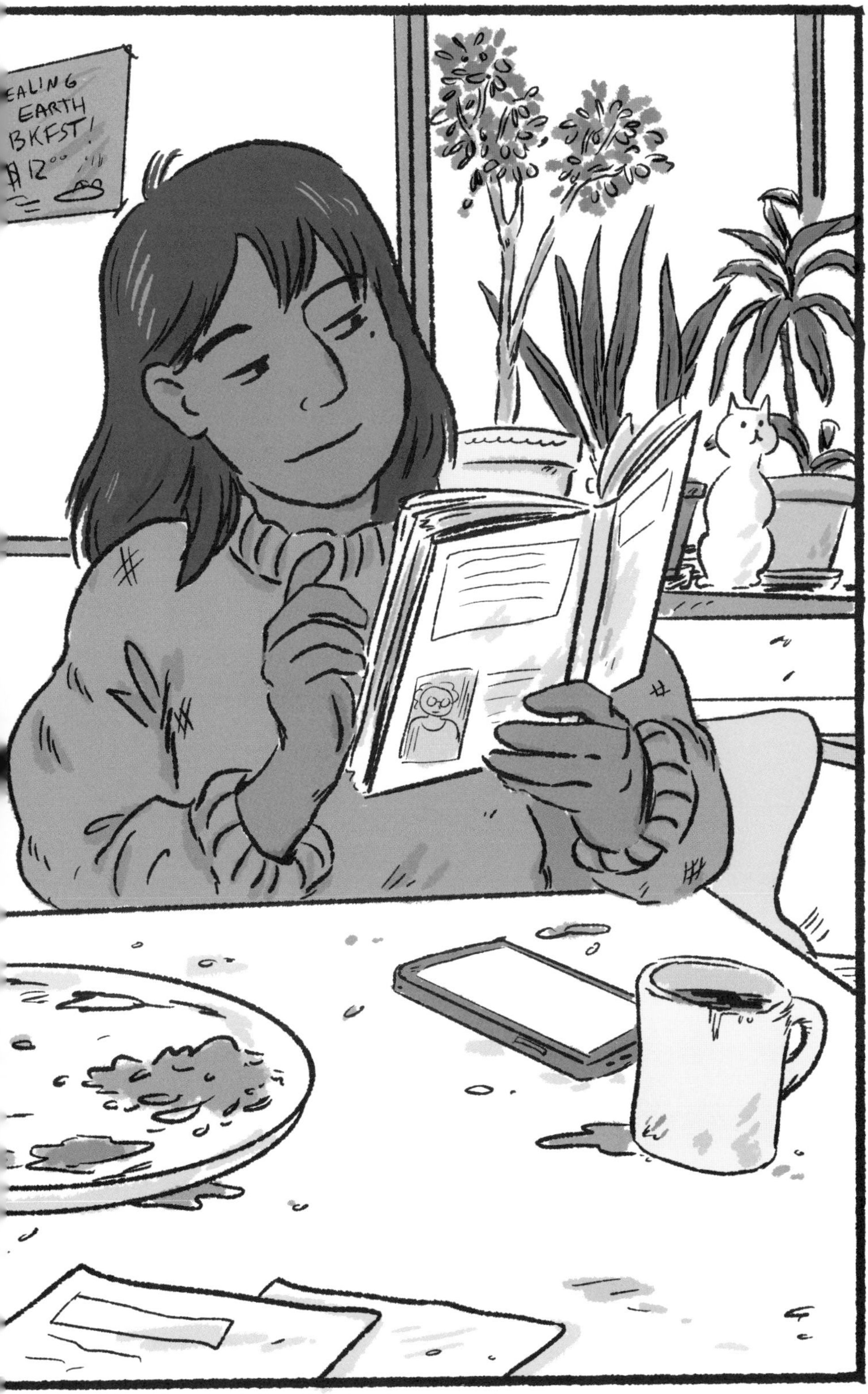
EALING
EARTH
BKFST!
$12

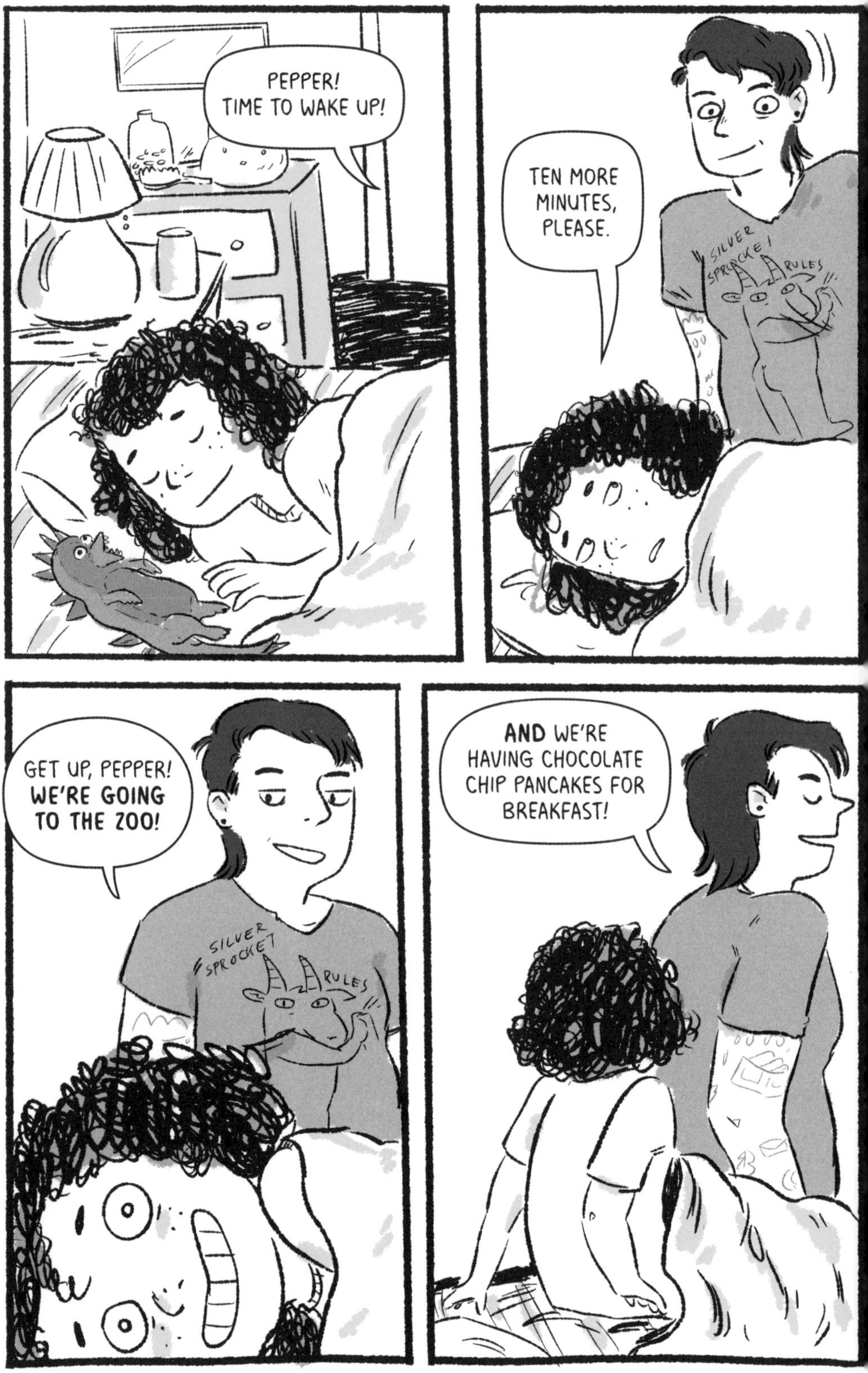
PEPPER! TIME TO WAKE UP!
TEN MORE MINUTES, PLEASE.
SILVER SPROCKET RULES
GET UP, PEPPER! **WE'RE GOING TO THE ZOO!**
SILVER SPROCKET RULES
AND WE'RE HAVING CHOCOLATE CHIP PANCAKES FOR BREAKFAST!

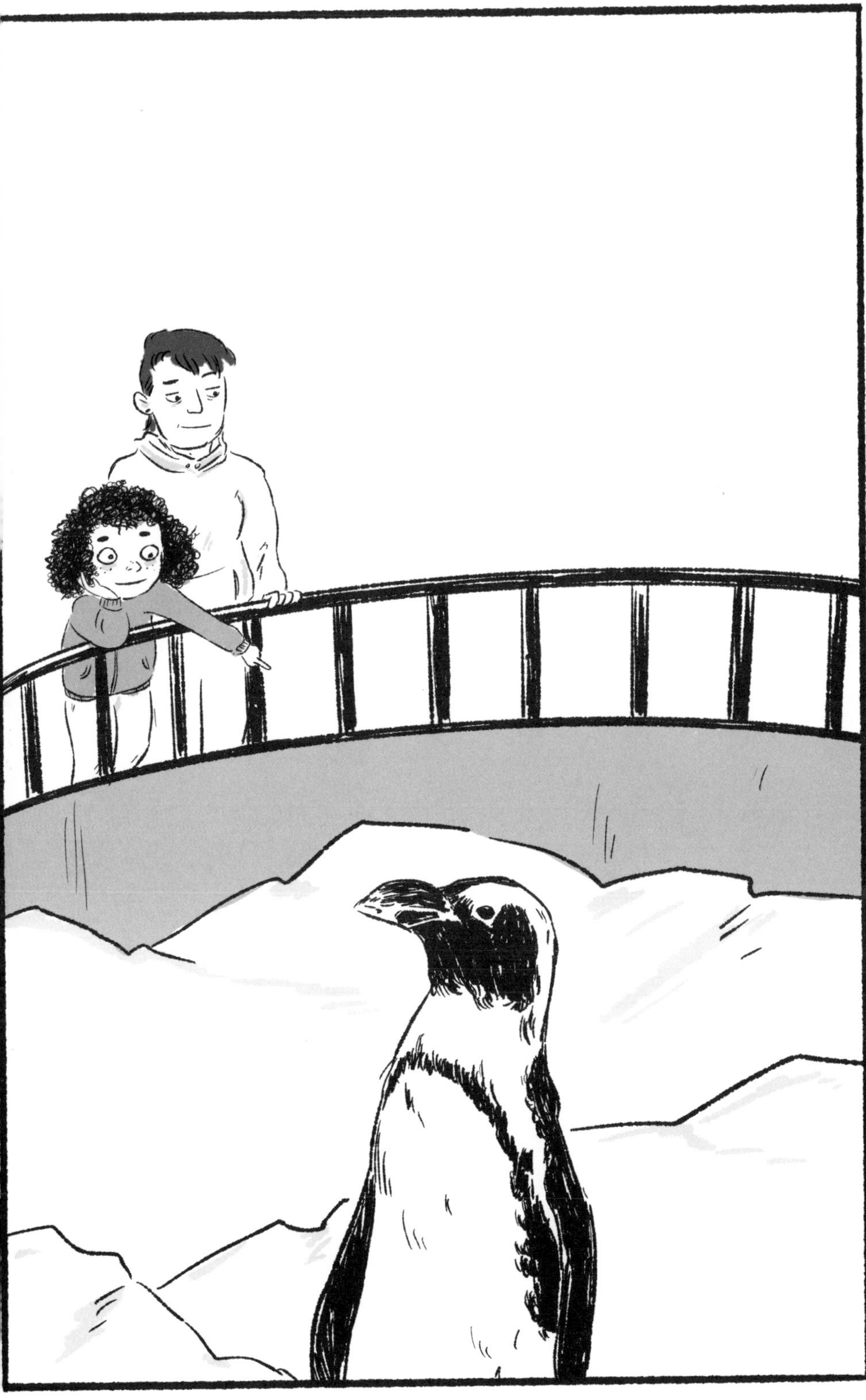

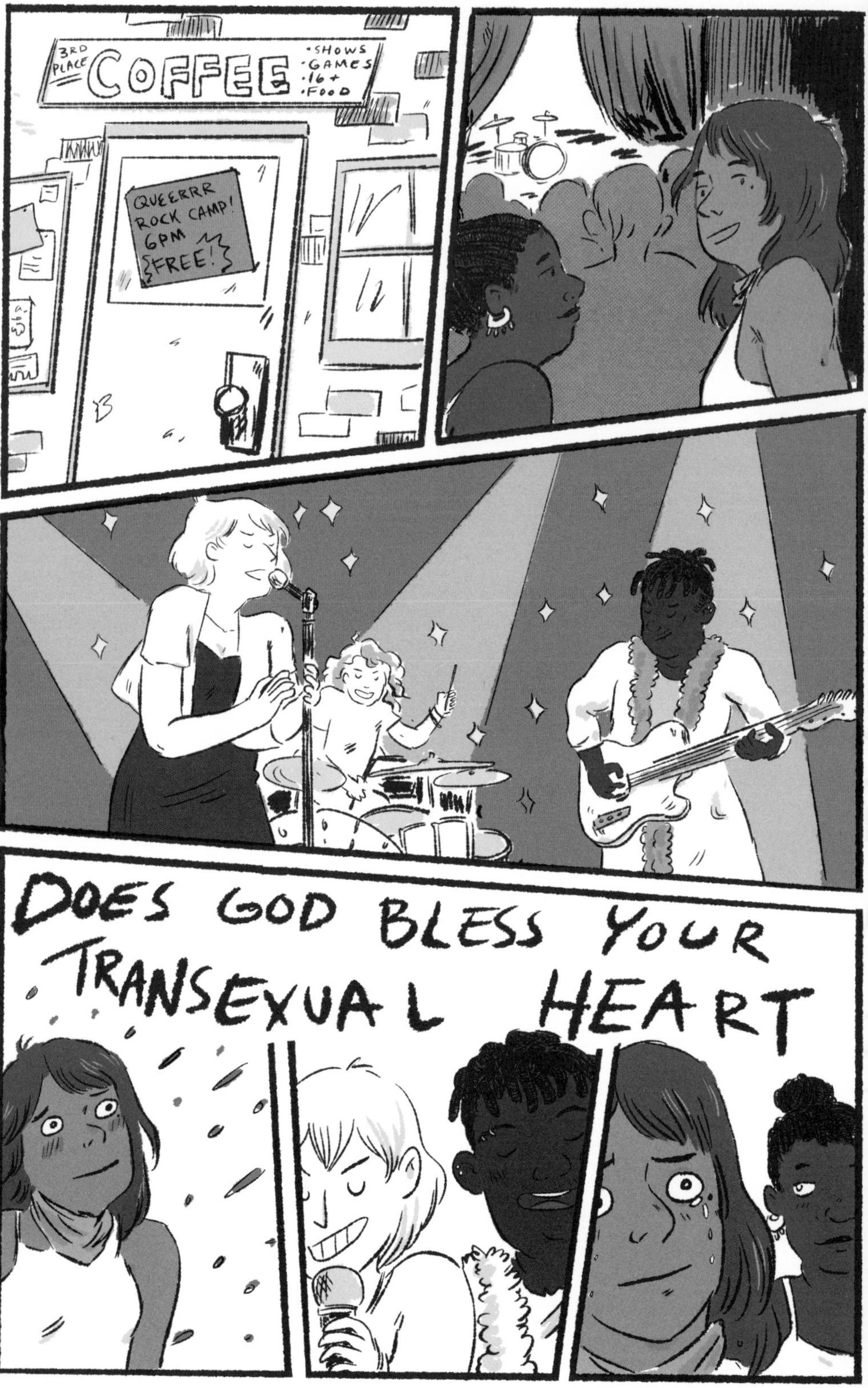
3RD PLACE
COFFEE
•SHOWS
•GAMES
•16+
•FOOD
QUEERRR ROCK CAMP! 6PM FREE!
DOES GOD BLESS YOUR TRANSEXUAL HEART

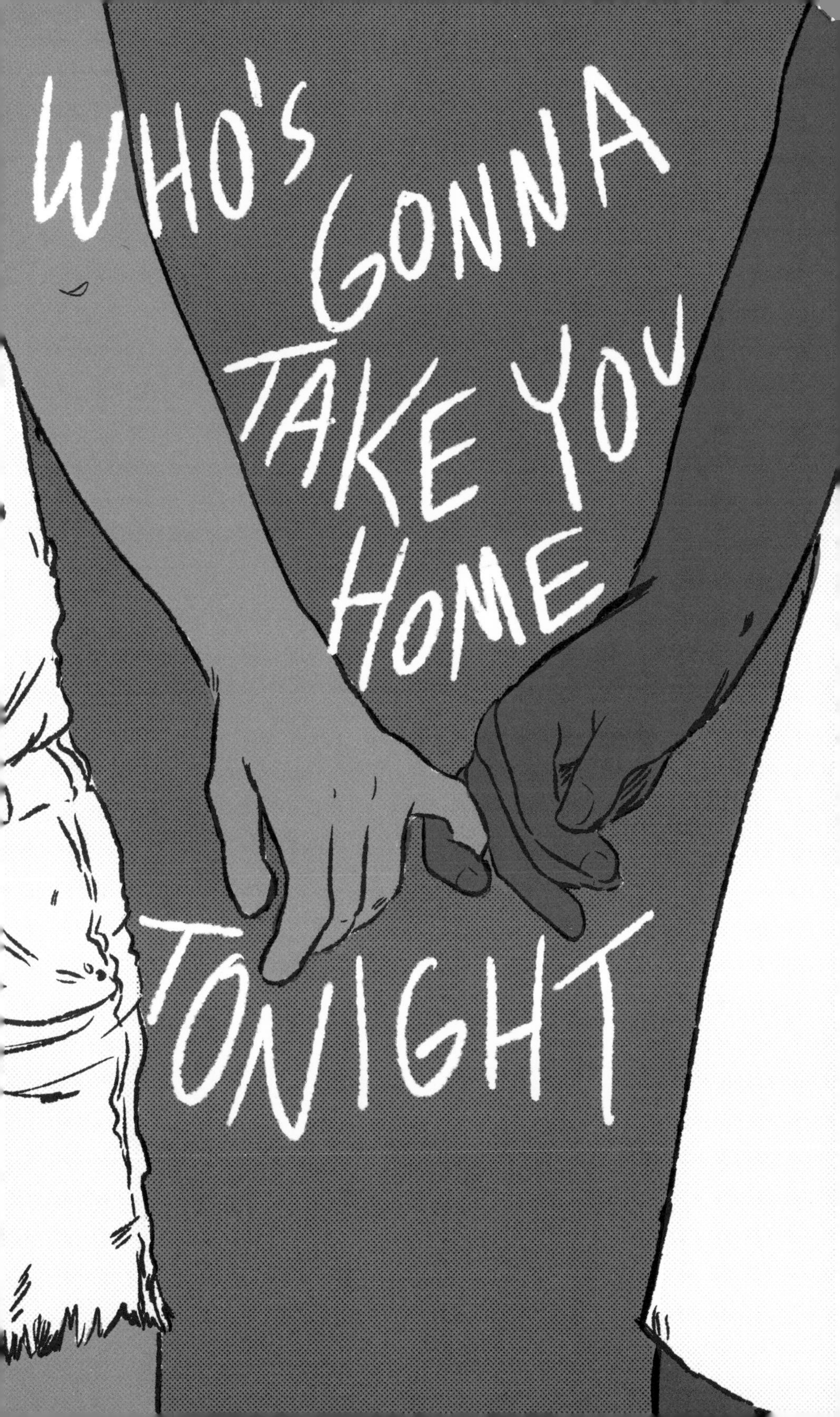
WHO'S GONNA TAKE YOU HOME TONIGHT

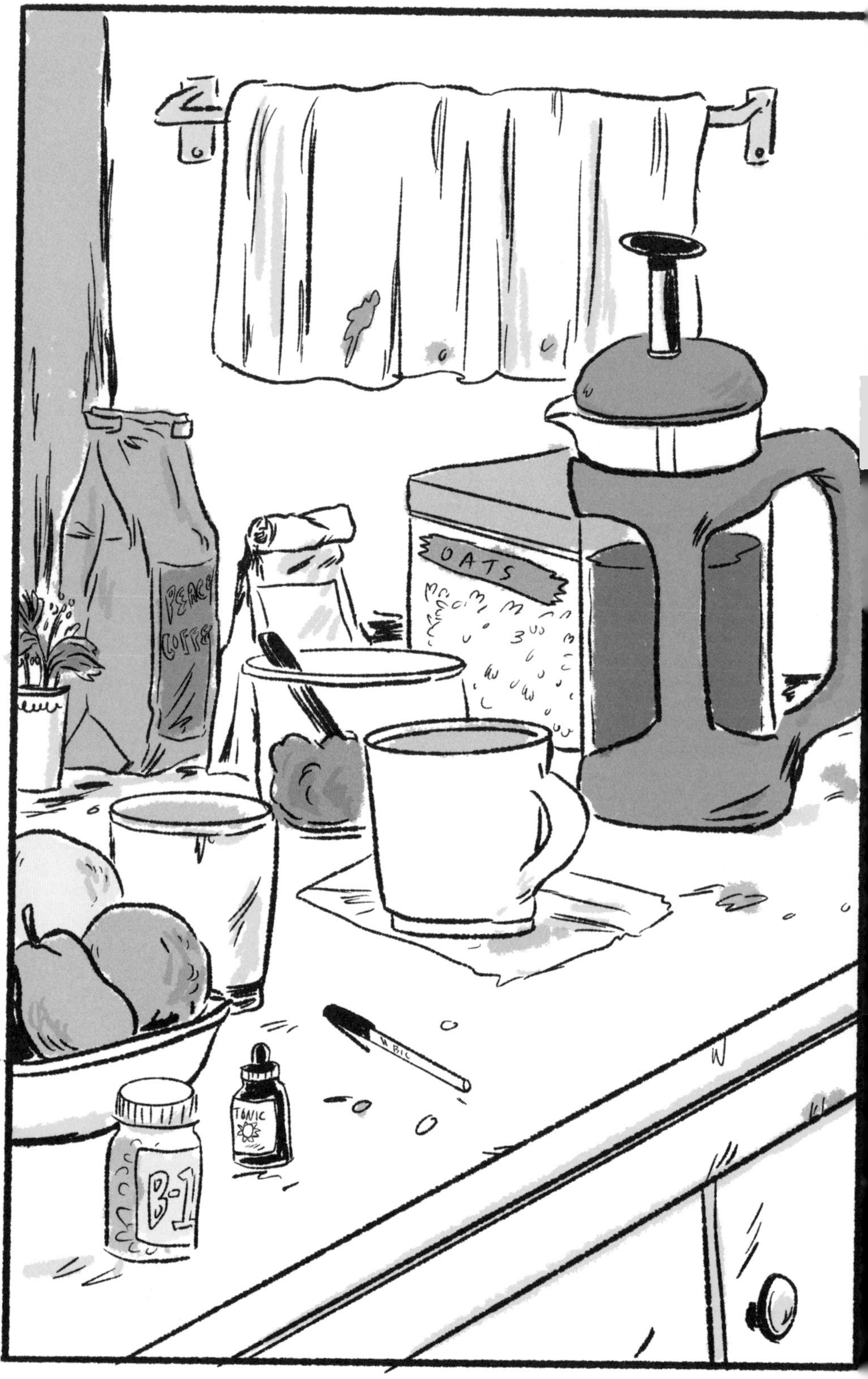
PEAC
COFFE
OATS
BIC
TONIC
B-1

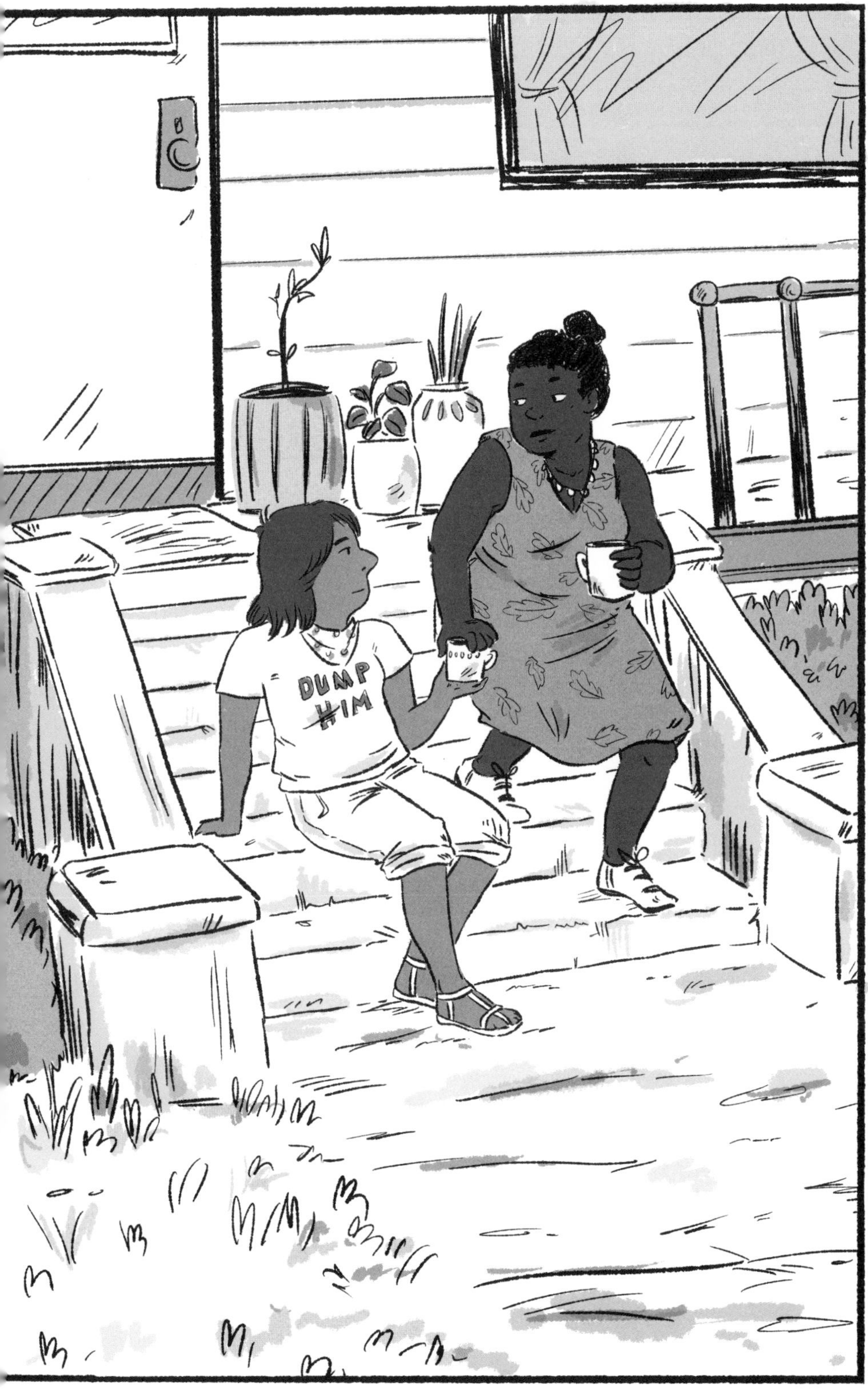
DUMP
HIM

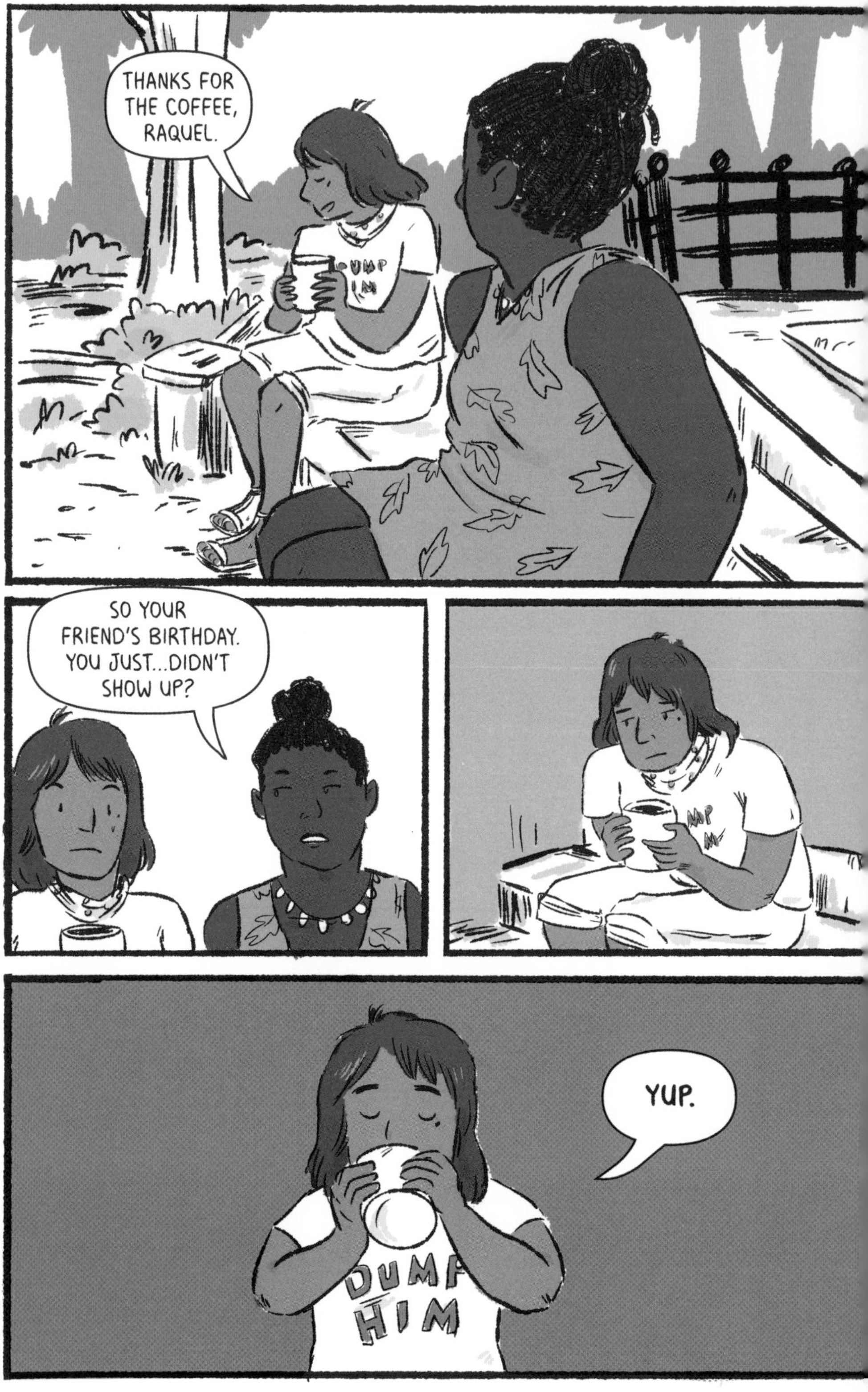

THANKS FOR THE COFFEE, RAQUEL.
SO YOUR FRIEND'S BIRTHDAY. YOU JUST...DIDN'T SHOW UP?
YUP.
DUMP HIM

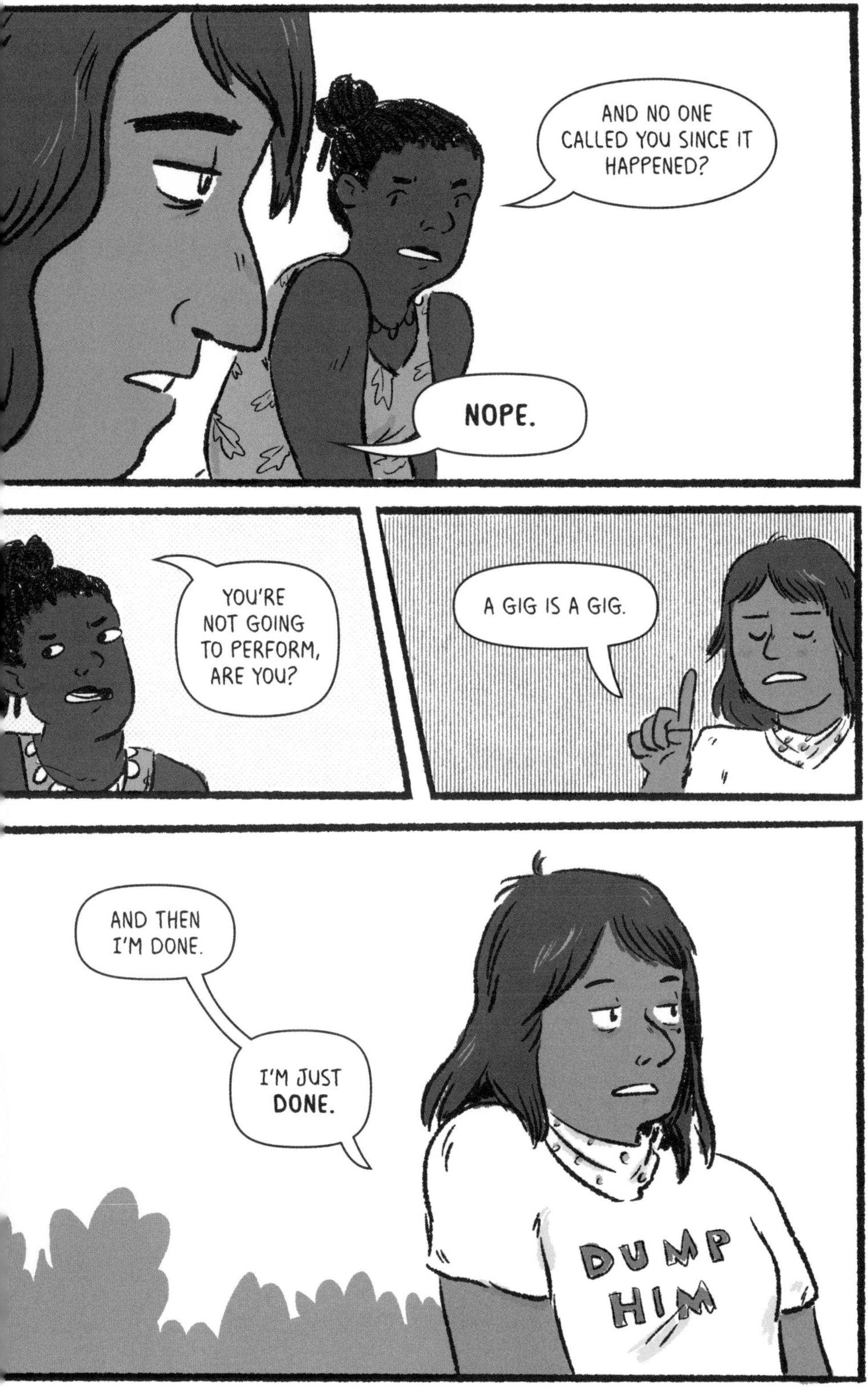
AND NO ONE CALLED YOU SINCE IT HAPPENED?
NOPE.
YOU'RE NOT GOING TO PERFORM, ARE YOU?
A GIG IS A GIG.
AND THEN I'M DONE.
I'M JUST **DONE.**
DUMP HIM

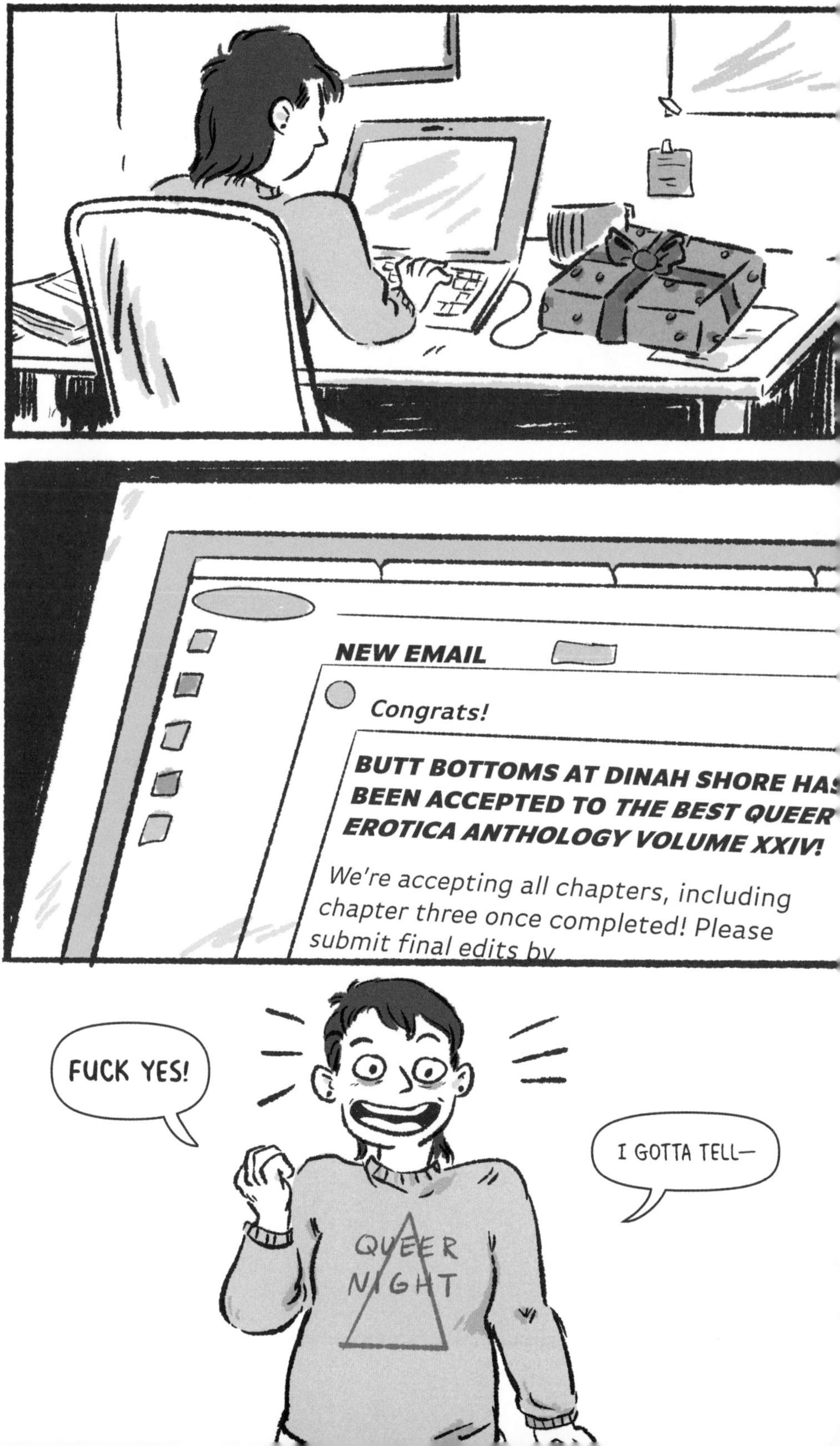
NEW EMAIL
Congrats!
BUTT BOTTOMS AT DINAH SHORE HAS BEEN ACCEPTED TO THE BEST QUEER EROTICA ANTHOLOGY VOLUME XXIV!
We're accepting all chapters, including chapter three once completed! Please submit final edits by
FUCK YES!
I GOTTA TELL—
QUEER NIGHT

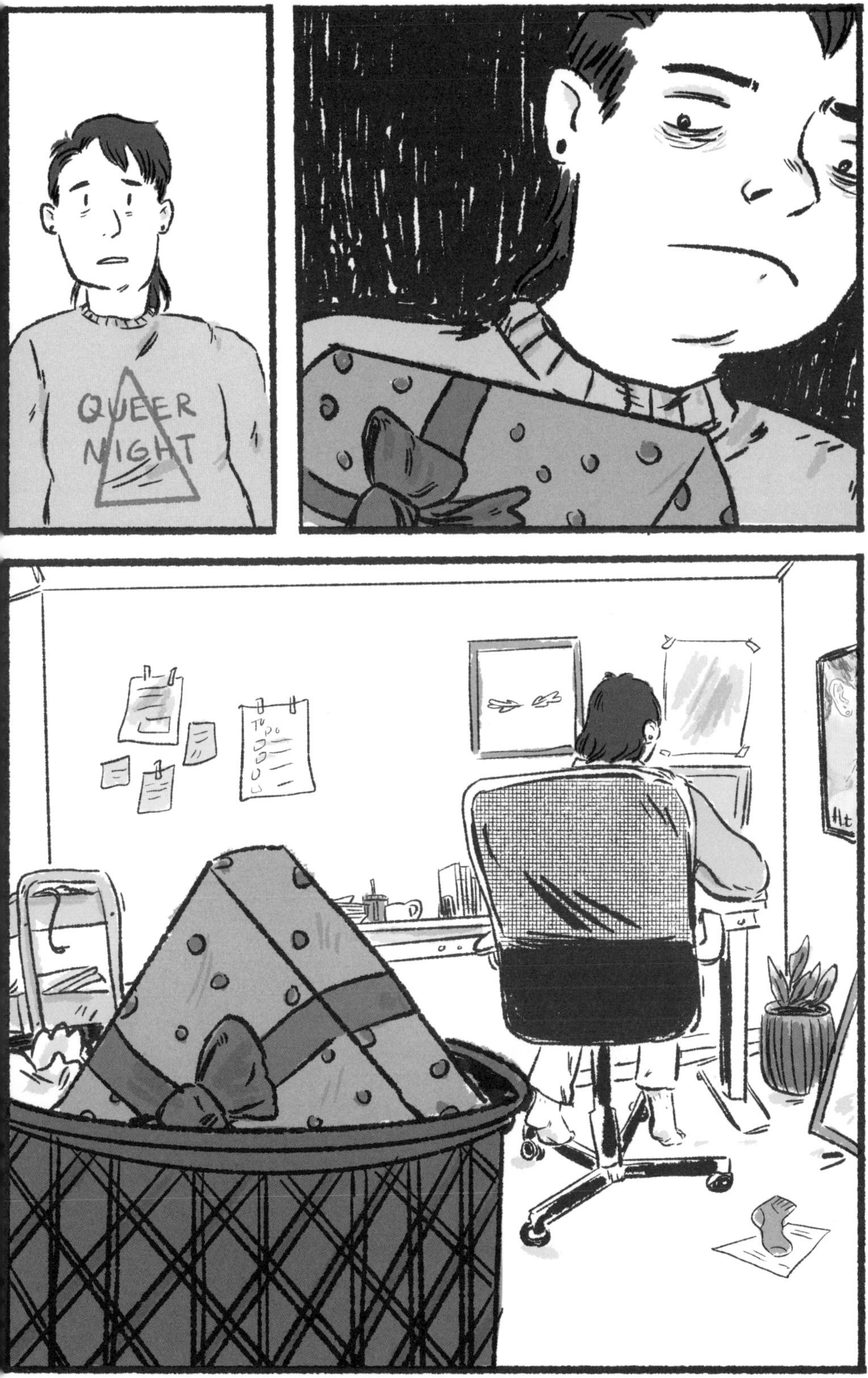
QUEER
NIGHT

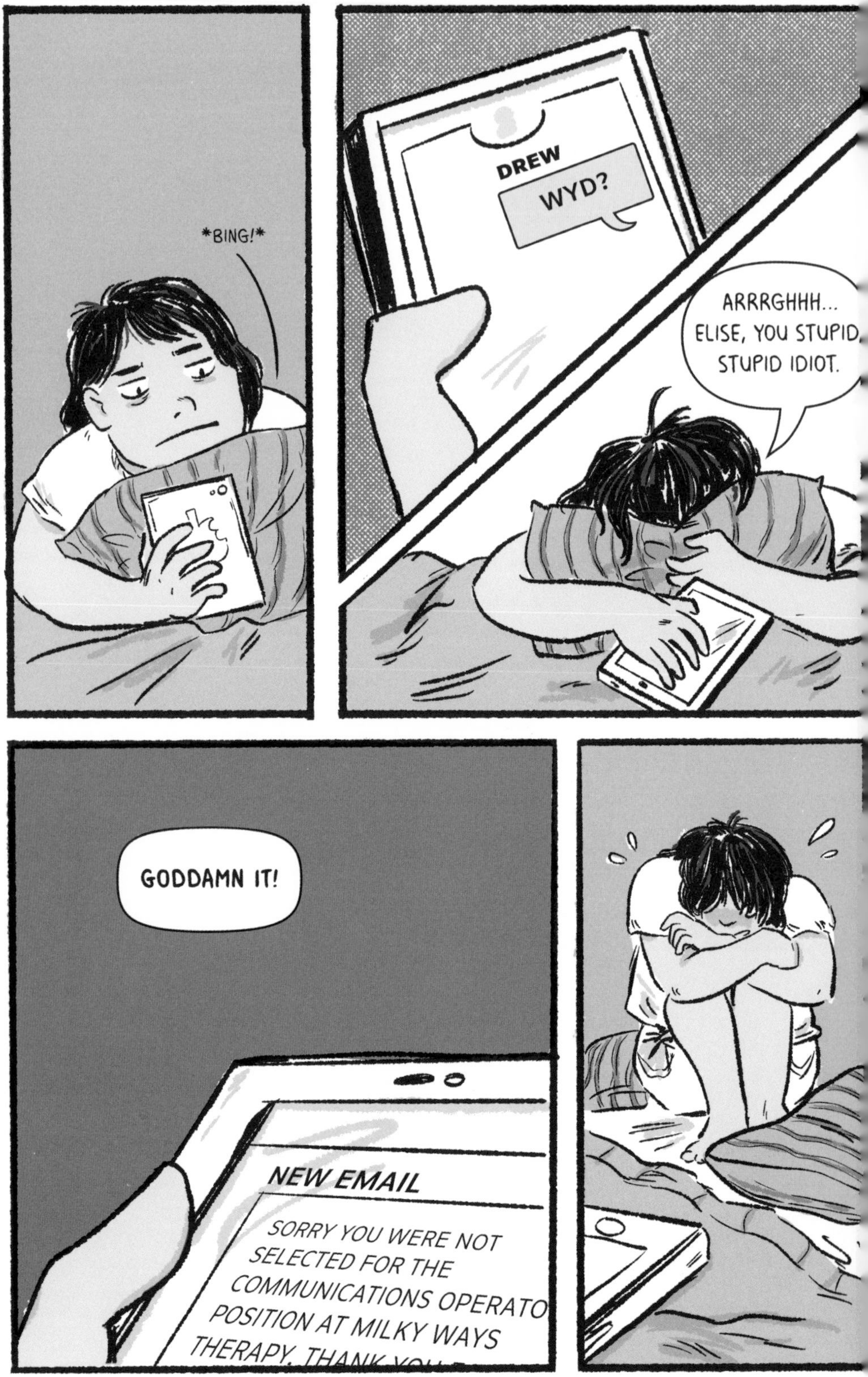
BING!
DREW
WYD?
ARRRGHHH... ELISE, YOU STUPID, STUPID IDIOT.
GODDAMN IT!
NEW EMAIL
SORRY YOU WERE NOT SELECTED FOR THE COMMUNICATIONS OPERATO
POSITION AT MILKY WAYS THERAPY.

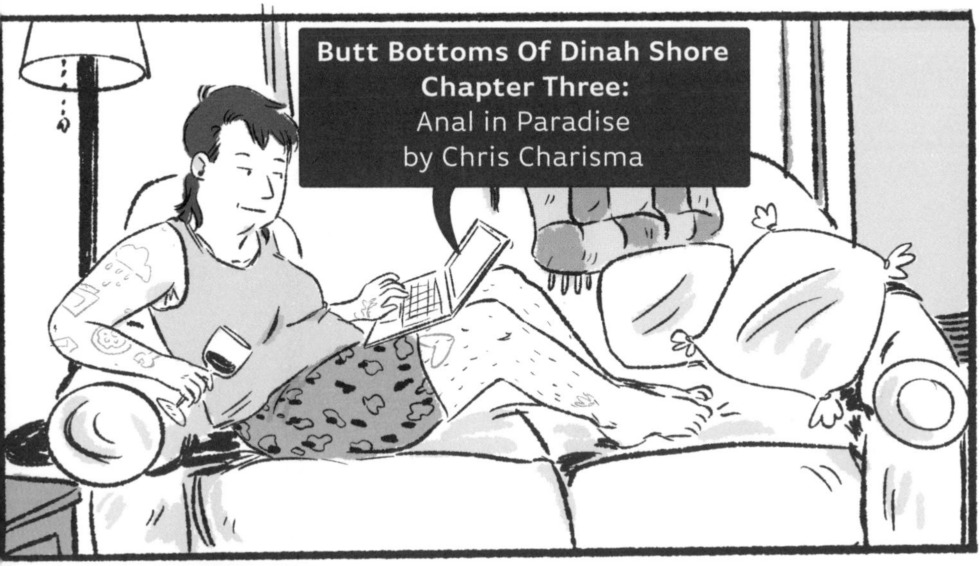
Butt Bottoms Of Dinah Shore
Chapter Three:
Anal in Paradise
by Chris Charisma

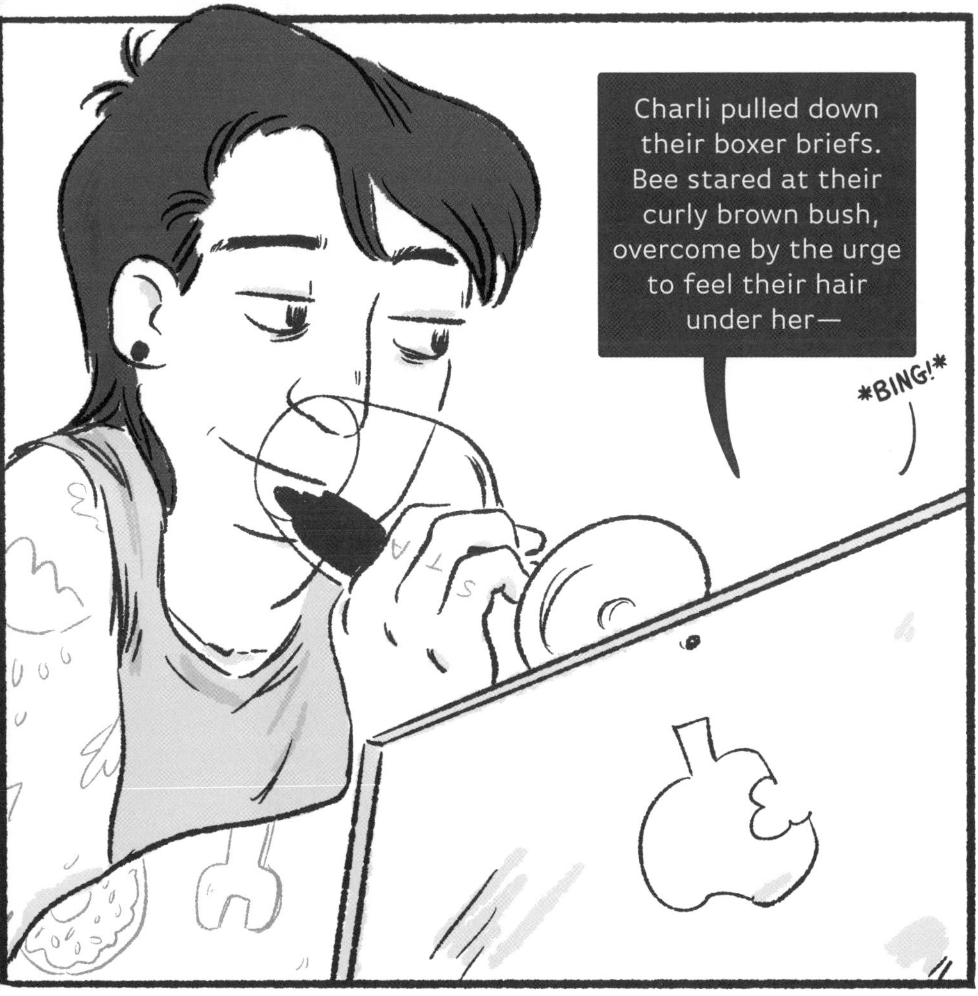
Charli pulled down their boxer briefs. Bee stared at their curly brown bush, overcome by the urge to feel their hair under her—
BING!

I WAS GETTING TO THE GOOD PART, FACEBOOK.

"REMINDER: YOU RSVPED AS GOING TO **GRIND TWO:** THE HOTTEST AND THIRSTIEST QUEER DANCE NIGHT FOR GAYS IN THEIR PRIME!"

AAAAAND THAT'S GONNA BE A "DECLINE" FROM ME, BRO.

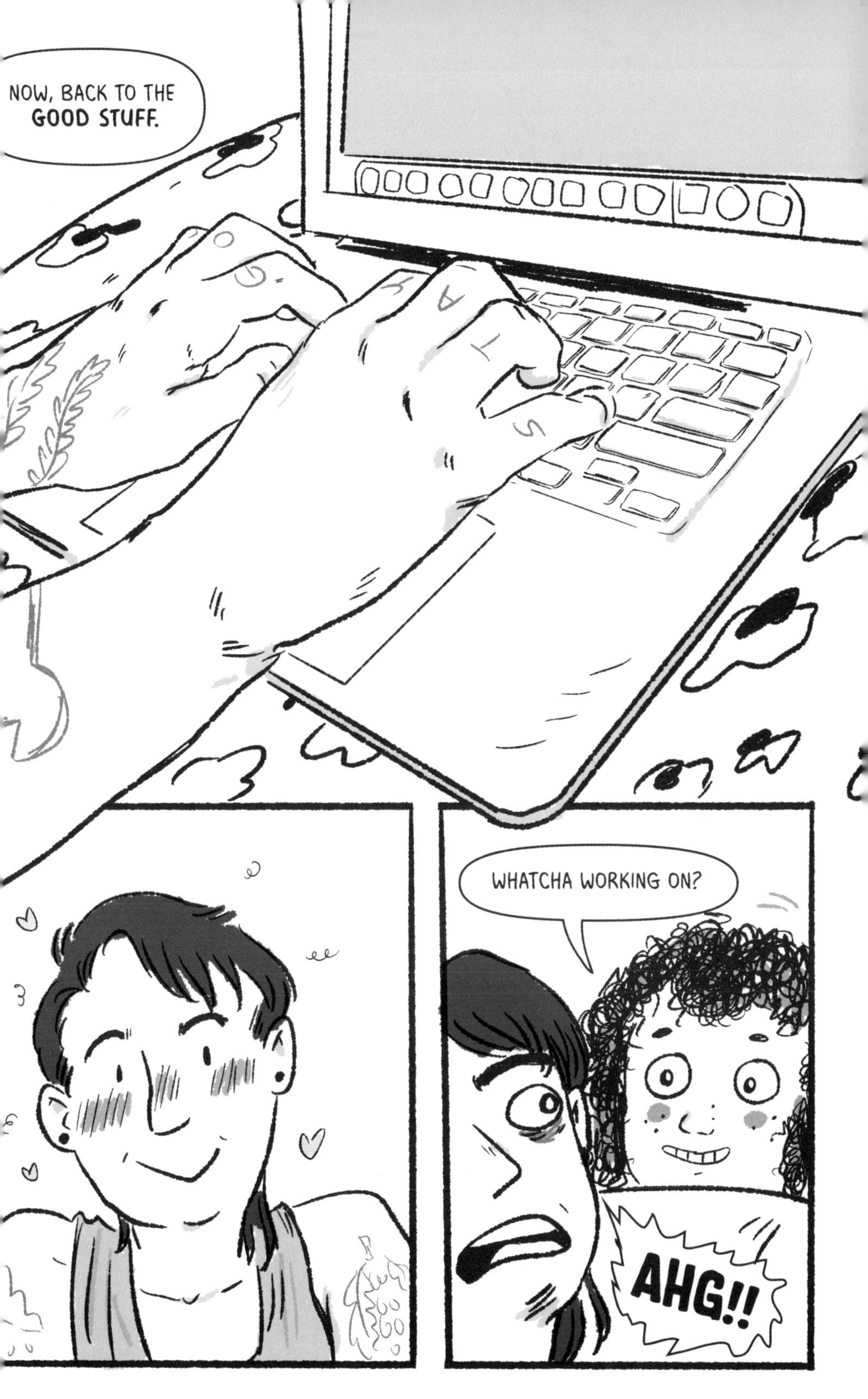
NOW, BACK TO THE **GOOD STUFF.**
WHATCHA WORKING ON?
AHG!!

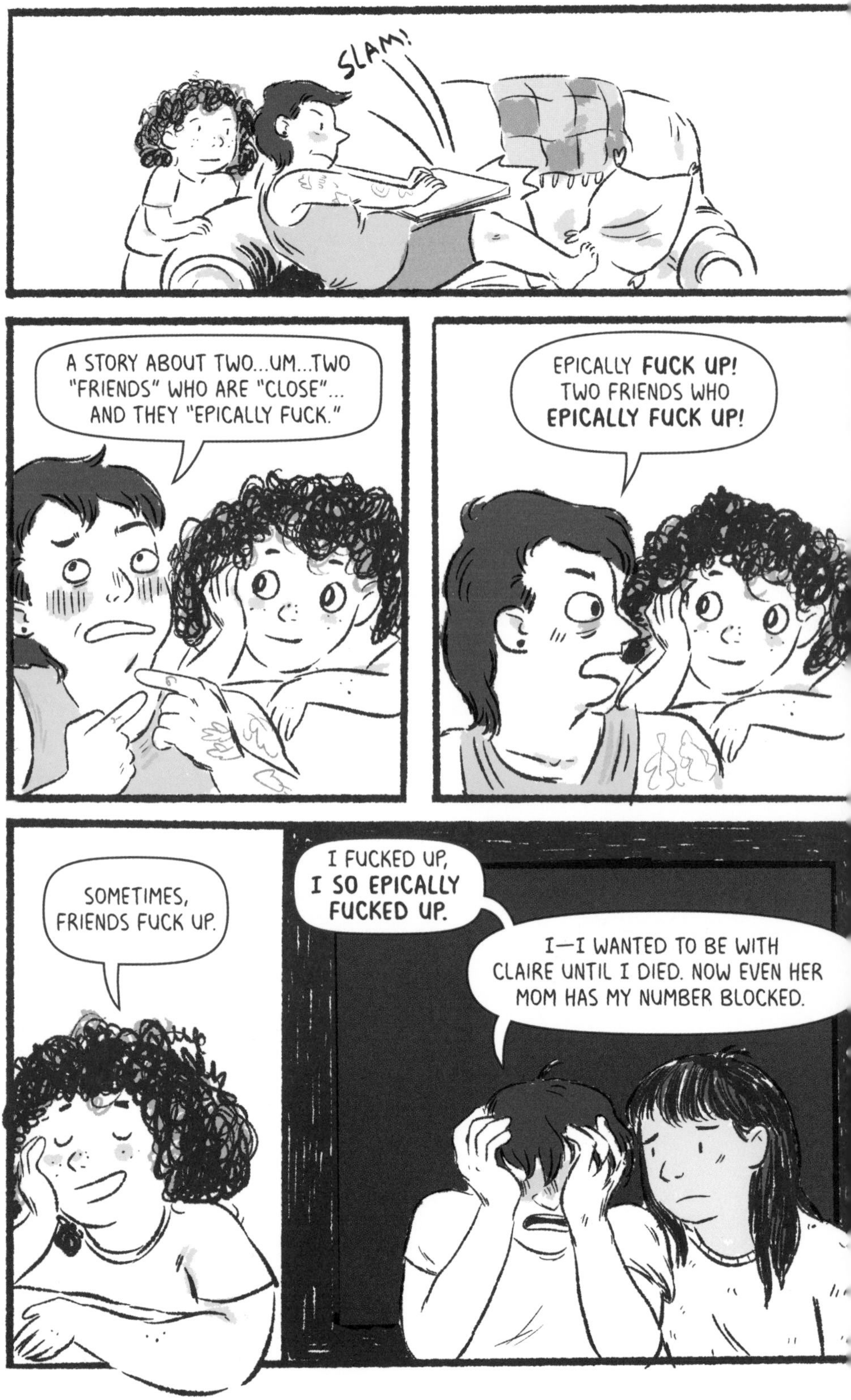
SLAM!
A STORY ABOUT TWO...UM...TWO "FRIENDS" WHO ARE "CLOSE"... AND THEY "EPICALLY FUCK."
EPICALLY **FUCK UP!** TWO FRIENDS WHO **EPICALLY FUCK UP!**
SOMETIMES, FRIENDS FUCK UP.
I FUCKED UP, **I SO EPICALLY FUCKED UP.**
I—I WANTED TO BE WITH CLAIRE UNTIL I DIED. NOW EVEN HER MOM HAS MY NUMBER BLOCKED.

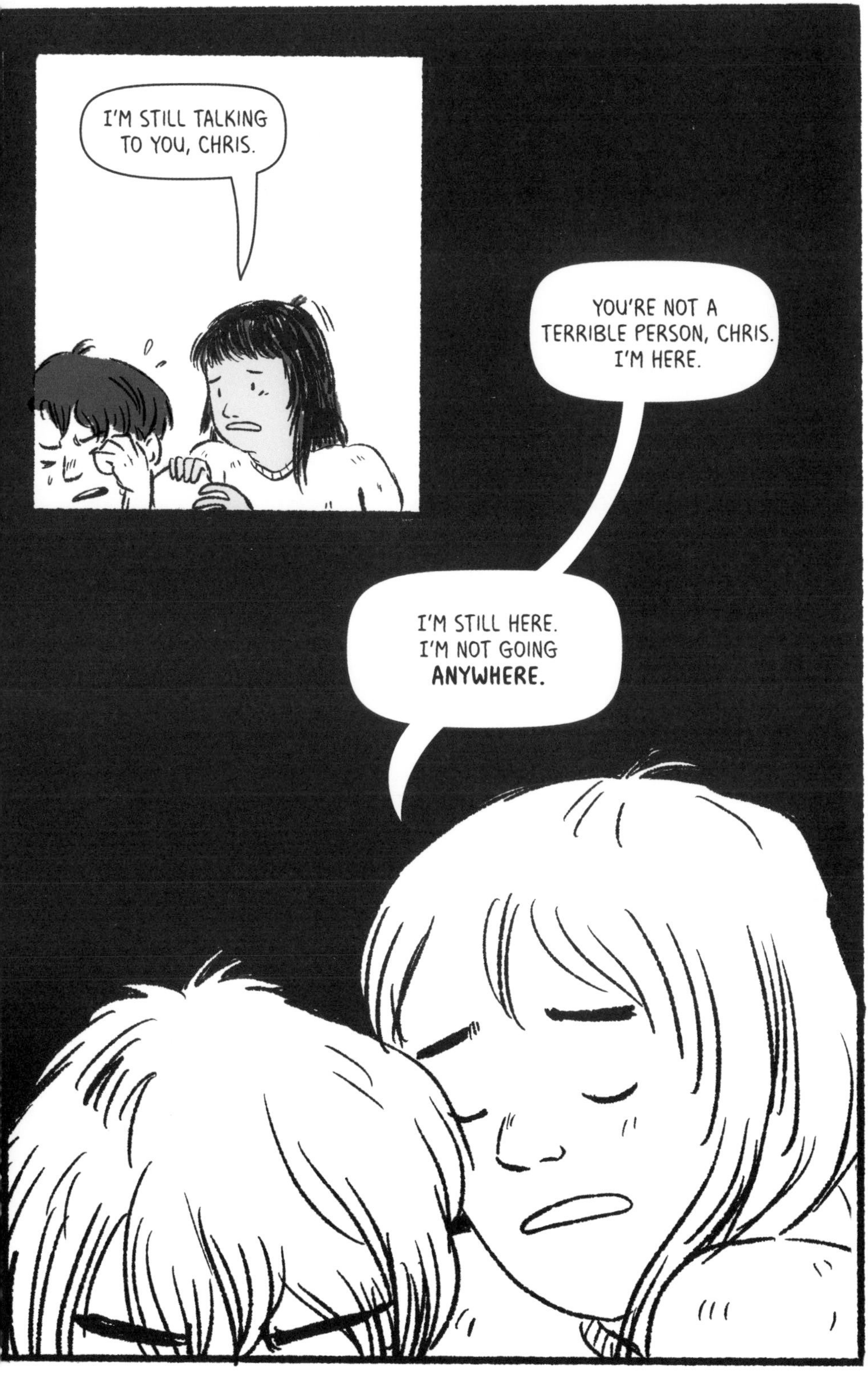
I'M STILL TALKING TO YOU, CHRIS.
YOU'RE NOT A TERRIBLE PERSON, CHRIS. I'M HERE.
I'M STILL HERE. I'M NOT GOING **ANYWHERE.**

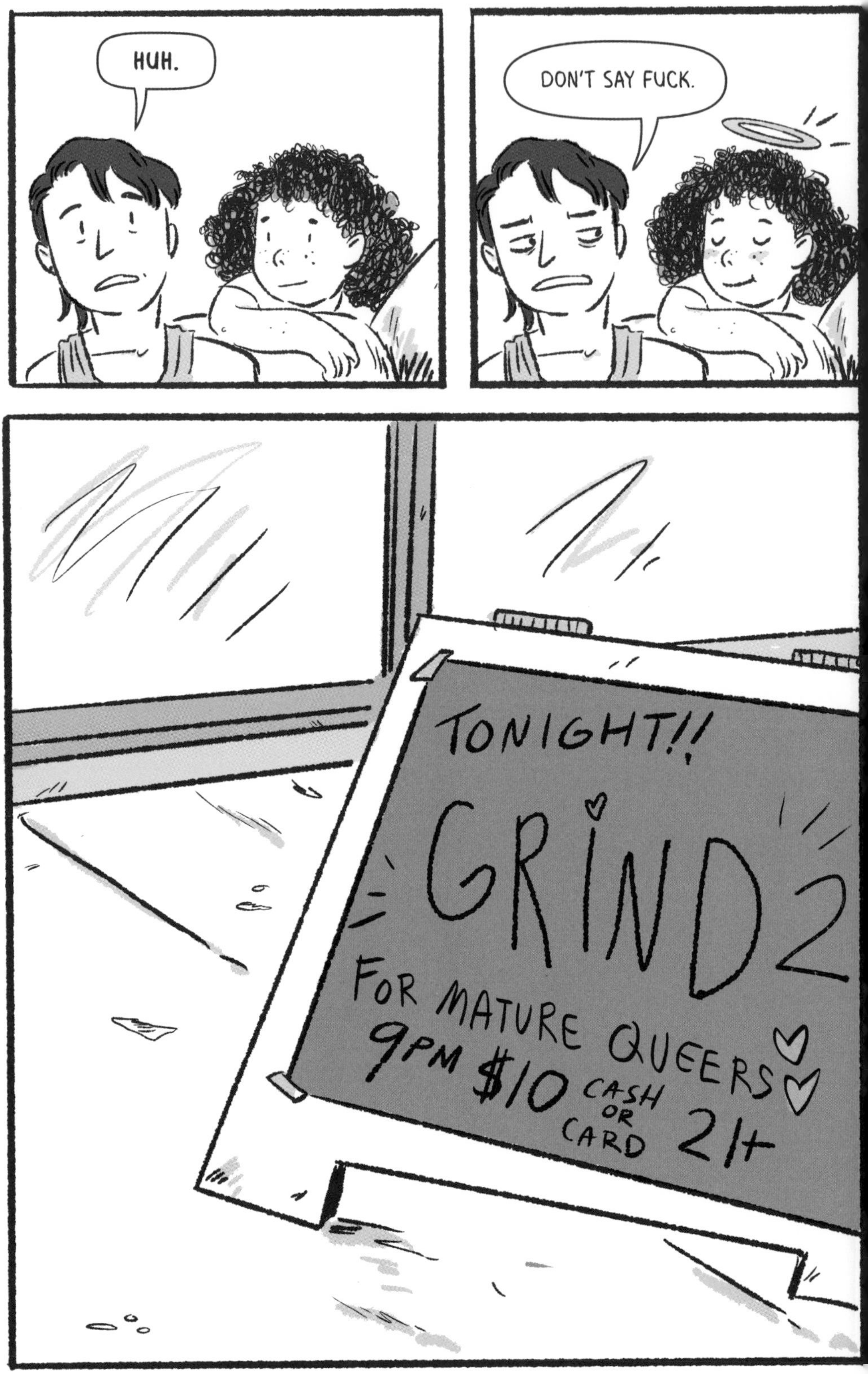
HUH.
DON'T SAY FUCK.
TONIGHT!!
GRIND 2
FOR MATURE QUEERS
9PM $10 CASH OR CARD 21+

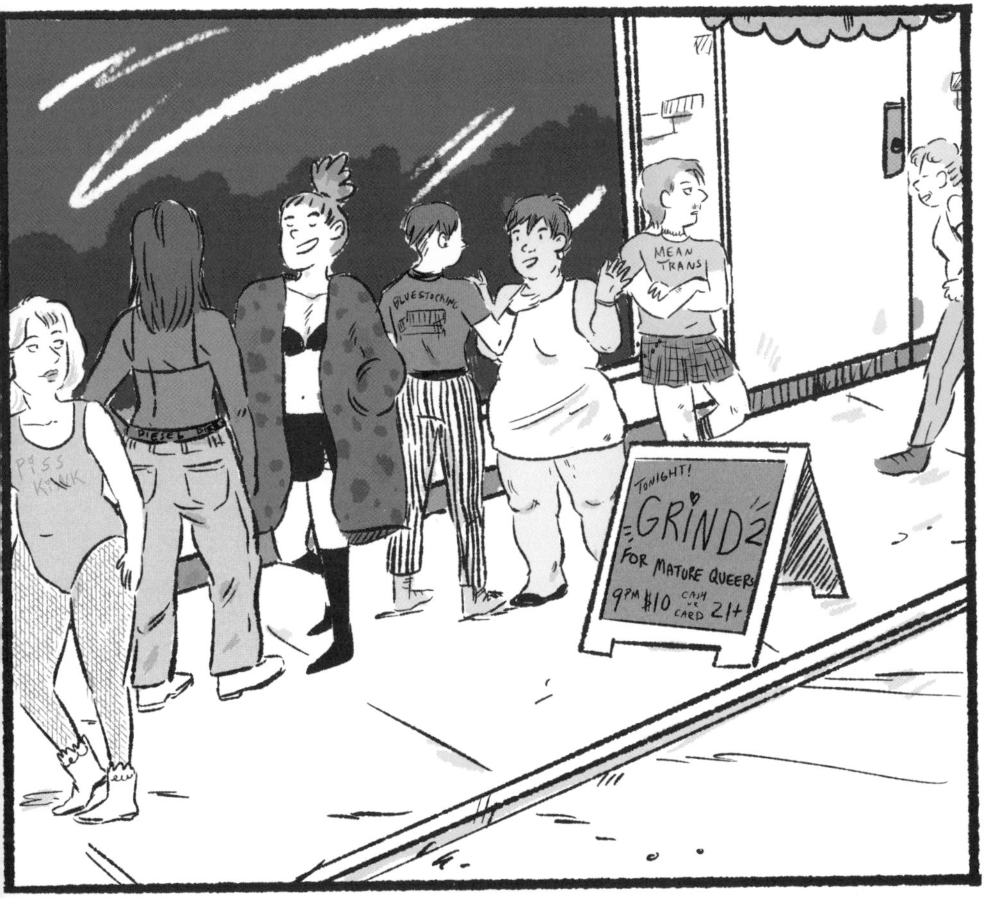
PISS KINK
DIESEL DIESEL
BLUESTOCKING
MEAN TRANS
TONIGHT!
GRIND2
FOR MATURE QUEERS
9PM $10 CASH OR CARD 21+

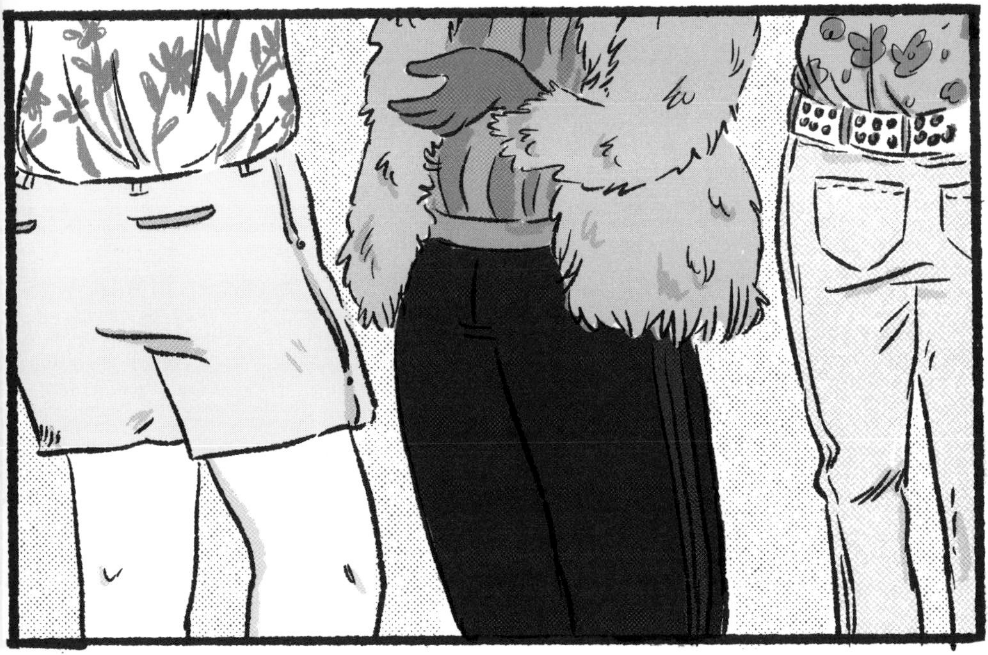

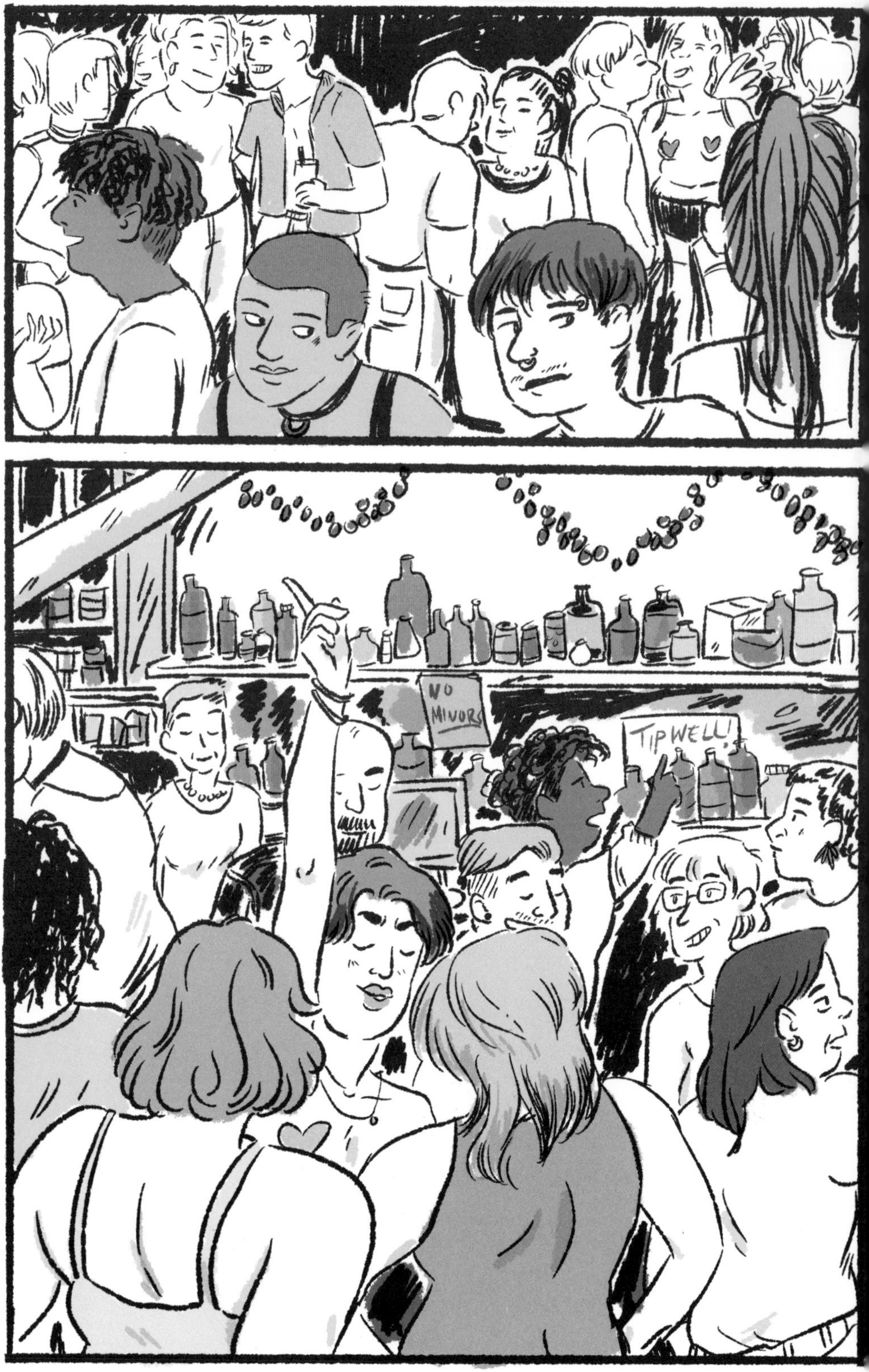
NO MINORS
TIP WELL!

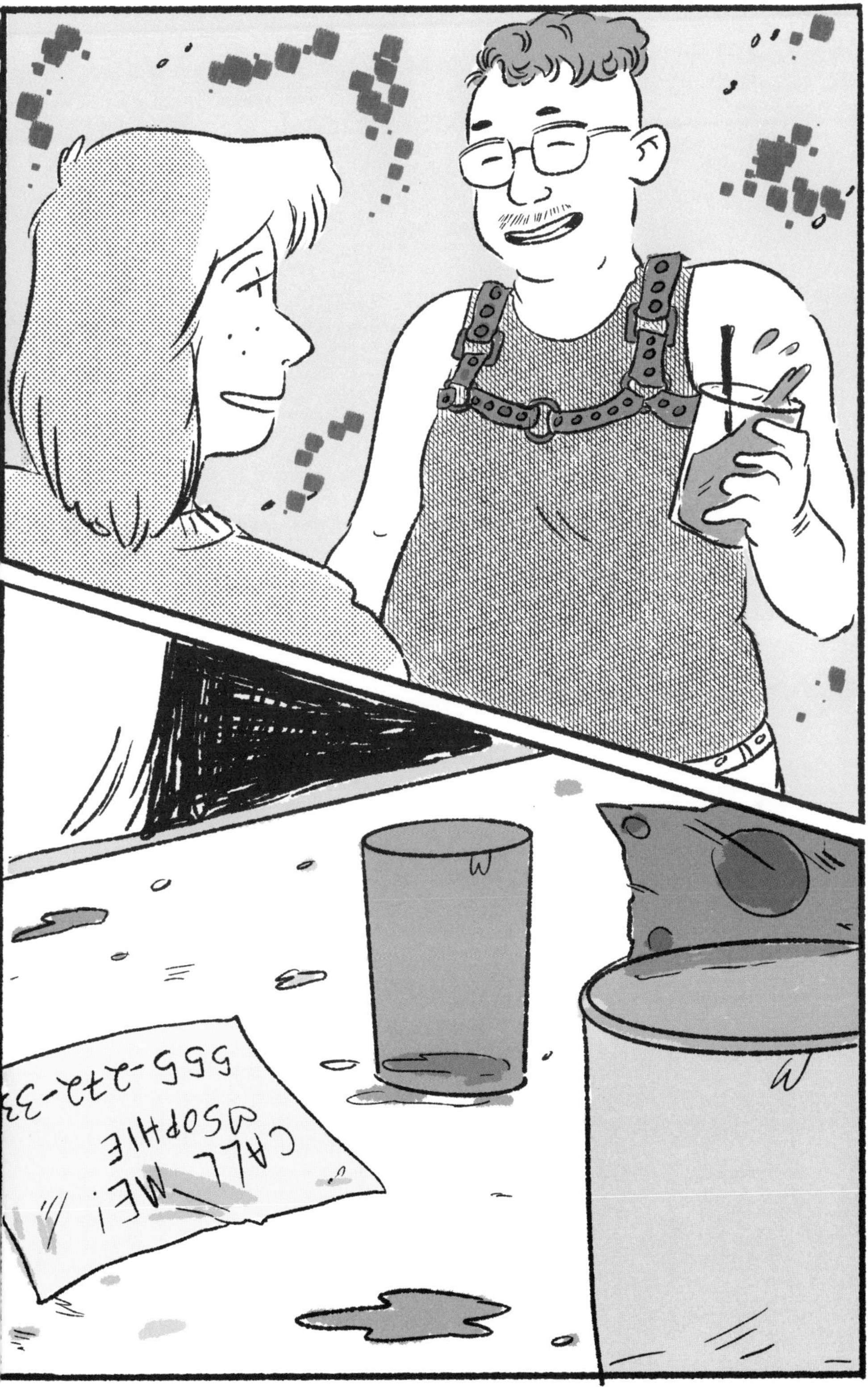
CALL ME!
♡SOPHIE
555-272-33

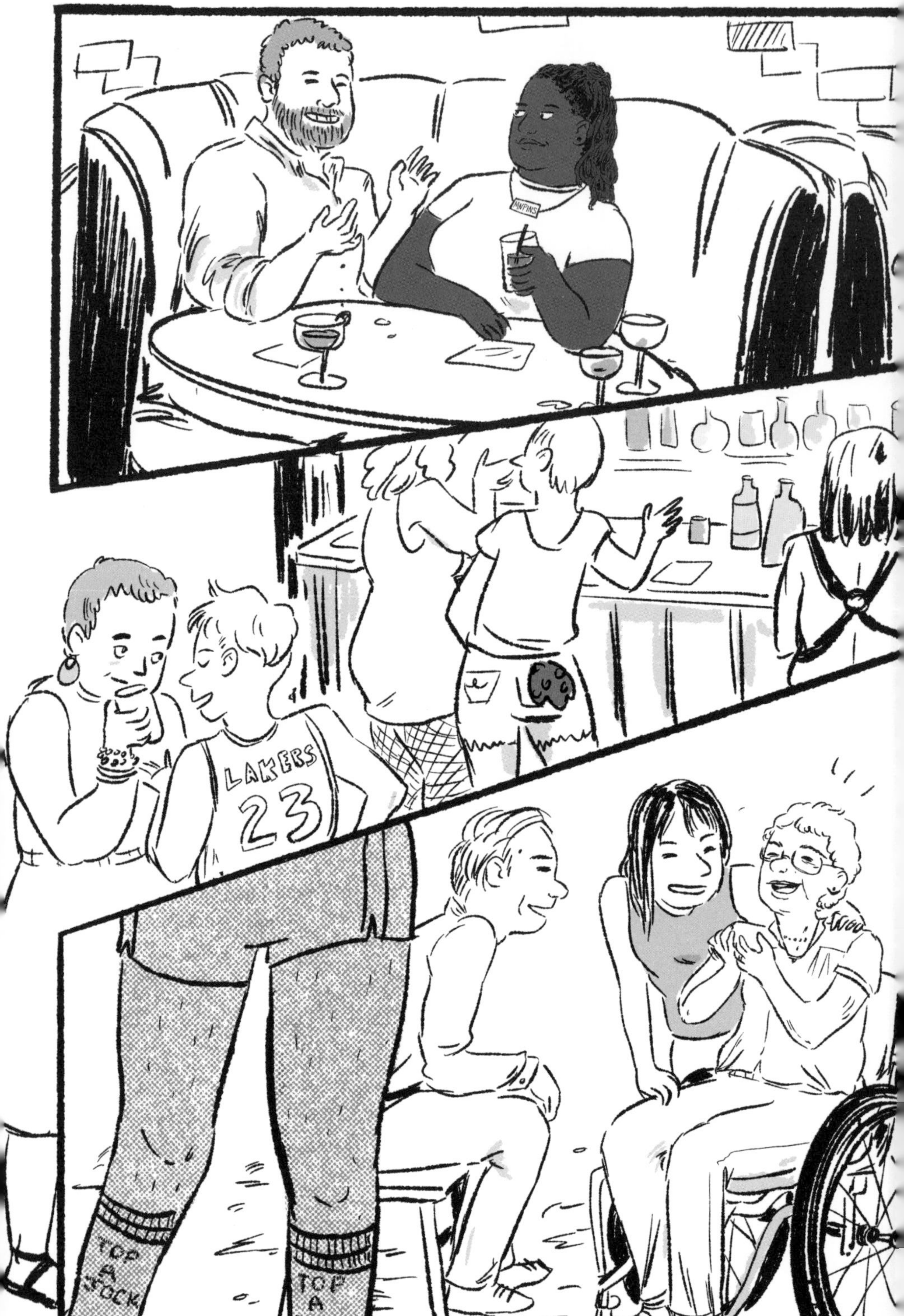
MNPINS
LAKERS
23
TOP A JOCK
TOP A JOCK

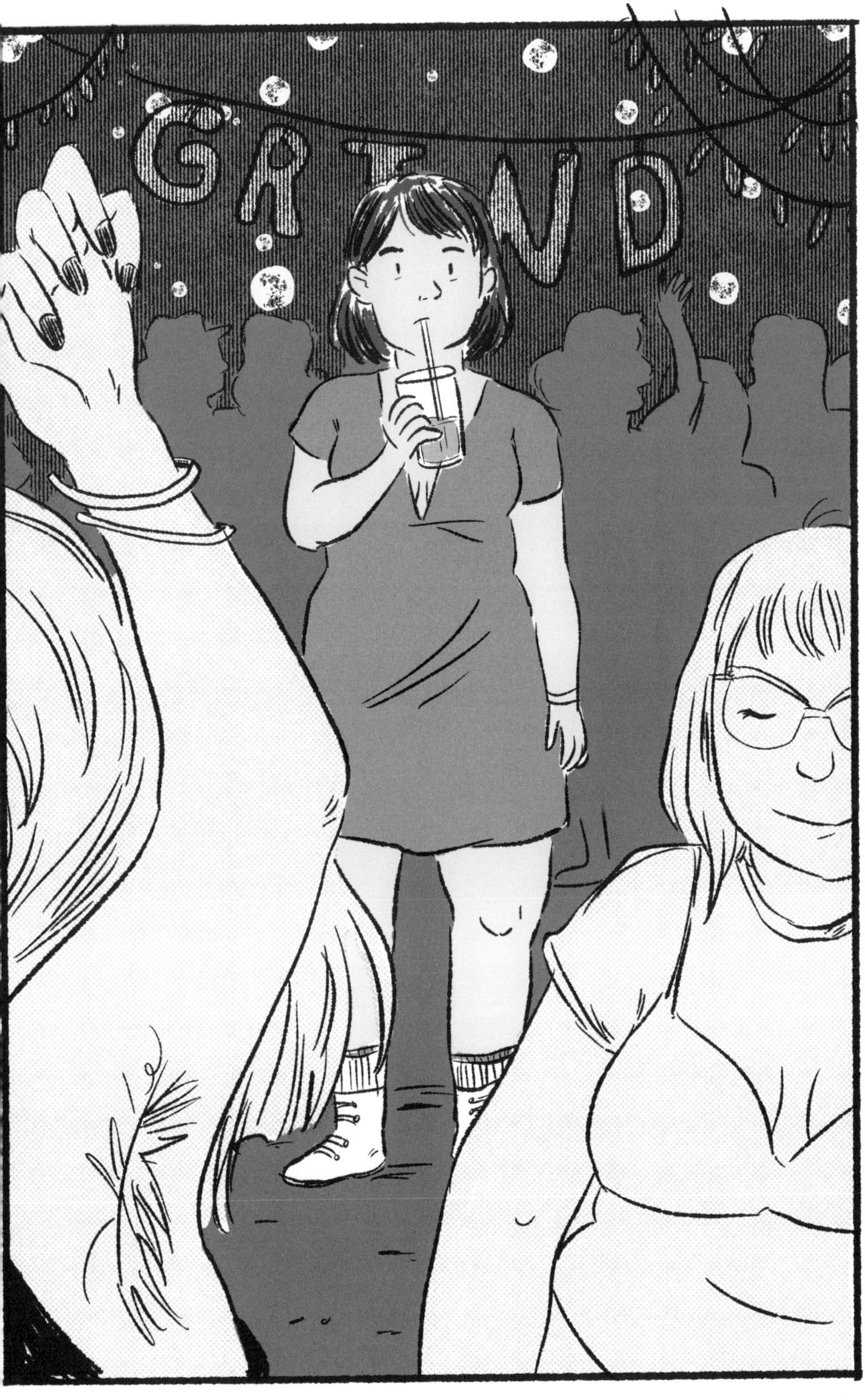

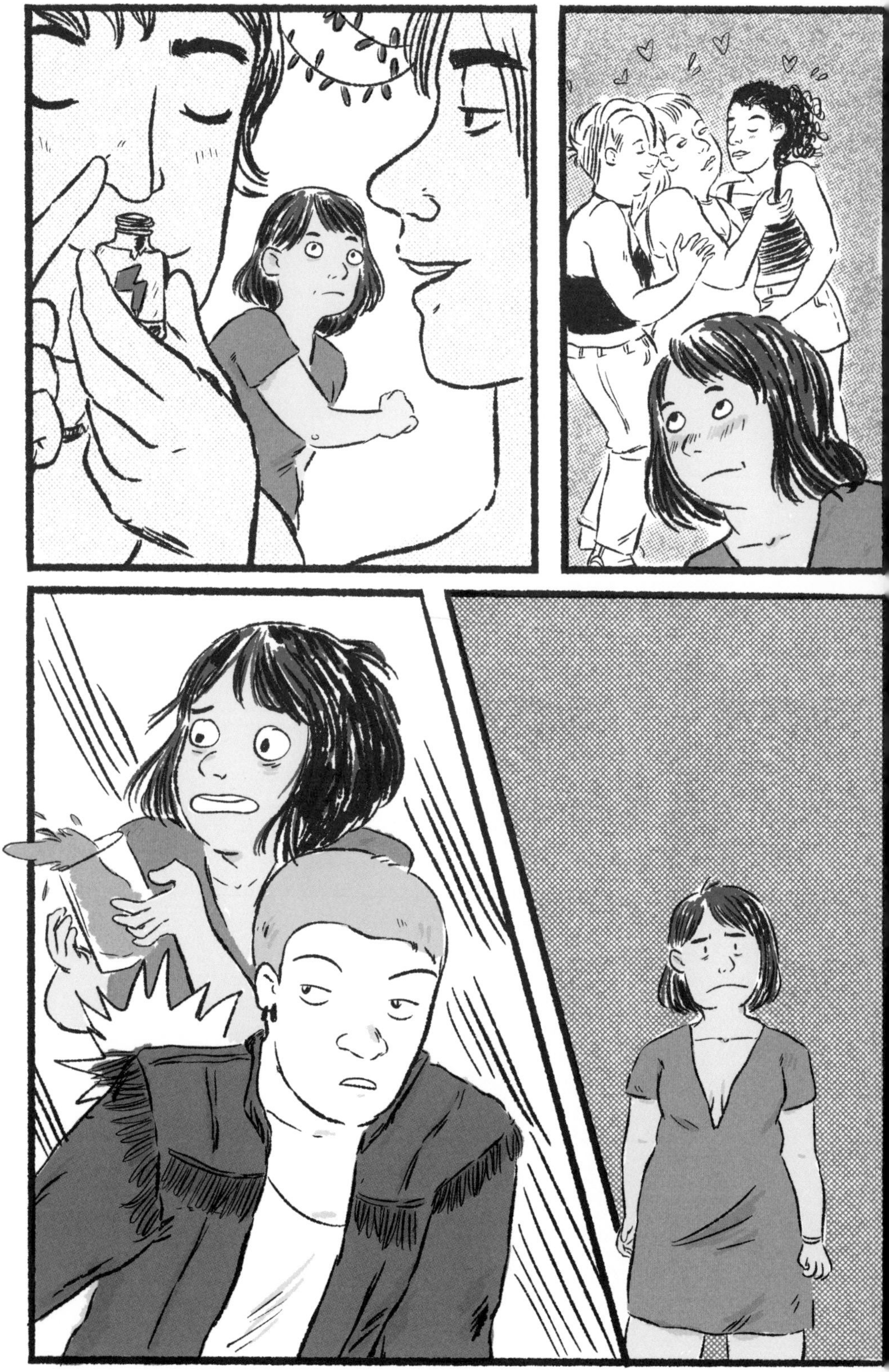

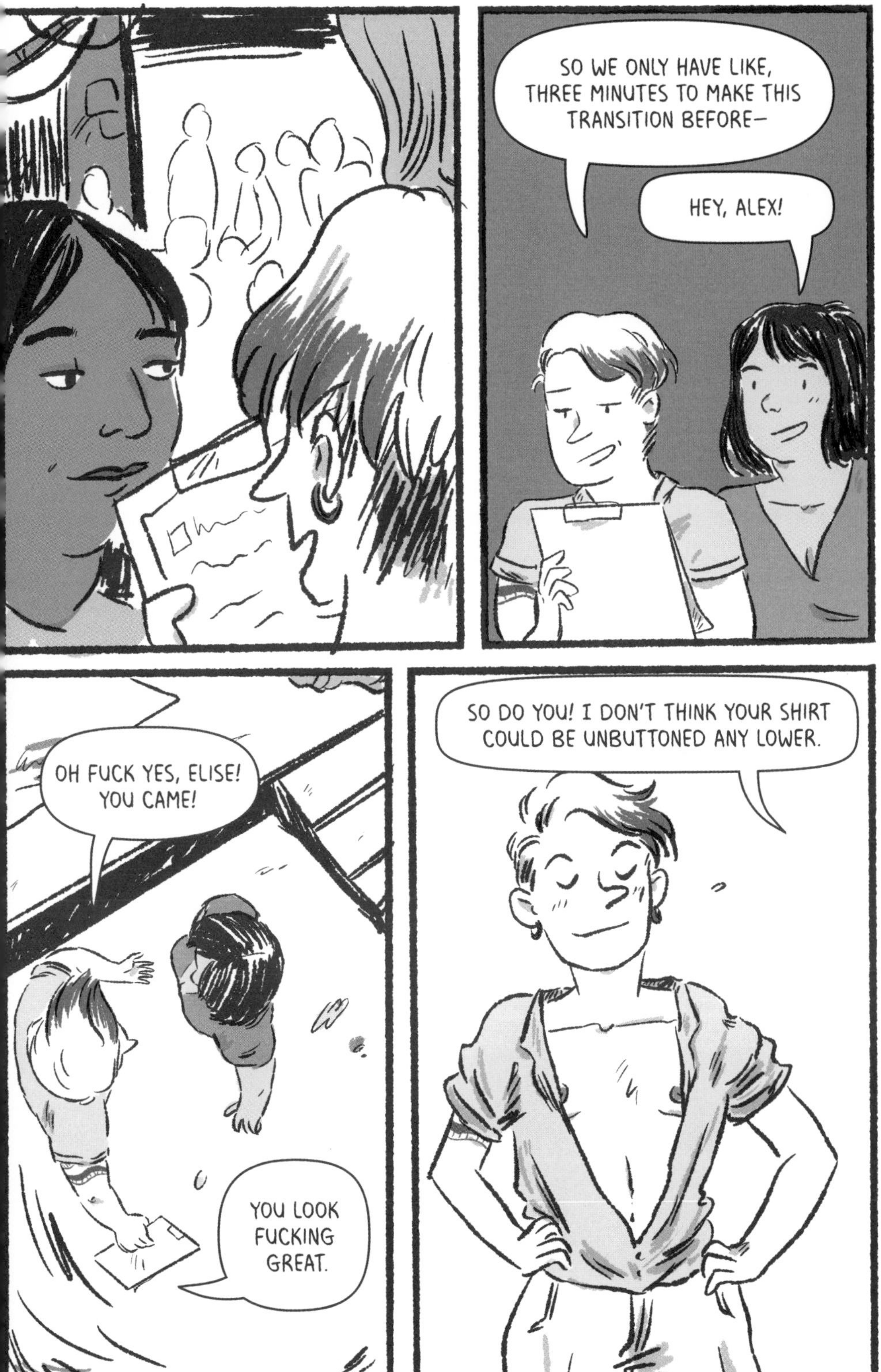
SO WE ONLY HAVE LIKE, THREE MINUTES TO MAKE THIS TRANSITION BEFORE–
HEY, ALEX!
OH FUCK YES, ELISE! YOU CAME!
YOU LOOK FUCKING GREAT.
SO DO YOU! I DON'T THINK YOUR SHIRT COULD BE UNBUTTONED ANY LOWER.

SO, HOW ARE YOU DOING?

ACTUALLY, PRETTY SHITTY.

I HAVEN'T TALKED TO CHRIS IN TWO WEEKS AND I KNOW I NEED TO GET OVER DREW BUT—

I AM SO SORRY ABOUT THAT, ELISE.

I CAN'T REALLY CHAT. I GOTTA HANDLE ALL THIS SHIT.

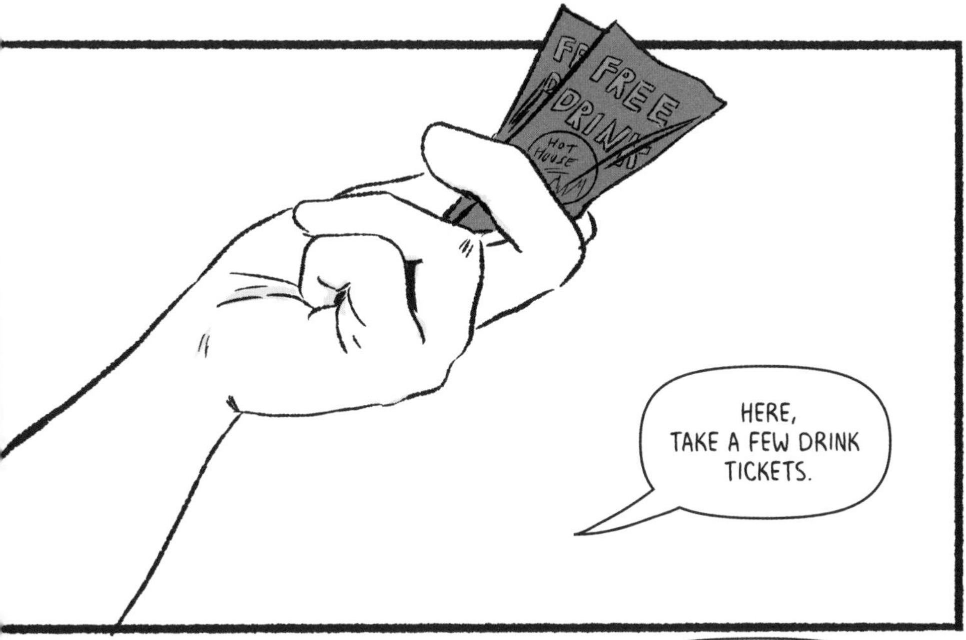
FREE
DRINK
HOT HOUSE
HERE,
TAKE A FEW DRINK
TICKETS.

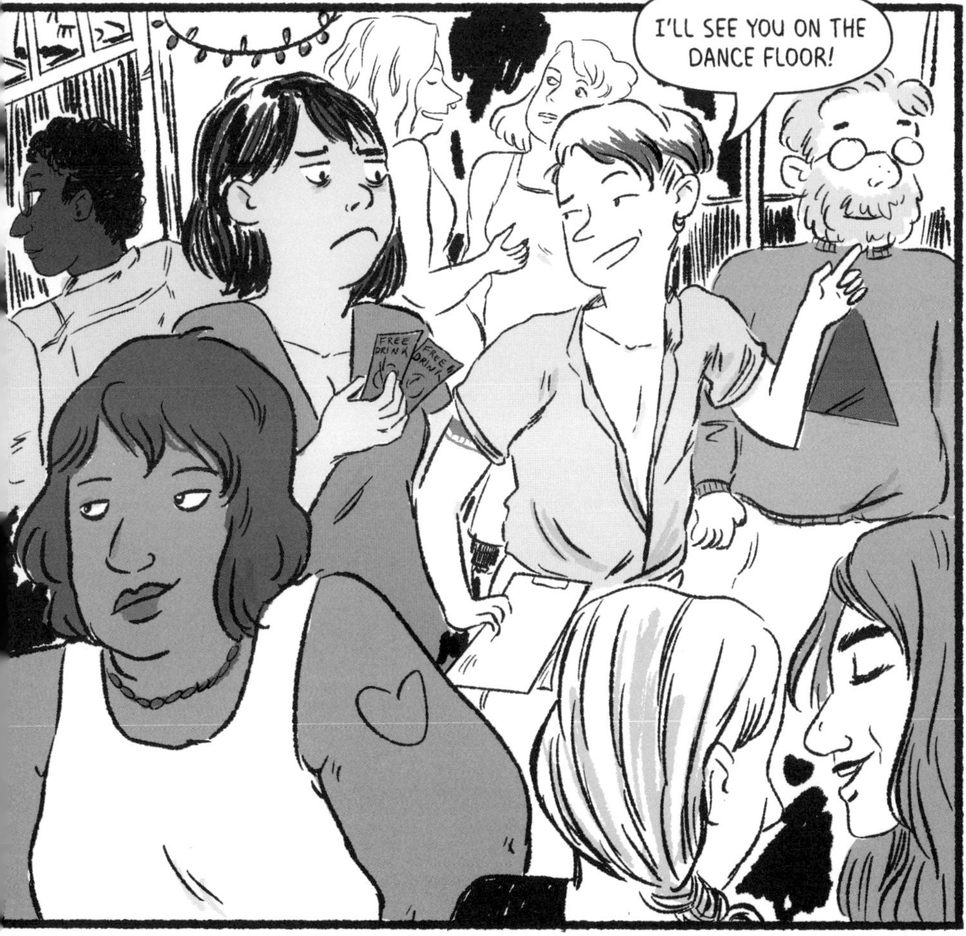
I'LL SEE YOU ON THE
DANCE FLOOR!
FREE
DRINK

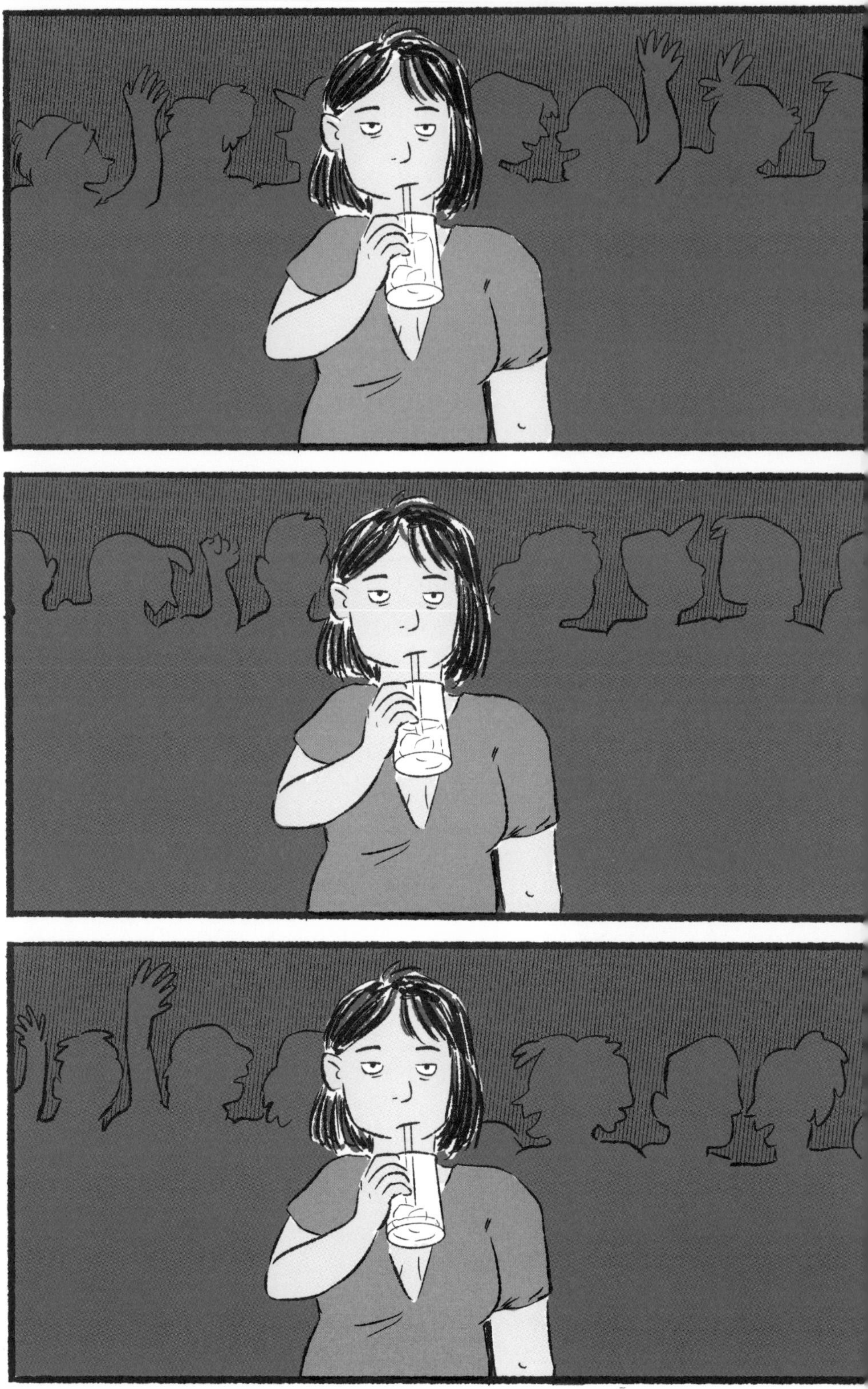

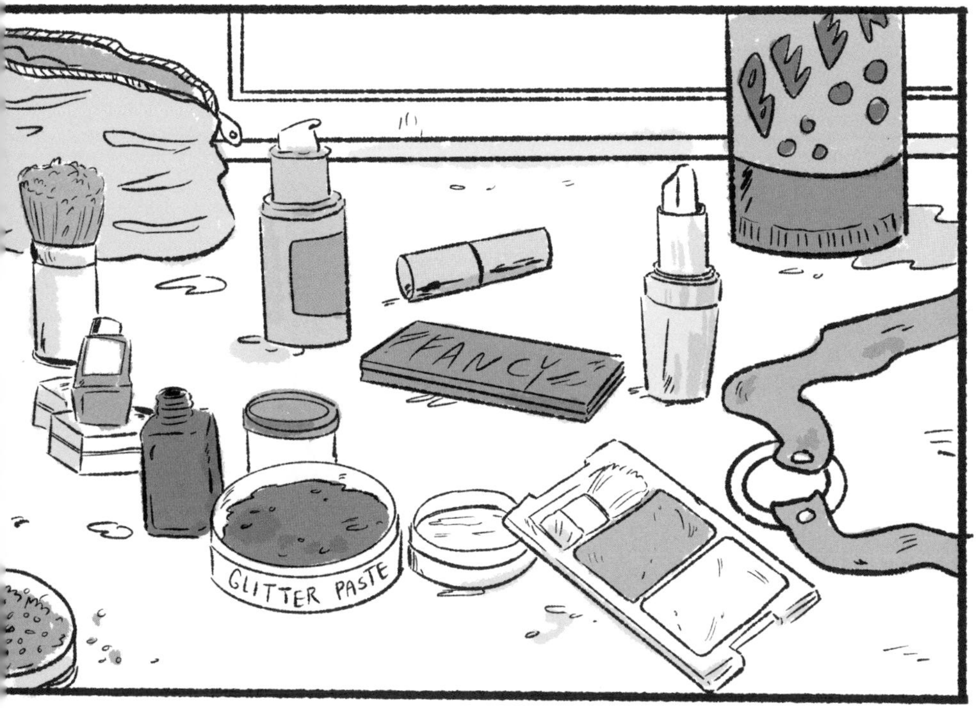

BEER
FANCY
GLITTER PASTE

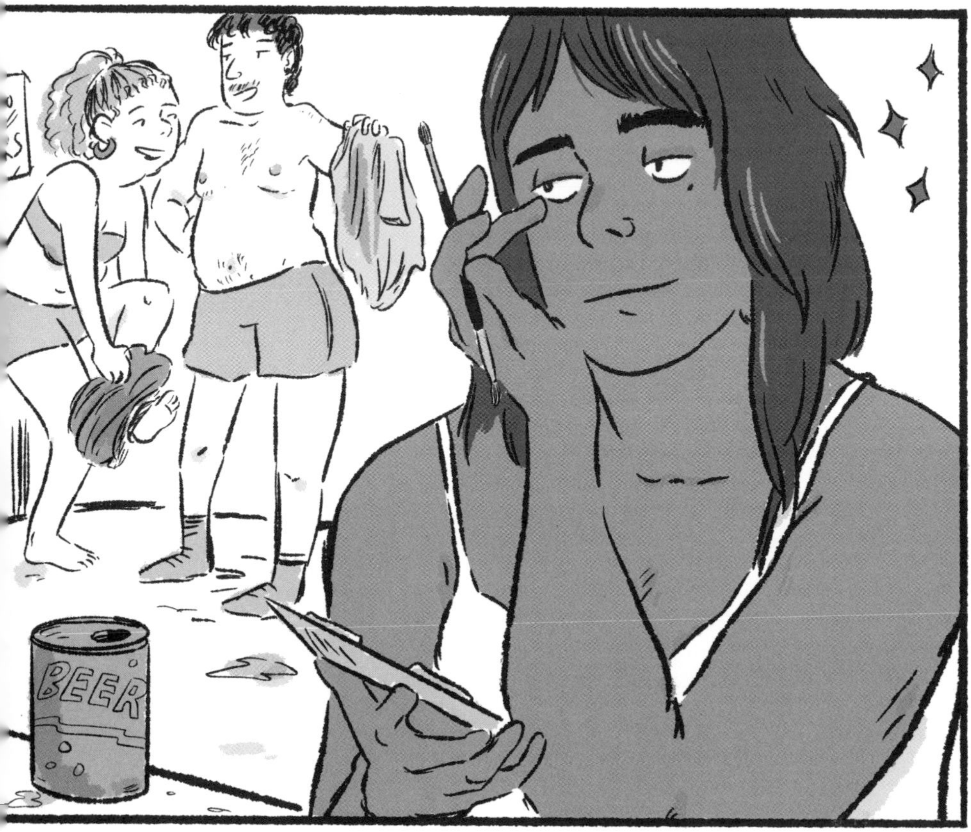

BEER

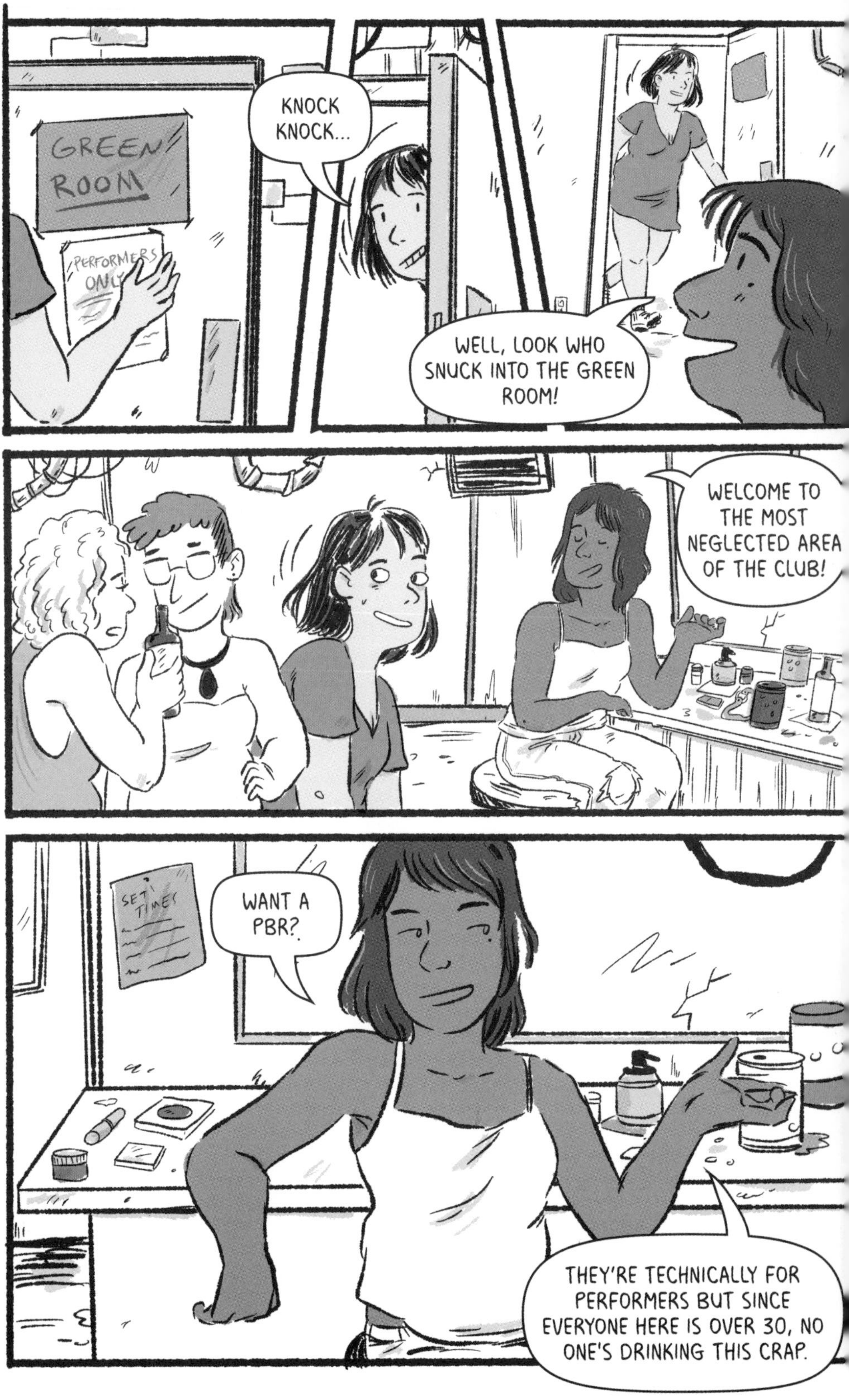
GREEN ROOM
PERFORMERS ONLY
KNOCK KNOCK...
WELL, LOOK WHO SNUCK INTO THE GREEN ROOM!
WELCOME TO THE MOST NEGLECTED AREA OF THE CLUB!
SET TIMES
WANT A PBR?
THEY'RE TECHNICALLY FOR PERFORMERS BUT SINCE EVERYONE HERE IS OVER 30, NO ONE'S DRINKING THIS CRAP.

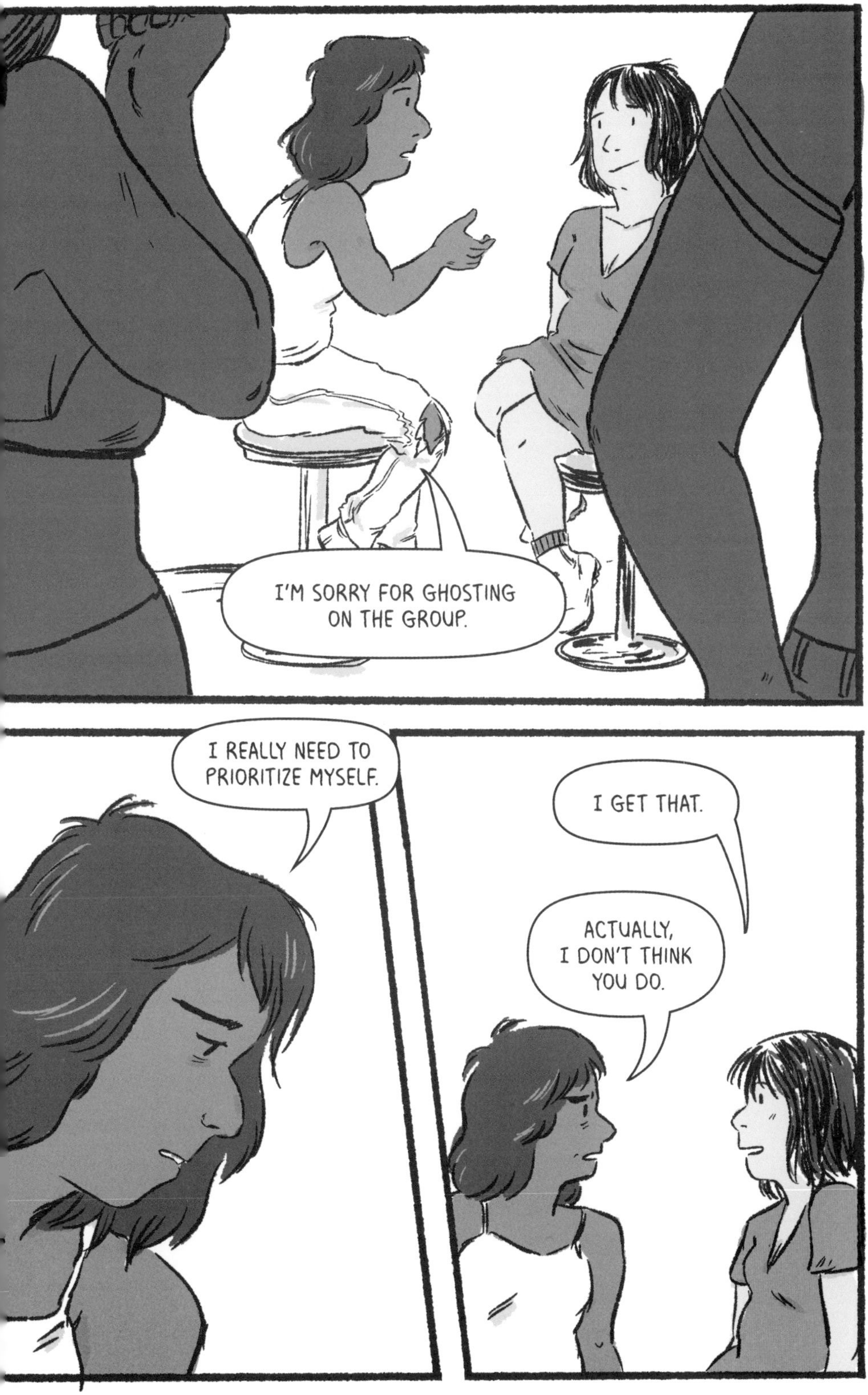
I'M SORRY FOR GHOSTING ON THE GROUP.
I REALLY NEED TO PRIORITIZE MYSELF.
I GET THAT.
ACTUALLY, I DON'T THINK YOU DO.

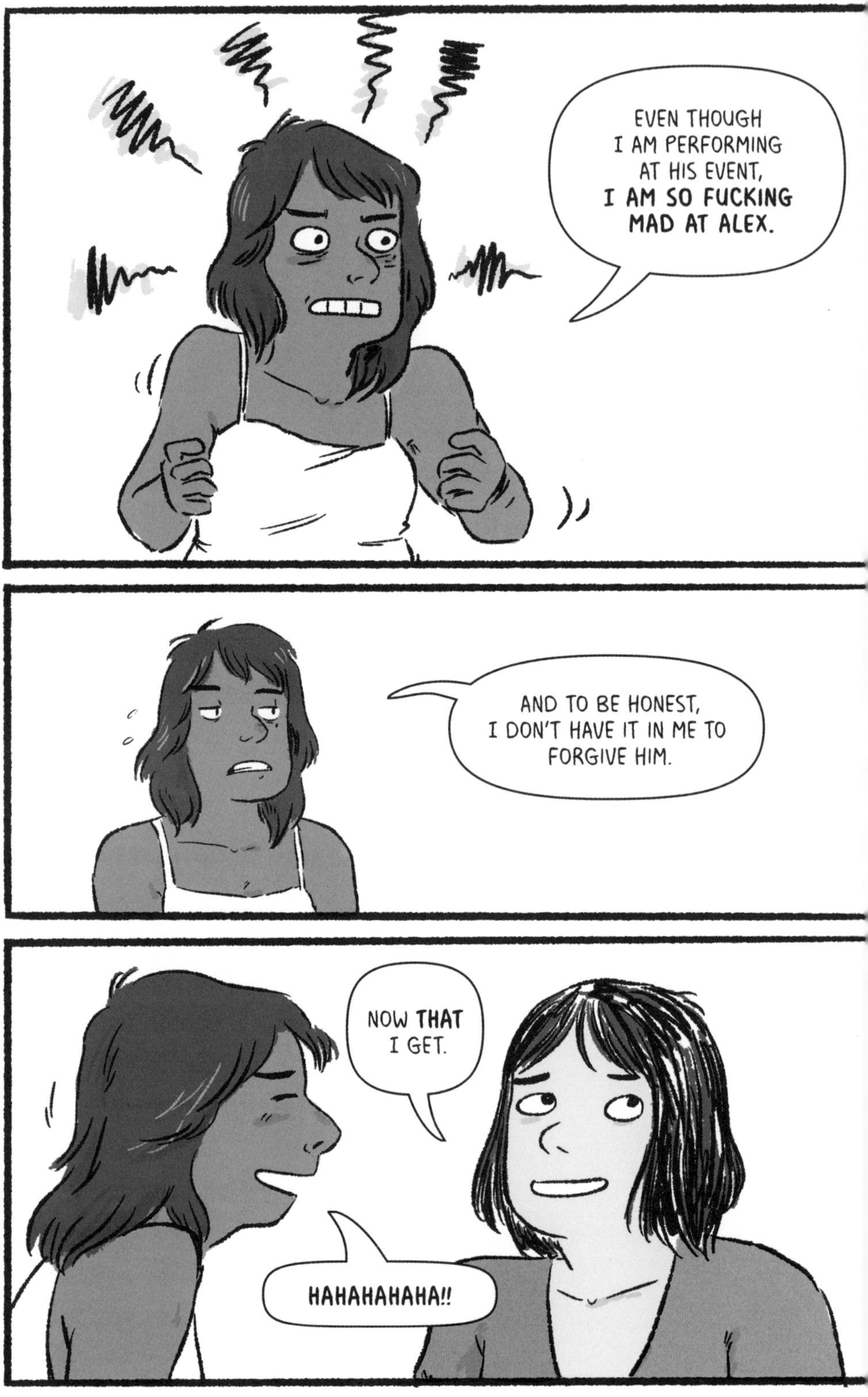
EVEN THOUGH I AM PERFORMING AT HIS EVENT, **I AM SO FUCKING MAD AT ALEX.**
AND TO BE HONEST, I DON'T HAVE IT IN ME TO FORGIVE HIM.
NOW **THAT** I GET.
HAHAHAHAHA!!

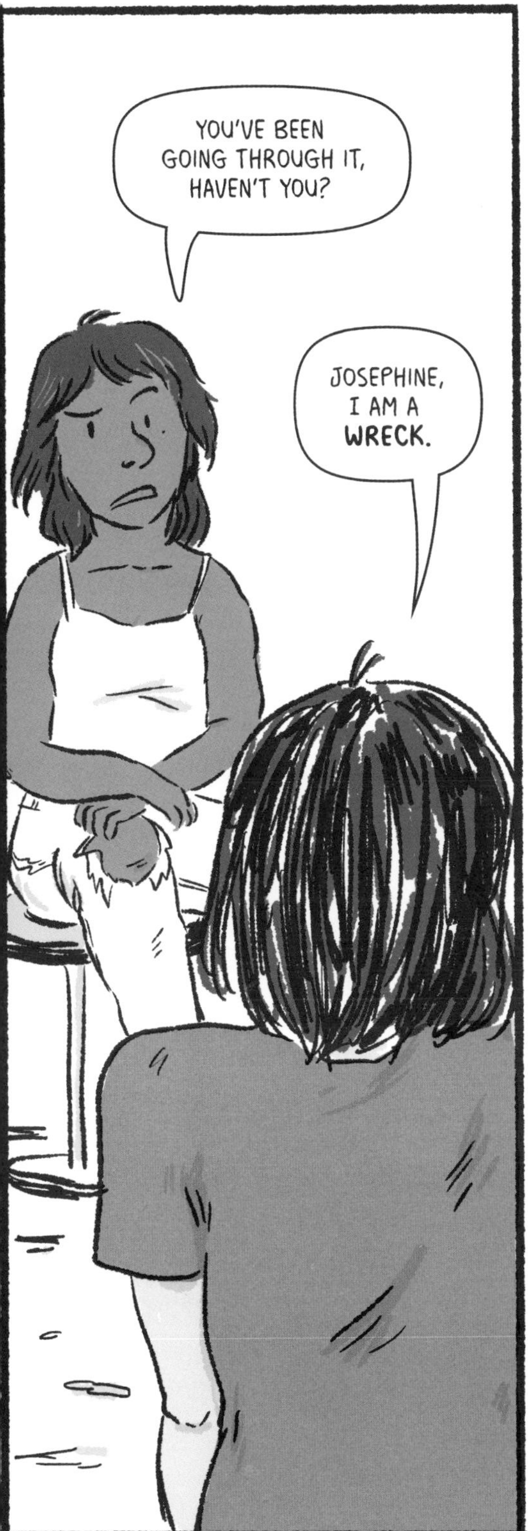
YOU'VE BEEN GOING THROUGH IT, HAVEN'T YOU?
JOSEPHINE, I AM A **WRECK.**

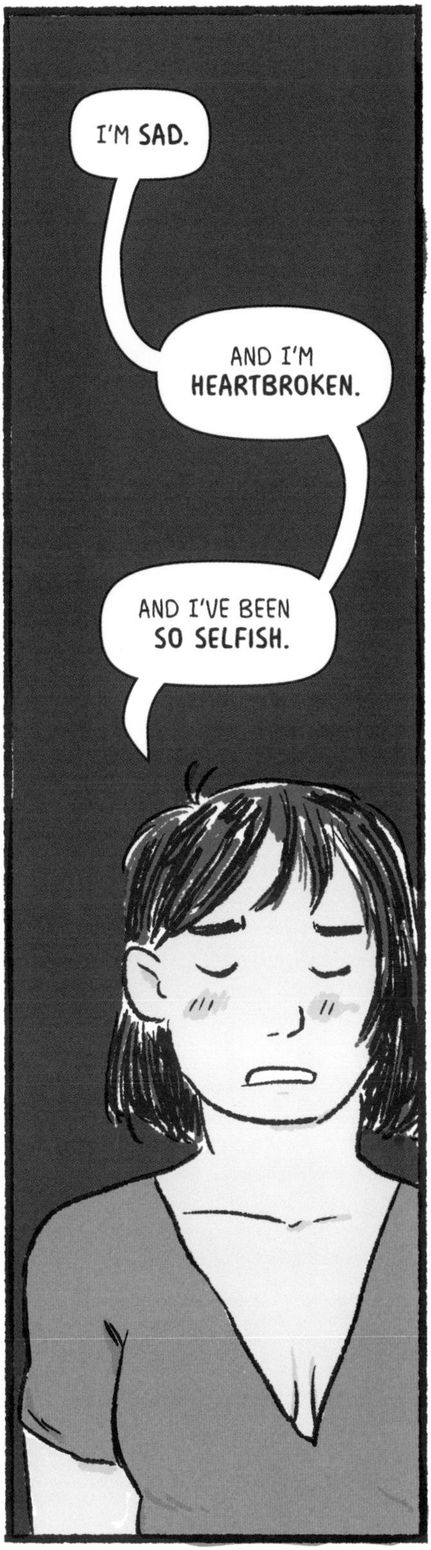
I'M **SAD.**
AND I'M **HEARTBROKEN.**
AND I'VE BEEN **SO SELFISH.**

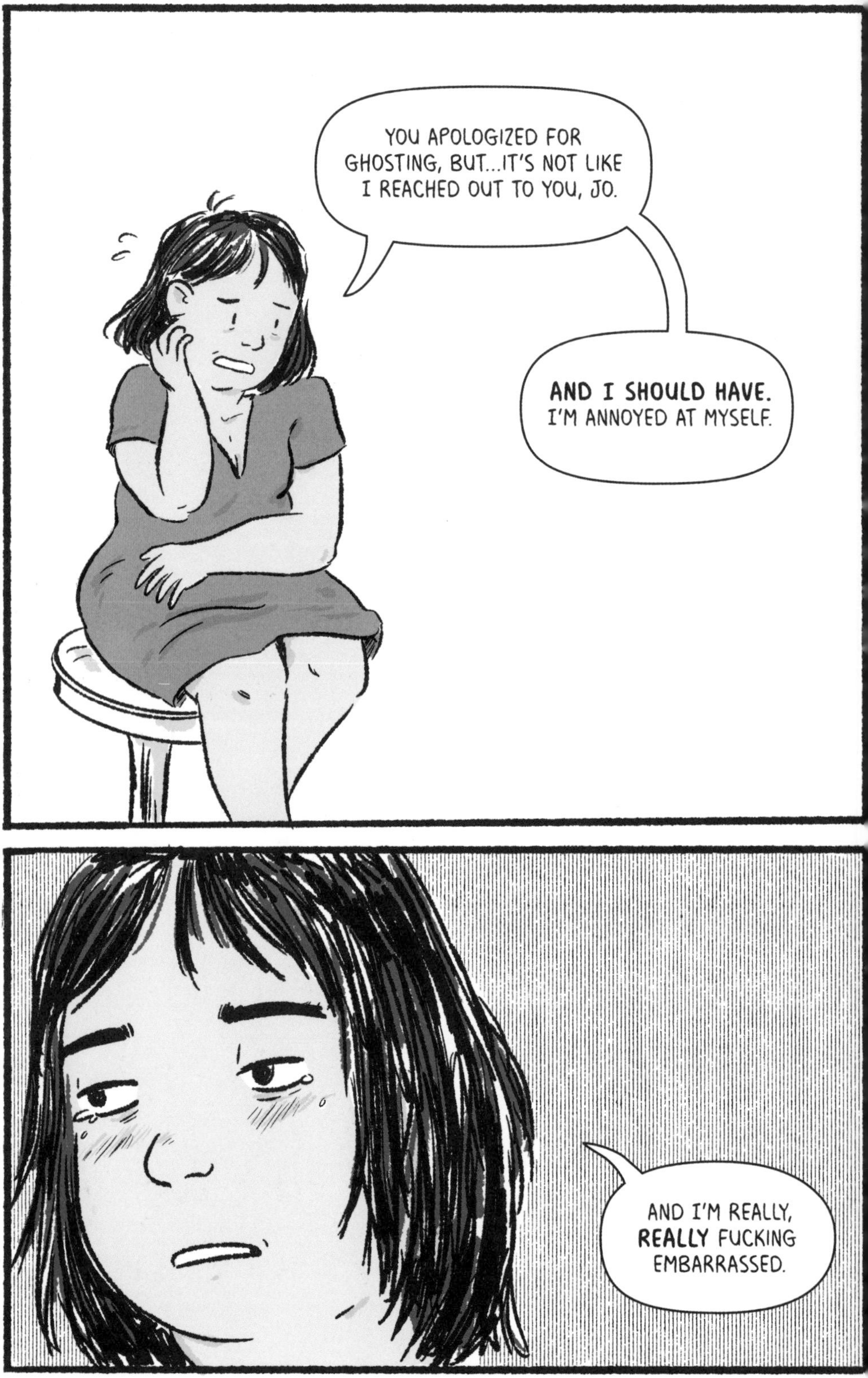
YOU APOLOGIZED FOR GHOSTING, BUT...IT'S NOT LIKE I REACHED OUT TO YOU, JO.
AND I SHOULD HAVE. I'M ANNOYED AT MYSELF.
AND I'M REALLY, REALLY FUCKING EMBARRASSED.

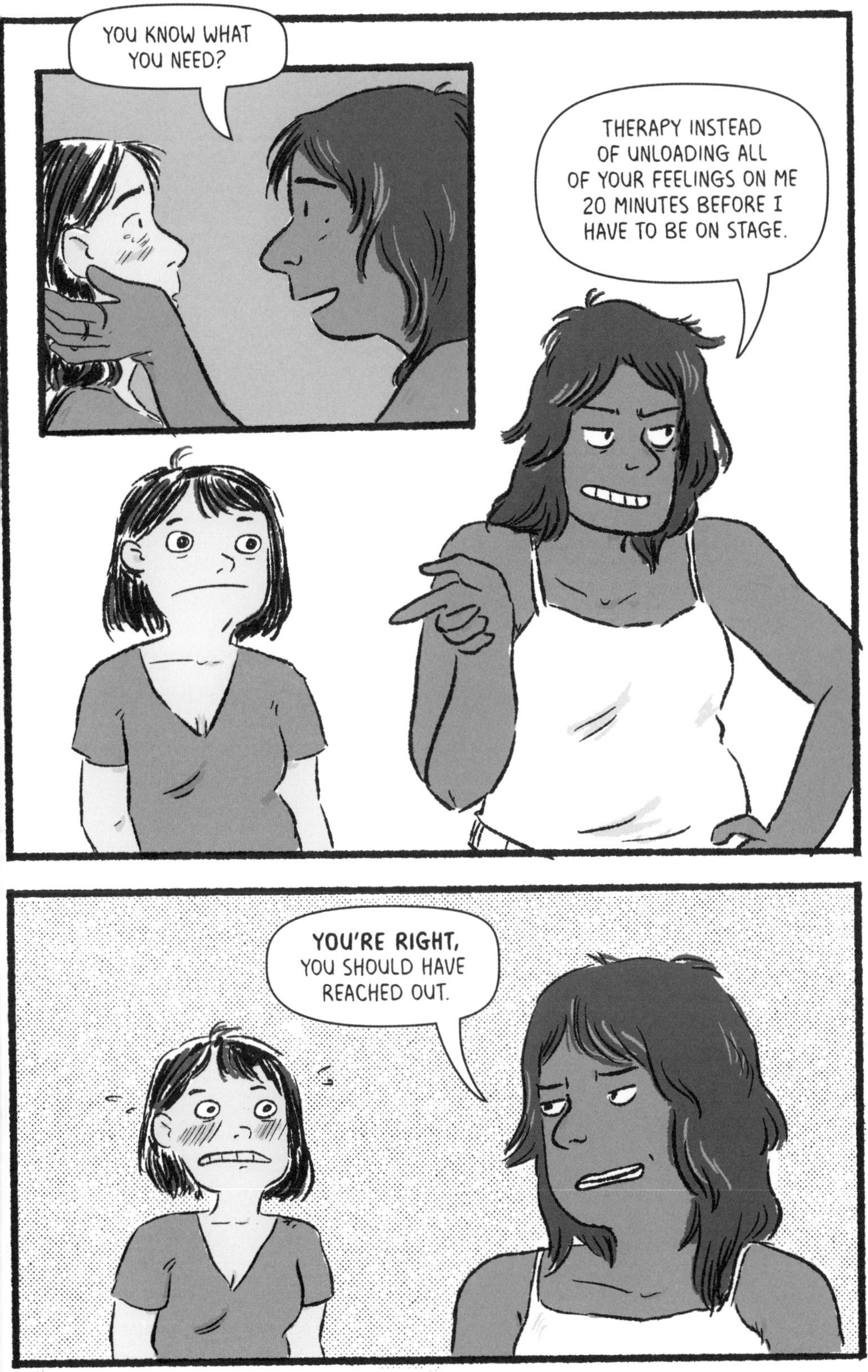

YOU KNOW WHAT YOU NEED?
THERAPY INSTEAD OF UNLOADING ALL OF YOUR FEELINGS ON ME 20 MINUTES BEFORE I HAVE TO BE ON STAGE.
YOU'RE RIGHT, YOU SHOULD HAVE REACHED OUT.

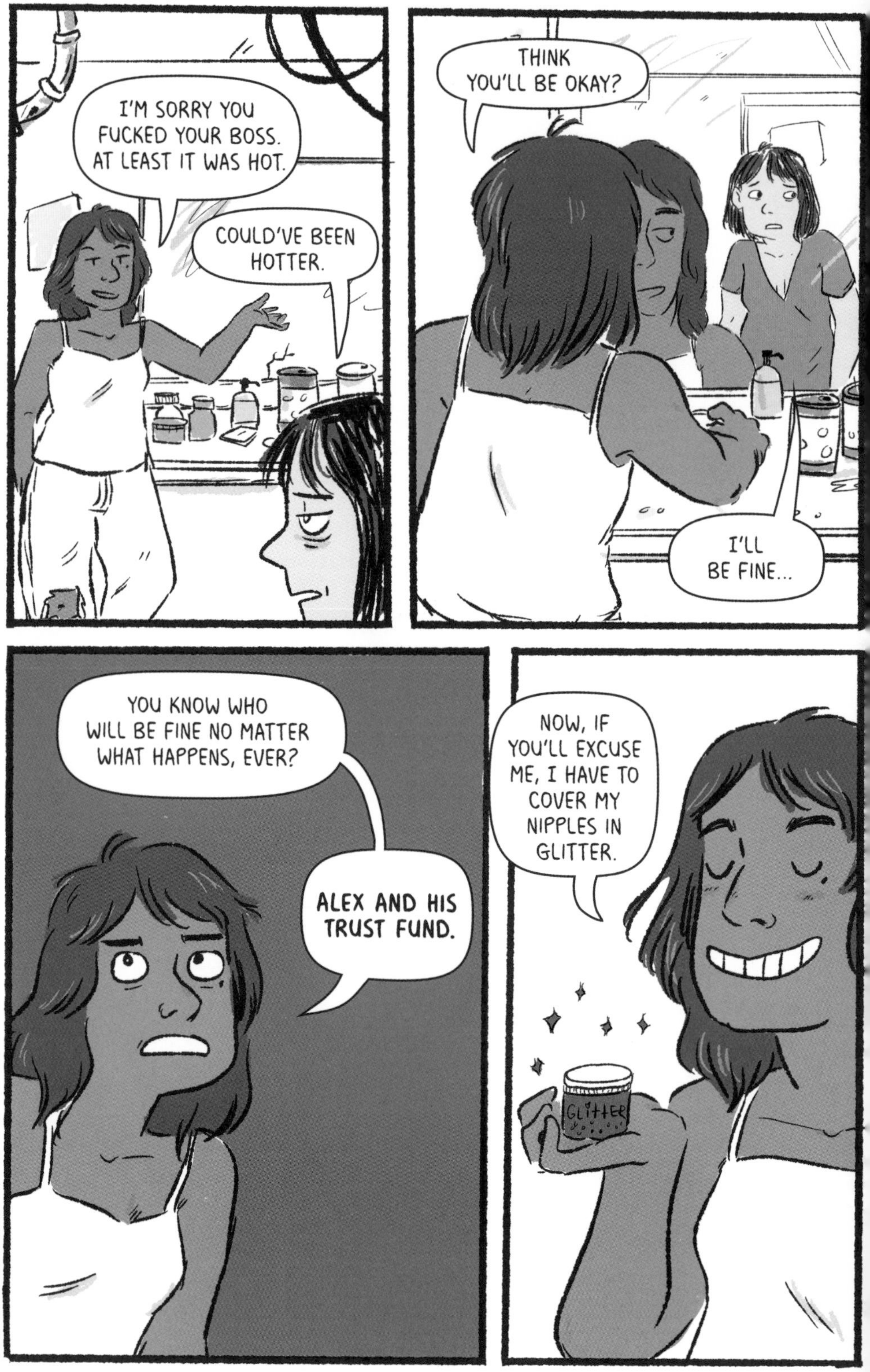
I'M SORRY YOU FUCKED YOUR BOSS. AT LEAST IT WAS HOT.
COULD'VE BEEN HOTTER.
THINK YOU'LL BE OKAY?
I'LL BE FINE...
YOU KNOW WHO WILL BE FINE NO MATTER WHAT HAPPENS, EVER?
ALEX AND HIS TRUST FUND.
NOW, IF YOU'LL EXCUSE ME, I HAVE TO COVER MY NIPPLES IN GLITTER.
GLITTER

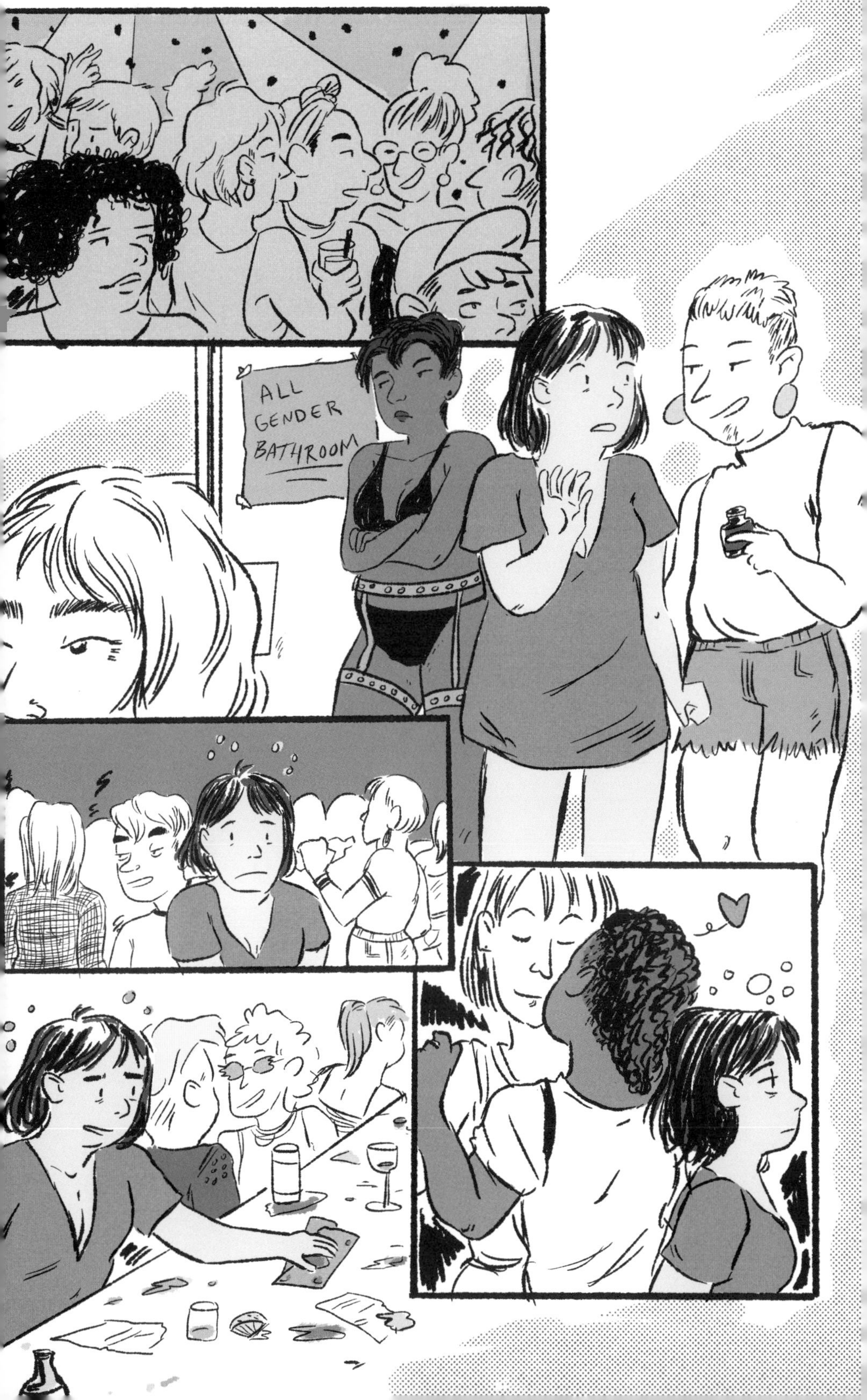
ALL
GENDER
BATHROOM

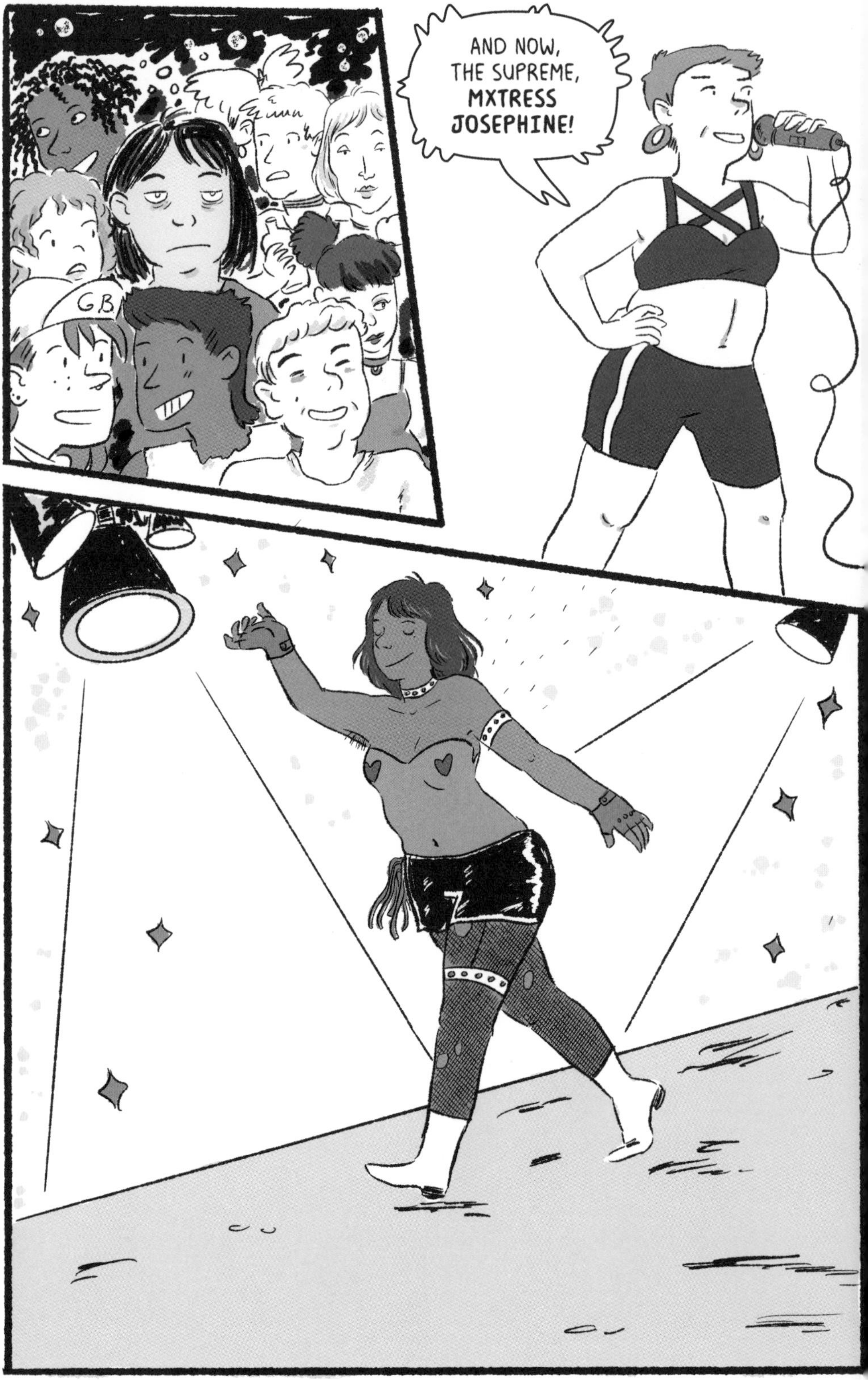
AND NOW, THE SUPREME, MXTRESS JOSEPHINE!
GB

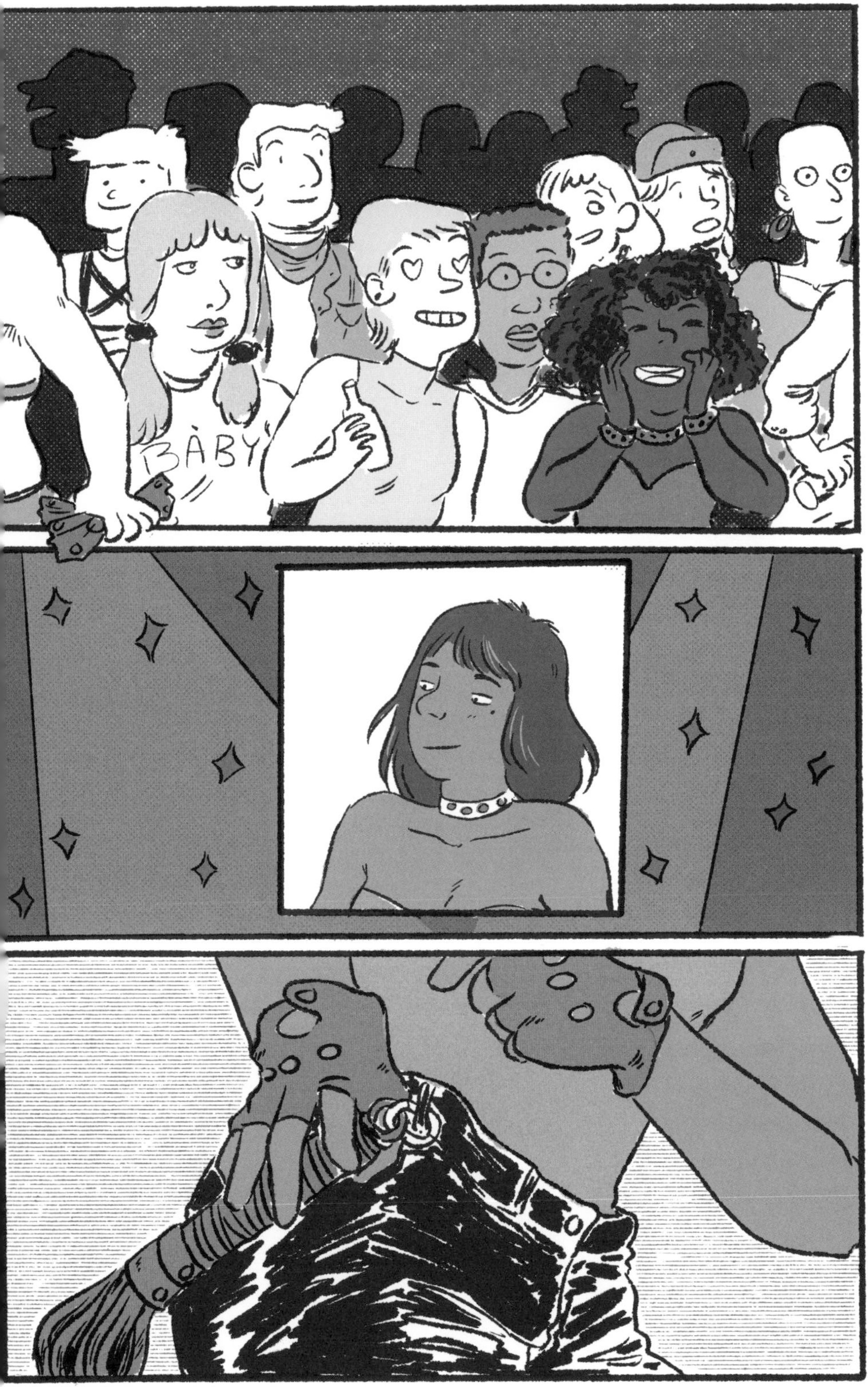
BABY

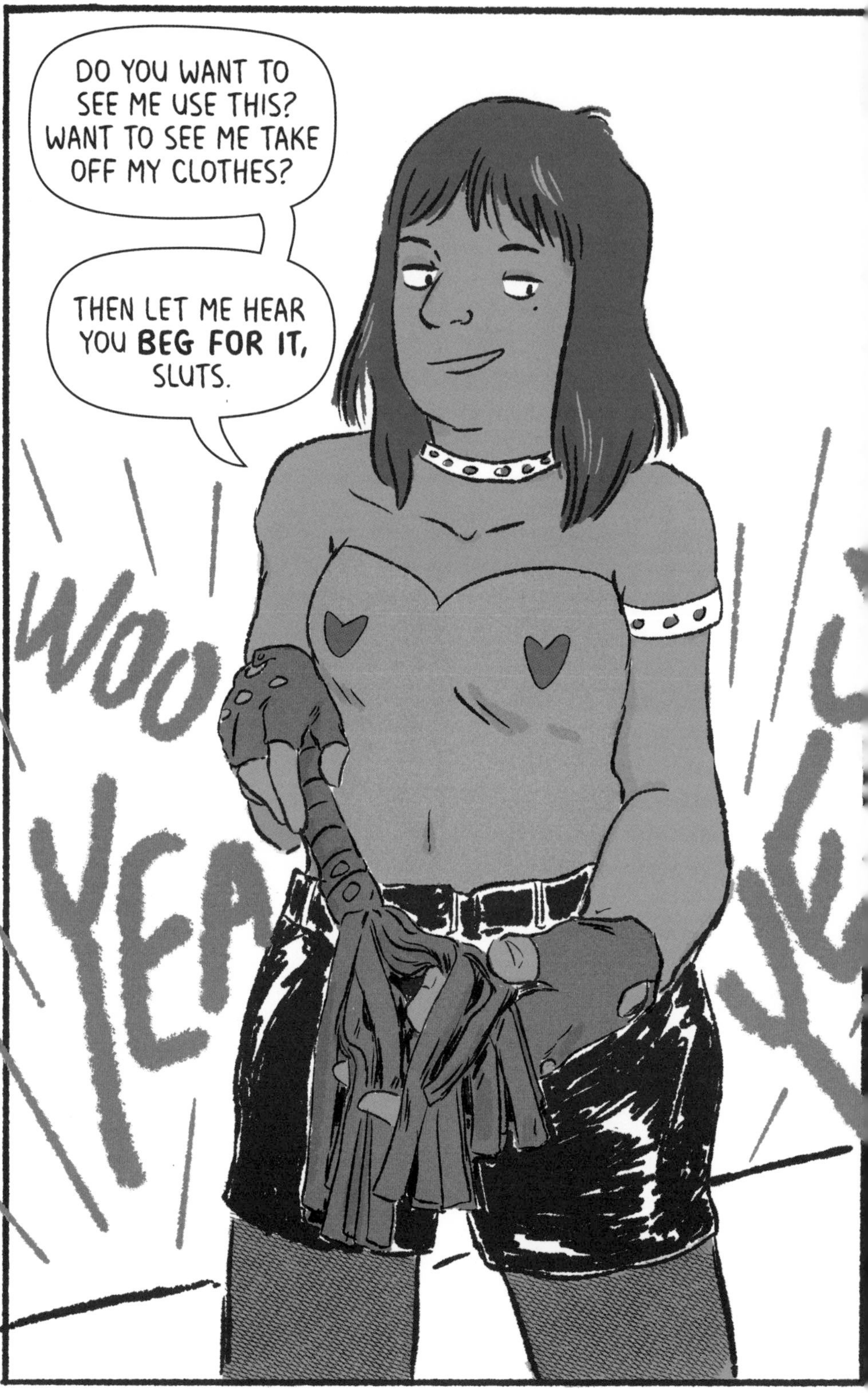
DO YOU WANT TO SEE ME USE THIS? WANT TO SEE ME TAKE OFF MY CLOTHES?
THEN LET ME HEAR YOU **BEG FOR IT,** SLUTS.
WOO
YEA

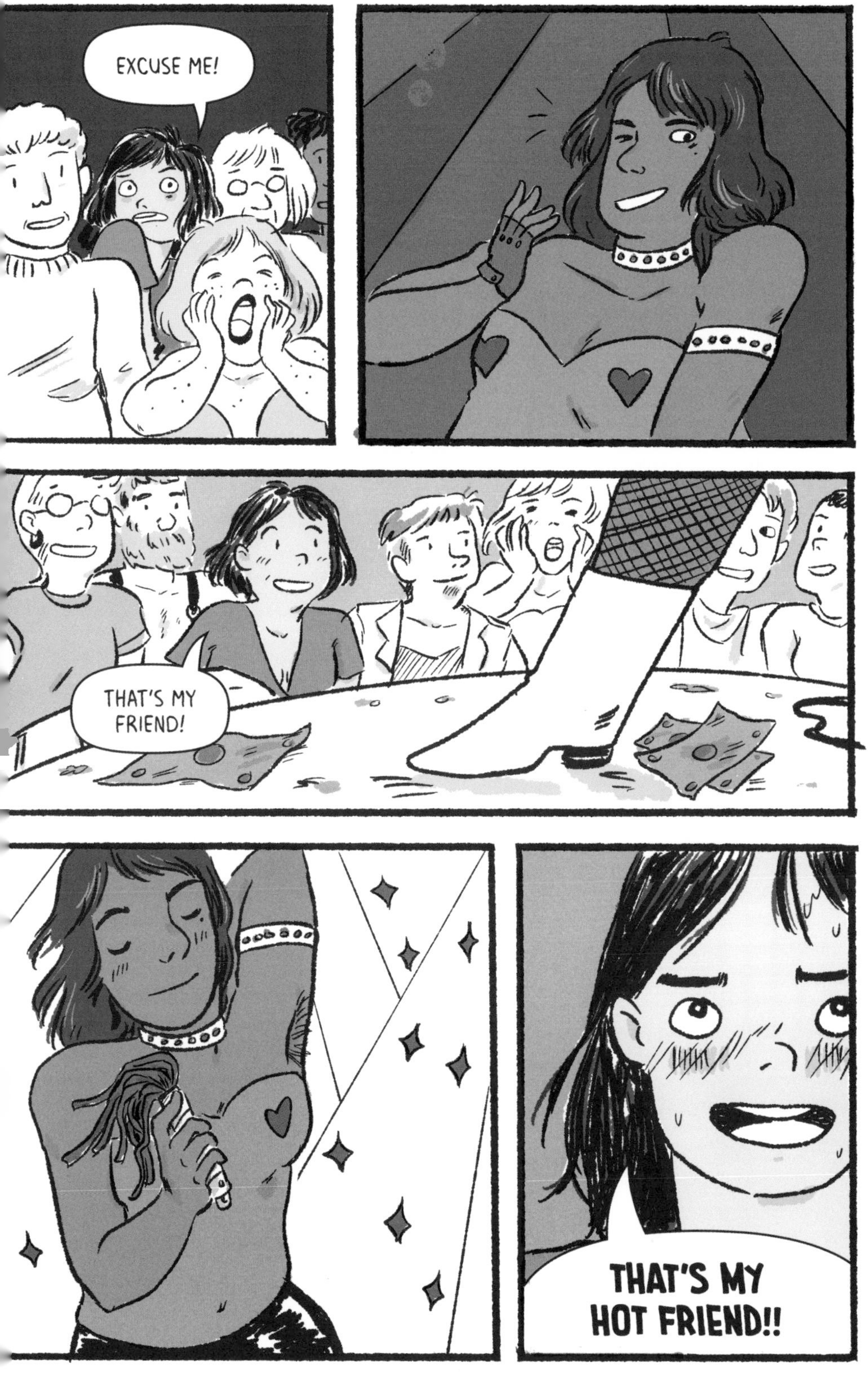
EXCUSE ME!
THAT'S MY FRIEND!
THAT'S MY HOT FRIEND!!

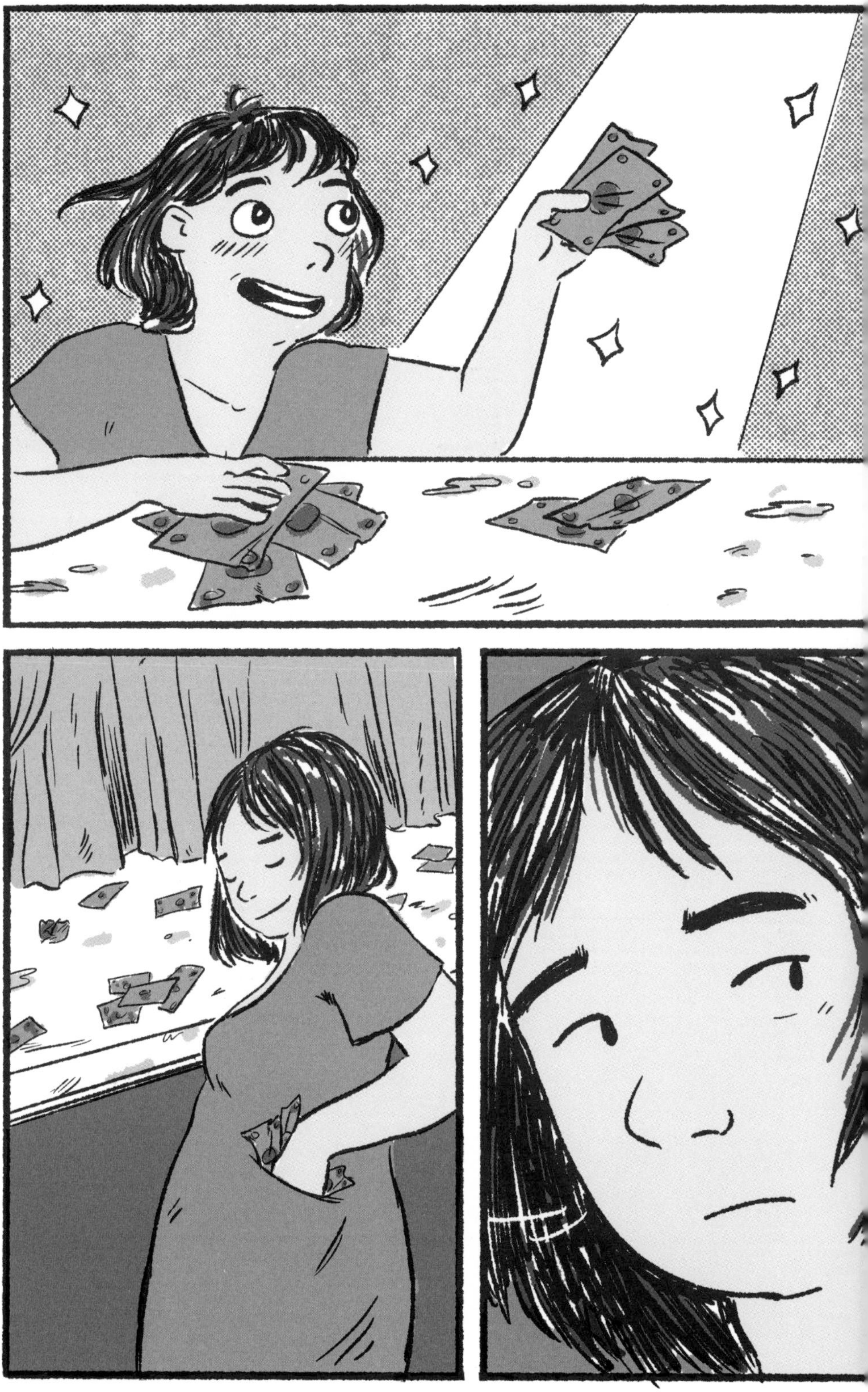

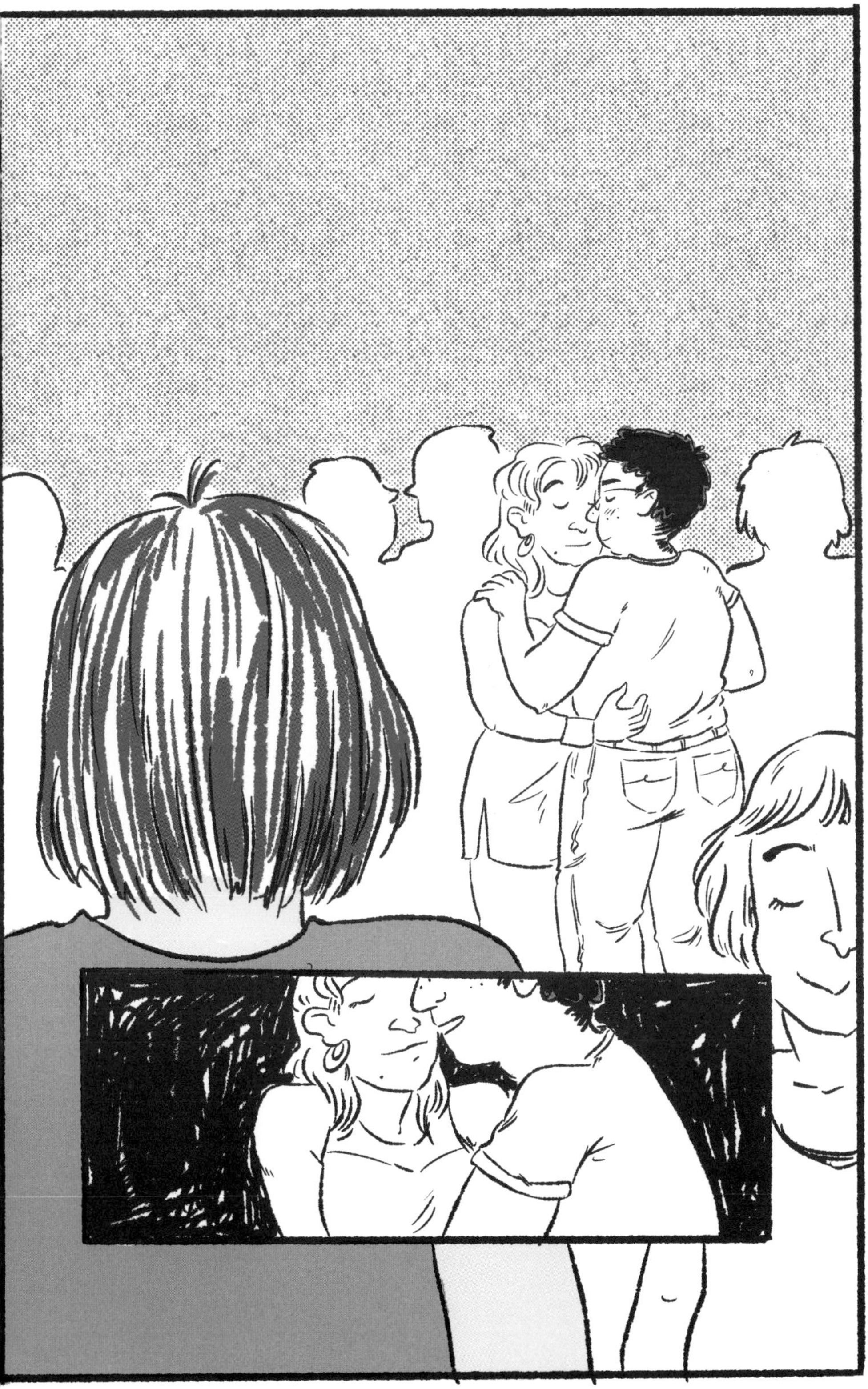

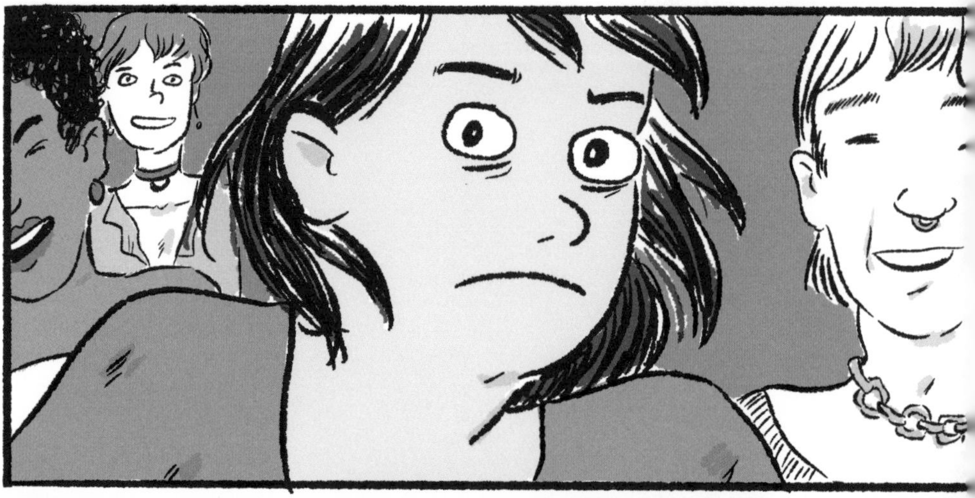

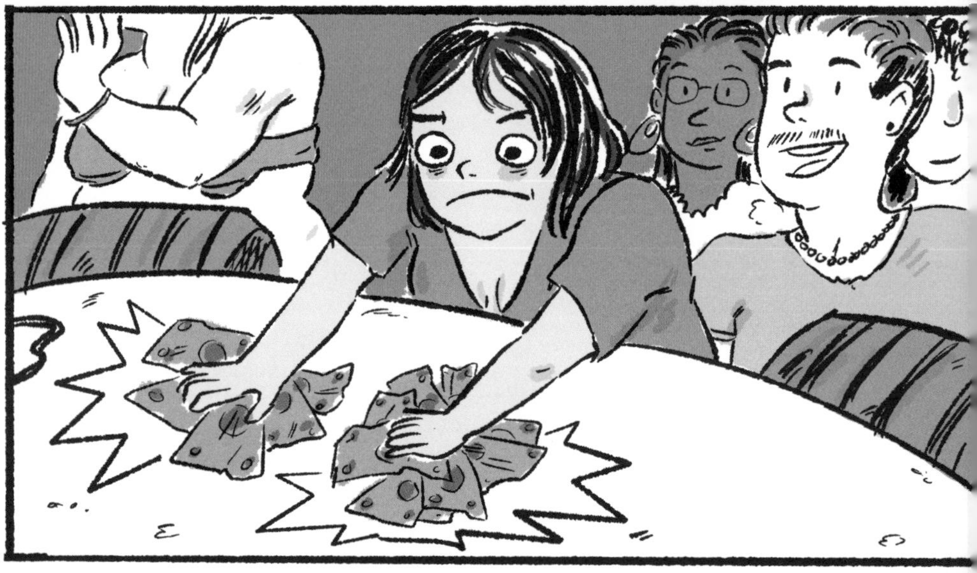

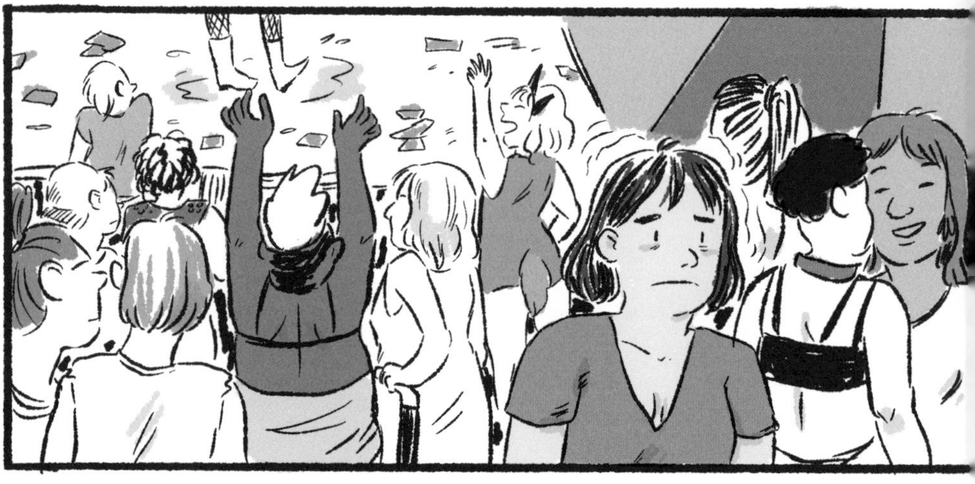

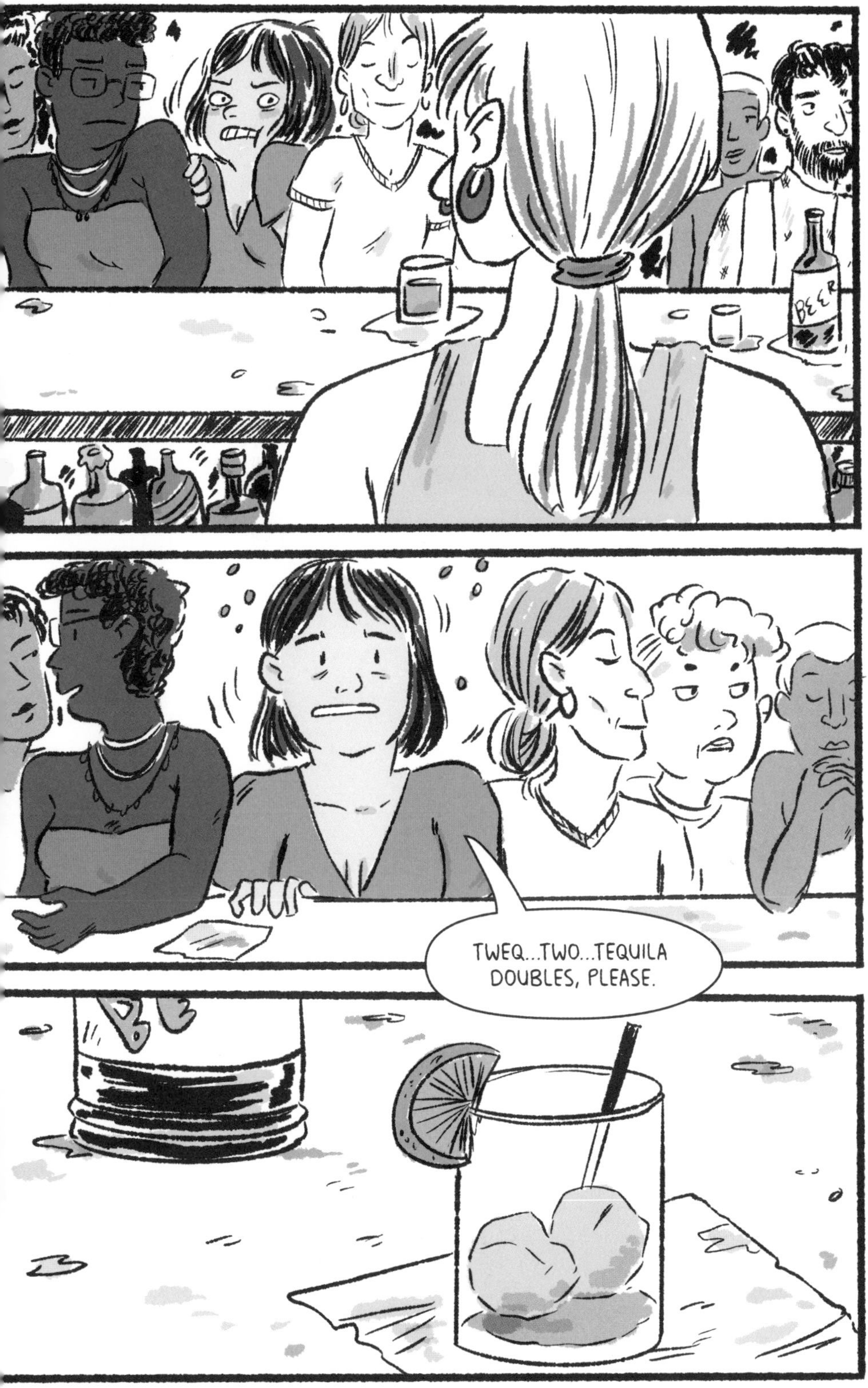
TWEQ...TWO...TEQUILA
DOUBLES, PLEASE.
BEER

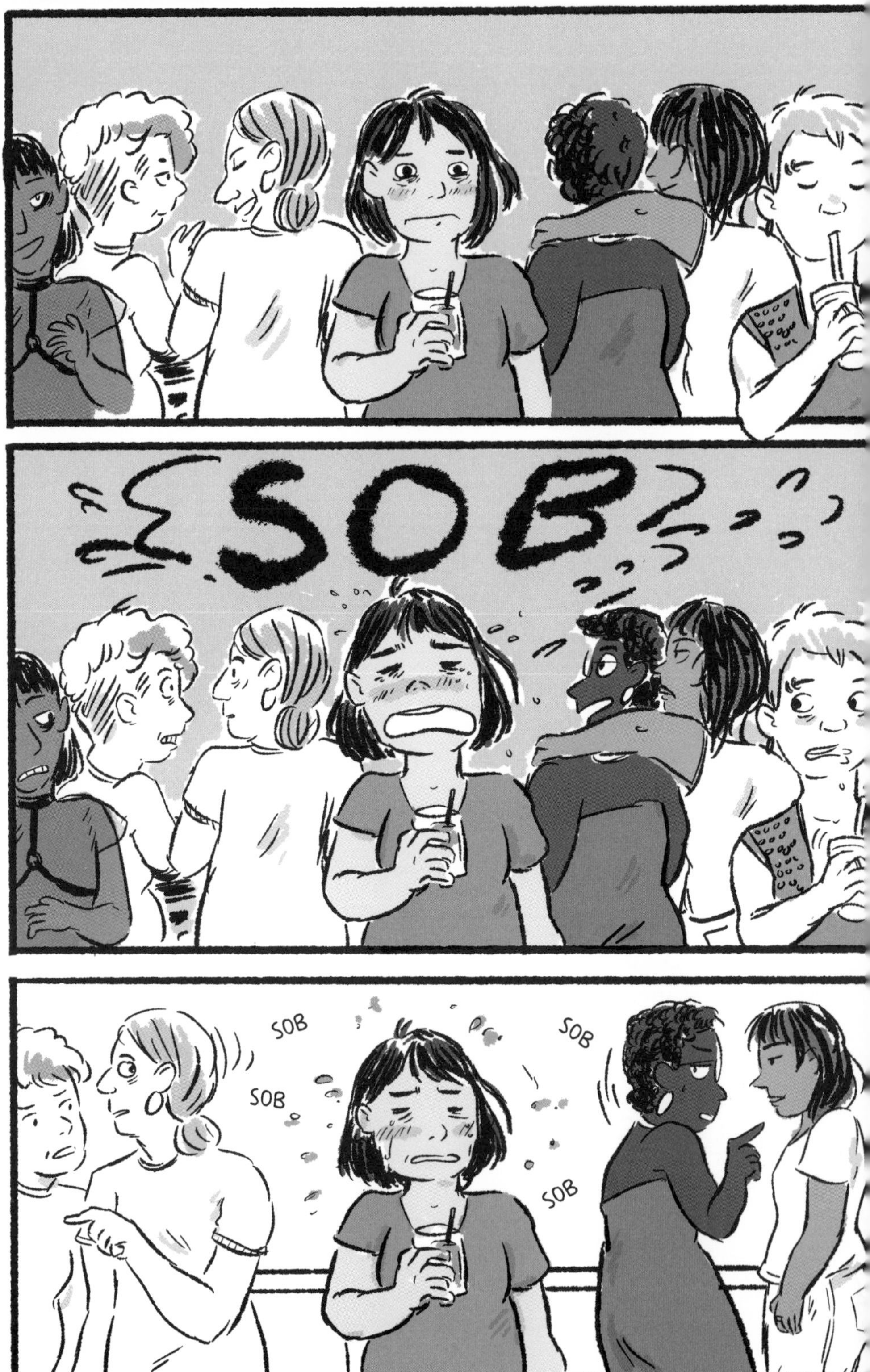
SOB
SOB
SOB
SOB
SOB

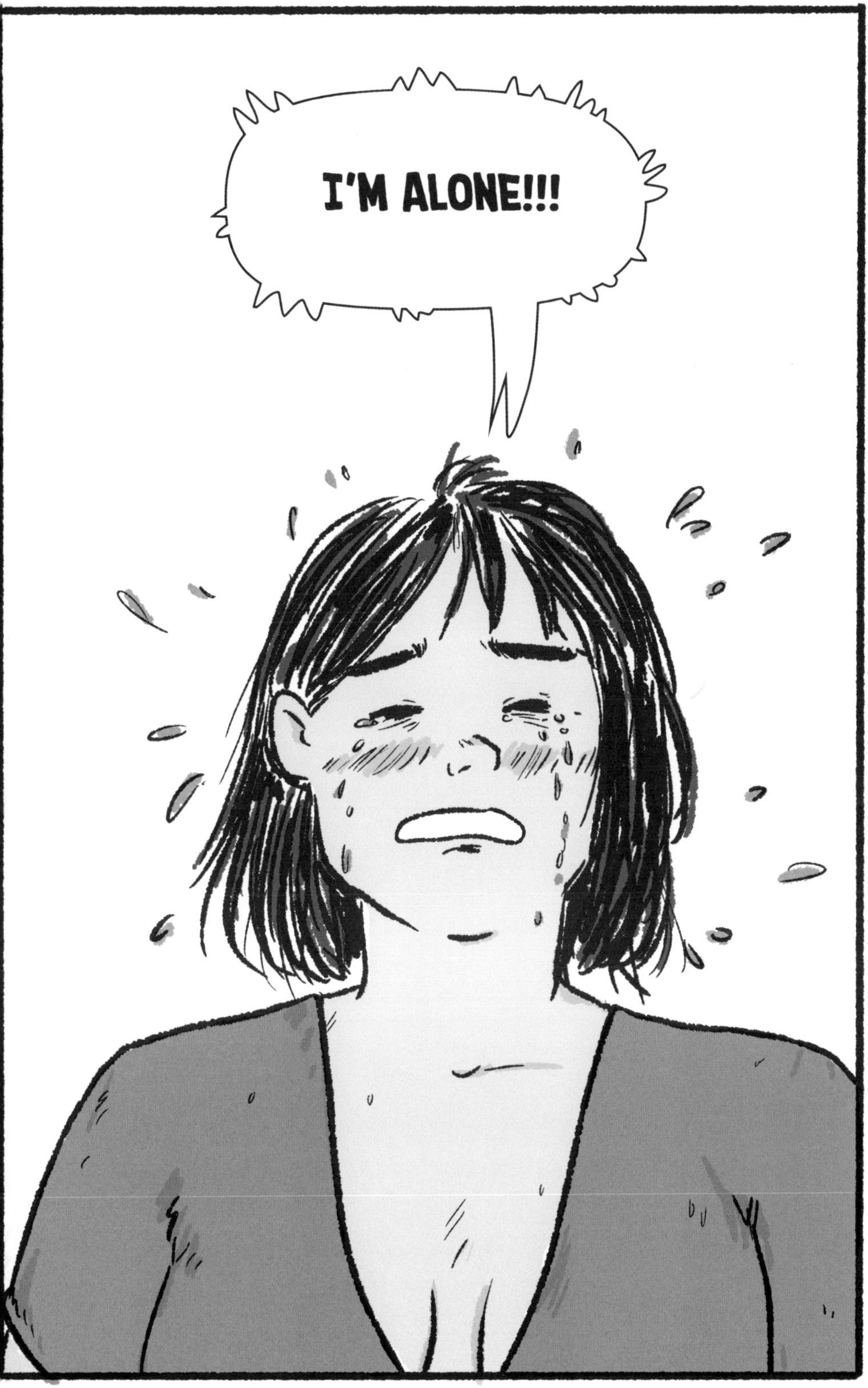
I'M ALONE!!!

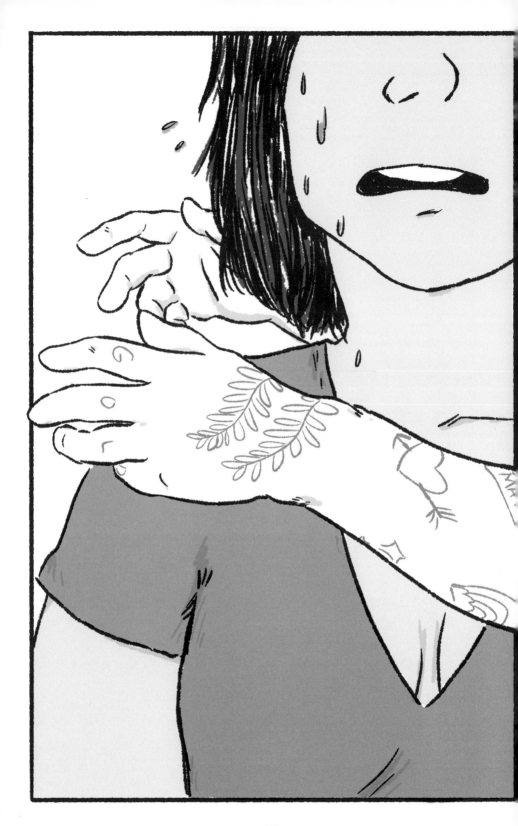

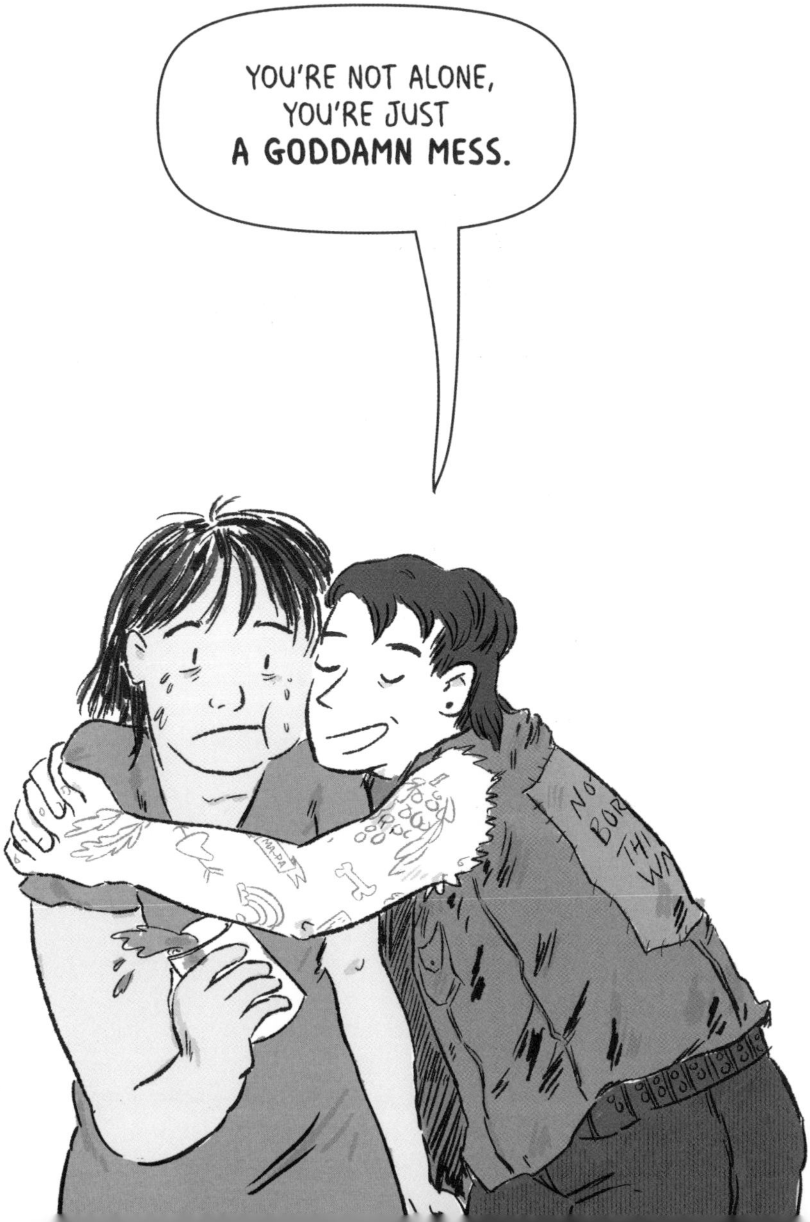
YOU'RE NOT ALONE, YOU'RE JUST **A GODDAMN MESS.**

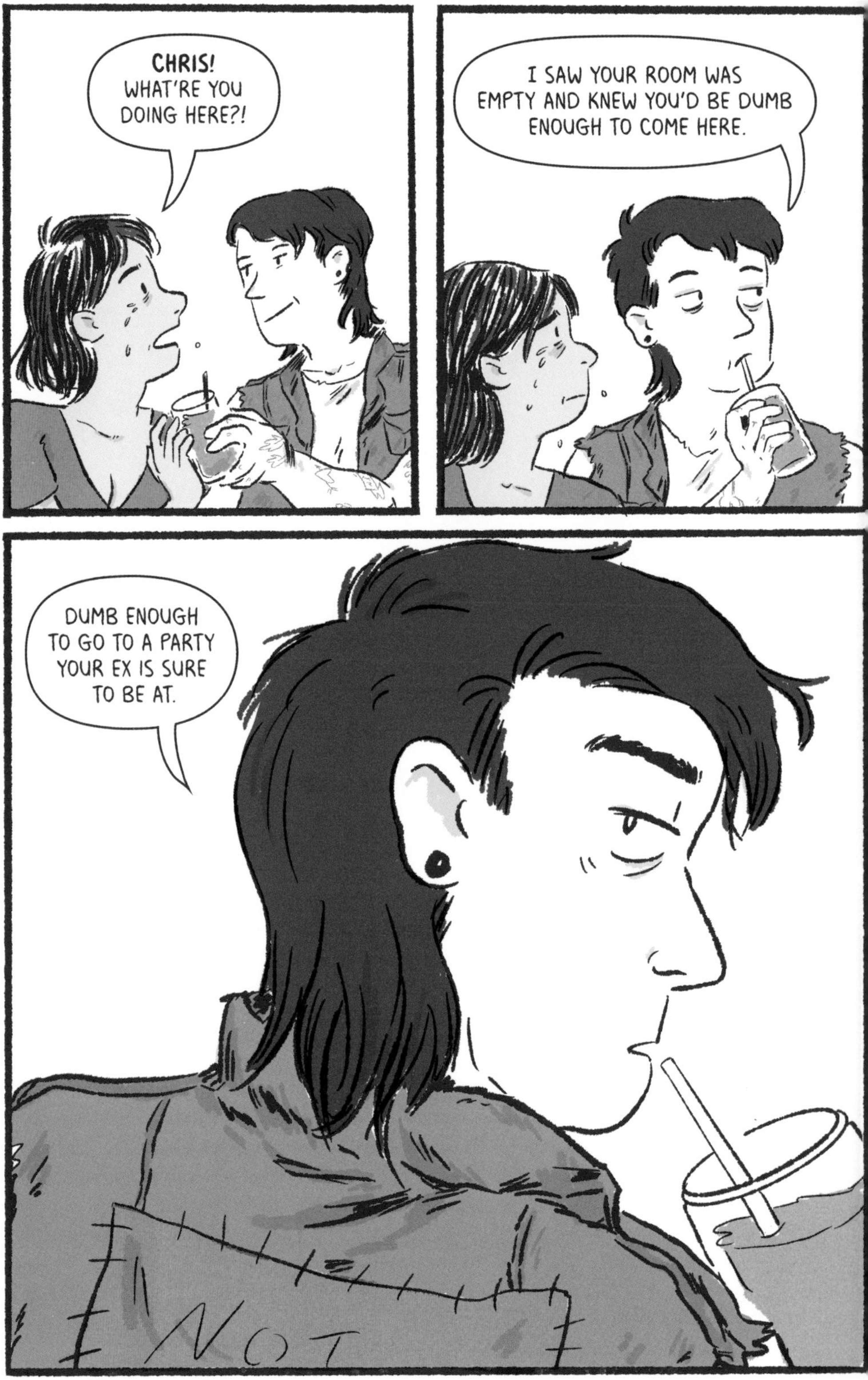
CHRIS! WHAT'RE YOU DOING HERE?!
I SAW YOUR ROOM WAS EMPTY AND KNEW YOU'D BE DUMB ENOUGH TO COME HERE.
DUMB ENOUGH TO GO TO A PARTY YOUR EX IS SURE TO BE AT.
NOT

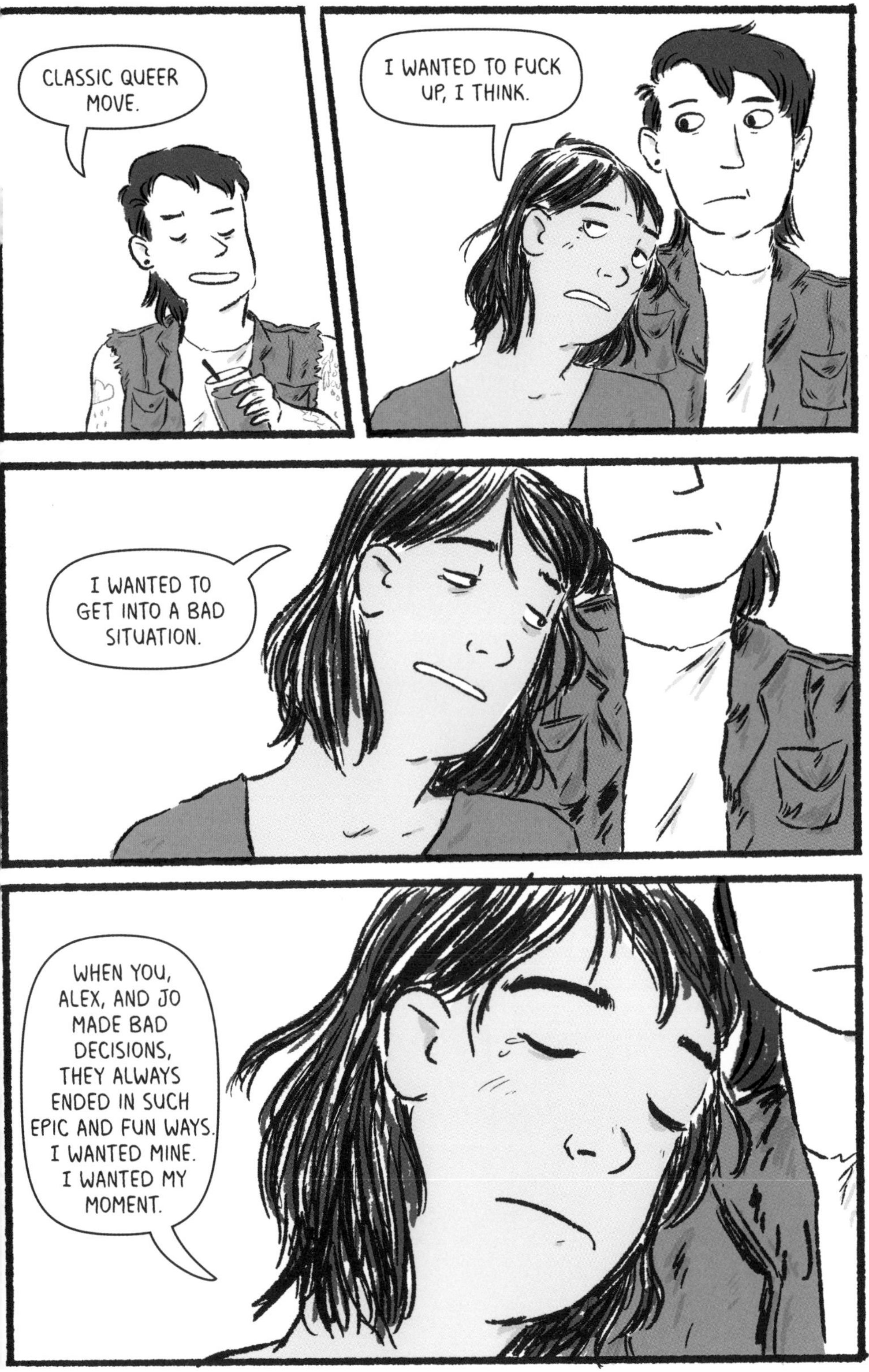

CLASSIC QUEER MOVE.
I WANTED TO FUCK UP, I THINK.
I WANTED TO GET INTO A BAD SITUATION.
WHEN YOU, ALEX, AND JO MADE BAD DECISIONS, THEY ALWAYS ENDED IN SUCH EPIC AND FUN WAYS. I WANTED MINE. I WANTED MY MOMENT.

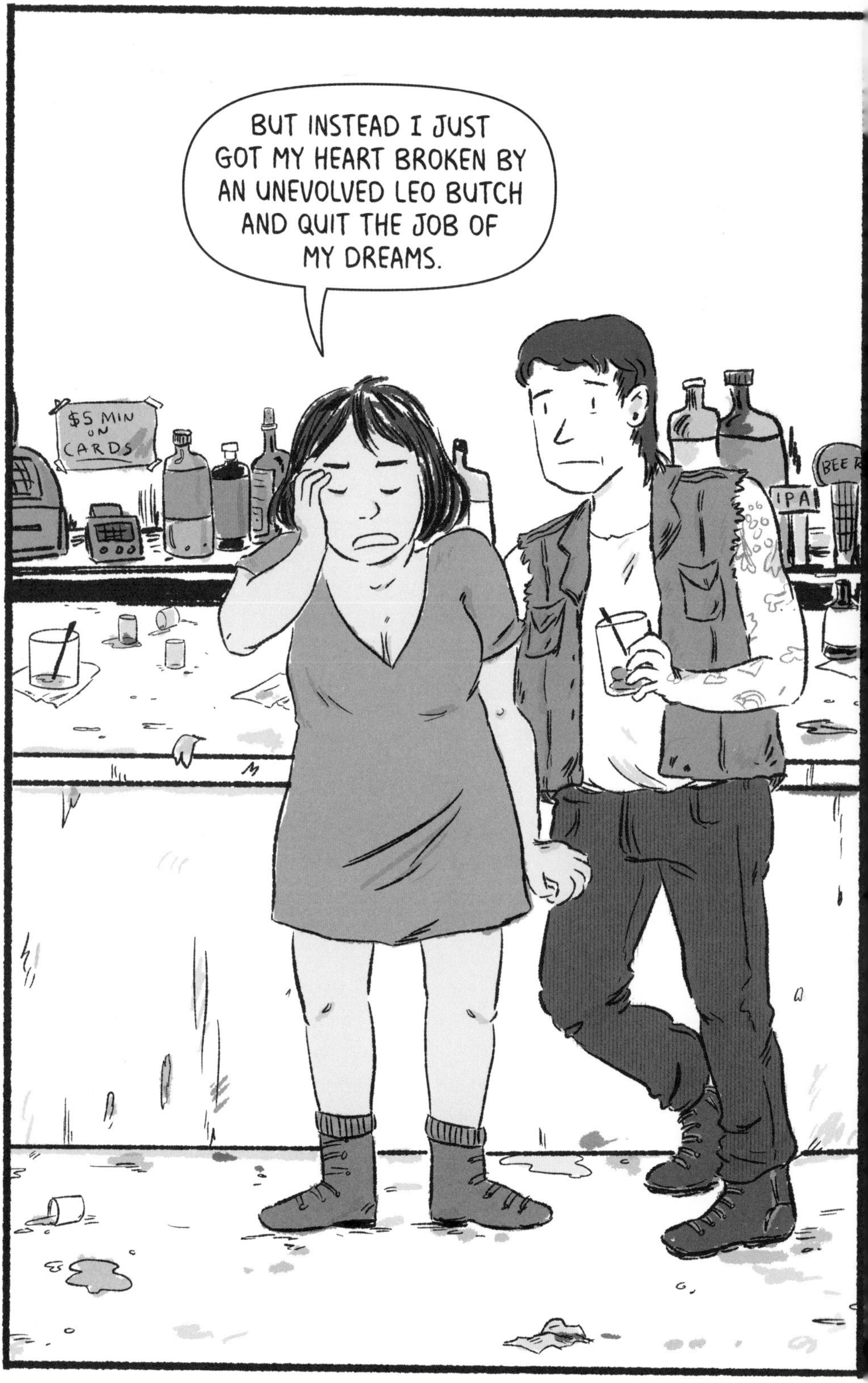
BUT INSTEAD I JUST GOT MY HEART BROKEN BY AN UNEVOLVED LEO BUTCH AND QUIT THE JOB OF MY DREAMS.
$5 MIN ON CARDS
IPA

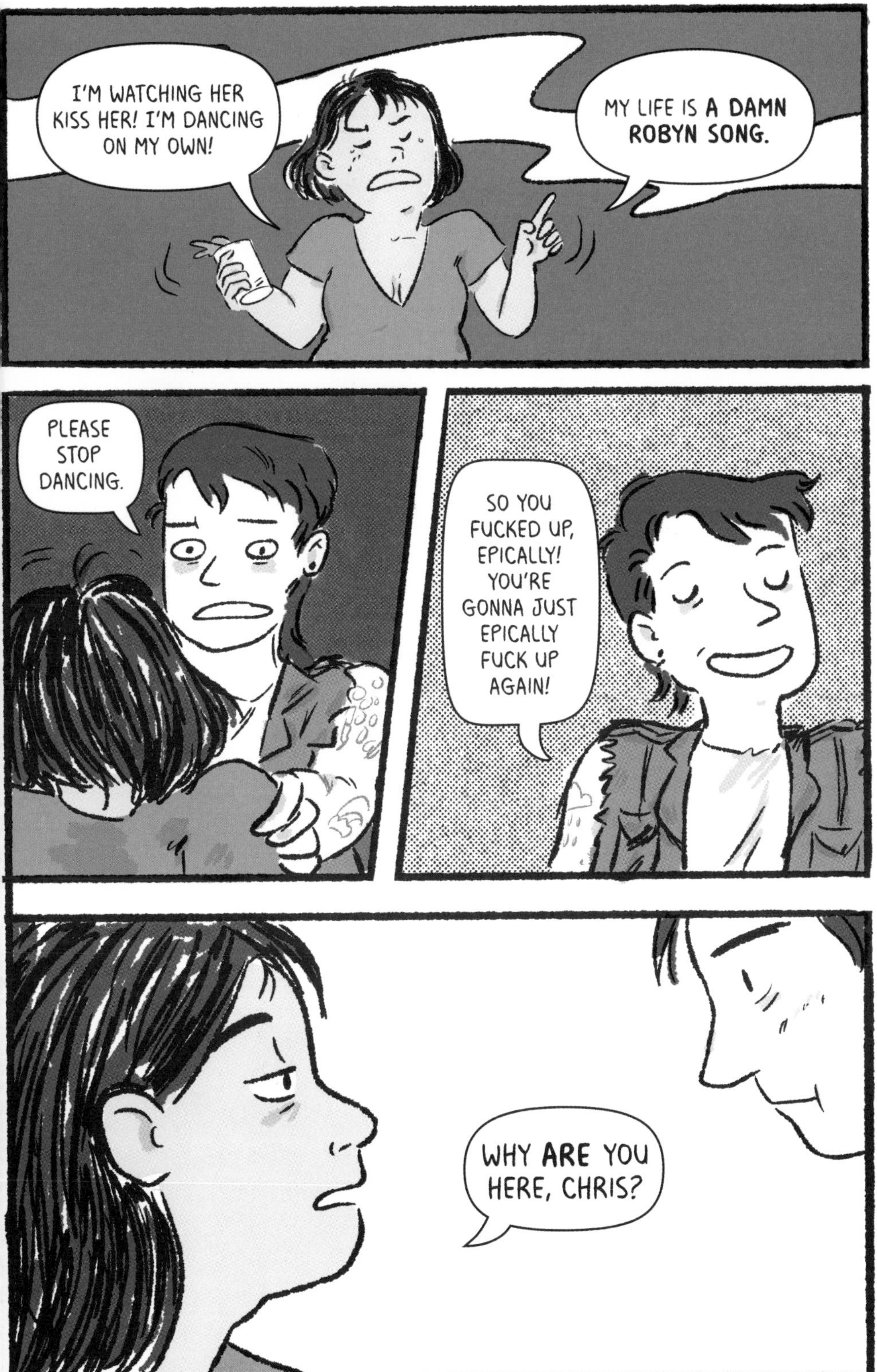
I'M WATCHING HER KISS HER! I'M DANCING ON MY OWN!
MY LIFE IS A DAMN ROBYN SONG.
PLEASE STOP DANCING.
SO YOU FUCKED UP, EPICALLY! YOU'RE GONNA JUST EPICALLY FUCK UP AGAIN!
WHY ARE YOU HERE, CHRIS?

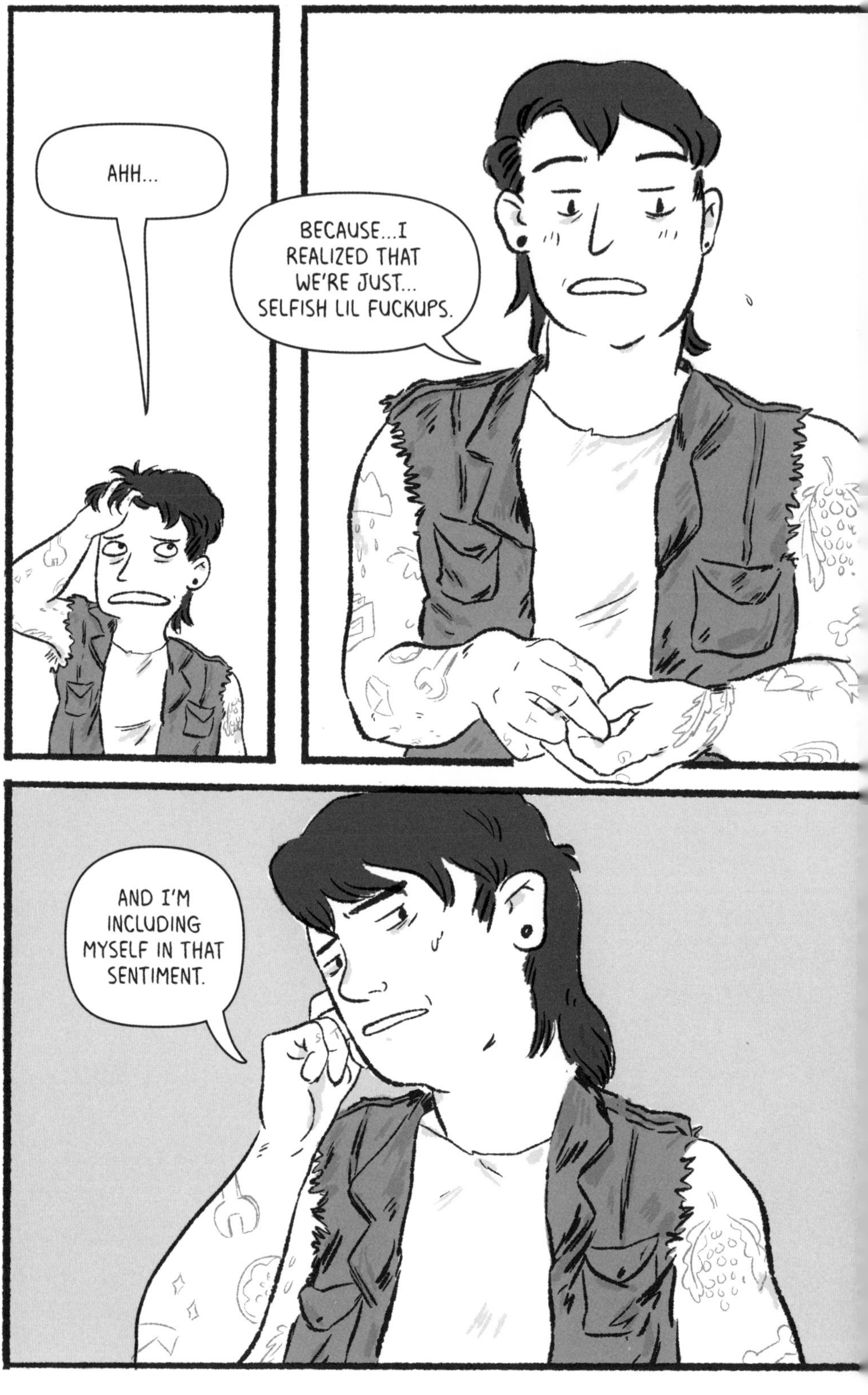
AHH...
BECAUSE...I REALIZED THAT WE'RE JUST... SELFISH LIL FUCKUPS.
AND I'M INCLUDING MYSELF IN THAT SENTIMENT.

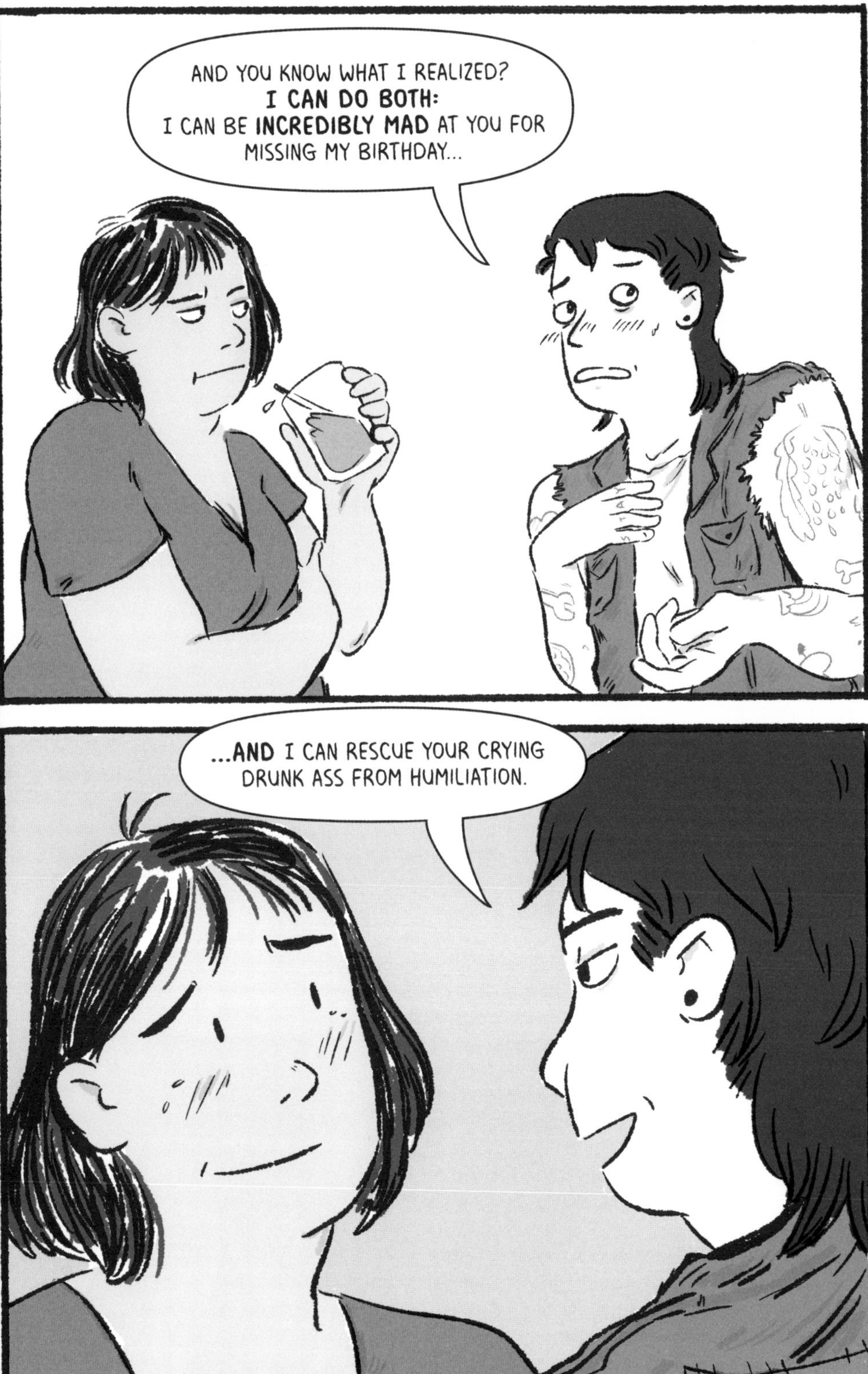
AND YOU KNOW WHAT I REALIZED? **I CAN DO BOTH:** I CAN BE **INCREDIBLY MAD** AT YOU FOR MISSING MY BIRTHDAY...
...**AND** I CAN RESCUE YOUR CRYING DRUNK ASS FROM HUMILIATION.

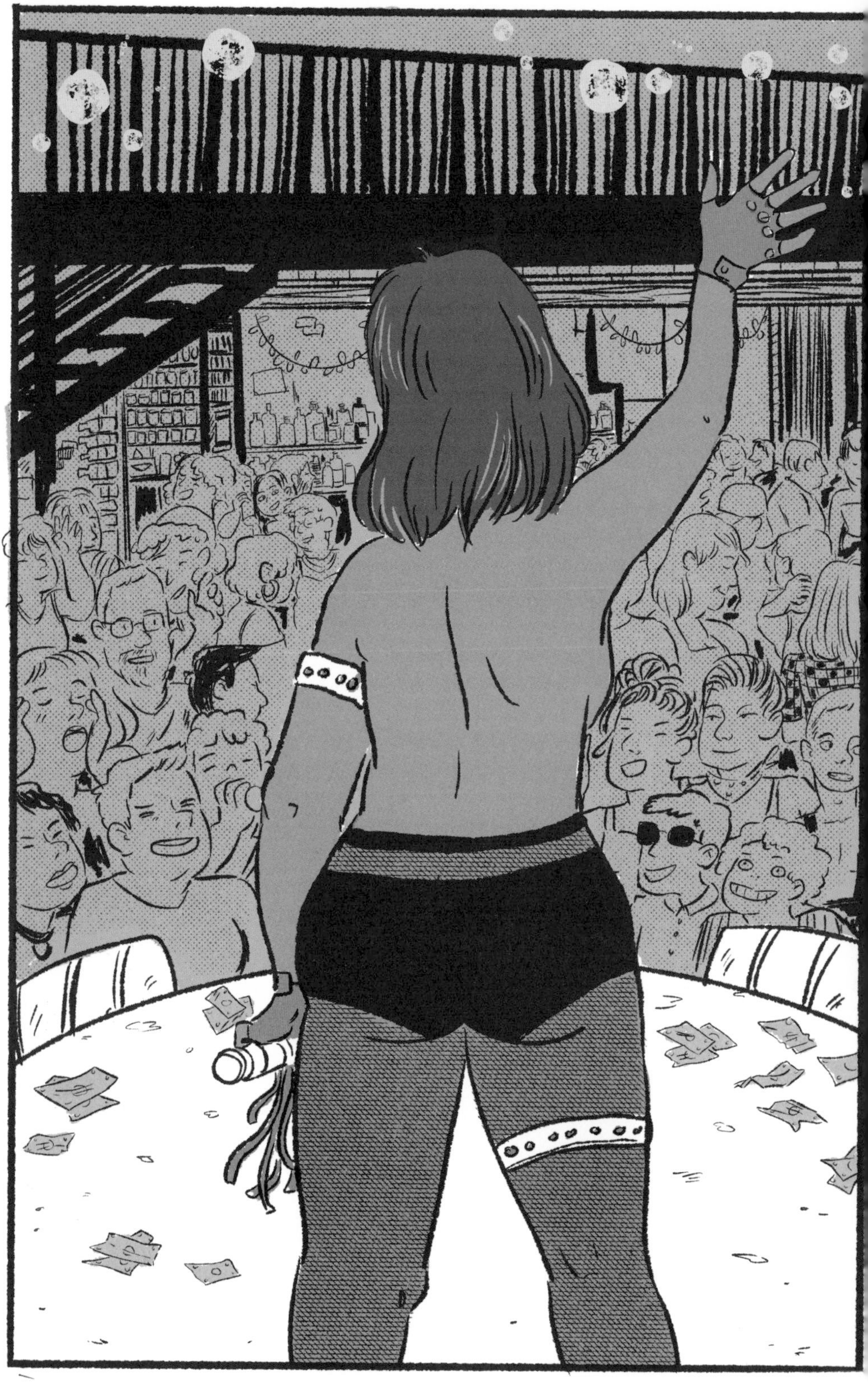

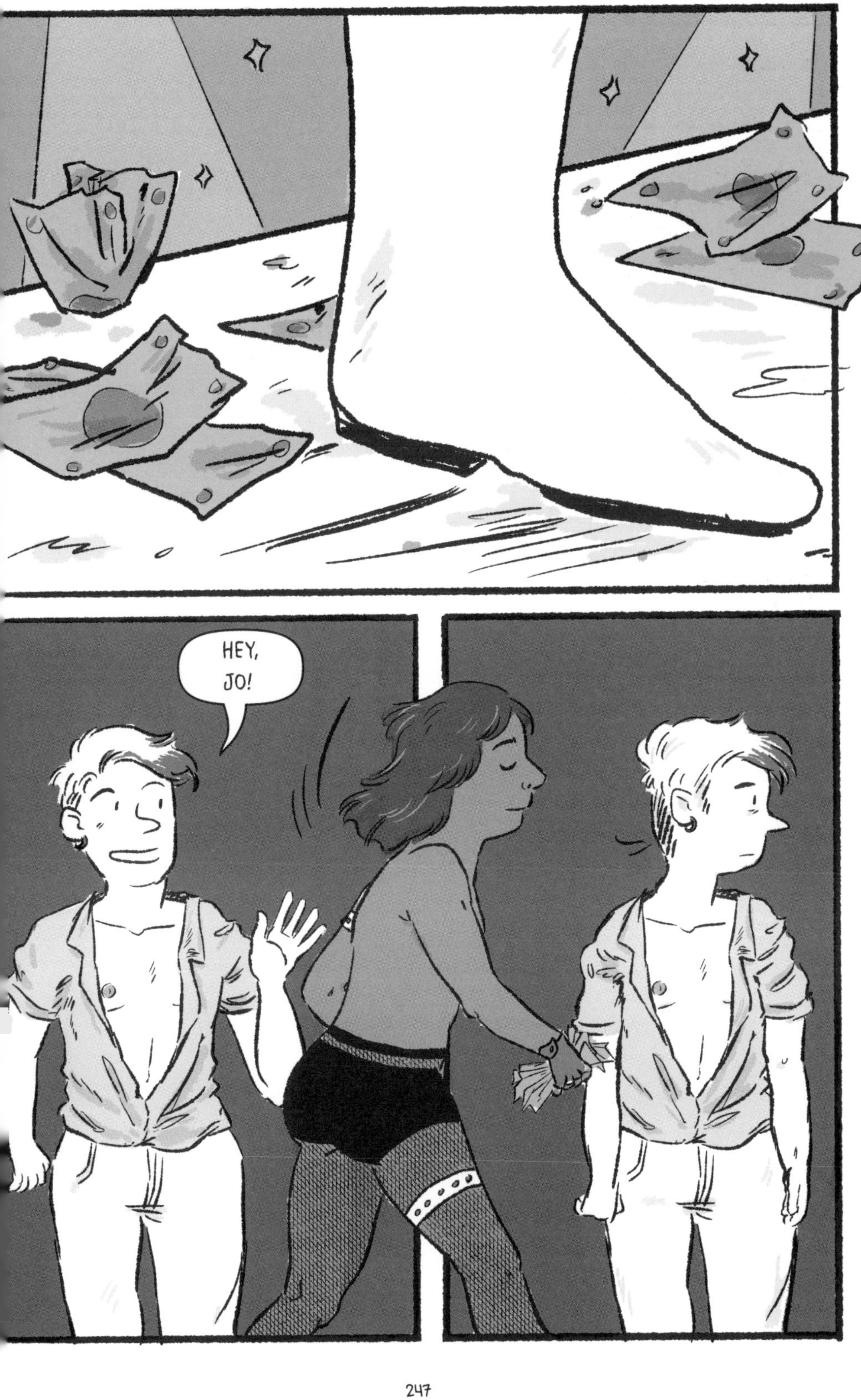
HEY,
JO!

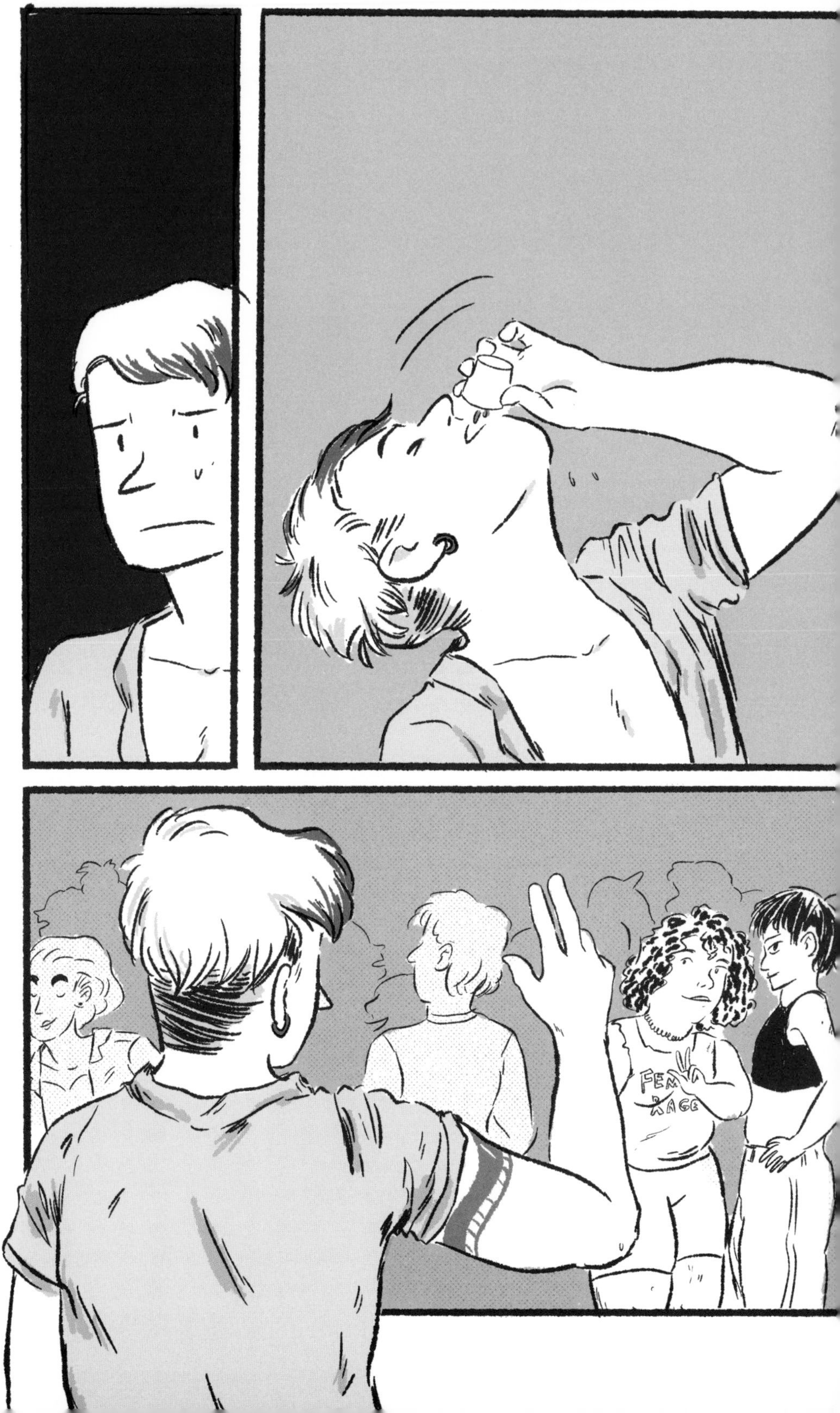

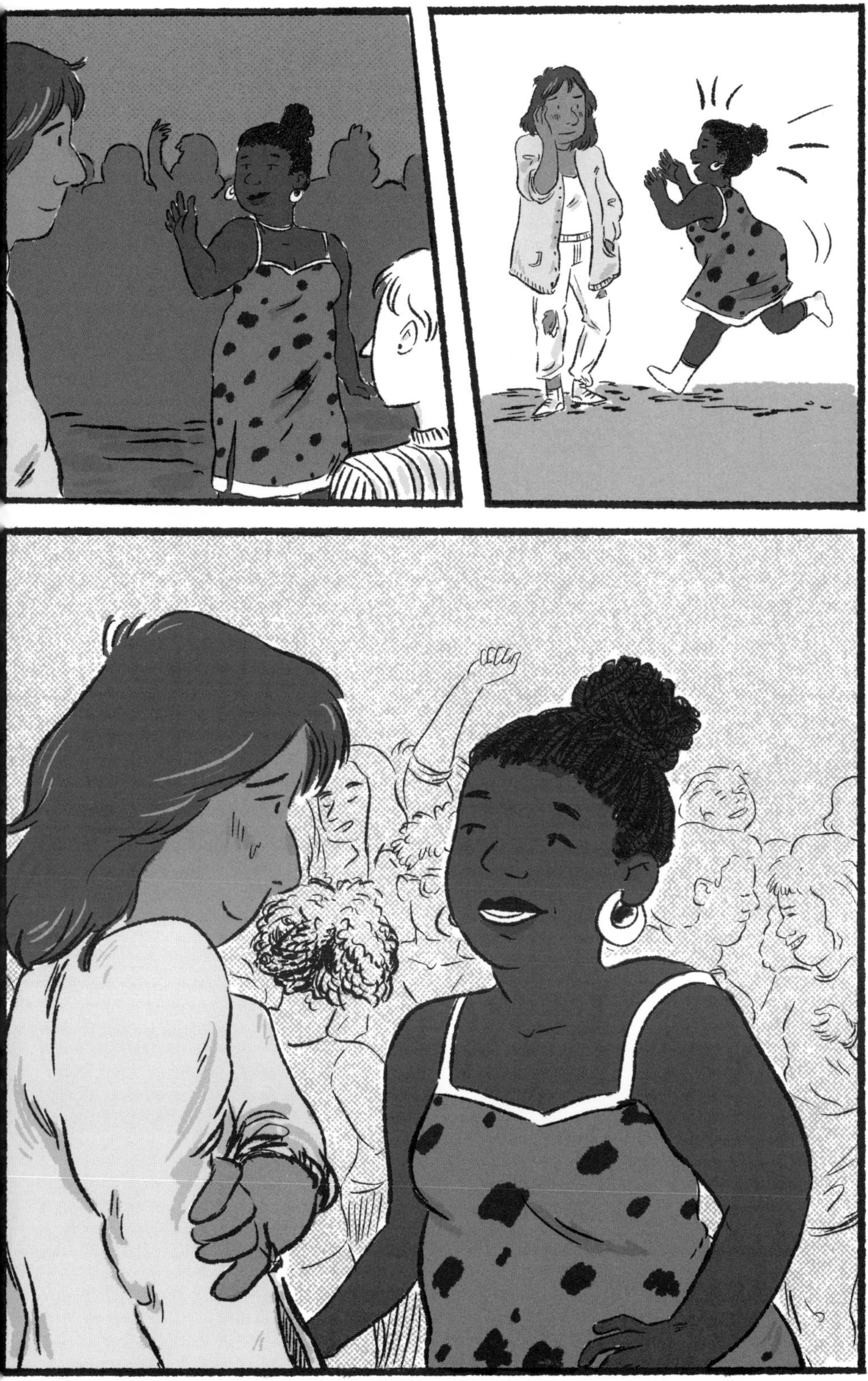

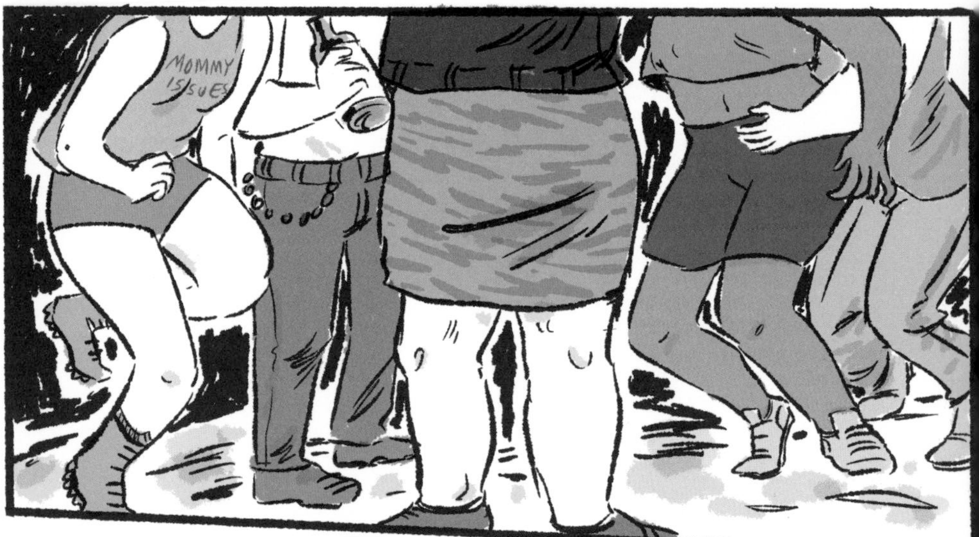
MOMMY ISSUES

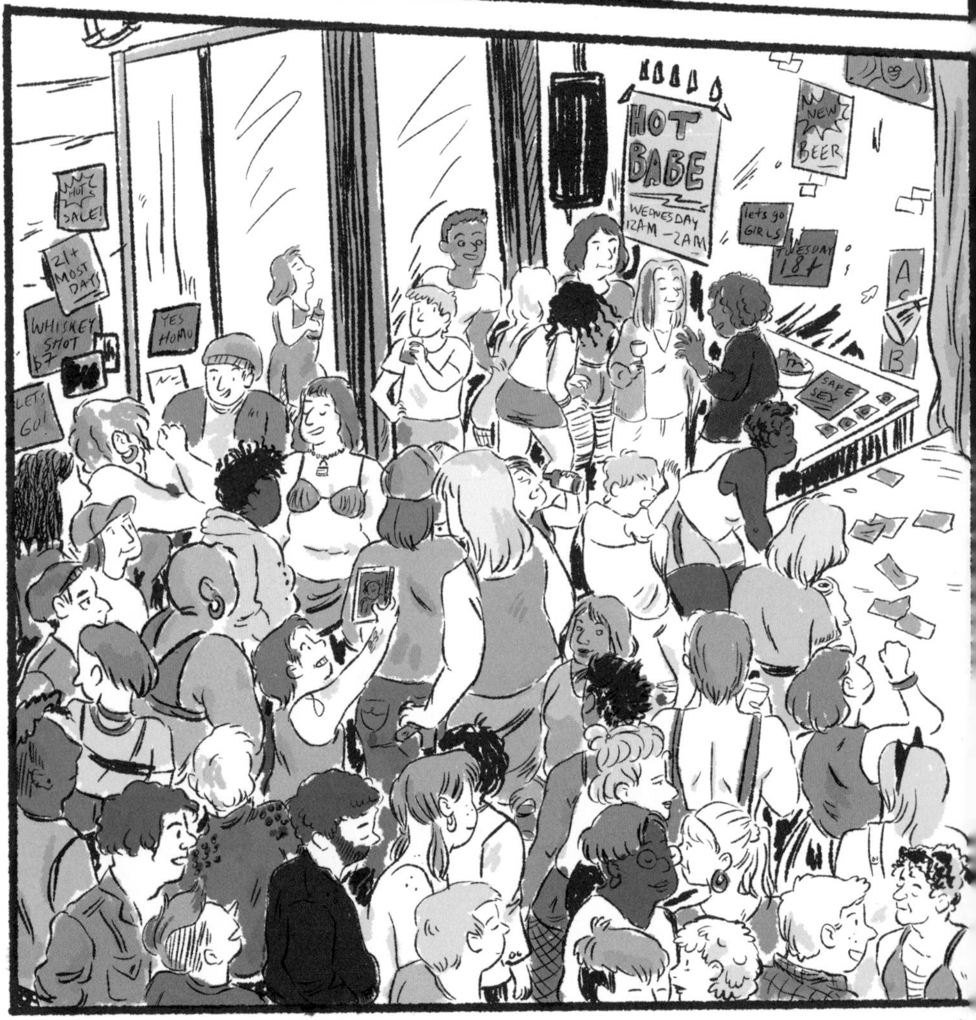
HOT BABE
WEDNESDAY 12AM-2AM
NEW BEER
lets go GIRLS
TUESDAY 18+
HOT SALE!
21+ MOST DAYS
WHISKEY SHOT $7
YES HOMO
LET'S GO!
SAFE SEX
A
B

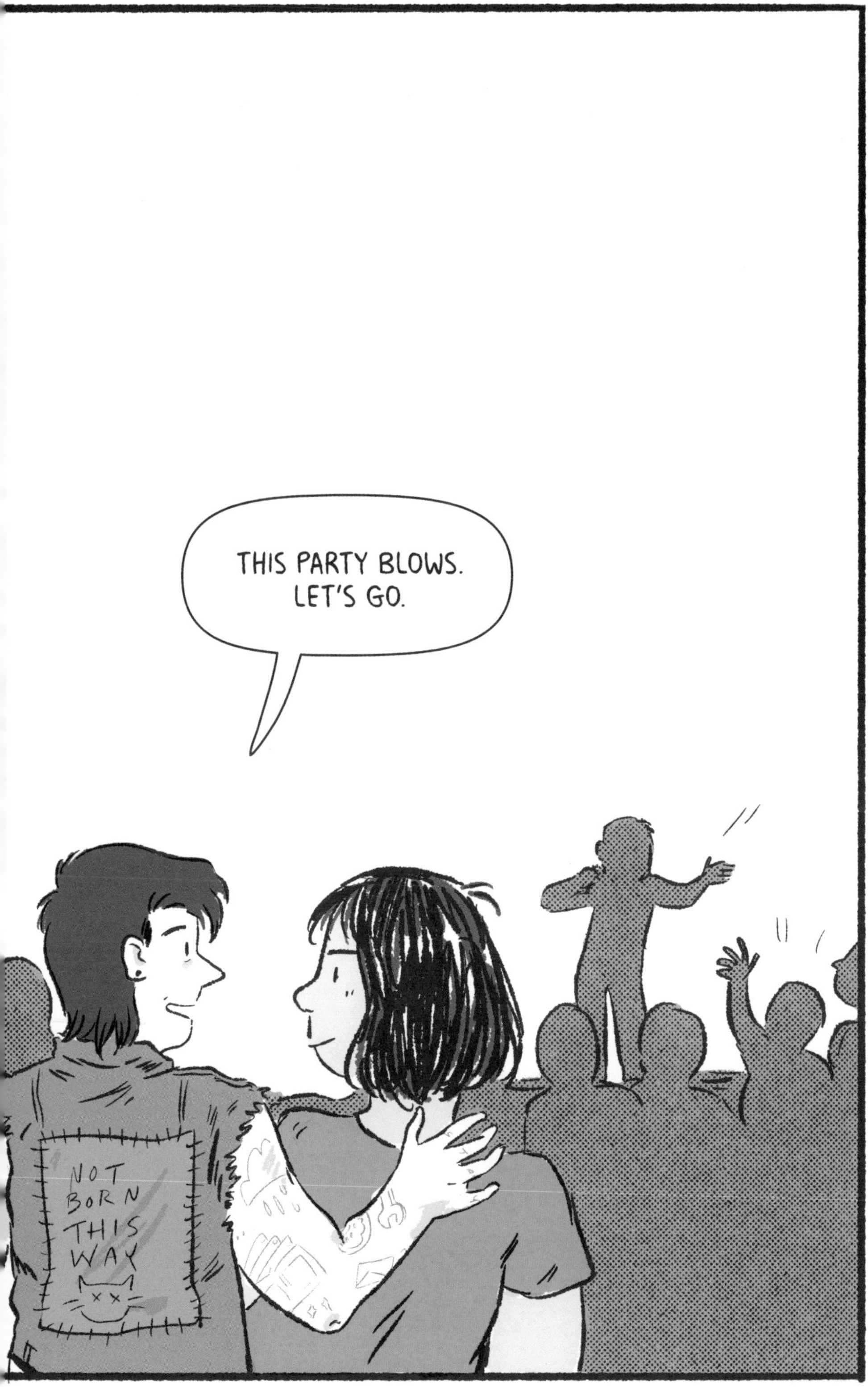
THIS PARTY BLOWS. LET'S GO.
NOT BORN THIS WAY

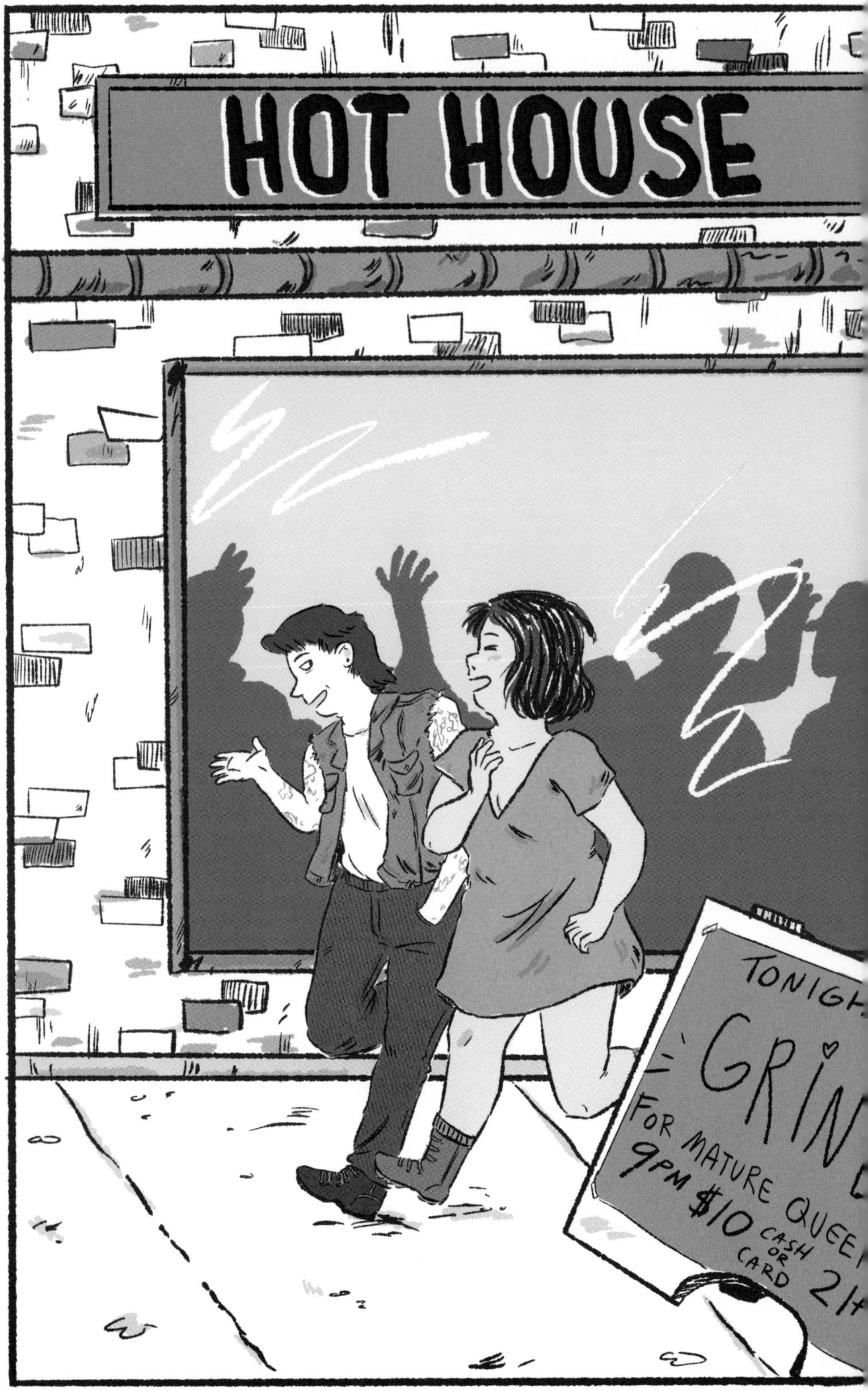
HOT HOUSE
TONIGH
GRIN
FOR MATURE QUEE
9PM $10 CASH OR CARD 21+

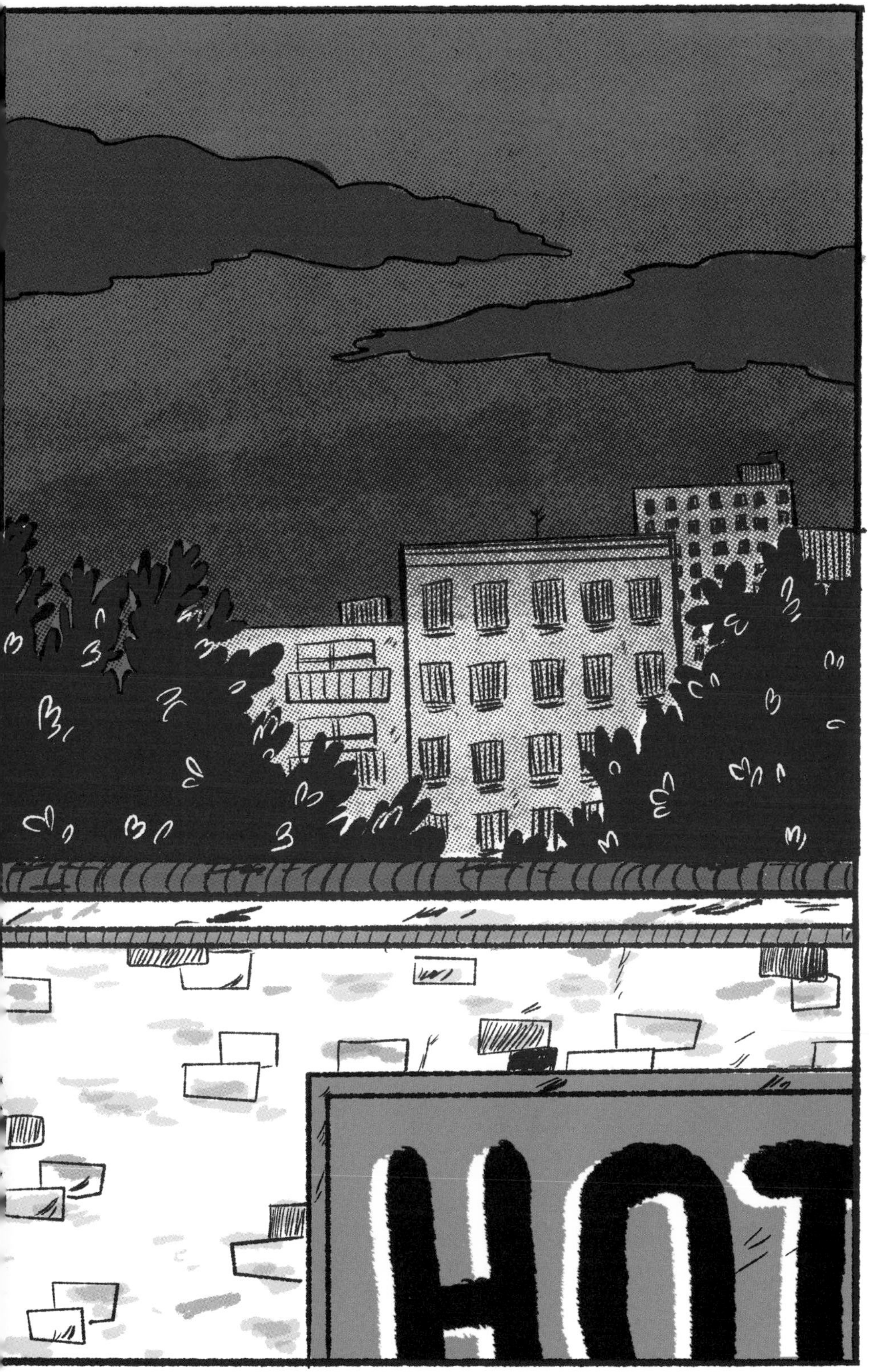
HOT

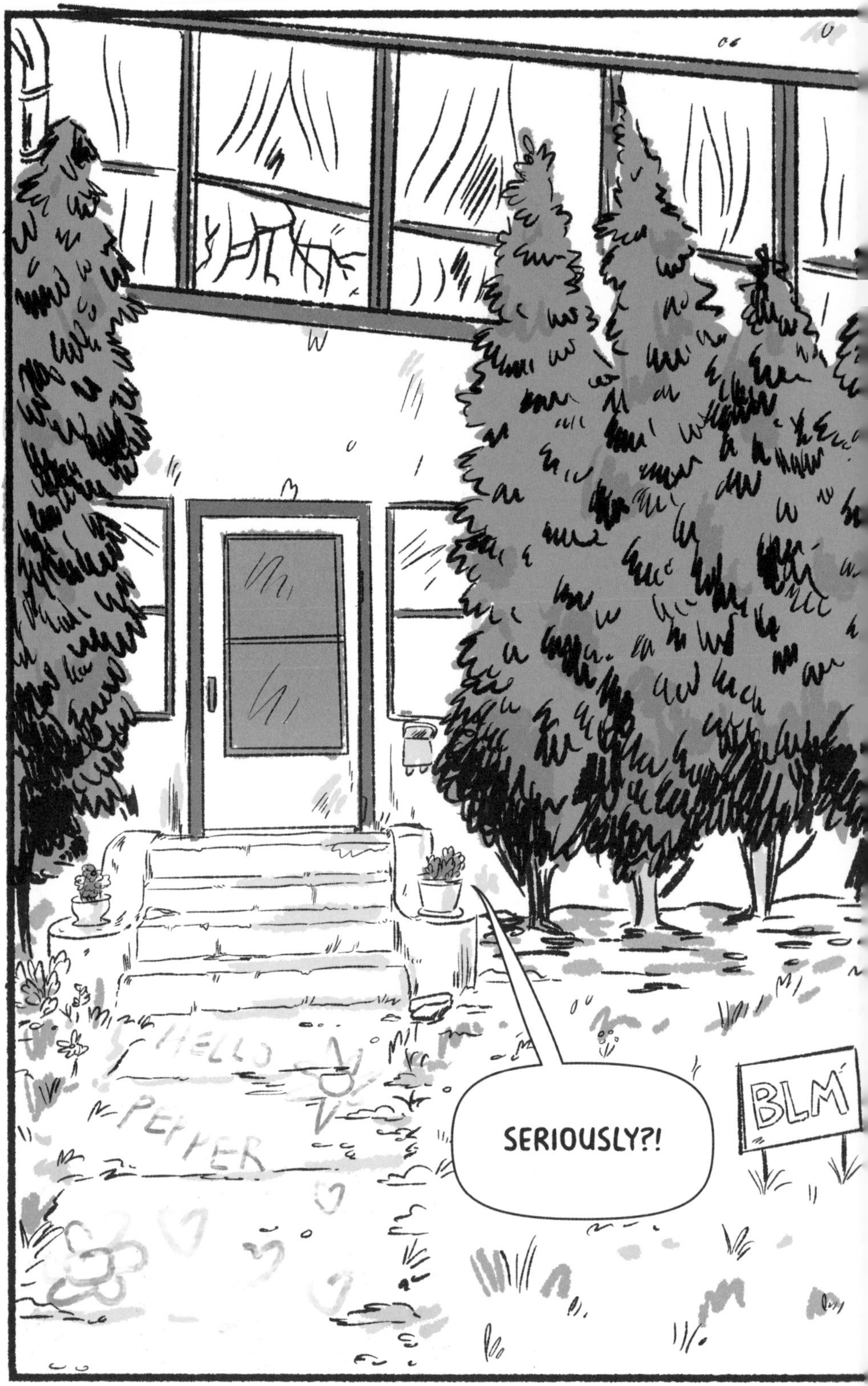

HELLO
PEPPER
SERIOUSLY?!
BLM

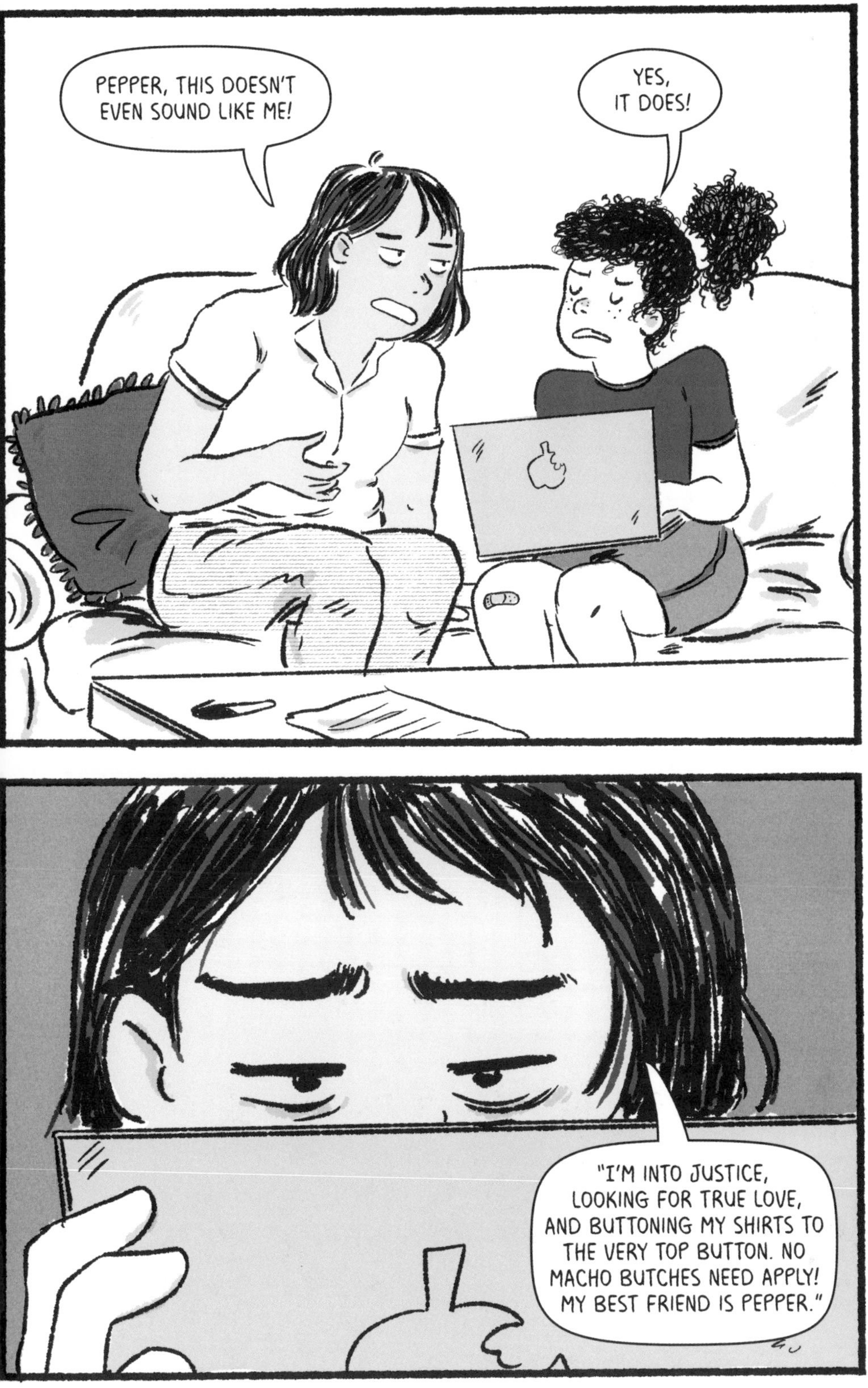
PEPPER, THIS DOESN'T EVEN SOUND LIKE ME!
YES, IT DOES!
"I'M INTO JUSTICE, LOOKING FOR TRUE LOVE, AND BUTTONING MY SHIRTS TO THE VERY TOP BUTTON. NO MACHO BUTCHES NEED APPLY! MY BEST FRIEND IS PEPPER."

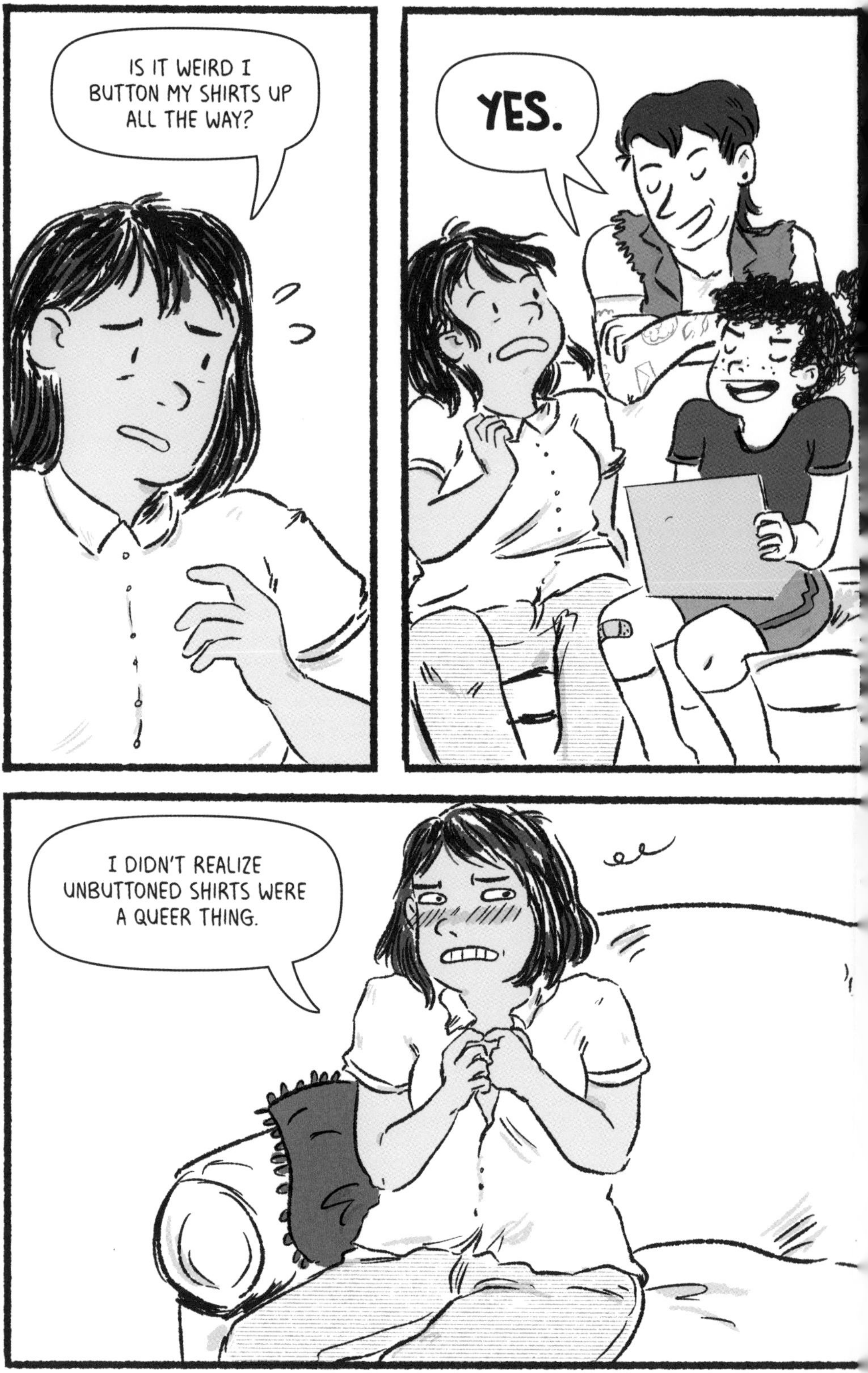
IS IT WEIRD I BUTTON MY SHIRTS UP ALL THE WAY?
YES.
I DIDN'T REALIZE UNBUTTONED SHIRTS WERE A QUEER THING.

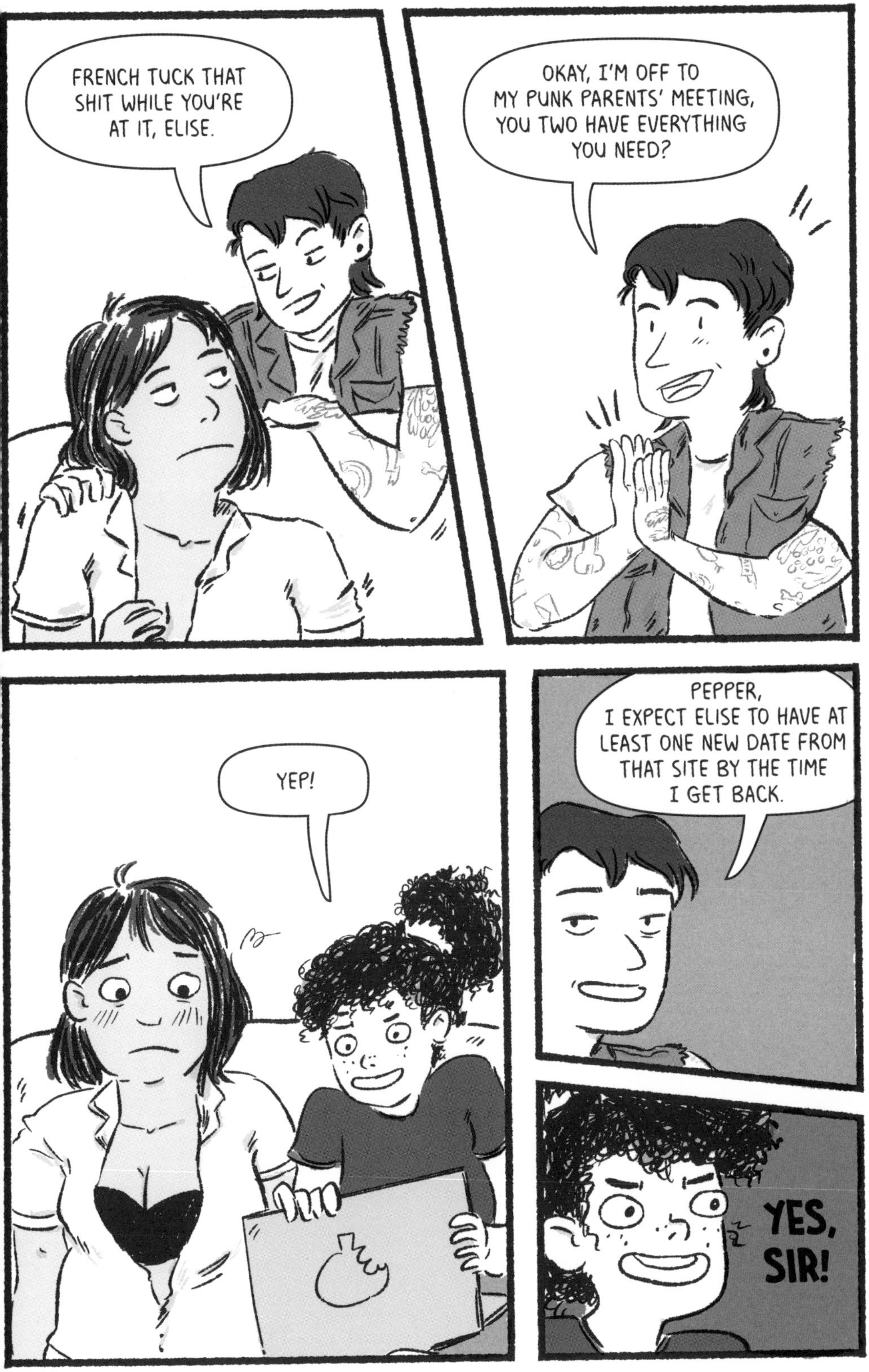

FRENCH TUCK THAT SHIT WHILE YOU'RE AT IT, ELISE.
OKAY, I'M OFF TO MY PUNK PARENTS' MEETING, YOU TWO HAVE EVERYTHING YOU NEED?
YEP!
PEPPER, I EXPECT ELISE TO HAVE AT LEAST ONE NEW DATE FROM THAT SITE BY THE TIME I GET BACK.
YES, SIR!

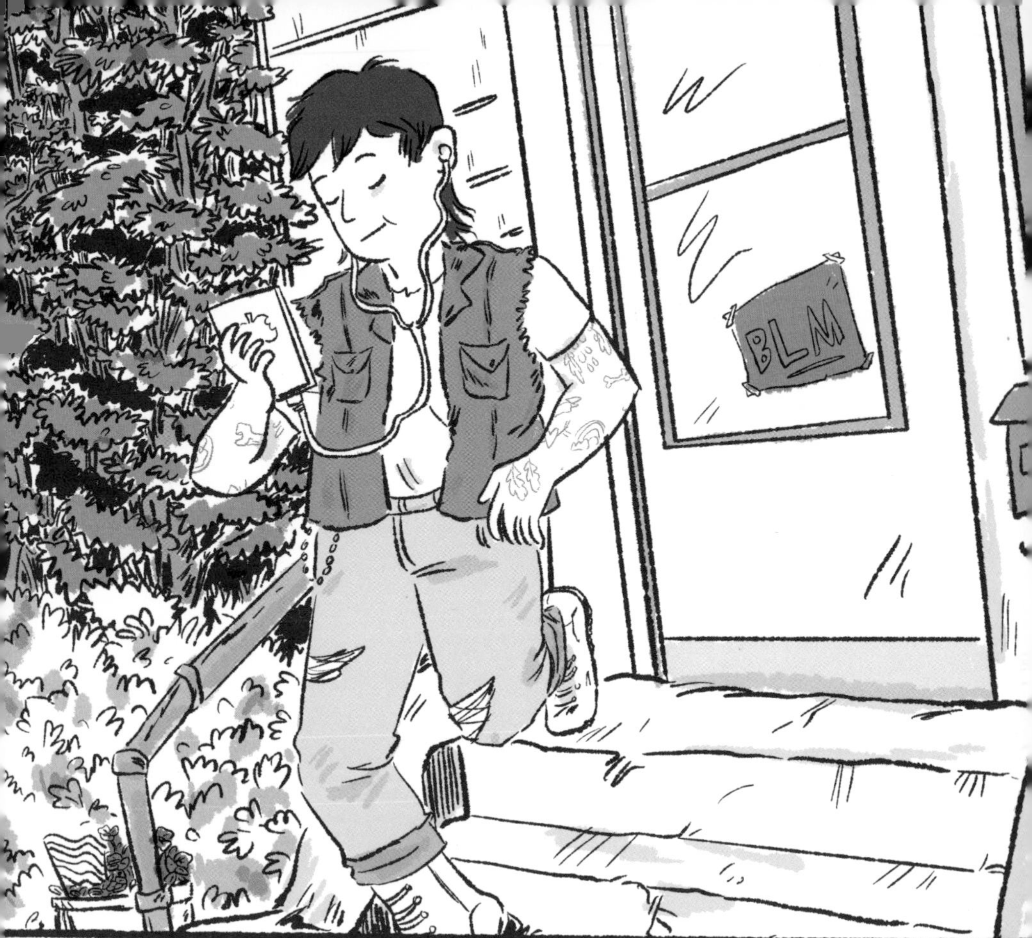
BLM

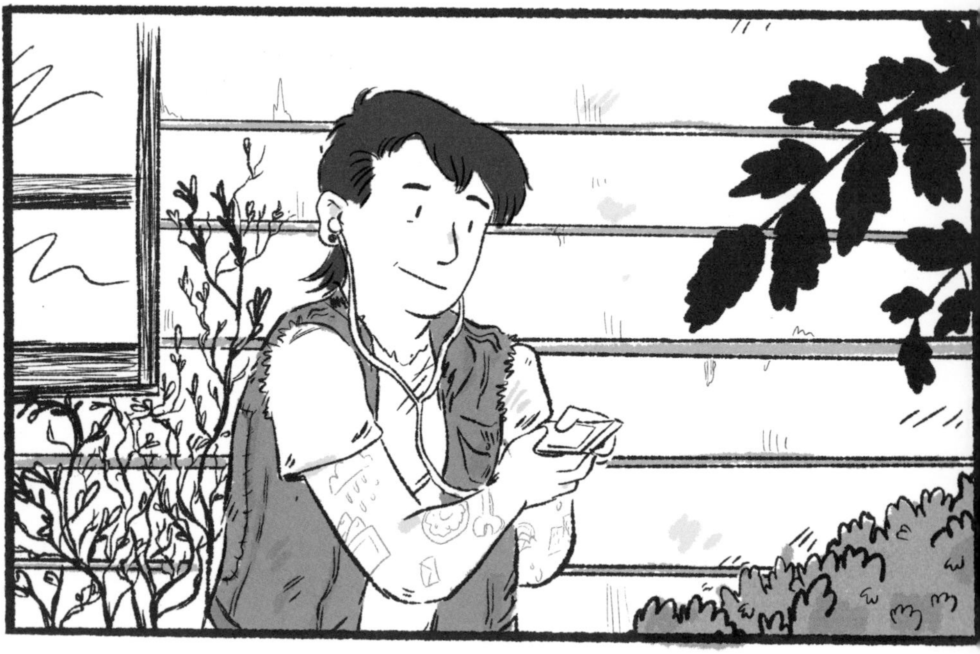

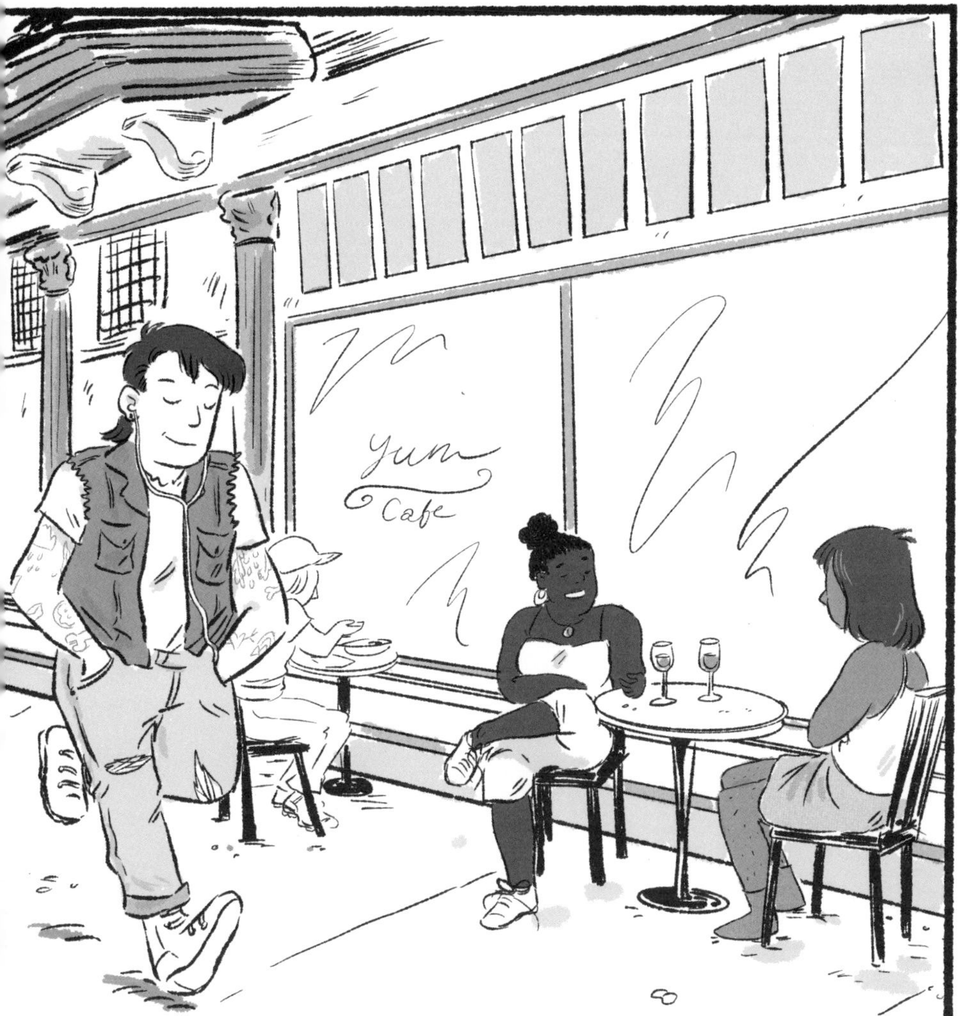
Yum
Cafe

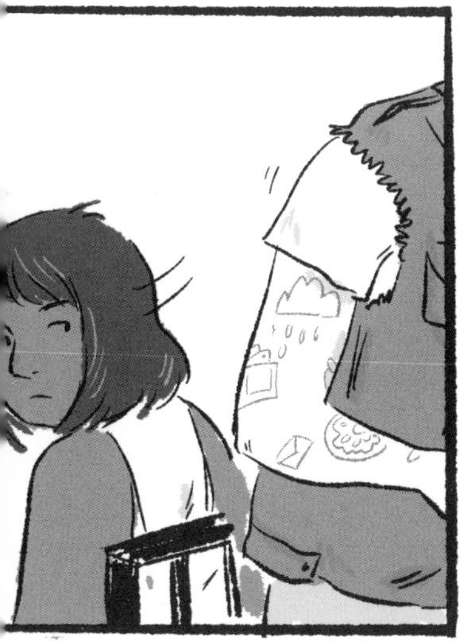

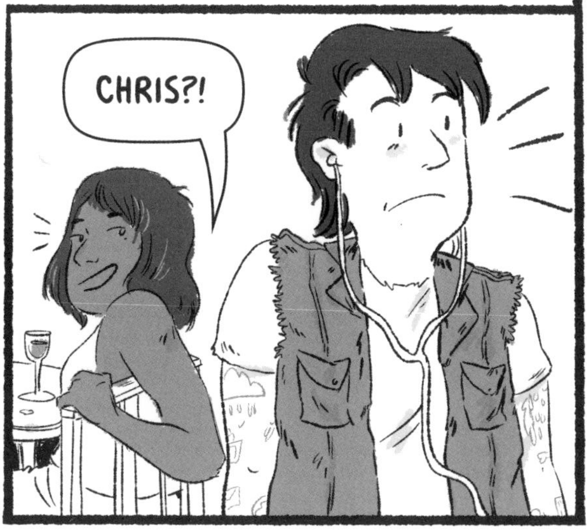
CHRIS?!

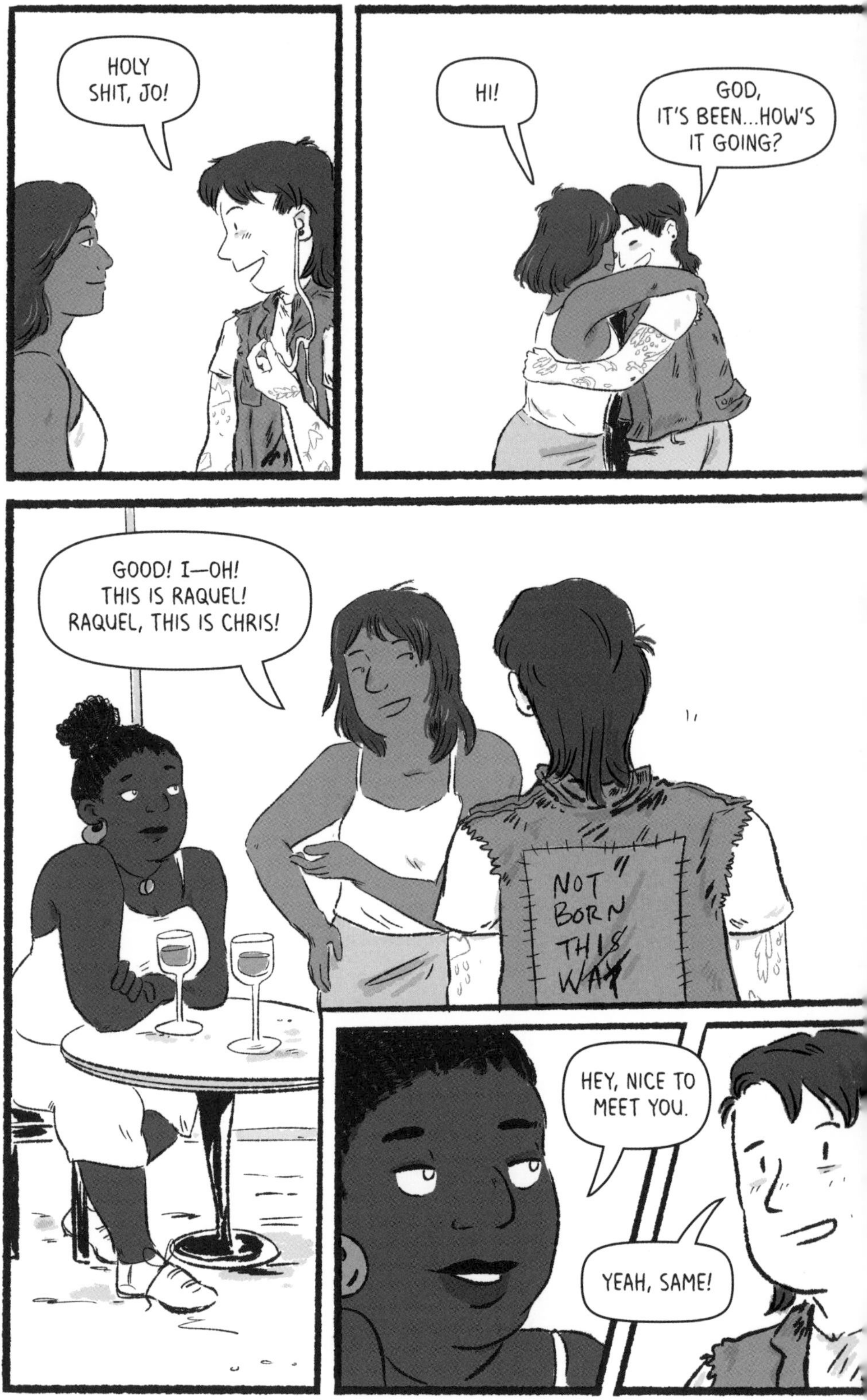
HOLY SHIT, JO!
HI!
GOD, IT'S BEEN...HOW'S IT GOING?
GOOD! I—OH! THIS IS RAQUEL! RAQUEL, THIS IS CHRIS!
NOT BORN THIS WAY
HEY, NICE TO MEET YOU.
YEAH, SAME!

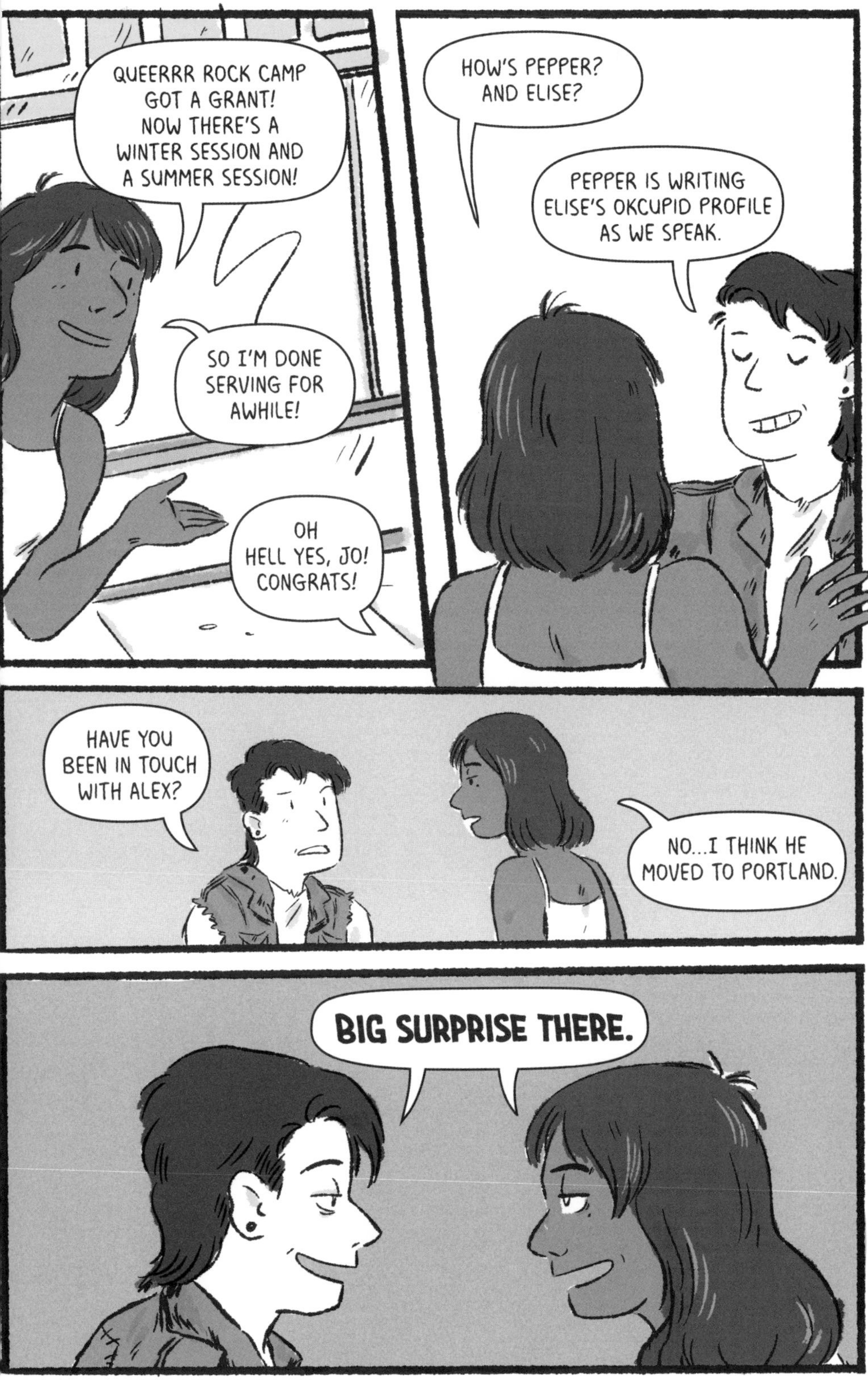
QUEERRR ROCK CAMP GOT A GRANT! NOW THERE'S A WINTER SESSION AND A SUMMER SESSION!
SO I'M DONE SERVING FOR AWHILE!
OH HELL YES, JO! CONGRATS!
HOW'S PEPPER? AND ELISE?
PEPPER IS WRITING ELISE'S OKCUPID PROFILE AS WE SPEAK.
HAVE YOU BEEN IN TOUCH WITH ALEX?
NO...I THINK HE MOVED TO PORTLAND.
BIG SURPRISE THERE.

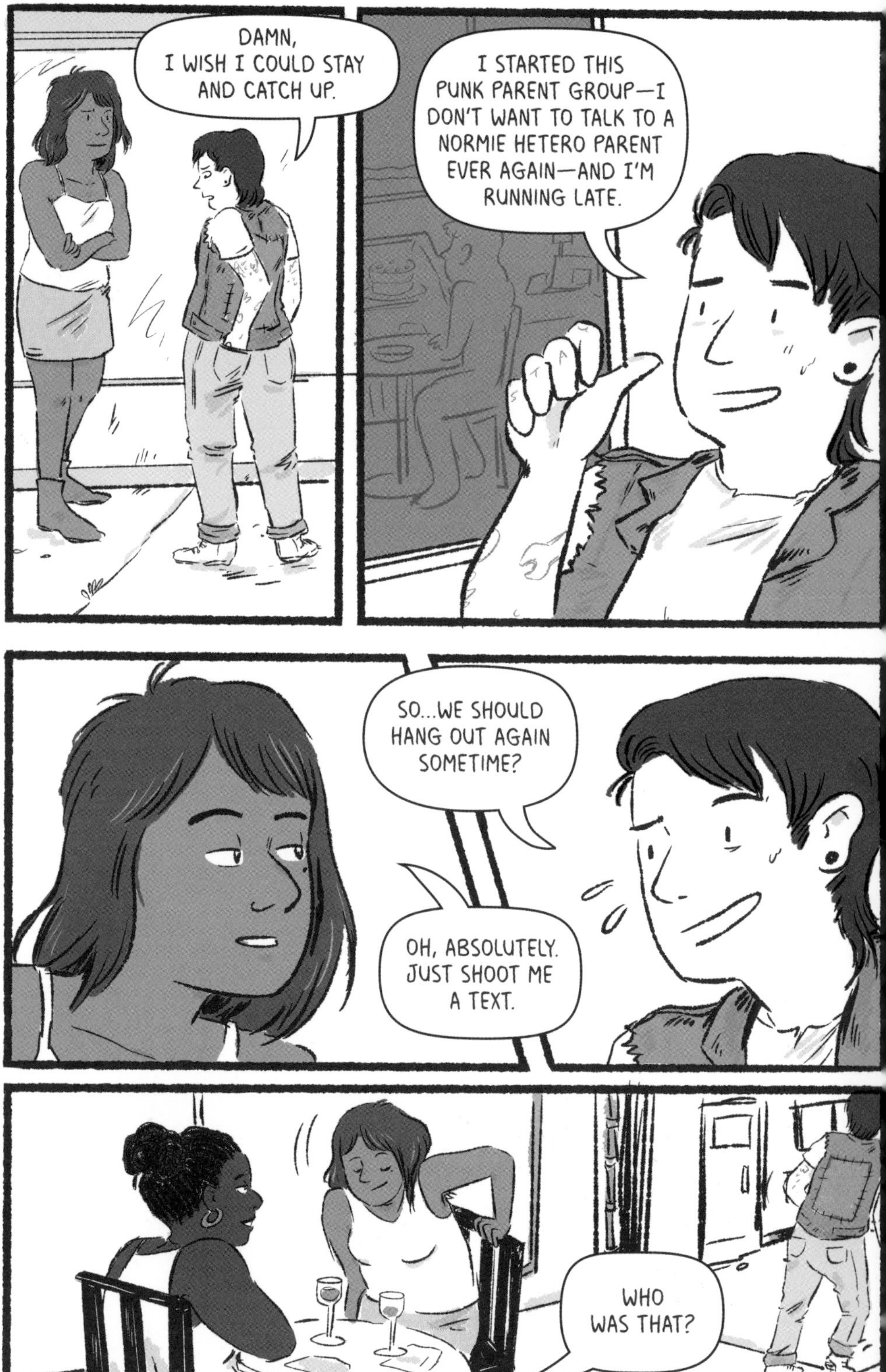
DAMN, I WISH I COULD STAY AND CATCH UP.
I STARTED THIS PUNK PARENT GROUP—I DON'T WANT TO TALK TO A NORMIE HETERO PARENT EVER AGAIN—AND I'M RUNNING LATE.
SO...WE SHOULD HANG OUT AGAIN SOMETIME?
OH, ABSOLUTELY. JUST SHOOT ME A TEXT.
WHO WAS THAT?

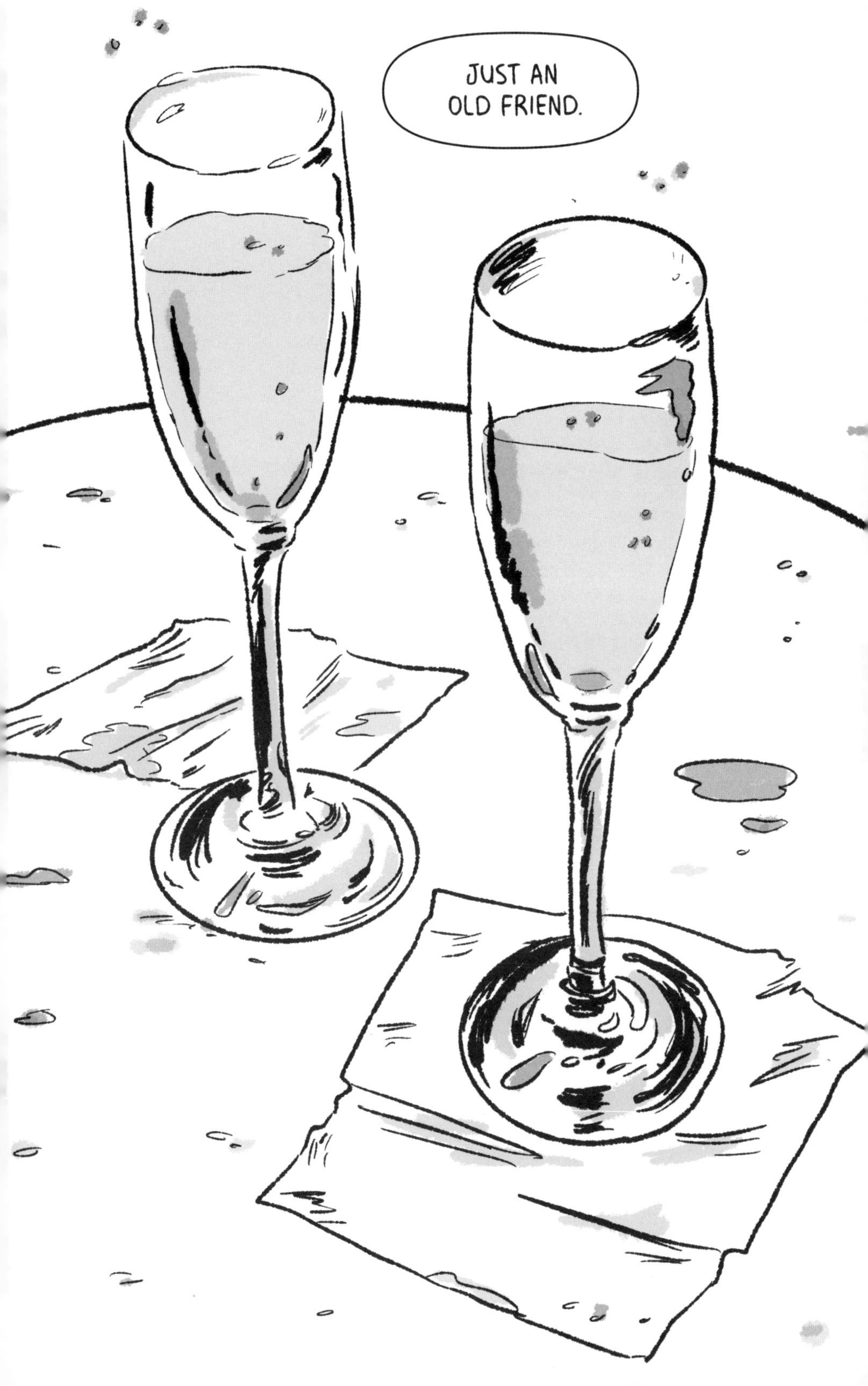
JUST AN OLD FRIEND.

ACKNOWLEDGMENTS

FIRST, I WANT TO THANK TREVOR KETNER AND BETH MARSHEA AT LADDERBIRD AGENCY FOR WORKING SO HARD TO ENSURE MY QUEER VISION NEVER GOT DILUTED BY ANY OUTSIDE PRESSURE. SECOND, I WANT TO GIVE A HUGE THANK-YOU TO CHARLOTTE GREENBAUM AND MARIKO TAMAKI FOR NEVER ASKING ME TO TONE DOWN MY CHARACTERS AND FOR SHEPHERDING *MIMOSA* INTO SOMETHING STRONGER THAN I COULD EVER IMAGINE. I NEED TO ACKNOWLEDGE THE INCREDIBLY TALENTED TEAM AT SURELY BOOKS, ESPECIALLY ANDY MILLER AND LAUREN WHITE-JACKSON, FOR ALL THEIR HARD WORK MAKING THIS BOOK LOOK AS AMAZING AS IT DOES. I ALSO WANT TO GIVE A GIANT THANK-YOU TO HAILEY KAAS FOR THE INSIGHT GIVEN WHEN *MIMOSA* WAS JUST A ROUGH SCRIPT.

WITHOUT JEN BARTEL AND THE FLAME CON MENTORSHIP, THIS BOOK WOULD NOT EXIST, SO THANK YOU FROM THE BOTTOM OF MY BIG GAY HEART FOR MAKING THIS HAPPEN. I OWE A HUGE AMOUNT OF GRATITUDE TO THE TIN HOUSE SUMMER WORKSHOP AND ALL THE ATTENDEES IN THE GRAPHIC NARRATIVE WORKSHOP WHO TENDERLY AND LOVINGLY CRITIQUED AND ENCOURAGED THIS PROJECT. I'D LIKE TO ESPECIALLY THANK MIRA JACOB FOR HER INSIGHT ON *MIMOSA* AND FOR CHANGING HOW I WRITE AND THINK ABOUT COMICS. I'M SO GRATEFUL FOR ISABELLA ROTMAN AND THE ENTIRE CARTOONIST CRIT CLUB FOR WELCOMING ME AND MY WORK INTO THEIR MONTHLY MEETINGS. THANKS TO MY INSTAGRAM FOLLOWERS (LOLLL)—YOUR ENTHUSIASM FOR ME AND MY LIFE AND MY WORK IS HONESTLY PRICELESS AND I DON'T CARE HOW CRINGE IT IS TO SAY IT! THANK YOU TO MY SUPPORTERS ON PATREON FOR FINANCIALLY HELPING ME EXIST AND CREATE AND GIVING ME A PLACE TO SHOWCASE WORK I CAN'T POST ELSEWHERE.

A GIANT THANK-YOU TO EVERYONE WHO LISTENED TO ME DAYDREAM, WHINE, AND CRY OVER THIS PROJECT—THERE ARE TOO MANY OF YOU TO LIST BUT KNOW THAT YOUR SUPPORT HAS BEEN INVALU-ABLE TO ME. I WANT TO GIVE A BIG THANK-YOU TO MY SISTERS, ELYSE AND KATHLEEN, FOR ALWAYS ANSWERING MY PHONE CALLS. YOU TWO KEPT MY ANXIETY IN CHECK FOR THE PAST FEW YEARS AND WITHOUT YOU I'D BE SIGNIFICANTLY LESS GROUNDED THAN I AM. THANK YOU, BRIE AND JESS, FOR ENCOURAGING THIS STORY RIGHT FROM INCEPTION! THANK YOU TO THE CUNT (RIP) FOR THE BEERS. THANK YOU, BABY GRANDMA, FOR FORCING ME TO STAY HOME AND WORK. SUSAN, TRISTAN, AND CHRISTINA—THANK YOU ALL FOR NOT JUST BEING CHEERLEADERS FOR MY WORK BUT FOR THE ABILITY YOU ALL HAVE TO SHOW UP AS WELL. THANK YOU MINNEAPOLIS FOR ALL THE PARTIES AND EVENTS AND QUEER NIGHTS AND QUEER SPACES AND THE ORGANIZERS WHO PUT SO MUCH ENERGY INTO MAKING THEM WHAT THEY ARE. FUCK A COAST, THIS PLACE IS THRIVING.

LASTLY, THANKS MOM AND DAD FOR ALWAYS BELIEVING I COULD BE A COMIC ARTIST, DESPITE KNOWING CARTOONISTS MAKE NO MONEY AND LIVE DERANGED LIVES, YOU CAUSED THIS AND I'M SO FUCKIN' GRATEFUL. MOM, YOU WOULD HAVE LOVED THIS ONE.